EPIC

CHINESE MYTHS & TALES

ANTHOLOGY OF CLASSIC TALES

Foreword by Davide Latini

FLAME TREE PUBLISHING

TALES

This is a FLAME TREE Book

Publisher & Creative Director: Nick Wells
Project Editor: Catherine Taylor

FLAME TREE PUBLISHING
6 Melbray Mews, Fulham,
London SW6 3NS, United Kingdom
www.flametreepublishing.com

First published 2018

18 20 22 21 19
1 3 5 7 9 10 8 6 4 2

ISBN: 978-1-78755-237-1

The cover image is created by Flame Tree Studio based on artwork by Slava Gerj and Gabor Ruszkai.

Incidental images by Shutterstock.com: Babin, John Lock (inspired by the mural painting of 60 gods by Daozi Wu, the celebrated painter of the Tang dynasty of China) and vectortatu.

A copy of the CIP data for this book is available from the British Library.

Printed and bound in China

EPIC

CHINESE MYTHS & TALES

ANTHOLOGY OF CLASSIC TALES

Foreword by Davide Latini

FLAME TREE PUBLISHING

TALES

Contents

Myths of the Stars

Myths of Thunder, Lightning, Wind & Rain

Myths of the Waters

Myths of Fire

Myths of Epidemics & Exorcism

Tales of the Goddess of Mercy

The Gods of China

Legends of Foxes and Other Animals

Ghostly Tales

Parables & Fairy Tales

Foreword

IF THERE IS ONE ELEMENT noticeably absent from the rich and varied early Chinese literary tradition, that is *epos*. Differently from other contemporary civilizations, ancient China seems to have never produced, in written form, a lengthy mythological narrative to which was attributed preeminent cultural importance. Instead, myths survived in fragments, quoted in philosophical works, alluded to in political treatises, commemorated in historical chronicles. This dearth, however, should not lead us to believe that myths were disregarded or relegated to marginal positions. On the contrary, the ubiquitous presence of splintered myths in texts of disparate genres attests to the extent to which the stories were ingrained in the social and cultural fabric. They mattered on so many different levels, in fact, that they transcended the ideological divergences between the doctrines they were summoned by, and their figurations crept deep into the crevices of artistic expression leaving indelible marks in the creative production of later centuries.

Through their narratives, myths explored existential themes like the origin of the world – when a primeval unwrought mass divided itself into two, generating Heaven and Earth – or the birth of humankind – shaped from clay by an ancestral goddess. More than in the material coming into being of things, though, the stories engaged in the shift from an untamed to an orderly world. The discoveries and inventions attributed to mythical heroes – fire, agriculture, calendrical arts, writing – played a major role in this civilizational process, together with rituals and rules of conduct, which constituted the ultimate gift from the sage rulers of old. The values embodied by these personages and their deeds nurtured the self-image of the Chinese world, providing a sense of belonging and a cultural identity. For this reason, the attainments granted by the intervention of mythical figures needed to be preserved and safeguarded, lest the cosmos plunge into chaos. Scores of unruly and rebellious figures – who threatened this system of values and embodied its diametric opposite – punctuate Chinese mythology. The most infamous specimen of this ilk is Chiyou, the belligerent and seditious inventor of weapons. His tremendous clash with the Yellow Emperor – archetype of the just sovereign – has been retold countless times as the typification of the triumph over evil. But the menace could even have the impersonal form of a cataclysm of massive proportions. The myth about the cosmic flood that plagued the reign of the emperors Yao and Shun is a conspicuous example. To prevent the inundation from engulfing everything and turn the world into an inhabitable swamp, Yu was appointed to quell the overflowing waters and guide them to the sea, an enterprise that required a complete reconfiguration of the morphology of the Chinese territory. Similarly, the mythical archer Yi is celebrated for having faced ten suns rising at once and scorching the earth. He shot down nine of them, reestablishing the normal activity of the remaining one. The defence against such antagonistic forces represented the need to periodically restore, confirm and ratify cultural values as well as conceptions about the nature of existence; in other words, to uphold a whole worldview.

Indeed, all these extraordinary feats performed by extraordinary characters adumbrate a profoundly human perspective. The motifs in these myths allude to the everlasting issues of the placement of humanity in the world and the preservation of the fragile relational balance with the environment humanity finds itself in. Dealing with these matters through myths and narratives allowed the ancient Chinese to carve out a niche for themselves in the world. This is true also for those tales that are not strictly linked to mythology, like the stories relating encounters with oddities, be they animal spirits, immortals, demons or ghosts. Coming in contact with the anomalous and the supernatural constituted a way of defining what it meant to be human and what was the role of humans in these interactions. Ultimately, the fact that fundamental beliefs and ideas were filtered through the medium of stories gives us a hint of the potency of narration. It is that same potency that we feel whenever we read these stories, which have the capacity to entertain us, entice us, and maybe to let us catch a glimpse of the contemplations weaved within them.

Davide Latini

Publisher's Note

Chinese myths, legends and fairy tales have been told and passed down over several thousand years, naturally evolving and mutating in the same way as those of any other culture. They will have originally been written down in one of many Chinese languages, and in fact up to around 220 AD this will have been in the form of Classical Chinese, a written form of Old Chinese, which then evolved into another traditional style known as Literary Chinese. All of these of course used a logographic (as opposed to a phonetic) script, and thus, when translating, in order for names and places to be rendered legible to Western readers they needed to be Romanized. There have been many systems for Romanizing Chinese throughout history, from Wade-Giles to Hanyu Pinyin, which tend to use accent marks with certain letters to clarify the pronunciation of individual sounds. However, the correct pronunciation of words can be hard to achieve even with some written explanation, as this needs to go hand in hand with proper appreciation of the mutual modifications of tone and rhythm, and so can only be properly acquired through oral instruction. Thus, due to this and the innate variation and inconsistency between the various sources used to compile this book, and the fact that some texts are direct translations from Chinese sources while others are inspired by traditional tales and written more simply, we have removed most of the accents in order for the reader to have an uncluttered and more accessible experience.

EPIC

CHINESE MYTHS & TALES

ANTHOLOGY OF CLASSIC TALES

Foreword by Davide Latini

FLAME TREE PUBLISHING

TALES

CHINESE MYTHOLOGY

Introduction

CHINA IS A VAST, SPRAWLING NATION, as geographically diverse as Europe and comparable to the European continent in size, containing at least one third of the world's population. It has always retained a mysterious and captivating appeal, and remains a country of rich contrasts and diverse cultural influences drawn from many different sources over the centuries.

Origins of Chinese Civilization

The origins of the Chinese civilization are to be found in the ancient cultures that arose along the fertile banks of the Yellow River in northern China where millet, hemp and mulberry trees were grown, and on the temperate flood plains of the Yangtze River in southern China that were conducive to fishing and the cultivation of rice and beans. These two societies which developed in Neolithic times were not the only ones to emerge in China but perhaps many of the enduring myths were first conceived there. In fact, archaeologists and social historians trace the origin of Chinese civilization back to the twelfth century BC, which is roughly the same date that Greek civilization emerged. Some of the earliest objects uncovered from excavated sites support the existence of a race of simple agriculturalists, known as the Shang, occupying the basin of the Yellow River in the north of the country at about this time.

Again, like their Greek counterparts, the Chinese evolved quickly into a sophisticated and efficient people, so that by the fourth century BC, they were able to boast a relatively civilized, structured society.

Unlike other European nations, China was not conquered by foreign invaders, with the result that she remained largely isolated from the West, and was able to preserve her own unique culture and traditions. That is not to say, however, that China remained immune to outside influences or that she was unduly possessive of her own traditions. More often than not, those invaders who landed on Chinese shores were surprised to encounter a society more developed than their own, and instead of wishing to subjugate it, ended up appropriating the country's values and practices. China, for her part, took what she considered worthwhile from foreign cultures and modified and assimilated it into her own. In this way, a mutually beneficial exchange was enacted.

The most significant external impact on the development of Chinese society was not made by would-be conquerors, however, but by tradesmen travelling the Rome-China Silk Road which was in commercial use by about 100 BC. At this time, India had cultivated an equally advanced society and the trade route allowed the two civilizations to meet without hostility. This encounter brought Buddhism to China, which of any other alien influence, had perhaps the most dramatic, long-term effect on her culture and literary heritage.

Origins of Chinese Myths

Chinese myths are as ancient as the culture itself: thousands of years in age and as varied as the people who contributed to the development of Chinese society. By the time they were put down in writing, many of them were already fragmentary and their significance half forgotten.

In common with many other nations, both Western and Eastern, the earliest mythology of the Chinese was in the oral tradition. Myths were very rare before 800 BC when fragments of tales with an astrological theme began to gain popularity. Subsequent Chinese myths and legends fall into several distinct groups. Though writing was developed by the Shang Dynasty (1520–1030 BC) in North China and further refined by the later Zhou Dynasty (1030–771 BC), myths were never used by the Chinese as the basis for great literary works, unlike in Indian or Mediterranean cultures. There are only enigmatic allusions to them in a few philosophical works, and by the time any serious attempt was made to record the myths, it is clear that many writers no longer believed in them or even understood them in full.

For many centuries after the introduction of writing, the Chinese took surprisingly little interest in their heritage of myths. The first work that includes any myths, and then only in passing, is the *Zhou Dynasty Classic of Poetry*, dating from around the sixth century BC. Two later works are far more important compilations of myths, the *Classic of Mountains and Seas* (third century BC) with its numerous accounts of over 200 mythical characters, and a chapter in the *Songs of Zhu* (fourth century BC) which records the sacred history of the Zhu polity in central China. Mention should be made of a few works written with philosophical intentions, the *Daoist Zhuangzi* text from 340 BC and the *Confucian Classic of History*, which was composed around the same time but restricts itself to myths concerning the origins of government and kingship. Apart from what can be gleaned from the tantalizing information given by these works, it was not until the compilation of the great medieval Imperial encyclopedias that any serious attempts were made to record the wealth of Chinese myths but by then many must have been lost forever.

Early Myths and Legends

The myths presented in the first two chapters of this book are all based on ancient tales arising from a highly fertile mythical period, up to and including the overthrow of the Yin dynasty and the establishment of the Zhou dynasty in 1122 BC. The later chapters offer a selection of popular fables spanning a number of later eras. It should be noted, however, that the period of antiquity in which these legends and fables are set is no indication of when they were actually first transcribed. The earliest myths, as we know them today, for example, the Creation Myths, have to be recognized as the reconstructions of a later, post-Confucian culture. These early tales, collected in different ancient books, such as the great historical annals, give only the most frugal biographical account of characters and events. In time, these tales were embellished with more detail, appearing in works like the Taoist *Shanghaijing (The Classic of Mountains and Seas)*, where a deeper sense of mystery and fantasy is woven around an existing historical record.

There are numerous Creation Myths, but several of these are worthy of note, each perhaps originating with one of the many different ethnic groups within ancient China. One of the best known concerns Nu Wa, a strange reptilian goddess who came to earth after it had been separated from the heavens. Some myths say that she created all things, including living beings, by going through seventy transformations. Others relate that although the natural world existed at that time, there were no humans in it. Feeling lonely, she saw a reflection of herself and took some mud and made a small copy of herself. When it came to life, she was delighted and began to create many thousands more, who populated the world while she remained as their teacher and protector.

Another well-known creation myth concerns Pan Gu (Coiled Antiquity), who was viewed as a primal deity or semi-divine human being. He was born from a primordial egg and when the egg split, the hard, opaque parts sank to become the earth while the soft, transparent parts became the heavens. Like Atlas, the Titan from Greek mythology, Pan Gu stood up and held the heaven and earth apart until they solidified in their present state. Exhausted by his labour, Pan Gu lay down and died. Each part of his body then became something in the natural world: his breath the wind and clouds; his eyes the sun and moon; his hair the stars; his bones and teeth the rocks and minerals; and so on. The very insects crawling on his dead body became human beings.

Other myths tell of the origin of the universe out of chaos, such as that of Hundun (Dense Chaos), who produced the world after he died after a misguided act of kindness, in which some fellow gods tried to carve him a face in return for his hospitality. The interplay of impersonal forces, such as the cosmic forces of the passive, dark, heavy feminine Yin and the active, sunny, light and masculine Yang, are also believed to have given rise to various elements in creation associated with their respective qualities.

Religious Schools of Thought

The imaginative minds of the ancient Chinese were crowded with Gods, giants, fairies, mortal heroes and devils, all of which ultimately appeared in their literature. Before Buddhism, Chinese religious practices were similar to those of the ancient Greeks, incorporating a huge number of deities who represented every aspect of nature, and a whole system of beliefs which attempted to explain the complexities of the universe in simple, human terms. The most important school of thought dominating China for thousands of years, was Confucianism, which devoted itself principally to the regulation of human relationships with a view to creating a practical social structure which would enable people to live in greater harmony together. Confucius favoured a more rational approach to life than that which he saw around him and discouraged the belief in the supernatural.

Co-existing with this methodical outlook, however, was the school of thought known as Taoism, seeking out the essential laws of nature which govern our lives, and in the age of Lao Tzu, the reputed founder of the Taoist religion, fresh myths began to appear. The period of the Warring States, 500 to 100 BC, again brought new impetus and greater emotional depth to mythological creation.

This era was followed by the advent of Buddhism which introduced to China many tales adapted from Indian mythology. To combat this foreign influence, Taoists invented newer characters and legends, mixing fact and fiction to a degree where the worlds of myth and reality become indistinguishable.

Broadly speaking, the diverse influences of Confucianism, Taoism and Buddhism resulted in a literature which was firmly rooted in the concept that everything on earth was in some way subject to divine authority. Order and peace exist on earth when Heaven's authority is acknowledged, but when it is ignored, natural calamities, such as floods and drought, are set to occur. According to the Taoist view, the supreme power of Heaven is administered by celestial government officials. Compared to the other splendours of creation, the mountains and streams, the forests and flowers, man's importance is diminished. Never before, in any other culture or early literature, was the emphasis on nature and humanity's communion with it, so crucial. Man's good fortune depended on his ability to behave in accordance with the dictates of Heaven. From ancient times onwards, the highest ambition he could aspire to was to determine the natural law of things and to behave in sympathy with it.

The Gods of the Cosmos

Unlike the mythologies of Mesopotamia, the Mediterranean and elsewhere, there is no structured pantheon of Chinese gods: literally hundreds are mentioned by name with brief myths associated with them in texts like the *Classic of Mountains and Seas*. Moreover, unlike other cultures, there are very few goddesses, perhaps reflecting the privileged status accorded to men in orthodox Chinese society.

The sun, moon and other heavenly bodies were of great significance to the ancient Chinese and their descendants and there are thus many gods associated with them. One of the best-known cycles of myths associated with the sun concerns the divine archer, Yi – originally a stellar god. Two goddesses are associated with the moon: Chang Xi (Constant Breath) and Chang E (Constant Sublime). Chang Xi gave birth to 12 moons, one for each month, while she dwelt in the wilderness of the west. It is said that she cared for her progeny by bathing them each night after their journey across the sky. Chang E, on the other hand, was the wife of the celestial archer Yi. Tales of these gods are found in the fourth and fifth chapters of this book, along with those of many others associated with the sun, moon and stars.

Gender in Chinese Myths

Many scholars believe that the earliest human societies worldwide were matriarchal in organization, but with the advent of the Bronze and Iron Ages, if not earlier, a shift seems to have occurred in many cultures to a patriarchal system that down-graded the female status. There are a few goddesses mentioned in Chinese mythology that hint at the former importance of women in society, such as Nu Wa, Chang Xi and Chang E, but the later male writers who compiled collections of myths seem to have done their best to undervalue the significance of the female in tune with the orthodox Confucian views of society. Nevertheless, apart from those mentioned above, other goddesses were important in ancient times as founders of early dynasties. Jian Di (Bamboo-slip Maiden) is mentioned as the progenitor of the first person of the Shang Dynasty, while Jiang the Originator was said to have been the mother of the first of the Zhou people. Like Hariti and other goddesses in India, disease and disaster is sometimes attributed to a female source in Chinese myth in the form of the Queen Mother of the West, a fierce and cruel being with tangled hair, tiger's fangs and a panther's tail, who was accompanied by other ferocious felines.

Catastrophe Myths

It is inevitable that a vast country like China should repeatedly witness natural disaster – droughts in the north and floods in the south. As with many other mythologies throughout the world, the Chinese have a range of catastrophe myths that tell of these events, perhaps distant memories of particularly devastating occasions when human survival itself may have seemed in doubt.

Four important flood myths, sometimes interlinked, have been preserved in early Chinese mythology, perhaps concerning different floods in various parts of the country or else the same event recorded by different people. One brief account relates how the world was saved from a combination of overwhelming floods and raging fires by the goddess Nu Wa who after restoring the sky then cuts the legs off a giant turtle and places them at the four corners of the earth to prop up the sky.

A second story tells of an ugly, misshapen god, Gong Gong, sometimes seen as the water god. Dissatisfied with his lesser status in the natural order of things, he challenged the fire god, the benevolent and wise ruler of the universe, and churned up the waters of the earth so that they crashed against the bulwarks of the sky. This resulted in catastrophic floods throughout the world. In some versions of this myth, this was the flood that Nu Wa averted.

A third myth speaks of a time when there was a world-threatening deluge. In order to deal with the situation, the gods nominated Gun (Giant Fish) to control the water. Two assistants were appointed to help him in this task: a divine eagle which knew the secrets of the sky and a divine turtle which knew the secrets of the waters, but their help is insufficient. Gun has to steal a magical 'breathing-earth' (a special type of earth of divine origin that had vitality) from the supreme god to control the flood waters and repair the world. Gun is punished for his theft and condemned to die on a mountain, but once dead his body does not rot and his son, Yu, is born from it.

Another important myth is known from two variants, involving the semi-divine Yu (Reptile Footprint), the son of Gun. In one version, Yu – unlike his father – was allowed to use the 'breathing earth' to repair the world and quell the floods; another version relates how Yu was commanded to deal with a devastating flood that had left everybody throughout China homeless by digging drainage channels.

Myths which deal with droughts are perhaps linked to the North China environment. One myth relates that when a drought afflicted the Shang lands for seven years, one of the mythical Shang kings, Tang, volunteered himself instead of the human sacrifices his people wanted to offer to the gods. Just as he was about to be burnt alive, a great downpour of rain fell in response to his selflessness.

Cultural Gods and Heroes

In contrast to many other mythologies, Chinese mythology is quite rich in accounts of beings who introduced cultural innovations into the world. These beings are often ambivalent in nature, either being semi-divine humans or gods. This ambivalence between the divine and the mortal realms was to become characteristic of later Chinese concepts of sages and emperors. Whether they were deified humans or gods demoted to human status, the mythical ancestors of various dynasties and tribes in China are said to have played a key role in introducing cultural innovations into the world.

A series of ten divine or semi-divine kings are associated with the earliest phase of the Zhou people, according to their accounts. The first of these was Fu Xi, sometimes associated with the goddess Nu Wa, who appears in a number of myths but who is particularly associated with the invention of writing. According to this myth, Fu Xi was the ruler of the universe and observed the markings and patterns found on various creatures. Based on his observations, he devised the Eight Trigrams that form the basis of the divinatory manual, the *Yi-jing* (this is also known as *I Ching*, and means Book of Changes). He is credited with the invention of music and also, after watching spiders at work, made fishing nets for humans. His successor, Shen Nung, was the farmer god who invented the plough and taught humans the art of agriculture. He also discovered the medicinal qualities of plants by pounding them with his whip and evaluating them by their smell and taste.

A later divine king was the famous Yellow Emperor, Huang Ti, who had over twenty sons, each of whom went on to sire important families of the Zhou dynasty. To him goes the credit for many innovations, such as the invention of the fire drill, by means of which he was able to clear forests and drive away wild animals using fire. Though he sometimes was viewed as a warrior god he was generally seen as peace-loving and had an ancient connection with healing; the Yellow Emperor's *Classic of Medicine*, which still forms the basis of traditional Chinese medical treatment, was attributed to him. One of Huang Ti's successors was Di Ku, who was married to the goddess Jiang Yuan. She became pregnant after accidentally treading on a footprint and gave birth to Hou-Ji. Thinking the child was unlucky, she tried on three occasions to rid herself of him by having him exposed to the elements, but each time he was saved. When the child grew up he made agricultural tools for the people and imparted the knowledge of crop cultivation, thereby guaranteeing the Chinese people a constant supply of food.

Hou-Ji was followed by the celebrated Yao, who was to be adopted in later times by the Confucians as the archetypal model of the sage – intelligent, accomplished, courteous and reverent. It was during his reign that the world was devastated by the catastrophic series of floods which required the intervention of Gun, as already mentioned. Yao wanted to appoint his chief minister as his successor but the latter refused so Yao turned his attention to Shun (Hibiscus), the low-class son of Gu Sou (Blind Man). Shun had come to the attention of Yao because Gu Sou was an obstinate reprobate who tried to kill Shun on three occasions. Shun had miraculously escaped each time. Through his filial piety, a virtue always esteemed by the Chinese, Shun eventually reforms his father's behaviour. After having put Shun through various tests, Yao retired and passed the throne to Shun. Shun, in his turn, was eventually replaced by Yu, the son of Gun.

The Chinese have always been fascinated by divination and in ancient times several techniques were of central importance to the rulers of the early dynasties. The Shang people made use of turtle shells and the shoulder blades of sheep and oxen in their divination. The question being put to the gods was written on the bone and heat was then applied with a heated rod to form cracks. It was from the pattern of these cracks that the will of the gods and the outcome of the question were known. The tens of thousands of these inscribed pieces of bone and shell which have been found date from the middle of the second millennium BC, providing the earliest examples of Chinese writing. Apart from these scratched questions, little else has survived from that period and scholars believe that writing was restricted to a handful of imperial diviners. An entirely different form of divination is associated with the agrarian Zhou dynasty, the use of the *Book of Changes (Yi-jing)* based on the sixty-four combinations that may be derived from the basic set of eight trigrams – patterns formed from three solid and broken lines. Though the Shang method of divination fell into disuse with the Shang people's demise, the Yi-jing is still widely consulted for divinatory purposes by many people.

The Chinese mythological tradition has furnished us with an extensive catalogue of ancient tales, several thousand in number. This volume is intended to provide an enjoyable and entertaining introduction to the most popular of those myths and fables and is in no way a comprehensive study of its subject. Nonetheless, it is hoped that the stories included will encourage the reader to explore further the fascinating world of Chinese mythology.

The Creation Myths

Introduction

THE EARLIEST CHINESE MYTHS, believed to have evolved in the primitive society of what is now northern China, are very old indeed, some of them dating back to the eighth century bc. They were passed on by word of mouth, by a simple people attempting to explain the origins of the cosmos and other astronomical phenomena beyond their comprehension.

The story of Pan Gu, although generally considered one of China's earliest legends, is actually from a much later period. Some scholars of Chinese mythology suggest that this myth was imported from Indo-China shortly before the advent of Buddhism in the first century BC. Other scholars attribute the tale specifically to the fourth century Taoist philosopher Ko Hung, author of the *Shen Hsien Chuan (Biographies of the Gods).*

But whatever his precise origins, the tale of how Pan Gu fashioned the universe is now very firmly established in Chinese folklore and a great number of Chinese people still trace their ancestry back to this particular god and his successor, the goddess Nu Wa. Ancient Chinese tales which centre on these two characters are commonly known as 'Creation Myths'.

Nu Wa and her consort, Fu Xi, were created to embellish the mythological notion of the origin of things. Again, the concept of Nu Wa is a very ancient one, first mentioned by Lieh Tzu in the fifth century BC. Nu Wa and Fu Xi are the great gentle protectors of humanity, while the God of Water, Gong Gong, is depicted as the destroyer of the earth. In these stories an interesting tension is introduced between the opposing forces of creativity and destruction.

Pan Gu and the Creation of the Universe

AT THE VERY BEGINNING of time, when only darkness and chaos existed and the heavens and the earth had not yet been properly divided up, the universe resembled the shape of a large egg. And at the centre of this egg, the first living creature one day came into being. After many thousands of years, when he had gathered sufficient strength and energy and had grown to the size of a giant, the creature, who gave himself the name of Pan Gu, awoke fully refreshed from his long rest and stood upright within his shell. He began to yawn very loudly and to stretch his enormous limbs, and as he did so, the walls of the egg were cracked open and separated into two even portions. The lighter, more fragile, part of the egg floated delicately upwards to form the white silken sheet of the sky, while the heavier, more substantial part, dropped downwards to form the earth's crusty surface.

Now when Pan Gu observed this, he was happy and proud to have created some light in place of the darkness and chaos out of which he had emerged. But at the same time, he began to fear that the skies and the earth might fuse once more, and he stood and scratched his huge head, pondering a solution to the problem. And after he had thought things through for quite a while, he decided that the only way to keep the two elements at a safe distance from each other was to place his own great bulk between them. So he took up his position, heaving and pushing upwards against the sky with his hands and pressing downwards into the earth with all the weight of his massive feet until a reasonable gap had been formed.

For the next eighteen thousand years, Pan Gu continued to push the earth and the sky apart, growing taller and taller every day until the gap measured some thirty thousand miles. And when this distance between them had been established, the sky grew firm and solid and the earth became securely fixed far beneath it. Pan Gu then looked around him and seeing that there was no longer any danger of darkness returning to the universe, he felt at last that he could lay down and rest, for his bones ached and he had grown old and frail over the years. Breathing a heavy sigh, he fell into an exhausted sleep from which he never awoke. But as he lay dying, the various parts of his vast body were miraculously transformed to create the world as we mortals know it today.

Pan Gu's head became the mountain ranges; his blood became the rivers and streams; the hairs on his head were changed into colourful and fragrant blossoms and his flesh was restored to become the trees and soil. His left eye was transformed into the sun and his right eye became the moon; his breath was revived in the winds and the clouds and his voice resounded anew as thunder and lightning. Even his sweat and tears were put to good use and were transformed into delicate droplets of rain and sweet-smelling morning dew.

And when people later came to inhabit the earth, they worshipped Pan Gu as a great creator and displayed the utmost respect for all the natural elements, believing them to be his sacred body spread out like a carpet before them beneath the blue arch of the heavens.

Nu Wa Peoples the Earth

WHEN THE UNIVERSE first emerged from chaos, mankind had not yet been created and the firmament and all the territories beneath it were inhabited by Gods or giants who had sprung forth from the body of Pan Gu. At that time, one particularly powerful Goddess appeared on earth in the company of her chosen heavenly companion. The Goddess's name was Nu Wa and her companion's name was Fu Xi. Together these deities set out to bring an even greater sense of order and regulation to the world.

And of all the other Gods residing in the heavens, Nu Wa was the strangest and most unusual in appearance, for the upper half of her body was shaped like a human being, while the lower part took the form of a snake. Nu Wa also possessed the unique ability to change her shape up to seventy times a day and she frequently appeared on earth in several different guises.

Although Nu Wa took great pleasure in the wondrous beauty of the new-born world she occupied, deep within she felt it to be a little too silent and she yearned to create something that would fill the empty stillness. One day shortly afterwards, as she walked along the banks of the great Yellow River, she began to imagine spending time in the company of other beings not unlike herself, animated creatures who might talk and laugh with her and with whom she could share her thoughts and feelings. Sitting herself down on the earth, she allowed her fingers to explore its sandy texture and without quite realizing it, began to mould the surrounding clay into tiny figures. But instead of giving them the lower bodies of reptiles, the Goddess furnished her creatures with little legs so they would stand upright. Pleased with the result, she placed the first of them beside her on the earth and was most surprised and overjoyed to see it suddenly come to life, dancing around her and laughing excitedly. She placed another beside it and again the same thing happened. Nu Wa was delighted with herself and with her own bare hands she continued to make more and more of her little people as she rested by the river bank.

But as the day wore on, the Goddess grew tired and it was then that she decided to make use of her supernatural powers to complete the task she had begun. So breaking off a length of wood from a nearby mulberry tree, she dredged it through the water until it was coated in mud. Then she shook the branch furiously until several hundred drops of mud landed on the ground and as each drop landed it was instantly transformed into a human being. Then Nu Wa pronounced that the beings she had shaped with her own hands should live to become the rich and fortunate people of the world, while those created out of the drops of mud should lead ordinary and humble lives. And realizing that her little creatures should themselves be masters of their own survival, Nu Wa separated them into sons and daughters and declared that they should marry and multiply until the whole wide world had become their home and they were free once and for all from the threat of extinction.

The War Between the Gods of Fire and Water

FOR A GREAT MANY YEARS after Nu Wa had created human beings, the earth remained a peaceful and joyous place and it was not until the final years of the Goddess's reign that mankind first encountered pain and suffering. For Nu Wa was extremely protective of the race she had created and considered it her supreme duty to shelter it from all harm and evil. People depended on Nu Wa for her guardianship and she, in turn, enabled them to live in comfort and security.

One day, however, two of the Gods who dwelt in the heavens, known as Gong Gong and Zhurong, became entangled in a fierce and bitter dispute. No one knew precisely why the two Gods began to shout and threaten one another, but before long they were resolved to do battle against each other and to remain fighting to the bitter end. Gong Gong, who was the God of Water, was well known as a violent and ambitious character and his bright red wavy hair perfectly mirrored his fiery and riotous spirit. Zhurong, the God of Fire, was equally belligerent when provoked and his great height and bulk rendered him no less terrifying in appearance.

Several days of fierce fighting ensued between the two of them during which the skies buckled and shifted under the strain of the combat. An end to this savage battle seemed to be nowhere in sight, as each God thrust and lunged with increasing fury and rage, determined to prove himself more powerful than the other. But on the fourth day, Gong Gong began to weary and Zhurong gained the upper hand, felling his opponent to the ground and causing him to tumble right out of the heavens.

Crashing to the earth with a loud bang, Gong Gong soon became acutely aware of the shame and disgrace of his defeat and decided that he would never again have the courage to face any of his fellow Gods. He was now resolved to end his own life and looked around him for some means by which he might perform this task honourably and successfully. And seeing a large mountain range in the distance rising in the shape of a giant pillar to the skies, Gong Gong ran towards it with all the speed he could muster and rammed his head violently against its base.

As soon as he had done this, a terrifying noise erupted from within the mountain, and gazing upwards, Gong Gong saw that a great wedge of rock had broken away from the peak, leaving behind a large gaping hole in the sky. Without the support of the mountain, the sky began to collapse and plummet towards the earth's surface, causing great crevasses to appear on impact. Many of these crevasses released intensely hot flames which instantly engulfed the earth's vegetation, while others spouted streams of filthy water which merged to form a great ocean. And as the flood and destruction spread throughout the entire world, Nu Wa's people no longer knew where to turn to for help. Thousands of them drowned, while others wandered the earth in terror and fear, their homes consumed by the raging flames and their crops destroyed by the swift-flowing water.

Nu Wa witnessed all of this in great distress and could not bear to see the race she had created suffer such appalling misery and deprivation. Though she was now old and looking forward to her time of rest, she decided that she must quickly take action to save her people, and it seemed that the only way for her to do this was to repair the heavens as soon as she possibly could with her very own hands.

Nu Wa Repairs the Sky

NU WA RAPIDLY set about gathering the materials she needed to mend the great hole in the sky. One of the first places she visited in her search was the river Yangtze where she stooped down and gathered up as many pebbles as she could hold in both arms. These were carefully chosen in a variety of colours and carried to a forge in the heavens where they were melted down into a thick, gravel-like paste. Once she had returned to earth, Nu Wa began to repair the damage, anxiously filling the gaping hole with the paste and smoothing whatever remained of it into the surrounding cracks in the firmament. Then she hurried once more to the river bank and, collecting together the tallest reeds, she built a large, smouldering fire and burnt the reeds until they formed a huge mound of ashes. With these ashes Nu Wa sealed the crevasses of the earth, so that water no longer gushed out from beneath its surface and the swollen rivers gradually began to subside.

After she had done this, Nu Wa surveyed her work, yet she was still not convinced that she had done enough to prevent the heavens collapsing again in the future. So she went out and captured one of the giant immortal tortoises which were known to swim among the jagged rocks at the deepest point of the ocean and brought it ashore to slaughter it. And when she had killed the creature, she chopped off its four sturdy legs and stood them upright at the four points of the compass as extra support for the heavens. Only now was the Goddess satisfied and she began to gather round her some of her frightened people in an attempt to reassure them that order had finally been restored.

To help them forget the terrible experiences they had been put through, Nu Wa made a flute for them out of thirteen sticks of bamboo and with it she began to play the sweetest, most soothing music. All who heard it grew calmer almost at once and the earth slowly began to emerge from the chaos and destruction to which it had been subjected. From that day forth, Nu Wa's people honoured her by calling her 'Goddess of music' and many among them took great pride in learning the instrument she had introduced them to.

But even though the heavens had been repaired, the earth was never quite the same again. Gong Gong's damage to the mountain had caused the skies to tilt permanently towards the north-west so that the Pole Star, around which the heavens revolved, was dislodged from its position directly overhead. The sun and the moon were also tilted, this time in the direction of the west, leaving a great depression in the south-east. And not only that, but the peak of the mountain which had crashed to the earth had left a huge hollow where it landed in the east into which the rivers and streams of the world flowed incessantly.

Nu Wa had done all she could to salvage the earth and shortly afterwards, she died. Her body was transformed into a thousand fairies who watched over the human race on her behalf. Her people believe that the reason China's rivers flow eastwards was because of Gong Gong's foolish collision with the mountain, a belief that is still shared by their ancestors today.

The Tradition of the Tea-Plant

"Good is the continence of the eye; Good is the continence of the ear; Good is the continence of the nostrils; Good is the continence of the tongue; Good is the continence of the body; Good is the continence of speech; Good is all...."

Again the Vulture of Temptation soared to the highest heaven of his contemplation, bringing his soul down, down, reeling and fluttering, back to the World of Illusion. Again the memory made dizzy his thought, like the perfume of some venomous flower. Yet he had seen the bayadere for an instant only, when passing through Kasi upon his way to China – to the vast empire of souls that thirsted after the refreshment of Buddha's law, as sun-parched fields thirst for the life-giving rain. When she called him, and dropped her little gift into his mendicant's bowl, he had indeed lifted his fan before his face, yet not quickly enough; and the penally of that fault had followed him a thousand leagues – pursued after him even into the strange land to which he had come to hear the words of the Universal Teacher. Accursed beauty! surely framed by the Tempter of tempters, by Mara himself, for the perdition of the just! Wisely had Bhagavat warned his disciples: "O ye Cramanas, women are not to be looked upon! And if ye chance to meet women, ye must not suffer your eyes to dwell upon them; but, maintaining holy reserve, speak not to them at all. Then fail not to whisper unto your own hearts, 'Lo, we are Cramanas, whose duty it is to remain uncontaminated by the corruptions of this world, even as the Lotos, which suffereth no vileness to cling unto its leaves, though it blossom amid the refuse of the wayside ditch.'" Then also came to his memory, but with a new and terrible meaning, the words of the Twentieth-and-Third of the Admonitions:

"Of all attachments unto objects of desire, the strongest indeed is the attachment to form. Happily, this passion is unique; for were there any other like unto it, then to enter the Perfect Way were impossible."

How, indeed, thus haunted by the illusion of form, was he to fulfil the vow that he had made to pass a night and a day in perfect and unbroken meditation? Already the night was beginning! Assuredly, for sickness of the soul, for fever of the spirit, there was no physic save prayer. The sunset was swiftly fading out. He strove to pray:

"O the Jewel in the Lotos!

"Even as the tortoise withdraweth its extremities into its shell, let me, O Blessed One, withdraw my senses wholly into meditation!

"O the Jewel in the Lotos!

"For even as rain penetrateth the broken roof of a dwelling long uninhabited, so may passion enter the soul uninhabited by meditation.

"O the Jewel in the Lotos!

"Even as still water that hath deposited all its slime, so let my soul, O Tathâgata, be made pure! Give me strong power to rise above the world, O Master, even as the wild bird rises from its marsh to follow the pathway of the Sun!

"O the Jewel in the Lotos!

"By day shineth the sun, by night shineth the moon; shineth also the warrior in harness of war; shineth likewise in meditations the Cramana. But the Buddha at all times, by night or by day, shineth ever the same, illuminating the world.

"O the Jewel in the Lotos!

"Let me cease, O thou Perfectly Awakened, to remain as an Ape in the World-forest, forever ascending and descending in search of the fruits of folly. Swift as the twining of serpents, vast as the growth of lianas in a forest, are the all-encircling growths of the Plant of Desire.

"O the Jewel in the Lotos!"

Vain his prayer, alas! vain also his invocation! The mystic meaning of the holy text – the sense of the Lotos, the sense of the Jewel – had evaporated from the words, and their monotonous utterance now served only to lend more dangerous definition to the memory that tempted and tortured him. O the jewel in her ear! What lotos-bud more dainty than the folded flower of flesh, with its dripping of diamond-fire! Again he saw it, and the curve of the cheek beyond, luscious to look upon as beautiful brown fruit. How true the Two Hundred and Eighty-Fourth verse of the Admonitions! – "So long as a man shall not have torn from his heart even the smallest rootlet of that liana of desire which draweth his thought toward women, even so long shall his soul remain fettered." And there came to his mind also the Three Hundred and Forty-Fifth verse of the same blessed book, regarding fetters:

"In bonds of rope, wise teachers have said, there is no strength; nor in fetters of wood, nor yet in fetters of iron. Much stronger than any of these is the fetter of concern for the jewelled earrings of women."

"Omniscient Gotama!" he cried, "all-seeing Tathagata! How multiform the Consolation of Thy Word! how marvellous Thy understanding of the human heart! Was this also one of Thy temptations? – one of the myriad illusions marshalled before Thee by Mara in that night when the earth rocked as a chariot, and the sacred trembling passed from sun to sun, from system to system, from universe to universe, from eternity to eternity?"

O the jewel in her ear! The vision would not go! Nay, each time it hovered before his thought it seemed to take a warmer life, a fonder look, a fairer form; to develop with his weakness; to gain force from his enervation. He saw the eyes, large, limpid, soft, and black as a deer's; the pearls in the dark hair, and the pearls in the pink mouth; the lips curling to a kiss, a flower-kiss; and a fragrance seemed to float to his senses, sweet, strange, soporific – a perfume of youth, an odor of woman. Rising to his feet, with strong resolve he pronounced again the sacred invocation; and he recited the holy words of the Chapter of Impermanency:

"Gazing upon the heavens and upon the earth ye must say, These are not permanent. Gazing upon the mountains and the rivers, ye must say, These are not permanent. Gazing upon the forms and upon the faces of exterior beings, and beholding their growth and their development, ye must say, These are not permanent."

And nevertheless! how sweet illusion! The illusion of the great sun; the illusion of the shadow-casting hills; the illusion of waters, formless and multiform; the illusion of – Nay, nay I what impious fancy! Accursed girl! yet, yet! why should he curse her? Had she ever done aught to merit the malediction of an ascetic? Never, never! Only her form, the memory of her, the beautiful phantom of her, the accursed phantom of her! What was she? An illusion creating illusions, a mockery, a dream, a shadow, a vanity, a vexation of spirit! The fault, the sin, was in himself, in his rebellious thought, in his untamed memory. Though mobile as water, intangible as vapor, Thought, nevertheless, may be tamed by the Will, may be harnessed to the chariot of Wisdom – must be! – that happiness be found. And he recited the blessed verses of the "Book of the Way of the Law":

"All forms are only temporary." When this great truth is fully comprehended by any one, then is he delivered from all pain. This is the Way of Purification.

"All forms are subject unto pain." When this great truth is fully comprehended by any one, then is he delivered from all pain. This is the Way of Purification.

"All forms are without substantial reality." When this great truth is fully comprehended by any one, then is he delivered from all pain. This is the way of ...

Her form, too, unsubstantial, unreal, an illusion only, though comeliest of illusions? She had given him alms! Was the merit of the giver illusive also, illusive like the grace of the supple fingers that gave? Assuredly there were mysteries in the Abhidharma impenetrable, incomprehensible!... It was a golden coin, stamped with the symbol of an elephant – not more of an illusion, indeed, than the gifts of Kings to the Buddha! Gold upon her bosom also, less fine than the gold of her skin. Naked between the silken sash and the narrow breast-corslet, her young waist curved glossy and pliant as a bow. Richer the silver in her voice than in the hollow pagals that made a moonlight about her ankles! But her smile! – the little teeth like flower-stamens in the perfumed blossom of her mouth!

O weakness! O shame! How had the strong Charioteer of Resolve thus lost his control over the wild team of fancy! Was this languor of the Will a signal of coming peril, the peril of slumber? So strangely vivid those fancies were, so brightly definite, as about to take visible form, to move with factitious life, to play some unholy drama upon the stage of dreams! "O Thou Fully Awakened!" he cried aloud, "help now thy humble disciple to obtain the blessed wakefulness of perfect contemplation! let him find force to fulfil his vow! suffer not Mara to prevail against him!" And he recited the eternal verses of the Chapter of Wakefulness:

"Completely and eternally awake are the disciples of Gotama! Unceasingly, by day and night, their thoughts are fixed upon the Law.
"Completely and eternally awake are the disciples of Gotama! Unceasingly, by day and night, their thoughts are fixed upon the Community.
"Completely and eternally awake are the disciples of Gotama! Unceasingly, by day and night, their thoughts are fixed upon the Body.
"Completely and eternally awake are the disciples of Gotama! Unceasingly, by day and night, their minds know the sweetness of perfect peace.
"Completely and eternally awake are the disciples of Gotama! Unceasingly, by day and night, their minds enjoy the deep peace of meditation."

There came a murmur to his ears; a murmuring of many voices, smothering the utterances of his own, like a tumult of waters. The stars went out before his sight; the heavens darkened their infinities: all things became viewless, became blackness; and the great murmur deepened, like the murmur of a rising tide; and the earth seemed to sink from beneath him. His feet no longer touched the ground; a sense of supernatural buoyancy pervaded every fibre of his body: he felt himself floating in obscurity; then sinking softly, slowly, like a feather dropped from the pinnacle of a temple. Was this death? Nay, for all suddenly, as transported by the Sixth Supernatural Power, he stood again in light – a perfumed, sleepy light, vapory, beautiful – that bathed the marvellous streets of some Indian city. Now the nature of the murmur became manifest to him; for he moved with a mighty throng, a people of pilgrims, a nation of worshippers. But these were not of his faith; they bore upon their foreheads the smeared symbols of obscene gods! Still, he could not escape from their midst; the mile-broad human torrent bore him irresistibly with it, as a leaf is swept by the waters of the Ganges. Rajahs were there with their trains, and princes riding upon elephants, and Brahmins robed in their vestments, and swarms of voluptuous dancing-girls, moving to chant of kabit and damâri. But whither, whither? Out of the city into the sun they passed, between avenues of banyan, down colonnades of palm. But whither, whither?

Blue-distant, a mountain of carven stone appeared before them – the Temple, lifting to heaven its wilderness of chiselled pinnacles, flinging to the sky the golden spray of its decoration. Higher it grew with approach, the blue tones changed to gray, the outlines sharpened in the light. Then each detail became visible: the elephants of the pedestals standing upon tortoises of rock; the great grim faces of the capitals; the serpents and monsters writhing among the friezes; the many-headed gods of basalt in their galleries of fretted niches, tier above tier; the pictured foulnesses, the painted lusts, the divinities of abomination. And, yawning in the sloping precipice of sculpture, beneath a frenzied swarming of gods and Gopia – a beetling pyramid of limbs and bodies interlocked – the Gate, cavernous and shadowy as the mouth of Siva, devoured the living multitude.

The eddy of the throng whirled him with it to the vastness of the interior. None seemed to note his yellow robe, none even to observe his presence. Giant aisles intercrossed their heights above him; myriads of mighty pillars, fantastically carven, filed away to invisibility behind the yellow illumination of torch-fires. Strange images, weirdly sensuous, loomed up through haze of incense. Colossal figures, that at a distance assumed the form of elephants or garuda-birds, changed aspect when approached, and revealed as the secret of their design an interplaiting of the bodies of women; while one divinity rode all the monstrous allegories – one divinity or demon, eternally the same in the repetition of the sculptor, universally visible as though self-multiplied. The huge pillars themselves were symbols, figures, carnalities; the orgiastic spirit of that worship lived and writhed in the contorted bronze of the lamps, the twisted gold of the cups, the chiselled marble of the tanks....

How far had he proceeded? He knew not; the journey among those countless columns, past those armies of petrified gods, down lanes of flickering lights, seemed longer than the voyage of a caravan, longer than his pilgrimage to China! But suddenly, inexplicably, there came a silence as of cemeteries; the living ocean seemed to have ebbed away from about him, to have been engulfed within abysses of subterranean architecture! He found himself alone in some strange crypt before a basin, shell-shaped and shallow, bearing in its centre a rounded column of less than human height, whose smooth and spherical summit was wreathed with flowers. Lamps similarly formed, and fed with oil of palm, hung above it. There was no other graven image, no visible divinity. Flowers of countless varieties lay heaped upon the pavement; they covered its surface like a carpet, thick, soft; they exhaled their ghosts beneath his feet. The perfume seemed to penetrate his brain – a perfume sensuous, intoxicating, unholy; an unconquerable languor mastered his will, and he sank to rest upon the floral offerings.

The sound of a tread, light as a whisper, approached through the heavy stillness, with a drowsy tinkling of pagals, a tintinnabulation of anklets. All suddenly he felt glide about his neck the tepid smoothness of a woman's arm. She, she! his Illusion, his Temptation; but how transformed, transfigured! – preternatural in her loveliness, incomprehensible in her charm! Delicate as a jasmine-petal the cheek that touched his own; deep as night, sweet as summer, the eyes that watched him. "Heart's-thief," her flower-lips whispered, "heart's-thief, how have I sought for thee! How have I found thee! Sweets I bring thee, my beloved; lips and bosom; fruit and blossom. Hast thirst? Drink from the well of mine eyes! Wouldst sacrifice? I am thine altar! Wouldst pray? I am thy God!"

Their lips touched; her kiss seemed to change the cells of his blood to flame. For a moment Illusion triumphed; Mara prevailed!... With a shock of resolve the dreamer awoke in the night – under the stars of the Chinese sky.

Only a mockery of sleep! But the vow had been violated, the sacred purpose unfulfilled! Humiliated, penitent, but resolved, the ascetic drew from his girdle a keen knife, and with unfaltering hands severed his eyelids from his eyes, and flung them from him. "O Thou Perfectly Awakened!" he prayed, "thy disciple hath not been overcome save through the feebleness of the body; and his vow hath been renewed. Here shall he linger, without food or drink, until the moment of its fulfilment." And having assumed the hieratic posture – seated himself with his lower limbs folded beneath him, and the palms of his hands upward, the right upon the left, the left resting upon the sole of his upturned foot – he resumed his meditation.

* * *

Dawn blushed; day brightened. The sun shortened all the shadows of the land, and lengthened them again, and sank at last upon his funeral pyre of crimson-burning cloud. Night came and glittered and passed. But Mara had tempted in vain. This time the vow had been fulfilled, the holy purpose accomplished.

And again the sun arose to fill the World with laughter of light; flowers opened their hearts to him; birds sang their morning hymn of fire worship; the deep forest trembled with delight; and far upon the plain, the eaves of many-storied temples and the peaked caps of the city-towers caught aureate glory. Strong in the holiness of his accomplished vow, the Indian pilgrim arose in the morning glow. He started for amazement as he lifted his hands to his eyes. What! was everything a dream? Impossible! Yet now his eyes felt no pain; neither were they lidless; not even so much as one of their lashes was lacking. What marvel had been wrought? In vain he looked for the severed lids that he had flung upon the ground; they had mysteriously vanished. But lo! there where he had cast them two wondrous shrubs were growing, with dainty leaflets eyelid-shaped, and snowy buds just opening to the East.

Then, by virtue of the supernatural power acquired in that mighty meditation, it was given the holy missionary to know the secret of that newly created plant – the subtle virtue of its leaves. And he named it, in the language of the nation to whom he brought the Lotos of the Good Law, "TE"; and he spake to it, saying:

"Blessed be thou, sweet plant, beneficent, life-giving, formed by the spirit of virtuous resolve! Lo! the fame of thee shall yet spread unto the ends of the earth; and the perfume of thy life be borne unto the uttermost parts by all the winds of heaven! Verily, for all time to come men who drink of thy sap shall find such refreshment that weariness may not overcome them nor languor seize upon them; – neither shall they know the confusion of drowsiness, nor any desire for slumber in the hour of duty or of prayer. Blessed be thou!"

* * *

And still, as a mist of incense, as a smoke of universal sacrifice, perpetually ascends to heaven from all the lands of earth the pleasant vapor of TE, created for the refreshment of mankind by the power of a holy vow, the virtue of a pious atonement.

Tales of the Five Emperors

Introduction

AFTER NU WA HAD peopled the earth, several of the heavenly gods began to take a greater interest in the world below them. The five most powerful of these gods descended to earth in due course and each was assigned various territories of the new world.

The Yellow Emperor (Huang Ti), the most important of the five sovereigns, is a part-mythical, part-historical figure who is reputed to have founded the Chinese nation around 4000 bc. During his 'historical' reign he is said to have developed a number of important astronomical instruments and mathematical theories, as well as introducing the first calendar to his people and a system for telling the time. He is always depicted as a figure who takes particular pride in humanity and one who consistently reveals a great love of nature and of peaceful existence.

Yet in order to achieve peace, the Yellow Emperor is forced, at one time or another, to battle against the other four gods. These include the Fiery or Red Emperor (Chih Ti), who is the Yellow Emperor's half-brother by the same mother, the White Emperor (Shao Hao), the Black Emperor (Zhuan Xu), and the Green Emperor (Tai Hou). The Yellow Emperor is victorious over all of these gods and he divides up the earth into four equal regions. The Red Emperor is placed in charge of the south, the White Emperor is in charge of the west, the Black Emperor rules the north, while the Green Emperor rules the east.

The Yellow Emperor's Earthly Kingdom

AFTER HE HAD GROWN for twenty-five months in his mother's womb, the infant God Huang Ti was safely delivered at last, bringing great joy to his celestial father, the God of Thunder. As soon as he appeared, Huang Ti had the gift of speech, and in each of his four faces the determination and energy of a born leader shone brightly for all to see. By the time the young God had grown to manhood, he alone among other deities had befriended every known spirit-bird, and a great many phoenixes travelled from afar simply to nest in his garden, or to perch themselves on the palace roof and terraces to serenade him with the sweetest of melodies.

When the five most powerful Gods decided to explore the earth, it was already in the minds of each that one among them should be assigned absolute and supreme control over the others. But the God of Fire, who was later known as the Red Emperor, was reluctant to share power with anyone, especially with his half-brother Huang Ti who seemed to be everyone else's natural choice. So when the time of the election came, the Red Emperor launched a vicious attack on the Yellow Emperor, instigating one of the fiercest battles the earth had ever witnessed. It was fought on the field of Banquan where the allies of Huang Ti, including wolves, leopards, bears and huge birds of prey, gathered together and rushed at the Red Emperor's troops until every last one of them lay slain.

Once this great battle was over and the Yellow Emperor had been acknowledged by all as supreme ruler, he set about building for himself a divine palace at the top of Mount Kunlun, which reached almost to the clouds. The magnificent royal residence, consisting of no less than five cities and twelve towers surrounded by solid walls of priceless jade, was flanked by nine fire-mountains which burnt day and night casting their warm red glow on the palace walls.

The front entrance faced eastwards and was guarded by the Kaiming, the loyal protector of the Gods, who had nine heads with human faces and the body of a giant panther. The exquisite gardens of the royal palace, where the Emperor's precious pearl trees and jade trees blossomed all year round, were protected by the three-headed God Li Zhu who sat underneath the branches never once allowing his three heads to sleep at the same time. This God was also guardian of the dan trees which bore five different exotic fruits once every five years, to be eaten exclusively by the Emperor himself.

From the largest garden, which was known as the Hanging Garden, a smooth path wound its way upwards to the heavens so that many of the most prestigious Gods and the rarest divine beasts chose to make the Emperor's wondrous kingdom their home, content that they had discovered earthly pleasures equal to their heavenly experience. And it was here, in this garden, that the supreme ruler particularly loved to sit each evening, taking time to admire his newly discovered world just as the setting sun bathed it in a gentle golden light. As he looked below him, he saw the reviving spring of Yaoshui flowing jubilantly into the crystal-clear waters of the Yaochi Lake. To the west he saw the great Emerald trees swaying delicately in the breeze, shedding a carpet of jewels on the earth beneath them. When he looked northwards his eyes were fixed upon the towering outline of Mount Zhupi where eagles and hawks soared merrily before their rest. The Yellow Emperor saw that all of this was good and knew that he would spend many happy years taking care of the earth.

The Fiery Emperor and the First Grain

THE FIERY EMPEROR, who ruled as God of the south, had the head of an ox and the body of a human being. He was also known as the God of the Sun and although in the past he had led his people in a disastrous rebellion against the Yellow Emperor, he was still much loved by his subjects and they held him in the highest esteem. The Fiery Emperor taught mankind how to control and make constructive use of fire through the art of forging, purifying and welding metals so that eventually his subjects were able to use it for cooking, lighting and for making domestic tools and hunting weapons. In those early times, the forests were filled with venomous reptiles and savage wild animals and the Fiery Emperor ordered his people to set fire to the undergrowth to drive away these dangerous and harmful creatures. He was also the first to teach them how to plant grain, together with a whole variety of medicinal herbs that could cure any ailment which might trouble them.

It was said that when the Fiery Emperor first appeared on earth he very wisely observed that there was not enough fruit on the trees, or vegetables in the ground to satisfy the appetite of his people. Knowing that mankind was forced to eat the flesh of other living creatures, the Emperor became unhappy and quickly set about instructing his subjects in the use of the plough and other tools of the land until they learned how to cultivate the soil around them. And when he saw that the soil was ready, the Emperor called for his people to pray aloud for a new and abundant food to rise up before them out of the ground.

As the people raised their faces to the heavens, a red bird carrying nine seedlings in its beak suddenly appeared through the clouds. As it swooped to the ground it began to scatter grains on to the upturned soil. After it had done this, the Fiery Emperor commanded the sun to warm the earth and from the seeds emerged five young cereal plants which began to multiply rapidly until a vast area of land was covered with luscious vegetation.

The fruits of these plants were harvested at the close of day to fill eight hundred wicker baskets. Then the Fiery Emperor showed his people how to set up market stalls and explained to them how to keep time according to the sun in order that they might barter among themselves in the future for whatever food they lacked. But even after having provided all of this, the Fiery Emperor was still not satisfied with his work. And so, taking his divine whip, he began to lash a number of the plants, which caused them to be endowed with healing properties, and he set them aside to be used by mankind whenever disease struck. The people, overjoyed that they were so well cared for, decided that the Fiery Emperor should henceforth go by the name of the Divine Peasant and they built in his honour a giant cauldron for boiling herbs and carried it to the summit of the Shenfu Mountains where it stands to this day.

The Bird and the Sea

THE FIERY EMPEROR had three daughters whom he loved and cared for very much, but it was his youngest daughter who had always occupied a special place in his heart. She was named Nu Wa, after the great Goddess who created mankind, and like her sisters she possessed a cheerful disposition and a powerful spirit of adventure.

One day Nu Wa went out in search of some amusement and seeing a little boat moored in the tiny harbour at a short distance from the palace gates, she went towards it, untied it and jumped aboard, allowing it to carry her out over the waves of the Eastern Sea. The young girl smiled happily to see the sun sparkle on the water and the graceful gulls circling overhead, but became so preoccupied in her joy that she failed to notice she had drifted out of sight, further and further towards the centre of the ocean. Suddenly, the wind picked up speed and the waves began to crash violently against the side of the boat. There was nothing Nu Wa could do to prevent herself being tossed overboard into the foaming spray and even though she struggled with every ounce of strength to save herself, she eventually lost the fight and was sadly drowned.

Just at that time, a small jingwei bird happened to approach the place where Nu Wa had fallen. And at that moment, her spirit, resentful of the fact that life had been cut short so unfairly, rose up in anger and entered the creature. Nu Wa now lived on in the form of a bird with a speckled head, white beak and red claws, and all day long she circled the skies angrily, vowing to take revenge on the sea which had deprived her of her life and left her father grieving for his beloved child.

It was not long before she conceived of a plan to fill up the sea with anything she could find, hoping that in time there would no longer be any room left for people to drown in it. So every day the little bird flew back and forth from the land out over the Eastern ocean until she grew weary with exhaustion. In her beak she carried pebbles, twigs, feathers and leaves which she dropped into the water below. But this was no easy task, and the sea laughed and jeered at the sight of the tiny bird labouring so strenuously:

"How do you imagine you will ever complete your work," hissed the waves mockingly. "Never in a million years will you be able to fill up the sea with twigs and stones, so why not amuse yourself somewhere else."

But the little jingwei would not be deterred: "If it takes me a hundred times a million years, I will not stop what I am doing. I will carry on filling you up until the end of the world, if necessary."

And although the sea continued to laugh even more loudly over the years, the jingwei never ceased to drop into the ocean whatever she managed to collect. Later, after she had found herself a mate and they had produced children together, a flock of jingwei birds circled above the water, helping to fill up the sea. And they continue to do so to this day in China, where their persistent courage and strength have won the admiration and applause of each and every Chinese citizen.

Tai Hou, the Green Emperor

EVEN IN THE WORLD OF DEITIES, the birth of the Green Emperor, God of the East, was judged quite an extraordinary affair. The story handed down among the other Gods was that the Emperor's mother, a beautiful young mortal named Hua Xu, lived originally in the ancient kingdom of Huaxushi, a place so remote and inaccessible, that many people had begun to question its very existence. Those who believed in this land, however, knew that its inhabitants possessed unique powers and gifts and often they were referred to as partial-Gods. They could move underwater as freely as they did above the earth, for example, and it was said that they could pass through fire without suffering any injury to the flesh. They walked through the air as easily as they walked on the ground and could see through the clouds as clearly as they could through glass.

One day the young girl Hua Xu was out walking across the northern plain of Leize, a name which means 'marshes of thunder', when she happened upon a gigantic footprint in the earth. She had never before encountered an imprint of its size and stooped to the ground to inspect it more closely. Imagining that a strange and wonderful being must have passed through the marshes, she grew very excited and found that she could not suppress the urge to compare the size of the footprint with her own. Slowly and carefully, Hua Xu placed her tiny foot in the enormous hollow and as she did so a strange vibration travelled up from the ground through the entire length of her body.

Shortly afterwards, the young girl found that she was pregnant and she was more than happy to be carrying a child, for there was no doubt in her mind that the Gods had intervened on that strange day to bring about her condition. After nine months Hua Xu gave birth to a son who bore the face of a man and the body of a snake. The elders of the people of Huanxushi advised that he should be named Tai Hou, a name fit for a supreme being they were convinced had been fathered by the God of Thunder.

Shao Hao, Son of the Morning Star

THE EMPEROR OF THE WEST, Shao Hao, was also said to have come into being as the result of a strange and wonderful union. His mother, who was considered to be one of the most beautiful females in the firmament, worked as a weaver-girl in the Palace of Heaven. And it was always the case that after she had sat weaving the whole day, she preferred nothing better than to cruise through the Milky Way in a raft of silver that had been specially built for her use. On these occasions, she would pause for rest underneath the old mulberry tree which reached more than ten thousand feet into the skies. The branches of this tree were covered in huge clusters of shining berries, hidden from the naked eye by delicately spiced, scarlet-coloured leaves. It was a well-known fact that whoever ate the fruit of this tree would immediately receive the gift of immortality and many had journeyed to the centre of the Milky Way with this purpose in mind.

At that time, a very handsome young star-God named Morning Star, who was also known as Prince of the White Emperor, regularly took it upon himself to watch over these berries. Often he came and sat under the Mulberry Tree where he played his stringed instrument and sang the most enchanting songs. One evening, however, Morning Star was surprised to find his usual place occupied by a strange and beautiful maiden. Timidly, he approached her, but there was hardly any need for such caution, for as the maiden raised her head, their eyes met and the two fell in love almost instantly.

The maiden invited the young God aboard her raft and together they floated off into the night sky, along the silver river of the Milky Way down towards the earth and the waves of the sea. And as Morning Star played his magical music, the maiden carved a turtledove from a precious piece of white jade and set it on the top of the mast where it stood as a joint symbol of their mutual love and their deep desire to be guided by each other through the various storms of life. The lovers drifted together over the earth's ocean as their immortal music echoed through the air. And from this joyful union a son was born whom the happy couple named Shao Hao, and it was the child's great destiny to become White Emperor of the western realms and to rule wisely over his people.

Zhuan Xu, Emperor of the North

THE YELLOW EMPEROR and his wife once had a son called Chang Yi who turned out to be a very disappointing and disobedient child. One day, Chang Yi committed a crime so terrible, even his own father could not bring himself to discuss it, and immediately banished his son to a remote corner of the world where he hoped he would never again set eyes on him. After a time, Chang Yi had a son of his own, a very foolish-looking creature it was said, with a long, thin neck, round, beady eyes, and a pig's snout where his mouth should have been. By some form of miracle, Chang Yi's son also managed to find a mate and eventually married a strong and wholesome woman named Ah Nu. From this marriage, the Yellow Emperor's great grandson, Zhuan Xu, was produced, a God who managed to redeem the family name and who, after a careful trial period, was appointed ruler of the earth's northern territories.

Following the Yellow Emperor's great battle against Chiyou, he began to look around for a successor, for he had grown extremely weary of the rebellion and discontent he had experienced during his long reign. His great-grandson had proven himself a faithful servant and everyone now agreed that Zhuan Xu should be the next God to ascend the divine throne.

Chiyou had brought widespread destruction and suffering to the earth which led Zhuan Xu to believe that the alliance between mortals and immortals must be dissolved to prevent an even greater disaster in the future. And so he set about the task of separating the people from the Gods and turned his attention first of all to the giant ladder which ran between heaven and earth. For in those days, it was not unusual for people to ascend the ladder to consult with the Gods when they were in trouble, and the Gods, in turn, often made regular visits to the earth's surface. Chiyou had made such a visit when he secretly plotted with the Maio tribe in the south to put an end to the Yellow Emperor's sovereignty. The bloodshed which followed would never again be tolerated by Zhaun Xu and he enlisted the aid of two Gods in his destruction of the ladder.

With their help, the world became an orderly place once more. The God Chong was assigned control of the heavens and his task was to ensure that immortals no longer descended to earth. The God Li, together with his son Yi, were put in charge of the earth. Yi had the face of a human but his feet grew out of his head to form a fan-shaped bridge to the heavens behind which the sun and the stars set each evening. Zhaun Xu supervised the work of the other Gods and took it upon himself to re-introduce discipline to a race which had become untamed. It was said that he banished all cruel instruments of war and taught mankind respect for his own kind once again. He forbade women to stand in the path of men and severely punished a sister and brother who lived together as husband and wife.

By the time Zhuan Xu died, the world was a much more peaceful place and on the day he passed away it was said that the elements rose up in a great lament. Jagged lightning lit up the skies and thunder clouds collided furiously with each other. The north wind howled fiercely and the underground streams burst to the surface in torrents of grief. Legend has it that Zhuan Xu was swept away by the water and his upper-half transformed into a fish so that he might remain on the earth in another form, ever watchful of mankind's progress.

Chiyou Challenges the Yellow Emperor

CHIYOU WAS A FEROCIOUS and ambitious God who had begun life as an aide and companion to the young deity, Huang Ti, in the days before he had risen to become Yellow Emperor on earth. During this time, the two had become firm friends and close confidants, but as soon as Huang Ti ascended the throne, this favourable relationship came to an abrupt end. For Chiyou could not bear to see his friend achieve the success he secretly longed for, and it became his obsession to find a way to reverse this situation and take the throne for himself.

Chiyou was the eldest of seventy-two brothers, all of them huge and powerful in stature. They each spoke the language of humans, but their bodies below the neckline were those of animals with cloven feet. Their heads were made of iron and their hideous copper faces contained four repulsive eyeballs protruding from mottled foreheads. These brothers ate all kinds of food, but they particularly liked to eat stones and chunks of metal, and their special skill was the manufacture of battle weapons, including sharp lances, spears, axes, shields and strong bows.

Now Chiyou had become convinced that he could easily overthrow the Yellow Emperor and so, gathering together his brothers and other minor Gods who were discontented with the Emperor's reign, he made an arrogant and boisterous descent to earth. First of all, however, he decided to establish a reputation for himself as a great warrior and immediately led a surprise attack on the ageing Fiery Emperor, knowing that he would seize power without a great deal of effort. The Fiery Emperor, who had witnessed his fair share of war, had no desire to lead his people into a climate of further suffering and torment, and soon fled from his home, leaving the way open for Chiyou to take control of the south. Shortly after this event, one of the largest barbarian tribes known as the Miao, who had been severely punished for their misdemeanours under the Fiery Emperor's authority, decided to take their revenge against the ruling monarchy and enthusiastically joined ranks of Chiyou and his brothers.

It was not long before the Yellow Emperor received word of the disturbances in the south, and hearing that it was his old friend who led the armies to rebellion, he at first tried to reason with him. But Chiyou refused to listen and insisted on war as the only path forward. The Yellow Emperor found that he had little choice but to lead his great army of Gods, ghosts, bears, leopards and tigers to the chosen battlefield of Zhuolu and here the terrible war began in earnest.

It was in Chiyou's nature to stop at nothing to secure victory against his opponent. Every subtle trick and sudden manoeuvre, no matter how underhanded, met with his approval and he had no hesitation in using his magic powers against the enemy. When he observed that his army had not made the progress he desired, he grew impatient and conjured up a thick fog which surrounded the Yellow Emperor and his men. The dense blanket of cloud swirled around them, completely obscuring their vision and they began to stab blindly with their weapons at the thin air. Then suddenly, the wild animals who made up a large part of the Emperor's forces started to panic and to flee in every direction straight into the arms of the enemy. The Yellow Emperor looked on desperately and, realizing that he was helpless to dispel the fog himself, he turned to his ministers and pleaded for help.

Fortunately, a little God named Feng Hou was among the Emperor's men, a deity renowned for his intelligence and inventiveness. And true to his reputation, Feng Hou began to puzzle a solution to the problem and within minutes he was able to offer a suggestion.

"I cannot banish from my mind an image of the Plough which appears in our skies at night-time and always points in the same direction," he informed the Emperor. "Now if only I could design something similar, we would be able to pinpoint our direction no matter which way we were forced to move through the mist."

And so Feng Hou set to work at once, using his magic powers to assist him, and within a very short time he had constructed a device, rather like a compass, which continued to point southwards, regardless of its position. And with this incredible new instrument, the Yellow Emperor finally managed to make his way out of the fog, through to the clear skies once more.

But the battle was far from over, and the Emperor began to plan his revenge for the humiliation Chiyou had brought upon his men. At once, he summoned another of his Gods before him, a dragon-shaped deity named Ying Long, who possessed the ability to make rain at will, and commanded him to produce a great flood that would overwhelm the enemy. But Chiyou had already anticipated that the Yellow Emperor would not gladly suffer his defeat, and before the dragon had even begun to prepare himself for the task ahead, Chiyou had called upon the Master of Wind and the Master of Rain who together brought heavy rains and howling winds upon the Yellow Emperor's army, leaving them close to defeat once more.

As a last desperate measure, the Emperor introduced one of his own daughters into the battlefield. Ba was not a beautiful Goddess, but she had the power to generate tremendous heat in her body, enough heat to dry up the rain which now threatened to overcome her father's legions. So Ba stood among them and before long, the rains had evaporated from the earth and the sun began to shine brilliantly through the clouds. Its bright rays dazzled Chiyou's men which enabled Ying Long to charge forward unnoticed, and as he did so, hundreds of enemy bodies were crushed beneath his giant feet, lying scattered behind him on the plains.

And seeing this result, the Yellow Emperor managed to recover some of his dignity and pride, but his army lay exhausted and the morale of his men was very low. He was worried also that they would not be able to withstand another onslaught, for although Chiyou had retreated, the Emperor was certain he would soon return with reinforcements. He knew that he must quickly find something to lift the spirits of his men, and after much thought it suddenly came to him.

What he needed most was to fill their ears with the sound of a victory drum, a drum which would resound with more power and volume than anyone had ever before imagined possible.

"With such a drum, I would bring fear to the enemy and hope to my own men," the Emperor thought to himself. "Two of my finest warriors must go out on my behalf and fetch a very special skin needed to produce this instrument."

And having decided that the great beast from the Liubo Mountain possessed the only skin which would suffice, the Yellow Emperor dispatched two of his messengers to kill the strange creature. It resembled an ox without horns, he told them, and they would find it floating on the waves of the Eastern Sea. Sometimes the beast was known to open its mouth to spit out great tongues of lightning, and its roar, it was said, was worse than that of any wild cat of the forests.

But in spite of the creature's terrifying description, the Emperor's men found the courage to capture and skin it without coming to any great harm. After they had done so, they carried the hide back to the battlefield where it was stretched over an enormous bamboo frame to create an impressively large drum. At first, the Yellow Emperor was satisfied with the result, but when his men began to beat upon it with their hands, he decided that the sound was not loud enough to please him. So again, he sent two of his finest warriors on an expedition, and this time they went in search of the God of Thunder, Lei Shen. They found the God sleeping peacefully and crept up on him to remove both his thigh bones as the Emperor had commanded them to do. With these thigh bones a suitable pair of drumsticks was made and handed over to the principal drummer who stood awaiting his signal to beat on the giant instrument.

At last, the drum was struck nine times, releasing a noise louder than the fiercest thunder into the air. Chiyou's men stood paralysed with terror and fear as all around them the earth began to quake and the mountains to tremble. But this was the opportunity the Yellow Emperor's men had waited for and they rushed forward with furious energy, killing as many of Chiyou's brothers and the Miao warriors as they could lay their hands on. And when the battlefield was stained with blood and the casualties were too heavy for Chiyou to bear much longer, he called for his remaining men to withdraw from the fighting.

Refusing to surrender to the Yellow Emperor, the defeated leader fled to the north of the country to seek the help of a group of giants who took particular delight in warfare. These giants were from a tribe known as the Kua Fu and with their help Chiyou revived the strength of his army and prepared himself for the next attack.

The Yellow Emperor Returns to the Heavens

CHIYOU HAD SPENT three days and three nights after his defeat at the battle of Zhuolu in the kingdom of the Kua Fu giants gathering rebel forces for his ongoing war against the Yellow Emperor. Both sides, it seemed, were now evenly matched once more and Chiyou relished the thought of a return to battle. But the Yellow Emperor saw that a renewal of conflict would only result in more loss of life and he was deeply disturbed and saddened by the prospect.

On the day before the second great battle was due to commence, the Emperor was sitting deep in thought in his favourite garden at the palace of Mount Kunlun when a strange Goddess suddenly appeared before him. She told him she was the Goddess of the Ninth Heaven and that she had been sent to help him in his plight.

"I fear for the lives of my men," the Yellow Emperor told her, "and I long for some new battle plan that will put an end to all this bloodshed."

So the Goddess sat down on the soft grass and began to reveal to him a number of new strategies conceived by the highest, most powerful Gods of the heavens. And having reassured the Emperor that his trouble would soon be at an end, she presented him with a shining new sword furnished of red copper that had been mined in the sacred Kunwu Mountains.

"Treat this weapon with respect," she told him as she disappeared back into the clouds, "and its magic powers will never fail you."

The next morning, the Emperor returned to the battlefield armed with his new strategies and the sacred weapon the Goddess had given him. And in battle after battle, he managed to overcome Chiyou's forces until at last they were all defeated and Chiyou himself was captured alive. The evil God was dragged in manacles and chains before the Yellow Emperor, but he showed no sign of remorse for the anguish he had caused and the destruction he had brought to the earth. The Yellow Emperor shook his head sadly, knowing that he now had little option but to order his prisoner's execution. The death sentence was duly announced, but Chiyou struggled so fiercely that the shackles around his ankles and wrists were stained crimson with blood.

When it was certain that he lay dead, Chiyou's manacles were cast into the wilderness where it is said they were transformed into a forest of maple trees whose leaves never failed to turn bright red each year, stained with the blood and anger of the fallen God.

And now that relative peace had been restored to the world once more, the Yellow Emperor spent his remaining time on earth re-building the environment around him. He taught the people how to construct houses for themselves where they could shelter from the rains; he brought them the gift of music and he also introduced them to the skill of writing. Mankind wanted to believe that the Yellow Emperor would always be with them on earth, but soon a divine dragon appeared in the skies, beckoning him back to the heavens. The time had arrived for the Yellow Emperor to answer this call and to acknowledge an end to the long reign of the Gods on earth. And so in the company of his fifty officials and all the other willing immortals whose stay had also run its course, he climbed on to the dragon's back and was carried up into the sky back to the heavens to take up his position again as crowned head of the celestial realms.

Giants in Early Chinese Legend

Introduction

IN CHINESE MYTHOLOGY, the earthly home, or 'Place of the Giant People', was said to have been in the region of the east sea, close to the Dayan Mountains. On top of Bogu Mountain lived the descendants of the dragons, giants who grew in the womb for thirty-six years before emerging fully matured and usually covered in long black hair. They could be up to fifty feet in height, with footprints six feet in length. Like their winged ancestors, they could fly before walking, and some lived as long as eighteen thousand years.

Xing Tian, the Headless Giant

ONCE THERE WAS A GIANT named Xing Tian who was full of ambition and great plans for his future. At one time, he had been an official of the Fiery Emperor, but when Chiyou had conquered the region, he had quickly switched loyalties and offered his services to the new, corrupt usurper of the south. It greatly disturbed the giant to hear reports of the bloody deaths of Chiyou's men at the hands of the Yellow Emperor and he wanted nothing less than to meet the Emperor face to face and challenge him to single combat until one of them lay dead.

So Xing Tian took up his axe and his shield and set off for the divine palace at the top of Mount Kunlun, seething with anger and rage as he thundered along. But the Yellow Emperor had received word of the giant's approach and seized his most precious sword ready to meet him head on. For days the two battled furiously, lashing out savagely with their weapons as they fought into the clouds and down the side of the mountain. They fought along all the great mountain ranges of northern China until eventually they reached the place known as the Long Sheep range in the north-east.

And it was here that the Yellow Emperor caught the giant off-guard and, raising his sword high into the air just at the level of the giant's shoulder, he slashed sideways with his blade until he had sliced off Xing Tian's head. A terrifying scream escaped the gaping, bloody mouth of the giant as his head began to topple forward, crashing with a loud thud to the ground and rolling down the hill like a massive boulder.

The giant stood frozen in absolute horror, and then he began feeling desperately with his hands around the hole above his shoulders where his head ought to have been. Soon panic had taken control of him and he thrashed about wildly with his weapon, carving up trees and tossing huge rocks into the air until the valleys began to shake and the sky began to cloud over with dust from the debris.

Seeing the giant's great fury, the Yellow Emperor grew fearful that Xing Tian might actually find his head and put it back on his shoulders again. So he swiftly drew his sword and sliced open the mountain underneath which the head had finally come to rest. Then he kicked the head into the chasm and sealed up the gap once more.

For ten thousand years afterwards the giant roamed the mountainside searching for his head. But in all that time he never found what he was looking for although he remained defiant that he would one day face the Yellow Emperor again. Some people say that the giant grew to be very resourceful, and to help him in his long search he used his two breasts for eyes and his navel for a mouth.

Kua Fu Chases the Sun

THE UNDERWORLD of the north where the most ferocious giants had lived since the dawn of time was centred around a wild range of black mountains. And underneath the tallest of these mountains the giant Kua Fu, gatekeeper of the dark city, had built for himself a home. Kua Fu was an enormous creature with three eyeballs and a snake hanging from each ear, yet in spite of his intimidating appearance he was said to be a fairly good-natured giant, though not the most intelligent of his race.

Kua Fu took great pleasure in everything to do with the sun. He loved to feel its warm rays on his great body, and nothing delighted him more than to watch the golden orb rise from its bed in the east each morning. He was never too keen, however, to witness it disappear below the horizon in the evenings and longed for the day when the sun would not have to sleep at night.

And as he sat watching the sun descend in the sky one particular evening, Kua Fu began thinking to himself:

"Surely I can do something to rid the world of this depressing darkness. Perhaps I could follow the sun and find out where it hides itself at night. Or better still, I could use my great height to catch it just as it begins to slide towards the west and fix it firmly in the centre of the sky so that it never disappears again."

So the following morning, Kua Fu set off in pursuit of the sun, stepping over mountains and rivers with his very long legs, all the time reaching upwards, attempting to grab hold of the shining sphere above him. Before long, however, evening had approached, and the sun began to glow a warm red, bathing the giant in a soothing, relaxing heat. Puffing and panting with exhaustion, Kua Fu stretched his huge frame to its full length in a last great effort to seize his prize. But as he did so, he was overcome by an unbearable thirst, the like of which he had never experienced before. He raced at once to a nearby stream and drank its entire contents down in one mouthful. Still his thirst had not been quenched, so he proceeded to the Weishui River and again gulped down the water until the river ran dry. But now he was even more thirsty and he felt as if he had only swallowed a single drop.

He began to chase all over the earth, pausing at every stream and lake, seeking to drown the fiery heat that raged within his body. Nothing seemed to have any effect on him, though he had by now covered a distance of eight thousand miles, draining the waters from every possible source he encountered. There was, however, one place that he had not yet visited where surely he would find enough water to satisfy him. That place was the great lake in the province of Henan where it was said the clearest, purest water flowed from the mountain streams into the lake's great cavern.

The giant summoned all his remaining strength and plodded along heavily in the direction of this last water hole. But he had only travelled a short distance before he collapsed to the ground, weak with thirst and exhaustion. The last golden rays of the sun curved towards his outstretched body, softening the creases on his weary forehead, and melting away his suffering. Kua Fu's eyelids began to droop freely and a smile spread its way across his face as he fell into a deep, deep, eternal sleep.

At dawn on the following morning, the sun rose as usual in the east, but the sleeping figure of the giant was no longer anywhere to be seen. In its place a great mountain had risen up towards the sky. And on the western side of the mountain a thick grove of trees had sprung up overnight. These trees were laden with the ripest, most succulent peaches whose sweet juices had the power to quench the most raging thirst of any passer-by. Many believe that the giant's body formed this beautiful site and that is why it is still named Kua Fu Mountain in his honour.

Myths of the Yin Nation

Introduction

THE STORIES OF THIS CHAPTER centre on the adventures of some of the most popular heroes of the ancient Yin nation, from Dijun and Xihe, to Yi, the indomitable archer; from Yao, the wise and benevolent Emperor, to Yu, the saviour of the human race. The welfare of the people is the dominant concern of Yao's reign, and the struggle to maintain order on earth when it is threatened by the hasty intervention of angry gods, or the foolish behaviour of lesser deities, is a recurring theme in these tales.

As with the earlier stories, many of the figures presented here are reputed to be genuinely historical. More often than not, however, characters are endowed with superhuman strength and magical skills, typical of the Chinese mythological tradition of blending fact and fiction, myth and history. Yu, for example, who succeeds Yao to the throne after the brief reign of Emperor Shun (2205–2197 BC) is an outstanding legendary hero, who first appears in the shape of a giant dragon and controls the great floodwaters on earth. He is at the same time, however, the historical founder of the Xia Dynasty, a powerful leader of the Chinese nation, ultimately responsible for the division of China into nine provinces.

The Ten Suns of Dijun and Xihe

THE GOD OF THE EAST, Dijun, had married the Goddess of the Sun, Xihe, and they lived together on the far eastern side of the world just at the edge of the great Eastern Ocean. Shortly after their marriage, the Goddess gave birth to ten suns, each of them a fiery, energetic, golden globe, and she placed the children lovingly in the giant Fusang tree close to the sea where they could frolic and bathe whenever they became overheated.

Each morning before breakfast, the suns took it in turns to spring from the enormous tree into the ocean below in preparation for their mother's visit when one of them would be lifted into her chariot and driven across the sky to bring light and warmth to the world. Usually the two remained together all day until they had travelled as far as the western abyss known as the Yuyuan. Then, when her sun had grown weary and the light had begun to fade from his body, Xihe returned him to the Fusang tree where he slept the night peacefully with his nine brothers. On the following morning, the Goddess would collect another of her suns, sit him beside her in her chariot, and follow exactly the same route across the sky. In this way, the earth was evenly and regularly heated, crops grew tall and healthy, and the people rarely suffered from the cold.

But one night, the ten suns began to complain among themselves that they had not yet been allowed to spend an entire day playing together without at least one of them being absent. And realizing how unhappy this situation made them feel, they decided to rebel against their mother and to break free of the tedious routine she insisted they follow. So the next morning, before the Goddess had arrived, all ten of them leapt into the skies at once, dancing joyfully above the earth, intent on making the most of their forbidden freedom. They were more than pleased to see the great dazzling light they were able to generate as they shone together, and made a solemn vow that they would never again allow themselves to become separated during the daytime.

The ten suns had not once paused to consider the disastrous consequences of their rebellion on the world below. For with ten powerful beams directed at the earth, crops began to wilt, rivers began to dry up, food became scarce and people began to suffer burns and wretched hunger pangs. They prayed for rains to drive away the suns, but none appeared. They called upon the great sorceress Nu Chou to perform her acts of magic, but her spells had no effect. They hid beneath the great trees of the forests for shade, but these were stripped of leaves and offered little or no protection. And now great hungry beasts of prey and dreaded monsters emerged from the wilderness and began to devour the human beings they encountered, unable to satisfy their huge appetites any longer. The destruction spread to every corner of the earth and the people were utterly miserable and filled with despair. They turned to their Emperor for help, knowing he was at a loss to know what to do, but he was their only hope, and they prayed that he would soon be visited by the God of Wisdom.

Yi, the Archer, is Summoned

TIJUN AND XIHE were horrified to see the effect their unruly children were having upon the earth and pleaded with them to return to their home in the Fusang tree. But in spite of their entreaties, the ten suns continued on as before, adamant that they would not return to their former lifestyle. Emperor Yao now grew very impatient, and summoning Dijun to appear before him, he demanded that the God teach his suns to behave. Dijun heard the Emperor's plea but still he could not bring himself to raise a hand against the suns he loved so dearly. It was eventually settled between them, however, that one of Yao's officials in the heavens, known as Yi, should quickly descend to earth and do whatever he must to prevent any further catastrophe.

Yi was not a God of very impressive stature, but his fame as one of the most gifted archers in the heavens was widespread, for it was well known that he could shoot a sparrow down in full flight from a distance of fifty miles. Now Dijun went to meet with Yi to explain the problem his suns had created, and he handed the archer a new red bow and a quiver of white arrows and advised him what he must do.

"Try not to hurt my suns any more than you need to," he told Yi, "but take this bow and ensure that you bring them under control. See to it that the wicked beasts devouring mankind are also slain and that order and calm are restored once more to the earth."

Yi readily accepted this challenge and, taking with him his wife Chang E, he departed the Heavenly Palace and made his descent to the world below. Emperor Yao was overjoyed to see the couple approach and immediately organized a tour of the land for them, where Yi witnessed for himself the devastation brought about by Dijun's children, as he came face to face with half-burnt, starving people roaming aimlessly over the scorched, cracked earth.

And witnessing all of this terrible suffering, Yi grew more and more furious with the suns of Dijun and it slipped his mind entirely that he had promised to treat them leniently. "The time is now past for reasoning or persuasion," Yi thought to himself, and he strode to the highest mountain, tightened the string of his powerful bow and took aim with the first of his arrows. The weapon shot up into the sky and travelled straight through the centre of one of the suns, causing it to erupt into a thousand sparks as it split open and spun out of control to the ground, transforming itself on impact into a strange three-legged raven.

Now there were only nine suns left in the sky and Yi fitted the next arrow to his bow. One after another the arrows flew through the air, expertly hitting their targets, until the earth slowly began to cool down. But when the Emperor saw that there were only two suns left in the sky and that Yi had already taken aim, he wisely remembered that at least one sun should survive to brighten the earth and so he crept up behind the archer and stole the last of the white arrows from his quiver.

Having fulfilled his undertaking to rid Emperor Yao of the nine suns, Yi turned his attention to the task of hunting down the various hideous monsters threatening the earth. Gathering a fresh supply of arrows, he made his way southwards to fight the man-eating monster of the marsh with six feet and a human head, known as Zao Chi. And with the help of his divine bow, he quickly overcame the creature, piercing his huge heart with an arrow of steel. Travelling northwards, he tackled a great many other ferocious beasts, including the nine-headed monster, Jiu Ying, wading into a deep, black pool and throttling the fiend with his own bare hands. After that, he moved onwards to the Quingqiu marshes of the east where he came upon the terrible vulture Dafeng, a gigantic bird of unnatural strength with a wing span so enormous that whenever the bird took to the air, a great typhoon blew up around it. And on this occasion, Yi knew that his single remaining arrow would only wound the bird, so he tied a long black cord to the shaft of the arrow before taking aim. Then as the creature flew past, Yi shot him in the chest and even though the vulture pulled strongly on the cord as it attempted to make towards a place of safety, Yi dragged it to the ground, plunging his knife repeatedly into its breast until all life had gone from it.

All over the earth, people looked upon Yi as a great hero, the God who had single-handedly rescued them from destruction. Numerous banquets and ceremonial feasts were held in his honour, all of them attended by the Emperor himself, who could not do enough to thank Yi for his assistance. Emperor Yao invited Yi to make his home on earth, promising to build him the a very fine palace overlooking Jade Mountain, but Yi was anxious to return to the heavens in triumph where he felt he rightly belonged and where, in any event, Dijun eagerly awaited an account of his exploits.

Chang E's Betrayal

AFTER YI, the great archer, had returned to the heavens with his wife, he immediately went in search of the God Dijun to report on the success of his mission on earth. He had managed to save mankind from the evil destruction of the ten suns, as Dijun had requested him, and was still basking in the glory of this mammoth achievement. Yi fully expected a reception similar to the one he had been given on earth, but instead he found an angry and unforgiving God waiting to receive him. Dijun did not welcome the archer with open arms, but walked forward and spoke only a few harsh words.

"I feel no warmth or gratitude in my heart towards you," he said to Yi in the bitterest of voices, "you have murdered all but one of my suns, and now I cannot bear to have you in my sight. So I have decided that from this day forth, you and your wife will be banished to the earth to live among the mortals you appear to have enjoyed serving so well. Because of the foul deed you have committed, it is my judgment that you no longer merit the status of Gods and neither of you will ever be permitted to enter the Heavens again."

And although Yi argued against his sentence, Dijun would not listen to a single word of his plea. Slowly, the archer made his way homewards, shocked and saddened by the breach of friendship and weighted down by the certain knowledge that his wife would not react well to the news.

And as expected, when Chang E had been told that she and her husband had been exiled to the earth, she was absolutely furious. Much more so than Yi, she revelled in the pleasures and privileges the Gods alone enjoyed, and throughout their married life together, she had never attempted to hide the fact that she had little or no tolerance for the inferior company of mortals. Now she began to regret ever tying herself in matrimony to the archer, for she felt strongly that she was being unduly punished for his hot-headed behaviour. Surely her banishment was totally unjust! And why was it that she was being punished for her husband's foolish actions? These thoughts circled around her head as she reluctantly gathered up her things, and she promised herself that she would never cease to reproach Yi, or allow him a day's rest, until he had made amends for what he had done to her.

The couple's earthly home was as comfortable as Yi could make it and all day long he trudged through the forests in search of the luxuries his wife demanded -- the most tender deer-flesh, or the most exotic, sun-ripened berries. But often when he would return exhausted with these items, Chang E would fling them away, declaring that she had no appetite for unsophisticated mortal food. And then she would begin to bemoan their dreadful misfortune, over and over again, while Yi sat there gloomily, his head in his hands, wishing that he had never set eyes on the suns of Dijun.

One evening, when Chang E had been thinking particularly long and hard about her miserable existence on earth, she went and stood before her husband and announced that she had made firm plans for their future.

"'I have had more than enough of this wretched place," she told Yi, "and I have no intention of dying here like a mortal and descending to the Underworld afterwards. If you want to keep me, Yi, you must do what I ask of you and go to the west, to the Mountain of Kunlun. For I have heard that the Queen Mother of the West, who lives there, keeps a very special substance. People call it the elixir of immortality and it is said that whoever takes this potion will be granted eternal life."

Now Yi had also heard a report of this strange queen and her magic medicine, and noticing that some of the old sparkle danced in his wife's eyes as she spoke about it, he could not find it in his heart to refuse her this request even though he knew that the journey ahead would be a treacherous one. For the Queen Mother of the West lived close to the earthly palace of the Yellow Emperor, a region encircled by fire mountains and a deep moat filled with boiling, hissing water which no mortal had ever yet penetrated. The Queen herself may have had the human face of a woman, but her teeth, it was said, were those of a tiger and her hair was long and matted, covering her ugly, scaly body which ended in a leopard's tail.

It was fortunate for Yi that he still possessed some of his God-like powers, since these enabled him to pass through the scorching flames and to swim through the intense heat of the water without coming to any harm. And having reached the opening of the cave where the queen rested, he decided that the best way to approach her was to greet her openly and honestly and tell her his story from start to finish in the hope that she might help him.

To the archer's immense relief, the Queen Mother of the West listened to all he had to say with an open mind, and certainly the image he painted of his innocent wife forced to suffer equal hardship because of what he had done, invited a genuine heartfelt sympathy. The queen suddenly reached into a copper box close by and withdrew a small leather pouch which she handed to Yi.

"The magic medicine inside of this pouch is very precious indeed," she told him. "It has been collected from the immortal trees on Mount Kunlun which flower only every three thousand years and bear fruit only every six thousand years. If two people eat this amount, which is all I have to give you, they will both have eternal life in the world of men. But if only one person swallows it all, that person will have the complete immortality of the Gods. Now take the medicine away with you and guard it well, for its value is beyond all measure."

And so Yi returned to his home and to his anxious wife, feeling as if a great burden had been lifted from his shoulders. For the first time in many years, his wife appeared happy to see him and she kissed his cheek as he presented her with the pouch and began to relate the entire story of his adventure, including everything the queen had told him about the magic potion. Chang E agreed with her husband that they should prepare a great feast to celebrate the end to their mortal lives and she took it upon herself to guard the medicine while her husband went in search of something very special for them to eat.

But as soon as Yi had disappeared into the trees, Chang E began to stare at the little pouch and her thoughts travelled to the days when she lived among the Gods in Heaven, breathing in the scent of beautiful flowers or reclining in the warm sunshine listening to the soothing tones of immortal music drifting gently on the breeze. A deep resentment against her husband rose up within her as she indulged this daydream of a divine kingdom she considered her rightful home and she knew that she would never be content simply with eternal life on earth. She could not let go of what Yi had trustingly told her, that there was only enough elixir to make one of them fully immortal again, and now she allowed her selfish desire to overcome her. Without hesitating a moment longer, Chang E quickly opened up the pouch and swallowed the entire contents all at once.

The effect of the medicine was almost immediate and Chang E felt her body become lighter and lighter until her feet began to lift themselves off the ground as they had done in the past so many times before.

"How glorious it is to be a Goddess again," she thought to herself as she floated happily towards the flickering stars in the direction of the heavens. She rose higher and higher through the air until the earth below resembled a tiny egg and the skies around her were completely silent and still. But now a sudden fear told hold of the Goddess, for it began to dawn on her that she was entirely alone, cut off from her husband Yi and other earthly mortals, yet not safely arrived in the world of deities. And as she thought more about her return to the Heavens it occurred to her for the first time that she may not necessarily receive a warm welcome there.

"How can I confront these other Gods," she said to herself, "when they will certainly scorn me for taking all of the elixir myself and for abandoning my poor husband. Perhaps it is not such a good idea to return straight to Heaven."

Chang E gazed around her and saw that she had must make an unhappy choice, either to return to the unwelcoming, grey earth, or move onwards towards the cold, silvery moon. "It is probably quite lonely on the moon," she thought, "still, it seems the best place to go to for a short length of time until the Gods have forgotten my crime." And so, she floated off towards the moon, determined that she would move on from here before too long.

But the moon was far more desolate and dispiriting than she had imagined possible, a cold, hostile place, totally uninhabited, apart from one rabbit who sat forlornly under a cassia tree. Chang E could not bear it a moment longer, and having decided that even a host of angry Gods presented a more desirable alternative, she attempted to rise again into the air. But she soon discovered that her powers had deserted her and that a strange metamorphosis was taking place in her body. Her back stiffened suddenly and then curved forwards. Her breasts separated and flattened, causing her stomach to bulge outwards. Small swellings began to appear all over her skin which lost its translucence and changed to a dull, murky green. Her mouth stretched wider and wider to the edge of her face where her ears once rested and her eyes grew larger and larger until they formed two ugly black rounds.

Once a beautiful and faithful wife, the greedy and disloyal Chang E had finally met with her punishment and was transformed into a giant toad. And in this form she remained until the end of time, doomed to keep a lonely watch over the earth below while yearning, every passing moment, to be with the husband she had so falsely deceived.

Hou-Ji, the Ice-Child

JIANG YUAN was one of four wives of Di Ku, God of the East. For many years the couple had tried to have a child together but they had not been successful and their marriage was not a very happy one as a result. One day, however, Jiang Yaun was walking along by the riverbank when she spotted a trail of large footprints in the earth. She was intrigued by them and began to follow where they led, placing her own tiny feet in the hollows of the ground. She was unaware that by doing this, she would conceive a child, and not long afterwards she gave birth to a son, an event which under normal circumstances would have brought her great joy.

But Jiang Yuan was filled with shame to see the tiny bundle wriggling in her arms, knowing that she had absolutely no knowledge of its father. And realizing that she would have great difficulty explaining the infant's birth to her husband, Jiang Yaun made up her mind to dispose of the child before she became a victim of scandalous gossip and derision. So she took the baby to a deserted country lane and left him to perish in the cold among the sheep and cattle. But then a strange thing happened. For instead of rejecting the baby and trampling him to death, the sheep and cattle treated him as one of their own, carrying him to a nearby barn where they nestled up close to him to keep him warm and suckled him with their own milk until he grew fit and strong.

Now Jiang Yuan had sent her scouts into the countryside to make sure that her unwanted child no longer lived. The news that he had survived and that he was being cared for by the animals of the pastures threw her into a fit of rage and she ordered her men to take the infant deep into the forests, to the most deserted spot they could find, where he was to be abandoned without any food or water. Jiang Yuan's messengers performed their duty exactly as they had been commanded, but again, fate intervened to save the child.

For one morning, a group of woodcutters who had travelled into the heart of the forest to find sturdier trees, spotted the child crawling through the undergrowth. Alarmed by his nakedness and grimy appearance, they immediately swept him up off the ground and carried him back to their village. Here, the woman Chingti, who was herself without child, took charge of the infant. She wrapped him in warm clothing and filled him with nourishing food until gradually he grew plump and healthy. His foster-mother doted on her son and it brought her great pleasure to see him thrive in her care.

But again, Jiang Yuan managed to track down the child and this time she was resolved to stop at nothing until she was certain of his destruction. And so, as a last resort, she carried him herself to a vast frozen river in the north where she stripped him naked and threw him on to the ice. For two years, the infant remained on the frozen waters, but from the very first day, he was protected from thc piercing cold by a flock of birds who took it in turn to fly down with morsels of food and to shelter him under their feathered wings.

The people grew curious to know why the birds swooped on to the icy surface of the river every day when clearly there were no fish to be had. Eventually a group of them set off across the ice to investigate further and soon they came upon the young child, curled up against the warm breast of a motherly seagull. They were amazed at the sight and took it as a sign that the child they had discovered was no ordinary mortal, but a very precious gift from the Gods. They rescued the young boy and named him Hou-Ji and as they watched him grow among them, his outstanding talents began to manifest themselves one by one.

Hou-Ji became an excellent farmer in time, but he did not follow any conventional model. He was a born leader and from a very early age he had learned to distinguish between every type of cereal and edible grain. He made agricultural tools for the people, such as hoes and spades, and soon the land delivered up every variety of crop, including wheat, beans, rice and large, succulent wild melons. The people had a bountiful supply of food and when the Emperor himself heard of Hou-Ji's great work he appointed him a minister of the state so that his knowledge of agriculture would spread throughout the nation.

When Hou-Ji died he left behind a 'Five-Crop-Stone' which guaranteed the Chinese people a constant supply of food even in times of famine. He was buried on the Duguang Plain, a magnificent region of rolling hills and clear-flowing rivers where the land has always remained exceptionally fertile.

Gun Battles the Great Flood

KING YAO, the first mortal emperor of China, was judged an outstanding monarch by his subjects, one of the wisest, most devoted rulers that had ever risen to power. Humble and charitable almost to a fault, Yao never allowed himself luxuries of any kind. He wore sackcloth in summer and only a deerskin during the winter months and spent his entire life making sure that his people had everything they could possibly need to keep them satisfied. If the Emperor spotted a man without clothes, he would remove the shirt from his own back and hand it over to the unfortunate person. If his people were short of food, he blamed himself for their suffering. If they committed a crime, he was immediately understanding and took personal responsibility for the breach of law and order.

Yet in spite of Yao's remarkably warm and tolerant nature, he was destined to suffer repeated misfortunes during his lifetime and his reign was plagued by disasters of every kind, including drought, starvation, disease and floods. But perhaps the worst period of the Emperor's rule came immediately after he had rid the earth of the suns of Dijun, when he had just breathed a sigh of relief and had set to work restoring the shattered morale of his nation.

During these days immediately following the destruction of the suns, when chaos still ruled the earth and the world of mortals failed to communicate a peaceful and harmonious atmosphere, the High God, Tiandi, happened to peer down from the Heavens and began to shake his head disappointedly. Everywhere the God looked, he saw people living miserable and wretched lives. Flames had devoured the homes of many and now they squabbled bitterly among themselves, desperate to secure basic food and provisions even by the most dishonest means.

Now Tiandi was not a God renowned for his patience and he saw only that mankind had begun to tread a path of wickedness and corruption. And taking swift action, he sent the God of Water to the earth's surface, commanding him to create a flood that would punish mankind for its debauched behaviour. This flood, he announced, would last for a period of no less than twenty-two years, after which time, it was hoped that the world would be properly cleansed of all evil.

So day after day the rains beat down upon the soil, pulverizing the crops which remained, flooding the houses, swelling the rivers to bursting point, until eventually the whole of the earth resembled one vast ocean. Those who were fortunate enough to avoid drowning, floated on the treacherous waters in search of tall trees or high mountains where they might come to rest. But even if they managed to reach dry land, they were then forced to compete with the fiercest beasts of the earth for food, so that many were mercilessly devoured even as they celebrated the fact that they had been saved.

Only one God among the deities of the heavens appeared to feel any sympathy for the innocent people suffering such appalling misery on earth. The God's name was Gun and he was the grandson of the Yellow Emperor. Now Gun took it upon himself to plead with Tiandi to put an end to the heavy rains, but the High God would not listen to a word of what he had to say and so Gun was forced to continue roaming the heavens, powerless to help the drowning people.

One day, however, as the young God sat alone dejectedly, pondering the destruction caused by the ongoing flood, he was approached by two of his friends, an eagle and a tortoise. And seeing their companion so downcast, the two enquired what they might do to lift his spirits.

"The only thing that would make me happy right now," Gun answered them, "would be to stop this water pouring out of the skies. But I have no idea how I can bring this about."

"It is not such a difficult task," replied the eagle, "if you feel you have courage enough to pay a visit to Tiandi's palace. For he is the keeper of the Shirang, a very precious substance which has exactly the same appearance of soil or clay. But if you can manage to drop some of this magical clay into the ocean, it will swell up to form a great dam that will hold back the flood waters."

It remains a great mystery to this day precisely how Gun overcame every obstacle to retrieve a handful of the magic soil, but he managed this task successfully and immediately departed for the earth where he flung the clay into the ocean. Almost at once, mountains began to spring up from the water and soon great stretches of land appeared everywhere as the huge waves began to subside. Filled with gratitude, the gaunt-faced people crawled down from the trees and out of their remote hiding places and began to hail Gun as the saviour of mankind.

But the High God, Tiandi, was not at all pleased with Gun's theft of the Shirang and its subsequent healing effect on the world below. Enraged by this challenge to his authority, he ordered the God of Fire, Zhurong, to go down to earth to murder the God who had betrayed him. The two met in combat on Mount Yushan, but Gun was no match for Zhurong and the God of Fire quickly overcame his opponent, striking him down without difficulty after they had exchanged only a few blows. And now the flood waters burst through the dam Gun had created, crashing on to the dried-out earth which became completely submerged once again.

Gun had sacrificed his life on Mount Yushan for the good of mankind, but he had died without completing his work and so his spirit refused to rest within the shell of his dead body. For three years, his remains lay in a special vault in the mountains, watched over by the people who greatly mourned his loss. But in all this time, Gun's body showed no sign of decomposing, for a new life had begun to grow inside of him, waiting for the day when it would be mature enough to emerge.

After these three years had passed and Gun's body had still not wasted away, Tiandi grew very concerned, fearing that the dead God was being transformed into an evil spirit destined to plague him for the rest of his days. So Tiandi sent one of his most trusted officials down to earth to carve up Gun's remains, presenting him with a divine sword called the Wudao. But a fantastic thing occurred as soon as the official's blade had slashed open Gun's belly. For instead of the blood he had anticipated would emerge from the opening, a large and mighty golden dragon sprung forth in its place. This dragon was Yu, the son of Gun, who had inherited all the strength and courage of his father and who had entered the world in all his magnificent glory to complete Gun's unfinished work.

Yu Controls the Flood

THE APPEARANCE of a great golden dragon in the skies, whose sole purpose it was to save mankind from destruction, encouraged the High God, Tiandi, to question whether or not the punishment he had meted out to the people below had been a little too severe. The mysterious creature was fiercely determined and persistent, he noticed, and to allow any further grievances between them was not the most prudent way forward. So Tiandi decided to yield to the dragon's wishes and put an end to the suffering on earth at long last.

Yu's mission so far had been an easy one. Tiandi not only ordered the God of Water to call a halt to the downpour, he also gave Yu enough Shirang to construct another great dam to hold back the flood waters. He sent the dragon Ying Long down to earth to assist him in repairing the widespread damage. Yu received this help gratefully and day and night channelled all his available energy into the task at hand.

Now all would have gone on smoothly, and the earth been restored to its original condition in little or no time, but for the God of Water, Gong Gong, who decided to cause as much trouble as possible for Yu. For it was Gong Gong who had originally created the flood and to see his great work undone by a mere boy-dragon was more than he could tolerate. No one had yet dared to disobey Yu's commands, but Gong Gong ignored every last one of them, entirely underestimating the dragon's strength and the powerful influence he exerted over his followers. And seeing that Gong Gong would not be reasoned with, Yu called together all the fairies, spirits and giants of the earth, so that not one remained to fight alongside Gong Gong. Then Yu challenged the God of Water to single combat, an encounter Gong Gong now wished he could avoid, for in no time, Yu had defeated him and skewered his ugly head upon his sword.

And after he had vanquished the God of Water, Yu went among the people handing them pieces of the magic clay so that they could decide for themselves where mountain ranges should appear and where stretches of land would flourish most. But it was not enough simply to rebuild the earth again, nor was the giant dam a permanent safeguard against flooding in the future. Yu realized that something more had to be done and so, dragging his great tail in the earth, he began to hollow out the soil, digging a long, tunnel-like structure through which the water could easily and swiftly flow, away from the land in the direction of the sea. Throughout the country, people followed his example and soon an entire network of shallow gullies began to appear, draining the surplus water from the plains. In this way, Yu brought the flood under control and created the great rivers of China that still flow eastwards towards the ocean to this very day.

The Marriage of Yu

YU HAD SPENT THIRTY YEARS on earth regulating the waters before it even occurred to him that he had earned a well-deserved rest and that perhaps the time had now arrived to make plans for his own future. Never in the past had he paused to consider the possibility that he might one day marry, but suddenly he felt lonely and in need of a wife who could love him and attend to him in old age. He had no idea how he might go about choosing a wife, however, and decided to put his trust in the Gods, waiting patiently for a sign from the divine powers above.

One morning, he observed a strange white fox with nine tails making its way towards him and he felt at once that the animal must be a heavenly messenger sent to help him in his quest. The fox approached and began to sing a strange little song which Yu listened to attentively, confident that its words would somehow enlighten him. The fox's song cheered him immensely and left him in little doubt that his search for a suitable wife was drawing to a close:

He who meets with the fox of nine tails
Will soon become king of the land.
He who weds the chief's daughter on Mount Tu
Will become a prosperous man.

Nu Jiao was reputed to be one of the most beautiful maidens in China and she dwelt in the distant valley of Tu on the summit of the great mountain. Ever since childhood, she had heard nothing but favourable reports of Yu and by now she was familiar with everything he had accomplished on earth. She had come to admire him from a distance as a God of legendary stature, and in her heart she had always entertained the hope that one day they would meet. And so when Yu appeared unexpectedly and asked for her hand in marriage, Nu Jiao could scarcely believe her good fortune and agreed at once to become his bride.

The two departed her father's kingdom and travelled southwards where they set up home and began a very happy married life together. It was not long before Nu Jiao became pregnant and the couple were overjoyed at the prospect of a son who would carry on his father's good work. For although the majority of the floods had been checked, the task of clearing the debris and ensuring that no similar disasters occurred in the future was still very much incomplete. And as the days passed by, the responsibility of overseeing more and more of this kind of work fell on Yu's experienced shoulders. Often he was forced to spend days away from home and occasionally he was away for several weeks at a time.

Now when the time was close at hand for Nu Jiao to deliver her child, Yu was unfortunately summoned to help restore the Huanyan Mountain which had begun to collapse and slide treacherously into the sea. And knowing that his wife would be anxious during his absence, Yu offered her the following words of comfort:

"If the task ahead were not so dangerous I would allow you to accompany me," he told her. "But I won't be very far away and I will take this drum with me and beat on it loudly when it is safe for you to join me."

Nu Jiao was relieved to hear this and she bade her husband farewell and watched him disappear into the forest.

As soon as he was within range of the great mountain, Yu transformed himself into a giant black bear with mighty claws and powerful shoulders in preparation for the gruelling work ahead. Then, after he had tied the drum to a tree behind him, he stooped to the ground and tossed a boulder high into a crevice of the mountain where he could see it had originally broken loose. One after another he tossed the huge boulders in the same direction until almost all the gaps in the mountain had been filled in and the towering structure took on a more solid appearance again. But just as his work was coming to an end, Yu allowed one of the boulders to slip from his upraised arms and it slid over his shoulder, striking the drum that remained tied to the tree.

At once, Nu Jiao prepared a small parcel of food for her husband and set off in the direction of Huanyan Mountain. Arriving at the place where the drum dangled in the breeze, she looked around for Yu, but was confronted instead by a terrifying black bear. Screaming in fright, Nu Jiao ran as fast as her legs would carry her towards her home, pursued by Yu who failed to realize that he had not changed back into his human shape. The young woman ran onwards in panic and dread, faster and faster, until all colour had drained from her face and her muscles grew stiff from the chase. At last, she dropped down to the earth, exhausted and beaten, and within seconds she was transformed into a stone.

Stunned and horrified by what had happened, Yu called out to his wife: "Give me my son, my only precious son." Immediately, the stone burst open and a small baby tumbled on to the earth. Yu named the child Qi, meaning 'cracked stone', and the story of his unusual birth earned him great fame even before he had grown to manhood.

MYTHS OF THE STARS

Introduction

ACCORDING TO CHINESE IDEAS, the sun, moon and planets influence sublunary events, especially the life and death of human beings, and changes in their colour tell of approaching calamities. Alterations in the appearance of the sun announce misfortunes to the State or its head, as revolts, famines, or the death of the emperor; when the moon waxes red, or turns pale, men should be in awe of the unlucky times foretold.

The sun and the moon are both included by the Chinese among the stars, the spirit of the sun king being 'Ch'ih-chiang of the Solar Palace', that of the moon queen 'Ch'ang O of the Lunar Palace'. The sun is symbolized by the figure of a raven in a circle, and the moon by a hare on its hind legs pounding rice in a mortar, or by a three-legged toad. The moon is a special object of worship in autumn, and moon cakes dedicated to it are sold at this season.

All the stars are ranged into constellations, and an emperor is installed over them, who resides at the North Pole; five monarchs also live in the five stars in Leo, where there is a palace called Wu Ti Tso, or 'Throne of the Five Emperors'. In this celestial government there are also an heir-apparent, empresses, sons and daughters, and tribunals, and the constellations receive the names of men, animals and other terrestrial objects. The Great Bear, or Dipper, is worshipped as the residence of the Fates, where the duration of life and other events relating to mankind are measured and meted out. Fears are excited by unusual phenomena among the heavenly bodies.

It is here that we also encounter T'ai Sui, the celestial spirit who presides over the year. He is the President of the Ministry of Time, a stellar god who corresponds to the planet Jupiter. This god is much to be feared. Whoever offends against him is sure to be destroyed. He strikes when least expected to.

The Herdsman and the Weaver Girl

MANY, MANY HUNDREDS OF YEARS AGO there lived in the palace of the High God in heaven a little weaver girl who spun and wove the most beautiful garments for the Gods, using colours and patterns more gorgeous than anything anyone had ever seen before. The High God was delighted with her efforts, but worried that she worked too hard, and for such long hours every day, and he decided to reward her diligence by giving her a rest from her labours. He determined to send her down to earth to live among mortals for a short time, to allow her to experience new and different pleasures. To ensure that the girl was well cared for, the High God chose for her a husband for her time on earth, a herdsman called Chen-Li, who lived with his two elder brothers on a farm by a great river.

The brothers had divided up the farm on their parents' death, and Chen-Li, being the youngest, had received nothing but an old ox, and the least fertile, most unproductive, piece of land. Here he built himself a rough home, and toiled day and night to make a living from the barren soil; although his life was hard he never complained, nor harboured a grudge against his brothers, for he was an honest youth of stout heart, which is indeed why the High God chose him for the weaver girl.

One evening Chen-Li was sitting watching the sun set over the distant mountains as his old ox munched the grass nearby. A feeling of great loneliness came over him, and he said to himself, "If only I had someone to share my life with, all my hard work would seem worthwhile." To his complete astonishment, the ox looked up and answered him, saying, "Do not be so sad, master. I can help you to find a wife who will bring you great joy." The ox then explained that it was really the Ox Star, sent to earth by the High God as a punishment, to work out its penance in labouring for mankind. It did not mention that it had also been given specific instructions regarding Chen-Li and the weaver girl, but went on to say: "If you go upstream you will find a beautiful, clear pool, shaded by willows and rushes. There the Heavenly Maidens bathe each afternoon; if you were to steal the clothes of one of them she would be unable to fly back to Heaven, and would have to, according to custom, become your wife."

Chen-Li did as the ox suggested, and the next afternoon he followed the river upstream, where he found the clear pool, shaded by willows. As he peered through the rushes, he saw the most beautiful girls he had ever set eyes on, laughing and splashing in the crystal waters. Spying their clothes piled on the banks of the pool, he leapt forward and snatched one of the piles; the noise disturbed the girls, who flew from the pool, took up their clothes, and soared away, up into the sky. Only one girl was left, naked in the pool, the little weaver girl, who looked shyly at Chen-Li and said, "Good Sir, if you would be generous enough to return my clothes, I will gladly come with you and become your wife." Chen-Li handed her clothes to her without hesitation, so strongly did he believe her promise. Then the girl dressed and, true to her word, followed him home and became his wife.

The couple were extremely happy in their simple existence, so much so that the weaver girl forgot all about the palace of the High God, and her place among the immortals. And in the fullness of time she bore the herdsman a fine son and a beautiful daughter, whom they loved dearly. However, the High God did not forget her, and grew impatient for her return. Eventually, when it became clear that she had no intention of leaving Chenh-Li, he sent down to earth his soldiers to bring her back. The weaver girl was distressed beyond all measure at leaving Chen-Li and her two children, but the soldiers were adamant, and carried her away, up into the sky. Chen-Li looked on in horror, unable to prevent this catastrophe, and he cried out in anguish, "What can I do? What can I do?"

The old ox saw his grief, and taking pity on Chen-Li said, "Master, my earthly form will die soon so that I can return to my celestial home; when I am dead, take off my hide and wrap it around you, and you will be able to follow your beloved." Saying this, the creature lay down and died at Chen-Li's feet, and, quickly, he did as the ox had instructed him. He picked up his son in one arm and his daughter in the other, and threw the leather hide around him. Instantly, all three soared up into the sky, and began to chase after the weaver girl, who was fast disappearing into the distance.

The High God watched this pursuit with much displeasure, and when he saw that Chen-Li would soon catch up with the weaver girl, he threw down his white silk scarf, which flowed and shimmered like fire between the lovers, forming a great river. Chen-Li called across the fiery torrent to his beloved, but to no avail, since neither could cross it. Defeated, he returned to his desolate home.

When the High God saw how much the weaver girl missed Chen-Li and her children, and how terribly they missed her, his anger abated, and he decreed that once a year, on the seventh day of the seventh month, all the magpies in the world would fly up into Heaven and form a bridge across the fiery river, so that the lovers could cross to each other and meet face to face. Whenever they met, the weaver girl would weep, and her tears fall to earth as drizzling rain; then all the women on earth would sorrow, and say, "Our sister is weeping again."

Chen-Li and the little weaver girl spent so much time in the sky, they eventually turned into stars; that is why, when we look up into the night sky, we can still see them both shining there. The fiery river is the Milky Way, on one side is Vega, the bright star that is the weaver girl, and on the other side shines Aquila, with two small stars beside it; which are Chen-Li and his two children. And if you look closely at the Milky Way on the night of the seventh day of the seventh month you will see these two stars meet as the two lovers are reunited for a few, precious hours, giving courage and hope to parted lovers throughout the world.

The Steep Summit

CH'IH-CHIANG LIVED in the reign of Hsien-yuan Huang-ti, who appointed him Director of Construction and Furnishing. When Hsien-yuan went on his visit to O-mei Shan, a mountain in Ssuch'uan, Ch'ih-chiang obtained permission to accompany him. Their object was to be initiated into the doctrine of immortality.

The Emperor was instructed in the secrets of the doctrine by T'ai-i Huang-jen, the spirit of this famous mountain, who, when he was about to take his departure, begged him to allow Ch'ih-chiang to remain with him. The new hermit went out every day to gather the flowering plants which formed the only food of his master, T'ai-i Huang-jen, and he also took to eating these flowers, so that his body gradually became spiritualized.

One day T'ai-i Huang-jen sent him to cut some bamboos on the summit of O-mei Shan, far away from the place where they lived. When he reached the base of the summit, all of a sudden three giddy peaks confronted him, so dangerous that even the monkeys and other animals dared not attempt to scale them. But he took his courage in his hands, climbed the steep slope and by sheer energy reached the summit. Having cut the bamboos, he tried to descend, but the rocks rose like a wall in sharp points all round him and he could not find a foothold anywhere. Then, though laden with the bamboos, he threw himself into the air and was borne on the wings of the wind. He came to earth safe and sound at the foot of the mountain and ran with the bamboos to his master. On account of this feat he was considered advanced enough to be admitted to instruction in the doctrine.

Shen I, the Divine Archer

THE EMPEROR YAO, one day, while walking in the streets of Huai-yang, met a man carrying a bow and arrows, the bow being bound round with a piece of red stuff. This was Ch'ih-chiang Tzu-yu. He told the Emperor he was a skilful archer and could fly in the air on the wings of the wind. Yao, to test his skill, ordered him to shoot one of his arrows at a pine-tree on the top of a neighbouring mountain. Ch'ih shot an arrow which transfixed the tree, and then jumped on to a current of air to go and fetch the arrow back. Because of this the Emperor named him Shen I, 'the Divine Archer', attached him to his suite, and appointed him Chief Mechanician of all Works in Wood. He continued to live only on flowers.

At this time terrible calamities began to lay waste the land. Ten suns appeared in the sky, the heat of which burnt up all the crops; dreadful storms uprooted trees and overturned houses; floods overspread the country. Near the Tung-t'ing Lake a serpent, a thousand feet long, devoured human beings, and wild boars of enormous size did great damage in the eastern part of the kingdom. Yao ordered Shen I to go and slay the devils and monsters who were causing all this mischief, placing three hundred men at his service for that purpose.

Shen I took up his post on Mount Ch'ing Ch'iu to study the cause of the devastating storms, and found that these tempests were released by Fei Lien, the Spirit of the Wind, who blew them out of a sack. The ensuing conflict ended in Fei Lien suing for mercy and swearing friendship to his victor, whereupon the storms ceased.

After this first victory Shen I led his troops to the banks of the Hsi Ho, West River, at Lin Shan. Here he discovered that on three neighbouring peaks nine extraordinary birds were blowing out fire and thus forming nine new suns in the sky. Shen I shot nine arrows in succession, pierced the birds, and immediately the nine false suns resolved themselves into red clouds and melted away. Shen I and his soldiers found the nine arrows stuck in nine red stones at the top of the mountain.

Shen I then led his soldiers to Kao-liang, where the river had risen and formed an immense torrent. He shot an arrow into the water, which thereupon withdrew to its source. In the flood he saw a man clothed in white, riding a white horse and accompanied by a dozen attendants. He quickly discharged an arrow, striking him in the left eye, and the horseman at once took to flight. He was accompanied by a young woman named Heng O, the younger sister of Ho Po, the Spirit of the Waters. Shen I shot an arrow into her hair. She turned and thanked him for sparing her life, adding: "I will agree to be your wife." After these events had been duly reported to the Emperor Yao, the wedding took place.

Three months later Yao ordered Shen I to go and kill the great Tung-t'ing serpent. An arrow in the left eye laid him out stark and dead. The wild boars also were all caught in traps and slain. As a reward for these achievements Yao canonized Shen I with the title of Marquis Pacifier of the Country.

Shen I Becomes Immortal

ABOUT THIS TIME T'ai-wu Fu-jen, the third daughter of Hsi Wang Mu, had entered a nunnery on Nan-min Shan, to the north of Lo-fou Shan, where her mother's palace was situated. She mounted a dragon to visit her mother, and all along the course left a streak of light in her wake. One day the Emperor Yao, from the top of Ch'ing-yun Shan, saw this track of light, and asked Shen I the cause of this unusual phenomenon. The latter mounted the current of luminous air, and letting it carry him whither it listed, found himself on Lo-fou Shan, in front of the door of the mountain, which was guarded by a great spiritual monster. On seeing Shen I this creature called together a large number of phoenixes and other birds of gigantic size and set them at Shen I. One arrow, however, settled the matter. They all fled, the door opened, and a lady followed by ten attendants presented herself. She was no other than Chin Mu herself. Shen I, having saluted her and explained the object of his visit, was admitted to the goddess's palace, and royally entertained.

"I have heard," said Shen I to her, "that you possess the pills of immortality; I beg you to give me one or two." "You are a well-known architect," replied Chin Mu; "please build me a palace near this mountain." Together they went to inspect a celebrated site known as Pai-yu-kuei Shan, 'White Jade-tortoise Mountain', and fixed upon it as the location of the new abode of the goddess. Shen I had all the spirits of the mountain to work for him. The walls were built of jade, sweet-smelling woods were used for the framework and wainscoting, the roof was of glass, the steps of agate. In a fortnight's time sixteen palace buildings stretched magnificently along the side of the mountain. Chin Mu gave to the architect a wonderful pill which would bestow upon him immortality as well as the faculty of being able at will to fly through the air. "But," she said, "it must not be eaten now: you must first go through a twelve-month preparatory course of exercise and diet, without which the pill will not have all the desired results." Shen I thanked the goddess, took leave of her, and, returning to the Emperor, related to him all that had happened.

On reaching home, the archer hid his precious pill under a rafter, lest anyone should steal it, and then began the preparatory course in immortality.

At this time there appeared in the south a strange man named Tso Ch'ih, 'Chisel-tooth'. He had round eyes and a long projecting tooth. He was a well-known criminal. Yao ordered Shen I and his small band of brave followers to deal with this new enemy. This extraordinary man lived in a cave, and when Shen I and his men arrived he emerged brandishing a padlock. Shen I broke his long tooth by shooting an arrow at it, and Tso Ch'ih fled, but was struck in the back and laid low by another arrow from Shen I. The victor took the broken tooth with him as a trophy.

Heng O, during her husband's absence, saw a white light which seemed to issue from a beam in the roof, while a most delicious odour filled every room. By the aid of a ladder she reached up to the spot whence the light came, found the pill of immortality, and ate it. She suddenly felt that she was freed from the operation of the laws of gravity and as if she had wings, and was just essaying her first flight when Shen I returned. He went to look for his pill, and, not finding it, asked Heng O what had happened.

The young wife, seized with fear, opened the window and flew out. Shen I took his bow and pursued her. The moon was full, the night clear, and he saw his wife flying rapidly in front of him, only about the size of a toad. Just when he was redoubling his pace to catch her up a blast of wind struck him to the ground like a dead leaf.

Heng O continued her flight until she reached a luminous sphere, shining like glass, of enormous size, and very cold. The only vegetation consisted of cinnamon-trees. No living being was to be seen. All of a sudden, she began to cough, and vomited the covering of the pill of immortality, which was changed into a rabbit as white as the purest jade. This was the ancestor of the spirituality of the yin, or female, principle. Heng O noticed a bitter taste in her mouth, drank some dew, and, feeling hungry, ate some cinnamon. She took up her abode in this sphere.

As to Shen I, he was carried by the hurricane up into a high mountain. Finding himself before the door of a palace, he was invited to enter, and found that it was the palace of Tung-hua Ti-chun, otherwise Tung Wang Kung, the husband of Hsi Wang Mu.

The God of the Immortals said to Shen I: "You must not be annoyed with Heng O. Everybody's fate is settled beforehand. Your labours are nearing an end, and you will become an Immortal. It was I who let loose the whirlwind that brought you here. Heng O, through having borrowed the forces which by right belong to you, is now an Immortal in the Palace of the Moon. As for you, you deserve much for having so bravely fought the nine false suns. As a reward, you shall have the Palace of the Sun. Thus, the yin and the yang will be united in marriage." This said, Tung-hua Ti-chun ordered his servants to bring a red Chinese sarsaparilla cake, with a lunar talisman.

"Eat this cake," he said; "it will protect you from the heat of the solar hearth. And by wearing this talisman you will be able at will to visit the lunar palace of Heng O; but the converse does not hold good, for your wife will not have access to the solar palace." This is why the light of the moon has its birth in the sun, and decreases in proportion to its distance from the sun, the moon being light or dark according as the sun comes and goes. Shen I ate the sarsaparilla cake, attached the talisman to his body, thanked the god, and prepared to leave. Tung Wang Kung said to him: "The sun rises and sets at fixed times; you do not yet know the laws of day and night; it is absolutely necessary for you to take with you the bird with the golden plumage, which will sing to advise you of the exact times of the rising, culmination, and setting of the sun." "Where is this bird to be found?" asked Shen I. "It is the one you hear calling Ia! Ia! It is the ancestor of the spirituality of the yang, or male, principle. Through having eaten the active principle of the sun, it has assumed the form of a three-footed bird, which perches on the fu-sang tree in the middle of the Eastern Sea. This tree is several thousands of feet in height and of gigantic girth. The bird keeps near the source of the dawn, and when it sees the sun taking his morning bath gives vent to a cry that shakes the heavens and wakes up all humanity. That is why I ordered Ling Chen-tzu to put it in a cage on T'ao-hua Shan, Peach-blossom Hill; since then its cries have been less harsh. Go and fetch it and take it to the Palace of the Sun. Then you will understand all the laws of the daily movements." He then wrote a charm which Shen I was to present to Ling Chen-tzu to make him open the cage and hand the golden bird over to him.

The charm worked, and Ling Chen-tzu opened the cage. The bird of golden plumage had a sonorous voice and majestic bearing. "This bird," he said, "lays eggs which hatch out nestlings with red combs, who answer him every morning when he starts crowing. He is usually called the cock of heaven, and the cocks down here which crow morning and evening are descendants of the celestial cock."

Shen I, riding on the celestial bird, traversed the air and reached the disk of the sun just at mid-day. He found himself carried into the centre of an immense horizon, as large as the earth, and did not perceive the rotatory movement of the sun. He then enjoyed complete happiness without care or trouble. The thought of the happy hours passed with his wife Heng O, however, came back to memory, and, borne on a ray of sunlight, he flew to the moon. He saw the cinnamon-trees and the frozen-looking horizon. Going to a secluded spot, he found Heng O there all alone. On seeing him she was about to run away, but Shen I took her hand and reassured her. "I am now living in the solar palace," he said; "do not let the past annoy you." Shen I cut down some cinnamon-trees, used them for pillars, shaped some precious stones, and so built a palace, which he named Kuang-han Kung, 'Palace of Great Cold'. From that time forth, on the fifteenth day of every moon, he went to visit her in her palace. That is the conjunction of the yang and yin, male and female principles, which causes the great brilliancy of the moon at that epoch.

Shen I, on returning to his solar kingdom, built a wonderful palace, which he called the Palace of the Lonely Park. From that time, the sun and moon each had their ruling sovereign.

When the old Emperor was informed that Shen I and his wife had both gone up to Heaven he was much grieved to lose the man who had rendered him such valuable service, and bestowed upon him the posthumous title of Tsung Pu, 'Governor of Countries'. In the representations of this god and goddess the former is shown holding the sun, the latter the moon.

A Victim of Ta Chi

PO I-K'AO WAS THE ELDEST SON of Wen Wang, and governed the kingdom during the seven years that the old King was detained as a prisoner of the tyrant Chou. He did everything possible to procure his father's release. Knowing the tastes of the cruel King, he sent him for his harem ten of the prettiest women who could be found, accompanied by seven chariots made of perfumed wood, and a white-faced monkey of marvellous intelligence. Besides these he included in his presents a magic carpet, on which it was necessary only to sit in order to recover immediately from the effects of drunkenness.

Unfortunately for Po I-k'ao, Chou's favourite concubine, Ta Chi, conceived a passion for him and had recourse to all sorts of ruses to catch him in her net; but his conduct was throughout irreproachable. Angered by his indifference, she tried slander in order to bring about his ruin. But at first this did not have the result she expected. Chou, after inquiry, was convinced of the innocence of Po. But an accident spoiled everything. In the middle of an amusing seance the monkey which had been given to the King by Po perceived some sweets in the hand of Ta Chi, and, jumping on to her body, snatched them from Her. The King and his concubine were furious, Chou had the monkey killed forthwith, and Ta Chi accused Po I-k'ao of having brought the animal into the palace with the object of making an attempt on the lives of the King and herself. But the Prince explained that the monkey, being only an animal, could not grasp even the first idea of entering into a conspiracy.

Shortly after this Po committed an unpardonable fault which changed the goodwill of the King into mortal enmity. He allowed himself to go so far as to suggest to the King that he should break off his relations with this infamous woman, the source of all the woes which were desolating the kingdom, and when Ta Chi on this account grossly insulted him he struck her with his lute.

For this offence, Ta Chi caused him to be crucified in the palace. Large nails were driven through his hands and feet, and his flesh was cut off in pieces. Not content with ruining Po I-k'ao, this wretched woman wished also to ruin Wen Wang. She therefore advised the King to have the flesh of the murdered man made up into rissoles and sent as a present to his father. If he refused to eat the flesh of his own son he was to be accused of contempt for the King, and there would thus be a pretext for having him executed. Wen Wang, being versed in divination and the science of the pa kua, Eight Trigrams, knew that these rissoles contained the flesh of his son, and to avoid the snare spread for him he ate three of the rissoles in the presence of the royal envoys. On their return the latter reported this to the King, who found himself helpless on learning of Wen Wang's conduct.

Po I-k'ao was canonized and appointed ruler of the constellation Tzu-wei of the North Polar heavens.

Legend of T'ai Sui

TAI SUI WAS THE SON of the Emperor Chou, the last of the Yin dynasty. His mother was Queen Chiang. When he was born he looked like a lump of formless flesh. The infamous Ta Chi, the favourite concubine of this wicked Emperor, at once informed him that a monster had been born in the palace, and the over-credulous sovereign ordered that it should immediately be cast outside the city. Shen Chen-jen, who was passing, saw the small abandoned one, and said: "This is an Immortal who has just been born." With his knife, he cut open the caul which enveloped it, and the child was exposed.

His protector carried him to the cave Shui Lien, where he led the life of a hermit, and entrusted the infant to Ho Hsien-ku, who acted as his nurse and brought him up.

The child's hermit-name was Yin Chiao meaning 'Yin the Deserted of the Suburb'. When he had reached an age when he was sufficiently intelligent, his nurse informed him that he was not her son, but really the son of the Emperor Chou, who, deceived by the calumnies of his favourite Ta Chi, had taken him for an evil monster and had him cast out of the palace. His mother had been thrown down from an upper storey and killed. Yin Chiao went to his rescuer and begged him to allow him to avenge his mother's death. The Goddess T'ien Fei, the Heavenly Concubine, picked out two magic weapons from the armoury in the cave, a battle-axe and club, both of gold, and gave them to Yin Chiao. When the Shang army was defeated at Mu Yeh, Yin Chiao broke into a tower where Ta Chi was, seized her, and brought her before the victor, King Wu, who gave him permission to split her head open with his battle-axe. But Ta Chi was a spiritual hen-pheasant. She transformed herself into smoke and disappeared. To reward Yin Chiao for his filial piety and bravery in fighting the demons, Yu Ti canonized him with the title T'ai Sui Marshal Yin.

T'ai Sui is the celestial spirit who presides over the year. He is the President of the Ministry of Time.

The Morning and the Evening Star

ONCE UPON A TIME there were two stars, sons of the Golden King of the Heavens. The one was named Tschen[1] and the other Shen. One day they quarreled, and Tschen struck Shen a terrible blow. Thereupon both stars made a vow that they would never again look upon each other. So Tschen only appears in the evening, and Shen only appears in the morning, and not until Tschen has disappeared is Shen again to be seen. And that is why people say: "When two brothers do not live peaceably with one another they are like Tschen and Shen."

Footnotes for 'The Morning and the Evening Star'

1. Tschen and Shen are Hesperus and Lucifer, the morning and evening stars. The tale is told in its traditional form.

Myths of Thunder, Lightning, Wind & Rain

Introduction

THE NUMBER OF SPIRITS and guardians associated with the elements in Chinese legend is vast. Each of these elements is managed by a Ministry in the Heavens, composed of a large number of celestial officials. Members of these ministries are the most powerful of the guardian spirits, since they control the unpredictable forces on earth, such as fire, thunder, lightning, wind and rain.

Natural disasters caused by these forces occur again and again in Chinese mythology. It is always crucial in these stories to maintain a favourable relationship with the God in charge. The Ministry of Thunder and Storms, to take but one example, has a complicated infrastructure. It is presided over by the Ancestor of Thunder, Lei Tsu, followed by other officials in order of seniority: Lei Kung, the Duke of Thunder, Tien Mu, the Mother of Lightning, Feng Po, the Count of Wind, Yu Shih, the Master of Rain and a string of other lesser Gods.

In temples Lei Tsu is placed in the centre with the other four to right and left. He is a divinity with three eyes, one in the middle of his forehead, from which, when open, a ray of white light streams to a distance of more than two feet. Mounted on a black unicorn, he can travel millions of miles in the twinkling of an eye.

The Spirit of Thunder is represented as an ugly, black, bat-winged demon with clawed feet, a monkey's head, and an eagle's beak, who holds a steel chisel in one hand and a spiritual hammer in the other, with which he beats numerous drums strung about him. This produces the terrific noise of thunder. According to the Chinese, it is the sound of these drums and not the lightning which causes death.

Wen Chung, Minister of Thunder

THIS STORY TELLS of Wen Chung, a minister of the tyrant king Chou who fought against the armies of the Chou dynasty. Being defeated, he fled to the mountains of Yen, Yen Shan, where he met Ch'ih Ching-tzu, one of the alleged discoverers of fire, and joined battle with him; the latter, however, flashed his yin-yang mirror at a unicorn and put it out of action. Lei Chen-tzu, one of Wu Wang's marshals, then struck the animal with his staff, severing it in two.

Wen Chung escaped in the direction of the mountains of Chueh-lung Ling, where another marshal, Yun Chung-tzu, barred his way. Yun's hands had the power of producing lightning, and eight columns of mysterious fire suddenly came out of the earth, completely enveloping Wen Chung. They were thirty feet high and ten feet in circumference. Ninety fiery dragons came out of each and flew away up into the air. The sky was like a furnace, and the earth shook with the awful claps of thunder. In this fiery prison Wen Chung died.

When the new dynasty finally proved victorious, Chiang Tzu-ya, by order of Yuan-shih T'ien-tsun, conferred on Wen Chung the supreme direction of the Ministry of Thunder, appointing him celestial prince and defender of the laws governing the distribution of clouds and rain. His full title was Celestial and Highly Honoured Head of the Nine Orbits of the Heavens, Voice of the Thunder, and Regulator of the Universe. His birthday is celebrated on the twenty-fourth day of the sixth moon.

Lei Kung, Duke of Thunder

THE DUKE OF THUNDER, Lei Kung, is represented in Chinese legend as an ugly black creature with clawed feet and a monkey's head. In his hand he holds a chisel which he uses to beat on a drum, producing the ferocious noise of thunder. A popular story about him recalls how one day, a youth who had been chopping firewood high in the mountains noticed a thunderstorm approaching and took shelter under a large tree. Suddenly a great fork of lightning struck the tree, trapping the Duke of Thunder underneath its great weight as it fell to the ground. Lei Kung begged the youth to release him, promising to reward him handsomely, until finally the terrified youth agreed to his request. In return for his help, the Duke of Thunder presented him with a book which would teach him to conjure up storms and tempests.

"When you need rain," the God told him, "call on one of my four brothers and they will come to your aid. But don't call on me unless it is really necessary because my mood is often unpredictable."

After he had said this, Lei Kung disappeared and the youth headed back to his village.

Within no time he had become a popular figure among the people who regularly took the opportunity to celebrate his great powers in the local inn. One night, however, the youth became so drunk and disorderly he was arrested and carried off by the police. The following morning, as he was led to court, he called upon the God of Thunder to save him from imprisonment. The God responded immediately and thundered through the air so loudly that the windows of the courthouse were shattered by the noise. Cowering to the floor in terror, the magistrate ordered the youth to be released and dismissed him from the court without imposing any sentence.

From this day onwards, the youth used his power to save many people. For whenever he saw that there was danger of the land becoming dried out, he ordered a great storm to appear overhead and the rains to saturate the soil below.

Lei Chen-tzu, Son of Thunder

LEI CHEN-TZU, Son of Thunder, was hatched from an egg after a clap of thunder and found by the soldiers of Wen Wang in some brushwood near an old tomb. The infant's chief characteristic was its brilliant eyes. Wen Wang, who already had ninety-nine children, adopted it as his hundredth, but gave it to a hermit named Yun Chung-tzu to rear as his disciple. The hermit showed him the way to rescue his adopted father from the tyrant who held him prisoner. In searching for a powerful weapon, the child found two apricots on the hillside and ate them both. He then noticed that wings had grown on his shoulders and was too ashamed to return home.

But the hermit, who knew intuitively what had happened, sent a servant to look for him. When they met the servant said: "Do you know that your face is completely altered?" The mysterious fruit had not only caused Lei Chen-tzu to grow wings, known as Wings of the Wind and Thunder, but his face had become green, his nose long and pointed, and two tusks protruded horizontally from each side of his mouth, while his eyes shone like mirrors.

Lei Chen-tzu now went and rescued Wen Wang, dispersing his enemies by means of his mystical power and bringing the old man back on his shoulders. Having brought him to safety, he returned to the hermit.

The Spirit of Lightning

TUNG WANG KUNG, the King of the Immortals, was playing at pitch-pot with Yu Nu. He lost; whereupon Heaven smiled and from its half-open mouth a ray of light came out. This was lightning; it is regarded as feminine because it is supposed to come from the earth, which is of the yin (or female) principle.

The Mother of Lightning is represented as a female figure, gorgeously dressed in blue, green, red, and white, holding in either hand a mirror from which streams two flashes of light. Lightning, say the Chinese, is caused by the rubbing together of the yin and the yang – just as sparks of fire may be produced by the friction of two substances.

Feng Po, God of the Wind

FENG PO, the God of the Wind, is represented as an old man with a white beard, yellow cloak, and blue and red cap. He holds a large sack, and directs the wind which comes from its mouth in any direction he pleases.

He is regarded as a stellar divinity under the control of the star Ch'i, because the wind blows at the time when the moon leaves that celestial mansion. He is also said to be a dragon called Fei Lien, at first one of the supporters of the rebel Ch'ih Yu, who was defeated by Huang Ti. Having been transformed into a spiritual monster, he stirred up tremendous winds in the southern regions. The Emperor Yao sent Shen I with three hundred soldiers to quiet the storms and appease Ch'ih Yu's relatives, who were wreaking their vengeance on the people. Shen I ordered the people to spread a long cloth in front of their houses, fixing it with stones. The wind, blowing against this, had to change its direction. Shen I then flew on the wind to the top of a high mountain, where he saw a monster at the base. It had the shape of a huge yellow and white sack and kept inhaling and exhaling in great gusts. Shen I, concluding that this was the cause of all these storms, shot an arrow and hit the monster, whereupon it took refuge in a deep cave. Here it turned on Shen I and, drawing a sword, dared him to attack the Mother of the Winds. Shen I, however, bravely faced the monster and discharged another arrow, this time hitting it in the knee. The monster immediately threw down its sword and begged that its life might be spared.

Yu Shih, Master of Rain

YU SHIH, the Master of Rain, clad in yellow scale-armour, with a blue hat and yellow busby, stands on a cloud and from a watering can pours rain upon the earth. Like many other gods, however, he is represented in various forms. Sometimes he holds a plate, on which is a small dragon, in his left hand, while with his right he pours down the rain.

Legend tells that the God of Rain is Ch'ih Sung-tzu, who appeared during a terrible drought in the reign of Shen Nung, and owing to his reputed magical power was requested by the latter to bring rain from the sky. "Nothing is easier," he replied; "pour a bottleful of water into an earthen bowl and give it to me." This being done, he plucked from a neighbouring mountain a branch of a tree, soaked it in the water, and with it sprinkled the earth. Immediately clouds gathered and rain fell in torrents, filling the rivers to overflowing. Ch'ih Sung-tzu was then honoured as the God of Rain, and his images show him holding the mystic bowl. He resides in the K'un-lun Mountains, and has many extraordinary peculiarities, such as the power to go through water without getting wet, to pass through fire without being burned and to float in space.

The One-Legged Bird

AT THE TIME WHEN Hsuan-ming Ta-jen instructed Fei Lien in the secrets of magic, the latter saw a wonderful bird which drew in water with its beak and blew it out again in the shape of rain. Fei Lien tamed it, and would take it about in his sleeve.

Later on a one-legged bird was seen in the palace of the Prince of Ch'i walking up and down and hopping in front of the throne. Being much puzzled, the Prince sent a messenger to Lu to inquire of Confucius concerning this strange behaviour. "This bird is a shang yang" said Confucius; "its appearance is a sign of rain. In former times the children used to amuse themselves by hopping on one foot, knitting their eyebrows, and saying: 'It will rain, because the shang yang is disporting himself.' Since this bird has gone to Ch'i, heavy rain will fall. The people should be told to dig channels and repair the dykes, for the whole country will be inundated." Not only Ch'i, but all the adjacent kingdoms were flooded; all sustained grievous damage except Ch'i, where the necessary precautions had been taken. This caused Duke Ching to exclaim: "Alas! How few listen to the words of the sages!"

Ma Yuan-shuai, Generalissimo of the West

MA YUAN-SHUAI is a three-eyed monster condemned by Ju Lai to reincarnation for excessive cruelty in the extermination of evil spirits.

In order to obey this command he entered the womb of Ma Chin-mu in the form of five globes of fire. Being a precocious youth, he could fight when only three days old and killed the Dragon king of the Eastern Sea. From his instructor he received a spiritual work dealing with wind and thunder, and a triangular piece of stone which he could change at will into anything he liked. By order of Yu Ti he subdued the Spirits of the Wind and Fire, the Blue Dragon, the King of the Five Dragons, and the Spirit of the Five Hundred Fire Ducks, all without injury to himself. For these and many other enterprises he was rewarded by Yu Ti with various magic articles and with the title of Generalissimo of the West, and is regarded as so successful an interceder with Yu Ti that he is prayed to for all sorts of benefits.

Myths of the Waters

Introduction

IN THE SPIRIT world there is a Ministry that controls all things connected with the waters on earth, salt or fresh. Its main divisions are the Department of Salt Waters, presided over by four Dragon-kings – those of the East, South, West and North – and the Department of Sweet Waters, presided over by the Four Kings (SSu- Tu) of the four great rivers – the Blue (Chiang), Yellow (Ho), Huai and Ch'I – and the Dragon spirits who control the Secondary Waters, the rivers, springs, lakes, pools, rapids.

The dragons are spirits of the waters. In a sense the dragon is the type of a man, self-controlled, and with powers that verge on the supernatural. In China the dragon is not a power for evil, instead he controls the rain, and so holds in his power prosperity and peace. He is the essence of the yang, or male, principle.

The dragon is also represented as the father of the great emperors of ancient times. His bones, teeth and saliva are employed as a medicine. He has the power of transformation and of rendering himself visible or invisible at will. In the spring he ascends to the skies and in the autumn buries himself in the watery depths. Some are wingless and rise into the air by their own inherent power. There is the celestial dragon, who guards the mansions of the gods and supports them so that they do not fall; the divine dragon, who causes the winds to blow and produces rain for the benefit of mankind; the earth dragon, who marks out the courses of rivers and streams; the dragon of the hidden treasures, who watches over the wealth concealed from mortals; and the five Sea Dragon Kings who live in gorgeous palaces in the depths of the sea.

The Foolish Dragon

THIS IS THE PART of the great Buddha legend referring to the dragon. In years gone by, a dragon living in the great sea saw that his wife's health was not good. He, seeing her colour fade away, said: "My dear, what shall I get you to eat?" Mrs. Dragon was silent. Just tell me and I will get it," pleaded the affectionate husband. "You cannot do it; why trouble?" she replied. "Trust me, and you shall have your heart's desire," said the dragon. "Well, I want a monkey's heart to eat." "Why, Mrs. Dragon, the monkeys live in the mountain forests! How can I get one of their hearts?" "Well, I am going to die; I know I am."

So the dragon went on shore, and, spying a monkey on the top of a tree, said: "Hail, shining one, are you not afraid you will fall?" "No, I have no such fear." "Why eat of one tree? Cross the sea, and you will find forests of fruit and flowers." "How can I cross?" "Get on my back." The dragon with his tiny load went seaward and then suddenly dived down. "Where are you going?" said the monkey with the salt water in his eyes and mouth. "Oh! My dear sir! my wife is very sad and ill and has taken a fancy to your heart." "What shall I do?" thought the monkey. He then spoke, "Illustrious friend, why did not you tell me? I left my heart on the top of the tree; take me back, and I will get it for Mrs. Dragon." The dragon returned to the shore. As the monkey was slow in coming down from the tree, the dragon said: "Hurry up, little friend, I am waiting." Then the monkey thought within himself, "What a fool this dragon is!"

Then Buddha said to his followers: "At this time I was the monkey."

An Unauthorized Portrait

PO SHIH, A TAOIST PRIEST, told Ch'in Shih Huang-ti, the First Emperor, that an enormous oyster vomited from the sea a mysterious substance which accumulated in the form of a tower and was known as 'the market of the sea'. Every year, at a certain period, the breath from his mouth was like the rays of the sun. The Emperor expressed a wish to see it, so Po Shih said he would write a letter to the God of the Sea and the next day the Emperor could witness the wonderful sight.

The Emperor then remembered a dream he had had the year before in which he saw two men fighting for the sun. The one killed the other and carried it off. He therefore wished to visit the country where the sun rose. Po Shih said that all that was necessary was to throw rocks into the sea and build a bridge across them. Immediately he rang his magic bell, the earth shook and rocks began to rise up; but as they moved too slowly he struck them with his whip and blood came from them, which left red marks in many places. The row of rocks extended as far as the shore of the sun country, but to build the bridge across them was found to be beyond the reach of human skill.

So Po Shih sent another messenger to the God of the Sea, requesting him to raise a pillar and place a beam across it which could be used as a bridge. The submarine spirits came and placed themselves at the service of the Emperor, who asked for an interview with the god. To this the god agreed on condition that no one should make a portrait of him, he being very ugly. Instantly a stone gangway one hundred thousand feet long rose out of the sea, and the Emperor, mounting his horse, went with his courtiers to the palace of the god. Among his followers was Lu Tung-shih, who tried to draw a portrait of the god by using his foot under the surface of the water. Detecting this manoeuvre, the god was incensed and said to the Emperor: "You have broken your word; did you bring Lu here to insult me? Retire at once, or evil will befall you." The Emperor, seeing that the situation was precarious, mounted his horse and galloped off. As soon as he reached the beach, the stone causeway sank and all his suite perished in the waves. One of the Court magicians said to the Emperor: "This god ought to be feared as much as the God of Thunder; then he could be made to help us. Today a grave mistake has been made." For several days after this incident the waves beat upon the beach with increasing fury. The Emperor then built a temple and a pagoda to the god on Chih-fu Shan and Wen-teng Shan respectively; by which he was apparently appeased.

The Shipwrecked Servant

ONCE THE EIGHT IMMORTALS were on their way to Ch'ang-li Shan to celebrate the birthday anniversary of Hsien Weng, the God of Longevity. They had with them a servant who bore the presents they intended to offer to the god. When they reached the seashore the Immortals walked on the waves without any difficulty, but Lan Ts'ai-ho remarked that the servant was unable to follow them and said that a means of transport must be found for him. So Ts'ao Kuo-chiu took a plank of cypress-wood and made a raft. But when they were in mid-ocean a typhoon arose and upset the raft and servant and presents sank to the bottom of the sea.

Regarding this as the hostile act of a water devil, the Immortals said they must demand an explanation from the Dragon King, Ao Ch'in. Li T'ieh-kuai took his gourd and, directing the mouth toward the bottom of the sea, created so brilliant a light that it illuminated the whole palace of the Sea King. Ao Ch'in, surprised, asked where this powerful light came from. He sent a messenger to ascertain its cause.

To this messenger the Immortals made their complaint. "All we want," they added, "is that the Dragon King shall restore to us our servant and the presents." On this being reported to Ao Ch'in he suspected his son of being the cause and, having established his guilt, severely reprimanded him. The young Prince took his sword and, followed by an escort, went to find those who had made the complaint to his father. As soon as he caught sight of the Immortals he began to inveigh against them.

Han Hsiang Tzu, not liking this undeserved abuse, changed his flute into a fishing line and as soon as the Dragon prince was within reach caught him on the hook, intending to keep him as a hostage. The Prince's escort returned at once and informed Ao Ch'in of what had happened. The latter declared that his son was in the wrong and proposed to restore the shipwrecked servant and the presents. The Court officers, however, held a different opinion. "These Immortals," they said, "dare to hold captive your Majesty's son merely on account of a few lost presents and a shipwrecked servant. This is a great insult, which we ask permission to avenge." Eventually they won over Ao Ch'in, and the armies of the deep gathered for the fray. The Immortals called to their aid the other Taoist Immortals and Heroes and thus two formidable armies found themselves face to face.

Several attempts were made by other divinities to avert the conflict, but without success. The battle was a strenuous one. Ao Ch'in received a ball of fire full on his head and his army was threatened with disaster when Tz'u-hang Ta-shih appeared with his bottle of lustral water. Using a willow-branch, he sprinkled the combatants with this magic fluid, causing all their magic powers to disappear.

Shui Kuan, the Ruler of the Watery Elements, then arrived and reproached Ao Ch'in; he assured him that if the matter were to come to the knowledge of Shang Ti, the Supreme Ruler, he would not only be severely punished but would risk losing his post. Ao Ch'in expressed penitence, restored the servant and the presents and made full apology to the Eight Immortals.

The Spirits of the Well

ONE DAY CHANG TAO-LING, the 'father of modern Taoism', was on Ho-ming Shan with his disciple Wang Ch'ang. "See," he said, "that shaft of white light on Yang Shan. There are undoubtedly some bad spirits there. Let us go and bring them to reason." When they reached the foot of the mountain they met twelve women who had the appearance of evil spirits. Chang Tao-ling asked them where the shaft of white light came from. They answered that it was the yin (female) principle of the earth. "Where is the source of the salt water?" he asked again. "That pond in front of you," they replied, "in which lives a very wicked dragon." Chang Tao-ling tried to force the dragon to come out, but without success. Then he drew a phoenix with golden wings on a charm and hurled it into the air over the pond. The dragon took fright and fled, the pond immediately drying up. After that Chang Tao-ling took his sword and stuck it in the ground. A well full of salt water appeared on the spot.

The twelve women each offered Chang Tao-ling a jade ring and asked that they might become his wives. He took the rings and, pressing them together in his hands, made one large single ring. "I will throw this ring into the well," he said, "and the one of you who recovers it shall be my wife." All the twelve women jumped into the well to get the ring. Then Chang Tao-ling put a cover over it and fastened it down, telling them that from now on they were the spirits of the well and would never be allowed to come out.

Shortly after this Chang Tao-ling met a hunter. He urged him not to kill living beings, but to change his occupation to that of a salt burner, instructing him how to draw out the salt from salt-water wells. The people of that district were helped both by being able to obtain the salt and by being no longer molested by the twelve female spirits. A temple, called Temple of the Prince of Ch'ing Ho, was built by them, and the territory of Ling Chou was given to Chang Tao-ling in recognition of the benefits he had granted the people.

The Dragon King's Daughter

THERE WAS ONCE a student named Liu Yi, who lived in the central region of China, near the great lakes. One day, as he was returning from the capital having successfully taken his examinations, he saw on the road ahead of him a young woman herding a flock of sheep. She was the most beautiful woman Liu had ever seen, but she was deeply distressed, tears coursing down her fair cheeks, her whole body shaking with sobs. Liu's heart went out to the girl, and he got down from his donkey and asked her if there was any way in which he could be of assistance. The girl thanked him through her tears, and explained the cause of her grief.

"My father is the Dragon King of Lake Dongting," she explained, "and many months ago he married me to the son of the God of the Jing river, whom I do not love. My husband is cruel to me, and his family torment me, but I cannot complain to my father as Lake Dongting is too far away for me to travel, and the family intercept my messages to him. I know my father would help if he but knew of my grief, but I am so utterly alone and friendless."

Liu was so touched by the girl's plight that he offered to take the message to her father himself, but he could not see how it could be done.

"Although the shores of Lake Dongting are my home," he said, "I am a mere human. How could I ever reach your father's palace in the terrifying depths of the lake?"

The girl replied, "If you are strong in heart, go to the sacred tangerine tree on the northern shore of the lake. Tie your sash around its trunk, and knock on it three times. From there you will be led to the palace."

Liu willingly agreed to undertake the journey, and the girl handed him a letter from the folds of her gown. As he remounted his donkey, he called out, "When you return to Dongting, I sincerely hope that we shall meet again." Then, spurring the animal on, he set off. After a few minutes he looked back, but the girl had disappeared together with her sheep.

Liu went straight to the northern shore of Lake Dongting, and finding the sacred tangerine tree, he tied his sash around its trunk and knocked on it three times as the girl had said. At once the waves of the lake parted, and a man rose up from the depths, and asked Liu what he wanted.

"I must talk to your king," Liu said. "It is a matter of the utmost importance."

The man nodded, and placed a blindfold over Liu's eyes. Liu became aware of a silence engulfing him, and his body became colder and colder, but he did not flinch. After a time, the blindfold was removed, and Liu found he was in a great palace, beautifully decorated with pearl and other precious stones, and all the warmth flooded back into his body. His guide showed him into a vast chamber, and there, on a mighty throne, sat the Dragon King.

Liu bowed low, and humbly proffered the girl's letter, explaining where and how he had met her on the road from the capital. The Dragon King read the letter, and as he did so great tears rolled down his face, and his huge hands shook. Then he instructed a servant to take the letter to the queen, and said to Liu, "I thank you for all your trouble. You have taken pity on my daughter, while I did nothing to save her from her suffering. I shall never forget your kindness to her, and your bravery in making this journey."

At that moment he was interrupted by a loud wailing from the queen's chamber, and the sound of weeping. "Quickly," ordered the king with a worried frown, "tell them to be quiet, or they will arouse Chiantang."

"Who is Chiantang?" asked Liu, surprised that anything should disturb such a mighty ruler.

The Dragon King explained that Chiantang was his younger brother, once ruler of Lake Chiantang. His quick temper had caused such floods and devastation, even threatening the Five Holy Peaks, that the High God had banished him from the lake, and forgiven him on the understanding that his brother guarantee his good behaviour. "This news would infuriate him, as he is extremely fond of his niece, and would instantly demand revenge."

As he spoke, there was a tremendous crash, and the chamber filled with smoke. In a tumult of lightning, thunder and rain, a huge red dragon tore through the hall, clouds streaming from his nostrils, and a mighty roar issuing from his throat. Liu fell to the ground in terror, but the dragon left as quickly as it had appeared.

"That was Chiantang," the Dragon King explained, helping the terrified Liu to his feet. "I must apologize for his frightening you like that." He called for wine and food, and graciously set them before Liu, who soon forgot his fear, as they talked about Liu's career, and life in the capital. A short while later, they were cut short by the arrival of the queen and her train, smiling and laughing amongst themselves. And Liu saw to his amazement that the Dragon King's daughter, whom he had met on the road, was in the group. The king embraced her, and he begged her forgiveness for allowing her to marry such a wretch, and she warmly thanked Liu for his help in rescuing her.

At that moment an elegant, dignified young man walked into the chamber and was introduced to Liu as Chiantang. Once he overcame his initial fear, Liu was delighted to find him a charming individual, courteously thanking Liu for his help, and toasting his health. Chiantang explained to his brother that he had fought the Jing River God and his men, and then visited the High God to explain his actions and apologize if he had done wrong. "He has generously forgiven me," he said, "and I now apologize to you, my brother for my fury in your palace, and to you, honoured guest, for scaring you."

"I am glad the High God has forgiven you," said the king. "And I willingly do so too, but you must be less hasty in future. And now tell me of the battle with the God of the Jing river."

"It was nothing," said Chiantang. "I slew six hundred thousand of his men, and destroyed two hundred square miles of his land, and the battle was as good as won."

"And what of my daughter's erstwhile husband?"

"I ate him," replied Chiantang casually, and the conversation was over.

The next day a great feast was held in Liu's honour; the Dragon King lavished gifts on him, and Chiantang drank to his health innumerable times. After much delicious food, and even more wine, Chiantang took Liu aside and said to him, "The king's daughter has been saved thanks to you. She is a fine woman, aware of how much she owes to you, and as it is clear that you are in love with her, I suggest that you marry her straight away."

Liu did not know what to say; although he was, as Chiantang had guessed, very much in love with the girl, marriage to the daughter of a God was not to be taken lightly. Nor was the suggestion of a rather drunken dragon to be taken too seriously, especially when Liu considered the possibility of Chiantang's anger at his presumption, if the dragon changed his mind when sober. So, regretfully, Liu talked the tipsy Chiantang out of his idea, and the next day left the palace for his home, laden with gifts, and accompanied by many servants. In his heart, though, he still longed for the Dragon Princess.

Months passed, and the now-wealthy Liu, knowing he could not pine for ever, married a local girl, but she was stricken with fever and soon died. To stave off his loneliness, Liu married again, but his second wife too caught the fever, and soon died. Despairing more and more, Liu married a girl from outside the region, who soon bore him a son. As time went by, Liu began to notice that his wife looked more and more like the Dragon Princess, the lost love of his youth, and after his second son had been born, the woman finally admitted that she was indeed the Dragon King's daughter. She had been bitterly disappointed when Liu turned down her uncle's suggestion, and kept remembering his last words to her on the road from the capital: 'When you return to Dongting, I sincerely hope that we shall meet again.' When Liu's second wife had died, she had seized her opportunity to become the third.

The couple lived together in great happiness, and raised a large family. They frequently visited the Dragon King's palace beneath the deep waters of Lake Dongting, and as Liu became older, they stayed there for longer and longer periods. Eventually they left the land of mortal men entirely, and took up residence with the immortal Dragon King and Queen, and Chiantang, in their immortal home beneath the waves.

The Old Mother of the Waters

THE OLD MOTHER of the Waters, Shui-mu Niang-niang, inundated the ancient city of Ssu-chou in Anhui almost every year. A report was presented to Yu Huang, Lord of the Skies, begging him to put an end to the menace who devastated the country and cost so many lives. The Lord of the Skies commanded the Great Kings of the Skies and their generals to raise troops and take the field in order to capture this goddess of the waters and deprive her of the power of doing further mischief. But her tricks triumphed over force and the city continued to be periodically devastated by inundations.

One day Shui-mu Niang-niang was seen near the city gate carrying two buckets of water. Li Lao-chun suspected some plot, but, an open attack being too risky, he preferred to adopt a ruse. He went and bought a donkey, led it to the buckets of water and let it drink their contents. Unfortunately the animal could not drink all the water, so that a little remained at the bottom of the buckets. Now these magical buckets contained the sources of the five great lakes, which held enough water to inundate the whole of China. Shui-mu Niang-niang overturned one of the buckets and the water that had remained in it was enough to cause a formidable flood, which submerged the unfortunate town, and buried it forever under the immense sheet of water called the Lake of Hung-tse.

So great a crime deserved an exemplary punishment and accordingly Yu Huang sent reinforcements to his armies and a pursuit of the goddess was planned.

Sun Hou-tzu, the Monkey Sun, the rapid courier – who in a single skip could travel thirty-six thousand miles – started in pursuit and caught her up, but the astute goddess was clever enough to slip through his fingers. Sun Hou-tzu, furious at this setback, went to ask Kuan-yin P'u-sa to come to his aid. She promised to do so. As one may imagine, the furious race she had had to escape from her enemy had given Shui-mu Niang-niang a good appetite. Exhausted with fatigue and with an empty stomach, she caught sight of a woman selling vermicelli, who had just prepared two bowls of it and was awaiting customers. Shui-mu Niang-niang went up to her and began to eat the strength-giving food with enthusiasm. No sooner had she eaten half of the vermicelli than it changed in her stomach into iron chains, which wound round her intestines. The end of the chain protruded from her mouth and the contents of the bowl became another long chain which welded itself to the end and stuck out beyond her lips. The vermicelli-seller was none other than Kuan-yin P'u-sa herself, who had conceived this idea as a means of ridding herself of this evil goddess. She ordered Sun Hou-tzu to take her down a deep well at the foot of a mountain in Hsu-i Hsien and to fasten her securely there. It is there that Shui-mu Niang-niang remains in her liquid prison. The end of the chain is to be seen when the water is low.

Hsu Sun, the Dragon Slayer

AT FORTY-ONE YEARS OF AGE, when Hsu Sun was Magistrate of Ching-yang, near the modern Chih-chiang Hsien, in Hupei, during times of drought he had only to touch a piece of tile to turn it into gold in order to relieve the people of their distress. He also saved many lives by curing sickness through the use of talismans and magic formulae.

During the period of the dynastic troubles, he resigned and joined the famous magician Kuo P'o. Together they went to the minister Wang Tun, who had risen against the Eastern Chin dynasty. Kuo P'o's remonstrance only irritated the minister, who cut off his head.

Hsu Sun then threw his chalice on the ridgepole of the room, causing it to be whirled into the air. As Wang Tun watched this unfold, Hsu disappeared and escaped. When he reached Lu-chiang K'ou, in Anhui, he boarded a boat, which two dragons towed into the offing and then raised into the air. In an instant they had borne it to the Lu Shan Mountains, to the south of Kiukiang, in Kiangsi. The perplexed boatman opened the window of his boat and looked out. The dragons, finding themselves discovered by an infidel, set the boat down on the top of the mountain and fled.

In this country was a dragon, or spiritual alligator, which transformed itself into a young man named Shen Lang. He married Chia Yu, daughter of the Chief Judge of T'an Chou. The young people lived in rooms below the official apartments. During spring and summer Shen Lang roamed in the rivers and lakes. One day Hsu met him, recognized him as a dragon and knew that he was the cause of the numerous floods that were devastating Kiangsi Province. He determined to find a means of getting rid of him.

Shen Lang, aware of the steps being taken against him, changed himself into a yellow ox and fled. Hsu at once transformed himself into a black ox and started in pursuit. The yellow ox jumped down a well to hide, but the black ox followed suit. The yellow ox then jumped out again and escaped to Ch'ang-sha, where he reassumed a human form.

Hsu Sun, returning to the town, hastened to the yamen and called to Shen Lang to come out and show himself, addressing him in a severe tone of voice: "Dragon, how dare you hide yourself there under a borrowed form?" Shen Lang then reassumed the form of a spiritual alligator and Hsu Sun ordered the spiritual soldiers to kill him. He then commanded his two sons to come out of their abode. By merely spurting a mouthful of water on them he transformed them into young dragons. Chia Yu was told to vacate the rooms at once and in the twinkling of an eye the whole yamen sank beneath the earth. Nothing but a lake remained where it had been.

After his victory over the dragon, Hsu Sun assembled the members of his family on Hsi Shan, outside the city of Nan-ch'ang Fu and all ascended to Heaven in full daylight, taking with them even the dogs and chickens. He was then 133 years old. Subsequently a temple was erected to him and he was canonized as Just Prince, Admirable and Beneficent.

The Building of Peking

WHEN THE MONGOL YUAN DYNASTY had been destroyed and the Emperor Hung Wu had succeeded in firmly establishing that of the Great Ming, Ta Ming, he made Chin-ling (the present Nanking) his capital and held his Court there with great splendour. Envoys from every province within the 'Four Seas' would assemble there to witness his greatness.

The Emperor had many sons and daughters by his different consorts and concubines, each mother in her inmost heart fondly hoping that her own son would be selected by his father to succeed him.

Although the Empress had a son, who was the heir-apparent, she felt envious of those ladies who had likewise been blessed with children for fear one of the princes should supplant her son in the affection of the Emperor and in the succession. This envy displayed itself on every occasion; she was greatly beloved by the Emperor and exerted all her influence with him to get the other young princes removed from Court. Through her means most of them were sent to the different provinces as governors.

One of the consorts of Hung Wu, the Lady Weng, had a son named Chu-ti. This young prince was very handsome and graceful; he was, moreover, of an amiable disposition. He was the fourth son of the Emperor and his pleasing manner had made him a great favourite, not only with his father, but with everyone about the Court. The Empress noticed the evident affection the Emperor had for this prince, so she plotted to get him removed from the Court as soon as possible. By a judicious use of flattery and cajolery, she ultimately persuaded the Emperor to appoint the prince governor of the Yen country. He was to be known as Yen Wang, Prince of Yen.

Soon afterwards the young Prince left Chin-ling to proceed to his post. As he left, however, a Taoist priest called Liu Po-wen, who had a great affection for the Prince, put a sealed packet into his hand and told him to open it when he found himself in difficulty, distress or danger; a glance at the first portion that came to his hand would invariably suggest some remedy for the evil, whatever it was. After doing so he was again to seal the packet, without further looking into its contents, till some other emergency arose necessitating advice or assistance, when he would again find it. The Prince departed on his journey and in time arrived safely at his destination.

When Chu-ti arrived in Yen it was a mere barren wilderness with very few inhabitants; those there lived in huts and scattered hamlets and there was no city to afford protection to the people and to defend then from robbers or would-be attackers.

When the Prince saw what a desolate looking place he had been appointed to – and thought of the long years he was probably destined to spend there – he grew very melancholy and nothing his attendants said or did could alleviate his sorrow.

All at once the Prince thought of the packet that the old Taoist priest had given him; he began to search for it – for in the bustle and excitement of travelling he had forgotten all about it – in hope that it might suggest something to better his prospects. Having found the packet, he quickly broke it open to see what instructions it contained; taking out the first paper which came to hand, he read the following:

"When you reach Pei-p'ing Fu (now Peking) you must build a city there and name it No-cha Ch'eng, the City of No-cha. But, as the work will be costly, you must issue a proclamation inviting the wealthy to subscribe the necessary funds for building it. At the back of this paper is a plan of the city; you must be careful to act according to the instructions accompanying it."

The Prince inspected the plan, carefully read the instructions and found even the minutest details fully explained. He was struck with the grandeur of the design of the proposed city and immediately acted on the instructions contained in the packet; proclamations were posted up and large sums were soon subscribed, ten of the wealthiest families who had accompanied him from Chin-ling being the largest contributors, supporting the plan not only with their purses, by giving immense sums, but by their influence among their less wealthy neighbours.

When enough money had been subscribed, a day was chosen on which to start building. Trenches where the foundations of the walls were to be were first dug out, according to the plan found in the packet. The foundations themselves consisted of layers of stone quarried from the western hills; bricks of an immense size were made and burnt in the neighbourhood; the moat was dug out and the earth from it used to fill in the centre of the walls; the whole circuit of the walls having battlements and embrasures. Above each of the nine gates of the city immense three-storied towers were built.

Near the front entrance of the city, facing each other, were built the Temples of Heaven and of Earth. Behind it the beautiful 'Coal Hill' (better known as 'Prospect Hill') was raised; while in the square in front of the Great Gate of the palace was buried an immense quantity of charcoal (that and the coal being stored as a precaution in case of siege).

The palace, containing many superb buildings, was built in a style of exceeding splendour; in the various enclosures were beautiful gardens and lakes; in the different courtyards, too, seventy-two wells were dug and thirty-six golden tanks placed. The whole of the buildings and grounds was surrounded by a lofty wall and a stone paved moat, in which the lotus and other beautiful flowers bloomed, and in the clear waters of which numerous gold and silver fish could be found.

The city was similar to that of Chin-ling. When everything was completed the Prince compared it with the plan and found that the city tallied with it in every respect. He was delighted and called for the ten wealthy persons who had been the chief contributors and gave each of them a pair of 'couchant dragon' silk- or satin-embroidered cuffs and allowed them great privileges. Up to the present time there is the common saying: "Since then the 'dragon-cuffed' gentlefolks have flourished."

All the people were loud in praise of the beauty and strength of the newly built city. Merchants from every province hastened to Peking, attracted by the news they heard of its magnificence and of the prospect of selling their wares. The people were prosperous and happy, food was plentiful, the troops brave, the monarch just, his ministers virtuous and all enjoyed the blessings of peace. All was tranquil.

However, one day one of the Prince's ministers reported that "the wells are thirsty and the rivers dried up" – there was no water and the people were all alarmed. At once the Prince called his counsellors together to devise some means of remedying this disaster and causing the water to return to the wells and springs, but no one could suggest a suitable plan.

The reason for the scarcity of water was that there was a dragon's cave outside the east gate of the city at a place called Lei-chen K'ou, 'Thunder-clap Mouth' or 'Pass'. The dragon had not been seen for many years, but it was well known that he lived there. In digging out the earth to build the wall, the workmen had broken into this dragon's cave, without knowing the consequences that would result. The dragon was angry and determined to move away from the new city, but the she-dragon said: "We have lived here thousands of years, and shall we suffer the Prince of Yen to drive us forth thus? If we do go we will collect all the water, place it in our baskets and at midnight we will appear in a dream to the Prince requesting permission to retire. If he gives us permission to do so and allows us also to take our baskets of water with us, he will fall into our trap – for we shall take the water with his own consent."

The two dragons then transformed themselves into an old man and an old woman, went to the chamber of the Prince, who was asleep, and appeared to him in a dream. Kneeling before him, they cried: "O Lord of a Thousand Years, we have come before you to beg leave to retire from this place and to beseech you out of your great bounty to give us permission to take these two baskets of water with us."

The Prince readily agreed, little dreaming of the danger he was facing. The dragons were delighted, and quickly left; they filled the baskets with all the water there was in Peking and carried them off with them.

When the Prince woke he paid no attention to his dream till he heard the report of the scarcity of water. Deciding there might be some hidden meaning in it, he opened the packet again and discovered that his dream visitors had been dragons who had taken the waters of Peking away with them in their magic baskets. He returned to the packet once more, which contained directions for the recovery of the water.

The Prince quickly donned his armour, mounted his black horse and, with spear in hand, dashed out of the west gate of the city. He soon caught up with the water-stealing dragons, who still retained the forms they had appeared to him in his dream. On a cart were the two identical baskets he had seen; in front of the cart, dragging it, was the old woman, while behind, pushing it, was the old man.

When the Prince saw them he galloped up to the cart and, without pausing, thrust his spear into one of the baskets, making a great hole, out of which the water rushed so rapidly that the Prince became frightened. He dashed off at full speed to save himself from being swallowed up by the waters, which in a very short time had risen more than thirty feet and had flooded the surrounding country. On galloped the Prince, followed by the roaring water, till he reached a hill, up which he urged his startled horse. When he reached the top he found that it stood out of the water like an island, completely surrounded; the water was seething and swirling round the hill in a frightful manner, but he could see neither of the dragons.

The Prince was alarmed at his perilous position, when suddenly a Buddhist priest appeared before him, with clasped hands and bent head, who told him not be alarmed, as with Heaven's assistance he would soon disperse the water. Then the priest recited a short prayer or spell and the waters receded as rapidly as they had risen, finally returning to their proper channels.

The broken basket became a large deep hole, in the centre of which was a fountain which threw up a vast body of clear water. From the midst of this arose a pagoda, which rose and fell with the water, floating on the top like a vessel; the spire thrusting itself far up into the sky, and swaying about like the mast of a ship in a storm.

The Prince returned to the city filled with wonder at what he had seen, and with joy at having so successfully carried out the directions contained in the packet. On all sides he was greeted by his delighted people, hailing him as the saviour of Peking. Since that time Peking has never had the misfortune to be without water.

The pagoda is called the Pagoda on the Hill of the Imperial Spring. The spring is still there and day and night its clear waters bubble up and flow eastward to Peking, which would now be a barren wilderness but for the Prince's pursuit of the water.

Kwang-Jui And The God of The River

CHINA IS A LAND where the great masses of the people have to toil and struggle incessantly in order to obtain even the bare necessities of daily existence. Unnumbered multitudes never enjoy a sufficiency of food, but have to be contented with whatever Heaven may send them; and profoundly thankful they are when they can be sure of two meals a day to stave off the pangs of hunger from themselves and their children.

How many there are who cannot by the severest toil obtain even these two meals is evident from the organized beggar communities, which are to be found in connection with every great city in the Empire, and from the vast numbers of tramps, who wander over the country on the highways and byways with pale and sodden faces and with garments nearly falling to pieces, picking up a scanty livelihood from the benevolent as they pass from village to village.

Whatever may be their inmost thoughts, the Chinese bear their terrible hardships and privations with a splendid heroism, with little complaining, with no widespread outbreaks of robbery, and with no pillaging of rice-shops and public granaries by organized mobs driven mad by hunger.

There is one beautiful feature about the Chinese that has been an important factor in steadying the nation. They are imbued with at least one great ideal, which touches their common life in every direction. Every man in the Empire, rich or poor, learned or unlearned, has a profound respect for what he calls Tien-Li, or Divine Righteousness. By this the Chinese judge all actions. It is the standard by which Kings and Princes and common people direct their conduct, whether in the highest affairs of state, or in the ordinary engagements of common every-day life.

In addition to this, the minds of the Chinese are filled with romance and poetry, so that to them the invisible world is peopled with fairies and all kinds of spirits, both good and bad, the former relieving in mysterious ways the dull greyness that sorrow and disaster often shed upon the lives of men.

The story of Kwang-Jui is a remarkable evidence of the unbounded faith which the Chinese have in the intervention of these mysterious beings to deliver men from calamities which would otherwise prove fatal to them.

When we first meet with Kwang-Jui, he is living with his widowed mother in a retired part of the country. His father had been dead for some time, and Kwang-Jui was now the only one upon whom the fortunes of the home could be built. He was a very studious lad, and was possessed of remarkable abilities, the result being that he successfully passed the various Imperial Examinations, even the final one in the capital, where the Sovereign himself presided as examiner.

After this last examination, as the men were waiting outside the Hall for the names of those who had satisfied the Emperor to be read out a considerable crowd had collected. Most of these people had come from mere curiosity to see the Imperial Edict, and to discover who the scholar was that stood first on the list. The excitement was intense, and speculation ran rife as to which of the candidates, who had come from almost every province in the Empire, was going to obtain the place of honour which was the dream and the ambition of every scholar in the land.

At last every breath was hushed, and every voice stilled in silence, as one of the high officials of the Palace, attended by an imposing retinue, came out of the great central doors, which had been flung wide open at his approach. In a clear voice he began to read the list. It was headed by the name of Kwang-Jui.

At this precise moment occurred an incident which was destined to change the whole current of Kwang-Jui's career. As he was standing overcome with emotion in consequence of the supreme honour which had been conferred upon him by the Emperor's Edict, a small round ball, beautifully embroidered, was thrown from an upper window of a house across the way, and struck him on the shoulder.

It may here be explained that it was a custom in the early days of the history of China to allow any young maiden who was reluctant to have her husband chosen for her by her parents, to make use of what was called "The throwing of the embroidered ball" in order to discover the man whom the gods intended her to marry. This ball was made of some soft material, wrapped round with a piece of red silk which was covered with variegated figures, worked by the damsel's own hands and emblematic of the love by which the hearts of husband and wife are bound indissolubly to each other. It was firmly believed by every maiden of this romantic type that the man who was struck by the ball from her fair hands was the one whom Heaven had selected as her husband; and no parent would ever dream of refusing to accept a choice made in this way.

Whilst Kwang-Jui was gazing in amused wonder at the symbol which he understood so well, a messenger from the house from which it had been thrown requested him in respectful tones to accompany him to his master, who desired to discuss with him a most important subject.

As Kwang-Jui entered the house, he discovered to his astonishment that it belonged to the Prime Minister, who received him with the utmost cordiality, and after a long conversation declared that he was prepared to submit to the will of the gods, and to accept him as his son-in-law. Kwang-Jui was of course in raptures at the brilliant prospects which were suddenly opening up before him. The day, indeed, was a red-letter one – an omen, he hoped, that fate was preparing to pour down upon him good fortune in the future. In one brief day he had been hailed as the most distinguished scholar in the Empire, and he had also been acknowledged as the son-in-law of the Empire's greatest official, who had the power of placing him in high positions where he could secure not only honours but also wealth sufficient to drive poverty away for ever from his home.

As there was no reason for delay, the hand of the beautiful daughter who had thrown the embroidered ball, and who was delighted that Heaven had chosen for her such a brilliant husband, was bestowed upon him by her parents. Times of great rejoicing succeeded, and when Kwang-Jui thought of the quiet and uninteresting days when he was still unknown to fame, and contrasted them with his present life, it seemed to him as though he were living in fairy-land. His wildest dreams in the past had never conjured up anything so grand as the life he was now leading. In one bound he had leaped from comparative poverty to fame and riches.

After a time, through the influence of his father-in-law, and with the hearty consent of the Emperor, who remembered what a brilliant student he had been, Kwang-Jui was appointed to be Prefect of an important district in the centre of China.

Taking his bride with him, he first of all proceeded to his old home, where his mother was waiting with great anxiety to welcome her now famous son. The old lady felt rather nervous at meeting her new daughter-in-law, seeing that the latter came from a family which was far higher in rank and far more distinguished than any in her own clan. As it was very necessary that Kwang-Jui should take up his office as Prefect without any undue delay, he and his mother and his bride set out in the course of a few days on the long journey to the distant prefecture, where their lives were destined to be marred by sorrow and disaster.

They had travelled the greater part of the way, and had reached a country market-town that lay on their route, when Kwang-Jui's mother, worn out with the toilsome journey, fell suddenly ill. The doctor who was called in shook his head and pronounced that she was suffering from a very serious complaint, which, whilst not necessarily fatal, would necessitate a complete rest for at least two or three months. Any further travelling must therefore be abandoned for the present, as it might be attended with the most serious consequences to the old lady.

Both husband and wife were greatly distressed at the unlucky accident which placed them in such an awkward position at this wayside inn. They were truly grieved at the serious sickness of their mother, but they were still more puzzled as to what course they should pursue in these most trying circumstances. The Imperial Rescript appointing Kwang-Jui to his office as Prefect commanded him to take up his post on a certain definite date. To delay until his mother would again be able to endure the fatigues of travel was out of the question, as disobedience to the Emperor's orders would be attended by his grave displeasure. Eventually his mother suggested that he and his wife should go on ahead, and that after taking up the duties of his office he should then delegate them for a time to his subordinates and return to take her home.

This advice Kwang-Jui decided to carry out; though with great reluctance, as he was most unwilling to abandon his mother to the care of strangers. He accordingly made all the arrangements he possibly could for her comfort whilst they were parted from each other; he had servants engaged to attend upon her, and he left sufficient money with her to meet all her expenses during his absence.

With a mind full of consideration for his mother, and wishing to show how anxious he was to give her pleasure, he went out into the market of the town to see if he could buy a certain kind of fish of which she was passionately fond. He had hardly got outside the courtyard of the inn, when he met a fisherman with a very fine specimen of the very fish that he wished to purchase.

As he was discussing the price with the man, a certain something about the fish arrested his attention. There was a peculiar look in its eyes that seemed full of pathos and entreaty. Its gaze was concentrated upon him, so human-like and with such intensity, that he instinctively felt it was pleading with him to do something to deliver it from a great disaster. This made him look at it more carefully, and to his astonishment the liquid eyes of the fish were still fixed upon him with a passionate regard that made him quiver with excitement.

"Fisherman," he said, "I want to buy this fish, and here is the price that you ask for it. I have but one stipulation to make, and that is that you take it to the river from which you caught it, and set it free to swim away wherever it pleases. Remember that if you fail to carry out this part of the bargain, great sorrow will come upon you and your home."

Little did either of them dream that the fish was the presiding God of the River, who for purposes of his own had transformed himself into this form, and who, while swimming up and down the stream had been caught in the net of the fisherman.

After travelling for some hours Kwang-Jui and his wife came to the bank of a considerable river, where they hired a large boat to convey them to their destination.

The boatman they engaged was a man of very low character. He had originally been a scholar and of good family, but, utterly depraved and immoral, he had gradually sunk lower and lower in society, until at last he had been compelled to fly from his home to a distant province, and there to engage in his present occupation in order to earn his living. The large amount of property which Kwang-Jui had with him seemed to arouse the worst passions in this man, and while the boat was being carried along by a fair wind and a flowing tide, he planned in his mind how he was to become the possessor of it. By the time that they reached the place where they were to anchor for the night, he had already decided what measures he should adopt.

A little after midnight, accordingly, he crept stealthily towards the place where Kwang-Jui was sleeping, stabbed him to the heart and threw his body into the fast-flowing river. He next threatened the wife that if she dared to utter a sound, he would murder her also and send her to join her husband in the Land of Shadows. Paralyzed with terror, she remained speechless, only a stifled sob and groan now and again breaking from her agonized heart. Her first serious idea was to commit suicide, and she was preparing to fling herself into the water that gurgled along the sides of the boat, when she was restrained by the thought that if she destroyed herself, she would never be able to avenge her husband's death or bring punishment upon the villain who had just murdered him.

It was not mere robbery, however, that was in the mind of the man who had committed this great crime. He had bigger ideas than that. He had noticed that in personal appearance he very much resembled his victim, so he determined to carry out the daring project of passing himself off as Kwang-Jui, the mandarin whom the Emperor had despatched to take up the appointment of Prefect.

Having threatened the widow that instant death would be her portion if she breathed a word to anyone about the true state of the case, and having arrayed himself in the official robes of the man whom he had stabbed to death, the boatman appeared at the yamen, where he presented the Imperial credentials and was duly installed in his office. It never entered his mind that it was not cowardice which kept the widow silent, but the stern resolve of a brave and high-minded woman that she would do her part to see that vengeance should in time fall upon the man who had robbed her of a husband whom she looked upon as the direct gift of Heaven.

Now, immediately after the body of Kwang-Jui had been cast into the water, the customary patrol sent by the God of the River to see that order was kept within his dominions, came upon it, and conveyed it with all speed into the presence of the god himself.

The latter looked at it intently for a moment, and then exclaimed in great excitement, "Why, this is the very person who only yesterday saved my life, when I was in danger of being delivered over to a cruel death! I shall now be able to show my gratitude by using all the power I possess to serve his interests. Bring him to the Crystal Grotto," he continued, "where only those who have distinguished themselves in the service of the State have ever been allowed to lie. This man has a claim upon me such as no one before him ever possessed. He is the saviour of my life, and I will tenderly care for him until the web of fate has been spun, and, the vengeance of Heaven having been wreaked upon his murderer, he shall once more rejoin the wife from whom he has been so ruthlessly torn."

With the passing of the months, the widow of Kwang-Jui gave birth to a son, the very image of his father. It was night-time when he was born, and not long after his birth, a mysterious voice, which could not be traced, was heard distinctly saying, "Let the child be removed without delay from the yamen, before the return of the Prefect, as otherwise its life will not be safe."

Accordingly, on the morrow, the babe, about whose destiny even Heaven itself seemed concerned, was carefully wrapped round with many coverings to protect it against the weather.

Inside the inmost dress, there was enclosed a small document, telling the child's tragic story and describing the danger from a powerful foe which threatened its life. In order to be able to identify her son, it might be after the lapse of many years, the mother cut off the last joint of the little finger of his left hand; and then, with tears and sighs, and with her heart full of unspoken agony, she took a last, lingering look upon the face of the little one.

A confidential slave woman carried him out of her room, and by devious ways and secret paths finally laid him on the river's bank. Casting a final glance at the precious bundle to see that no danger threatened it, she hurried back in the direction of the city, with the faint cries of the abandoned infant still sounding in her ears.

And now the child was in the hands of Heaven. That this was so was evident from the fact that in a few minutes the abbot of the monastery, which could be seen crowning the top of a neighbouring hill, passed along the narrow pathway by the side of the river. Hearing a baby's cry, he hastened towards the place from which the sounds came, and picking up the little bundle, and realizing that the infant had been deserted, he carried it up to the monastery and made every arrangement for its care and comfort. Fortunately he was a man of a deeply benevolent nature, and no more suitable person could have been found to take charge of the child.

We must now allow eighteen years to pass by. The child that had been left on the margin of the river had grown up to be a fine, handsome lad. The abbot had been his friend ever since the day when his heart had been touched by his cries, and his love for the little foundling had grown with the years. The boy had become a kind of son to him, and in order not to be parted from him he had taught him the temple duties, so that he was now a qualified priest in the service of the gods.

One morning the young man, whose name was Sam-Choang, came to the abbot with a restless, dissatisfied look on his face, and begged to be told who his father was, and who his mother. The old priest, who had long been aware of the tragic story of Kwang-Jui's murder, felt that the time had come when the lad ought to know what he had hitherto concealed from him. Taking out the document which he had found upon him as a baby, he read it to him, and then the great secret was out. After this a long and serious discussion took place between the two as to the wisest methods to be adopted for bringing the Prefect to justice and delivering the lad's mother from the humiliating position which she had so heroically borne for all these eighteen years.

The next day a young priest, with shaven head and dressed in the usual slate-coloured gown, appeared at the yamen of the Prefect to solicit subscriptions for the neighbouring monastery. As the Prefect was absent on some public business, he was ushered into the reception-room, where he was received by his mother, who had always been a generous supporter of the Goddess of Mercy.

At the first sight of this striking-looking young bonze, she found her heart agitated in a strange and powerful way, such as she had not experienced for many a long year; and when she noticed that the little finger on his left hand was without the last joint, she trembled with the utmost excitement.

After a few words about the object for which he had come, the young priest slipped into her hand the very paper which she had written eighteen years ago; and as she looked at her own handwriting and then gazed into his face and saw the striking likeness to the man at whom she had thrown the embroidered ball, the mother-instinct within her flashed suddenly out, and she recognized that this handsome lad was her own son. The joy of the mother as she looked upon the face of Sam-Choang was reflected in the sparkling eyes and glowing look of pleasure that lit up his whole countenance.

Retiring for a short time his mother returned with a letter which she handed to him. In a low voice she told him that it was to her father, who still lived in the capital, and to whom he was to take it without any delay. In order to prevent suspicion on the part of the Prefect, he was to travel as a priest, who was endeavouring to obtain subscriptions for his monastery. He was to be sure, also, to visit the place where his grandmother had been left, and to try and find out what had become of her. In order to defray his expenses she gave him a few bars of gold, which he could exchange for the current money at the banks on the way.

When Sam-Choang arrived at the inn where his father had parted with his grandmother, he could find no trace of her. A new landlord was in possession, who had never even heard her name; but on enquiring amongst the shopkeepers in the neighbourhood, he found to his horror that she was now a member of the beggars' camp, and that her name was enrolled amongst that degraded fraternity.

On reaching the wretched hovel where she was living, he discovered that when her money was exhausted and no remittance came to her from her son, she had been driven out on to the street by the innkeeper, and from that time had tramped the country, living on the scraps and bits which were bestowed upon her by the benevolent. Great was her joy when her grandson led her away to the best inn in the place, and on his departure gave her an ample supply of money for all her needs until they should meet again.

When Sam-Choang reached the capital and handed his mother's letter to his grandfather, the most profound excitement ensued. As soon as the Emperor was officially informed of the case, he determined that the severest punishment should be inflicted upon the man who had not only committed a cruel murder, but through it had dared to usurp a position which could only be held at the Sovereign's command. An Imperial Edict was accordingly issued ordering the Prime Minister to take a considerable body of troops and proceed with all possible speed to the district where such an unheard-of crime had been committed, and there to hand over the offender to immediate execution.

By forced marches, so as to outstrip any private intelligence that might have been sent from the capital, the avenging force reached the city a little before the break of day. Here they waited in silence outside the city gates, anxiously listening for the boom of the early gun which announces the dawn, and at the same time causes the gates to be flung wide open for the traffic of the day to commence.

As soon as the warders had admitted the waiting crowd outside, the soldiers, advancing at a run, quickly reached the yamen, and arrested the Prefect. Without form of trial but simply with a curt announcement from the Prime Minister that he was acting upon instructions from the Emperor, the mandarin was dragged unceremoniously through the gaping crowds that rushed from their doors to see the amazing spectacle.

The feet of Fate had marched slowly but with unerring certainty, and had at last reached the wretched criminal.

But where was he being taken? This road did not lead to the execution ground, where malefactors were doomed to end their careers in shame. Street after street was passed, and still the stern-faced soldiers forced the mandarin down the main thoroughfares, whose sides had often been lined with respectful crowds as he swept by with his haughty retinue. At last they reached the city gate, through which they marched, and then on towards the river, which could be seen gleaming like a silver thread in the distance.

Arrived at its bank, the troops formed into a square with the prisoner in the centre. Addressing him, the Prime Minister said, "I have selected this spot rather than the public execution ground where criminals are put to death. Your crime has been no common one; and so to-day, in the face of high Heaven whose righteousness you have dared to violate, and within sound of the flowing waters of the stream that witnessed the murder, you shall die."

Half a dozen soldiers then threw him violently to the ground, and in a few minutes the executioner had torn his bleeding heart from his bosom. Then, standing with it still in his hand, he waited by the side of the Prime Minister, who read out to the great multitude the indictment which had been drawn up against the Prefect. In this he described his crimes, and at the same time appealed to Heaven and to the God of the River to take measures to satisfy and appease the spirit of him who had been cut off in the prime of life by the man who had just been executed.

As soon as the reading of the document had been concluded, it was set fire to and allowed to burn until only the blackened ashes remained. These, together with the criminal's heart, were then cast into the river. They were thus formally handed over to the god, who would see that in the Land of Shadows there should come a further retribution on the murderer for the crimes he had committed on earth.

The water patrol happened to pass by soon after the ashes and heart had been flung into the river, and picking them up most carefully, they carried them to the official residence of the god. The indictment was at once formally entered amongst the archives of the office, to be used as evidence when the case was in due time brought before the notice of Yam-lo: and after looking at the heart with the intensest scrutiny for some little time, the god exclaimed, "And so the murderer has at last received some part of the punishment he so richly deserved. It is now time for me to awake the sleeping husband, so that he may be restored to the wife from whom he has been separated for eighteen years."

Passing into the Crystal Grotto, where the unconscious form of Kwang-Jui had reposed for so many years, the god touched the body gently with his hand, and said: "Friend, arise! Your wife awaits you, and loving ones who have long mourned you. Many years of happiness are still before you, and the honours that your Sovereign will bestow upon you shall place you amongst the famous men of the State. Arise, and take your place once more amongst the living!"

The Prime Minister was sitting with his daughter, listening to the sad story of the years of suffering through which she had passed, when the door was silently opened, and the figure of her long-lost husband glided in. Both started up in fear and amazement, for they believed that what they saw was only a restless spirit which had wandered from the Land of Shadows and would speedily vanish again from their sight. In this, however, they were delightfully disappointed. Kwang-Jui and his wife were once more reunited, and for many a long year their hearts were so full of gladness and contentment, that the sorrows which they had endured gradually became effaced from their memories. They always thought with the deepest gratitude of the God of the River, who for eighteen years had kept the unconscious husband alive and had finally restored him to his heart-broken wife.

Sam-Chung And The Water Demon

SAM-CHUNG WAS ONE of the most famous men in the history of the Buddhist Church, and had distinguished himself by the earnestness and self-denial with which he had entered on the pursuit of eternal life. His mind had been greatly exercised and distressed at the pains and sorrows which mankind were apparently doomed to endure. Even those, however, terrible as they were, he could have managed to tolerate had they not ended, in the case of every human being, in the crowning calamity which comes upon all at the close of life.

Death was the great mystery which cast its shadow on every human being. It invaded every home. The sage whose virtues and teachings were the means of uplifting countless generations of men came under its great law. Men of infamous and abandoned character seemed often to outlive the more virtuous of their fellow-beings; but they too, when the gods saw fit, were hurried off without any ceremony. Even the little ones, who had never violated any of the laws of Heaven, came under this universal scourge; and many of them, who had only just commenced to live were driven out into the Land of Shadows by this mysterious force which dominates all human life.

Accordingly Sam-Chung wanted to be freed from the power of death, so that its shadow should never darken his life in the years to come.

After careful enquiry, and through friendly hints from men who, he had reason to believe, were fairies in disguise and had been sent by the Goddess of Mercy to help those who aspired after a higher life, he learned that it was possible by the constant pursuit of virtue to arrive at that stage of existence in which death would lose all its power to injure, and men should become immortal. This boon of eternal life could be won by every man or woman who was willing to pay the price for so precious a gift. It could be gained by great self-denial, by willingness to suffer, and especially by the exhibition of profound love and sympathy for those who were in sorrow of any kind. It appeared, indeed, that the one thing most imperatively demanded by the gods from those who aspired to enter their ranks was that they should be possessed of a divine compassion, and that their supreme object should be the succouring of distressed humanity. Without this compassion any personal sacrifice that might be made in the search for immortality would be absolutely useless.

Sam-Chung was already conscious that he was a favourite of the gods, for they had given him two companions, both with supernatural powers, to enable him to contend against the cunning schemes of the evil spirits, who are ever planning how to thwart and destroy those whose hearts are set upon higher things.

One day, accompanied by Chiau and Chu, the two attendants commissioned by the Goddess of Mercy to attend upon him, Sam-Chung started on his long journey for the famous Tien-ho river, to cross which is the ambition of every pilgrim on his way to the land of the Immortals. They endured many weeks of painful travelling over high mountains and through deep valleys which lay in constant shadow, and across sandy deserts where men perished of thirst or were struck down by the scorching heat of the sun, before they met any of the infernal foes that they expected to be lying in wait for them.

Weary and footsore, they at last arrived one evening on the shores of the mighty Tien-ho, just as the sun was setting. The glory of the clouds in the west streamed on to the waters of the river, and made them sparkle with a beauty which seemed to our wearied travellers to transform them into something more than earthly. The river here was so wide that it looked like an inland sea. There was no sign of land on the distant horizon, nothing but one interminable vista of waters, stretching away as far as the eye could reach.

One thing, however, greatly disappointed Sam-Chung and his companions, and that was the absence of boats. They had planned to engage one, and by travelling across the river during the night, they hoped to hurry on their way and at the same time to rest and refresh themselves after the fatigues they had been compelled to endure on their long land journey.

It now became a very serious question with them where they were to spend the night. There was no sign of any human habitation round about. There was the sandy beach along which they were walking, and there was the wide expanse of the river, on which the evening mists were slowly gathering; but no appearance of life. Just as they were wondering what course they should pursue, the faint sound of some musical instruments came floating on the air and caught their ear. Hastening forward in the direction from which the music came, they ascended a piece of rising ground, from the top of which they were delighted to see a village nestling on the hillside, and a small temple standing on the very margin of the river.

With hearts overjoyed at the prospect of gaining some place where they could lodge for the night, they hurried forward to the hamlet in front of them. As they drew nearer, the sounds of music became louder and more distinct. They concluded that some festival was being observed, or that some happy gathering amongst the people had thrown them all into a holiday mood. Entering the village, they made their way to a house which stood out prominently from the rest, and which was better built than any others they could see. Besides, it was the one from which the music issued, and around its doors was gathered a number of people who had evidently been attending some feast inside.

As the three travellers came up to the door, a venerable-looking old man came out to meet them. Seeing that they were strangers, he courteously invited them to enter; and on Sam-Chung asking whether they could be entertained for the night, he assured them that there was ample room for them in the house, and that he gladly welcomed them to be his guests for as long as it was their pleasure to remain.

"In the meanwhile you must come in," he said, "and have some food, for you must be tired and hungry after travelling so far, and the tables are still covered with the good things which were prepared for the feast to-day."

After they had finished their meal, they began to talk to the old gentleman who was so kindly entertaining them. They were greatly pleased with his courtesy and with the hearty hospitality which he had pressed upon them. They noticed, however, that he was very absent-minded, and looked as if some unpleasant thought lay heavy on his heart.

"May I ask," said Sam-Chung, "what was the reason for the great gathering here to-day? There is no festival in the Chinese calendar falling on this date, so I thought I would take the liberty of enquiring what occasion you were really commemorating."

"We were not commemorating anything," the old man replied with a grave face. "It was really a funeral service for two of my grand-children, who, though they are not yet dead, will certainly disappear out of this life before many hours have passed."

"But how can such a ceremony be performed over persons who are still alive?" asked Sam-Chung with a look of wonder in his face.

"When I have explained the circumstances to you, you will then be no longer surprised at this unusual service," replied the old man.

"You must know," he continued, "that this region is under the control of a Demon of a most cruel and bloodthirsty disposition. He is not like the ordinary spirits, whose images are enshrined in our temples, and whose main aim is to protect and guard their worshippers. This one has no love for mankind, but on the contrary the bitterest hatred, and his whole life seems to be occupied in scheming how he may inflict sorrow and disaster on them. His greatest cruelty is to insist that every year just about this time two children, one a boy and the other a girl, shall be conveyed to his temple by the river side to be devoured by him. Many attempts have been made to resist this barbarous demand, but they have only resulted in increased suffering to those who have dared to oppose him. The consequence is that the people submit to this cruel murder of their children, though many a heart is broken at the loss of those dearest to them."

"But is there any system by which the unfortunate people may get to know when this terrible sacrifice is going to be demanded from them?" asked Sam-Chung.

"Oh yes," replied the man. "The families are taken in rotation, and when each one's turn comes round, their children are prepared for the sacrifice. Moreover, that there may be no mistake, the Demon himself appears in the home a few days before, and gives a threatening command to have the victims ready on such a date. Only the day before yesterday, this summons came to us to have our children ready by tomorrow morning at break of day. That is why we had a feast to-day, and performed the funeral rites for the dead, so that their spirits may not be held under the control of this merciless Damon, but may in time be permitted to issue from the Land of Shadows, and be born again under happier circumstances into this world, which they are leaving under such tragic circumstances."

"But what is the Demon like?" enquired Sam-Chung.

"Oh, no one can ever tell what he is like," said the man. "He has no bodily form that one can look upon. His presence is known by a strong blast of wind which fills the place with a peculiar odour, and with an influence so subtle that you feel yourself within the grip of a powerful force, and instinctively bow your head as though you were in the presence of a being who could destroy you in a moment were he so disposed."

"One more question and I have finished," said Sam-Chung. "Where did this Demon come from, and how is it that he has acquired such an overmastering supremacy over the lives of men, that he seems able to defy even Heaven itself, and all the great hosts of kindly gods who are working for the salvation of mankind?"

"This Demon," the man replied, "was once an inhabitant of the Western Heaven, and under the direct control of the Goddess of Mercy. He must, however, have been filled with evil devices and fiendish instincts from the very beginning, for he seized the first opportunity to escape to earth, and to take up his residence in the grottoes and caverns that lie deep down beneath the waters of the Tien-ho. Other spirits almost as bad as himself have also taken up their abode there, and they combine their forces to bring calamity and disaster upon the people of this region."

Sam-Chung, whose heart was filled with the tenderest feelings of compassion for all living things, so much so that his name was a familiar one even amongst the Immortals in the far-off Western Heaven, felt himself stirred by a mighty indignation when he thought of how innocent childhood had been sacrificed to minister to the unnatural passion of this depraved Demon. Chiau and Chu were as profoundly indignant as he, and a serious consultation ensued as to the best methods to be adopted to save the little ones who were doomed to destruction on the morrow, and at the same time to break the monster's rule so that it should cease for ever.

Chiau, who was the more daring of the two whom I the goddess had deputed to protect Sam-Chung, at length cried out with flashing eyes, "I will personate the boy, Chu shall act the girl, and together we will fight the Demon and overthrow and kill him, and so deliver the people from his dreadful tyranny."

Turning to the old man, he said, "Bring the children here so that we may see them, and make our plans so perfect that the Demon with all his cunning will not be able to detect or frustrate them."

In a few moments the little ones were led in by their grandfather. The boy was seven and the girl was one year older. They were both of them nervous and shy, and clung timidly to the old man as if for protection.

They were very interesting-looking children. The boy was a proud, brave-spirited little fellow, as one could see by the poise of his head as he gazed at the strangers. If anything could be predicted from his looks, he would one day turn out to be a man of great power, for he had in his youthful face all the signs which promise a life out of the common. The girl was a shy little thing, with her hair done up in a childlike fashion that well became her. She was a dainty little mortal. Her eyes were almond-shaped, and with the coyness of her sex she kept shooting out glances from the corners of them at the three men who were looking at her. Her cheeks were pale, with just a suspicion of colour painted into them by the deft hand of nature; whilst her lips had been touched with the faintest dash of carmine, evidently just a moment ago, before she left her mother's side.

"Now, my boy," said Chiau to the little fellow, "keep your eyes fixed on me, and never take them from me for a moment; and you, little sister," addressing the girl, "do the same to the man next to me, and you will see something that will make you both laugh."

The eyes of them both were at once riveted on the two men, and a look of amazement slowly crept into their faces. And no wonder, for as they gazed they saw the two men rapidly changing, and becoming smaller and smaller, until they were the exact size and image of themselves. In their features and dress, and in every minute detail they were the precise pattern of the children, who with staring eyes were held spellbound by the magic change which had taken place in front of them.

"Now," said Chiau to the old gentleman, "the transformation is complete. Take the children away and hide them in the remotest and most inaccessible room that you have in your house. Let them be seen by no chattering woman or servant who might divulge our secret, so that in some way or other it might reach the ears of the Demon, and put him on his guard. Remember that from this moment these little ones are not supposed to exist, but that we are your grand-children who are to be taken to the temple tomorrow morning at break of day."

Just as the eastern sky showed the first touch of colour, two sedan-chairs were brought up to the door to carry the two victims away to be devoured by the Demon. A few frightened-looking neighbours peered through the gloom to catch a last glimpse of the children, but not one of them had the least suspicion that the boy and girl were really fairies who were about to wage a deadly battle with the Demon in order to deliver them from the curse under which they lived.

No sooner had the children been put into the temple, where a dim rush-light did but serve to disclose the gloom, and the doors had been closed with a bang, than the chair-bearers rushed away in fear for their very lives.

An instant afterwards a hideous, gigantic form emerged from an inner room and advanced towards the children. The Demon was surprised, however, to find that on this occasion the little victims did not exhibit any signs of alarm, as had always been the case hitherto, but seemed to be calmly awaiting his approach. There was no symptom of fear about them, and not a cry of terror broke from their lips; but with a fearless and composed mien they gazed upon him as he advanced.

Hesitating for a moment, as if to measure the foe which he began to fear might lie concealed beneath the figures of the boy and girl before him, the Demon's great fiery eyes began to flash with deadly passion as he saw the two little ones gradually expand in size, until they were transformed into beings as powerful and as mighty as himself. He knew at once that he had been outwitted, and that he must now battle for his very life; so, drawing a sword which had always stood him in good stead, he rushed upon the two who faced him so calmly and with such apparent confidence in themselves.

Chiau and Chu were all ready for the fray, and with weapons firmly gripped and with hearts made strong by the consciousness of the justice of their cause, they awaited the onslaught of the Demon.

And what a battle it was that then ensued in the dim and shadowy temple! It was a conflict of great and deadly significance, waged on one side for the deliverance of helpless childhood, and on the other for the basest schemes that the spirits of evil could devise. It was a battle royal, in which no quarter was either asked or given. The clash of weapons, and sounds unfamiliar to the human ear, and groans and cries which seemed to come from a lost soul, filled the temple with their hideous uproar.

At last the Demon, who seemed to have been grievously wounded, though by his magic art he had caused his wounds to be instantly healed, began to see that the day was going against him. One more mighty lunge with his broadsword, and one more furious onset, and his craven heart failed him. With a cry of despair he fled from the temple, and plunged headlong into the river flowing by its walls.

Great were the rejoicings when Chiau and Chu returned to report to Sam-Chung the glorious victory they had gained over the Demon. Laughter and rejoicing were heard in every home, and men and women assembled in front of their doors and at the corners of the narrow alley-ways to congratulate each other on the great deliverance which that day had come to them and to their children. The dread of the Demon had already vanished, and a feeling of freedom so inspired the men of the village that as if by a common impulse, they rushed impetuously down to where the temple stood, and in the course of a few hours every vestige of it had disappeared beneath the waters into which the Demon had plunged.

After his great defeat the baffled spirit made his way to the grotto beneath the waters, where he and the other demons had taken up their abode. A general council was called to devise plans to wipe out the disgrace which had been sustained, and to regain the power that had slipped from the Demon's grasp. They wished also to visit Sam-Chung with condign punishment which would render him helpless for the future.

"We must capture him," said one wicked-looking imp, who always acted as counsellor to the rest. "I have been told that to devour some of his flesh would ensure the prolongation of life for more than a thousand years."

The suggestion to seize Sam-Chung was unanimously accepted as a very inspiration of genius, and the precise measures which were to be adopted in order to capture him were agreed to after a long discussion.

On the very next morning, a most violent snowstorm set in, so that the face of the river and the hills all round about, and the very heavens themselves were lost in the blinding snow-drifts that flew before the gale. Gradually the cold became so intense that the Ice King laid his grip upon the waters of the Tien-ho, and turned the flowing stream into a crystal highway, along which men might travel with ease and safety. Such a sight had never been seen before by any of the people who lived upon its banks, and many were the speculations as to what such a phenomenon might mean to the welfare of the people of the region. It never occurred to any one that this great snow-storm which had turned into ice a river that had never been known to freeze before, was all the work of demons determined on the destruction of Sam-Chung.

Next day the storm had passed, but the river was one mass of ice which gleamed and glistened in the morning rays. Much to the astonishment of Sam-Chung and his two companions, they caught sight of a number of people, who appeared to be merchants, moving about on the bank of the river, together with several mules laden with merchandise. The whole party seemed intent on their preparations for crossing the river, which they were observed to test in various places to make sure that it was strong enough to bear their weight. This they seemed satisfied about, for in a short time the men and animals set forward on their journey across the ice.

Sam-Chung immediately insisted upon following their example, though the plan was vigorously opposed by the villagers, who predicted all kinds of dangers if he entered on such an uncertain and hazardous enterprise. Being exceedingly anxious to proceed on his journey, however, and seeing no prospect of doing so if he did not take advantage of the present remarkable condition of the river, he hastened to follow in the footsteps of the merchants, who by this time had already advanced some distance on the ice.

He would have been less anxious to enter on this perilous course, had he known that the innocent-looking traders who preceded him were every one of them demons who had changed themselves into the semblance of men in order to lure him to his destruction.

Sam-Chung and his companions had not proceeded more than five or six miles, when ominous symptoms of coming disaster began to manifest themselves. The extreme cold in the air suddenly ceased, and a warm south wind began to blow. The surface of the ice lost its hardness. Streamlets of water trickled here and there, forming great pools which made walking exceedingly difficult.

Chiau, whose mind was a very acute and intelligent one, became terrified at these alarming symptoms of danger, especially as the ice began to crack, and loud and prolonged reports reached them from every direction. Another most suspicious thing was the sudden disappearance of the company of merchants, whom they had all along kept well in sight. There was something wrong, he was fully convinced, and so with all his wits about him, he kept himself alert for any contingency. It was well that he did this, for before they had proceeded another mile, the ice began to grow thinner, and before they could retreat there was a sudden crash and all three were precipitated into the water.

Hardly had Chiau's feet touched the river, than with a superhuman effort he made a spring into the air, and was soon flying with incredible speed in the direction of the Western Heaven, to invoke the aid of the Goddess of Mercy to deliver Sam-Chung from the hands of an enemy who would show him no quarter.

In the meanwhile Sam-Chung and Chu were borne swiftly by the demons, who were eagerly awaiting their immersion in the water, to the great cave that lay deep down at the bottom of the mighty river. Chu, being an immortal and a special messenger of the Goddess, defied all the arts of the evil spirits to injure him, so that all they could do was to imprison him in one of the inner grottoes and station a guard over him to prevent his escape. Sam-Chung, however, was doomed to death, and the Demon, in revenge for the disgrace he had brought upon him, and in the hope of prolonging his own life by a thousand years, decided that on the morrow he would feast upon his flesh. But he made his plans without taking into consideration the fact that Sam-Chung was an especial favourite with the Goddess.

During the night a tremendous commotion occurred. The waters of the river fled in every direction as before the blast of a hurricane, and the caverns where the demons were assembled were illuminated with a light so brilliant that their eyes became dazzled, and for a time were blinded by the sudden blaze that flashed from every corner. Screaming with terror, they fled in all directions. Only one remained, and that was the fierce spirit who had wrought such sorrow amongst the people of the land near by. He too would have disappeared with the rest, had not some supernatural power chained him to the spot where he stood.

Soon the noble figure of the Goddess of Mercy appeared, accompanied by a splendid train of Fairies who hovered round her to do her bidding. Her first act was to release Sam-Chung, who lay bound ready for his death, which but for her interposition would have taken place within a few hours. He and his two companions were entrusted to the care of a chosen number of her followers, and conveyed with all speed across the river.

The Goddess then gave a command to some who stood near her person, and in a moment, as if by a flash of lightning, the cowering, terrified Demon had vanished, carried away to be confined in one of the dungeons where persistent haters of mankind are kept imprisoned, until their hearts are changed by some noble sentiment of compassion and the Goddess sees that they are once more fit for liberty.

And then the lights died out, and the sounds of fairy voices ceased. The waters of the river, which had been under a divine spell, returned to their course, and the Goddess with her magnificent train of beneficent spirits departed to her kingdom in the far-off Western Heaven.

The Queen of Heaven

THE QUEEN OF HEAVEN,[1] who is also known as the Holy Mother, was in mortal life a maiden of Fukien, named Lin. She was pure, reverential and pious in her ways and died at the age of seventeen. She shows her power on the seas and for this reason the seamen worship her. When they are unexpectedly attacked by wind and waves, they call on her and she is always ready to hear their pleas.

There are many seamen in Fukien, and every year people are lost at sea. And because of this, most likely, the Queen of Heaven took pity on the distress of her people during her lifetime on earth. And since her thoughts are uninterruptedly turned toward aiding the drowning in their distress, she now appears frequently on the seas.

In every ship that sails a picture of the Queen of Heaven hangs in the cabin, and three paper talismans are also kept on shipboard. On the first she is painted with crown and scepter, on the second as a maiden in ordinary dress, and on the third she is pictured with flowing hair, barefoot, standing with a sword in her hand. When the ship is in danger the first talisman is burnt, and help comes. But if this is of no avail, then the second and finally the third picture is burned. And if no help comes then there is nothing more to be done.

When seamen lose their course among wind and waves and darkling clouds, they pray devoutly to the Queen of Heaven. Then a red lantern appears on the face of the waters. And if they follow the lantern they will win safe out of all danger. The Queen of Heaven may often be seen standing in the skies, dividing the wind with her sword. When she does this the wind departs for the North and South, and the waves grow smooth.

A wooden wand is always kept before her holy picture in the cabin. It often happens that the fish-dragons play in the seas. They are two giant fish who spout up water against one another till the sun in the sky is obscured, and the seas are shrouded in profound darkness. And often, in the distance, one may see a bright opening in the darkness. If the ship holds a course straight for this opening it will win through, and is suddenly floating in calm waters again. Looking back, one may see the two fishes still spouting water, and the ship will have passed directly beneath their jaws. But a storm is always near when the fish dragons swim; therefore it is well to burn paper or wool so that the dragons do not draw the ship down into the depths. Or the Master of the Wand may burn incense before the wand in the cabin. Then he must take the wand and swing it over the water three times, in a circle. If he does so the dragons will draw in their tails and disappear.

When the ashes in the censer fly up into the air without any cause, and are scattered about, it is a sign that great danger is threatening.

Nearly two-hundred years ago an army was fitted out to subdue the island of Formosa. The captain's banner had been dedicated with the blood of a white horse. Suddenly the Queen of

Heaven appeared at the tip of the banner-staff. In another moment she had disappeared, but the invasion was successful.

On another occasion, in the days of Kien Lung, the minister Dschou Ling was ordered to install a new king in the Liu-Kiu Islands. When the fleet was sailing by south of Korea, a storm arose, and his ship was driven toward the Black Whirlpool. The water had the color of ink, sun and moon lost their radiance, and the word was passed about that the ship had been caught in the Black Whirlpool, from which no living man had ever returned. The seaman and travelers awaited their end with lamentations. Suddenly an untold number of lights, like red lanterns, appeared on the surface of the water. Then the seamen were overjoyed and prayed in the cabins. "Our lives are saved!" they cried, "the Holy Mother has come to our aid!" And truly, a beautiful maiden with golden earrings appeared. She waved her hand in the air and the winds became still and the waves grew even. And it seemed as though the ship were being drawn along by a mighty hand. It moved plashing through the waves, and suddenly it was beyond the limits of the Black Whirlpool.

Dschou Ling on his return told of this happening, and begged that temples be erected in honor of the Queen of Heaven, and that she be included in the list of the gods. And the emperor granted his prayer.

Since then temples of the Queen of Heaven are to be found in all sea-port towns, and her birthday is celebrated on the eighth day of the fourth month with spectacles and sacrifices.

Footnotes for 'The Queen of Heaven'

1. 'The Queen of Heaven', whose name is Tian Hou, or more exactly, Tian Fe Niang Niang, is a Taoist goddess of seamen, generally worshiped in all coast towns.

The Dragon-Princess

IN THE SEA OF DUNGTING there is a hill, and in that hill there is a hole, and this hole is so deep that it has no bottom.

Once a fisherman was passing there who slipped and fell into the hole. He came to a country full of winding ways which led over hill and dale for several miles. Finally he reached a dragon-castle lying in a great plain. There grew a green slime which reached to his knees. He went to the gate of the castle. It was guarded by a dragon who spouted water which dispersed in a fine mist. Within the gate lay a small hornless dragon who raised his head, showed his claws, and would not let him in.

The fisherman spent several days in the cave, satisfying his hunger with the green slime, which he found edible and which tasted like rice-mush. At last he found a way out again. He told the district mandarin what had happened to him, and the latter reported the matter to the emperor. The emperor sent for a wise man and questioned him concerning it.

The wise man said: "There are four paths in this cave. One path leads to the south-west shore of the Sea of Dungting, the second path leads to a valley in the land of the four rivers, the third path ends in a cave on the mountain of Lo-Fu and the fourth in an island of the Eastern Sea. In this cave dwells the seventh daughter of the Dragon-King of the Eastern Sea,[1] who guards his pearls and his treasure. It happened once in the ancient days, that a fisherboy dived into the water and brought up a pearl from beneath the chin of a black dragon. The dragon was asleep, which was the reason the fisherboy brought the pearl to the surface without being harmed. The treasure which the daughter of the Dragon-King has in charge is made up of thousands and millions of such jewels. Several thousands of small dragons watch over them in her service. Dragons have the peculiarity of fighting shy of wax. But they are fond of beautiful jade-stones, and of kung-tsing, the hollowgreen wood, and like to eat swallows. If one were to send a messenger with a letter, it would be possible to obtain precious pearls."

The emperor was greatly pleased, and announced a large reward for the man who was competent to go to the dragon-castle as his messenger.

The first man to come forward was named So Pi-Lo. But the wise man said: "A great-great-great-great-grandfather of yours once slew more than a hundred of the dragons of the Eastern Sea, and was finally himself slain by the dragons. The dragons are the enemies of your family and you cannot go."

Then came a man from Canton, Lo-Dsi-Tschun, with his two brothers, who said that his ancestors had been related to the Dragon-King. Hence they were well liked by the dragons and well known to them. They begged to be entrusted with the message.

The wise man asked: "And have you still in your possession the stone which compels the dragons to do your will?"

"Yes," said they, "we have brought it along with us."

The wise man had them show him the stone; then he spoke: "This stone is only obeyed by the dragons who make clouds and send down the rain. It will not do for the dragons who guard the pearls of the sea-king." Then he questioned them further: "Have you the dragon-brain vapor?"

When they admitted that they had not, the wise man said: "How then will you compel the dragons to yield their treasure?"

And the emperor said: "What shall we do?"

The wise man replied: "On the Western Ocean sail foreign merchants who deal in dragon-brain vapor. Someone must go to them and seek it from them. I also know a holy man who is an adept in the art of taming dragons, and who has prepared ten pounds of the dragon-stone. Someone should be sent for that as well."

The emperor sent out his messengers. They met one of the holy man's disciples and obtained two fragments of dragon-stone from him.

Said the wise man: "That is what we want!"

Several more months went by, and at last a pill of dragon-brain vapor had also been secured. The emperor felt much pleased and had his jewelers carve two little boxes of the finest jade. These were polished with the ashes of the Wutung-tree. And he had an essence prepared of the very best hollowgreen wood, pasted with sea-fish lime, and hardened in the fire. Of this two vases were made. Then the bodies and the clothing of the messengers were rubbed with tree-wax, and they were given five hundred roasted swallows to take along with them.

They went into the cave. When they reached the dragon-castle, the little dragon who guarded the gate smelled the tree-wax, so he crouched down and did them no harm. They gave him a hundred roasted swallows as a bribe to announce them to the daughter of the Dragon-King. They were admitted to her presence and offered her the jade caskets, the vases and the four hundred roasted swallows as gifts. The dragon's daughter received them graciously, and they unfolded the emperor's letter.

In the castle there was a dragon who was over a thousand years old. He could turn himself into a human being, and could interpret the language of human beings. Through him the dragon's daughter learned that the emperor was sending her the gifts, and she returned them with a gift of three great pearls, seven smaller pearls and a whole bushel of ordinary pearls. The messengers took leave, rode off with their pearls on a dragon's back, and in a moment they had reached the banks of the Yangtze-kiang. They made their way to Nanking, the imperial capital, and there handed over their treasure of gems.

The emperor was much pleased and showed them to the wise man. He said: "Of the three great pearls one is a divine wishing-pearl of the third class, and two are black dragon-pearls of medium quality. Of the seven smaller pearls two are serpent-pearls, and five are mussel-pearls. The remaining pearls are in part sea-crane pearls, in part snail and oyster-pearls. They do not approach the great pearls in value, and yet few will be found to equal them on earth."

The emperor also showed them to all his servants. They, however, thought the wise man's words all talk, and did not believe what he said.

Then the wise man said: "The radiance of wishing-pearls of the first class is visible for forty miles, that of the second class for twenty miles, and that of the third for ten miles. As far as their radiance carries, neither wind nor rain, thunder nor lightning, water, fire nor weapons may reach. The pearls of the black dragon are nine-colored and glow by night. Within the circle of their light the poison of serpents and worms is powerless. The serpent-pearls are seven-colored, the mussel-pearls five-colored. Both shine by night. Those most free from spots are the best. They grow within the mussel, and increase and decrease in size as the moon waxes and wanes."

Someone asked how the serpent and sea-crane pearls could be told apart, and the wise man answered: "The animals themselves recognize them."

Then the emperor selected a serpent-pearl and a sea-crane pearl, put them together with a whole bushel of ordinary pearls, and poured the lot out in the courtyard. Then a large yellow serpent and a black crane were fetched and placed among the pearls. At once the crane took up a sea-crane pearl in his bill and began to dance and sing and flutter around. But the serpent snatched at the serpent-pearl, and wound himself about it in many coils. And when the people saw this they acknowledged the truth of the wise man's words. As regards the radiance of the larger and smaller pearls it turned out, too, just as the wise man had said.

In the dragon-castle the messengers had enjoyed dainty fare, which tasted like flowers, herbs, ointment and sugar. They had brought a remnant of it with them to the capital; yet exposed to the air it had become as hard as stone. The emperor commanded that these fragments be preserved in the treasury. Then he bestowed high rank and titles on the three brothers, and made each one of them a present of a thousand rolls of fine silk stuff. He also had investigated why it was that the fisherman, when he chanced upon the cave, had not been destroyed by the dragons. And it turned out that his fishing clothes had been soaked in oil and tree-wax. The dragons had dreaded the odor.

Footnotes for 'The Dragon-Princess'

1. As regards the Dragon-King of the Eastern Sea, see 'Notscha' (page 175) and 'The Ape Sun Wu Kung' (page 192). The pearl under the dragon's chin comes from Dschuang Dsi. With regard to So Pi-Lo and Lo-Dsi-Tschun, see 'Help in Need' (page 108).

Help in Need

SOME TWENTY MILES east of Gingdschou lies the Lake of the Maidens. It is several miles square and surrounded on all sides by thick green thickets and tall forests. Its waters are clear and dark-blue. Often all kinds of wondrous creatures show themselves in the lake. The people of the vicinity have erected a temple there for the Dragon Princess. And in times of drought all make pilgrimage there to offer up prayers.

West of Gingdschou, two hundred miles away, is another lake, whose god is named Tschauna, and who performs many miracles. During the time of the Tang dynasty there lived in Gingdschou a mandarin by name of Dschou Bau. While he was in office it chanced that in the fifth month clouds suddenly arose in the sky, piling themselves up like mountains, among which wriggled dragons and serpents; they rolled up and down between the two seas. Tempest and rain, thunder and lightning arose so that houses fell to pieces, trees were torn up by the roots, and much damage was done the crops. Dschou Bau took the blame upon himself,[1] and prayed to the heavens that his people might be pardoned.

On the fifth day of the sixth month he sat in his hall of audience and gave judgment; and suddenly he felt quite weary and sleepy. He took off his hat and laid down on the cushions. No sooner had he closed his eyes than he saw a warrior in helmet and armor, with a halberd in his hand, standing on the steps leading to the hall, who announced: "A lady is waiting outside who wishes to enter!" Dschou Bau asked him: "Who are you?" The answer was: "I am your door-keeper. In the invisible world I already have been performing this duty for many years." Meanwhile two figures clad in green came up the steps, knelt before him and said: "Our mistress has come to visit you!" Dschou Bau rose. He beheld lovely clouds, from which fell a fine rain, and strange fragrances enchanted him. Suddenly he saw a lady clad in a simple gown, but of surpassing beauty, float down from on high, with a retinue of many female servants. These were all neat and clean in appearance, and waited upon the lady as though she were a princess. When the latter entered the hall she raised her arms in greeting. Dschou Bau came forward to meet her and invited her to be seated. From all sides bright-colored clouds came floating in, and the courtyard was filled with a purple ether. Dschou Bau had wine and food brought and entertained them all in the most splendid way. But the goddess sat staring straight before her with wrinkled brows, and seemed to feel very sad. Then she rose and said with a blush: "I have been living in this neighborhood for many years. A wrong which has been done me, permits me to pass the bounds of what is fitting, and encourages me to ask a favor of you. Yet I do not know whether you wish to save me!"

"May I hear what it is all about," answered Dschou Bau. "If I can help you, I will be glad to place myself at your disposal."

The goddess said: "For hundreds of years my family has been living in the depth of the Eastern Sea. But we were unfortunate in that our treasures excited the jealousy of men. The ancestor of Pi-Lo nearly destroyed our entire clan by fire. My ancestors had to fly and hide themselves. And not long ago, our enemy Pi-Lo himself wanted to deliver an imperial letter in the cave of the Sea of Dungting. Under the pretext of begging for pearls and treasures, he wished to enter the dragon-castle and destroy our family. Fortunately a wise man saw through his treacherous purpose, and Lo-Dsi-Tschun and his brothers were sent in his stead. Yet my people did not feel safe from future attacks. For this reason they withdrew to the distant West. My father has done much good to mankind and hence is highly honored there. I am his ninth daughter. When I was sixteen I was wedded to the youngest son of the Rock-Dragon. But my good husband had a fiery temper, which often caused him to offend against the laws of courtesy, and in less than a year's time the punishment of heaven was his portion. I was left alone and returned to the home of my parents. My father wished me to marry again; but I had promised to remain true to the memory of my husband, and made a vow not to comply with my father's wish. My parents grew angry, and I was obliged to retire to this place in view of their anger. That was three years ago. Who could imagine that the contemptible dragon Tschauna, who was seeking a wife for his youngest brother, would try to force the wedding-gift upon me? I refused to accept it; but Tschauna knew how to gain his point with my father, and was determined to carry out his intention. My father, regardless of my wishes, promised me to him. And then the dragon Tschauna appeared with his youngest brother and wanted to carry me off by sheer force of arms. I encountered him with fifty faithful followers, and we fought on the meadow before the city. We were defeated, and I am more than ever afraid that Tschauna will attempt to drag me off. So I have plucked up courage to beg you to lend me your mercenaries so that I may beat off my foes and remain as I am. If you will help me I will be grateful to you till the end of my days."

Dschou Bau answered: "You come from a noble family. Have you no kinsfolk who will hasten to help you in your need, that you are compelled to turn to a mortal man?"

"It is true that my kinsfolk are far-famed and numerous. If I were to send out letters and they came to my aid, they would rub out that scaly scoundrel Tschauna as one might rub garlic. But my deceased husband offended the high heavens and he has not yet been pardoned. And my parents' will, too, is opposed to mine, so that I dare not call upon my kinsfolk for help. You will understand my need." Then Dschou Bau promised to help her, and the princess thanked him and departed.

When he awoke, he sighed long thinking over his strange experience. And the following day he sent off fifteen hundred soldiers to stand guard by the Lake of the Maidens.

On the seventh day of the sixth month Dschou Bau rose early. Darkness still lay before the windows, yet it seemed to him as though he could glimpse a man before the curtain. He asked who it might be. The man said: "I am the princess's adviser. Yesterday you were kind enough to send soldiers to aid us in our distress. But they were all living men, and such cannot fight against invisible spirits. You will have to send us soldiers of yours who have died, if you wish to aid us."

Dschou Bau reflected for a time, and then it occurred to him that of course such must be the case. So he had his field-secretary examine the roster to see how many of his soldiers had fallen in battle. And the latter counted up to some two thousand foot-soldiers and five-hundred horsemen. Dschou Bau appointed his deceased officer Mong Yuan as their leader, and wrote his commands on a paper which he burned, in order thus to place them at the princess's disposal. The living soldiers he recalled. When they were being reviewed in the courtyard after their return, a soldier suddenly fell unconscious. It was not until early the following morning that he came to his senses again. He was questioned and replied: "I saw a man clad in red who approached me and said: 'Our princess is grateful for the aid your master has so kindly given her. Yet she still has a request to make and has asked me to call you.' I followed him to the temple. The princess bade me come forward and said to me: 'I thank your master from my heart for sending me the ghost soldiers, but Mong Yuan, their leader is incapable. Yesterday the robbers came with three thousand men, and Mong Yuan was beaten by them. When you return and again see your master, say that I earnestly beg him to send me a good general. Perhaps that will save me in my need.' Then she had me led back again and I regained consciousness."

When Dschou Bau had heard these words, which seemed to fit strangely well with what he had dreamed, he thought he would try to see if this were really the case. Therefore he chose his victorious general Dschong Tschong-Fu to take the place of Mong Yuan. That evening he burned incense, offered wine and handed over to the princess this captain's soul.

On the twenty-sixth of the month news came from the general's camp that he had suddenly died at midnight on the thirteenth. Dschou Bau was frightened, and sent a man to bring him a report. The latter informed him that the general's heart had hardly ceased to beat, and that, in spite of the hot summer weather, his body was free from any trace of decay. So the order was given not to bury him.

Then one night an icy, spectral wind arose, which whirled up sand and stones, broke trees and tore down houses. The standing corn in the fields was blown down. The storm lasted all day. Finally, the crash of a terrific thunderbolt was heard, and then the skies cleared and the clouds scattered. That very hour the dead general began to breathe painfully on his couch, and when his attendants came to him, he had returned to life again.

They questioned him and he told them: "First I saw a man in a purple gown riding a black horse, who came up with a great retinue. He dismounted before the door. In his hand he held a decree of appointment which he gave me, saying: 'Our princess begs you most respectfully to become her general. I hope that you will not refuse.' Then he brought forth gifts and heaped them up before the steps. Jade-stones, brocades, and silken garments, saddles, horses, helmets and suits of mail – he heaped them all up in the courtyard. I wished to decline, but this he would not allow, and urged me to enter his chariot with him. We drove a hundred miles and met a train of three-hundred armored horsemen who had ridden out to escort me. They led me to a great city, and before the city a tent had been erected in which played a band of musicians. A high official welcomed me. When I entered the city the onlookers were crowded together like walls. Servants ran to and fro bearing orders. We passed through more than a dozen gates before we reached the princess. There I was requested to dismount and change my clothes in order to enter the presence of the princess, for she wished to receive me as her guest. But I thought this too great an honor and greeted her below, on the steps. She, however, invited me to seat myself near her in the hall. She sat upright in all her incomparable beauty, surrounded by female attendants adorned with the richest jewels. These plucked lute-strings and played flutes. A throng of servitors stood about in golden girdles with purple tassels, ready to carry out her commands. Countless crowds were assembled before the palace. Five or six visitors sat in a circle about the princess, and a general led me to my place. The princess said to me: 'I have begged you to come here in order to entrust the command of my army to you. If you will break the power of my foe I will reward you richly.' I promised to obey her. Then wine was brought in, and the banquet was served to the sound of music. While we were at table a messenger entered: 'The robber Tschauna has invaded our land with ten thousand footmen and horsemen, and is approaching our city by various roads. His way is marked by columns of fire and smoke!' The guests all grew pale with terror when they heard the news. And the princess said: 'This is the foe because of whom I have sought your aid. Save me in my hour of need!' Then she gave me two chargers, a suit of golden armor, and the insignia of a commander-in-chief, and bowed to me. I thanked her and went, called together the captains, had the army mustered and rode out before the city. At several decisive points I placed troops in ambush. The enemy was already approaching in great force, careless and unconcerned, intoxicated by his former victories. I sent out my most untrustworthy soldiers in advance, who allowed themselves to be beaten in order to lure him on. Light-armed men then went out against him, and retreated in skirmish order. And thus he fell into my ambush. Drums and kettledrums sounded together,[2] the ring closed around them on all sides and the robber army suffered a grievous defeat. The dead lay about like hemp-stalks, but little Tschauna succeeded in breaking through the circle. I sent out the light horsemen after him, and they seized him before the tent of the enemy's commanding general. Hastily I sent word to the princess, and she reviewed the prisoners before the palace. All the people, high and low, streamed together, to acclaim her. Little Tschauna was about to be executed in the market place when a messenger came spurring up with a command from the princess's father to pardon him. The princess did not dare to disobey. So he was dismissed to his home after he had sworn to give up all thought of realizing his traitorous plans. I was loaded with benefits as a reward for my victory. I was invested with an estate with three thousand peasants, and was given a palace, horses and wagons, all sorts of jewels, men-servants and women-servants, gardens and forests, banners and suits of mail. And my subordinate officers, too, were duly rewarded. On the following day a banquet was held, and the princess herself filled a goblet, sent it to me by one of her attendants, and said: 'Widowed early in life, I opposed the wishes of my stern father and fled to this spot. Here the infamous Tschauna harassed me and well-nigh put me to shame. Had not your master's great kindness and your own courage come to my assistance, hard would have been my lot!' Then she began to thank me and her tears of emotion flowed like a stream. I bowed and begged her to grant me leave of absence, so that I might look after my family. I was given a month's leave and the following day she dismissed me with a splendid retinue. Before the city a pavilion had been erected in which I drank the stirrup-cup. Then I rode away and when I arrived before our own gate a thunder-peal crashed and I awoke."

Thereupon the general wrote an account of what had happened to Dschou Bau, in which he conveyed the princess's thanks. Then he paid no further heed to worldly matters, but set his house in order and turned it over to his wife and son. When a month had passed, he died without any sign of illness.

That same day one of his officers was out walking. Suddenly he saw a heavy cloud of dust rising along the highway, while flags and banners darkened the sun. A thousand knights were escorting a man who sat his horse proudly and like a hero. And when the officer looked at his face, it was the general Dschong Tschong-Fu. Hastily he stepped to the edge of the road, in order to allow the cavalcade to pass, and watched it ride by. The horsemen took the way to the Lake of the Maidens, where they disappeared.

Footnotes for 'Help in Need'

1. The expression: "Dschou Bau took the blame upon himself" is explained by the fact that the territorial mandarin is responsible for his district, just as the emperor is for the whole empire. Since extraordinary natural phenomena are the punishment of heaven, their occurrence supposed the guilt of man.

2. "Drums and kettledrums sounded together": the kettledrums sounded the attack, and the drums the retreat. The simultaneous sounding of both signals was intended to throw the enemy's army into disorder.

The Disowned Princess

AT THE TIME that the Tang dynasty was reigning there lived a man named Liu I, who had failed to pass his examinations for the doctorate. So he traveled home again. He had gone six or seven miles when a bird flew up in a field, and his horse shied and ran ten miles before he could stop him. There he saw a woman who was herding sheep on a hillside. He looked at her and she was lovely to look upon, yet her face bore traces of hidden grief. Astonished, he asked her what was the matter.

The woman began to sob and said: "Fortune has forsaken me, and I am in need and ashamed. Since you are kind enough to ask I will tell you all. I am the youngest daughter of the Dragon-King of the Sea of Dungting, and was married to the second son of the Dragon-King of Ging Dschou. Yet my husband ill-treated and disowned me. I complained to my step-parents, but they loved their son blindly and did nothing. And when I grew insistent they both became angry, and I was sent out here to herd sheep." When she had done, the woman burst into tears and lost all control of herself. Then she continued: "The Sea of Dungting is far from here; yet I know that you will have to pass it on your homeward journey. I should like to give you a letter to my father, but I do not know whether you would take it."

Liu I answered: "Your words have moved my heart. Would that I had wings and could fly away with you. I will be glad to deliver the letter to your father. Yet the Sea of Dungting is long and broad, and how am I to find him?"

"On the southern shore of the Sea stands an orange-tree," answered the woman, "which people call the tree of sacrifice. When you get there you must loosen your girdle and strike the tree with it three times in succession. Then someone will appear whom you must follow. When you see my father, tell him in what need you found me, and that I long greatly for his help."

Then she fetched out a letter from her breast and gave it to Liu I. She bowed to him, looked toward the east and sighed, and, unexpectedly, the sudden tears rolled from the eyes of Liu I as well. He took the letter and thrust it in his bag.

Then he asked her: "I cannot understand why you have to herd sheep. Do the gods slaughter cattle like men?"

"These are not ordinary sheep," answered the woman; "these are rain-sheep."

"But what are rain-sheep?"

"They are the thunder-rams," replied the woman.

And when he looked more closely he noticed that these sheep walked around in proud, savage fashion, quite different from ordinary sheep.

Liu I added: "But if I deliver the letter for you, and you succeed in getting back to the Sea of Dungting in safety, then you must not use me like a stranger."

The woman answered: "How could I use you as a stranger? You shall be my dearest friend."

And with these words they parted.

In course of a month Liu I reached the Sea of Dungting, asked for the orange-tree and, sure enough, found it. He loosened his girdle, and struck the tree with it three times. At once a warrior emerged from the waves of the sea, and asked: "Whence come you, honored guest?"

Liu I said: "I have come on an important mission and want to see the King."

The warrior made a gesture in the direction of the water, and the waves turned into a solid street along which he led Liu I. The dragon-castle rose before them with its thousand gates, and magic flowers and rare grasses bloomed in luxurious profusion. The warrior bade him wait at the side of a great hall.

Liu I asked: "What is this place called?"

"It is the Hall of the Spirits," was the reply.

Liu I looked about him: all the jewels known to earth were there in abundance. The columns were of white quartz, inlaid with green jade; the seats were made of coral, the curtains of mountain crystal as clear as water, the windows of burnished glass, adorned with rich lattice-work. The beams of the ceiling, ornamented with amber, rose in wide arches. An exotic fragrance filled the hall, whose outlines were lost in darkness.

Liu I had waited for the king a long time. To all his questions the warrior replied: "Our master is pleased at this moment to talk with the priest of the sun up on the coral-tower about the sacred book of the fire. He will, no doubt, soon be through."

Liu I went on to ask: "Why is he interested in the sacred book of the fire?"

The reply was: "Our master is a dragon. The dragons are powerful through the power of water. They can cover hill and dale with a single wave. The priest is a human being. Human beings are powerful through fire. They can burn the greatest palaces by means of a torch. Fire and water fight each other, being different in their nature. For that reason our master is now talking with the priest, in order to find a way in which fire and water may complete each other."

Before they had quite finished there appeared a man in a purple robe, bearing a scepter of jade in his hand.

The warrior said: "This is my master!"

Liu I bowed before him.

The king asked: "Are you not a living human being? What has brought you here?"

Liu I gave his name and explained: "I have been to the capital and there failed to pass my examination. When I was passing by the Ging Dschou River, I saw your daughter, whom you love, herding sheep in the wilderness. The winds tousled her hair, and the rain drenched her. I could not bear to see her trouble and spoke to her. She complained that her husband had cast her out and wept bitterly. Then she gave me a letter for you. And that is why I have come to visit you, O King!"

With these words he fetched out his letter and handed it to the king. When the latter had read it, he hid his face in his sleeve and said with a sigh: "It is my own fault. I picked out a worthless husband for her. Instead of securing her happiness I have brought her to shame in a distant land. You are a stranger and yet you have been willing to help her in her distress, for which I am very grateful to you." Then he once more began to sob, and all those about him shed tears. Thereupon the monarch gave the letter to a servant who took it into the interior of the palace; and soon the sound of loud lamentations rose from the inner rooms.

The king was alarmed and turned to an official: "Go and tell them within not to weep so loudly! I am afraid that Tsian Tang may hear them."

"Who is Tsian Tang?" asked Liu I.

"He is my beloved brother," answered the king. "Formerly he was the ruler of the Tsian-Tang River, but now he has been deposed."

Liu I asked: "Why should the matter be kept from him?"

"He is so wild and uncontrollable," was the reply, "that I fear he would cause great damage. The deluge which covered the earth for nine long years in the time of the Emperor Yau was the work of his anger. Because he fell out with one of the kings of heaven, he caused a great deluge that rose and covered the tops of five high mountains. Then the king of heaven grew angry with him, and gave him to me to guard. I had to chain him to a column in my palace."

Before he had finished speaking a tremendous turmoil arose, which split the skies and made the earth tremble, so that the whole palace began to rock, and smoke and clouds rose hissing and puffing. A red dragon, a thousand feet long, with flashing eyes, blood-red tongue, scarlet scales and a fiery beard came surging up. He was dragging along through the air the column to which he had been bound, together with its chain. Thunders and lightnings roared and darted around his body; sleet and snow, rain and hail-stones whirled about him in confusion. There was a crash of thunder, and he flew up to the skies and disappeared.

Liu I fell to earth in terror. The king helped him up with his own hand and said: "Do not be afraid! That is my brother, who is hastening to Ging Dschou in his rage. We will soon have good news!"

Then he had food and drink brought in for his guest. When the goblet had thrice made the rounds, a gentle breeze began to murmur and a fine rain fell. A youth clad in a purple gown and wearing a lofty hat entered. A sword hung at his side. His appearance was manly and heroic. Behind him walked a girl radiantly beautiful, wearing a robe of misty fragrance. And when Liu I looked at her, lo, it was the dragon-princess whom he had met on his way! A throng of maidens in rosy garments received her, laughing and giggling, and led her into the interior of the palace. The king, however, presented Liu I to the youth and said: "This is Tsian Tang, my brother!"

Tsian Tang thanked him for having brought the message. Then he turned to his brother and said: "I have fought against the accursed dragons and have utterly defeated them!"

"How many did you slay?"

"Six hundred thousand."

"Were any fields damaged?"

"The fields were damaged for eight hundred miles around."

"And where is the heartless husband?"

"I ate him alive!"

Then the king was alarmed and said: "What the fickle boy did was not to be endured, it is true. But still you were a little too rough with him; in future you must not do anything of the sort again." And Tsian Tang promised not to.

That evening Liu I was feasted at the castle. Music and dancing lent charm to the banquet. A thousand warriors with banners and spears in their hands stood at attention. Trombones and trumpets resounded, and drums and kettledrums thundered and rattled as the warriors danced a war-dance. The music expressed how Tsian Tang had broken through the ranks of the enemy, and the hair of the guest who listened to it rose on his head in terror. Then, again, there was heard the music of strings, flutes and little golden bells. A thousand maidens in crimson and green silk danced around. The return of the princess was also told in tones. The music sounded like a song of sadness and plaining, and all who heard it were moved to tears. The King of the Sea of Dungting was filled with joy. He raised his goblet and drank to the health of his guest, and all sorrow departed from them. Both rulers thanked Liu I in verses, and Liu I answered them in a rimed toast. The crowd of courtiers in the palace-hall applauded. Then the King of the Sea of Dungting drew forth a blue cloud-casket in which was the horn of a rhinoceros, which divides the water. Tsian Tang brought out a platter of red amber on which lay a carbuncle. These they presented to their guest, and the other inmates of the palace also heaped up embroideries, brocades and pearls by his side. Surrounded by shimmer and light Liu I sat there, smiling, and bowed his thanks to all sides. When the banquet was ended he slept in the Palace of Frozen Radiance.

On the following day another banquet was held. Tsian Tang, who was not quite himself, sat carelessly on his seat and said: "The Princess of the Dungting Sea is handsome and delicately fashioned. She has had the misfortune to be disowned by her husband, and to-day her marriage is annulled. I should like to find another husband for her. If you were agreeable it would be to your advantage. But if you were not willing to marry her, you may go your way, and should we ever meet again we will not know each other."

Liu I was angered by the careless way in which Tsian Tang spoke to him. The blood rose to his head and he replied: "I served as a messenger, because I felt sorry for the princess, but not in order to gain an advantage for myself. To kill a husband and carry off a wife is something an honest man does not do. And since I am only an ordinary man, I prefer to die rather than do as you say."

Tsian Tang rose, apologized and said: "My words were over-hasty. I hope you will not take them ill!" And the King of the Dungting Sea also spoke kindly to him, and censured Tsian Tang because of his rude speech. So there was no more said about marriage.

On the following day Liu I took his leave, and the Queen of the Dungting Sea gave a farewell banquet in his honor.

With tears the queen said to Liu I: "My daughter owes you a great debt of gratitude, and we have not had an opportunity to make it up to you. Now you are going away and we see you go with heavy hearts!"

Then she ordered the princess to thank Liu I.

The princess stood there, blushing, bowed to him and said: "We will probably never see each other again!" Then tears choked her voice.

It is true that Liu I had resisted the stormy urging of her uncle, but when he saw the princess standing before him in all the charm of her loveliness, he felt sad at heart; yet he controlled himself and went his way. The treasures which he took with him were incalculable. The king and his brother themselves escorted him as far as the river.

When, on his return home, he sold no more than a hundredth part of what he had received, his fortune already ran into the millions, and he was wealthier than all his neighbors. He decided to take a wife, and heard of a widow who lived in the North with her daughter. Her father had become a Taoist in his later years and had vanished in the clouds without ever returning. The mother lived in poverty with the daughter; yet since the girl was beautiful beyond measure she was seeking a distinguished husband for her.

Liu I was content to take her, and the day of the wedding was set. And when he saw his bride unveiled on the evening of her wedding day, she looked just like the dragon-princess. He asked her about it, but she merely smiled and said nothing.

After a time heaven sent them a son. Then she told her husband: "To-day I will confess to you that I am truly the Princess of Dungting Sea. When you had rejected my uncle's proposal and gone away, I fell ill of longing, and was near death. My parents wanted to send for you, but they feared you might take exception to my family. And so it was that I married you disguised as a human maiden. I had not ventured to tell you until now, but since heaven has sent us a son, I hope that you will love his mother as well."

Then Liu I awoke as though from a deep sleep, and from that time on both were very fond of each other.

One day his wife said: "If you wish to stay with me eternally, then we cannot continue to dwell in the world of men. We dragons live ten thousand years, and you shall share our longevity. Come back with me to the Sea of Dungting!"

Ten years passed and no one knew where Liu I, who had disappeared, might be. Then, by accident, a relative went sailing across the Sea of Dungting. Suddenly a blue mountain rose up out of the water.

The seamen cried in alarm: "There is no mountain on this spot! It must be a water-demon!"

While they were still pointing to it and talking, the mountain drew near the ship, and a gaily-colored boat slid from its summit into the water. A man sat in the middle, and fairies stood at either side of him. The man was Liu I. He beckoned to his cousin, and the latter drew up his garments and stepped into the boat with him. But when he had entered the boat it turned into a mountain. On the mountain stood a splendid castle, and in the castle stood Liu I, surrounded with radiance, and with the music of stringed instruments floating about him.

They greeted each other, and Liu I said to his cousin: "We have been parted no more than a moment, and your hair is already gray!"

His cousin answered: "You are a god and blessed: I have only a mortal body. Thus fate has decreed."

Then Liu I gave him fifty pills and said: "Each pill will extend your life for the space of a year. When you have lived the tale of these years, come to me and dwell no longer in the earthly world of dust, where there is nothing but toil and trouble."

Then he took him back across the sea and disappeared.

His cousin, however, retired from the world, and fifty years later, and when he had taken all the pills, he disappeared and was never seen again.

How the River-God's Wedding Was Broken Off

AT THE TIME of the seven empires there lived a man by the name of Si-Men Bau[1] who was a governor on the Yellow River. In this district the river-god was held in high honor. The sorcerers and witches who dwelt there said: "Every year the river-god looks for a bride, who must be selected from among the people. If she be not found then wind and rain will not come at the proper seasons, and there will be scanty crops and floods!" And then, when a girl came of age in some wealthy family, the sorcerers would say that she should be selected. Whereupon her parents, who wished to protect their daughter, would bribe them with large sums of money to look for someone else, till the sorcerers would give in, and order the rich folk to share the expense of buying some poor girl to be cast into the river. The remainder of the money they would keep for themselves as their profit on the transaction. But whoever would not pay, their daughter was chosen to be the bride of the river-god, and was forced to accept the wedding gifts which the sorcerers brought her. The people of the district chafed grievously under this custom.

Now when Si-Men entered into office, he heard of this evil custom. He had the sorcerers come before him and said: "See to it that you let me know when the day of the river-god's wedding comes, for I myself wish to be present to honor the god! This will please him, and in return he will shower blessings on my people." With that he dismissed them. And the sorcerers were full of praise for his piety.

So when the day arrived they gave him notice. Si-Men dressed himself in his robes of ceremony, entered his chariot and drove to the river in festival procession. The elders of the people, as well as the sorcerers and the witches were all there. And from far and near men, women and children had flocked together in order to see the show. The sorcerers placed the river-bride on a couch, adorned her with her bridal jewels, and kettledrums, snaredrums and merry airs vied with each other in joyful sound.

They were about to thrust the couch into the stream, and the girl's parents said farewell to her amid tears. But Si-Men bade them wait and said: "Do not be in such a hurry! I have appeared in person to escort the bride, hence everything must be done solemnly and in order. First someone must go to the river-god's castle, and let him know that he may come himself and fetch his bride."

And with these words he looked at a witch and said: "You may go!" The witch hesitated, but he ordered his servants to seize her and thrust her into the stream. After which about an hour went by.

"That woman did not understand her business," continued Si-Men, "or else she would have been back long ago!" And with that he looked at one of the sorcerers and added: "Do you go and do better!" The sorcerer paled with fear, but Si-Men had him seized and cast into the river. Again half-an-hour went by.

Then Si-Men pretended to be uneasy. "Both of them have made a botch of their errand," said he, "and are causing the bride to wait in vain!" Once more he looked at a sorcerer and said: "Do you go and hunt them up!" But the sorcerer flung himself on the ground and begged for mercy. And all the rest of the sorcerers and witches knelt to him in a row, and pleaded for grace. And they took an oath that they would never again seek a bride for the river-god.

Then Si-Men held his hand, and sent the girl back to her home, and the evil custom was at an end forever.

Footnotes for 'How the River-God's Wedding Was Broken Off'

1. Si-Men Bau was an historical personage, who lived five centuries before Christ.

The Spirits of the Yellow River

THE SPIRITS OF the Yellow River are called Dai Wang – Great King. For many hundreds of years past the river inspectors had continued to report that all sorts of monsters show themselves in the waves of the stream, at times in the shape of dragons, at others in that of cattle and horses, and whenever such a creature makes an appearance a great flood follows. Hence temples are built along the river banks. The higher spirits of the river are honored as kings, the lower ones as captains, and hardly a day goes by without their being honored with sacrifices or theatrical performances. Whenever, after a dam has been broken, the leak is closed again, the emperor sends officials with sacrifices and ten great bars of Tibetan incense. This incense is burned in a great sacrificial censer in the temple court, and the river inspectors and their subordinates all go to the temple to thank the gods for their aid. These river gods, it is said, are good and faithful servants of former rulers, who died in consequence of their toil in keeping the dams unbroken. After they died their spirits became river-kings; in their physical bodies, however, they appear as lizards, snakes and frogs.

The mightiest of all the river-kings is the Golden Dragon-King. He frequently appears in the shape of a small golden snake with a square head, low forehead and four red dots over his eyes. He can make himself large or small at will, and cause the waters to rise and fall. He appears and vanishes unexpectedly, and lives in the mouths of the Yellow River and the Imperial Canal. But in addition to the Golden Dragon-King there are dozens of river-kings and captains, each of whom has his own place. The sailors of the Yellow River all have exact lists in which the lives and deeds of the river-spirits are described in detail.

The river-spirits love to see theatrical performances. Opposite every temple is a stage. In the hall stands the little spirit-tablet of the river-king, and on the altar in front of it a small bowl of golden lacquer filled with clean sand. When a little snake appears in it, the river-king has arrived. Then the priests strike the gong and beat the drum and read from the holy books. The official is at once informed and he sends for a company of actors. Before they begin to perform the actors go up to the temple, kneel, and beg the king to let them know which play they are to give. And the river-god picks one out and points to it with his head; or else he writes signs in the sand with his tail. The actors then at once begin to perform the desired play.

The river-god cares naught for the fortunes or misfortunes of human beings. He appears suddenly and disappears in the same way, as best suits him.

Between the outer and the inner dam of the Yellow River are a number of settlements. Now it often happens that the yellow water moves to the very edge of the inner walls. Rising perpendicularly, like a wall, it gradually advances. When people see it coming they hastily burn incense, bow in prayer before the waters, and promise the river-god a theatrical performance. Then the water retires and the word goes round: "The river-god has asked for a play again!"

In a village in that section there once dwelt a wealthy man. He built a stone wall, twenty feet high, around the village, to keep away the water. He did not believe in the spirits of the river, but trusted in his strong wall and was quite unconcerned.

One evening the yellow water suddenly rose and towered in a straight line before the village. The rich man had them shoot cannon at it. Then the water grew stormy, and surrounded the wall to such a height that it reached the openings in the battlements. The water foamed and hissed, and seemed about to pour over the wall. Then everyone in the village was very much frightened. They dragged up the rich man and he had to kneel and beg for pardon. They promised the river-god a theatrical performance, but in vain; but when they promised to build him a temple in the middle of the village and give regular performances, the water sank more and more and gradually returned to its bed. And the village fields suffered no damage, for the earth, fertilized by the yellow slime, yielded a double crop.

Once a scholar was crossing the fields with a friend in order to visit a relative. On their way they passed a temple of the river-god where a new play was just being performed. The friend asked the scholar to go in with him and look on. When they entered the temple court they saw two great snakes upon the front pillars, who had wound themselves about the columns, and were thrusting out their heads as though watching the performance. In the hall of the temple stood the altar with the bowl of sand. In it lay a small snake with a golden body, a green head and red dots above his eyes. His neck was thrust up and his glittering little eyes never left the stage. The friend bowed and the scholar followed his example.

Softly he said to his friend: "What are the three river-gods called?"

"The one in the temple," was the reply, "is the Golden Dragon-King. The two on the columns are two captains. They do not dare to sit in the temple together with the king."

This surprised the scholar, and in his heart he thought: "Such a tiny snake! How can it possess a god's power? It would have to show me its might before I would worship it."

He had not yet expressed these secret thoughts before the little snake suddenly stretched forth his head from the bowl, above the altar. Before the altar burned two enormous candles. They weighed more than ten pounds and were as thick as small trees. Their flame burned like the flare of a torch. The snake now thrust his head into the middle of the candle-flame. The flame must have been at least an inch broad, and was burning red. Suddenly its radiance turned blue, and was split into two tongues. The candle was so enormous and its fire so hot that even copper and iron would have melted in it; but it did not harm the snake.

Then the snake crawled into the censer. The censer was made of iron, and was so large one could not clasp it with both arms. Its cover showed a dragon design in open-work. The snake crawled in and out of the holes in this cover, and wound his way through all of them, so that he looked like an embroidery in threads of gold. Finally all the openings of the cover, large and small, were filled by the snake. In order to do so, he must have made himself several dozen feet long. Then he stretched out his head at the top of the censer and once more watched the play.

Thereupon the scholar was frightened, he bowed twice, and prayed: "Great King, you have taken this trouble on my account! I honor you from my heart!"

No sooner had he spoken these words than, in a moment, the little snake was back in his bowl, and just as small as he had been before.

In Dsiningdschou they were celebrating the river god's birthday in his temple. They were giving him a theatrical performance for a birthday present. The spectators crowded around as thick as a wall, when who should pass but a simple peasant from the country, who said in a loud voice: "Why, that is nothing but a tiny worm! It is a great piece of folly to honor it like a king!"

Before ever he had finished speaking the snake flew out of the temple. He grew and grew, and wound himself three times around the stage. He became as thick around as a small pail, and his head seemed like that of a dragon. His eyes sparkled like golden lamps, and he spat out red flame with his tongue. When he coiled and uncoiled the whole stage trembled and it seemed as though it would break down. The actors stopped their music and fell down on the stage in prayer. The whole multitude was seized with terror and bowed to the ground. Then some of the old men came along, cast the peasant on the ground, and gave him a good thrashing. So he had to cast himself on his knees before the snake and worship him. Then all heard a noise as though a great many firecrackers were being shot off. This lasted for some time, and then the snake disappeared.

East of Shantung lies the city of Dongschou. There rises an observation-tower with a great temple. At its feet lies the water-city, with a sea-gate at the North, through which the flood-tide rises up to the city. A camp of the boundary guard is established at this gate.

Once upon a time there was an officer who had been transferred to this camp as captain. He had formerly belonged to the land forces, and had not yet been long at his new post. He gave some friends of his a banquet, and before the pavilion in which they feasted lay a great stone shaped somewhat like a table. Suddenly a little snake was seen crawling on this stone. It was spotted with green, and had red dots on its square head. The soldiers were about to kill the little creature, when the captain went out to look into the matter. When he had looked he laughed and said: "You must not harm him! He is the river-king of Dsiningdschou. When I was stationed in Dsiningdschou he sometimes visited me, and then I always gave sacrifices and performances in his honor. Now he has come here expressly in order to wish his old friend luck, and to see him once more."

There was a band in camp; the bandsmen could dance and play like a real theatrical troupe. The captain quickly had them begin a performance, had another banquet with wine and delicate foods prepared, and invited the river-god to sit down to the table.

Gradually evening came and yet the river-god made no move to go.

So the captain stepped up to him with a bow and said: "Here we are far removed from the Yellow River, and these people have never yet heard your name spoken. Your visit has been a great honor for me. But the women and fools who have crowded together chattering outside, are afraid of hearing about you. Now you have visited your old friend, and I am sure you wish to get back home again."

With these words he had a litter brought up; cymbals were beaten and fire-works set off, and finally a salute of nine guns was fired to escort him on his way. Then the little snake crawled into the litter, and the captain followed after. In this order they reached the port, and just when it was about time to say farewell, the snake was already swimming in the water. He had grown much larger, nodded to the captain with his head, and disappeared.

Then there were doubts and questionings: "But the river-god lives a thousand miles away from here, how does he get to this place?"

Said the captain: "He is so powerful that he can get to any place, and besides, from where he dwells a waterway leads to the sea. To come down that way and swim to sea is something he can do in a moment's time!"

Myths of Fire

Introduction

THE CELESTIAL organization of Fire is the fifth Ministry, which is presided over by a President, Lo Hsuan, 'Stellar Sovereign of the Fire-virtue', with five subordinate ministers, four of whom are star-gods, and the fifth a 'celestial prince who receives fire': Chieh-huo T'ien-chun. Like so many other Chinese deities, the five were all ministers of the tyrant emperor Chou.

Lo Hsuan and the Ministry of Fire

IT IS BELIEVED that Lo Hsuan was originally a Taoist priest known as Yen-chung Hsien, of the island Huo-lung, meaning 'Fire-dragon'. His face was the colour of ripe fruit of the jujube-tree, his hair and beard red, the former done up in the shape of a fish-tail. He is also said to have had three eyes. He wore a red cloak ornamented with the pa kua; his horse snorted flames from its nostrils and fire darted from its hoofs.

While fighting in the service of the son of the tyrant emperor, Lo Hsuan suddenly changed himself into a giant with three heads and six arms. In each of his hands he held a magic weapon. These were a seal which reflected the heavens and the earth, a wheel of the five fire-dragons, a gourd containing ten thousand fire-crows, and, in the other hands, two swords which floated like smoke and a tall column of smoke enclosing swords of fire.

Having arrived at the city of Hsi Ch'i, Lo Hsuan sent forth his smoke-column and the air was filled with swords of fire. The ten thousand fire-crows, emerging from the gourd, spread themselves over the town and a terrible fire broke out, the whole place being ablaze in just a few minutes.

It was then that Princess Lung Chi, daughter of Wang-mu Niang-niang appeared in the sky. She spread her shroud of mist and dew over the city and the fire was extinguished by a heavy downpour of rain. All the mysterious mechanisms of Lo Hsuan lost their power and the magician took to his heels down the side of the mountain. There he was met by Li, the Pagoda-bearer, who threw his golden pagoda into the air. The pagoda fell on Lo Hsuan's head and broke his skull.

The Legend of Ch'ih Ching-tzu

OF THE VARIOUS FIRE-GODS, Ch'ih Ching-tzu, the principle of spiritual fire, is one of the five spirits representing the Five Elements. He is Fire personified, which has its birth in the south on Mount Shih-t'ang. He himself and everything connected with him – his skin, hair, beard, trousers and cloak of leaves – are all of the colour of fire, though he is sometimes represented with a blue cap resembling the blue tip of a flame.

He appeared in the presence of Huang Lao in a fire cloud. It was he who obtained fire from the wood of the mulberry tree. The heat of this fire, joined with the moisture of water, developed the germs of terrestrial beings.

The Red Emperor

CHU JUNG WAS a legendary emperor who made his first appearance in the time of Hsien Yuan. In his youth he asked Kuang-shou Lao-jen, 'Old Longevity', to grant him immortality. "The time has not yet come," replied Old Longevity; "before it does you have to become an emperor. I will give you the means of reaching the end you desire. Give orders that after you are dead you are to be buried on the southern slope of the sacred mountain Heng Shan; there you will learn the doctrine of Ch'ih Ching-tzu and will become immortal."

The Emperor Hsien Yuan, having abdicated the throne, sent for Chu Jung and bestowed upon him the crown. Chu Jung, having become emperor, taught the people the use of fire and the advantages to be derived from it.

In those early times the forests were filled with venomous reptiles and savage animals; he ordered the peasants to set fire to the brushwood to drive away these dangerous neighbours and keep them at a distance. He also taught his subjects the art of purifying, forging and welding metals by the action of fire. He was nicknamed Ch'ih Ti, 'the Red Emperor'. He reigned for more than two hundred years, and became an Immortal. His capital was the ancient city of Kuei, north-east of Hsin-cheng Hsien. His tomb is on the southern slope of Heng Shan. The peak is known as Chu Jung Peak. His descendants, who went to live in the south, were the ancestors of the Directors of Fire.

Hui Lu, God of Fire

THE MOST POPULAR God of Fire is Hui Lu, a celebrated magician who lived some time before the reign of Ti K'u, the father of Yao the Great, and had a mysterious bird named Pi Fang and a hundred other fire birds shut up in a gourd. He had only to let them out to set up an extensive fire that would extend over the whole country.

Huang Ti ordered Chu Jung to fight Hui Lu and also to subdue the rebel Chih Yu. Chu Jung had a large bracelet of pure gold – a most wonderful and effective weapon. He hurled it into the air and it fell on Hui Lu's neck, throwing him to the ground and rendering him incapable of moving. Finding resistance impossible, he asked for mercy from his victor and promised to be his follower in the spiritual contests. Subsequently he always called himself Huo-shih Chih T'u, 'the Disciple of the Master of Fire'.

Shen Nung, the Fire Emperor

WHEN SHEN NUNG, the God of Agriculture, succeeded the Emperor Fu Hsi on the throne he adopted fire as the emblem of his government, just as Huang Ti adopted the symbol of Earth. He came to be called Huo Ti, the 'Fire emperor'.

Shen Nung taught his subjects the use of fire for smelting metals and making implements and weapons, and the use of oil in lamps. All the divisions of his official hierarchy were connected in some way with this element – there were the Ministers of Fire generally, the officers of Fire of the North, South, etc. He subsequently become doubly the patron of fire and a second fire symbol was added to his name, changing it from Huo Ti, 'Fire Emperor', to Yen Ti, 'Blazing Emperor'.

The Fire-God

LONG BEFORE THE TIME of Fu Hi, Dschu Yung, the Magic Welder, was the ruler of men. He discovered the use of fire, and succeeding generations learned from him to cook their food. Hence his descendants were intrusted with the preservation of fire, while he himself was made the Fire-God. He is a personification of the Red Lord, who showed himself at the beginning of the world as one of the Five Ancients. The Fire-God is worshiped as the Lord of the Holy Southern Mountain.[1] In the skies the Fiery Star,[2] the southern quarter of the heavens and the Red Bird[3] belong to his domain. When there is danger of fire the Fiery Star glows with a peculiar radiance. When countless numbers of fire-crows fly into a house, a fire is sure to break out in it.

In the land of the four rivers[4] there dwelt a man who was very rich. One day he got into his wagon and set out on a long journey. And he met a girl, dressed in red, who begged him to take her with him. He allowed her to get into the wagon, and drove along for half-a-day without even looking in her direction. Then the girl got out again and said in farewell: "You are truly a good and honest man, and for that reason I must tell you the truth. I am the Fire-God. Tomorrow a fire will break out in your house. Hurry home at once to arrange your affairs and save what you can!" Frightened, the man faced his horses about and drove home as fast as he could. All that he possessed in the way of treasures, clothes and jewels, he removed from the house. And, when he was about to lie down to sleep, a fire broke out on the hearth which could not be quenched until the whole building had collapsed in dust and ashes. Yet, thanks to the Fire-God, the man had saved all his movable belongings.

Footnotes for 'The Fire God'

1. The Holy Southern Mountain is Sung-Schan in Huan.
2. The Fiery Star is Mars.
3. The constellations of the southern quarter of the heavens are grouped by the Chinese as under the name of the "Red Bird".
4. The "land of the four rivers" is Setchuan, in the western part of present-day China.

Myths of Epidemics & Exorcism

Introduction

WHERE WE ENCOUNTER some of the more interesting tales of the gods of Epidemics and of Exorcism, who belong to a number of celestial Ministries.

The composition of the Ministry of Epidemics is arranged differently in different historical works as Epidemics (regarded as epidemics on earth, but as demons in Heaven) of the Centre, Spring, Summer, Autumn and Winter, or as the marshals clothed in yellow, green, red, white and blue respectively, or as the Officers of the East, West, South and North, with two additional members: a Taoist who quells the plague and the Grand Master who urges people to do right.

The Ministry of Exorcism, on the other hand, is a Taoist invention and is composed of seven chief ministers, whose duty is to expel evil spirits from dwellings and generally to counteract the annoyances of infernal demons. The two gods usually referred to in the popular legends are P'an Kuan and Chung K'uei. The first is the Guardian of the Living and the Dead in the Otherworld. He was originally a scholar named Ts'ui Chio, who became the Minister of Ceremonies. After his death he was appointed to the spiritual post mentioned above. His best-known achievement is his prolongation of the life of the Emperor T'ai Tsung of the T'ang dynasty by twenty years by changing i, 'one', into san, 'three', in the life register kept by the gods. However, the original P'an Kuan, 'the Decider of Life in Hades', has been gradually supplanted in popular favour by Chung K'uei, 'the Protector against Evil Spirits'.

The Five Spirits of the Plague

WITH REGARD TO the Ministry of Seasonal Epidemics, it is told that in the sixth moon of the eleventh year of the reign of Kao Tsu, founder of the Sui dynasty, five men appeared in the air, clothed in robes of five colours, each carrying different objects in his hands: the first a spoon and earthenware vase, the second a leather bag and sword, the third a fan, the fourth a club, the fifth a jug of fire.

The Emperor asked his Grand Historiographer who these were and if they were benevolent or evil spirits. The official answered: "These are the five powers of the five directions. Their appearance indicates the imminence of epidemics, which will last throughout the four seasons of the year." "What remedy is there, and how am I to protect the people?" inquired the Emperor. "There is no remedy," replied the official, "for epidemics are sent by Heaven." During that year the mortality was very great. The Emperor built a temple to the five men and granted them the title of Marshals to the Five Spirits of the Plague. During that and the following dynasty sacrifices were offered to them on the fifth day of the fifth moon.

The Legend of Lu Yueh

LU YUEH, the President of the Ministry of Epidemics was an old Taoist hermit living at Chiu-lung Tao ('Nine-dragon Island') who became an Immortal. The four members of the Ministry were his disciples. He wore a red garment had a blue face, red hair, long teeth and three eyes. His war horse was named the Myopic Camel. He carried a magic sword and was in the service of Chou Wang, whose armies were concentrated at Hsi Ch'i. In a duel with Mu-cha, brother of No-cha, he had his arm severed by a sword. In another battle with Huang T'ien-hua, son of Huang Fei-hu, he appeared with three heads and six arms. In his many hands he held the celestial seal, plague microbes, the flag of plague, the plague sword and two mysterious swords. His faces were green and large teeth protruded from his mouths. Huang T'ien-hua threw his magic weapon and hit him on the leg. Just at that moment Chiang Tzu-ya arrived with his whip and felled him with a blow. However, he was able to rise again and took to flight.

Resolved to avenge his defeat, he joined General Hsu Fang who was commanding an army corps at Ch'uan-yun Kuan. Round the mountain he organized a system of entrenchments and of infection against their enemies. Yang Chien released his celestial hound which bit Lu Yueh on the crown of his head. Then Yang Jen, armed with his magic fan, pursued Lu Yueh and compelled him to retreat to his fortress. Lu Yueh mounted the central raised part of the embattled wall and opened all his plague-disseminating umbrellas, with the intent of infecting Yang Jen, but the latter, simply by waving his fan, reduced all the umbrellas to dust and also burned the fort, and with it Lu Yueh.

The Five Graduates

THERE IS AN INTERESTING LEGEND concerning five other gods of epidemics. These gods are called the Wu Yueh, 'Five Mountains', and are worshipped in the temple San-i Ko at Ju-kao, especially in outbreaks of contagious diseases and fevers. A sufferer goes to the temple and promises offerings to the gods in the event of recovery. The customary offering is five small wheaten loaves (called shao ping) and a pound of meat.

The Wu Yueh are stellar devils whom Yu Huang sent to be reincarnated on earth. Their names were T'ien Po-hsueh, Tung Hung-wen, Ts'ai Wen-chu, Chao Wu-chen, and Huang Ying-tu. They were all noted for their brilliant intellects and were clever scholars who successfully passed their graduate's examination.

The story goes that when Li Shih-min ascended the throne he called together all the literati of the Empire to take the Doctor's Examination in the capital. Our five graduates started for the metropolis, but, losing their way, were robbed and had to beg help in order to reach the end of their journey. By good luck they all met in the San-i Ko temple and told each other the various hardships they had endured. But when they eventually reached the capital the examination was over and they were out in the streets without resources. So they took an oath of brotherhood for life and death. They pawned some of the few clothes they possessed and bought some musical instruments, turning themselves into a band of strolling musicians. The first bought a drum, the second a seven-stringed guitar, the third a mandolin, the fourth a clarinet and the fifth and youngest composed songs.

They went through the streets of the capital giving their concerts, and Fate decreed that Li Shih-min should hear their melodies. Charmed with the sweet sounds, he asked Hsu Mao-kung where this band of exceptional musicians came from. Having made inquiries, the minister related their experiences to the Emperor. Li Shih-min ordered them to be brought to him and after hearing them play and sing he appointed them to his private suite. They were to accompany him wherever he went.

Meanwhile, the Emperor bore malice toward Chang T'ien-shih, the Master of the Taoists, because he refused to pay the taxes on his property and conceived a plan to bring about his destruction. He caused a spacious subterranean chamber to be dug under the reception hall of his palace. A wire passed through the ceiling to where the Emperor sat. This was so that the signal for the music to begin or stop could be given at will. Having stationed the five musicians in this subterranean chamber, he summoned the Master of the Taoists and invited him to a banquet. During the course of this he pulled the wire and a subterranean babel began.

The Emperor pretended to be terrified and allowed himself to fall to the ground. Then, addressing himself to the T'ien-shih, he said: "I know that you can at will catch the devilish hobgoblins which molest human beings. You can hear for yourself the infernal row they make in my palace. I order you under penalty of death to put a stop to their pranks and to exterminate them."

Having said this, the Emperor left. The Master of the Taoists brought his projecting mirror and began to seek for the evil spirits. In vain he inspected the palace and its precincts; he could discover nothing. In despair threw his mirror on the floor of the reception hall.

A minute later, sad and pensive, he stooped to pick it up; when he saw reflected in it the subterranean room and the musicians! At once he drew five talismans on yellow paper, burned them and ordered his celestial general, Chao Kung-ming, to take his sword and kill the five musicians. The order was promptly executed, but when the T'ien-shih informed the Emperor, he could not believe it was true. He went to his seat and pulled the wire, but all remained silent. A second and third time he gave the signal, but without response. He then ordered his Grand Officer to ascertain what had happened. The officer found the five graduates bathed in their blood and lifeless.

The Emperor, furious, reproached the Master of the Taoists. "But," replied the T'ien-shih, "was it not your Majesty who ordered me under pain of death to exterminate the authors of this pandemonium?" Li Shih-min could not reply. He dismissed the Master of the Taoists and ordered the five victims to be buried.

After the funeral ceremonies, apparitions appeared at night in the place where they had been killed, and the palace became a babel. The spirits threw bricks and broke the tiles on the roofs.

The Emperor ordered his uncomfortable visitors to go to the T'ien-shih who had murdered them. They obeyed and, seizing the garments of the Master of the Taoists, swore not to allow him any rest if he would not restore them to life.

To appease them the Taoist said: "I am going to give each of you a wonderful object. You are then to return and spread epidemics among wicked people, beginning in the imperial palace and with the Emperor himself, with the object of forcing him to canonize you."

One received a fan, another a gourd filled with fire, the third a metallic ring to encircle people's heads, the fourth a stick made of wolves' teeth and the fifth a cup of lustral water.

The spirit graduates left full of joy and made their first experiment on Li Shih-min. The first gave him feverish chills by waving his fan, the second burned him with the fire from his gourd, the third encircled his head with the ring, causing him violent headache, the fourth struck him with his stick and the fifth poured out his cup of lustral water on his head.

The same night a similar tragedy took place in the palace of the Empress and the two chief imperial concubines.

T'ai-po Chin-hsing, however, informed Yu Huang what had happened and, touched with compassion, he sent three Immortals with pills and talismans which cured the Empress and the ladies of the palace.

Li Shih-min, having also recovered his health, summoned the five deceased graduates and expressed his regret for the unfortunate series of events. He said to them: "To the south of the capital is the temple San-i Ko. I will change its name to Hsiang Shan Wu Yueh Shen, 'Fragrant Hill of the Five Mountain Spirits'. On the twenty-eighth day of the ninth moon betake yourselves to that temple to receive the seals of your canonization." He granted them the title of Ti, 'Emperor'.

The Exorcism of Emptiness and Devastation

THIS LEGEND tells of the Emperor Ming Huang of the T'ang dynasty who, after an expedition to Mount Li in Shensi, was attacked by fever. During a nightmare he saw a small demon fantastically dressed in red trousers, with a shoe on one foot but not on the other and a shoe hanging from his girdle.

Having broken through a bamboo gate, the demon took possession of an embroidered box and a jade flute and then began to make a tour of the palace. The Emperor grew angry and questioned him. "Your humble servant," replied the little demon, "is named Hsu Hao, 'Emptiness and Devastation'," "I have never heard of such a person," said the Emperor. The demon replied, "Hsu means to desire Emptiness, because in Emptiness one can fly just as one wishes; Hao, 'Devastation', changes people's joy to sadness."

The Emperor, irritated by this flippancy, was about to call his guard, when suddenly a great devil appeared wearing a tattered head-covering and a blue robe. He had a horn clasp on his belt and official boots on his feet. The devil went up to the sprite, tore out one of his eyes, crushed it up and ate it. The Emperor asked the newcomer who he was. "Your humble servant," he replied, "is Chung K'uei, Physician of Tung-nan Shan in Shensi. In the reign-period Wu Te of the Emperor Kao Tsu of the T'ang dynasty I was rejected and unjustly defrauded of a first class in the public examinations. Overwhelmed with shame, I committed suicide on the steps of the imperial palace. The Emperor ordered me to be buried in a green robe [reserved for members of the imperial clan], and out of gratitude for that favour I swore to protect the sovereign in any part of the Empire against the evil plots of the demon Hsu Hao." At these words the Emperor awoke and found that the fever had left him.

His Majesty called for Wu Tao-tzu (one of the most celebrated Chinese artists) to paint the portrait of the person he had seen in his dream. The work was so well done that the Emperor recognized it as the actual demon he had seen in his sleep and rewarded the artist handsomely. The portrait is said to have been still in the imperial palace during the Sung dynasty.

Tales of the Goddess of Mercy

Introduction

THE MOST POPULAR Goddess of the Buddhist faith is the beautiful Kuan Yin, a deity originally represented as a man. This transition from a male deity into a female one seems to have emerged sometime during the Northern Sung Dynasty (AD 960–1126) and is reflected in Kuan Yin's miraculous appearance in human form in the saga of Miao Shan that follows.

According to the ancient myth, Kuan Yin was about to enter Heaven when she heard a cry of anguish from the earth beneath her and could not prevent herself from investigating its source. Hence her name translates as 'one who hears the cries of the world'.

Kuan Yin is the patron saint of Tibetan Buddhism, the patron Goddess of mothers, the guardian of the storm-tossed fisherman and the overall protector of mankind. If, in the midst of a fire she is called upon, the fire ceases to burn. If during a battle her name is called, the sword and spear of the enemy prove harmless. If prone to evil thoughts, the heart is immediately purified when she is summoned. Her image is that of a Madonna figure with a child in her arms. All over China this Goddess is revered and it is this image that appears not only in temples of worship but also in households and other public places.

The Birth of Miao Shan

IN THE TWENTY-FIRST YEAR of the reign of Ta Hao (the Great Great One) of the Golden Heavenly Dynasty, a man named P'o Chia, whose first name was Lo Yu – an enterprising kinglet of Hsi Yii – seized the throne for twenty years after fighting a war for three years. His kingdom was known as Hsing Lin and the title of his reign as Miao Chuang.

The kingdom of Hsing Lin was situated between India on the west, the kingdom of T'ien Cheng on the south and the kingdom of Siam on the north. Of this kingdom the two pillars of State were the Grand Minister Chao Chen and the General Ch'u Chieh. The Queen Pao Te, whose maiden name was Po Ya, and the King Miao Chuang had lived nearly half a century without having a son to succeed to the throne. This was a source of great grief to them. Po Ya suggested to the King that the God of Hua Shan, the sacred mountain in the west, had the reputation of being always willing to help; and that if he prayed to him and asked his pardon for having shed so much blood during the wars which preceded his accession to the throne he might obtain an heir.

Welcoming this suggestion, the King sent for Chao Chen and ordered him to dispatch the two Chief Ministers of Ceremonies, Hsi Heng-nan and Chih Tu, to the temple of Hua Shan with instructions to request fifty Buddhist and Taoist priests to pray for seven days and seven nights in order that the King might obtain a son. When that period was over, the King and Queen would go in person to offer sacrifices in the temple.

The envoys took with them many rare and valuable presents and for seven days and seven nights the temple resounded with the sound of drums, bells and all kinds of instruments, intermingled with the voices of the praying priests. On their arrival the King and Queen offered sacrifices to the god of the sacred mountain.

But the God of Hua Shan knew that the King had been deprived of a male heir as a punishment for the extensive loss of life during his three years' war. The priests, however, interceded for him, urging that the King had come in person to offer the sacrifices, so the God could not altogether reject his prayer. So he ordered Ch'ien-li Yen, 'Thousand-li Eye', and Shun-feng Erh, 'Favourable-wind Ear', to go quickly and find out if there were not some worthy person who was on the point of being reincarnated into this world.

The two messengers shortly returned and stated that in India, in the village of Chih-shu Yuan in the Chiu Ling Mountains, there lived a good man named Shih Ch'in-ch'ang whose ancestors had observed all the ascetic rules of the Buddhists for three generations. This man was the father of three children – the eldest Shih Wen, the second Shih Chin and the third Shih Shan – all worthy followers of the great Buddha.

Meanwhile, Wang Che, a bandit chief and thirty of his band of men, finding themselves pursued and harassed by the Indian soldiers, without provisions or shelter and dying of hunger, went to Shih Wen and begged for something to eat. Knowing that they were evildoers, Shih Wen and his two brothers refused to give them anything; if they starved, they said, the peasants would no longer suffer from their attacks. So the robbers decided that it was a case of life for life and broke into the house of a rich family of the name of Tai, burning their home, killing a hundred men, women and children, and carrying off everything they possessed.

The local t'u-ti (or Local God) made a report to Yu Huang at once.

"This Shih family," replied the god, "for three generations has given itself up to good works, and certainly the robbers were not deserving of any pity. However, it is impossible to deny that the three brothers Shih, in refusing them food, morally compelled them to loot the Tai family's house, putting all to the sword or flames. Is this not the same as if they had committed the crime themselves? Let them be arrested and put in chains in the celestial prison and let them never see the light of the sun again."

"Since," said the messenger to the God of Hua Shan, "your gratitude toward Miao Chuang compels you to grant him an heir, why not ask Yu Huang to pardon their crime and reincarnate them in the womb of the Queen Po Ya, so that they may begin a new terrestrial existence and give themselves up to good works?" As a result, the God of Hua Shan called the Spirit of the Wind and gave him a message for Yu Huang.

The message was as follows: "King Miao Chuang has offered sacrifice to me and begged me to grant him an heir. But since by his wars he has caused the deaths of a large number of human beings, he does not deserve to have his request granted. Now these three brothers Shih have offended your Majesty by forcing Wang Che to be guilty of murder and robbery. I pray you to take into account their past good works and pardon their crime, giving them an opportunity of expiating it by causing them all three to be reborn, but of the female sex, in the womb of Po Ya the Queen. In this way they will be able to atone for their crime and save many souls." Yu Huang was pleased to comply and he ordered the Spirit of the North Pole to release the three captives and take their souls to the palace of King Miao Chuang, where in three years' time they would be changed into females in the womb of Queen Po Ya.

The King, who was anxiously expecting the birth of an heir, was informed one morning that a daughter had been born to him. She was named Miao Ch'ing. A year went by and another daughter was born. This one was named Miao Yin. When, at the end of the third year, another daughter was born, the King, beside himself with rage, called his Grand Minister Chao Chen and said to him, "I am past fifty, and have no male child to succeed me on the throne. My dynasty will therefore become extinct. Of what use have been all my labours and all my victories?" Chao Chen tried to console him, saying, "Heaven has granted you three daughters: no human power can change this divine decree. When these princesses have grown up, we will choose three sons-in-law for your Majesty, and you can elect your successor from among them. Who will dare to dispute his right to the throne?"

The King named the third daughter Miao Shan. She became noted for her modesty and many other good qualities and scrupulously observed all the tenets of the Buddhist doctrines. Virtuous living seemed, indeed, to be like second nature.

Miao Shan's Ambition

ONE DAY, when the three daughters of King Miao Chuang were playing in the palace garden of Perpetual Spring, Miao Shan said to her sisters, "Riches and glory are like the rain in spring or the morning dew; a little while, and all is gone. Kings and emperors think to enjoy to the end the good fortune which places them in a rank apart from other human beings; but sickness lays them low in their coffins, and all is over. Where are now all those powerful dynasties which have laid down the law to the world? As for me, I desire nothing more than a peaceful retreat on a lone mountain, there to attempt the attainment of perfection. If someday I can reach a high degree of goodness, then, borne on the clouds of Heaven, I will travel throughout the universe, passing in the twinkling of an eye from east to west. I will rescue my father and mother, and bring them to Heaven; I will save the miserable and afflicted on earth; I will convert the spirits which do evil, and cause them to do good. That is my only ambition."

No sooner had she finished speaking than a lady of the Court came to announce that the King had found sons-in-law for his two elder daughters. The wedding feast was to be the very next day. "Be quick," she added, "and prepare your presents, your dresses and so forth, for the King's order is imperative." The husband chosen for Miao Ch'ing was a First Academician named Chao K'uei. His personal name was Te Ta, and he was the son of a celebrated minister of the reigning dynasty. Miao Yin's husband-to-be was a military officer named Ho Feng, whose personal name was Ch'ao Yang. He had passed first in the examination for the Military Doctorate. The marriage ceremonies were magnificent. Festivity followed festivity; the newlyweds were duly installed in their palaces and general happiness prevailed.

There now remained only Miao Shan. The King and Queen wished to find for her a man famous for knowledge and virtue, capable of ruling the kingdom and worthy of being the successor to the throne. So the King called her and explained to her all his plans regarding her and how all his hopes rested on her.

"It is a crime," she replied, "for me not to comply with my father's wishes; but you must pardon me if my ideas differ from yours."

"Tell me what your ideas are," said the King. "I do not wish to marry," she said. "I wish to attain to perfection and to Buddhahood. Then I promise that I will not be ungrateful to you."

"Wretch of a daughter," cried the King in anger, "you think you can teach me, the head of the State and ruler of so great a people! Has anyone ever known a daughter of a king become a nun? Can a good woman be found in that class? Put aside all these mad ideas of a nunnery and tell me at once if you will marry a First Academician or a Military First Graduate."

"Who is there," answered the girl, "who does not love the royal dignity? What person who does not aspire to the happiness of marriage? However, I wish to become a nun. With respect to the riches and glory of this world, my heart is as cold as a dead cinder and I feel a keen desire to make it ever purer and purer."

The King was furious and wished to cast her out from his presence. Miao Shan, knowing she could not openly disobey his orders, took another course. "If you absolutely insist upon my marrying," she said, "I will consent; only I must marry a physician."

"A physician!" growled the King. "Are men of good family and talents wanting in my kingdom? What an absurd idea, to want to marry a physician!"

"My wish is," said Miao Shan, "to heal humanity of all its ills; of cold, heat, lust, old age and all infirmities. I wish to equalize all classes, putting rich and poor on the same footing, to have community of goods, without distinction of persons. If you will grant me my wish, I can still in this way become a Buddha, a Saviour of Mankind. There is no necessity to call in the diviners to choose an auspicious day. I am ready to be married now."

At these words the King was mad with rage. "Wicked imbecile!" he cried, "What diabolical suggestions are these that you dare to make in my presence?" Without further ado he called Ho T'ao, who on that day was officer of the palace guard. When he had arrived and kneeled to receive the King's commands, the latter said: "This wicked nun dishonours me. Take from her her Court robes and drive her from my presence. Take her to the Queen's garden and let her perish there of cold: that will be one care less for my troubled heart."

Miao Shan fell on her face and thanked the King. She went with the officer to the Queen's garden, where she began to lead her retired hermit life with the moon for companion and the wind for friend, content to see all obstacles overthrown on her way to Nirvana – the highest state of spiritual bliss – and glad to exchange the pleasures of the palace for the sweetness of solitude.

The Nunnery of The White Bird

AFTER MANY FUTILE ATTEMPTS to dissuade Miao Shan from her purpose, one day the King and Queen sent Miao Hung and Ts'ui Hung to make a last attempt to bring their misguided daughter to her senses. Miao Shan, annoyed at this renewed attempt, ordered them never again to come and torment her with their silly prattle. "I have found out," she added, "that there is a well-known temple at Ju Chou in Lung-shu Hsien. This Buddhist temple is known as the Nunnery of the White Bird. In it five hundred nuns give themselves up to the study of the true doctrine and the way of perfection. Go then and ask the Queen to obtain the King's permission for me to retire there. If you can do me this favour, I will not fail to reward you later."

Miao Chuang summoned the messengers and inquired the result of their efforts. "She is more unapproachable than ever," they replied; "she has even ordered us to ask the Queen to obtain your Majesty's permission to retire to the Nunnery of the White Bird in Lung-shu Hsien."

The King gave his permission, but sent strict orders to the nunnery instructing the nuns to do all in their power to dissuade the Princess from remaining.

This Nunnery of the White Bird had been built by Huang Ti and the five hundred nuns who lived in it had as Superior a lady named I Yu, who was remarkable for her virtue. On receipt of the royal mandate, she had summoned Cheng Cheng-ch'ang, the choir mistress, and informed her that Princess Miao Shan would shortly arrive at the temple. She requested her to receive the visitor courteously, but at the same time to do all she could to dissuade her from adopting the life of a nun. Having given these instructions, the Superior, accompanied by two novices went to meet Miao Shan at the gate of the temple. On her arrival they saluted her. The Princess returned the salute, but said: "I have just left the world in order to place myself under your orders: why do you come and salute me on my arrival? I beg you to be so good as to take me into the temple, in order that I may pay my respects to the Buddha." I Yu led her into the principal hall and instructed the nuns to light incense sticks, ring the bells and beat the drums. The visit to the temple finished, she went into the preaching hall, where she greeted her instructresses. The latter obeyed the King's command and tried to persuade the Princess to return to her home but, as none of their arguments had any effect, they decided to give her a trial. She was to be put in charge of the kitchen, where she could prepare the food for the nunnery and generally be at the service of all. If she did not do a good job, they could dismiss her.

Miao Shan joyfully agreed, and went to make her humble submission to the Buddha. She knelt before Ju Lai and made offering to him, praying: "Great Buddha, full of goodness and mercy, your humble servant wishes to leave the world. Grant that I may never yield to the temptations which will be sent to try my faith." Miao Shan further promised to observe all the regulations of the nunnery and to obey the superiors.

This generous self-sacrifice touched the heart of Yu Huang, the Master of Heaven, who summoned the Spirit of the North Star and instructed him as follows:

"Miao Shan, the third daughter of King Miao Chuang, has renounced the world in order to devote herself to the attainment of perfection. Her father has consigned her to the Nunnery of the White Bird. She has happily undertaken the burden of all the work in the nunnery. If she is left without help, who is there who will be willing to adopt the virtuous life? Go quickly and order the Three Agents, the Gods of the Five Sacred Peaks, the Eight Ministers of the Heavenly Dragon, Ch'ieh Lan and the t'u-ti to send her help at once. Tell the Sea Dragon to dig her a well near the kitchen, a tiger to bring her firewood, birds to collect vegetables for the nuns and all the spirits of Heaven to help her in her duties, so that she may give herself up without disturbance to the pursuit of perfection. See that my commands are promptly obeyed." The Spirit of the North Star complied without delay.

Seeing all these gods arrive to help the novice, the Superior, I Yu, spoke with the choir mistress, saying: "We assigned to the Princess the burdensome work of the kitchen because she refused to return to the world; but since she began her duties the gods of the eight caves of Heaven have come to offer her fruit, Ch'ieh Lan sweeps the kitchen, the dragon has dug a well, the God of the Hearth and the tiger bring her fuel, birds collect vegetables for her, the nunnery bell every evening at dusk booms of itself, as if struck by some mysterious hand. Obviously miracles are being performed. Hasten and fetch the King and beg his Majesty to recall his daughter."

Cheng Cheng-ch'ang travelled to the palace and informed the King of all that had happened. The King called Hu Pi-li, the chief of the guard, and ordered him to go the Nunnery of the White Bird and burn it to the ground, together with the nuns. When he reached the place the commander surrounded the nunnery with his soldiers and set fire to it. The five hundred doomed nuns invoked the aid of Heaven and earth, and then, addressing Miao Shan, said: "It is you who have brought upon us this terrible disaster."

"It is true," said Miao Shan. "I alone am the cause of your destruction." She then knelt down and prayed to Heaven: "Great Sovereign of the Universe, your servant is the daughter of King Miao Chuang; you are the grandson of King Lun. Will you not rescue your younger sister? You have left your palace; I also have left mine. You in former times took yourself to the snowy mountains to attain perfection; I came here with the same object. Will you not save us from this fiery destruction?"

Her prayer ended, Miao Shan took a bamboo hairpin from her hair. She pricked the roof of her mouth with it and spat the flowing blood toward Heaven. Immediately great clouds gathered in all parts of the sky and sent down heavy rain, which put out the fire that threatened the nunnery. The nuns threw themselves on their knees and thanked her for having saved their lives.

The Execution of Miao Shan

AFTER WITNESSING the extraordinary event at the Nunnery of the White Bird, Hu Pi-li rushed back to inform the King. The King was enraged. He ordered Hu Pi-li to go back at once and bring his daughter in chains. He was to behead her on the spot.

But the Queen, who had heard of this new plot, begged the King to grant her daughter one last chance. "If you will give permission," she said, "I will have a magnificent pavilion built at the side of the road where Miao Shan will pass in chains on the way to her execution. We will go there with our two other daughters and our sons-in-law. As she passes we will have music, songs and feasting – everything likely to impress her and make her contrast our luxurious life with her miserable plight. This will surely make her repent."

"I agree," said the King, "to counter-order her execution until your preparations are complete." Nevertheless, when the time came, Miao Shan showed nothing but disdain for all this worldly show, and to all advances replied only: "I love not these pompous vanities; I swear that I prefer death to the so-called joys of this world." She was then led to the place of execution. All the Court was present. Sacrifices were made to her as to one already dead. In the midst of all this the Queen appeared. She ordered the officials to return to their posts, so that she might once more urge her daughter to repent. But Miao Shan only listened in silence with downcast eyes.

The King felt great disgust at the thought of shedding his daughter's blood. He ordered her to be imprisoned in the palace so that he might make a last effort to save her. "I am the King," he said; "my orders cannot be lightly set aside. Disobedience to them involves punishment and in spite of my paternal love for you, if you persist in your present attitude, you will be executed tomorrow in front of the palace gate."

The t'u-ti, hearing the King's verdict, immediately went to Yu Huang and reported to him the sentence that had been pronounced against Miao Shan. Yu Huang exclaimed: "Save Buddha, there is none in the west so noble as this Princess. Tomorrow, at the appointed hour, go to the scene of execution, break the swords and splinter the lances they will use to kill her. See that she suffers no pain. At the moment of her death transform yourself into a tiger and bring her body to the pine wood. Having deposited it in a safe place, put a magic pill in her mouth to arrest decay. Her triumphant soul on its return from the lower regions must find it in a perfect state of preservation in order to be able to re-enter it and animate it afresh. After that she must go to Hsiang Shan on P'u T'o Island, where she will reach the highest state of perfection."

On the appointed day, Commander Hu Pi-li led the condemned Princess to the place of execution. Troops had been stationed there to maintain order. The t'u-ti was in attendance at the palace gates. Miao Shan was radiant with joy. "Today," she said, "I leave the world for a better life. Hasten to take my life, but beware of mutilating my body."

The King's warrant arrived, and suddenly the sky became overcast and darkness fell upon the earth. A bright light surrounded Miao Shan, and when the sword of the executioner fell upon the neck of the victim it was broken in two. Then they thrust at her with a spear, but the weapon fell to pieces. After that the King ordered that she be strangled with a silken cord. A few moments later a tiger leapt into the execution ground, dispersed the executioners, put the body of Miao Shan on his back and disappeared into the pine forest. Hu Pi-li rushed to the palace. He told the King full all that had happened and received a reward of two ingots of gold.

Meanwhile, Miao Shan's soul, which remained unhurt, was carried on a cloud. She awoke, as from a dream, lifted her head and looked round but she could not see her body. "My father has just had me strangled," she sighed. "How is it that I find myself in this place? Here are neither mountains, nor trees, nor vegetation; no sun, moon, nor stars; no habitation, no sound, no cackling of a fowl nor barking of a dog. How can I live in this desolate region?"

Suddenly a young man appeared carrying a large banner. He was dressed in blue, shining with a brilliant light. He said to her: "By order of Yen Wang, the King of the Hells, I come to take you to the eighteen infernal regions."

"What is this cursed place where I am now?" asked Miao Shan.

"This is the lower world, Hell," he replied. "Your refusal to marry, and the magnanimity with which you chose death rather than break your resolutions, deserve the recognition of Yu Huang.

The ten gods of the lower regions, impressed by your eminent virtue, have sent me to you. Fear nothing and follow me."

So Miao Shan began her visit to all the infernal regions. The Gods of the Ten Hells came to congratulate her. "Who am I," asked Miao Shan, "that you should take the trouble to show me such respect?"

"We have heard," they replied, "that when you recite your prayers all evil disappears as if by magic. We should like to hear you pray."

"I consent," replied Miao Shan, "on condition that all the condemned ones in the ten infernal regions be released from their chains in order to listen to me."

At the appointed time the condemned were led in by Niu T'ou ('Ox-head') and Ma Mien ('Horse-face'), the two chief constables of Hell, and Miao Shan began her prayers. No sooner had she finished than Hell was suddenly transformed into a paradise of joy, and the instruments of torture into lotus-flowers.

P'an Kuan, the keeper of the Register of the Living and the Dead, presented a memorial to Yen Wang stating that since Miao Shan's arrival there was no more pain in Hell; and all the condemned were beside themselves with happiness. "Since it has always been decreed," he added, "that, in justice, there must be both a Heaven and a Hell, if you do not send this saint back to earth, there will no longer be any Hell, but only a Heaven."

"Since that is so," said Yen Wang, "let forty-eight flag bearers escort her across the Styx Bridge so that she may be taken to the pine forest to re-enter her body and resume her life in the upper world."

The King of the Hells, having paid his respects to her, asked the youth in blue to take her soul back to her body, which she found lying under a pine tree. Having re-entered it, Miao Shan found herself alive again. A bitter sigh escaped from her lips. "I remember," she said, "all that I saw and heard in Hell. I sigh for the moment which will find me free of all impediments, and yet my soul has re-entered my body. Here, without any lonely mountain on which to give myself up to the pursuit of perfection, what will become of me?" Great tears welled from her eyes.

Just then Ju Lai Buddha appeared. "Why have you come to this place?" he asked. Miao Shan explained why the King had put her to death and how after her descent into Hell her soul had re-entered her body. "I greatly pity your misfortune," Ju Lai said, "but there is no one to help you. I also am alone. Why should we not marry? We could build ourselves a hut and pass our days in peace. What say you?" "Sir," she replied, "you must not make impossible suggestions. I died and came to life again. How can you speak so lightly? Do me the pleasure of withdrawing from my presence."

"Well," said the visitor, "he to whom you are speaking is no other than the Buddha of the West. I came to test your virtue. This place is not suitable for your devotional exercises; I invite you to come to Hsiang Shan."

Miao Shan threw herself on her knees and said: "My bodily eyes deceived me. I never thought that your Majesty would come to a place like this. Pardon my seeming want of respect. Where is this Hsiang Shan?"

"Hsiang Shan is a very old monastery," Ju Lai replied, "built in the earliest historical times. It is inhabited by Immortals. It is situated in the sea, on P'u T'o Island. There you will be able to reach the highest perfection."

"How far off is this island?" Miao Shan asked. "More than a thousand miles," Ju Lai replied. "I fear," she said, "I could not bear the fatigue of so long a journey." "Calm yourself," he replied. "I have brought with me a magic peach, of a kind not to be found in any earthly orchard. Once you have eaten it, you will experience neither hunger nor thirst; old age and death will have no power over you: you will live for ever."

Miao Shan ate the magic peach, left Ju Lai and started on the way to Hsiang Shan. From the clouds the Spirit of the North Star saw her making her way toward P'u T'o. He called the Guardian of the Soil of Hsiang Shan and said to him: "Miao Shan is on her way to your country; the way is long and difficult. I ask you take the form of a tiger and carry her to her journey's end."

The t'u-ti transformed himself into a tiger and stationed himself in the middle of the road along which Miao Shan must pass. As Miao Shan approached the tiger she said, "I am a poor girl devoid of filial piety. I have disobeyed my father's commands; devour me, and make an end of me."

The tiger then spoke, saying: "I am not a real tiger, but the Guardian of the Soil of Hsiang Shan. I have received instructions to carry you there. Get on my back."

"Since you have received these instructions," said the girl, "I will obey, and when I have attained to perfection I will not forget your kindness."

The tiger went off like a flash of lightning, and in the twinkling of an eye Miao Shan found herself at the foot of the rocky slopes of P'u T'o Island.

Miao Shan Attains Perfection

AFTER NINE YEARS in the retreat of P'u T'o Island Miao Shan had reached the pinnacle of perfection. Ti-tsang Wang then came to Hsiang Shan, and was so astonished at her virtue that he inquired of the local t'u-ti as to what had brought about this wonderful result. "With the exception of Ju Lai, in all the west no one equals her in dignity and perfection. She is the Queen of the three thousand P'u-sa's and of all the beings on earth who have skin and blood. We regard her as our sovereign in all things. Therefore, on the nineteenth day of the eleventh moon we will enthrone her."

The t'u-ti sent out his invitations for the ceremony. The Dragon king of the Western Sea, the Gods of the Five Sacred Mountains, the one hundred and twenty Emperor saints, the thirty-six officials of the Ministry of Time, the celestial functionaries in charge of wind, rain, thunder and lightning, the Three Causes, the Five Saints, the Eight Immortals, the Ten Kings of the Hells – all were present on the appointed day. Miao Shan took her seat on the lotus throne and the assembled gods proclaimed her sovereign of Heaven and earth and a Buddha. Furthermore, they decided that it was not right that she should remain alone at Hsiang Shan; so they begged her to choose a worthy young man and a virtuous young woman to serve her in the temple.

The t'u-ti was entrusted with the task of finding them. In his search he met a young priest named Shan Ts'ai. After the death of his parents he had become a hermit on Ta-hua Shan and was still a novice in the science of perfection. Miao Shan ordered him to be brought to her. "Who are you?" she asked.

"I am a poor orphan priest of no merit," he replied. "From my earliest youth I have led the life of a hermit. I have been told that your power is equalled only by your goodness, so I have ventured to come to pray you to show me how to attain to perfection."

"My only fear," replied Miao Shan, "is that your desire for perfection may not be sincere."

"I have now no parents," the priest continued, "and I have come a very long way to find you. How can I be wanting in sincerity?"

"What special degree of ability have you attained during your course of perfection?" asked Miao Shan.

"I have no skill," replied Shan Ts'ai, "but I rely for everything on your great pity, and under your guidance I hope to reach the required ability."

"Very well," said Miao Shan, "take up your station on the top of yonder peak, and wait till I find a means of transporting you."

Miao Shan called the t'u-ti and asked him to go and beg all the Immortals to disguise themselves as pirates and to besiege the mountain, waving torches and threatening with swords and spears to kill her. "Then I will seek refuge on the summit, and will leap over the precipice to prove Shan Ts'ai's fidelity and affection."

A minute later a ferocious gang of robbers rushed up to the temple of Hsiang Shan. Miao Shan cried for help, rushed up the steep incline, missed her footing and rolled down into the ravine. Shan Ts'ai, seeing her fall into the abyss, without hesitation flung himself after her in order to rescue her. When he reached her, he asked: "What have you to fear from the robbers? You have nothing for them to steal; why throw yourself over the precipice, exposing yourself to certain death?"

Miao Shan saw that he was weeping, and wept too. "I must comply with the wish of Heaven," she said.

Shan Ts'ai, inconsolable, prayed Heaven and earth to save his protectress. Miao Shan said to him: "You should not have risked your life by throwing yourself over the precipice, I have not yet transformed you. But you did a brave thing and I know that you have a good heart. Now, look down there." "Oh," said he, "if I am not mistaken, that is a corpse." "Yes," she replied, "that is your former body. Now you are transformed you can rise at will and fly in the air." Shan Ts'ai bowed low to thank her. She said to him: "From now on you must say your prayers by my side and not leave me for a single day."

'Brother and Sister'

WITH HER SPIRITUAL SIGHT Miao Shan perceived at the bottom of the Southern Sea the third son of Lung Wang, who, in carrying out his father's orders, was making his way through the waves in the form of a carp. While doing so, he was caught in a fisherman's net and taken to the market at Yueh Chou where he was offered for sale. Miao Shan at once sent her faithful Shan Ts'ai, disguised as a servant, to buy him. She gave him the money to purchase the fish, which he was to take to the foot of the rocks at P'u T'o and set free in the sea. The son of Lung Wang heartily thanked his deliverer, and on his return to the palace he told his father what had occurred. The King said: "As a reward, make her a present of a luminous pearl, so that she may recite her prayers by its light at night time."

Lung Nu, the daughter of Lung Wang's third son, asked her grandfather's permission to take the gift to Miao Shan and beg that she might be allowed to study the doctrine of the sages under her guidance. After having proved her sincerity, she was accepted as a pupil. Shan Ts'ai called her his sister, and Lung Nu reciprocated by calling him her dear brother. Both lived as brother and sister by Miao Shan's side.

The King's Punishment

AFTER KING MIAO CHUANG had burned the Nunnery of the White Bird and killed his daughter, Ch'ieh Lan Buddha presented a petition to Yu Huang praying that the crime be not allowed to go unpunished. Yu Huang, justly irritated, ordered P'an Kuan to consult the Register of the Living and the Dead to see how long this homicidal King had yet to live. P'an Kuan turned over the pages of his register and saw that according to the divine ordinances the King's reign on the throne of Hsing Lin should last for twenty years, but that this period had not yet expired. "That which has been decreed is unable to be changed," said Yu Huang, "but I will punish him by sending him illness." He called the God of Epidemics, and ordered him to afflict the King's body with ulcers, of a kind which could not be healed except by remedies to be given him by his daughter Miao Shan.

The order was promptly executed and the King could get no rest by day or by night. His two daughters and their husbands spent their time feasting while he tossed about in agony on his sickbed. The most famous physicians were called in but the pain only grew worse. Despair took hold of the patient. He then proclaimed that he would grant the succession to the throne to any person who would provide him with an effectual remedy to restore him to health.

Miao Shan had learnt all that was taking place at the palace. She assumed the form of a priest doctor, clothed herself in a priest's gown and attached to her girdle a gourd containing pills and other medicines. Then she went straight to the palace gate, read the royal edict posted there, and tore it down. Some members of the palace guard seized her, and inquired angrily: "Who are you that you should dare to tear down the royal proclamation?"

"I, a poor priest, am also a doctor," she replied. "I read the edict posted on the palace gates. The King is looking for a doctor who can heal him. I am a doctor of an old cultured family and propose to restore him to health."

"If you are of a cultured family, why did you become a priest?" they asked. "Would it not have been better to gain your living honestly in practising your art than to shave your head and go loafing about the world? Besides, all the highest physicians have tried in vain to cure the King; do you imagine that you will be more skilful than all the aged practitioners?"

"Set your minds at ease," she replied. "I have received from my ancestors the most effective remedies and I guarantee that I shall restore the King to health," The palace guard informed the King and in the end the priest was admitted. Having reached the royal bed chamber, he sat still awhile in order to calm himself before feeling the pulse, and to have complete control of all his faculties while examining the King. When he felt quite sure of himself, he approached the King's bed, took the King's hand, felt his pulse, carefully diagnosed the nature of the illness and assured himself that it was easily curable.

One serious difficulty, however, presented itself, and that was that the right medicine was almost impossible to obtain. The King showed his displeasure by saying: "For every illness there is a medical prescription and for every prescription a specific medicine; how can you say that the diagnosis is easy, but that there is no remedy?"

"Your Majesty," replied the priest, "the remedy for your illness is not to be found in any pharmacy, and no one would agree to sell it."

The King became angry and ordered those about him to drive away the priest, who left smiling.

The following night the King dreamt of an old man who said to him: "This priest alone can cure your illness and, if you ask him, he himself will give you the right remedy." The King awoke as soon as these words had been uttered and begged the Queen to recall the priest. When the priest returned the King related his dream and begged him to give him the remedy required. "What, after all, is this remedy that I must have in order to be cured?" he asked.

"There must be the hand and eye of a living person, from which to compound the ointment which alone can save you," answered the priest.

The King called out: "This priest is fooling me! Who would ever give his hand or his eye? Even if anyone would, I could never have the heart to make use of them."

"Nevertheless," said the priest, "there is no other effective remedy."

"Then where can I obtain this remedy?" asked the King.

"Your Majesty must send your ministers, who must observe the Buddhist rules of abstinence, to Hsiang Shan, where they will be given what is required."

"Where is Hsiang Shan, and how far from here?"

"About a thousand or more miles, but I myself will indicate the route to be followed. In a very short time they will return."

The King, who was suffering terribly, was more contented when he heard that the journey could be made quickly. He called his two ministers, Chao Chen and Liu Ch'in, and instructed them to lose no time in starting for Hsiang Shan. They were warned to scrupulously observe the Buddhist rules of abstinence. Meanwhile, the king ordered the Minister of Ceremonies to detain the priest in the palace until their return.

The two sons-in-law of the King, Ho Feng and Chao K'uei, had already made secret preparations to succeed to the throne as soon as the King should breathe his last. They were surprised to learn that the priest had hopes of curing the King's illness and that he was waiting in the palace until the remedy was brought to him. Fearing that they might be disappointed in their ambition, and that after his recovery the King would give the crown to the priest, they entered into a conspiracy with an unscrupulous courtier named Ho Li. They needed to act quickly because the ministers would soon be back. That same night Ho Li was to give to the King a poisoned drink made, he would say, by the priest to numb the King's pain until the return of his two ministers. Shortly after, an assassin, Su Ta, was to murder the priest. Both the King and the priest would meet their death and the kingdom would pass to the King's two sons-in-law.

Miao Shan had returned to Hsiang Shan, leaving the bodily form of the priest in the palace. She saw the two traitors preparing the poison and was aware of their wicked intentions. Calling the spirit Yu I, she told him to fly to the palace and change the poison about to be administered to the King into a harmless soup and to bind the assassin hand and foot.

At midnight Ho Li carried the poisoned drink and knocked at the door of the royal apartment. He said to the Queen that the priest had prepared a soothing potion while waiting for the return of the ministers. "I come," he said, "to offer it to his Majesty." The Queen took the bowl in her hands and was about to give it to the King, when Yu I arrived unannounced. Quickly he snatched the bowl from the Queen and poured the contents on the ground; at the same moment he knocked over those present in the room, so that they all rolled on the floor.

At the same time, the assassin Su Ta entered the priest's room and struck him with his sword. Instantly the assassin, without knowing how, found himself wrapped up in the priest's robe and thrown to the ground. He struggled and tried to free himself but found that his hands had been rendered useless by some mysterious power and that there was no escape. The spirit Yu I then returned to Hsiang Shan and reported to Miao Shan.

The next morning, the two sons-in-law of the King heard of the turn things had taken during the night. The whole palace was in a state of great confusion.

When he was informed that the priest had been killed, the King called Ch'u Ting-lieh and ordered him to have the murderer arrested. Su Ta was tortured and confessed all that he knew. Together with Ho Li he was condemned to be cut into a thousand pieces.

The two sons-in-law were seized and executed. It was only through the Queen's intervention that their wives were spared. The infuriated King, however, ordered that his two daughters should be imprisoned in the palace.

In the meantime, Chao Chen and Liu Ch'in had reached Hsiang Shan. When they were brought to Miao Shan the ministers took out the King's letter and read it to her.

"I, Miao Chuang, King of Hsing Lin, have learned that there dwells at Hsiang Shan an Immortal whose power and compassion have no equal in the whole world. I have passed my fiftieth year, and am afflicted with ulcers that all remedies have failed to cure. Today a priest has assured me that at Hsiang Shan I can obtain the hand and eye of a living person, with which he will prepare an ointment able to restore me to health. Relying on his word and on the goodness of the Immortal to whom he has directed me, I venture to beg that those two parts of a living body necessary to heal my ulcers be sent to me. I assure you of my everlasting gratitude, fully confident that my request will not be refused."

The next morning Miao Shan urged the ministers to take a knife and cut off her left hand and gouge out her left eye. Liu Ch'in took the knife but did not dare to obey the order. "Be quick," urged the Immortal; "you have been commanded to return as soon as possible; why do you hesitate as if you were a young girl?" Liu Ch'in was forced to do it. He plunged in the knife, and the red blood flooded the ground, spreading an odour like sweet incense. The hand and eye were placed on a golden plate, and, having paid their grateful respects to the Immortal, the envoys left.

After they had gone, Miao Shan – who had transformed herself in order to allow the envoys to remove her hand and eye – told Shan Ts'ai that she was now going to prepare the ointment that would cure the King. "Should the Queen," she added, "send for another eye and hand, I will transform myself again and you can give them to her." No sooner had she finished speaking than she mounted a cloud and disappeared in space. The two ministers reached the palace and presented the Queen with the gruesome remedy. She wept, overcome with gratitude and emotion. "What Immortal," she asked, "can have been so charitable as to sacrifice a hand and eye for the King's benefit?" Then suddenly she uttered a great cry, as she recognized the hand of her daughter.

"Who else, in fact, but his child," she continued amid her sobs, "could have had the courage to give her hand to save her father's life?" "What are you saying?" said the King. "In the world there are many hands like this." Just then the priest entered the King's apartment. "This great Immortal has long devoted herself to the attainment of perfection," he said. "She has healed a great many people. Give me the hand and eye." He took them and quickly produced an ointment which, he told the King, was to be applied to his left side. No sooner had it touched his skin than the pain on his left side disappeared as if by magic; no sign of ulcers was to be seen on that side, but his right side remained as swollen and painful as before.

"Why is it," asked the King, "that this remedy, which is so effective for the left side, should not be applied to the right?" "Because," replied the priest, "the left hand and eye of the saint cures only the left side. If you wish to be completely cured, you must send your officers to obtain the right eye and right hand also." The King accordingly dispatched his envoys again with a letter of thanks, and begging as a further favour that the cure should be completed by the healing of his right side.

On the arrival of the envoys Shan Ts'ai met them in the mutilated form of Miao Shan. He told them to cut off his right hand, pluck out his right eye and put them on a plate. At the sight of the four bleeding wounds, Liu Ch'in could not stop himself from calling out indignantly: "This priest is a wicked man to make a martyr of a woman in order to obtain the succession!"

Having said this, he left with his companion for the kingdom of Hsing Lin. On their return the King was overwhelmed with joy. The priest quickly prepared the ointment, and the King applied it to his right side. At once the ulcers disappeared like the darkness of night before the rising sun. The whole Court congratulated the King and praised the priest. The King gave the latter the title Priest of the Brilliant Eye. He fell on his face to return thanks and added: "I, a poor priest, have left the world, and have only one wish, namely, that your Majesty should govern your subjects with justice and sympathy and that all the officials of the realm should prove themselves men of integrity. As for me, I am used to roaming about. I have no desire for any royal estate. My happiness exceeds all earthly joys."

The priest then waved the sleeve of his cloak and a cloud descended from Heaven. Seating himself on it, the priest disappeared in the sky. From the cloud a note containing the following words was seen to fall: "I am one of the Teachers of the West. I came to cure the King's illness, and so to glorify the True Doctrine."

All who witnessed this miracle exclaimed with one voice: "This priest is the Living Buddha, who is going back to Heaven!" The note was taken to King Miao Chuang, who exclaimed: "Who am I that I should deserve that one of the rulers of Heaven should deign to descend and cure me by the sacrifice of hands and eyes?"

"What was the face of the saintly person like who gave you the remedy?" he then asked Chao Chen.

"It was like that of your deceased daughter, Miao Shan," he replied.

"When you removed her hands and eyes did she seem to suffer?"

"I saw a great flow of blood, and my heart failed, but the face of the victim seemed radiant with happiness."

"This certainly must be my daughter Miao Shan, who has attained to perfection," said the King. "Who but she would have given hands and eyes? Purify yourselves and observe the rules of abstinence. Go quickly to Hsiang Shan to return thanks to the saint for this favour. I myself will soon make a pilgrimage there to return thanks in person."

The King's Repentance

THREE YEARS LATER the King and Queen, with the noblemen of their Court, set out to visit Hsiang Shan. On the way the monarchs were captured by the Green Lion, or God of Fire, and the White Elephant, or Spirit of the Water – the two guardians of the Temple of Buddha – who transported them to a dark cavern in the mountains. A terrific battle then took place between the evil spirits on the one side and some hosts of heavenly genii, who had been summoned to the rescue, on the other. While its issue was still uncertain, reinforcements under the Red Child Devil, who could resist fire, and the Dragon king of the Eastern Sea, who could subdue water, finally defeated the enemy and the prisoners were released.

The King and Queen now resumed their pilgrimage, and Miao Shan instructed Shan Ts'ai to receive the monarchs when they arrived to offer incense. She herself took up her place on the altar, her eyes torn out, her hands cut off and her wrists all dripping with blood. The King recognized his daughter and bitterly reproached himself; the Queen fell swooning at her feet. Miao Shan then spoke and tried to comfort them. She told them of all that she had experienced since the day when she had been executed and how she had attained to immortal perfection. She then went on: "In order to punish you for having caused the deaths of all those who perished in the wars preceding your accession to the throne and also to avenge the burning of the Nunnery of the White Bird, Yu Huang afflicted you with those terrible ulcers. It was then that I changed myself into a priest in order to heal you and gave my eyes and hands, with which I prepared the ointment that cured you. It was I, moreover, who secured your liberty from Buddha when you were imprisoned in the cave by the Green Lion and the White Elephant."

At these words the King threw himself with his face on the ground, offered incense, worshipped Heaven, earth, the sun and the moon, saying with a voice broken by sobs: "I committed a great crime in killing my daughter, who has sacrificed her eyes and hands in order to cure my sickness."

No sooner were these words uttered than Miao Shan reassumed her normal form and, descending from the altar, approached her parents and sisters. Her body had again its original completeness; and in the presence of its perfect beauty and finding themselves reunited as one family, all wept for joy.

"Well," said Miao Shan to her father, "will you now force me to marry and prevent my devoting myself to the attainment of perfection?"

"Speak no more of that," replied the King. "I was in the wrong. If you had not reached perfection, I should not now be alive. I have made up my mind to exchange my sceptre for the pursuit of the perfect life, which I wish to lead together with you."

Then he addressed his Grand Minister Chao Chen, saying: "Your devotion to the service of the State has rendered you worthy to wear the crown: I surrender it to you." The Court proclaimed Chao Chen King of Hsing Lin, said farewell to Miao Chuang and set out for their kingdom accompanied by their new sovereign.

Buddha had summoned the White Elephant and the Green Lion, and was on the point of sentencing them to eternal damnation when the compassionate Miao Shan interceded for them. "Certainly you deserve no forgiveness," he said, "but I cannot refuse a request made by Miao Shan, whose clemency is without limit. I give you over to her, to serve and obey her in everything. Follow her."

Miao Shan Becomes a Buddha

THE GUARDIAN SPIRIT on duty that day then announced the arrival of a messenger from Yu Huang. It was T'ai-po Chin-hsing, who was the bearer of a divine decree, which he handed to Miao Shan. It read as follows: "I, the august Emperor, make known to you this decree: Miao Chuang, King of Hsing Lin, forgetful alike of Heaven and Hell, the six virtues, and metempsychosis, has led a blameworthy life; but your nine years of penitence, the filial piety which caused you to sacrifice your own body to effect his cure, in short, all your virtues, have redeemed his faults. Your eyes can see and your ears can hear all the good and bad deeds and words of men. You are the object of my especial regard. Therefore I make proclamation of this decree of canonization.

"Miao Shan will have the title of Very Merciful and Very Compassionate P'u-sa, Saviour of the Afflicted, Miraculous and Always Helpful Protectress of Mortals. On your lofty precious lotus-flower throne, you will be the Sovereign of the Southern Seas and of P'u T'o Isle. Your two sisters, until now tainted with earthly pleasures, will gradually progress till they reach true perfection. Miao Ch'ing will have the title of Very Virtuous P'u-sa, the Completely Beautiful, Rider of the Green Lion. Miao Yin will be honoured with the title of Very Virtuous and Completely Resplendent P'u-sa, Rider of the White Elephant. King Miao Chuang is raised to the dignity of Virtuous Conquering P'u-sa, Surveyor of Mortals. Queen Po Ya receives the title of P'u-sa of Ten Thousand Virtues, Surveyor of Famous Women. Shan Ts'ai has the title of Golden Youth. Lung Nu has the title of Jade Maiden." Finally he said, "During all time incense is to be burned before all the members of this canonized group."

THE GODS OF CHINA

Introduction

THE ORDINARY CHINESE people seemed to have had little difficulty amalgamating and absorbing a number of different religious beliefs, resulting in popular superstitions that convey the diverse influences of Confucianism, Taoism and Buddhism.

Confucius was a pragmatic man, whose main concern was for the smooth running of the state where individuals took personal responsibility for the creation of a harmonious atmosphere on earth, reflecting that of the Heavens. Taoism argued that there was a natural order in the world determining the behaviour of all things and that even inanimate objects had an existence of their own. Buddhism contributed to society the concept of the transmigration of souls and introduced the notion of an Underworld, presided over by the gatekeeper, Yen Wang. Overall, Chinese people believed that there was a great deal of communication between heaven and earth. It was widely believed that the Gods lived on earth in the capacity of divine officials, and returned to the heavens regularly to report on the progress of humanity.

The dualistic idea of the Otherworld being a replica of this one is nowhere more clearly illustrated than in the nine celestial Ministries or official Boards, with their chiefs and staffs presiding over the spiritual hierarchies. Generally, the functions of the officers of the celestial Boards are to protect mankind from the evils represented in the title of the Board. In all cases the duties seem to be remedial. As the God of War is the God who protects people from the evils of war, so the vast hierarchy of these various divinities is conceived as functioning for the good of mankind.

But besides the Gods who hold definite official posts in these various Ministries, there are also a very large number who are protecting patrons of the people.

Mr. Redcoat, the God of Good Luck

DURING THE T'ANG DYNASTY, in the reign-period Chien Chung (AD 780–84) of the Emperor Te Tsung, the Princess T'ai Yin noticed that Lu Ch'i, a native of Hua Chou, had the bones of an Immortal and wanted to marry him.

Her neighbour, Ma P'o, introduced him one day into the Crystal Palace for an interview with his future wife. The Princess gave him the choice of three careers: to live in the Dragon Prince's Palace with the guarantee of immortal life, to enjoy immortality among the people on the earth, or to have the honour of becoming a minister of the Empire. Lu Ch'i first answered that he would like to live in the Crystal Palace. The young lady was overjoyed and said to him: "I am Princess T'ai Yin. I will inform Shang Ti, the Supreme Ruler, at once." A moment later the arrival of a celestial messenger was announced. Two officers bearing flags preceded him and took him to the foot of the flight of steps. The messenger presented himself as Chu I, the envoy of Shang Ti.

Addressing himself to Lu Ch'i, he asked: "Do you wish to live in the Crystal Palace?" The latter did not reply. T'ai Yin urged him to give his answer, but he remained silent. In despair the Princess went to her apartment and brought out five pieces of precious cloth, which she presented to the divine envoy, begging him to have patience and wait a little longer for the answer. After some time, Chu I repeated his question. Then Lu Ch'i in answered a firm voice: "I have devoted my life to the hard labour of study and wish to attain to the dignity of minister on this earth."

T'ai Yin ordered Ma P'o to lead Lu Ch'i from the palace. From that day his face became transformed: he developed the lips of a dragon, the head of a panther and the green face of an Immortal. He took his degree and was promoted to be Director of the Censorate. The Emperor, appreciating the good sense shown in his advice, appointed him a minister of the Empire.

From this legend it would seem that Chu I is the purveyor of official posts. However, in practice, he is more generally seen as the protector of weak candidates, as the God of Good Luck for those who present themselves at examinations with a somewhat light understanding of literary knowledge. The special legend relating to this role is known everywhere in China. It is as follows:

An examiner, busily correcting the essays of the candidates, after a superficial look of one of the essays, put it on one side as obviously inferior. He is quite determined not to pass the candidate who has written it. Then the essay, moved by some mysterious power, was replaced in front of his eyes, as if to invite him to examine it more closely. At the same time an old man, clothed in a red garment, suddenly appeared before him and by a nod of his head made him understand that he should pass the essay. The examiner, surprised at the novelty of the incident and fortified by the approval of his supernatural visitor, admitted the author of the essay to the literary degree.

Chu I is invoked by the literati as a powerful protector and aid to success. When anyone with a poor chance of passing presents himself at an exam, his friends encourage him by the popular saying: "Who knows but that Mr. Redcoat will nod his head?"

Kuan Ti, the God of War

A YOUNG MAN whose name was Yun-chang was born near Chieh Liang in Ho Tung (now the town of Chieh Chou in Shansi). The boy had a difficult nature and, having exasperated his parents, he was shut up in a room from which he escaped by breaking through the window. In one of the neighbouring houses he heard a young lady and an old man weeping. Running to the foot of the wall of the compound, he asked the reason for their grief. The old man replied that though his daughter was already engaged, the uncle of the local official, smitten by her beauty, wished to make her his concubine. His petitions to the official had only been rejected with curses.

Beside himself with rage, the youth seized a sword and went and killed both the official and his uncle. He escaped through the T'ung Kuan, the pass to Shensi. Having successfully avoided capture by the barrier officials, he knelt down at the side of a brook to wash his face. As he did so he discovered his appearance was completely transformed. His complexion had become reddish-grey and he was absolutely unrecognizable. He then presented himself with assurance before the officers, who asked him his name. "My name is Kuan," he replied. It was by that name that he was then known.

One day Kuan arrived at the town of Chu-chou, in Chihli. There he met Chang Fei, a butcher who had been selling his meat all morning. At noon the butcher lowered what remained of his meat into a well. He placed a stone weighing twenty-five pounds over the mouth of the well and said with a sneer: "If anyone can lift that stone and take my meat, I will make him a present of it!" Kuan Yu, going up to the edge of the well, lifted the stone with the same ease as he would a tile, took the meat and made off. Chang Fei pursued him and eventually the two came to blows, but no one dared to separate them. Just then Liu Pei, a hawker of straw shoes arrived, and put a stop to the fight. The community of ideas which they found they possessed soon gave rise to a firm friendship between the three men.

Another account represents Liu Pei and Chang Fei as having entered a village inn to drink wine, when a man of gigantic stature pushing a wheelbarrow stopped at the door to rest. As he sat himself down he hailed the waiter, saying: "Bring me some wine quickly, because I have to rush to the town to enlist in the army."

Liu Pei looked at this man, nine feet in height, with a beard two feet long. His face was the colour of the fruit of the jujube tree and his lips were carmine. Eyebrows like sleeping silkworms shaded his phoenix eyes, which were a scarlet red. Terrible was his appearance.

"What is your name?" asked Liu Pei. "My family name is Kuan, my own name is Yu, my surname Yun Chang," he replied. "I am from the Ho Tung country. For the last five or six years I have been wandering around the world as a fugitive to escape from my pursuers, because I killed a powerful man of my country who was oppressing the poor people. I hear that they are collecting a body of troops to crush the brigands, and I should like to join the expedition."

Chang Fei (also named Chang I Te), is described as eight feet in height, with round shining eyes in a panther's head and a pointed chin bristling with a tiger's beard. His voice resembled the rumbling of thunder. His enthusiasm was like that of a fiery steed. He was a native of Cho Chun, where he owned some fertile farms. He was a butcher and wine merchant.

Liu Pei, surnamed Hsuan Te, (otherwise Hsien Chu), was the third member of the group.

The three men went to Chang Fei's farm. The following day they met in his peach orchard and sealed their friendship with an oath. Having bought a black ox and a white horse, with the various accessories to perform a sacrifice, they killed the victims, burnt the incense of friendship, and after twice prostrating themselves took this oath:

"We three, Liu Pei, Kuan Yu, and Chang Fei, already united by mutual friendship, although belonging to different clans, now bind ourselves by the union of our hearts and join our forces in order to help each other in times of danger. We wish to pay to the State our debt of loyal citizens and give peace to our black-haired compatriots. We do not inquire if we were born in the same year, the same month or on the same day, but we desire only that the same year, the same month and the same day may find us united in death. May Heaven our King and Earth our Queen see clearly our hearts! If any one of us violate justice or forget benefits, may Heaven and Man unite to punish him!"

The oath having been formally taken, Liu Pei was saluted as elder brother, Kuan Yu as the second and Chang Fei as the youngest. Their sacrifice to Heaven and earth over, they killed an ox and served a feast, to which they invited over three hundred of the soldiers from the district. They all drank copiously until they were intoxicated. Liu Pei enrolled the peasants; Chang Fei bought them horses and arms; and then they set out to make war on the Yellow Turbans (Huang Chin Tsei).

Kuan Yu proved himself worthy of the affection which Liu Pei showed him; brave and generous, he never turned aside from danger. His fidelity was shown especially on one occasion when, having been taken prisoner by Ts'ao Ts'ao, together with two of Liu Pei's wives and having been allotted a common sleeping apartment with his fellow captives, he preserved the ladies' reputation and his own trustworthiness by standing at the door of the room all night with a lighted lantern in his hand.

Kuan Yu remained faithful to his oath, even though tempted with a marquisate by the great Ts'ao Ts'ao, but he was eventually captured by Sun Ch'uan and put to death in AD 219. Long celebrated as the most renowned of China's military heroes, he was ennobled in AD 1120 as Faithful and Loyal Duke. Eight years later he was given the still more glorious title of Magnificent Prince and Pacificator. The Emperor Wen of the Yuan dynasty added the appellation Warrior Prince and Civilizer and, finally, the Emperor Wan Li of the Ming dynasty, in 1594, gave him the title of Faithful and Loyal Great Ti, Supporter of Heaven and Protector of the Kingdom. He therefore became a god, a ti, and has ever since received worship as Kuan Ti or Wu Ti, the God of War.

Temples erected in his honour are to be seen in all parts of the country. He is one of the most popular gods of China. During the last half-century of the Manchu Period his fame greatly increased. In 1856 he is said to have appeared in the heavens and successfully turned the tide of battle in favour of the Imperialists. His portrait hangs in every tent but his worship is not confined to the officials and the army. Many trades and professions have elected him as a patron saint. The sword of the public executioner used to be kept within the precincts of his temple and after an execution the presiding magistrate would stop there to worship for fear the ghost of the criminal might follow him home. He knew that the spirit would not dare to enter Kuan Ti's presence.

The Diamond Kings of Heaven

ON THE RIGHT AND LEFT SIDES of the entrance hall of Buddhist temples, two on each side, are the gigantic figures of the four great Ssu Ta Chin-kang or T'ien-wang, the Diamond Kings of Heaven. They are the protectors or governors of the continents lying in the direction of the four cardinal points from Mount Sumeru, the centre of the world. They are four brothers named respectively Mo-li Ch'ing (Pure), or Tseng Chang, Mo-li Hung (Vast), or Kuang Mu, Mo-li Hai (Sea), or To Wen, and Mo-li Shou (Age), or Ch'ih Kuo. They are said to bestow all kinds of happiness on those who honour the Three Treasures, Buddha, the Law and the Priesthood.

Kings and nations who neglect the Law lose their protection. They are described as follows:

Mo-li Ch'ing, the eldest, is twenty-four feet tall. He has a beard, the hairs of which are like copper wire. He carries a magnificent jade ring and a spear and always fights on foot. He also has a magic sword, 'Blue Cloud', on the blade of which are engraved the characters Ti, Shui, Huo, Feng (Earth, Water, Fire, Wind). When brandished, the magic sword causes a black wind which produces tens of thousands of spears. These spears pierce the bodies of men and turn them to dust. The wind is followed by a fire which fills the air with tens of thousands of golden fiery serpents. A thick smoke also rises out of the ground which blinds and burns men, none being able to escape.

Mo-li Hung carries in his hand an umbrella called the Umbrella of Chaos, formed of pearls with spiritual properties. Opening this marvellous implement causes the heavens and earth to be covered with thick darkness. Turning it upside down produces violent storms of wind and thunder and universal earthquakes.

Mo-li Hai holds a four-stringed guitar, the twanging of which supernaturally affects the earth, water, fire or wind. When it is played all the world listens and the camps of the enemy take fire.

Mo-li Shou has two whips and a panther-skin bag, the home of a creature resembling a white rat, known as Hua-hu Tiao. When at large this creature assumes the form of a white winged elephant, which devours men. He sometimes also has a snake or other man-eating creature, always ready to obey his commands.

The legend of the Four Diamond Kings goes that at the time of the consolidation of the Chou dynasty in the twelfth and eleventh centuries BC, Chiang Tzu-ya (chief counsellor to Wen Wang) and General Huang Fei-hu were defending the town and mountain of Hsi-ch'i. The supporters of the house of Shang appealed to the four genii Mo, who lived at Chia-meng Kuan, praying for them to come to their aid. They agreed and raised an army of one hundred thousand celestial soldiers. They travelled through towns, fields and mountains and arrived at the north gate of Hsi-ch'i in less than a day, where Mo-li Ch'ing pitched his camp and entrenched his soldiers.

Hearing of this, Huang Fei-hu hurried to warn Chiang Tzu-ya of the danger that threatened him. "The four great generals who have just arrived at the north gate," he said, "are marvellously powerful genii, experts in all the mysteries of magic and use of wonderful charms. It is feared that we will not be able to resist them."

Many fierce battles ensued. At first these went in favour of the Chin-kang, thanks to their magical weapons and especially to Mo-li Shou's Hua-hu Tiao, who terrorized the enemy by devouring their bravest warriors.

Unfortunately for the Chin-kang, the brute attacked and swallowed Yang Chien, the nephew of Yu Huang. This genie, on entering the body of the monster, split his heart apart and cut him in two. Then, as he could transform himself at will, he assumed the shape of Hua-hu Tiao and went off to Mo-li Shou, who unsuspectingly put him back into his bag.

The Four Kings held a festival to celebrate their triumph and having drunk copiously soon fell asleep. During the night Yang Chien came out of the bag with the intention stealing the three magical weapons of the Chin-kang. But he succeeded only in carrying off the umbrella of Mo-li Hung. In a subsequent battle No-cha, the son of Vadjrâ-pani (the God of Thunder), broke the jade ring of Mo-li Ch'ing. Misfortune followed misfortune. Deprived of their magical weapons, the Chin-kang began to lose heart. To complete their embarrassment, Huang T'ien Hua brought a matchless magical weapon to the attack called the 'Heart-piercer'. This was a spike seven-and-a-half inches long, enclosed in a silk sheath. It projected a ray of light so strong that eyes were blinded by it.

Huang T'ien Hua, hard pressed by Mo-li Ch'ing, drew the mysterious spike from its sheath and hurled it at his adversary. It entered his neck and with a deep groan the giant fell dead.

Mo-li Hung and Mo-li Hai hastened to avenge their brother, but before they could come within striking distance of Huang Ti'en Hua his formidable spike reached their hearts and they lay prone at his feet.

The one remaining hope for the sole survivor was in Hua-hu Tiao. Mo-li Shou, not knowing that the creature had been slain, put his hand into the bag to pull him out. Immediately after which Yang Chien, who had re-entered the bag, bit his hand off at the wrist. There remained nothing but a stump of bone. In this moment of intense agony Mo-li Shou fell an easy prey to Huang T'ien Hua. The magical spike pierced his heart and he fell bathed in his own blood. So perished the last of the Chin-kang.

The Three Pure Ones

TURNING TO THE GODS OF TAOISM, we find that the triad or trinity consists of three Supreme Gods, each in his own Heaven. These three Heavens, the San Ch'ing ('Three Pure Ones'), were formed from the three airs, which are subdivisions of the one primordial air.

The first Heaven is Yu Ch'ing. In it reigns the first member of the Taoist triad. He inhabits the Jade Mountain. The entrance to his palace is named the Golden Door. He is the source of all truth, as the sun is the source of all light.

Various authorities give his name differently – Yuan-shih T'ien-tsun, or Lo Ching Hsin, and call him T'ien Pao (meaning 'the Treasure of Heaven'). Some state that the name of the ruler of this first Heaven is Yu Huang and it is he who occupies this supreme position. The Three Pure Ones are above him in rank, but he (the Pearly Emperor) is entrusted to oversee the world. He has all the power of Heaven and earth in his hands. He is the correlative of Heaven, or rather Heaven itself.

The second Heaven, Shang Ch'ing, is ruled by the second person of the triad, named Ling-pao T'ien-tsun, or Tao Chun. He is the custodian of the sacred books. He has existed from the beginning of the world. He calculates time, dividing it into different periods. He occupies the upper pole of the world. He determines the movements and interaction, or regulates the relations of the yin and the yang – the two great principles of nature.

In the third Heaven, T'ai Ch'ing, the Taoists place Lao Tzu, the promulgator of the true doctrine drawn up by Ling-pao T'ien-tsun. He is alternatively called Shen Pao ('the Treasure of the Spirits') and T'ai-shang Lao-chun ('the Most Eminent Aged Ruler'). Under various assumed names he appears as the teacher of kings and emperors, the reformer of successive generations.

This three-storied Taoist Heaven, or three Heavens, is the result of Taoists' desire not to be out-rivalled by the Buddhists. For Buddha, the Law and the Priesthood they substitute the Tao (or Reason), the Classics and the Priesthood.

With regards to the organization of the Taoist Heavens, Yu Huang has the names of eight hundred Taoist divinities and a multitude of Immortals on his register. These are all divided into three categories: Saints (Sheng-jen), Heroes (Chen-jen), and Immortals (Hsien-jen), occupying the three Heavens respectively in that order.

The Three Causes

CONNECTED WITH TAOISM (but not exclusively associated with that religion) is the worship of the Three Causes, the deities presiding over three departments of physical nature – Heaven, earth and water. They are known by various names: San Kuan ('the Three Agents'), San Yuan ('the Three Origins'), San Kuan Ta Ti ('the Three Great Emperor Agents') and T'ai Shang San Kuan ('the Three Supreme Agents'). This worship has passed through four main phases, as follows.

The first comprises Heaven, earth and water, or T'ien, Ti, Shui – the sources of happiness, forgiveness of sins and deliverance from evil, respectively. Their names, written on labels and offered to Heaven (on a mountain), earth (by burial) and water (by immersion), are supposed to cure sickness. This idea dates from the Han dynasty, being first noted about AD 172.

The second, San Yuan dating from AD 407 under the Wei dynasty, identified the Three Agents with three dates of which they were respectively made the patrons. The year was divided into three unequal parts: the first to the seventh moon, the seventh to the tenth and the tenth to the twelfth. Of these, the fifteenth day of the first, seventh and tenth moons, respectively became the three principal dates of these periods. The Agent of Heaven became the principal patron of the first division, honoured on the fifteenth day of the first moon, and so on.

The third phase, San Kuan, resulted from the first two being found too complicated for popular favour. The San Kuan were the three sons of a man, Ch'en Tzu-ch'un, who was so handsome and intelligent that the three daughters of Lung Wang, the Dragon King, fell in love with him and went to live with him. The eldest girl was the mother of the Superior Cause, the second of the Medium Cause and the third of the Inferior Cause. All these were gifted with supernatural powers. Yuan-shih T'ien-tsun canonized them as the Three Great Emperor Agents of Heaven, earth and water, governors of all beings, devils or gods in the three regions of the universe. As in the first phase, the T'ien Kuan confers happiness, the Ti Kuan grants remission of sins and the Shui Kuan delivers from evil or misfortune.

The fourth phase consisted simply in the substitution by the priests for the abstract or time-principles of the three great sovereigns of ancient times, Yao, Shun, and Yu. The literati, proud of the achievements of their ancient rulers, were quick to offer incense to them. Temples, or San Yuan Kung, sprang up in many parts of the Empire.

The First Cause

YUAN-SHIH T'IEN-TSUN (or the First Cause), the Highest in Heaven, is generally placed at the head of the Taoist triad. He is said never to have existed but in the fertile imagination of the Lao Tzuist sectarians. According to them Yuan-shih T'ien-tsun had neither origin nor master, but is himself the cause of all beings, which is why he is called the First Cause. The name assigned to him is Lo Ching Hsin.

As first member of the triad and sovereign ruler of the First Heaven, he is raised in rank above all the other gods. He was born before all beginnings. His substance is imperishable. It is formed essentially of uncreated air, invisible and without perceptible limits. No one has been able to penetrate to the beginnings of his existence. The source of all truth, he at each renovation of the worlds gives out the mysterious doctrine that confers immortality. All who reach this knowledge achieve eternal life, become refined like the spirits, or instantly become Immortals, even while on earth.

Originally, Yuan-shih T'ien-tsun was not a member of the Taoist triad. He resided above the Three Heavens, above the Three Pure Ones, surviving the destructions and renovations of the universe, as an immovable rock in the midst of a stormy sea. He set the stars in motion and caused the planets to revolve. The chief of his secret police was Tsao Chun, the Kitchen-god, who rendered to him an account of the good and evil deeds of each family. His executive agent was Lei Tsu, the God of Thunder, and his subordinates. The seven stars of the North Pole were the palace of his ministers, whose offices were on the various sacred mountains. Nowadays, however, Yuan-shih T'ien-tsun is generally neglected for Yu Huang.

Yu Huang, the Jade Emperor

YU HUANG means 'the Jade Emperor', or 'the Pure August One', jade symbolizing purity. He is also known by the name Yu-huang Shang-ti, 'the Pure August Emperor on High'.

The history of this deity, who later received many titles and became the most popular god, a very Chinese Jupiter, seems to be somewhat as follows: In AD 1005 the Emperor Ch'eng Tsung of the Sung dynasty was forced to sign a disgraceful peace with the Tunguses or Kitans and the dynasty was in danger of losing the support of the nation. In order to hoodwink the people the Emperor announced with great pomp and ceremony that he was in direct communication with the gods of Heaven. In doing this he was following the advice of his crafty and unreliable minister Wang Ch'in-jo, who had often tried to persuade him that the pretended revelations attributed to Fu Hsi, Yu Wang and others were only pure inventions to induce obedience.

The Emperor, having studied his part well, assembled his ministers in the tenth moon of the year 1012, and made the following declaration to them: "In a dream I had a visit from an Immortal, who brought me a letter from Yu Huang, the purpose of which was as follows: 'I have already sent you by your ancestor Chao (T'ai Tsu) two celestial letters. Now I am going to send him in person to visit you.'" A little while later his ancestor T'ai Tsu, the founder of the dynasty, came according to Yu Huang's promise and Ch'eng Tsung quickly informed his ministers of it. This is the origin of Yu Huang. He was born of a fraud and came ready made from the brain of an emperor.

Fearing of being admonished for the fraud by another of his ministers, the scholar Wang Tan, the Emperor decided to put a golden gag in his mouth. So one day, having invited him to a banquet, he overwhelmed him with flattery and made him drunk with good wine. "I would like the members of your family also to taste this wine," he added, "so I am making you a present of a cask of it." When Wang Tan returned home, he found the cask filled with precious pearls. Out of gratitude to the Emperor he kept silent as to the fraud and made no further opposition to his plans. However on his death bed he asked that his head be shaved like a priest's and that he be dressed in priestly robes so that he might make amends for his crime of feebleness before the Emperor.

K'ang Hsi, the great Emperor of the Ch'ing dynasty, who had already declared that if it is wrong to impute deceit to a man it is still more reprehensible to impute a fraud to Heaven, stigmatized him as follows: "Wang Tan committed two faults: the first was in showing himself a vile flatterer of his Prince during his life; the second was in becoming a worshipper of Buddha at his death."

History side, the legend of Yu Huang relates that in ancient times there was a kingdom named Kuang Yen Miao Lo Kuo, whose king was Ching Te and whose queen was Pao Yueh. Though getting on in years, the Queen had no son. The Taoist priests were summoned to the palace to perform their rites. They recited prayers in the hope of obtaining an heir to the throne.

During the ensuing night the Queen had a vision. Lao Chun appeared to her, riding a dragon and carrying a male child in his arms. He floated down through the air in her direction. The Queen begged him to give her the child as an heir to the throne. "I am quite willing," he said. "Here it is." She fell on her knees and thanked him. When she awoke, she found herself pregnant. At the end of a year the Prince was born. From an early age he was compassionate and generous to the poor. On the death of his father he ascended the throne, but after reigning only a few days he abdicated in favour of his chief minister and became a hermit at P'u-ming, in Shensi, and also on Mount Hsiu Yen, in Yunnan. Having attained to perfection, he passed the rest of his days curing sickness and saving life; and it was in the exercise of these charitable deeds that he died. The emperors Ch'eng Tsung and Hui Tsung, of the Sung dynasty, loaded him with all the various titles associated with his name today.

Both Buddhists and Taoists claim him as their own, the former identifying him with Indra, in which case Yu Huang is a Buddhist deity incorporated into the Taoist pantheon. He has also been taken to be the subject of a 'nature myth'. The Emperor Ching Te, his father, is the sun, the Queen Pao Yueh the moon, and the marriage symbolizes the rebirth of the vivifying power which clothes nature with green plants and beautiful flowers.

The Legend of T'ung-t'ien Chiao-chu

IN MODERN TAOISM T'ung-t'ien Chiao-chu is regarded as the first of the Patriarchs and one of the most powerful genii of the sect. His master was Hung-chun Lao-tsu. He wore a red robe embroidered with white cranes and rode a k'uei niu – a monster resembling a buffalo, with one long horn like a unicorn. His palace, the Pi Yu Kung, was situated on Mount Tzu Chih Yai.

This genie took the part of Chou Wang and helped him to resist Wu Wang's armies. First, he sent his disciple To-pao Tao-jen to Chieh-p'ai Kuan. He gave him four precious swords and the plan of a fort which he was to construct and to name Chu-hsien Chen, 'the Citadel of all the Immortals'.

To-pao Tao-jen carried out his orders, but he had to fight a battle with Kuang Ch'eng-tzu, and the latter, armed with a celestial seal, struck his adversary so hard that he fell to the ground and had to take refuge in flight.

T'ung-t'ien Chiao-chu came to the defence of his disciple and to restore the morale of his forces. Unfortunately, a posse of gods arrived to aid Wu Wang's powerful general, Chiang Tzu-ya. The first who attacked T'ung-t'ien Chiao-chu was Lao Tzu, who struck him several times with his stick. Then came Chun T'i, armed with his cane. The buffalo of T'ung-t'ien Chiao-chu stamped him under foot, and Chun T'i was thrown to the earth. He only just had time to rise quickly and mount into the air amid a great cloud of dust.

There could be no doubt that the fight was going against T'ung-t'ien Chiao-chu; to complete his feeling of unease Jan-teng Tao-jen split the air and fell on him unexpectedly. With a violent blow of his staff he cast him down and compelled him to give up the struggle.

T'ung-t'ien Chiao-chu then prepared plans for a new fortified camp beyond T'ung Kuan. He tried to take the offensive once more, but again Lao Tzu stopped him with a blow of his stick. Yuan-shih T'ien-tsun wounded his shoulder with his precious stone Ju-i, and Chun-t'i Tao-jen waved his 'Branch of the Seven Virtues'. Immediately the magic sword of T'ung-t'ien Chiao-chu was reduced to splinters and he saved himself only by flight.

Hung-chun Lao-tsu, the master of these three genii, seeing his three beloved disciples in the melee, resolved to make peace between them. He assembled all three in a tent in Chiang Tzu-ya's camp, made them kneel before him, then reproached T'ung-t'ien Chiao-chu for having taken the part of the tyrant Chou, and recommended them to live in harmony in future. After finishing his speech, he produced three pills and ordered each of the genii to swallow one. When they had done so, Hung-chun Lao-tsu said to them: "I have given you these pills to ensure an absolute truce among you. Know that the first who entertains a thought of discord in his heart will find that the pill will explode in his stomach and cause his instant death."

Hung-chun Lao-tsu then took T'ung-t'ien Chiao-chu away with him on his cloud to Heaven.

The Immortals

AN IMMORTAL, according to the Taoist, is a solitary man of the mountains. He appears to die, but does not. After 'death' his body retains all the qualities of the living. The body or corpse is for him only a means of transition, a phase of metamorphosis – a cocoon or chrysalis, the temporary home of the butterfly. To reach this state a hygienic regimen both of the body and mind must be observed. All luxury, greed and ambition must be avoided. But negation is not enough. In the system of nourishment all the elements which strengthen the essence of the constituent yin and yang principles must be found by means of medicine, chemistry and exercise. When the maximum vital force has been acquired the means of preserving it and keeping it from the attacks of death and disease must be discovered; in a word, he must spiritualize himself – render himself completely independent of matter.

Mu Kung or Tung Wang Kung, the God of the Immortals, was also called I Chun Ming and Yu Huang Chun, the Prince Yu Huang. Legend has it that the primitive vapour congealed, remained inactive for a time and then produced living beings, beginning with the formation of Mu Kung, the purest substance of the Eastern Air and sovereign of the active male principle yang and of all the countries of the East. His palace is in the misty heavens, violet clouds form its dome, blue clouds its walls. Hsien T'ung, 'the Immortal Youth', and Yu Nu, 'the Jade Maiden', are his servants. He keeps the register of all the Immortals, male and female.

Similarly, Hsi Wang Mu was formed of the pure quintessence of the Western Air, in the legendary continent of Shen Chou. She is often called the Golden Mother of the Tortoise. Her family name is variously given as Hou, Yang and Ho. Her own name was Hui, and first name Wan-chin. She had nine sons and twenty-four daughters.

As Mu Kung, formed of the Eastern Air, is the active principle of the male air and sovereign of the Eastern Air, so Hsi Wang Mu, born of the Western Air, is the passive or female principle (yin) and sovereign of the Western Air. These two principles, co-operating, give rise to Heaven and earth and all the beings of the universe, and therefore become the two principles of life and of the subsistence of all that exists. She is the head of the troop of genii dwelling on the K'un-lun Mountains (the Taoist equivalent of the Buddhist Sumeru).

Hsi Wang Mu's palace is situated in the high mountains of the snowy K'un-lun. It is about 333 miles in circuit; a rampart of massive gold surrounds its battlements of precious stones. Its right wing rises on the edge of the Kingfishers' River. It is the usual abode of the Immortals, who are divided into seven special categories according to the colour of their garments – red, blue, black, violet, yellow, green and 'nature colour'. There is a marvellous fountain built of precious stones, where the periodical banquet of the Immortals is held. This feast is called P'an-t'ao Hui, 'the Feast of Peaches'. It takes place on the borders of the Yao Ch'ih (Lake of Gems) and is attended by both male and female Immortals. Besides several superfine meats, they are served with bears' paws, monkeys' lips, dragons' liver, phoenix marrow and peaches gathered in the orchard, endowed with the mystic virtue of granting longevity on all who have the good luck to taste them. It was by these peaches that the date of the banquet was fixed. The tree put forth leaves once every three thousand years, and it required three thousand years after that for the fruit to ripen. These were Hsi Wang Mu's birthdays, when all the Immortals assembled for the great feast.

The Eight Immortals

DURING THE MONGOL or Yuan Dynasty in the thirteenth century, a group of Taoist deities who were known as the 'Eight Immortals', or Pa Hsien, became the new focus of a whole catalogue of Chinese legends, achieving a rapid and widespread popularity. Partly historical and partly mythical figures, the Eight Immortals were said to share a home together in the Eastern Paradise on the isles of Peng-lai. Characters similar to these Gods were celebrated in earlier Taoist tales, but now for the first time they appeared as a group, whose different personalities were intended to represent the whole spectrum of society ranging from young to old, rich to poor, whether male or female in gender. The Chinese were very fond of these characters and their numerous eccentricities, and increasingly they became a favourite subject for artists. They appeared together frequently in paintings, or on pottery and elaborate tapestries, or as statuettes and larger sculptures.

The most famous of the Eight Immortals was known as Li Tiehkuai, a name which means 'Li of the Iron Crutch'. Among the group, he was perhaps the most gifted disciple of Taoism, an immortal reputed to have acquired his great wisdom from the spirit of Lao Tzu himself. After the course of instruction had been completed, it was said that the Great Master summoned Li to the Heavens to assess his ability more closely. Li willingly answered the call and his soul left his body and journeyed upwards towards the firmament.

But before Li departed the earth, he placed one of his own pupils, known as Lang Ling, in charge of his body, ordering him to guard it well for a period of seven days until he returned to reclaim it. After only six days had elapsed, however, the student was called to his mother's deathbed, and because he was reluctant to leave the body exposed to scavengers, he decided to cremate it before he departed.

When Li returned to earth he found only a mound of ashes where his body once lay and his spirit was forced to wander about in search of another host. Fortunately, however, a beggar had just died of starvation in the nearby woods, and Li entered the body without any further delay. But as soon as he had done so, he began to regret his decision, for the deceased beggar had only had one leg, his head was ugly and pointed, and the hair around his face was long and dishevelled. Li wished to leave the vile body he had entered, but Lao Tzu advised him that this would not be wise. So instead, the Great Master of the Heavens sent him a gold band to keep his matted hair in place and an iron crutch to help him move about more easily.

And one of the first benevolent acts Li performed in this human body was to visit the home of his negligent pupil, where he poured the contents of his gourd into the mouth of Lang Ling's dead mother, bringing her back to life instantly. For two hundred years Li roamed the earth in this way, converting people to Taoism and healing them with his medicine. He represents the sick and his emblems are an iron stick and a gourd.

The second of the Eight Immortals was called Han Chung-li, a powerful military figure, who in his younger days rose to become Marshal of the Empire. After Han became converted to Taoism, however, he chose to live the life of a hermit in Yang-chio Mountain. Here, he studied the ways of immortality and stored whatever secrets he discovered in a large jade casket within his cave. Some say that Han Chung-li was highly skilled in the ways of alchemy and that during the great famine he changed base metals, such as copper and pewter, into silver which he then distributed to the poor, saving thousands of lives. A fan of feathers, or the peach of immortality are his emblems, and he is associated with military affairs.

During a visit to Yang-chio Mountain, Lu Tung-pin, the son of a high-ranking government official and a clever young scholar, met with Han Chung-li, who invited him into his cave to share some rice wine with him. Tired from his journey, Lu Tung-pin readily accepted the invitation, but as soon as he tasted the wine he fell into a deep sleep. And while he slept, he had an unpleasant dream which altered the course of his life.

He dreamt that he had married well, fathered several healthy children, and that he had risen to a position of great prominence in his work before his fiftieth year. After this time, he looked forward to a peaceful retirement, but for some reason, he was exiled in disgrace and his family put to death for his misdemeanours. For the rest of his days, he was condemned to a futile and lonely existence from which he could find no escape. Lu awoke from his dream with a start and began to interpret its meaning. At length, he became convinced of the vanity of worldly dignities and begged Han Chung-li to accept him as a disciple in order that he might train to be one of the Eight Immortals. He is commonly associated with scholars and is always portrayed carrying a sword.

The fourth Immortal, Chang-kuo Lao, was also a famous hermit who lived in the Heng Chou Mountains. He usually appeared seated on a white donkey which he was able to fold up like a piece of paper and which would resume its former shape once he had sprinkled water on it. Chang-kuo Lao claimed that he was a descendant of Emperor Yao and his special magical powers enabled him to bring fertility to young couples. His emblem is a white mule, or a phoenix feather, and he represents the old.

Tsao Kuo-chiu, who is associated with the nobility and whose emblem is a scribe's tablet, became an Immortal after he renounced the wickedness of his worldly life. Tsao was the eldest of two brothers whose sister was married to the Emperor, Jen Tsung. One day the Empress invited a young graduate and his wife to dine with her at the palace, but disaster struck when the younger brother, Ching-chih, who was notorious for his bad behaviour, allowed himself to become besotted by the lady and decided to murder her husband. After he had committed this crime, the soul of the husband demanded justice from the God Pao and Ching-chih was immediately thrown in prison. Knowing his brother would inevitably face the death penalty, Tsao Kuo-chiu encouraged him to kill the graduate's wife so that no evidence of his crime would remain. But the wife escaped to inform Pao of this second attack and Tsao Kuo-chiu was also thrown in prison to face execution.

Eventually, the Empress intervened on her brothers' behalf and begged the Emperor to grant them both an amnesty. As soon as this happened, Tsao was so grateful he decided to abandon his life of luxury and to live by the doctrines of Taoism. For the remainder of his days Tsao Kuo-chiu lived as a hermit devoting himself to the practice of perfection.

The sixth and seventh Immortals were very young men. Han Hsiang Tzu was the grand-nephew of one of the greatest poets of the Tang Dynasty, and from an early age he was schooled by his uncle in the ways of poetry until eventually his ability far surpassed that of the older man. Shortly afterwards, the youth became a disciple of Lu Tung-pin and at the end of his instruction he was required to climb to the top of the Immortalizing Peach Tree. As he did so, he lost his balance and fell dead to the ground. Miraculously, however, he came to life once more, for he had attained the gift of immortality during the descent. Han Hsiang Tzu is always depicted carrying either a flower-basket or a peach and he represents cultured society.

Lan Tsai-ho, a strolling actor and singer of about sixteen years of age, dressed himself in a tattered blue gown and a black wooden belt, and always wore only one shoe. His life was spent urging people to convert to Taoism and he denounced the material comforts of mortals. When given money, he either strung it on a cord and used it as an instrument to beat time as he sang, or scattered it to the ground for the poor to pick up. His emblem is a lute and he represents the poor.

Only one of the Eight Immortals, Ho Hsien-Ku was a woman and she was always depicted holding a lotus flower or the peach of immortality, presented to her by Lu Tung-pin after she had lost her way through the mountains. While still very young, she chose to live a simple life of celibacy and prayer on Yunmu Ling Mountain. Here, she found a stone known as the Yunmu Shih, 'mother-of-pearl', and was told in a dream to powder the stone and to swallow its dust should she wish to become an Immortal. Ho Hsien-Ku followed this instruction and spent the rest of her days floating around the mountains, picking wild berries which she carried to her mother. Her emblem is a lotus and she represents young, unmarried girls.

Chang Tao-ling, the Heavenly Teacher

CHANG TAO-LING, the first Taoist pope, was born in AD 35, in the reign of the Emperor Kuang Wu Ti of the Han dynasty. His birthplace is variously given as the T'ien-mu Shan, 'Eye of Heaven Mountain', in Lin-an Hsien, in Chekiang, and Feng-yang Fu, in Anhui. He devoted himself wholly to study and meditation, declining all offers to enter the service of the State. He preferred to live in the mountains of Western China, where he persevered in the study of alchemy and in cultivating the virtues of purity and mental abstraction. From the hands of Lao Tzu he received a mystic treatise. Any by following the instructions in it he was successful in his search for the elixir of life.

One day when he was engaged in experimenting with the 'Dragon-tiger elixir' a spiritual being appeared to him and said: "On Po-sung Mountain is a stone house in which are concealed the writings of the Three Emperors of antiquity and a canonical work. By obtaining these you may ascend to Heaven, if you undergo the course of discipline they prescribe."

Chang Tao-ling found these works and by means of them he obtained the power of flying, of hearing distant sounds and of leaving his body. After going through a thousand days of discipline and after receiving instruction from a goddess, who taught him to walk about among the stars, he began to fight with the king of the demons, to divide mountains and seas and to command the wind and thunder. All the demons fled before him. On account of the immense slaughter of demons by this hero, the wind and thunder were reduced to subjection, and various divinities hurried to acknowledge their faults. In nine years he gained the power to ascend to Heaven.

Chang Tao-ling may rightly be considered as the true founder of modern Taoism. The recipes for the pills of immortality contained in the mysterious books, and the invention of talismans for the cure of all sorts of diseases, not only elevated him to the high position he has since occupied in the minds of his numerous disciples, but enabled them in turn to successfully exploit this new source of power and wealth. From that time the Taoist sect began to specialize in the art of healing. Protecting or curing talismans bearing the Master's seal were purchased for enormous sums. It is therefore seen that he was after all a deceiver of the people, and unbelievers or rival partisans of other sects have dubbed him a 'rice thief'.

He is generally represented as dressed in richly decorated garments, brandishing his magic sword with his right hand, holding a cup containing the draught of immortality in his left, and riding a tiger which in one paw grasps his magic seal and with the others tramples down the five venomous creatures: lizard, snake, spider, toad and centipede. Pictures of him with these accessories are pasted up in houses on the fifth day of the fifth moon to protect from calamity and sickness.

Another legend relating to Chang Tao-ling is that, not wishing to ascend to Heaven too soon, he took of only half of the pill of immortality, dividing the other half among several of his admirers. Also that he had at least two selves or personalities, one of which used to amuse itself in a boat on a small lake in front of his house. The other self would receive his visitors, entertaining them with food, drink and conversation.

On one occasion this self said to them: "You are unable to quit the world altogether as I can, but by imitating my example in the matter of family relations you could obtain a medicine which would prolong your lives by several centuries. I have given the crucible in which Huang Ti prepared the draught of immortality to my disciple Wang Ch'ang. Later on, a man will come from the East, who will also make use of it. He will arrive on the seventh day of the first moon."

Exactly on that day a man named Chao Sheng arrived from the East. Chang then led all three hundred of his disciples to the highest peak of the Yun-t'ai. Below them they saw a peach tree growing near a pointed rock, stretching out its branches like arms above a fathomless abyss. It was a large tree, covered with ripe fruit.

Chang said to his disciples: "I will communicate a spiritual formula to the one among you who will dare to gather the fruit of that tree." They all leaned over to look, but each declared the feat to be impossible. Chao Sheng alone had the courage to rush out to the point of the rock and up the tree stretching out into space. He stood and gathered the peaches, placing them in the folds of his cloak, as many as it would hold, but when he wished to climb back up the precipitous slope, his hands slipped on the smooth rock and all his attempts were in vain. So he threw the peaches, three hundred and two in all, one by one up to Chang Tao-ling, who distributed them. Each disciple ate one, as did Chang, who reserved the remaining one for Chao Sheng, whom he helped to climb up again. To do this Chang extended his arm to a length of thirty feet, everyone present marvelling at the miracle.

After Chao had eaten his peach Chang stood on the edge of the precipice and said with a laugh, "Chao Sheng was brave enough to climb out to that tree and his foot never tripped. I too will make the attempt. If I succeed I will have a big peach as a reward."

Having said this, he leapt into space and jumped into the branches of the peach tree. Wang Ch'ang and Chao Sheng also jumped into the tree and stood one on each side of him. There Chang communicated to them the mysterious formula. Three days later they returned to their homes; then, having made final arrangements, they returned once more to the mountain peak. From here, in the presence of the other disciples, who followed them with their eyes until they had completely disappeared from view, all three ascended to Heaven in broad daylight.

The name of Chang Tao-ling, the Heavenly Teacher, is a household name in China. He is the earthly representative of the Pearly Emperor in Heaven and the Commander-in-Chief of the hosts of Taoism. He, the chief of the wizards, the 'true man', as he is known, wields an immense spiritual power throughout the land. The present pope boasts of an unbroken line for many generations. His family obtained possession of the Dragon-tiger Mountain in Kiangsi around AD 1000.

T'ai I, the Great One

TEMPLES ARE FOUND in various parts of China dedicated to T'ai I, the Great One, or Great Unity.

When Emperor Wu Ti (140–86 BC) of the Han dynasty was in search of the secret of immortality, and various suggestions had proved unsatisfactory, he turned to a Taoist priest named Miao Chi. The priest told the Emperor that his lack of success was due to his omission to sacrifice to T'ai I, the first of the celestial spirits. The Emperor, believing his word, ordered the Grand Master of Sacrifices to re-establish this worship at the capital.

He carefully followed the prescriptions of Miao Chi. This enraged the literati, who resolved to ruin him. One day, when the Emperor was about to drink one of his potions, one of the chief courtiers seized the cup and drank the contents himself. The Emperor was about to have him slain, when he said: "Your Majesty's order is unnecessary; if the potion confers immortality, I cannot be killed; if, on the other hand, it does not, your Majesty should reward me for disproving the pretensions of the Taoist priest." The Emperor, however, was not convinced.

One account represents T'ai I as having lived in the time of Shen Nung, the Divine Husbandman, who visited him to consult with him on the subjects of diseases and fortune. He was Hsien Yuan's medical teacher. His medical knowledge was handed down to future generations. He was one of those who, with the Immortals, was invited to the great Peach Assembly of the Western Royal Mother.

As the spirit of the star T'ai I he resides in the Eastern Palace, listening for the cries of sufferers in order to save them. With a boat of lotus flowers of nine colours he ferries men over to the shore of salvation. Holding in his hand a willow branch, he scatters from it the dew of the doctrine.

T'ai I is variously represented as the Ruler of the Five Celestial Sovereigns, Cosmic Matter before it congealed into concrete shapes, the Triune Spirit of Heaven, earth, and T'ai I as three separate entities, an unknown Spirit, and the Spirit of the Pole Star.

Tou Mu, Goddess of the North Star

TOU MU, THE BUSHEL MOTHER, or Goddess of the North Star, worshipped by both Buddhists and Taoists, is the Indian Maritchi, and was made a stellar divinity by the Taoists.

She is said to have been the mother of the nine Jen Huang or Human Sovereigns of fabulous antiquity, who succeeded the lines of Celestial and Terrestrial Sovereigns. In the Taoist religion she occupies the same relative position as Kuan Yin, who may be said to be the heart of Buddhism. Having attained to a profound knowledge of celestial mysteries, she shone with heavenly light, could cross the seas, and pass from the sun to the moon. She also had a kind heart for the sufferings of humanity. The King of Chou Yu, in the north, married her on hearing of her many virtues. They had nine sons. Yuan-shih T'ien-tsun came to earth to invite her, her husband and nine sons to enjoy the delights of Heaven. He placed her in the palace Tou Shu, the Pivot of the Pole, because all the other stars revolve round it, and gave her the title of Queen of the Doctrine of Primitive Heaven. Her nine sons have their palaces in the neighbouring stars.

Tou Mu wears the Buddhist crown, is seated on a lotus throne, has three eyes, eighteen arms, and holds various precious objects in her numerous hands, such as a bow, spear, sword, flag, dragon's head, pagoda, five chariots, sun's disk, moon's disk, etc. She has control of the books of life and death, and all who wish to prolong their days worship at her shrine. Her devotees abstain from animal food on the third and twenty-seventh day of every month.

Of her sons, two are the Northern and Southern Bushels; the latter, dressed in red, rules birth; the former, in white, rules death. "A young Esau once found them on the South Mountain, under a tree, playing chess, and by an offer of venison his lease of life was extended from nineteen to ninety-nine years."

Snorter and Blower

AT THE TIME of the overthrow of the Shang and establishment of the Chou dynasty in 1122 BC there lived two marshals, Cheng Lung and Ch'en Ch'i. These were Heng and Ha, the Snorter and Blower respectively. The former was the chief superintendent of supplies for the armies of the tyrant emperor Chou, the Nero of China. The latter was in charge of obtaining food for the same army.

Legend has it that from his master, Tu O, the celebrated Taoist magician of the K'un-lun Mountains, Heng acquired a marvellous power. When he snorted, his nostrils emitted two white columns of light, which destroyed his enemies, body and soul. It was through him the Chou gained numerous victories. One day he was captured, bound and taken to the general of Chou. His life was spared and he was made general superintendent of army stores as well as generalissimo of five army corps.

Later on he found himself face to face with the Blower. The latter had learned from the magician how to store a supply of yellow gas in his chest which, when he blew it out, annihilated anyone it struck. By this means he caused large gaps to be made in the ranks of the enemy.

Being opposed to each other, one snorting out great streaks of white light, the other blowing streams of yellow gas, the battle continued until the Blower was wounded in the shoulder by No-cha, of the Chou army, and pierced in the stomach with a spear by Huang Fei-hu, Yellow Flying Tiger.

The Snorter in turn was slain in this fight by Marshal Chin Ta-sheng, 'Golden Big Pint', an ox spirit who was blessed with the mysterious power of producing the celebrated niu huang, ox-yellow, or bezoar. Facing the Snorter, with a noise like thunder he spat a piece of bezoar as large as a rice bowl in his face. It struck him on the nose and split his nostrils. He fell to the earth and was cut in two by a blow from his victor's sword.

After the Chou dynasty had been fully established Chiang Tzu-ya canonized the two marshals Heng and Ha, and granted them the offices of guardians of the Buddhist temple gates, where their gigantic images may be seen.

Blue Dragon and White Tiger

THE FUNCTIONS CARRIED OUT by Heng and Ha at the gates of Buddhist temples are in Taoist temples done by Blue Dragon and White Tiger. The former, the Spirit of the Blue Dragon Star, was Teng Chiu-kung, one of the chief generals of the last emperor of the Yin dynasty. He had a son named Teng Hsiu and a daughter named Ch'an-yu.

The story goes that the army of Teng Chiu-kung was camped at San-shan Kuan, when he received orders to go to the battle then taking place at Hsi Ch'i. There, in standing up to No-cha and Huang Fei-hu, he had his left arm broken by the former's magic bracelet. Fortunately for him, his subordinate, T'u Hsing-sun, a renowned magician, gave him a remedy which quickly healed the fracture.

His daughter then came on the scene to avenge her father. She had a magic weapon, the Five-fire Stone, which she hurled full in the face of Yang Chien. But the Immortal was not wounded. His celestial dog jumped at Ch'an-yu and bit her neck, so that she was forced to flee. T'u Hsing-sun, however, healed the wound.

After a banquet, Teng Chiu-kung promised his daughter in marriage to T'u Hsing-sun if he would gain him the victory at Hsi Ch'i. Chiang Tzu-ya then persuaded T'u's magic master, Chu Liu-sun, to call his disciple over to his camp, where he asked him why he was fighting against the new dynasty. "Because," he replied, "Chiu-kung has promised me his daughter in marriage as a reward of success."

So Chiang Tzu-ya promised to obtain the bride and sent a force to seize her. As a result of the fighting that ensued, Chiu-kung was beaten and retreated in confusion, leaving Ch'an-yu in the hands of the victors. During the next few days the marriage was celebrated with great ceremony in the victor's camp. According to custom, the bride returned for some days to her father's house, and while there she strongly urged Chiu-kung to submit. Following her advice, he went over to Chiang Tzu-ya's party.

In the ensuing battles he fought valiantly on the side of his former enemy and killed many famous warriors, but he was eventually attacked by the Blower, from whose mouth a column of yellow gas struck him, throwing him from his horse. He was held prisoner and executed by order of General Ch'iu Yin. Chiang Tzu-ya granted him the kingdom of the Blue Dragon Star.

The Spirit of the White Tiger Star is Yin Ch'eng-hsiu. His father, Yin P'o-pai, a high courtier of the tyrant Chou Wang, was sent to negotiate peace with Chiang Tzu-ya, but was seized and put to death by Marquis Chiang Wen-huan. His son, attempting to avenge his father's murder, was pierced by a spear. His head was cut off and carried in triumph to Chiang Tzu-ya.

As compensation he was canonized as the Spirit of the White Tiger Star.

The City God

CH'ENG-HUANG IS the Celestial Mandarin or City god. Every fortified city or town in China is surrounded by a wall, or ch'eng, composed usually of two battlemented walls, the space between which is filled with earth. This earth is dug from the ground outside, making a ditch, or huang, running parallel with the ch'eng. The Ch'eng-huang is the spiritual official of the city or town. All the numerous Ch'eng-huang constitute a celestial Ministry of Justice, presided over by a Ch'eng-huang-in-chief.

The origin of the worship of the Ch'eng-huang dates back to the time of the great Emperor Yao (2357 BC), who instituted a sacrifice called Pa Cha in honour of eight spirits, of whom the seventh, Shui Yung corresponded to the dyke and rampart known later as Ch'eng-huang. Since the Sung dynasty sacrifices have been offered to the Ch'eng-huang all over the country, though now and then some towns have adopted another or special god as their Ch'eng-huang, such as Chou Hsin, adopted as the Ch'eng-huang of Hangchou, the capital of Chekiang Province.

Concerning Chou Hsin, who had a 'face of ice and iron', and was so much dreaded for his severity that old and young fled at his approach, it is told that once when he was trying a case a storm blew some leaves on to his table. In spite of diligent search the tree to which this kind of leaf belonged could not be found anywhere in the neighbourhood, but was eventually discovered in a Buddhist temple a long way off. The judge declared that the priests of this temple must be guilty of murder. By his order the tree was felled, and in its trunk was found the body of a woman who had been assassinated. The priests were convicted of the murder.

The City God of Yen Ch'eng

THE CH'ENG-HUANG P'U-SA is the patron god of a city, his position in the unseen world similar to that of a chih hsien (district magistrate) among men, if the city under his care is a hsien; but if the city hold the rank of a fu, it has (or used to have) two Ch'eng-huang P'u-sas, one a prefect, and the other a district magistrate.

One part of his duty consists of sending small demons to carry off the spirits of the dying, of which spirits he then acts as ruler and judge. He is supposed to exercise special care over the k'u kuei, or spirits which have no descendants to worship and offer sacrifices to them. During the Seventh Month Festival he is carried around the city in his chair to maintain order among them, while the people offer food to them and burn paper money for their benefit. He is also carried in procession at the Ch'ing Ming Festival and on the first day of the tenth month.

This is the legend of the Ch'eng-huang P'u-sa of the city of Yen Ch'eng (Salt City), who is in the extremely unfortunate predicament of having no skin to his face.

Once upon a time in Yen Ch'eng lived an orphan boy who was brought up by his uncle and aunt. He was just entering his teens when his aunt lost a gold hairpin and accused him of having stolen it. The boy, whose conscience was clear in this matter, thought of a plan that might prove his innocence.

"Let's go tomorrow to Ch'eng-huang P'u-sa's temple," he said, "and I will swear an oath before the god, so that he may show my innocence." So they went to the temple, and the boy, solemnly addressing the idol, said "If I have taken my aunt's gold pin, may my foot twist, and may I fall as I go out of your temple door!"

However, as he stepped over the threshold his foot did twist and he fell to the ground. Of course, everybody was firmly convinced of his guilt and what could the poor boy say when his own appeal to the god had turned against him?

After such a proof of his wickedness his aunt had no room in her house for her orphan nephew. And he himself no longer wanted to stay with people who suspected him of theft. So he left the home that had sheltered him for years and wandered out alone into the cold hard world. The boy encountered many hardships, but with rare bravery he persevered in his studies and at the age of twenty odd years became a mandarin.

In course of time our hero returned to Yen Ch'eng to visit his uncle and aunt. While he was there he took himself to the temple of the deity who had dealt so harshly with him and prayed for a revelation as to the whereabouts of the lost hairpin. He slept that night in the temple and was rewarded by a vision in which the Ch'eng-huang P'u-sa told him that the pin would be found under the floor of his aunt's house.

He rushed back and informed his relatives, who took up the boards in the place indicated, and lo and behold there lay the long-lost pin! The women of the house then remembered that the pin had been used in pasting together the various layers of the soles of shoes and, when night came, had been carelessly left on the table. No doubt rats, attracted by the smell of the paste which clung to it, had carried it off to their domains under the floor.

The young mandarin joyfully returned to the temple and offered sacrifices by way of thanksgiving to the Ch'eng-huang P'u-sa for bringing his innocence to light, but he could not stop himself from giving the god a gentle reproach: "You made me fall down and so led people to think I was guilty, and now you accept my gifts. Aren't you ashamed to do such a thing? You have no face!" As he uttered the words all the plaster fell from the face of the idol and was smashed into fragments.

From that day forward the Ch'eng-huang P'u-sa of Yen Ch'eng has had no skin on his face. People have tried to patch up the disfigured features, but in vain: the plaster always falls off and the face remains skinless.

Some try to defend the Ch'eng-huang P'u-sa by saying that he was not at home on the day when his temple was visited by the accused boy and his relatives, and that one of the little demons employed by him to carry off dead people's spirits perpetrated a practical joke on the poor boy out of sheer mischief.

In that case it is certainly hard that his skin should so persistently testify against him by refusing to remain on his face!

The Kitchen God

TSAO CHUN, THE KITCHEN GOD, is said to be a Taoist invention, but is universally worshipped by all families in China. Traditionally about sixty million pictures of him were regularly worshipped twice a month, at the new and full moon.

His temple was a small niche above the kitchen stove where an incense stick burned continuously. From this position, the Kitchen God kept an account of how well the family behaved, compiling his annual report for the attention of the Supreme Being of the Heavens. At New Year, he was destined to return to the firmament to present his report and he was sent on his way with a great deal of ceremony. Firecrackers were lit and a lavish meal prepared to improve his mood. His mouth was smeared with honey, so that only 'sweet' words would escape his lips when he stood before the Supreme Being. He was entrusted with the power to punish and reward members of the family under his supervision. He is also called 'the God of the Stove'.

The origin of his worship, according to the legend, is that a Taoist priest named Li Shao-chun obtained from the Kitchen god the double favour of exemption from growing old and of being able to live without eating. He then went to the Emperor Hsiao Wu-ti of the Han dynasty, and promised him that he would benefit by the powers of the god provided that he would consent to patronize and encourage his religion. It was by this means, he added, that the Emperor Huang Ti obtained his knowledge of alchemy, which enabled him to make gold.

The Emperor asked the priest to bring him his divine patron, and one night the image of Tsao Chun appeared to him. Deceived by this trick, dazzled by the ingots of gold which he too should obtain, and determined to risk everything for the pill of immortality which was among the benefits promised, the Emperor made a solemn sacrifice to the God of the Kitchen. This was the first time that a sacrifice had been officially offered to this new deity.

Li Shao-chun gradually lost the confidence of the Emperor and, at his wits' end, conceived the plan of writing some phrases on a piece of silk and then forcing them to be swallowed by an ox. This done, he announced that a wonderful script would be found in the animal's stomach. The ox was killed and the script was found there as predicted, but Li's unlucky star decreed that the Emperor should recognize his handwriting, and he was put to death. Nevertheless, the worship of the Kitchen god continued and increased.

The God of Happiness

THE GOD OF HAPPINESS, Fu Shen, owes his origin to the fondness of the Emperor Wu Ti of the Liang dynasty for dwarfs as servants and comedians in his palace. The number levied from the Tao Chou district in Hunan became greater and greater until one day a Criminal Judge of Tao

Chou named Yang Hsi-chi represented to the Emperor that, according to law, the dwarfs were his subjects but not his slaves. Being touched by this remark, the Emperor ordered the levy to be stopped.

Overjoyed at their liberation from this hardship, the people of that district set up images of Yang and offered sacrifices to him. He was revered as the Spirit of Happiness. It was in this simple way that there became a god is worshipped almost as universally as the God of Riches.

The God of Riches

AS WITH MANY OTHER CHINESE GODS, the God of Wealth, Ts'ai Shen, has been ascribed to several different people. The original and best known until later times was Chao Kung-ming. The accounts of him also differ but the following is the most popular.

When Chiang Tzu-ya was fighting for the Chou dynasty against the last of the Shang emperors, Chao Kung-ming, then a hermit on Mount O-mei, took the part of the latter.

He performed many wonderful feats. He could ride a black tiger and hurl pearls which burst like bombshells. But he was eventually overcome by the form of witchcraft known in Wales as Ciurp Creadh. Chiang Tzu-ya made a straw image of him, wrote his name on it, burned incense and worshipped before it for twenty days. On the twenty-first day he shot arrows made of peach wood into its eyes and heart. At that same moment Kung-ming, then in the enemy's camp, felt ill and fainted, and uttering a cry gave up the ghost.

Later on Chiang Tzu-ya persuaded Yuan-shih T'ien-tsun to release the spirits of the heroes who had died in battle from the Otherworld, and when Chao Kung-ming was led into his presence he praised his bravery and canonized him as President of the Ministry of Riches and Prosperity.

The God of Riches is universally worshipped in China. Talismans, trees of which the branches are strings of cash, and the fruits ingots of gold, to be obtained merely by shaking them down, a magic inexhaustible casket full of gold and silver – these and other spiritual sources of wealth are associated with this much-adored deity. He is represented in the guise of a visitor accompanied by a crowd of attendants laden down with all the treasures that the hearts of men, women and children could desire.

The God of Longevity

THE GOD OF LONGEVITY, Shou Hsing, was first a stellar deity and only later represented in human form. It was a constellation formed of the two star-groups Chio and K'ang, the first two on the list of twenty-eight constellations. Hence it was called the Star of Longevity.

When it appears the nation enjoys peace. When it disappears there will be war. Ch'in Shih Huang-ti, the First Emperor, was the first to offer sacrifices to this star, the Old Man of the South Pole, at She Po, in 246 BC. Since then the worship has been continued regularly until modern times.

But desire for something personal than a star led to this god being represented as an old man. Connected with this is a long legend which turns on the point that after the father of Chao Yen had been told that his son would not live beyond the age of nineteen, the transposition from shih-chiu (nineteen) to chiu-shih (ninety) was made by one of two gamblers, who turned out to be the Spirit of the North Pole. He is the one who fixes the time of death, as the Spirit of the South Pole does of birth.

The deity is a domestic god, usually spoken of as Shou Hsing Lao T'ou Tzu, 'Longevity Star Old-pate'. He is represented as riding a stag, with a flying bat above his head. He holds a large peach in his hand, and attached to his long staff are a gourd and a scroll. The stag and the bat both indicate fu, happiness. The peach, gourd and scroll are symbols of longevity.

The Door Gods

IT WAS THE IMPORTANT TASK of these Gods to ward off undesirable visitors and evil spirits from Chinese households and often pictures of ferocious warriors were pinned on either side of the door for this purpose. In the more modern version of this legend, these pictures represented two war ministers of the Emperor T'ai Tsung of the Tang dynasty. These two ministers of outstanding ability were deified after death to become the Door Gods.

The story unfolds that one day the Emperor fell gravely ill with a high fever and during the night he imagined he heard demons in the passageway attempting to gain entry to his chamber. The Emperor grew increasingly delirious and everyone became concerned for his health. Eventually it was decided that two of his finest warriors, Chin Shu-pao and Hu Ching-te, should stand guard overnight outside his door.

For the first time in many weeks, the Emperor slept soundly and peacefully. Next morning, he thanked his men heartily and from that time onwards his health continued to improve. Soon he felt well enough to release his men from their nocturnal duty, but he ordered them to have their portraits painted, looking as fierce as they possibly could, so that he could paste these on his bedroom door to keep evil spirits away in the future.

Yang Oerlang

THE SECOND DAUGHTER of the Ruler of Heaven once came down upon the earth and secretly became the wife of a mortal man named Yang. And when she returned to Heaven she was blessed with a son. But the Ruler of Heaven was very angry at this desecration of the heavenly halls. He banished her to earth and covered her with the Wu-I hills. Her son, however, Oerlang by name, the nephew of the Ruler of Heaven, was extraordinarily gifted by nature. By the time he was full grown he had learned the magic art of being able to control eight times nine transformations. He could make himself invisible, or could assume the shape of birds and beasts, grasses, flowers, snakes and fishes, as he chose. He also knew how to empty out seas and remove mountains from one place to another. So he went to the Wu-I hills and rescued his mother, whom he took on his back and carried away. They stopped to rest on a flat ledge of rock.

Then the mother said: "I am very thirsty!"

Oerlang climbed down into the valley in order to fetch her water, and some time passed before he returned. When he did his mother was no longer there. He searched eagerly, but on the rock lay only her skin and bones, and a few blood-stains. Now you must know that at that time there were still ten suns in the heavens, glowing and burning like fire. The Daughter of Heaven, it is true, was divine by nature; yet because she had incurred the anger of her father and had been banished to earth, her magic powers had failed her. Then, too, she had been imprisoned so long beneath the hills in the dark that, coming out suddenly into the sunlight, she had been devoured by its blinding radiance.

When Oerlang thought of his mother's sad end, his heart ached. He took two mountains on his shoulders, pursued the suns and crushed them to death between the mountains. And whenever he had crushed another sun-disk, he picked up a fresh mountain. In this way he had already slain nine of the ten suns, and there was but one left. And as Oerlang pursued him relentlessly, he hid himself in his distress beneath the leaves of the portulacca plant. But there was a rainworm close by who betrayed his hiding-place, and kept repeating: "There he is! There he is!"

Oerlang was about to seize him, when a messenger from the Ruler of the Heaven suddenly descended from the skies with a command: "Sky, air and earth need the sunshine. You must allow this one sun to live, so that all created beings may live. Yet, because you rescued your mother, and showed yourself to be a good son, you shall be a god, and be my bodyguard in the Highest Heaven, and shall rule over good and evil in the mortal world, and have power over devils and demons." When Oerlang received this command he ascended to Heaven.

Then the sun-disk came out again from beneath the portulacca leaves, and out of gratitude, since the plant had saved him, he bestowed upon it the gift of a free-blooming nature, and ordained that it never need fear the sunshine. To this very day one may see on the lower side of the portulacca leaves quite delicate little white pearls. They are the sunshine that remained hanging to the leaves when the sun hid under them. But the sun pursues the rainworm, when he ventures forth out of the ground, and dries him up as a punishment for his treachery.

Since that time Yang Oerlang has been honored as a god. He has oblique, sharply marked eyebrows, and holds a double-bladed, three-pointed sword in his hand. Two servants stand beside him, with a falcon and a hound; for Yang Oerlang is a great hunter. The falcon is the falcon of the gods, and the hound is the hound of the gods. When brute creatures gain possession of magic powers or demons oppress men, he subdues them by means of the falcon and hound.

Notscha

THE OLDEST DAUGHTER of the Ruler of Heaven had married the great general Li Dsing.[1] Her sons were named Gintscha, Mutscha and Notscha. But when Notscha was given her, she dreamed at night that a Taoist priest came into her chamber and said: "Swiftly receive the Heavenly Son!" And straightway a radiant pearl glowed within her. And she was so frightened at her dream that she awoke. And when Notscha came into the world, it seemed as though a ball of flesh were turning in circles like a wheel, and the whole room was filled with strange fragrances and a crimson light.

Li Dsing was much frightened, and thought it was an apparition. He clove the circling ball with his sword, and out of it leaped a small boy whose whole body glowed with a crimson radiance. But his face was delicately shaped and white as snow. About his right arm he wore a golden armlet and around his thighs was wound a length of crimson silk, whose glittering shine dazzled the eyes. When Li Dsing saw the child he took pity on him and did not slay him, while his wife began to love the boy dearly.

When three days had passed, all his friends came to wish him joy. They were just sitting at the festival meal when a Taoist priest entered and said: "I am the Great One.[2] This boy is the bright Pearl of the Beginning of Things, bestowed upon you as your son. Yet the boy is wild and unruly, and will kill many men. Therefore I will take him as my pupil to gentle his savage ways." Li Dsing bowed his thanks and the Great One disappeared.

When Notscha was seven years old he once ran away from home. He came to the river of nine bends, whose green waters flowed along between two rows of weeping-willows. The day was hot, and Notscha entered the water to cool himself. He unbound his crimson silk cloth and whisked it about in the water to wash it. But while Notscha sat there and whisked about his scarf in the water, it shook the castle of the Dragon-King[3] of the Eastern Sea to its very foundations. So the Dragon-King sent out a Triton, terrible to look upon, who was to find out what was the matter. When the Triton saw the boy he began to scold. But the latter merely looked up and said: "What a strange-looking beast you are, and you can actually talk!" Then the Triton grew enraged, leaped up and struck at Notscha with his ax. But the latter avoided the blow, and threw his golden armlet at him. The armlet struck the Triton on the head and he sank down dead.

Notscha laughed and said: "And there he has gone and made my armlet bloody!" And he once more sat down on a stone, in order to wash his armlet. Then the crystal castle of the dragon began to tremble as though it were about to fall apart. And a watchman also came and reported that the Triton had been slain by a boy. So the Dragon-King sent out his son to capture the boy. And the son seated himself on the water-cleaving beast, and came up with a thunder of great waves of water. Notscha straightened up and said: "That is a big wave!" Suddenly he saw a creature rise out of the waves, on whose back sat an armed man who cried in a loud voice: "Who has slain my Triton?" Notscha answered: "The Triton wanted to slay me so I killed him. What difference does it make?" Then the dragon assailed him with his halberd. But Notscha said: "Tell me who you are before we fight." "I am the son of the Dragon-King," was the reply. "And I am Notscha, the son of General Li Dsing. You must not rouse my anger with your violence, or I will skin you, together with that old mud-fish, your father!" Then the dragon grew wild with rage, and came storming along furiously. But Notscha cast his crimson cloth into the air, so that it flashed like a ball of fire, and cast the dragon-youth from his breast. Then Notscha took his golden armlet and struck him on the forehead with it, so that he had to reveal himself in his true form as a golden dragon, and fall down dead.

Notscha laughed and said: "I have heard tell that dragon-sinews[4] make good cords. I will draw one out and bring it to my father, and he can tie his armor together with it." And with that he drew out the dragon's back sinew and took it home.

In the meantime the Dragon-King, full of fury, had hastened to Notscha's father Li Dsing and demanded that Notscha be delivered up to him. But Li Dsing replied: "You must be mistaken, for my boy is only seven years old and incapable of committing such misdeeds." While they were still quarreling Notscha came running up and cried: "Father, I'm bringing along a dragon's sinew for you, so that you may bind up your armor with it!" Now the dragon broke out into tears and furious scolding. He threatened to report Li Dsing to the Ruler of the Heaven, and took himself off, snorting with rage.

Li Dsing grew very much excited, told his wife what had happened, and both began to weep. Notscha, however, came to them and said: "Why do you weep? I will just go to my master, the Great One, and he will know what is to be done." And no sooner had he said the words than he had disappeared. He came into his master's presence and told him the whole tale. The latter said: "You must get ahead of the dragon, and prevent him from accusing you in Heaven!" Then he did some magic, and Notscha found himself set down by the gate of Heaven, where he waited for the dragon. It was still early in the morning; the gate of Heaven had not yet been opened, nor was the watchman at his post. But the dragon was already climbing up. Notscha, whom his master's magic had rendered invisible, threw the dragon to the ground with his armlet, and began to pitch into him. The dragon scolded and screamed. "There the old worm flounders about," said Notscha, "and does not care how hard he is beaten! I will scratch off some of his scales." And with these words he began to tear open the dragon's festal garments, and rip off some of the scales beneath his left arm, so that the red blood dripped out. Then the dragon could no longer stand the pain and begged for mercy. But first he had to promise Notscha that he would not complain of him, before the latter would let him go. And then the dragon had to turn himself into a little green snake, which Notscha put into his sleeve and took back home with him. But no sooner had he drawn the little snake from his sleeve than it assumed human shape. The dragon then swore that he would punish Li Dsing in a terrible manner, and disappeared in a flash of lightning.

Li Dsing was now angry with his son in earnest. Therefore Notscha's mother sent him to the rear of the house to keep out of his father's sight. Notscha disappeared and went to his master, in order to ask him what he should do when the dragon returned. His master advised him and Notscha went back home. And all the Dragon Kings of the four seas were assembled, and had bound his parents, with cries and tumult, in order to punish them. Notscha ran up and cried with a loud voice: "I will take the punishment for whatever I have done! My parents are blameless! What is the punishment you wish to lay upon me?" "Life for life!" said the dragon. "Very well then, I will destroy myself!" And so he did and the dragons went off satisfied; while Notscha's mother buried him with many tears.

But the spiritual part of Notscha, his soul,[5] fluttered about in the air, and was driven by the wind to the cave of the Great One. He took it in and said to it: "You must appear to your mother! Forty miles distant from your home rises a green mountain cliff. On this cliff she must build a shrine for you. And after you have enjoyed the incense of human adoration for three years, you shall once more have a human body." Notscha appeared to his mother in a dream, and gave her the whole message, and she awoke in tears. But Li Dsing grew angry when she told him about it. "It serves the accursed boy right that he is dead! It is because you are always thinking of him that he appears to you in dreams. You must pay no attention to him." The woman said no more, but thenceforward he appeared to her daily, as soon as she closed her eyes, and grew more and more urgent in his demand. Finally all that was left for her to do was to erect a temple for Notscha without Li Dsing's knowledge.

And Notscha performed great miracles in his temple. All prayers made in it were granted. And from far away people streamed to it to burn incense in his honor.

Thus half a year passed. Then Li Dsing, on the occasion of a great military drill, once came by the cliff in question, and saw the people crowding thickly about the hill like a swarm of ants. Li Dsing inquired what there were to see upon the hill. "It is a new god, who performs so many miracles that people come from far and near to honor him." "What sort of a god is he?" asked Li Dsing. They did not dare conceal from him who the god was. Then Li Dsing grew angry. He spurred his horse up the hill and, sure enough, over the door of the temple was written: "Notscha's Shrine." And within it was the likeness of Notscha, just as he had appeared while living. Li Dsing said: "While you were alive you brought misfortune to your parents. Now that you are dead you deceive the people. It is disgusting!" With these words he drew forth his whip, beat Notscha's idolatrous likeness to pieces with it, had the temple burned down, and the worshipers mildly reproved. Then he returned home.

Now Notscha had been absent in the spirit upon that day.[6] When he returned he found his temple destroyed; and the spirit of the hill gave him the details. Notscha hurried to his master and related with tears what had befallen him. The latter was roused and said: "It is Li Dsing's fault. After you had given back your body to your parents, you were no further concern of his. Why should he withdraw from you the enjoyment of the incense?" Then the Great One made a body of lotus-plants, gave it the gift of life, and enclosed the soul of Notscha within it. This done he called out in a loud voice: "Arise!" A drawing of breath was heard, and Notscha leaped up once more in the shape of a small boy. He flung himself down before his master and thanked him. The latter bestowed upon him the magic of the fiery lance, and Notscha thenceforward had two whirling wheels beneath his feet: The wheel of the wind and the wheel of fire. With these he could rise up and down in the air. The master also gave him a bag of panther-skin in which to keep his armlet and his silken cloth.

Now Notscha had determined to punish Li Dsing. Taking advantage of a moment when he was not watched, he went away, thundering along on his rolling wheels to Li Dsing's dwelling. The latter was unable to withstand him and fled. He was almost exhausted when his second son, Mutscha, the disciple of the holy Pu Hain, came to his aid from the Cave of the White Crane. A violent quarrel took place between the brothers; they began to fight, and Mutscha was overcome; while Notscha once more rushed in pursuit of Li Dsing. At the height of his extremity, however, the holy Wen Dschu of the Hill of the Five Dragons, the master of Gintscha, Li Dsing's oldest son, stepped forth and hid Li Dsing in his cave. Notscha, in a rage, insisted that he be delivered up to him; but Wen Dschu said: "Elsewhere you may indulge your wild nature to your heart's content, but not in this place."

And when Notscha in the excess of his rage turned his fiery lance upon him, Wen Dschu stepped back a pace, shook the seven-petaled lotus from his sleeve, and threw it into the air. A whirlwind arose, clouds and mists obscured the sight, and sand and earth were flung up from the ground. Then the whirlwind collapsed with a great crash. Notscha fainted, and when he regained consciousness found himself bound to a golden column with three thongs of gold, so that he could no longer move. Wen Dschu now called Gintscha to him and ordered him to give his unruly brother a good thrashing. And this he did, while Notscha, obliged to stand it, stood grinding his teeth. In his extremity he saw the Great One floating by, and called out to him: "Save me, O Master!" But the latter did not notice him; instead he entered the cave and thanked Wen Dschu for the severe lesson which he had given Notscha. Finally they called Notscha in to them and ordered him to be reconciled to his father. Then they dismissed them both and seated themselves to play chess. But no sooner was Notscha free than he again fell into a rage, and renewed his pursuit of his father. He had again overtaken Li Dsing when still another saint came forward to defend the latter. This time it was the old Buddha of the Radiance of the Light. When Notscha attempted to battle with him he raised his arm, and a pagoda shaped itself out of red, whirling clouds and closed around Notscha. Then Radiance of Light placed both his hands on the pagoda and a fire arose within it which burned Notscha so that he cried loudly for mercy. Then he had to promise to beg his father's forgiveness and always to obey him in the future. Not till he had promised all this did the Buddha let him out of the pagoda again. And he gave the pagoda to Li Dsing; and taught him a magic saying which would give him the mastery over Notscha. It is for this reason that Li Dsing is called the Pagoda-bearing King of Heaven.

Later on Li Dsing and his three sons, Gintscha, Mutscha and Notscha, aided King Wu of the Dschou dynasty to destroy the tyrant Dschou-Sin.

None could withstand their might. Only once did a sorcerer succeed in wounding Notscha in the left arm. Any other would have died of the wound. But the Great One carried him into his cave, healed his wound and gave him three goblets of the wine of the gods to drink, and three fire-dates to eat. When Notscha had eaten and drunk he suddenly heard a crash at his left side and another arm grew out from it. He could not speak and his eyes stood out from their sockets with horror. But it went on as it had begun: six more arms grew out of his body and two more heads, so that finally he had three heads and eight arms. He called out to his Master: "What does all this mean?" But the latter only laughed and said: "All is as it should be. Thus equipped you will really be strong!" Then he taught him a magic incantation by means of which he could make his arms and heads visible or invisible as he chose. When the tyrant Dschou-Sin had been destroyed, Li Dsing and his three sons, while still on earth, were taken up into heaven and seated among the gods.

Footnotes for 'Notscha'

1. Li Dsing, the Pagoda-bearing King of Heaven, may be traced back to Indra, the Hindu god of thunder and lightning. The Pagoda might be an erroneous variant of the thunderbolt Vadjra. In such case Notscha would be a personification of the thunder.
2. The Great One (Tai I), is the condition of things before their separation into the active and passive principles.
3. The Dragon-King of the Eastern Sea also occurs in 'The Ape Sun Wu Kung' (*see* page 192).
4. "Dragon sinew" means the spinal cord, the distinction between nerves and sinews not being carefully observed.
5. "Three spirits and seven souls": man has three spirits, usually above his head, and seven animal souls.
6. "Notscha had been absent in the spirit upon that day": the idol is only the seat of the godhead, which the latter leaves or inhabits as he chooses. Therefore the godhead must be summoned when prayers are offered, by means of bells and incense. When the god is not present, his idol is merely a block of wood or stone.

The Halos of the Saints

THE TRUE GODS all have halos around their heads. When the lesser gods and demons see these halos, they hide and dare not move. The Master of the Heavens[1] on the Dragon-Tiger Mountain meets the gods at all times. One day the God of War came down to the mountain while the mandarin of the neighboring district was visiting the Master of the Heavens. The latter advised the mandarin to withdraw and hide himself in an inner chamber. Then he went out to receive the God of War. But the mandarin peeped through a slit in the door, and he saw the red face and green garment of the God of War as he stood there, terrible and awe-inspiring. Suddenly a red halo flashed up above his head, whose beams penetrated into the inner chamber so that the mandarin grew blind in one eye. After a time the God of War went away again, and the Master of the Heavens accompanied him. Suddenly Guan Di said, with alarm: "Confucius is coming! The halo he wears illumines the whole world. I cannot endure its radiance even a thousand miles away, so I must hurry and get out of the way!" And with that he stepped into a cloud and disappeared. The Master of the Heavens then told the mandarin what had happened, and added: "Fortunately you did not see the God of War face to face! Whoever does not possess the greatest virtue and the greatest wisdom, would be melted by the red glow of his halo." So saying he gave him a pill of the elixir of life to eat, and his blind eye gradually regained its sight.

It is also said that scholars wear a red halo around their heads which devils, foxes and ghosts fear when they see it.

There was once a scholar who had a fox for a friend. The fox came to see him at night, and went walking with him in the villages. They could enter the houses, and see all that was going on, without people being any the wiser. But when at a distance the fox saw a red halo hanging above a house he would not enter it. The scholar asked him why not.

"Those are all celebrated scholars," answered the fox. "The greater the halo, the more extensive is their knowledge. I dread them and do not dare enter their houses."

Then the man said: "But I am a scholar, too! Have I no halo which makes you fear me, instead of going walking with me?"

"There is only a black mist about your head," answered the fox. "I have never yet seen it surrounded by a halo."

The scholar was mortified and began to scold him; but the fox disappeared with a horse-laugh.

Footnotes for 'The Halos of the Saints'

1. This tale is told as traditionally handed down. The Master of the Heavens, Tian Schi, who dwells on the Lung Hu Schan, is the so-called Taoist pope.

Laotsze

LAOTSZE IS REALLY OLDER than heaven and earth put together. He is the Yellow Lord or Ancient, who created this world together with the other four. At various times he has appeared on earth,[1] under various names. His most celebrated incarnation, however, is that of Laotsze, "The Old Child", which name he was given because he made his appearance on earth with white hair.

He acquired all sorts of magic powers by means of which he extended his life-span. Once he hired a servant to do his bidding. He agreed to give him a hundred pieces of copper daily; yet he did not pay him, and finally he owed him seven million, two hundred thousand pieces of copper. Then he mounted a black steer and rode to the West. He wanted to take his servant along. But when they reached the Han-Gu pass, the servant refused to go further, and insisted on being paid. Yet Laotsze gave him nothing.

When they came to the house of the guardian[2] of the pass, red clouds appeared in the sky. The guardian understood this sign and knew that a holy man was drawing near. So he went out to meet him and took him into his house. He questioned him with regard to hidden knowledge, but Laotsze only stuck out his tongue at him and would not say a word. Nevertheless, the guardian of the pass treated him with the greatest respect in his home. Laotsze's servant told the servant of the guardian that his master owed him a great deal of money, and begged the latter to put in a good word for him. When the guardian's servant heard how large a sum it was, he was tempted to win so wealthy a man for a son-in-law, and he married him to his daughter. Finally the guardian heard of the matter and came to Laotsze together with the servant. Then Laotsze said to his servant: "You rascally servant. You really should have been dead long ago. I hired you, and since I was poor and could give you no money, I gave you a life-giving talisman to eat. That is how you still happen to be alive. I said to you: 'If you will follow me into the West, the land of Blessed Repose, I will pay you your wages in yellow gold. But you did not wish to do this.'" And with that he patted his servant's neck. Thereupon the latter opened his mouth, and spat out the life-giving talisman. The magic signs written on it with cinnabar, quite fresh and well-preserved, might still be seen. But the servant suddenly collapsed and turned into a heap of dry bones. Then the guardian of the pass cast himself to earth and pleaded for him. He promised to pay the servant for Laotsze and begged the latter to restore him to life. So Laotsze placed the talisman among the bones and at once the servant came to life again. The guardian of the pass paid him his wages and dismissed him. Then he adored Laotsze as his master, and the latter taught him the art of eternal life, and left him his teachings, in five thousand words, which the guardian wrote down. The book which thus came into being is the Tao Teh King, "The Book of the Way and Life." Laotsze then disappeared from the eyes of men. The guardian of the pass however, followed his teachings, and was given a place among the immortals.

Footnotes for 'Laotsze'

1. The Taoists like to assert that Laotsze's journey to the West was undertaken before the birth of Buddha, who, according to many, is only a reincarnation of Laotsze.
2. The guardian of the Han-Gu pass is mentioned by the name of Guan Yin Hi, in the Lia Dsi and the Dschuang Dsi.

Legends of Foxes and Other Animals

Introduction

AMONG THE MANY many animals worshipped by the Chinese, those at times seen emerging from coffins or graves naturally hold a prominent place. They are supposed to be the transmigrated souls of deceased human beings. We should therefore expect animals such as the fox, stoat and weasel to be closely associated with the worship of ghosts and spirits and that they should be the subjects of, or included in, a large number of Chinese legends. This we find. Of these animals, the fox is mentioned in Chinese legends perhaps more often than any other.

Generally, the fox is a creature of ill omen, long-lived (living to eight hundred or even a thousand years), with a peculiar virtue in every part of his body, able to produce fire by striking the ground with his tail, cunning, cautious, sceptical, able to see into the future, to transform himself (usually into old men, scholars or pretty young maidens) and fond of playing pranks and tormenting mankind.

Of course, there are many other animals that crop up in traditional Chinese tales, whether because they hold special significance for the Chinese in some aspect or because their characteristics help serve a useful function in the story, and several are featured in this chapter. The tiger, for instance, is a significant animal in Chinese culture, revered as having many symbolic associations and as being powerful and protective force. Dogs too are an important motif, whether by virtue of being one of the zodiacal signs or because myth has them as being the first providers of grain – so it is not surprising to see them emerge as the hero in two of the stories included in this chapter.

Friendship with Foxes

A CERTAIN MAN had an enormous stack of straw, as big as a hill, in which his servants, taking what they needed, had made quite a large hole. In this hole a fox made his home and would often show himself to the master of the house under the form of an old man. One day the old man invited the master to come into his home. At first he declined, but after being pressed, he accepted. When he got inside he saw a long suite of handsome apartments.

The pair sat down and exquisitely perfumed tea and wine were brought. But the place was so gloomy that there was no difference between night and day. Once the entertainment was over, the guest took his leave. But as he left he looked back and found that the beautiful rooms and their contents had all disappeared. The old man himself was in the habit of going away in the evening and returning with the first streaks of morning light; and as no one was able to follow him, one day the master of the house asked him where he went. The old man replied that a friend invited him to drink wine. The master begged to be allowed to accompany him, a proposal to which the old man very reluctantly consented. However, he seized the master by the arm and away they went as though riding on the wings of the wind.

They soon reached a city and walked into a restaurant, where there were a number of people drinking together and making a great noise. The old man led his companion to a gallery above, from which they could look down on the feasters below. He himself went down and brought back all kinds of nice food and wine from the tables, without appearing to be seen or noticed by any of the company.

After a while a man dressed in red garments came forward and laid some exquisite dishes on the table. At once the master asked the old man to go down and get him some of these. "Ah," replied the old man, "that is an upright man: I cannot approach him." Considering this, the master said to himself, "By seeking the companionship of a fox, I am deflected from the true course. From now on I too will be an upright man."

No sooner had he formed this resolution than he suddenly lost all control of his body. He fell from the gallery down among the revellers below. These gentlemen were astonished. Looking up, he himself saw there was no gallery to the house – only a large beam on which he had been sitting. He told the revellers the story of how he had come to be in the restaurant. Those present made up a purse for him to pay his travelling expenses; for he was at Yu-t'ai – a thousand li from home.

The Marriage Lottery

A CERTAIN LABOURER, named Ma T'ien-jung, lost his wife when he was just twenty years of age, and was too poor to take another. One day, when out hoeing in the fields, he watched a nice looking young lady leave the path and come tripping across the furrows toward him. She had such a refined look that Ma concluded she must have lost her way and began to make some playful remarks. "You go along home," cried the young lady, "and I'll be with you before long."

Ma doubted this rather extraordinary promise, but she vowed and declared she would not break her word; and then Ma went off, telling her that his front door faced the north. At midnight the young lady arrived. Ma saw that her hands and face were covered with fine hair, which quickly made him suspect that she was a fox. She did not deny the accusation; and accordingly Ma said to her, "If you really are one of those wonderful creatures you will be able to get me anything I want; and I should be much obliged if you would start by giving me some money to relieve my poverty." The young lady said she would.

The following evening when she came again, Ma asked her where the money was. "Dear me!" replied she, "I forgot it." As she was going away Ma reminded her of what he wanted, but on the following evening she made precisely the same excuse, promising to bring it another day. A few nights afterwards, Ma asked her once more for the money. This time she drew two pieces of silver from her sleeve, each weighing about five or six ounces. They were both of fine quality. Ma was very pleased. He stored them away in a cupboard.

Some months later Ma happened to need some money, so he took out these pieces. However the person he showed them to said they were only pewter, and easily bit off a portion of one of them with his teeth. Ma was alarmed and put the pieces away. When evening came he confronted the young lady. "It's all your bad luck," she retorted.

"Real gold would be too much for your inferior destiny." There was an end of that; but Ma went on to say, "I always heard that fox girls were of surpassing beauty; how is it you are not?" "Oh," replied the young lady, "we always adapt ourselves to our company. Now you haven't the luck of an ounce of silver to call your own; and what would you do, for instance, with a beautiful princess? My beauty may not be good enough for the aristocracy; but among your big-footed, bent-backed rustics, why, it may safely be called 'surpassing'!"

A few months went by, and then one day the young lady came and gave Ma three ounces of silver, saying, "You have often asked me for money, but in consequence of your bad luck I have always refrained from giving you any. Now, however, your marriage is at hand, and I here give you the cost of a wife, which you may also regard as a parting gift from me." Ma replied that he was not engaged, to which the young lady answered that in a few days a go-between would visit him to arrange the affair. "And what will she be like?" asked Ma. "Why, as your aspirations are for 'surpassing' beauty," replied the young lady, "of course she will be possessed of surpassing beauty." "I hardly expect that," said Ma; "at any rate, three ounces of silver will not be enough to get a wife." "Marriages," explained the young lady, "are made in the moon; mortals have nothing to do with them." "And why must you be going away like this?" inquired Ma. "Because," answered she, "for us to meet only by night is not the proper thing. I had better get you another wife and have done with you." Then when morning came she departed, giving Ma a pinch of yellow powder, saying, "In case you are ill after we are separated, this will cure you."

Sure enough, the next day a go-between did come. Ma immediately asked what the proposed bride was like; to which the go-between replied that she was very passable looking. Four or five ounces of silver was fixed as the marriage present. Ma had no difficulty on that score, but declared he must have a peep at the young lady. The go-between said she was a respectable girl and would never allow herself to be seen. However, it was arranged that they should go to the house together, and wait for a good opportunity.

So off they went, Ma remaining outside while the go-between went in, returning in a little while to tell him it was alright. "A relative of mine lives in the same court. Just now I saw the young lady sitting in the hall. We have only got to pretend we are going to see my relative and you will be able to catch a glimpse of her." Ma agreed and so they went through the hall, where he saw the young lady sitting down with her head bent forward while someone was scratching her back. She seemed to be all that the go-between had said; but when they came to discuss the money it appeared that the young lady only wanted one or two ounces of silver, just to buy herself a few clothes. Ma thought this was a very small amount, so he gave the go-between a present for her trouble, which just finished up the three ounces his fox friend had given him. An auspicious day was chosen and the young lady came over to his house. Ma was shocked to discover the girl was humpbacked and pigeon-breasted, with a short neck like a tortoise and feet which were ten inches long! The meaning of his fox friend's remarks then flashed upon him.

The Magnanimous Girl

AT CHIN-LING THERE LIVED a talented young man named Ku, who was very poor. Having an elderly mother he was reluctant to leave home, so he employed himself in writing or painting for people. Ku always gave his mother the proceeds – going on this way until he was twenty-five years of age without taking a wife. Opposite to their house was another building, which had long been unoccupied. One day an old woman and a young girl moved in, but there being no gentleman with them young Ku did not make any inquiries as to who they were or where they had come from.

Then one day, just as Ku was entering his house he observed a young lady come out of his mother's door. She was about eighteen or nineteen years old, very clever and refined looking and when she noticed Mr. Ku she did not run away, but seemed quite self-possessed.

"It was the young lady over the way; she came to borrow my scissors and measure," said his mother, "and she told me that there is only her mother and herself. They don't seem to belong to the lower classes. I asked her why she didn't get married, to which she replied that her mother was old. I must go and call on her tomorrow and find out how the land lies. If she doesn't expect too much, you could take care of her mother for her."

So the next day Ku's mother went over to the girl's house. She discovered that the girl's mother was deaf and that they were evidently poor, apparently not having a day's food in the house. Ku's mother asked how they were able to survive and the old lady said they trusted for food to her daughter's ten fingers. She then threw out some hints about uniting the two families, to which the old lady seemed to agree. The daughter, however, would not consent. Mrs. Ku returned home and told her son, saying, "Perhaps she thinks we are too poor. She doesn't speak or laugh, is very nice looking, and as pure as snow; truly no ordinary girl." That was the end of that.

Until one day, Ku was sitting in his study when a young man arrived at his door. The stranger said he was from a neighbouring village and employed Ku to draw a picture for him. The two youths soon struck up a firm friendship and met regularly. Later it happened that the stranger happened to see the young lady of over the way. "Who is that?" he said, following her with his eyes. Ku told him and then he said, "She is certainly pretty, but rather stern in her appearance."

One day Ku's mother told him the girl had come to beg a little rice, as they had had nothing to eat all day. "She's a good daughter," said his mother, "and I'm very sorry for her. We must try and help them a little." So Ku picked up a sack of rice and, knocking at their door, presented it with his mother's compliments. The young lady took the rice, but said nothing. After that she got into the habit of coming over and helping Ku's mother with her work and household affairs, almost as if she had been her daughter-in-law, for which Ku was very grateful to her. Whenever he had anything nice he always sent some of it in to her mother, though the young lady herself never once took the trouble to thank him.

So things went on until Ku's mother got an abscess on her leg. She lay writhing in agony day and night. Then the young lady devoted herself to the invalid, waiting on her and giving her medicine with such care and attention that at last the sick woman cried out, "Oh that I could secure such a daughter-in-law as you to see this old body into its grave!" The young lady soothed her and replied, "Your son is a hundred times more filial than I, a poor widow's only daughter." "But even a filial son makes a bad nurse," answered the patient; "besides, I am now drawing toward the evening of my life, when my body will be exposed to the mists and the dews, and I am deeply saddened about our ancestral worship and the continuance of our line." As she was speaking Ku walked in. His mother, weeping, said, "I am deeply indebted to this young lady; do not forget to repay her goodness." Ku made a low bow, but the young lady said, "Sir, when you were kind to my mother, I did not thank you; why then thank me?" Ku was becoming more attached to her than ever, but could never get her to show him the slightest warmth from her cold demeanour toward him. One day, however, he managed to squeeze her hand, after which she told him never to do so again. Then for some time he neither saw nor heard anything of her.

She had taken a violent dislike to the young stranger who had befriended Ku. One evening, when he was sitting talking with Ku, the young lady appeared. After a while she got angry at something he said. She drew from her robe a glittering knife about a foot long. The young man, seeing her do this, ran out in terror. She ran after him, only to find that he had vanished. She then threw her dagger up into the air, and with a streak of light like a rainbow, something came tumbling down with a flop. Ku grabbed a light and ran to see what it was. There lay a white fox, head in one place and body in another. "There is your friend," cried the girl, "I knew he would cause me to destroy him sooner or later." Ku dragged it into the house and said, "Let's wait until tomorrow to talk it over; we will be calmer then."

When the young lady arrived the following day Ku inquired about her knowledge of the black art. She told Ku not to trouble himself about such things and to keep it secret or it might be prejudicial to his happiness. Ku then pleaded with her to consent to their union, to which she replied that she had already been as it were a daughter-in-law to his mother, and there was no need to push the thing further. "Is it because I am poor?" asked Ku. "Well, I am not rich," she answered, "but the fact is I had rather not." Then she left. The next evening when Ku went across to their house to try once more to persuade her the young lady had disappeared, and was never seen again.

The Boon-Companion

ONCE UPON A TIME there was a young man named Ch'e, who was not particularly well off, but at the same time very fond of his wine; so much so that without his three cups of liquor every night he was quite unable to sleep. Bottles were seldom absent from the head of his bed.

One night he had woken up and was turning over and over, when he imagined someone was in the bed with him. But then, thinking it was only the clothes that had slipped off, he put out his hand to feel and in doing so touched something silky like a cat. Striking a light, he found it was a fox, lying in a drunken sleep like a dog. Then looking at his wine bottle he saw that it had been emptied. "A boon-companion," he said laughing. To avoid startling the animal, he covered it up and lay down to sleep with his arm across it, leaving the candle alight so as to see what transformation it might undergo. About midnight the fox stretched itself and Ch'e cried, "Well, to be sure, you've had a nice sleep!" He then drew off the clothes and saw an elegant young man in a scholar's dress; but the young man jumped up, and, bowing low, returned his host many thanks for not cutting off his head. "Oh," replied Ch'e, "I am not averse to liquor myself; in fact they say I'm too much given to it. If you have no objection, we'll be a pair of drinking chums." So they lay down and went to sleep again, Ch'e urging the young man to visit him often, saying that they must have faith in each other. The fox agreed to this, but when Ch'e awoke in the morning his bedfellow had already disappeared.

That evening he prepared a goblet of first-rate wine in expectation of his friend's arrival. At nightfall sure enough he came. They then sat together drinking and the fox cracked so many jokes that Ch'e said he regretted he had not known him before. "And truly I don't know how to repay your kindness," replied the fox, "in preparing all this nice wine for me." "Oh," said Ch'e, "what's a pint or so of wine? Nothing worth speaking of." "Well," replied the fox, "you are only a poor scholar and money isn't so easy to get. I must see if I can't secure a little wine capital for you." The next evening when he arrived he said to Ch'e, "Two miles down toward the south-east you will find some silver lying by the wayside. Go early in the morning and get it." So in the morning Ch'e set off and actually obtained two lumps of silver, with which he bought some choice morsels to help them out with their wine that evening. The fox now told him that there was a vault in his backyard which he ought to open; and when he did so he found more than a hundred strings of cash. "Now then," cried Ch'e, delighted, "I shall have no more anxiety about funds for buying wine with all this in my purse!" "Ah," replied the fox, "the water in a puddle is not inexhaustible. I must do something further for you." Some days afterward the fox said to Ch'e, "Buckwheat is very cheap in the market just now. Something is to be done in that line." Accordingly Ch'e bought over forty tons, much to the ridicule of others; but before long there was a bad drought and all kinds of grain and beans were spoilt. Only buckwheat would grow, and Ch'e sold off his stock at a profit of one thousand per cent. With his wealth beginning to increase, he bought two hundred acres of rich land and always planted his crops – corn, millet, or what not – on the advice of the fox secretly given to him beforehand. The fox looked on Ch'e's wife as a sister and on Ch'e's children as his own, but when Ch'e later died it never came to the house again.

Chia Tzu-lung Finds the Stone

AT CH'ANG-AN there lived a scholar named Chia Tzu-lung, who one day noticed a very refined looking stranger. After making inquiries about him, Chia learned that he was a Mr. Chen who had taken lodgings nearby. Accordingly, Chia called on him the next day and sent in his card, but did not see Chen, who happened to be out at the time. The same thing happened three times and eventually Chia employed someone to watch and let him know when Mr. Chen was at home.

However, even then the latter would not come out to receive his guest and Chia had to go in and find him. The two then entered into conversation and soon became mutually charmed with each other.

Before long Chia sent off a servant to bring wine from a neighbouring wine shop. Mr. Chen proved himself a pleasant companion, and when the wine was nearly finished he went to a box and took some wine cups from it and a large and beautiful jade tankard. Into the tankard he poured a single cup of wine and immediately it was filled to the brim. They then began to help themselves from the tankard; but however much they took out, the contents never seemed to diminish. Chia was astonished at this and begged Mr. Chen to tell him how it was done. "Ah," replied Mr. Chen, "I tried to avoid making your acquaintance solely because of your one bad quality – avarice. The art I practise is a secret known only to the Immortals: how can I divulge it to you?" "You do me wrong," rejoined Chia, "in attributing avarice to me. The avaricious, indeed, are always poor." Mr. Chen laughed, and they separated for that day; but from that time they were constantly together, and all ceremony between them was laid aside.

Whenever Chia wanted money Mr. Chen would bring out a black stone and, muttering a charm, would rub it on a tile or a brick, which was instantly changed into a lump of silver. This silver he would give to Chia. It was always just as much as he actually needed, no more no less; and if ever Chia asked for more Mr. Chen would rally him on the subject of avarice.

Finally Chia determined to try to get possession of this stone; and one day, when Mr. Chen was sleeping off the fumes of a drinking bout, he tried to extract it from his clothes. However, Chen detected him at once and declared that they could no longer be friends. The next day he left the place altogether.

About a year later Chia was wandering by the riverbank, when he saw a handsome looking stone, similar to that in the possession of Mr. Chen. He picked it up and carried it home with him at once. After a few days had passed, suddenly Mr. Chen himself arrived at Chia's house. He explained that the stone in question possessed the property of changing anything into gold, and that it had been given to him long before by a certain Taoist priest whom he had followed as a disciple. "Alas!" he added, "I got tipsy and lost it; but divination told me where it was, and if you will now restore it to me I will take care to repay your kindness." "You have divined rightly," Chia replied; "the stone is with me; but remember, if you please, that the poor Kuan Chung shared the wealth of his friend Pao Shu." At this hint Mr. Chen said he would give Chia one hundred ounces of silver. Chia replied that one hundred ounces was a fair offer, but that he would far sooner have Mr. Chen teach him the formula to utter when rubbing the stone on anything, so that he might try the thing once himself. But Mr. Chen was afraid to do this.

Chia cried out, "You are an Immortal yourself; you must know well enough that I would never deceive a friend." So Mr. Chen was persuaded to teach him the formula. Chia would have tried the art on the immense stone washing block which was lying close at hand had Mr. Chen not seized his arm and begged him not to do anything so outrageous. Chia then picked up half a brick and laid it on the washing block, saying to Mr. Chen, "This little piece is not too much, surely?" Accordingly Mr. Chen relaxed his hold and let Chia proceed, which he did by promptly ignoring the half brick and quickly rubbing the stone on the washing block. Mr. Chen turned pale when he saw him do this. He made a dash forward to get hold of the stone, but it was too late; the washing-block was already a solid mass of silver. Chia quietly handed him back the stone. "Alas! Alas!" cried Mr. Chen in despair, "What is to be done now? For, having granted such wealth on a mortal, Heaven will surely punish me. Oh, if you would save me, give away one hundred coffins and one hundred suits of wadded clothes." "My friend," replied Chia, "my object in getting money was not to hoard it up like a miser." Mr. Chen was delighted at this.

During the next three years Chia engaged in trade, always taking care to fulfil his promise to Mr. Chen. Then one day Mr Chen reappeared and, grasping Chia's hand, said to him, "Trustworthy and noble friend, when we last parted the Spirit of Happiness impeached me before God and my name was erased from the list of angels. But now that you have carried out my request that sentence has been rescinded. Go on as you have begun, without ceasing." Chia asked Mr. Chen what office he filled in Heaven; to which the latter replied that he was only a fox who, by a sinless life, had finally attained to that clear perception of the truth which leads to immortality. Wine was then brought, and the two friends enjoyed themselves together as of old; and even when Chia had passed ninety years of age the fox still used to visit him from time to time.

The Fox and the Tiger

ONCE A FOX MET A TIGER. The latter bared his teeth, stretched out his claws, and was about to devour him. But the fox spoke and said: "My dear sir, you must not think that you are the only king of beasts. Your courage does not compare with my own. Let us walk together, and do you keep behind me. And if men catch sight of me and do not fear me, then you may devour me." The tiger was willing, and so the fox led him along a broad highway. But the travelers, when they saw the tiger in the distance, were all frightened and ran away.

Then the fox said: "How about it? I went in advance, and the men saw me and had not as yet seen you."

And thereupon the tiger drew in his tail and ran away himself.

The tiger had remarked quite well that the men were afraid of the fox, but he had not noticed that the fox had borrowed the terror he inspired from him.

Fox-Fire

ONCE UPON A TIME there was a strong young farmer who came home late one evening from market. His way led him past the gardens of a wealthy gentleman, in which stood a number of tall buildings. Suddenly he saw something shining floating in the air inside the gardens, something which glowed like a ball of crystal. He was astonished, and climbed the wall around the gardens, but there was not a human being in sight; all he saw was, at a distance, something which appeared to be a dog, looking up at the moon. And whenever it blew its breath out a ball of fire came out of its mouth, and rose to the moon. And whenever it drew its breath in the ball sank down again, and it caught it in its jaws. And so it went on without a stop. Then the farmer realized that it was a fox, who was preparing the elixir of life.[1] He hid in the grass and waited until the ball of fire came down again, at about the height of his own head. Then he stepped hastily from his hiding-place, took it away and at once swallowed it. And he could feel it glow as it passed down his throat into his stomach. When the fox saw what had happened he grew angry. He looked furiously at the farmer, but feared his strength. For this reason he did not dare attack him, but went angrily on his way.

From that time on the farmer-boy could make himself invisible, was able to see ghosts and devils, and had intercourse with the spirit-world. In cases of sickness, when people lay unconscious, he could call back their souls, and if someone had committed a sin he could plead for them. He earned much money owing to these gifts.

When he reached his fiftieth year, he withdrew from all things and would no longer exercise his arts. One summer evening he was sitting in his courtyard, enjoying the cool air. While there he drank a number of goblets of wine, and by midnight had fallen fast asleep. Suddenly he awoke, feeling ill. It seemed as though someone were patting him on the back, and before he knew it, the ball of fire had leaped out from his throat. At once a hand reached for it and a voice said: "For thirty long years you kept my treasure from me, and from a poor farmer-lad you have grown to be a wealthy man. Now you have enough, and I would like to have my fire-ball back again!"

Then the man knew what had happened, but the fox was gone.

Footnotes for 'Fox-Fire'

1. The thought underlying the story is the belief that the fox prepares the elixir of life out of his own breath, which he allows to rise to the moon. If a thief can rob him of the elixir he gains supernatural powers.

The Talking Silver Foxes

THE SILVER FOXES[1] resemble other foxes, but are yellow, fire-red or white in color. They know how to influence human beings, too. There is a kind of silver fox which can learn to speak like a man in a year's time. These foxes are called "Talking Foxes".

South-west of the bay of Kaiutschou there is a mountain by the edge of the sea, shaped like a tower, and hence known as Tower Mountain. On the mountain there is an old temple with the image of a goddess, who is known as the Old Mother of Tower Mountain.[2] When children fall ill in the surrounding villages, the magicians often give orders that paper figures of them be burned at her altar, or little lime images of them be placed around it. And for this reason the altar and its surroundings are covered with hundreds of figures of children made in lime. Paper flowers, shoes and clothing are also brought to the Old Mother, and lie in a confusion of colors. The pilgrimage festivals take place on the third day of the third month, and the ninth day of the ninth month, and then there are theatrical performances, and the holy writings are read. And there is also an annual fair. The girls and women of the neighborhood burn incense and pray to the goddess. Parents who have no children go there and pick out one of the little children made of lime, and tie a red thread around its neck, or even secretly break off a small bit of its body, dissolve it in water and drink it. Then they pray quietly that a child may be sent them.

Behind the temple is a great cave where, in former times, some talking foxes used to live. They would even come out and seat themselves on the point of a steep rock by the wayside. When a wanderer came by they would begin to talk to him in this fashion: "Wait a bit, neighbor; first smoke a pipe!" The traveler would look around in astonishment, to see where the voice came from, and would become very much frightened. If he did not happen to be exceptionally brave, he would begin to perspire with terror, and run away. Then the fox would laugh: "Hi hi!"

Once a farmer was plowing on the side of the mountain. When he looked up he saw a man with a straw hat, wearing a mantle of woven grass and carrying a pick across his shoulder coming along the way.

"Neighbor Wang," said he, "first smoke a pipeful and take a little rest! Then I will help you plow."

Then he called out "Hu!" the way farmers do when they talk to their cattle.

The farmer looked at him more closely and saw then that he was a talking fox. He waited for a favorable opportunity, and when it came gave him a lusty blow with his ox-whip. He struck home, for the fox screamed, leaped into the air and ran away. His straw hat, his mantle of woven grass and the rest he left lying on the ground. Then the farmer saw that the straw hat was just woven out of potato-leaves; he had cut it in two with his whip. The mantle was made of oak-leaves, tied together with little blades of grass. And the pick was only the stem of a kau-ling plant, to which a bit of brick had been fastened.

Not long after, a woman in a neighboring village became possessed. A picture of the head priest of the Taoists[3] was hung up in her room, but the evil spirit did not depart. Since there were none who could exorcise devils in the neighborhood, and the trouble she gave was unendurable, the woman's relatives decided to send to the temple of the God of War and beg for aid.

But when the fox heard of it he said: "I am not afraid of your Taoist high-priest nor of your God of War; the only person I fear is your neighbor Wang in the Eastern village, who once struck me cruelly with his whip."

This suited the people to a T. They sent to the Eastern village, and found out who Wang was. And Wang took his ox-whip and entered the house of the possessed woman.

Then he said in a deep voice: "Where are you? Where are you? I have been on your trail for a long time. And now, at last, I have caught you!"

With that he snapped his whip.

The fox hissed and spat and flew out of the window.

They had been telling stories about the talking fox of Tower Mountain for more than a hundred years when one fine day, a skilful archer came to that part of the country who saw a creature like a fox, with a fiery-red pelt, whose back was striped with gray. It was lying under a tree. The archer aimed and shot off its hind foot.

At once it said in a human voice: "I brought myself into this danger because of my love for sleep; but none may escape their fate! If you capture me you will get at the most no more than five thousand pieces of copper for my pelt. Why not let me go instead? I will reward you richly, so that all your poverty will come to an end."

But the archer would not listen to him. He killed him, skinned him and sold his pelt; and, sure enough, he received five thousand pieces of copper for it.

From that time on the fox-spirit ceased to show itself.

Footnotes for 'The Talking Silver Foxes'

1. The silver fox is known in Chinese as "Pi", the same word also being used for "panthers", since this legendary beast partakes of the nature of both animals.

2. "The Old Mother" is really the mother-goddess of the Taischan. But in other localities she is chiefly honored as a child-giving goddess.
3. "A picture of the head priest of the Taoists": Talismans painted by the head priest of the Taoists or the Taoist pope, the so-called "Master of the Heavens," (Tian Schi) have special virtues against all kinds of sorcery and enchantment. The war god Guan Di also is appealed to as a savior in all sorts of emergencies.

The Ape Sun Wu Kung

FAR, FAR AWAY to the East, in the midst of the Great Sea there is an island called the Mountain of Flowers and Fruits. And on this mountain there is a high rock. Now this rock, from the very beginning of the world, had absorbed all the hidden seed power of heaven and earth and sun and moon, which endowed it with supernatural creative gifts. One day the rock burst, and out came an egg of stone. And out of this stone egg a stone ape was hatched by magic power. When he broke the shell he bowed to all sides. Then he gradually learned to walk and to leap, and two streams of golden radiance broke from his eyes which shot up to the highest of the castles of heaven, so that the Lord of the Heavens was frightened. So he sent out the two gods, Thousandmile-Eye and Fine-Ear, to find out what had happened. The two gods came back and reported: "The rays shine from the eyes of the stone ape who was hatched out of the egg which came from the magic rock. There is no reason for uneasiness."

Little by little the ape grew up, ran and leaped about, drank from the springs in the valleys, ate the flowers and fruits, and time went by in unconstrained play.

One day, during the summer, when he was seeking coolness, together with the other apes on the island, they went to the valley to bathe. There they saw a waterfall which plunged down a high cliff. Said the apes to each other: "Whoever can force his way through the waterfall, without suffering injury, shall be our king." The stone ape at once leaped into the air with joy and cried: "I will pass through!" Then he closed his eyes, bent down low and leaped through the roar and foam of the waters. When he opened his eyes once more he saw an iron bridge, which was shut off from the outer world by the waterfall as though by a curtain.

At its entrance stood a tablet of stone on which were graven the words: "This is the heavenly cave behind the water-curtain on the Blessed Island of Flowers and Fruits." Filled with joy, the stone ape leaped out again through the waterfall and told the other apes what he had found. They received the news with great content, and begged the stone ape to take them there. So the tribe of apes leaped through the water on the iron bridge, and then crowded into the cave castle where they found a hearth with a profusion of pots, cups and platters. But all were made of stone. Then the apes paid homage to the stone ape as their king, and he was given the name of Handsome King of the Apes. He appointed long-tailed, ring-tailed and other monkeys to be his officials and counselors, servants and retainers, and they led a blissful life on the Mountain, sleeping by night in their cave castle, keeping away from birds and beasts, and their king enjoyed untroubled happiness. In this way some three hundred years went by.

One day, when the King of the Apes sat with his subjects at a merry meal, he suddenly began to weep. Frightened, the apes asked him why he so suddenly grew sad amid all his bliss. Said the

King: "It is true that we are not subject to the law and rule of man, that birds and beasts do not dare attack us, yet little by little we grow old and weak, and some day the hour will strike when Death, the Ancient, will drag us off! Then we are gone in a moment, and can no longer dwell upon earth!" When the apes heard these words, they hid their faces and sobbed. But an old ape, whose arms were connected in such a way that he could add the length of one to that of the other, stepped forth from the ranks. In a loud tone of voice he said: "That you have hit upon this thought, O King, shows the desire to search for truth has awakened you! Among all living creatures, there are but three kinds who are exempt from Death's power: the Buddhas, the blessed spirits and the gods. Whoever attains one of these three grades escapes the rod of re-birth, and lives as long as the Heavens themselves."

The King of the Apes said: "Where do these three kinds of beings live?" And the old ape replied: "They live in caves and on holy mountains in the great world of mortals." The King was pleased when he heard this, and told his apes that he was going to seek out gods and sainted spirits in order to learn the road to immortality from them. The apes dragged up peaches and other fruits and sweet wine to celebrate the parting banquet, and all made merry together.

On the following morning the Handsome King of the Apes rose very early, built him a raft of old pine trees and took a bamboo staff for a pole. Then he climbed on the raft, quite alone, and poled his way through the Great Sea. Wind and waves were favorable and he reached Asia. There he went ashore. On the strand he met a fisherman. He at once stepped up to him, knocked him down, tore off his clothes and put them on himself. Then he wandered around and visited all famous spots, went into the market-places, the densely populated cities, learned how to conduct himself properly, and how to speak and act like a well-bred human being. Yet his heart was set on learning the teaching of the Buddhas, the blessed spirits and the holy gods. But the people of the country in which he was were only concerned with honors and wealth. Not one of them seemed to care for life. Thus he went about until nine years had passed by unnoticed. Then he came to the strand of the Western Sea and it occurred to him: "No doubt there are gods and saints on the other side of the sea!" So he built another raft, floated it over the Western Sea and reached the land of the West. There he let his raft drift, and went ashore. After he had searched for many days, he suddenly saw a high mountain with deep, quiet valleys. As the Ape King went toward it, he heard a man singing in the woods, and the song sounded like one the blessed spirits might sing. So he hastily entered the wood to see who might be singing. There he met a wood-chopper at work. The Ape King bowed to him and said: "Venerable, divine master, I fall down and worship at your feet!" Said the wood-chopper: "I am only a workman; why do you call me divine master?" "Then, if you are no blessed god, how comes it you sing that divine song?" The wood-chopper laughed and said: "You are at home in music. The song I was singing was really taught me by a saint." "If you are acquainted with a saint," said the Ape King, "he surely cannot live far from here. I beg of you to show me the way to his dwelling." The wood-chopper replied: "It is not far from here. This mountain is known as the Mountain of the Heart. In it is a cave where dwells a saint who is called 'The Discerner'. The number of his disciples who have attained blessedness is countless. He still has some thirty to forty disciples gathered about him. You need only follow this path which leads to the South, and you cannot miss his dwelling." The Ape King thanked the wood-chopper and, sure enough, he came to the cave which the latter had described to him. The gate was locked and he did not venture to knock. So he leaped up into a pine tree, picked pine-cones and devoured the seed. Before long one of the saint's disciples came and opened the door and said: "What sort of a beast is it that is making such a noise?" The Ape King leaped down from his tree, bowed, and said: "I have come in search of truth. I did not venture to knock." Then the disciple had to laugh and said: "Our master was seated lost in meditation, when he told me to lead in the seeker after truth who stood without the gate, and here you really are. Well, you may come along with me!" The Ape King smoothed his clothes, put his hat on straight, and stepped in. A long passage led past magnificent buildings and quiet hidden huts to the place where the master was sitting upright on a seat of white marble. At his right and left stood his disciples, ready to serve him. The Ape King flung himself down on the ground and greeted the master humbly. In answer to his questions he told him how he had found his way to him. And when he was asked his name, he said: "I have no name. I am the ape who came out of the stone." So the master said: "Then I will give you a name. I name you Sun Wu Kung." The Ape King thanked him, full of joy, and thereafter he was called Sun Wu Kung. The master ordered his oldest disciple to instruct Sun Wu Kung in sweeping and cleaning, in going in and out, in good manners, how to labor in the field and how to water the gardens. In the course of time he learned to write, to burn incense and read the sutras. And in this way some six or seven years went by.

One day the master ascended the seat from which he taught, and began to speak regarding the great truth. Sun Wu Kung understood the hidden meaning of his words, and commenced to jerk about and dance in his joy. The master reproved him: "Sun Wu Kung, you have still not laid aside your wild nature! What do you mean by carrying on in such an unfitting manner?" Sun Wu Kung bowed and answered: "I was listening attentively to you when the meaning of your words was disclosed to my heart, and without thinking I began to dance for joy. I was not giving way to my wild nature." Said the master: "If your spirit has really awakened, then I will announce the great truth to you. But there are three hundred and sixty ways by means of which one may reach this truth. Which way shall I teach you?" Said Sun Wu Kung: "Whichever you will, O Master!" Then the Master asked: "Shall I teach you the way of magic?" Said Sun Wu Kung: "What does magic teach one?" The Master replied: "It teaches one to raise up spirits, to question oracles, and to foretell fortune and misfortune." "Can one secure eternal life by means of it?" inquired Sun Wu Kung. "No," was the answer. "Then I will not learn it." "Shall I teach you the sciences?" "What are the sciences?" "They are the nine schools of the three faiths. You learn how to read the holy books, pronounce incantations, commune with the gods, and call the saints to you." "Can one gain eternal life by means of them?" "No." "Then I will not learn them." "The way of repose is a very good way." "What is the way of repose?" "It teaches how to live without nourishment, how to remain quiescent in silent purity, and sit lost in meditation." "Can one gain eternal life in this way?" "No." "Then I will not learn it." "The way of deeds is also a good way." "What does that teach?" "It teaches one to equalize the vital powers, to practise bodily exercise, to prepare the elixir of life and to hold one's breath." "Will it give one eternal life?" "Not so." "Then I will not learn it! I will not learn it!" Thereupon the Master pretended to be angry, leaped down from his stand, took his cane and scolded: "What an ape! This he will not learn, and that he will not learn! What are you waiting to learn, then?" With that he gave him three blows across the head, retired to his inner chamber, and closed the great door after him.

The disciples were greatly excited, and overwhelmed Sun Wu Kung with reproaches. Yet the latter paid no attention to them, but smiled quietly to himself, for he had understood the riddle which the Master had given him to solve. And in his heart he thought: "His striking me over the head three times meant that I was to be ready at the third watch of the night. His withdrawing to his inner chamber and closing the great door after him, meant that I was to go in to him by the back door, and that he would make clear the great truth to me in secret." Accordingly he waited until evening, and made a pretense of lying down to sleep with the other disciples. But when the third watch of the night had come he rose softly and crept to the back door. Sure enough it stood ajar. He slipped in and stepped before the Master's bed. The Master was sleeping with his face turned toward the wall, and the ape did not venture to wake him, but knelt down in front of the bed. After a time the Master turned around and hummed a stanza to himself:

"A hard, hard grind,Truth's lesson to expound.One talks oneself deaf, dumb and blind,Unless the right man's found."

Then Sun Wu Kung replied: "I am waiting here reverentially!"

The Master flung on his clothes, sat up in bed and said harshly: "Accursed ape! Why are you not asleep? What are you doing here?"

Sun Wu Kung answered: "Yet you pointed out to me yesterday that I was to come to you at the third watch of the night, by the back door, in order to be instructed in the truth. Therefore I have ventured to come. If you will teach me in the fulness of your grace, I will be eternally grateful to you."

Thought the Master to himself: "There is real intelligence in this ape's head, to have made him understand me so well." Then he replied: "Sun Wu Kung, it shall be granted you! I will speak freely with you. Come quite close to me, and then I will show you the way to eternal life."

With that he murmured into his ear a divine, magical incantation to further the concentration of his vital powers, and explained the hidden knowledge word for word. Sun Wu Kung listened to him eagerly, and in a short time had learned it by heart. Then he thanked his teacher, went out again and lay down to sleep. From that time forward he practised the right mode of breathing, kept guard over his soul and spirit, and tamed the natural instincts of his heart. And while he did so three more years passed by. Then the task was completed.

One day the Master said to him: "Three great dangers still threaten you. Everyone who wishes to accomplish something out of the ordinary is exposed to them, for he is pursued by the envy of demons and spirits. And only those who can overcome these three great dangers live as long as the heavens."

Then Sun Wu Kung was frightened and asked: "Is there any means of protection against these dangers?"

Then the Master again murmured a secret incantation into his ear, by means of which he gained the power to transform himself seventy-two times.

And when no more than a few days had passed Sun Wu Kung had learned the art.

One day the Master was walking before the cave in the company of his disciples. He called Sun Wu Kung up to him and asked: "What progress have you made with your art? Can you fly already?"

"Yes, indeed," said the ape.

"Then let me see you do so."

The ape leaped into the air to a distance of five or six feet from the ground. Clouds formed beneath his feet, and he was able to walk on them for several hundred yards. Then he was forced to drop down to earth again.

The Master said with a smile: "I call that crawling around on the clouds, not floating on them, as do the gods and saints who fly over the whole world in a single day. I will teach you the magic incantation for turning somersaults on the clouds. If you turn one of those somersaults you advance eighteen thousand miles at a clip."

Sun Wu Kung thanked him, full of joy, and from that time on he was able to move without limitation of space in any direction.

One day Sun Wu Kung was sitting together with the other disciples under the pine-tree by the gate, discussing the secrets of their teachings. Finally they asked him to show them some of his transforming arts. Sun Wu Kung could not keep his secret to himself, and agreed to do so.

With a smile he said: "Just set me a task! What do you wish me to change myself into?"

They said: "Turn yourself into a pine-tree."

So Sun Wu Kung murmured a magic incantation, turned around – and there stood a pine-tree before their very eyes. At this they all broke out into a horse-laugh. The Master heard the noise and came out of the gate, dragging his cane behind him.

"Why are you making such a noise?" he called out to them harshly.

Said they: "Sun Wu Kung has turned himself into a pine-tree, and this made us laugh."

"Sun Wu Kung, come here!" said the Master. "Now just tell me what tricks you are up to? Why do you have to turn yourself into a pine-tree? All the work you have done means nothing more to you than a chance to make magic for your companions to wonder at. That shows that your heart is not yet under control."

Humbly Sun Wu Kung begged his forgiveness.

But the Master said: "I bear you no ill will, but you must go away."

With tears in his eyes Sun Wu Kung asked him: "But where shall I go?"

"You must go back again whence you came," said the Master. And when Sun Wu Kung sadly bade him farewell, he threatened him: "Your savage nature is sure to bring down evil upon you some time. You must tell no one that you are my pupil. If you so much as breathe a word about it, I will fetch your soul and lock it up in the nethermost hell, so that you cannot escape for a thousand eternities."

Sun Wu Kung replied: "I will not say a word! I will not say a word!"

Then he once more thanked him for all the kindness shown him, turned a somersault and climbed up to the clouds.

Within the hour he had passed the seas, and saw the Mountain of Flowers and Fruits lying before him. Then he felt happy and at home again, let his cloud sink down to earth and cried: "Here I am back again, children!" And at once, from the valley, from behind the rocks, out of the grass and from amid the trees came his apes. They came running up by thousands, surrounded and greeted him, and inquired as to his adventures. Sun Wu Kung said: "I have now found the way to eternal life, and need fear Death the Ancient no longer." Then all the apes were overjoyed, and competed with each other in bringing flowers and fruits, peaches and wine, to welcome him. And again they honored Sun Wu Kung as the Handsome Ape King.

Sun Wu Kung now gathered the apes about him and questioned them as to how they had fared during his absence.

Said they: "It is well that you have come back again, great king! Not long ago a devil came here who wanted to take possession of our cave by force. We fought with him, but he dragged away many of your children and will probably soon return."

Sun Wu Kung grew very angry and said: "What sort of a devil is this who dares be so impudent?"

The apes answered: "He is the Devil-King of Chaos. He lives in the North, who knows how many miles away. We only saw him come and go amid clouds and mist."

Sun Wu Kung said: "Wait, and I will see to him!" With that he turned a somersault and disappeared without a trace.

In the furthest North rises a high mountain, upon whose slope is a cave above which is the inscription: "The Cave of the Kidneys." Before the door little devils were dancing. Sun Wu Kung called harshly to them: "Tell your Devil-King quickly that he had better give me my children back again!" The little devils were frightened, and delivered the message in the cave. Then the Devil-King reached for his sword and came out. But he was so large and broad that he could not even see Sun Wu Kung. He was clad from head to foot in black armor, and his face was as black as the bottom of a kettle. Sun Wu Kung shouted at him: "Accursed devil, where are your eyes, that you cannot see the venerable Sun?" Then the devil looked to the ground and saw a stone ape standing before him, bare-headed, dressed in red, with a yellow girdle and black boots. So the Devil-King laughed and said: "You are not even four feet high, less than thirty years of age, and weaponless, and yet you venture to make such a commotion." Said Sun Wu Kung: "I am not too small for you; and I can make myself large at will. You scorn me because I am without a weapon, but my two fists can thresh to the very skies." With that he stooped, clenched his fists and began to give the devil a beating. The devil was large and clumsy, but Sun Wu Kung leaped about nimbly. He struck him between the ribs and between the wind and his blows fell ever more fast and furious. In his despair the devil raised his great knife and aimed a blow at Sun Wu Kung's head. But the latter avoided the blow, and fell back on his magic powers of transformation. He pulled out a hair, put it in his mouth, chewed it, spat it out into the air and said: "Transform yourself!" And at once it turned into many hundreds of little apes who began to attack the devil. Sun Wu Kung, be it said, had eighty-four thousand hairs on his body, every single one of which he could transform. The little apes with their sharp eyes, leaped around with the greatest rapidity. They surrounded the Devil-King on all sides, tore at his clothes, and pulled at his legs, until he finally measured his length on the ground. Then Sun Wu Kung stepped up, tore his knife from his hand, and put an end to him. After that he entered the cave and released his captive children, the apes. The transformed hairs he drew to him again, and making a fire, he burned the evil cave to the ground. Then he gathered up those he had released, and flew back with them like a storm-wind to his cavern on the Mountain of Flowers and Fruits, joyfully greeted by all the apes.

After Sun Wu Kung had obtained possession of the Devil-King's great knife, he exercised his apes every day. They had wooden swords and lances of bamboo, and played their martial music on reed pipes. He had them build a camp so that they would be prepared for all dangers. Suddenly the thought came to Sun Wu Kung: "If we go on this way, perhaps we may incite some human or animal king to fight with us, and then we would not be able to withstand him with our wooden swords and bamboo lances!" And to his apes he said: "What should be done?" Four baboons stepped forward and said: "In the capital city of the Aulai empire there are warriors without number. And there coppersmiths and steelsmiths are also to be found. How would it be if we were to buy steel and iron and have those smiths weld weapons for us?"

A somersault and Sun Wu Kung was standing before the city moat. Said he to himself: "To first buy the weapons would take a great deal of time. I would rather make magic and take some." So he blew on the ground. Then a tremendous storm-wind arose which drove sand and stones before it, and caused all the soldiers in the city to run away in terror. Then Sun Wu Kung went to the armory, pulled out one of his hairs, turned it into thousands of little apes, cleared out the whole supply of weapons, and flew back home on a cloud.

Then he gathered his people about him and counted them. In all they numbered seventy-seven thousand. They held the whole Mountain in terror, and all the magic beasts and spirit princes who dwelt on it. And these came forth from seventy-two caves and honored Sun Wu Kung as their head.

One day the Ape King said: "Now you all have weapons; but this knife which I took from the Devil-King is too light, and no longer suits me. What should be done?"

Then the four baboons stepped forward and said: "In view of your spirit powers, O king, you will find no weapon fit for your use on all the earth! Is it possible for you to walk through the water?"

The Ape King answered: "All the elements are subject to me and there is no place where I cannot go."

Then the baboons said: "The water at our cave here flows into the Great Sea, to the castle of the Dragon-King of the Eastern Sea. If your magic power makes it possible, you could go to the Dragon-King and let him give you a weapon."

This suited the Ape King. He leaped on the iron bridge and murmured an incantation. Then he flung himself into the waves, which parted before him and ran on till he came to the palace of water-crystal. There he met a Triton who asked who he was. He mentioned his name and said: "I am the Dragon-King's nearest neighbor, and have come to visit him." The Triton took the message to the castle, and the Dragon-King of the Eastern Sea came out hastily to receive him. He bade him be seated and served him with tea.

Sun Wu Kung said: "I have learned the hidden knowledge and gained the powers of immortality. I have drilled my apes in the art of warfare in order to protect our mountain; but I have no weapon I can use, and have therefore come to you to borrow one."

The Dragon-King now had General Flounder bring him a great spear. But Sun Wu Kung was not satisfied with it. Then he ordered Field-Marshal Eel to fetch in a nine-tined fork, which weighed three thousand six hundred pounds. But Sun Wu Kung balanced it in his hand and said: "Too light! Too light! Too light!"

Then the Dragon-King was frightened, and had the heaviest weapon in his armory brought in. It weighed seven thousand two hundred pounds. But this was still too light for Sun Wu Kung. The Dragon-King assured him that he had nothing heavier, but Sun Wu Kung would not give in and said: "Just look around!"

Finally the Dragon-Queen and her daughter came out, and said to the Dragon-King: "This saint is an unpleasant customer with whom to deal. The great iron bar is still lying here in our sea; and not so long ago it shone with a red glow, which is probably a sign it is time for it to be taken away."

Said the Dragon-King: "But that is the rod which the Great Yu used when he ordered the waters, and determined the depth of the seas and rivers. It cannot be taken away."

The Dragon-Queen replied: "Just let him see it! What he then does with it is no concern of ours."

So the Dragon-King led Sun Wu Kung to the measuring rod. The golden radiance that came from it could be seen some distance off. It was an enormous iron bar, with golden clamps on either side.

Sun Wu Kung raised it with the exertion of all his strength, and then said: "It is too heavy, and ought to be somewhat shorter and thinner!"

No sooner had he said this than the iron rod grew less. He tried it again, and then he noticed that it grew larger or smaller at command. It could be made to shrink to the size of a pin. Sun Wu Kung was overjoyed and beat about in the sea with the rod, which he had let grow large again, till the waves spurted mountain-high and the dragon-castle rocked on its foundations. The Dragon-King trembled with fright, and all his tortoises, fishes and crabs drew in their heads.

Sun Wu Kung laughed, and said: "Many thanks for the handsome present!" Then he continued: "Now I have a weapon, it is true, but as yet I have no armor. Rather than hunt up two or three other households, I think you will be willing to provide me with a suit of mail."

The Dragon-King told him that he had no armor to give him.

Then the ape said: "I will not leave until you have obtained one for me." And once more he began to swing his rod.

"Do not harm me!" said the terrified Dragon-King, "I will ask my brothers."

And he had them beat the iron drum and strike the golden gong, and in a moment's time all the Dragon-King's brothers came from all the other seas. The Dragon-King talked to them in private and said: "This is a terrible fellow, and we must not rouse his anger! First he took the rod with the golden clamps from me, and now he also insists on having a suit of armor. The best thing to do would be to satisfy him at once, and complain of him to the Lord of the Heavens later."

So the brothers brought a magic suit of golden mail, magic boots and a magic helmet.

Then Sun Wu Kung thanked them and returned to his cave. Radiantly he greeted his children, who had come to meet him, and showed them the rod with the golden clamps. They all crowded up and wished to pick it up from the ground, if only a single time; but it was just as though a dragon-fly had attempted to overthrow a stone column, or an ant were trying to carry a great mountain. It would not move a hair's breadth. Then the apes opened their mouths and stuck out their tongues, and said: "Father, how is it possible for you to carry that heavy thing?" So he told them the secret of the rod and showed them its effects. Then he set his empire in order, and appointed the four baboons field-marshals; and the seven beast-spirits, the ox-spirit, the dragon-spirit, the bird-spirit, the lion-spirit and the rest also joined him.

One day he took a nap after dinner. Before he did so he had let the bar shrink, and had stuck it in his ear. While he was sleeping he saw two men come along in his dream, who had a card on which was written "Sun Wu Kung." They would not allow him to resist, but fettered him and led his spirit away. And when they reached a great city the Ape King gradually came to himself. Over the city gate he saw a tablet of iron on which was engraved in large letters: "The Nether World."

Then all was suddenly clear to him and he said: "Why, this must be the dwelling-place of Death! But I have long since escaped from his power, and how dare he have me dragged here!" The more he reflected the wilder he grew. He drew out the golden rod from his ear, swung it and let it grow large. Then he crushed the two constables to mush, burst his fetters, and rolled his bar before him into the city. The ten Princes of the Dead were frightened, bowed before him and asked: "Who are you?"

Sun Wu Kung answered: "If you do not know me then why did you send for me and have me dragged to this place? I am the heaven-born saint Sun Wu Kung of the Mountain of Flowers and Fruits. And now, who are you? Tell me your names quickly or I will strike you!"

The ten Princes of the Dead humbly gave him their names.

Sun Wu Kung said: "I, the Venerable Sun, have gained the power of eternal life! You have nothing to say to me! Quick, let me have the Book of Life!"

They did not dare defy him, and had the scribe bring in the Book. Sun Wu Kung opened it. Under the head of "Apes," No. 1350, he read: "Sun Wu Kung, the heaven-born stone ape. His years shall be three hundred and twenty-four. Then he shall die without illness."

Sun Wu Kung took the brush from the table and struck out the whole ape family from the Book of Life, threw the Book down and said: "Now we are even! From this day on I will suffer no impertinences from you!"

With that he cleared a way for himself out of the Nether World by means of his rod, and the ten Princes of the Dead did not venture to stay him, but only complained of him afterward to the Lord of the Heavens.

When Sun Wu Kung had left the city he slipped and fell to the ground. This caused him to wake, and he noticed he had been dreaming. He called his four baboons to him and said: "Splendid, splendid! I was dragged to Death's castle and I caused considerable uproar there. I had them give me the Book of Life, and I struck out the mortal hour of all the apes!" And after that time the apes on the Mountain no longer died, because their names had been stricken out in the Nether World.

But the Lord of the Heavens sat in his castle, and had all his servants assembled about him. And a saint stepped forward and presented the complaint of the Dragon-King of the Eastern Sea. And another stepped forward and presented the complaint of the ten Princes of the Dead. The Lord of the Heavens glanced through the two memorials. Both told of the wild, unmannerly conduct of Sun Wu Kung. So the Lord of the Heavens ordered a god to descend to earth and take him prisoner. The Evening Star came forward, however, and said: "This ape was born of the purest powers of heaven and earth and sun and moon. He has gained the hidden knowledge and has become an immortal. Recall, O Lord, your great love for all that which has life, and forgive him his sin! Issue an order that he be called up to the heavens, and be given a charge here, so that he may come to his senses. Then, if he again oversteps your commands, let him be punished without mercy." The Lord of the Heavens was agreeable, had the order issued, and told the Evening Star to take it to Sun Wu Kung. The Evening Star mounted a colored cloud and descended on the Mountain of Flowers and Fruits.

He greeted Sun Wu Kung and said to him: "The Lord had heard of your actions and meant to punish you. I am the Evening Star of the Western Skies, and I spoke for you. Therefore he has commissioned me to take you to the skies, so that you may be given a charge there."

Sun Wu Kung was overjoyed and answered: "I had just been thinking I ought to pay Heaven a visit some time, and sure enough, Old Star, here you have come to fetch me!"

Then he had his four baboons come and said to them impressively: "See that you take good care of our Mountain! I am going up to the heavens to look around there a little!"

Then he mounted a cloud together with the Evening Star and floated up. But he kept turning his somersaults, and advanced so quickly that the Evening Star on his cloud was left behind. Before he knew it he had reached the Southern Gate of Heaven and was about to step carelessly through. The gate-keeper did not wish to let him enter, but he did not let this stop him. In the midst of their dispute the Evening Star came up and explained matters, and then he was allowed to enter the heavenly gate. When he came to the castle of the Lord of the Heavens, he stood upright before it, without bowing his head.

The Lord of the Heavens asked: "Then this hairy face with the pointed lips is Sun Wu Kung?"

He replied: "Yes, I am the Venerable Sun!"

All the servants of the Lord of the Heavens were shocked and said: "This wild ape does not even bow, and goes so far as to call himself the Venerable Sun. His crime deserves a thousand deaths!"

But the Lord said: "He has come up from the earth below, and is not as yet used to our rules. We will forgive him."

Then he gave orders that a charge be found for him. The marshal of the heavenly court reported: "There is no charge vacant anywhere, but an official is needed in the heavenly stables." Thereupon the Lord made him stablemaster of the heavenly steeds. Then the servants of the Lord of the Heavens told him he should give thanks for the grace bestowed on him. Sun Wu Kung called out aloud: "Thanks to command!" took possession of his certificate of appointment, and went to the stables in order to enter upon his new office.

Sun Wu Kung attended to his duties with great zeal. The heavenly steeds grew sleek and fat, and the stables were filled with young foals. Before he knew it half a month had gone by. Then his heavenly friends prepared a banquet for him.

While they were at table Sun Wu Kung asked accidentally: "Stablemaster? What sort of a title is that?"

"Why, that is an official title," was the reply.

"What rank has this office?"

"It has no rank at all," was the answer.

"Ah," said the ape, "is it so high that it outranks all other dignities?"

"No, it is not high, it is not high at all," answered his friends. "It is not even set down in the official roster, but is quite a subordinate position. All you have to do is to attend to the steeds. If you see to it that they grow fat, you get a good mark; but if they grow thin or ill, or fall down, your punishment will be right at hand."

Then the Ape King grew angry: "What, they treat me, the Venerable Sun, in such a shameful way!" and he started up. "On my Mountain I was a king, I was a father! What need was there for him to lure me into his heaven to feed horses? I'll do it no longer! I'll do it no longer!"

Hola, and he had already overturned the table, drawn the rod with the golden clamps from his ear, let it grow large and beat a way out for himself to the Southern gate of Heaven. And no one dared stop him.

Already he was back in his island Mountain and his people surrounded him and said: "You have been gone for more than ten years, great king! How is it you do not return to us until now?"

The Ape King said: "I did not spend more than about ten days in Heaven. This Lord of the Heavens does not know how to treat his people. He made me his stablemaster, and I had to feed his horses. I am so ashamed that I am ready to die. But I did not put up with it, and now I am here once more!"

His apes eagerly prepared a banquet to comfort him. While they sat at table two horned devil-kings came and brought him a yellow imperial robe as a present. Filled with joy he slipped into it, and appointed the two devil-kings leaders of the vanguard. They thanked him and began to flatter him: "With your power and wisdom, great king, why should you have to serve the Lord of the Heavens? To call you the Great Saint who is Heaven's Equal would be quite in order."

The ape was pleased with this speech and said: "Good, good!" Then he ordered his four baboons to have a flag made quickly, on which was to be inscribed: "The Great Saint Who Is Heaven's Equal." And from that time on he had himself called by that title.

When the Lord of the Heavens learned of the flight of the ape, he ordered Li Dsing,[2] the pagoda-bearing god, and his third son, Notscha, to take the Ape King prisoner. They sallied forth at the head of a heavenly warrior host, laid out a camp before his cave, and sent a brave warrior to challenge him to single combat. But he was easily beaten by Sun Wu Kung and obliged to flee, and Sun Wu Kung even shouted after him, laughing: "What a bag of wind! And he calls himself a heavenly warrior! I'll not slay you. Run along quickly and send me a better man!"

When Notscha saw this he himself hurried up to do battle.

Said Sun Wu Kung to him: "To whom do you belong, little one? You must not play around here, for something might happen to you!"

But Notscha cried out in a loud voice: "Accursed ape! I am Prince Notscha, and have been ordered to take you prisoner!" And with that he swung his sword in the direction of Sun Wu Kung.

"Very well," said the latter, "I will stand here and never move."

Then Notscha grew very angry, and turned into a three-headed god with six arms, in which he held six different weapons. Thus he rushed on to the attack.

Sun Wu Kung laughed. "The little fellow knows the trick of it! But easy, wait a bit! I will change shape, too!"

And he also turned himself into a figure with three heads and with six arms, and swung three gold-clamp rods. And thus they began to fight. Their blows rained down with such rapidity that it seemed as though thousands of weapons were flying through the air. After thirty rounds the combat had not yet been decided. Then Sun Wu Kung hit upon an idea. He secretly pulled out one of his hairs, turned it into his own shape, and let it continue the fight with Notscha. He himself, however, slipped behind Notscha, and gave him such a blow on the left arm with his rod that his knees gave way beneath him with pain, and he had to withdraw in defeat.

So Notscha told his father Li Dsing: "This devil-ape is altogether too powerful! I cannot get the better of him!" There was nothing left to do but to return to the Heavens and admit their overthrow. The Lord of the Heavens bowed his head, and tried to think of some other hero whom he might send out.

Then the Evening Star once more came forward and said: "This ape is so strong and so courageous, that probably not one of us here is a match for him. He revolted because the office of stablemaster appeared too lowly for him. The best thing would be to temper justice with mercy, let him have his way, and appoint him Great Saint Who Is Heaven's Equal. It will only be necessary to give him the empty title, without combining a charge with it, and then the matter would be settled." The Lord of the Heavens was satisfied with this suggestion, and once more sent the Evening Star to summon the new saint. When Sun Wu Kung heard that he had arrived, he said: "The old Evening Star is a good fellow!" and he had his army draw up in line to give him a festive reception. He himself donned his robes of ceremony and politely went out to meet him.

Then the Evening Star told him what had taken place in the Heavens, and that he had his appointment as Great Saint Who Is Heaven's Equal with him.

Thereupon the Great Saint laughed and said: "You also spoke in my behalf before, Old Star! And now you have again taken my part. Many thanks! Many thanks!"

Then when they appeared together in the presence of the Lord of the Heavens the latter said: "The rank of Great Saint Who Is Heaven's Equal is very high. But now you must not cut any further capers."

The Great Saint expressed his thanks, and the Lord of the Heavens ordered two skilled architects to build a castle for him East of the peach-garden of the Queen-Mother of the West. And he was led into it with all possible honors.

Now the Saint was in his element. He had all that heart could wish for, and was untroubled by any work. He took his ease, walked about in the Heavens as he chose, and paid visits to the gods. The Three Pure Ones and the Four Rulers he treated with some little respect; but the planetary gods and the lords of the twenty-eight houses of the moon, and of the twelve zodiac signs, and the other stars he addressed familiarly with a "Hey, you!" Thus he idled day by day, without occupation among the clouds of the Heavens. On one occasion one of the wise said to the Lord of the Heavens: "The holy Sun is idle while day follows day. It is to be feared that some mischievous thoughts may occur to him, and it might be better to give him some charge."

So the Lord of the Heavens summoned the Great Saint and said to him: "The life-giving peaches in the garden of the Queen-Mother will soon be ripe. I give you the charge of watching over them. Do your duty conscientiously!"

This pleased the Saint and he expressed his thanks. Then he went to the garden, where the caretakers and gardeners received him on their knees.

He asked them: "How many trees in all are there in the garden?"

"Three thousand six hundred," replied the gardener. "There are twelve-hundred trees in the foremost row. They have red blossoms and bear small fruit, which ripens every three thousand years. Whoever eats it grows bright and healthy. The twelve hundred trees in the middle row have double blossoms and bear sweet fruit, which ripens every six thousand years. Whoever eats of it is able to float in the rose-dawn without aging. The twelve hundred trees in the last row bear red-striped fruit with small pits. They ripen every nine thousand years. Whoever eats their fruit lives eternally, as long as the Heavens themselves, and remains untouched for thousands of eons."

The Saint heard all this with pleasure. He checked up the lists and from that time on appeared every day or so to see to things. The greater part of the peaches in the last row were already ripe. When he came to the garden, he would on each occasion send away the caretakers and gardeners under some pretext, leap up into the trees, and gorge himself to his heart's content with the peaches.

At that time the Queen-Mother of the West was preparing the great peach banquet to which she was accustomed to invite all the gods of the Heavens. She sent out the fairies in their garments of seven colors with baskets, that they might pick the peaches. The caretaker said to them: "The garden has now been entrusted to the guardianship of the Great Saint Who is Heaven's Equal, so you will first have to announce yourselves to him." With that he led the seven fairies into the garden. There they looked everywhere for the Great Saint, but could not find him. So the fairies said: "We have our orders and must not be late. We will begin picking the peaches in the meantime!" So they picked several baskets full from the foremost row. In the second row the peaches were already scarcer. And in the last row there hung only a single half-ripe peach. They bent down the bough and picked it, and then allowed it to fly up again.

Now it happened that the Great Saint, who had turned himself into a peach-worm, had just been taking his noon-day nap on this bough. When he was so rudely awakened, he appeared in his true form, seized his rod and was about to strike the fairies.

But the fairies said: "We have been sent here by the Queen-Mother. Do not be angry, Great Saint!"

Said the Great Saint: "And who are all those whom the Queen-Mother has invited?"

They answered: "All the gods and saints in the Heavens, on the earth and under the earth."

"Has she also invited me?" said the Saint.

"Not that we know of," said the fairies.

Then the Saint grew angry, murmured a magic incantation and said: "Stay! Stay! Stay!"

With that the seven fairies were banned to the spot. The Saint then took a cloud and sailed away on it to the palace of the Queen-Mother.

On the way he met the Bare-Foot God and asked him: "Where are you going?"

"To the peach banquet," was the answer.

Then the Saint lied to him, saying: "I have been commanded by the Lord of the Heavens to tell all the gods and saints that they are first to come to the Hall of Purity, in order to practise the rites, and then go together to the Queen-Mother."

Then the Great Saint changed himself into the semblance of the Bare-Foot God and sailed to the palace of the Queen-Mother. There he let his cloud sink down and entered quite unconcerned. The meal was ready, yet none of the gods had as yet appeared. Suddenly the Great Saint caught the aroma of wine, and saw well-nigh a hundred barrels of the precious nectar standing in a room to one side. His mouth watered. He tore a few hairs out and turned them into sleep-worms. These worms crept into the nostrils of the cup-bearers so that they all fell asleep. Thereupon he enjoyed the delicious viands to the full, opened the barrels and drank until he was nearly stupefied. Then he said to himself: "This whole affair is beginning to make me feel creepy. I had better go home first of all and sleep a bit." And he stumbled out of the garden with uncertain steps. Sure enough, he missed his way, and came to the dwelling of Laotzse. There he regained consciousness. He arranged his clothing and went in. There was no one to be seen in the place, for at the moment Laotzse was at the God of Light's abode, talking to him, and with him were all his servants, listening. Since he found no one at home the Great Saint went as far as the inner chamber, where Laotzse was in the habit of brewing the elixir of life. Beside the stove stood five gourd containers full of the pills of life which had already been rolled. Said the Great Saint: "I had long since intended to prepare a couple of these pills. So it suits me very well to find them here." He poured out the contents of the gourds, and ate up all the pills of life. Since he had now had enough to eat and drink he thought to himself: "Bad, bad! The mischief I have done cannot well be repaired. If they catch me my life will be in danger. I think I had better go down to earth again and remain a king!" With that he made himself invisible, went out at the Western Gate of Heaven, and returned to the Mountain of Flowers and Fruits, where he told his people who received him the story of his adventures.

When he spoke of the wine-nectar of the peach garden, his apes said: "Can't you go back once more and steal a few bottles of the wine, so that we too may taste of it and gain eternal life?"

The Ape King was willing, turned a somersault, crept into the garden unobserved, and picked up four more barrels. Two of them he took under his arms and two he held in his hands. Then he disappeared with them without leaving a trace and brought them to his cave, where he enjoyed them together with his apes.

In the meantime the seven fairies, whom the Great Saint had banned to the spot, had regained their freedom after a night and a day. They picked up their baskets and told the Queen-Mother what had happened to them. And the cup-bearers, too, came hurrying up and reported the destruction which someone unknown had caused among the eatables and drinkables. The Queen-Mother went to the Lord of the Heavens to complain. Shortly afterward Laotzse also came to him to tell about the theft of the pills of life. And the Bare-Foot God came along and reported that he had been deceived by the Great Saint Who Is Heaven's Equal; and from the Great Saint's palace the servants came running and said that the Saint had disappeared and was nowhere to be found. Then the Lord of the Heavens was frightened, and said: "This whole mess is undoubtedly the work of that devilish ape!"

Now the whole host of Heaven, together with all the star-gods, the time-gods and the mountain-gods was called out in order to catch the ape. Li Dsing once more was its commander-in-chief. He invested the entire Mountain, and spread out the sky-net and the earth-net, so that no one could escape. Then he sent his bravest heroes into battle. Courageously the ape withstood all attacks from early morn till sundown. But by that time his most faithful followers had been captured. That was too much for him. He pulled out a hair and turned it into thousands of Ape-Kings, who all hewed about them with golden-clamped iron rods. The heavenly host was vanquished, and the ape withdrew to his cave to rest.

Now it happened that Guan Yin[4] had also gone to the peach banquet in the garden, and had found out what Sun Wu Kung had done. When she went to visit the Lord of the Heavens, Li Dsing was just coming in, to report the great defeat which he had suffered on the Mountain of Flowers and Fruits. Then Guan Yin said to the Lord of the Heavens: "I can recommend a hero to you who will surely get the better of the ape. It is your grandson Yang Oerlang. He has conquered all the beast and bird spirits, and overthrown the elves in the grass and the brush. He knows what has to be done to get the better of such devils."

So Yang Oerlang was brought in, and Li Dsing led him to his camp. Li Dsing asked Yang Oerlang how he would go about getting the better of the ape.

Yang Oerlang laughed and said: "I think I will have to go him one better when it comes to changing shapes. It would be best for you to take away the sky-net so that our combat is not disturbed." Then he requested Li Dsing to post himself in the upper air with the magic spirit mirror in his hand, so that when the ape made himself invisible, he might be found again by means of the mirror. When all this had been arranged, Yang Oerlang went out in front of the cave with his spirits to give battle.

The ape leaped out, and when he saw the powerful hero with the three-tined sword standing before him he asked: "And who may you be?"

The other said: "I am Yang Oerlang, the grandson of the Lord of the Heavens!"

Then the ape laughed and said: "Oh yes, I remember! His daughter ran away with a certain Sir Yang, to whom heaven gave a son. You must be that son!"

Yang Oerlang grew furious, and advanced upon him with his spear. Then a hot battle began. For three hundred rounds they fought without decisive results. Then Yang Oerlang turned himself into a giant with a black face and red hair.

"Not bad," said the ape, "but I can do that too!"

So they continued to fight in that form. But the ape's baboons were much frightened. The beast and planet spirits of Yang Oerlang pressed the apes hard. They slew most of them and the others hid away. When the ape saw this his heart grew uneasy. He drew the magic giant-likeness in again, took his rod and fled. But Yang Oerlang followed hard on his heels. In his urgent need the ape thrust the rod, which he had turned into a needle, into his ear, turned into a sparrow, and flew up into the crest of a tree. Yang Oerlang who was following in his tracks, suddenly lost sight of him. But his keen eyes soon recognized that he had turned himself into a sparrow. So he flung away spear and crossbow, turned himself into a sparrow-hawk, and darted down on the sparrow. But the latter soared high into the air as a cormorant. Yang Oerlang shook his plumage, turned into a great sea-crane, and shot up into the clouds to seize the cormorant. The latter dropped, flew into a valley and dove beneath the waters of a brook in the guise of a fish. When Yang Oerlang reached the edge of the valley, and had lost his trail he said to himself: "This ape has surely turned himself into a fish or a crab! I will change my form as well in order to catch him." So he turned into a fish-hawk and floated above the surface of the water. When the ape in the water caught sight of the fish-hawk, he saw that he was Yang Oerlang. He swiftly swung around and fled, Yang Oerlang in pursuit. When the latter was no further away than the length of a beak, the ape turned, crept ashore as a water-snake and hid in the grass. Yang Oerlang, when he saw the water-snake creep from the water, turned into an eagle and spread his claws to seize the snake. But the water-snake sprang up and turned into the lowest of all birds, a speckled buzzard, and perched on the steep edge of a cliff. When Yang Oerlang saw that the ape had turned himself into so contemptible a creature as a buzzard, he would no longer play the game of changing form with him. He reappeared in his original form, took up his crossbow and shot at the bird. The buzzard slipped and fell down the side of the cliff. At its foot the ape turned himself into the chapel of a field-god. He opened his mouth for a gate, his teeth became the two wings of the door, his tongue the image of the god, and his eyes the windows. His tail was the only thing he did not know what to do with. So he let it stand up stiffly behind him in the shape of a flagpole. When Yang Oerlang reached the foot of the hill he saw the chapel, whose flagpole stood in the rear. Then he laughed and said: "That ape is really a devil of an ape! He wants to lure me into the chapel in order to bite me. But I will not go in. First I will break his windows for him, and then I will stamp down the wings of his door!" When the ape heard this he was much frightened. He made a bound like a tiger, and disappeared without a trace in the air. With a single somersault he reached Yang Oerlang's own temple. There he assumed Yang Oerlang's own form and stepped in. The spirits who were on guard were unable to recognize him. They received him on their knees. So the ape then seated himself on the god's throne, and had the prayers which had come in submitted to him.

When Yang Oerlang no longer saw the ape, he rose in the air to Li Dsing and said: "I was vying with the ape in changing shape. Suddenly I could no longer find him. Take a look in the mirror!" Li Dsing took a look in the magic spirit mirror and then he laughed and said: "The ape has turned himself into your likeness, is sitting in your temple quite at home there, and making mischief." When Yang Oerlang heard this he took his three-tined spear, and hastened to his temple. The door-spirits were frightened and said: "But father came in only this very minute! How is it that another one comes now?" Yang Oerlang, without paying attention to them, entered the temple and aimed his spear at Sun Wu Kung. The latter resumed his own shape, laughed and said: "Young sir, you must not be angry! The god of this place is now Sun Wu Kung." Without uttering a word Yang Oerlang assailed him. Sun Wu Kung took up his rod and returned the blows. Thus they crowded out of the temple together, fighting, and wrapped in mists and clouds once more gained the Mountain of Flowers and Fruits.

In the meantime Guan Yin was sitting with Laotzse, the Lord of the Heavens and the Queen-Mother in the great hall of Heaven, waiting for news. When none came she said: "I will go with Laotzse to the Southern Gate of Heaven and see how matters stand." And when they saw that the struggle had still not come to an end she said to Laotzse: "How would it be if we helped Yang Oerlang a little? I will shut up Sun Wu Kung in my vase."

But Laotzse said: "Your vase is made of porcelain. Sun Wu Kung could smash it with his iron rod. But I have a circlet of diamonds which can enclose all living creatures. That we can use!" So he flung his circlet through the air from the heavenly gate, and struck Sun Wu Kung on the head with it. Since he had his hands full fighting, the latter could not guard himself against it, and the blow on the forehead caused him to slip. Yet he rose again and tried to escape. But the heavenly hound of Yang Oerlang bit his leg until he fell to the ground. Then Yang Oerlang and his followers came up and tied him with thongs, and thrust a hook through his collar-bone so that he could no longer transform himself. And Laotzse took possession of his diamond circlet again, and returned with Guan Yin to the hall of Heaven. Sun Wu Kung was now brought in in triumph, and was condemned to be beheaded. He was then taken to the place of execution and bound to a post. But all efforts to kill him by means of ax and sword, thunder and lightning were vain. Nothing so much as hurt a hair on his head.

Said Laotzse: "It is not surprising. This ape has eaten the peaches, has drunk the nectar and also swallowed the pills of life. Nothing can harm him. The best thing would be for me to take him along and thrust him into my stove in order to melt the elixir of life out of him again. Then he will fall into dust and ashes."

So Sun Wu Kung's fetters were loosed, and Laotzse took him with him, thrust him into his oven, and ordered the boy to keep up a hot fire.

But along the edge of the oven were graven the signs of the eight elemental forces.[5] And when the ape was thrust into the oven he took refuge beneath the sign of the wind, so that the fire could not injure him; and the smoke only made his eyes smart. He remained in the oven seven times seven days. Then Laotzse had it opened to take a look. As soon as Sun Wu Kung saw the light shine in, he could no longer bear to be shut up, but leaped out and upset the magic oven. The guards and attendants he threw to the ground and Laotzse himself, who tried to seize him, received such a push that he stuck his legs up in the air like an onion turned upside down. Then Sun Wu Kung took his rod out of his ear, and without looking where he struck, hewed everything to bits, so that the star-gods closed their doors and the guardians of the Heavens ran away. He came to the castle of the Lord of the Heavens, and the guardian of the gate with his steel whip was only just in time to hold him back. Then the thirty-six thunder gods were set at him, and surrounded him, though they could not seize him.

The Lord of the Heavens said: "Buddha[6] will know what is to be done. Send for him quickly!"

So Buddha came up out of the West with Ananada and Kashiapa, his disciples. When he saw the turmoil he said: "First of all, let weapons be laid aside and lead out the Saint. I wish to speak with him!" The gods withdrew. Sun Wu Kung snorted and said: "Who are you, who dare to speak to me?" Buddha smiled and replied: "I have come out of the blessed West, Shakiamuni Amitofu. I have heard of the revolt you have raised, and am come to tame you!"

Said Sun Wu Kung: "I am the stone ape who has gained the hidden knowledge. I am master of seventy-two transformations, and will live as long as Heaven itself. What has the Lord of the Heavens accomplished that entitles him to remain eternally on his throne? Let him make way for me, and I will be satisfied!"

Buddha replied with a smile: "You are a beast which has gained magic powers. How can you expect to rule here as Lord of the Heavens? Be it known to you that the Lord of the Heavens has toiled for eons in perfecting his virtues. How many years would you have to pass before you could attain the dignity he has gained? And then I must ask you whether there is anything else you can do, aside from playing your tricks of transformation?"

Said Sun Wu Kung: "I can turn cloud somersaults. Each one carries me eighteen thousand miles ahead. Surely that is enough to entitle me to be the Lord of the Heavens?"

Buddha answered with a smile: "Let us make a wager. If you can so much as leave my hand with one of your somersaults, then I will beg the Lord of the Heavens to make way for you. But if you are not able to leave my hand, then you must yield yourself to my fetters."

Sun Wu Kung suppressed his laughter, for he thought: "This Buddha is a crazy fellow! His hand is not a foot long; how could I help but leap out of it?" So he opened his mouth wide and said: "Agreed!"

Buddha then stretched out his right hand. It resembled a small lotus-leaf. Sun Wu Kung leaped up into it with one bound. Then he said: "Go!" And with that he turned one somersault after another, so that he flew along like a whirlwind. And while he was flying along he saw five tall, reddish columns towering to the skies. Then he thought: "That is the end of the world! Now I will turn back and become Lord of the Heavens. But first I will write down my name to prove that I was there." He pulled out a hair, turned it into a brush, and wrote with great letters on the middle column: "The Great Saint Who Is Heaven's Equal." Then he turned his somersaults again until he had reached the place whence he had come. He leaped down from the Buddha's hand laughing and cried: "Now hurry, and see to it that the Lord of the Heavens clears his heavenly castle for me! I have been at the end of the world and have left a sign there!"

Buddha scolded: "Infamous ape! How dare you claim that you have left my hand? Take a look and see whether or not 'The Great Saint Who Is Heaven's Equal', is written on my middle finger!"

Sun Wu Kung was terribly frightened, for at the first glance he saw that this was the truth. Yet outwardly he pretended that he was not convinced, said he would take another look, and tried to make use of the opportunity to escape. But Buddha covered him with his hand, shoved him out of the gate of Heaven, and formed a mountain of water, fire, wood, earth and metal, which he softly set down on him to hold him fast. A magic incantation pasted on the mountain prevented his escape.

Here he was obliged to lie for hundreds of years, until he finally reformed and was released, in order to help the Monk of the Yangtze-kiang[7] fetch the holy writings from out of the West. He honored the Monk as his master, and thenceforward was known as the Wanderer. Guan Yin, who had released him, gave the Monk a golden circlet. Sun Wu Kung was induced to put it on, and it at once grew into his flesh so that he could not remove it. And Guan Yin gave the Monk a magic formula by means of which the ring could be tightened, should the ape grow disobedient. But from that time on he was always polite and well-mannered.

Footnotes for 'The Ape Sun Wu Kung'

1. This tale, like 'The Pilgrim's Progress', is an allegory, the ape symbolizing the human heart.
2. As regards Li Dsing and Notscha, see 'Notscha' (page 175).
3. As regards Yang Oerlang, see 'Yang Oerlang' (page 174).
4. Guan Yin is generally worshipped throughout China as the Feminine goddess. The motive of the magic flight is found frequently in fairy-tales the world over. Guan Yin is often represented holding a vase, Bau Ping. Laotzse's circlet or ring is the Tao.
5. The eight elemental powers, i.e., Ba Gua.
6. Buddha: while Sun Wu Kung is equipped to struggle against all external powers, he is conquered by Buddha, who does not combat him, but subdues him by his omnipresence.
7. The Monk of the Yangtze-kiang is Huan Dschuang, see 'The Monk of the Yangtze-Kiang' (page 414).

The Frog Princess

THERE WHERE THE Yangtze-kiang has come about half-way on its course to the sea, the Frog King is worshiped with great devotion. He has a temple there and frogs by the thousand are to be found in the neighborhood, some of them of enormous size. Those who incur the wrath of the god are apt to have strange visitations in their homes. Frogs hop about on tables and beds, and in extreme cases they even creep up the smooth walls of the room without falling. There are various kinds of omens, but all indicate that some misfortune threatens the house in question. Then the people living in it become terrified, slaughter a cow and offer it as a sacrifice. Thus the god is mollified and nothing further happens.

In that part of the country there once lived a youth named Sia Kung-Schong. He was handsome and intelligent. When he was some six or seven years of age, a serving-maid dressed in green entered his home. She said that she was a messenger from the Frog King, and declared that the Frog King wished to have his daughter marry young Sia. Old Sia was an honest man, not very bright, and since this did not suit him, he declined the offer on the plea that his son was still too young to marry. In spite of this, however, he did not dare look about for another mate for him.

Then a few years passed and the boy gradually grew up. A marriage between him and a certain Mistress Giang was decided upon.

But the Frog King sent word to Mistress Giang: "Young Sia is my son-in-law. How dare you undertake to lay claim to what does not belong to you!" Then Father Giang was frightened, and took back his promise.

This made Old Sia very sad. He prepared a sacrifice and went to his temple to pray. He explained that he felt unworthy of becoming the relation of a god. When he had finished praying a multitude of enormous maggots made their appearance in the sacrificial meat and wine, and crawled around. He poured them out, begged forgiveness, and returned home filled with evil forebodings. He did not know what more he could do, and had to let things take their course.

One day young Sia went out into the street. A messenger stepped up to him and told him, on the part of the Frog King that the latter urgently requested Sia to come to him. There was no help for it; he had to follow the messenger. He led him through a red gateway into some magnificent, high-ceilinged rooms. In the great hall sat an ancient man who might have been some eighty years of age. Sia cast himself down on the ground before him in homage. The old man bade him rise, and assigned him a place at the table. Soon a number of girls and women came crowding in to look at him. Then the old man turned to them and said: "Go to the room of the bride and tell her that the bridegroom has arrived!"

Quickly a couple of maids ran away, and shortly after an old woman came from the inner apartments, leading a maiden by the hand, who might have been sixteen years of age, and was incomparably beautiful. The old man pointed to her and said: "This is my tenth little daughter. It seemed to me that you would make a good pair. But your father has scorned us because of our difference in race. Yet one's marriage is a matter that is of life-long importance. Our parents can determine it only in part. In the end it rests mainly with one's self."

Sia looked steadily at the girl, and a fondness for her grew in his heart. He sat there in silence. The old man continued: "I knew very well that the young gentleman would agree. Go on ahead of us, and we will bring you your bride!"

Sia said he would, and hurried to inform his father. His father did not know what to do in his excitement. He suggested an excuse and wanted to send Sia back to decline his bride with thanks. But this Sia was not willing to do. While they were arguing the matter, the bride's carriage was already at the door. It was surrounded by a crowd of greencoats, and the lady entered the house, and bowed politely to her parents-in-law. When the latter saw her they were both pleased, and the wedding was announced for that very evening.

The new couple lived in peace and good understanding. And after they had been married their divine parents-in-law often came to their house. When they appeared dressed in red, it meant that some good fortune was to befall them; when they came dressed in white, it signified that they were sure to make some gain. Thus, in the course of time, the family became wealthy.

But since they had become related to the gods the rooms, courtyards and all other places were always crowded with frogs. And no one ventured to harm them. Sia Kung-Schong alone was young and showed no consideration. When he was in good spirits he did not bother them, but when he got out of sorts he knew no mercy, and purposely stepped on them and killed them.

In general his young wife was modest and obedient; yet she easily lost her temper. She could not approve her husband's conduct. But Sia would not do her the favor to give up his brutal habit. So she scolded him because of it and he grew angry.

"Do you imagine," he told her, "that because your parents can visit human beings with misfortune, that a real man would be afraid of a frog?"

His wife carefully avoided uttering the word "frog," hence his speech angered her and she said: "Since I have dwelt in your house your fields have yielded larger crops, and you have obtained the highest selling prices. And that is something after all. But now, when young and old, you are comfortably established, you wish to act like the fledgling owl, who picks out his own mother's eyes as soon as he is able to fly!"

Sia then grew still more angry and answered: "These gifts have been unwelcome to me for a long time, for I consider them unclean. I could never consent to leave such property to sons and grandsons. It would be better if we parted at once!"

So he bade his wife leave the house, and before his parents knew anything about it, she was gone. His parents scolded him and told him to go at once and bring her back. But he was filled with rage, and would not give in to them.

That same night he and his mother fell sick. They felt weak and could not eat. The father, much worried, went to the temple to beg for pardon. And he prayed so earnestly that his wife and son recovered in three days' time. And the Frog Princess also returned, and they lived together happily and contented as before.

But the young woman sat in the house all day long, occupied solely with her ornaments and her rouge, and did not concern herself with sewing and stitching. So Sia Kung-Schong's mother still had to look out for her son's clothes.

One day his mother was angry and said: "My son has a wife, and yet I have to do all the work! In other homes the daughter-in-law serves her mother-in-law. But in our house the mother-in-law must serve the daughter-in-law."

This the princess accidentally heard. In she came, much excited, and began: "Have I ever omitted, as is right and proper, to visit you morning and evening? My only fault is that I will not burden myself with all this toil for the sake of saving a trifling sum of money!" The mother answered not a word, but wept bitterly and in silence because of the insult offered her.

Her son came along and noticed that his mother had been weeping. He insisted on knowing the reason, and found out what had happened. Angrily he reproached his wife. She raised objections and did not wish to admit that she had been in the wrong. Finally Sia said: "It is better to have no wife at all than one who gives her mother-in-law no pleasure. What can the old frog do to me after all, if I anger him, save call misfortunes upon me and take my life!" So he once more drove his wife out of the house.

The princess left her home and went away. The following day fire broke out in the house, and spread to several other buildings. Tables, beds, everything was burned.

Sia, in a rage because of the fire, went to the temple to complain: "To bring up a daughter in such a way that she does not please her parents-in-law shows that there is no discipline in a house. And now you even encourage her in her faults. It is said the gods are most just. Are there gods who teach men to fear their wives? Incidentally, the whole quarrel rests on me alone. My parents had nothing to do with it. If I was to be punished by the ax and cord, well and good. You could have carried out the punishment yourself. But this you did not do. So now I will burn your own house in order to satisfy my own sense of justice!"

With these words he began piling up brush-wood before the temple, struck sparks and wanted to set it ablaze. The neighbors came streaming up, and pleaded with him. So he swallowed his rage and went home.

When his parents heard of it, they grew pale with a great fear. But at night the god appeared to the people of a neighboring village, and ordered them to rebuild the house of his son-in-law. When day began to dawn they dragged up building-wood and the workmen all came in throngs to build for Sia. No matter what he said he could not prevent them. All day long hundreds of workmen were busy. And in the course of a few days all the rooms had been rebuilt, and all the utensils, curtains and furniture were there as before. And when the work had been completed the princess also returned. She climbed the stairs to the great room, and acknowledged her fault with many tender and loving words. Then she turned to Sia Kung-Schong, and smiled at him sideways. Instead of resentment joy now filled the whole house. And after that time the princess was especially peaceable. Two whole years passed without an angry word being said.

But the princess had a great dislike for snakes. Once, by way of a joke, young Sia put a small snake into a parcel, which he gave her and told her to open. She turned pale and reproached him. Then Sia-Kung-Schong also took his jest seriously, and angry words passed.

At last the princess said: "This time I will not wait for you to turn me out. Now we are finally done with one another!" And with that she walked out of the door.

Father Sia grew very much alarmed, beat his son himself with his staff, and begged the god to be kind and forgive. Fortunately there were no evil consequences. All was quiet and not a sound was heard.

Thus more than a year passed. Sia-Kung-Schong longed for the princess and took himself seriously to task. He would creep in secret to the temple of the god, and lament because he had lost the princess. But no voice answered him. And soon afterward he even heard that the god had betrothed his daughter to another man. Then he grew hopeless at heart, and thought of finding another wife for himself. Yet no matter how he searched he could find none who equalled the princess. This only increased his longing for her, and he went to the home of the Yuans, to a member of which family it was said she had been promised. There they had already painted the walls, and swept the courtyard, and all was in readiness to receive the bridal carriage. Sia was overcome with remorse and discontent. He no longer ate, and fell ill. His parents were quite stunned by the anxiety they felt on his account, and were incapable of helpful thought.

Suddenly while he was lying there only half-conscious, he felt someone stroke him, and heard a voice say: "And how goes it with our real husband, who insisted on turning out his wife?"

He opened his eyes and it was the princess.

Full of joy he leaped up and said: "How is it you have come back to me?" The princess answered: "To tell the truth, according to your own habit of treating people badly, I should have followed my father's advice and taken another husband. And, as a matter of fact, the wedding gifts of the Yuan family have been lying in my home for a long time. But I thought and thought and could not bring myself to do so. The wedding was to have been this evening and my father thought it shameful to have the wedding gifts carried back. So I took the things myself and placed them before the Yuan's door. When I went out my father ran out beside me: 'You insane girl,' he said, 'so you will not listen to what I say! If you are ill-treated by Sia in the future I wash my hands of it. Even if they kill you you shall not come home to me again!'"

Moved by her faithfulness the tears rolled from Sia's eyes. The servants, full of joy, hurried to the parents to acquaint them with the good news. And when they heard it they did not wait for the young people to come to them, but hastened themselves to their son's rooms, took the princess by the hand and wept. Young Sia, too, had become more settled by this time, and was no longer so mischievous. So he and his wife grew to love each other more sincerely day by day.

Once the princess said to him: "Formerly, when you always treated me so badly, I feared that we would not keep company into our old age. So I never asked heaven to send us a child. But now that all has changed, and I will beg the gods for a son."

And, sure enough, before long Sia's parents-in-law appeared in the house clad in red garments, and shortly after heaven sent the happy pair two sons instead of one.

From that time on their intercourse with the Frog-King was never interrupted. When someone among the people had angered the god, he first tried to induce young Sia to speak for him, and sent his wife and daughter to the Frog Princess to implore her aid. And if the princess laughed, then all would be well.

The Sia family has many descendants, whom the people call "the little frog men."[1] Those who are near them do not venture to call them by this name, but those standing further off do so.

Footnotes for 'The Frog Princess'

1. "Little frog men", Wa Dsi, is the derogatory name which the North Chinese give the Chinese of the South on occasion.

The Cave Of The Beasts

ONCE UPON A TIME there was a family in which there were seven daughters. One day when the father went out to gather wood, he found seven wild duck eggs. He brought them home, but did not think of giving any to his children, intending to eat them himself, with his wife. In the evening the oldest daughter woke up, and asked her mother what she was cooking. The mother said: "I am cooking wild duck eggs. I will give you one, but you must not let your sisters know." And so she gave her one. Then the second daughter woke up, and asked her mother what she was cooking. She said: "Wild duck eggs. If you will not tell your sisters, I'll give you one." And so it went. At last the daughters had eaten all the eggs, and there were none left.

In the morning the father was very angry with the children, and said: "Who wants to go along to grandmother?" But he intended to lead the children into the mountains, and let the wolves devour them there. The older daughters suspected this, and said: "We are not going along!" But the two younger ones said: "We will go with you." And so they drove off with their father. After they had driven a good ways, they asked: "Will we soon get to grandmother's house?" "Right away," said their father. And when they had reached the mountains he told them: "Wait here. I will drive into the village ahead of you, and tell grandmother that you are coming." And then he drove off with the donkey-cart. They waited and waited, but their father did not come. At last they decided that their father would not come back to fetch them, and that he had left them alone in the mountains. So they went further and further into the hills seeking a shelter for the night. Then they spied a great stone. This they selected for a pillow, and rolled it over to the place where they were going to lie down to sleep. And then they saw that the stone was the door to a cave. There was a light in the cave, and they went into it. The light they had seen came from the many precious stones and jewels of every sort in the cave, which belonged to a wolf and a fox. They had a number of jars of precious stones and pearls that shone by night. The girls said: "What a lovely cave this is! We will lie right down and go to bed." For there stood two golden beds with gold-embroidered covers. So they lay down and fell asleep. During the night the wolf and fox came home. And the wolf said: "I smell human flesh!" But the fox replied: "Oh, nonsense! There are no human beings who can enter our cave. We lock it up too well for that." The wolf said: "Very well, then let us lie down in our beds and sleep." But the fox answered: "Let us curl up in the kettles on the hearth. They still hold a little warmth from the fire." The one kettle was of gold and the other of silver, and they curled up in them.

When the girls rose early in the morning, they saw the wolf and the fox lying there, and were much frightened. And they put the covers on the kettles and heaped a number of big stones on them, so that the wolf and the fox could not get out again. Then they made a fire. The wolf and the fox said: "Oh, how nice and warm it is this morning! How does that happen?" But at length it grew too hot for them. Then they noticed that the two girls had kindled a fire and they cried: "Let us out! We will give you lots of precious stones, and lots of gold, and will do you no harm!" But the girls would not listen to them, and kept on making a bigger fire. So that was the end of the wolf and the fox in the kettles.

Then the girls lived happily for a number of days in the cave. But their father was seized with a longing for his daughters, and he went into the mountains to look for them. And he sat right down on the stone in front of the cave to rest, and tapped his pipe against it to empty the ashes. Then the girls within called out: "Who is knocking at our door?" And the father said: "Are those not my daughters' voices?" While the daughters replied: "Is that not our father's voice?" Then they pushed aside the stone and saw that it was their father, and their father was glad to see them once more. He was much surprised to think that they should have chanced on this cave full of precious stones, and they told him the whole story. Then their father fetched people to help him carry home the jewels. And when they got home, his wife wondered where he had obtained all these treasures. So the father and daughters told her everything, and they became a very wealthy family, and lived happily to the end of their days.

The Golden Beetle, or Why the Dog Hates the Cat

"WHAT WE SHALL eat tomorrow, I haven't the slightest idea!" said Widow Wang to her eldest son, as he started out one morning in search of work.

"Oh, the gods will provide. I'll find a few coppers somewhere," replied the boy, trying to speak cheerfully, although in his heart he also had not the slightest idea in which direction to turn.

The winter had been a hard one: extreme cold, deep snow, and violent winds. The Wang house had suffered greatly. The roof had fallen in, weighed down by heavy snow. Then a hurricane had blown a wall over, and Ming-li, the son, up all night and exposed to a bitter cold wind, had caught pneumonia. Long days of illness followed, with the spending of extra money for medicine. All their scant savings had soon melted away, and at the shop where Ming-li had been employed his place was filled by another. When at last he arose from his sick-bed he was too weak for hard labour and there seemed to be no work in the neighbouring villages for him to do. Night after night he came home, trying not to be discouraged, but in his heart feeling the deep pangs of sorrow that come to the good son who sees his mother suffering for want of food and clothing.

"Bless his good heart!" said the poor widow after he had gone. "No mother ever had a better boy. I hope he is right in saying the gods will provide. It has been getting so much worse these past few weeks that it seems now as if my stomach were as empty as a rich man's brain. Why, even the rats have deserted our cottage, and there's nothing left for poor Tabby, while old Blackfoot is nearly dead from starvation."

When the old woman referred to the sorrows of her pets, her remarks were answered by a pitiful mewing and woebegone barking from the corner where the two unfed creatures were curled up together trying to keep warm.

Just then there was a loud knocking at the gate. When the widow Wang called out, "Come in!" she was surprised to see an old bald-headed priest standing in the doorway. "Sorry, but we have nothing," she went on, feeling sure the visitor had come in search of food. "We have fed on scraps these two weeks – on scraps and scrapings – and now we are living on the memories of what we used to have when my son's father was living. Our cat was so fat she couldn't climb to the roof. Now look at her. You can hardly see her, she's so thin. No, I'm sorry we can't help you, friend priest, but you see how it is."

"I didn't come for alms," cried the clean-shaven one, looking at her kindly, "but only to see what I could do to help you. The gods have listened long to the prayers of your devoted son. They honour him because he has not waited till you die to do sacrifice for you. They have seen how faithfully he has served you ever since his illness, and now, when he is worn out and unable to work, they are resolved to reward him for his virtue. You likewise have been a good mother and shall receive the gift I am now bringing."

"What do you mean?" faltered Mrs. Wang, hardly believing her ears at hearing a priest speak of bestowing mercies. "Have you come here to laugh at our misfortunes?"

"By no means. Here in my hand I hold a tiny golden beetle which you will find has a magic power greater than any you ever dreamed of. I will leave this precious thing with you, a present from the god of filial conduct."

"Yes, it will sell for a good sum," murmured the other, looking closely at the trinket, "and will give us millet for several days. Thanks, good priest, for your kindness."

"But you must by no means sell this golden beetle, for it has the power to fill your stomachs as long as you live."

The widow stared in open-mouthed wonder at the priest's surprising words.

"Yes, you must not doubt me, but listen carefully to what I tell you. Whenever you wish food, you have only to place this ornament in a kettle of boiling water, saying over and over again the names of what you want to eat. In three minutes take off the lid, and there will be your dinner, smoking hot, and cooked more perfectly than any food you have ever eaten."

"May I try it now?" she asked eagerly.

"As soon as I am gone."

When the door was shut, the old woman hurriedly kindled a fire, boiled some water, and then dropped in the golden beetle, repeating these words again and again:

"Dumplings, dumplings, come to me,
I am thin as thin can be.
Dumplings, dumplings, smoking hot,
Dumplings, dumplings, fill the pot."

Would those three minutes never pass? Could the priest have told the truth? Her old head was nearly wild with excitement as clouds of steam rose from the kettle. Off came the lid! She could wait no longer. Wonder of wonders! There before her unbelieving eyes was a pot, full to the brim of pork dumplings, dancing up and down in the bubbling water, the best, the most delicious dumplings she had ever tasted. She ate and ate till there was no room left in her greedy stomach, and then she feasted the cat and the dog until they were ready to burst.

"Good fortune has come at last," whispered Blackfoot, the dog, to Whitehead, the cat, as they lay down to sun themselves outside. "I fear I couldn't have held out another week without running away to look for food. I don't know just what's happened, but there's no use questioning the gods."

Mrs. Wang fairly danced for joy at the thought of her son's return and of how she would feast him.

"Poor boy, how surprised he will be at our fortune – and it's all on account of his goodness to his old mother."

When Ming-li came, with a dark cloud overhanging his brow, the widow saw plainly that disappointment was written there.

"Come, come, lad!" she cried cheerily, "clear up your face and smile, for the gods have been good to us and I shall soon show you how richly your devotion has been rewarded." So saying, she dropped the golden beetle into the boiling water and stirred up the fire.

Thinking his mother had gone stark mad for want of food, Ming-li stared solemnly at her. Anything was preferable to this misery. Should he sell his last outer garment for a few pennies and buy millet for her? Blackfoot licked his hand comfortingly, as if to say, "Cheer up, master, fortune has turned in our favour." Whitehead leaped upon a bench, purring like a sawmill.

Ming-li did not have long to wait. Almost in the twinkling of an eye he heard his mother crying out,

"Sit down at the table, son, and eat these dumplings while they are smoking hot."

Could he have heard correctly? Did his ears deceive him? No, there on the table was a huge platter full of the delicious pork dumplings he liked better than anything else in all the world, except, of course, his mother.

"Eat and ask no questions," counselled the Widow Wang. "When you are satisfied I will tell you everything."

Wise advice! Very soon the young man's chopsticks were twinkling like a little star in the verses. He ate long and happily, while his good mother watched him, her heart overflowing with joy at seeing him at last able to satisfy his hunger. But still the old woman could hardly wait for him to finish, she was so anxious to tell him her wonderful secret.

"Here, son!" she cried at last, as he began to pause between mouthfuls, "look at my treasure!" And she held out to him the golden beetle.

"First tell me what good fairy of a rich man has been filling our hands with silver?"

"That's just what I am trying to tell you," she laughed, "for there was a fairy here this afternoon sure enough, only he was dressed like a bald priest. That golden beetle is all he gave me, but with it comes a secret worth thousands of cash to us."

The youth fingered the trinket idly, still doubting his senses, and waiting impatiently for the secret of his delicious dinner. "But, mother, what has this brass bauble to do with the dumplings, these wonderful pork dumplings, the finest I ever ate?"

"Baubles indeed! Brass! Fie, fie, my boy! You little know what you are saying. Only listen and you shall hear a tale that will open your eyes."

She then told him what had happened, and ended by setting all of the left-over dumplings upon the floor for Blackfoot and Whitehead, a thing her son had never seen her do before, for they had been miserably poor and had had to save every scrap for the next meal.

Now began a long period of perfect happiness. Mother, son, dog and cat – all enjoyed themselves to their hearts' content. All manner of new foods such as they had never tasted were called forth from the pot by the wonderful little beetle. Bird-nest soup, shark's fins, and a hundred other delicacies were theirs for the asking, and soon Ming-li regained all his strength, but, I fear, at the same time grew somewhat lazy, for it was no longer necessary for him to work. As for the two animals, they became fat and sleek and their hair grew long and glossy.

But alas! according to a Chinese proverb, pride invites sorrow. The little family became so proud of their good fortune that they began to ask friends and relatives to dinner that they might show off their good meals. One day a Mr. and Mrs. Chu came from a distant village. They were much astonished at seeing the high style in which the Wangs lived. They had expected a beggar's meal, but went away with full stomachs.

"It's the best stuff I ever ate," said Mr. Chu, as they entered their own tumble-down house.

"Yes, and I know where it came from," exclaimed his wife. "I saw Widow Wang take a little gold ornament out of the pot and hide it in a cupboard. It must be some sort of charm, for I heard her mumbling to herself about pork and dumplings just as she was stirring up the fire."

"A charm, eh? Why is it that other people have all the luck? It looks as if we were doomed forever to be poor."

"Why not borrow Mrs. Wang's charm for a few days until we can pick up a little flesh to keep our bones from clattering? Turn about's fair play. Of course, we'll return it sooner or later."

"Doubtless they keep very close watch over it. When would you find them away from home, now that they don't have to work any more? As their house only contains one room, and that no bigger than ours, it would be difficult to borrow this golden trinket. It is harder, for more reasons than one, to steal from a beggar than from a king."

"Luck is surely with us," cried Mrs. Chu, clapping her hands. "They are going this very day to the Temple fair. I overheard Mrs. Wang tell her son that he must not forget he was to take her about the middle of the afternoon. I will slip back then and borrow the little charm from the box in which she hid it."

"Aren't you afraid of Blackfoot?"

"Pooh! he's so fat he can do nothing but roll. If the widow comes back suddenly, I'll tell her I came to look for my big hair-pin, that I lost it while I was at dinner."

"All right, go ahead, only of course we must remember we're borrowing the thing, not stealing it, for the Wangs have always been good friends to us, and then, too, we have just dined with them."

So skilfully did this crafty woman carry out her plans that within an hour she was back in her own house, gleefully showing the priest's charm to her husband. Not a soul had seen her enter the Wang house. The dog had made no noise, and the cat had only blinked her surprise at seeing a stranger and had gone to sleep again on the floor.

Great was the clamour and weeping when, on returning from the fair in expectation of a hot supper, the widow found her treasure missing. It was long before she could grasp the truth. She went back to the little box in the cupboard ten times before she could believe it was empty, and the room looked as if a cyclone had struck it, so long and carefully did the two unfortunates hunt for the lost beetle.

Then came days of hunger which were all the harder to bear since the recent period of good food and plenty. Oh, if they had only not got used to such dainties! How hard it was to go back to scraps and scrapings!

But if the widow and her son were sad over the loss of the good meals, the two pets were even more so. They were reduced to beggary and had to go forth daily upon the streets in search of stray bones and refuse that decent dogs and cats turned up their noses at.

One day, after this period of starvation had been going on for some time, Whitehead began suddenly to frisk about in great excitement.

"Whatever is the matter with you?" growled Blackfoot. "Are you mad from hunger, or have you caught another flea?"

"I was just thinking over our affairs, and now I know the cause of all our trouble."

"Do you indeed?" sneered Blackfoot.

"Yes, I do indeed, and you'd better think twice before you mock me, for I hold your future in my paw, as you will very soon see."

"Well, you needn't get angry about nothing. What wonderful discovery have you made – that every rat has one tail?"

"First of all, are you willing to help me bring good fortune back to our family?"

"Of course I am. Don't be silly," barked the dog, wagging his tail joyfully at the thought of another good dinner. "Surely! surely! I will do anything you like if it will bring Dame Fortune back again."

"All right. Here is the plan. There has been a thief in the house who has stolen our mistress's golden beetle. You remember all our big dinners that came from the pot? Well, every day I saw our mistress take a little golden beetle out of the black box and put it into the pot. One day she held it up before me, saying, 'Look, puss, there is the cause of all our happiness. Don't you wish it was yours?' Then she laughed and put it back into the box that stays in the cupboard."

"Is that true?" questioned Blackfoot. "Why didn't you say something about it before?"

"You remember the day Mr. and Mrs. Chu were here, and how Mrs. Chu returned in the afternoon after master and mistress had gone to the fair? I saw her, out of the tail of my eye, go to that very black box and take out the golden beetle. I thought it curious, but never dreamed she was a thief. Alas! I was wrong! She took the beetle, and if I am not mistaken, she and her husband are now enjoying the feasts that belong to us."

"Let's claw them," growled Blackfoot, gnashing his teeth.

"That would do no good," counselled the other, "for they would be sure to come out best in the end. We want the beetle back – that's the main thing. We'll leave revenge to human beings; it is none of our business."

"What do you suggest?" said Blackfoot. "I am with you through thick and thin."

"Let's go to the Chu house and make off with the beetle."

"Alas, that I am not a cat!" moaned Blackfoot. "If we go there I couldn't get inside, for robbers always keep their gates well locked. If I were like you I could scale the wall. It is the first time in all my life I ever envied a cat."

"We will go together," continued Whitehead. "I will ride on your back when we are fording the river, and you can protect me from strange animals. When we get to the Chu house, I will climb over the wall and manage the rest of the business myself. Only you must wait outside to help me to get home with the prize."

No sooner arranged than done. The companions set out that very night on their adventure. They crossed the river as the cat had suggested, and Blackfoot really enjoyed the swim, for, as he said, it took him back to his puppyhood, while the cat did not get a single drop of water on her face. It was midnight when they reached the Chu house.

"Just wait till I return," purred Whitehead in Blackfoot's ear.

With a mighty spring she reached the top of the mud wall, and then jumped down to the inside court. While she was resting in the shadow, trying to decide just how to go about her work, a slight rustling attracted her attention, and pop! one giant spring, one stretch-out of the claws, and she had caught a rat that had just come out of his hole for a drink and a midnight walk.

Now, Whitehead was so hungry that she would have made short work of this tempting prey if the rat had not opened its mouth and, to her amazement, begun to talk in good cat dialect.

"Pray, good puss, not so fast with your sharp teeth! Kindly be careful with your claws! Don't you know it is the custom now to put prisoners on their honour? I will promise not to run away."

"Pooh! what honour has a rat?"

"Most of us haven't much, I grant you, but my family was brought up under the roof of Confucius, and there we picked up so many crumbs of wisdom that we are exceptions to the rule. If you will spare me, I will obey you for life, in fact, will be your humble slave." Then, with a quick jerk, freeing itself, "See, I am loose now, but honour holds me as if I were tied, and so I make no further attempt to get away."

"Much good it would do you," purred Whitehead, her fur crackling noisily, and her mouth watering for a taste of rat steak. "However, I am quite willing to put you to the test. First, answer a few polite questions and I will see if you're a truthful fellow. What kind of food is your master eating now, that you should be so round and plump when I am thin and scrawny?"

"Oh, we have been in luck lately, I can tell you. Master and mistress feed on the fat of the land, and of course we hangers-on get the crumbs."

"But this is a poor tumble-down house. How can they afford such eating?"

"That is a great secret, but as I am in honour bound to tell you, here goes. My mistress has just obtained in some manner or other, a fairy's charm– "

"She stole it from our place," hissed the cat, "I will claw her eyes out if I get the chance. Why, we've been fairly starving for want of that beetle. She stole it from us just after she had been an invited guest! What do you think of that for honour, Sir Rat? Were your mistress's ancestors followers of the sage?"

"Oh, oh, oh! Why, that explains everything!" wailed the rat. "I have often wondered how they got the golden beetle, and yet of course I dared not ask any questions."

"No, certainly not! But hark you, friend rat – you get that golden trinket back for me, and I will set you free at once of all obligations. Do you know where she hides it?"

"Yes, in a crevice where the wall is broken. I will bring it to you in a jiffy, but how shall we exist when our charm is gone? There will be a season of scanty food, I fear; beggars' fare for all of us."

"Live on the memory of your good deed," purred the cat. "It is splendid, you know, to be an honest beggar. Now scoot! I trust you completely, since your people lived in the home of Confucius. I will wait here for your return. Ah!" laughed Whitehead to herself, "luck seems to be coming our way again!"

Five minutes later the rat appeared, bearing the trinket in its mouth. It passed the beetle over to the cat, and then with a whisk was off for ever. Its honour was safe, but it was afraid of Whitehead. It had seen the gleam of desire in her green eyes, and the cat might have broken her word if she had not been so anxious to get back home where her mistress could command the wonderful kettle once more to bring forth food.

The two adventurers reached the river just as the sun was rising above the eastern hills.

"Be careful," cautioned Blackfoot, as the cat leaped upon his back for her ride across the stream, "be careful not to forget the treasure. In short, remember that even though you are a female, it is necessary to keep your mouth closed till we reach the other side."

"Thanks, but I don't think I need your advice," replied Whitehead, picking up the beetle and leaping on to the dog's back.

But alas! just as they were nearing the farther shore, the excited cat forgot her wisdom for a moment. A fish suddenly leaped out of the water directly under her nose. It was too great a temptation. Snap! went her jaws in a vain effort to land the scaly treasure, and the golden beetle sank to the bottom of the river.

"There!" said the dog angrily, "what did I tell you? Now all our trouble has been in vain – all on account of your stupidity."

For a time there was a bitter dispute, and the companions called each other some very bad names – such as turtle and rabbit. Just as they were starting away from the river, disappointed and discouraged, a friendly frog who had by chance heard their conversation offered to fetch the treasure from the bottom of the stream. No sooner said than done, and after thanking this accommodating animal profusely, they turned homeward once more.

When they reached the cottage the door was shut, and, bark as he would, Blackfoot could not persuade his master to open it. There was the sound of loud wailing inside.

"Mistress is broken-hearted," whispered the cat, "I will go to her and make her happy."

So saying, she sprang lightly through a hole in the paper window, which, alas! was too small and too far from the ground for the faithful dog to enter.

A sad sight greeted the gaze of Whitehead. The son was lying on the bed unconscious, almost dead for want of food, while his mother, in despair, was rocking backwards and forwards wringing her wrinkled hands and crying at the top of her voice for someone to come and save them.

"Here I am, mistress," cried Whitehead, "and here is the treasure you are weeping for. I have rescued it and brought it back to you."

The widow, wild with joy at sight of the beetle, seized the cat in her scrawny arms and hugged the pet tightly to her bosom.

"Breakfast, son, breakfast! Wake up from your swoon! Fortune has come again. We are saved from starvation!"

Soon a steaming hot meal was ready, and you may well imagine how the old woman and her son, heaping praises upon Whitehead, filled the beast's platter with good things, but never a word did they say of the faithful dog, who remained outside sniffing the fragrant odours and waiting in sad wonder, for all this time the artful cat had said nothing of Blackfoot's part in the rescue of the golden beetle.

At last, when breakfast was over, slipping away from the others, Whitehead jumped out through the hole in the window.

"Oh, my dear Blackfoot," she began laughingly, "you should have been inside to see what a feast they gave me! Mistress was so delighted at my bringing back her treasure that she could not give me enough to eat, nor say enough kind things about me. Too bad, old fellow, that you are hungry. You'd better run out into the street and hunt up a bone."

Maddened by the shameful treachery of his companion, the enraged dog sprang upon the cat and in a few seconds had shaken her to death.

"So dies the one who forgets a friend and who loses honour," he cried sadly, as he stood over the body of his companion.

Rushing out into the street, he proclaimed the treachery of Whitehead to the members of his tribe, at the same time advising that all self-respecting dogs should from that time onwards make war upon the feline race.

And that is why the descendants of old Blackfoot, whether in China or in the great countries of the West, have waged continual war upon the children and grandchildren of Whitehead, for a thousand generations of dogs have fought them and hated them with a great and lasting hatred.

The Strange Tale of Doctor Dog

FAR UP IN the mountains of the Province of Hunan in the central part of China, there once lived in a small village a rich gentleman who had only one child. This girl, like the daughter of Kwan-yu in the story of the Great Bell, was the very joy of her father's life.

Now Mr. Min, for that was this gentleman's name, was famous throughout the whole district for his learning, and, as he was also the owner of much property, he spared no effort to teach Honeysuckle the wisdom of the sages, and to give her everything she craved. Of course this was enough to spoil most children, but Honeysuckle was not at all like other children. As sweet as the flower from which she took her name, she listened to her father's slightest command, and obeyed without ever waiting to be told a second time.

Her father often bought kites for her, of every kind and shape. There were fish, birds, butterflies, lizards and huge dragons, one of which had a tail more than thirty feet long. Mr. Min was very skilful in flying these kites for little Honeysuckle, and so naturally did his birds and butterflies circle round and hover about in the air that almost any little western boy would have been deceived and said, "Why, there is a real bird, and not a kite at all!" Then again, he would fasten a queer little instrument to the string, which made a kind of humming noise, as he waved his hand from side to side. "It is the wind singing, Daddy," cried Honeysuckle, clapping her hands with joy; "singing a kite-song to both of us." Sometimes, to teach his little darling a lesson if she had been the least naughty, Mr. Min would fasten queerly twisted scraps of paper, on which were written many Chinese words, to the string of her favourite kite.

"What are you doing, Daddy?" Honeysuckle would ask. "What can those queer-looking papers be?"

"On every piece is written a sin that we have done."

"What is a sin, Daddy?"

"Oh, when Honeysuckle has been naughty; that is a sin!" he answered gently. "Your old nurse is afraid to scold you, and if you are to grow up to be a good woman, Daddy must teach you what is right."

Then Mr. Min would send the kite up high – high over the house-tops, even higher than the tall Pagoda on the hillside. When all his cord was let out, he would pick up two sharp stones, and, handing them to Honeysuckle, would say, "Now, daughter, cut the string, and the wind will carry away the sins that are written down on the scraps of paper."

"But, Daddy, the kite is so pretty. Mayn't we keep our sins a little longer?" she would innocently ask.

"No, child; it is dangerous to hold on to one's sins. Virtue is the foundation of happiness," he would reply sternly, choking back his laughter at her question. "Make haste and cut the cord."

So Honeysuckle, always obedient – at least with her father – would saw the string in two between the sharp stones, and with a childish cry of despair would watch her favourite kite, blown by the wind, sail farther and farther away, until at last, straining her eyes, she could see it sink slowly to the earth in some far-distant meadow.

"Now laugh and be happy," Mr. Min would say, "for your sins are all gone. See that you don't get a new supply of them."

Honeysuckle was also fond of seeing the puppet show, for, you must know, this old-fashioned amusement for children was enjoyed by little folks in China, perhaps three thousand years before your great-grandfather was born. It is even said that the great Emperor, Mu, when he saw these little dancing images for the first time, was greatly enraged at seeing one of them making eyes at his favourite wife. He ordered the showman to be put to death, and it was with difficulty the poor fellow persuaded his Majesty that the dancing puppets were not really alive at all, but only images of cloth and clay.

No wonder then Honeysuckle liked to see the puppets if the Son of Heaven himself had been deceived by their queer antics into thinking them real people of flesh and blood.

But we must hurry on with our story, or some of our readers will be asking, "But where is Dr. Dog? Are you never coming to the hero of this tale?" One day when Honeysuckle was sitting inside a shady pavilion that overlooked a tiny fish-pond, she was suddenly seized with a violent attack of colic. Frantic with pain, she told a servant to summon her father, and then without further ado, she fell over in a faint upon the ground.

When Mr. Min reached his daughter's side, she was still unconscious. After sending for the family physician to come post haste, he got his daughter to bed, but although she recovered from her fainting fit, the extreme pain continued until the poor girl was almost dead from exhaustion.

Now, when the learned doctor arrived and peered at her from under his gigantic spectacles, he could not discover the cause of her trouble. However, like some of our western medical men, he did not confess his ignorance, but proceeded to prescribe a huge dose of boiling water, to be followed a little later by a compound of pulverized deer's horn and dried toadskin.

Poor Honeysuckle lay in agony for three days, all the time growing weaker and weaker from loss of sleep. Every great doctor in the district had been summoned for consultation; two had come from Changsha, the chief city of the province, but all to no avail. It was one of those cases that seem to be beyond the power of even the most learned physicians. In the hope of receiving the great reward offered by the desperate father, these wise men searched from cover to cover in the great Chinese Cyclopedia of Medicine, trying in vain to find a method of treating the unhappy maiden. There was even thought of calling in a certain foreign physician from England, who was in a distant city, and was supposed, on account of some marvellous cures he had brought to pass, to be in direct league with the devil. However, the city magistrate would not allow Mr. Min to call in this outsider, for fear trouble might be stirred up among the people.

Mr. Min sent out a proclamation in every direction, describing his daughter's illness, and offering to bestow on her a handsome dowry and give her in marriage to whoever should be the means of bringing her back to health and happiness. He then sat at her bedside and waited, feeling that he had done all that was in his power. There were many answers to his invitation. Physicians, old and young, came from every part of the Empire to try their skill, and when they had seen poor Honeysuckle and also the huge pile of silver shoes her father offered as a wedding gift, they all fought with might and main for her life; some having been attracted by her great beauty and excellent reputation, others by the tremendous reward.

But, alas for poor Honeysuckle! Not one of all those wise men could cure her! One day, when she was feeling a slight change for the better, she called her father, and, clasping his hand with her tiny one said, "Were it not for your love I would give up this hard fight and pass over into the dark wood; or, as my old grandmother says, fly up into the Western Heavens. For your sake, because I am your only child, and especially because you have no son, I have struggled hard to live, but now I feel that the next attack of that dreadful pain will carry me away. And oh, I do not want to die!"

Here Honeysuckle wept as if her heart would break, and her old father wept too, for the more she suffered the more he loved her.

Just then her face began to turn pale. "It is coming! The pain is coming, father! Very soon I shall be no more. Good-bye, father! Good-bye; good– ." Here her voice broke and a great sob almost broke her father's heart. He turned away from her bedside; he could not bear to see her suffer. He walked outside and sat down on a rustic bench; his head fell upon his bosom, and the great salt tears trickled down his long grey beard.

As Mr. Min sat thus overcome with grief, he was startled at hearing a low whine. Looking up he saw, to his astonishment, a shaggy mountain dog about the size of a Newfoundland. The huge beast looked into the old man's eyes with so intelligent and human an expression, with such a sad and wistful gaze, that the greybeard addressed him, saying, "Why have you come? To cure my daughter?"

The dog replied with three short barks, wagging his tail vigorously and turning toward the half-opened door that led into the room where the girl lay.

By this time, willing to try any chance whatever of reviving his daughter, Mr. Min bade the animal follow him into Honeysuckle's apartment. Placing his forepaws upon the side of her bed, the dog looked long and steadily at the wasted form before him and held his ear intently for a moment over the maiden's heart. Then, with a slight cough he deposited from his mouth into her outstretched hand, a tiny stone. Touching her wrist with his right paw, he motioned to her to swallow the stone.

"Yes, my dear, obey him," counselled her father, as she turned to him inquiringly, "for good Dr. Dog has been sent to your bedside by the mountain fairies, who have heard of your illness and who wish to invite you back to life again."

Without further delay the sick girl, who was by this time almost burned away by the fever, raised her hand to her lips and swallowed the tiny charm. Wonder of wonders! No sooner had it passed her lips than a miracle occurred. The red flush passed away from her face, the pulse resumed its normal beat, the pains departed from her body, and she arose from the bed well and smiling.

Flinging her arms about her father's neck, she cried out in joy, "Oh, I am well again; well and happy; thanks to the medicine of the good physician."

The noble dog barked three times, wild with delight at hearing these tearful words of gratitude, bowed low, and put his nose in Honeysuckle's outstretched hand.

Mr. Min, greatly moved by his daughter's magical recovery, turned to the strange physician, saying, "Noble Sir, were it not for the form you have taken, for some unknown reason, I would willingly give four times the sum in silver that I promised for the cure of the girl, into your possession. As it is, I suppose you have no use for silver, but remember that so long as we live, whatever we have is yours for the asking, and I beg of you to prolong your visit, to make this the home of your old age – in short, remain here for ever as my guest – nay, as a member of my family."

The dog barked thrice, as if in assent. From that day he was treated as an equal by father and daughter. The many servants were commanded to obey his slightest whim, to serve him with the most expensive food on the market, to spare no expense in making him the happiest and best-fed dog in all the world. Day after day he ran at Honeysuckle's side as she gathered flowers in her garden, lay down before her door when she was resting, guarded her Sedan chair when she was carried by servants into the city. In short, they were constant companions; a stranger would have thought they had been friends from childhood.

One day, however, just as they were returning from a journey outside her father's compound, at the very instant when Honeysuckle was alighting from her chair, without a moment's warning, the huge animal dashed past the attendants, seized his beautiful mistress in his mouth, and before anyone could stop him, bore her off to the mountains. By the time the alarm was sounded, darkness had fallen over the valley and as the night was cloudy no trace could be found of the dog and his fair burden.

Once more the frantic father left no stone unturned to save his daughter. Huge rewards were offered, bands of woodmen scoured the mountains high and low, but, alas, no sign of the girl could be found! The unfortunate father gave up the search and began to prepare himself for the grave. There was nothing now left in life that he cared for – nothing but thoughts of his departed daughter. Honeysuckle was gone for ever.

"Alas!" said he, quoting the lines of a famous poet who had fallen into despair:

"My whiting hair would make an endless rope,
Yet would not measure all my depth of woe."

Several long years passed by; years of sorrow for the ageing man, pining for his departed daughter. One beautiful October day he was sitting in the very same pavilion where he had so often sat with his darling. His head was bowed forward on his breast, his forehead was lined with grief. A rustling of leaves attracted his attention. He looked up. Standing directly in front of him was Dr. Dog, and lo, riding on his back, clinging to the animal's shaggy hair, was Honeysuckle, his long-lost daughter; while standing near by were three of the handsomest boys he had ever set eyes upon!

"Ah, my daughter! My darling daughter, where have you been all these years?" cried the delighted father, pressing the girl to his aching breast. "Have you suffered many a cruel pain since you were snatched away so suddenly? Has your life been filled with sorrow?"

"Only at the thought of your grief," she replied, tenderly, stroking his forehead with her slender fingers; "only at the thought of your suffering; only at the thought of how I should like to see you every day and tell you that my husband was kind and good to me. For you must know, dear father, this is no mere animal that stands beside you. This Dr. Dog, who cured me and claimed me as his bride because of your promise, is a great magician. He can change himself at will into a thousand shapes. He chooses to come here in the form of a mountain beast so that no one may penetrate the secret of his distant palace."

"Then he is your husband?" faltered the old man, gazing at the animal with a new expression on his wrinkled face.

"Yes; my kind and noble husband, the father of my three sons, your grandchildren, whom we have brought to pay you a visit."

"And where do you live?"

"In a wonderful cave in the heart of the great mountains; a beautiful cave whose walls and floors are covered with crystals, and encrusted with sparkling gems. The chairs and tables are set with jewels; the rooms are lighted by a thousand glittering diamonds. Oh, it is lovelier than the palace of the Son of Heaven himself! We feed of the flesh of wild deer and mountain goats, and fish from the clearest mountain stream. We drink cold water out of golden goblets, without first boiling it, for it is purity itself. We breathe fragrant air that blows through forests of pine and hemlock. We live only to love each other and our children, and oh, we are so happy! And you, father, you must come back with us to the great mountains and live there with us the rest of your days, which, the gods grant, may be very many."

The old man pressed his daughter once more to his breast and fondled the children, who clambered over him rejoicing at the discovery of a grandfather they had never seen before.

From Dr. Dog and his fair Honeysuckle are sprung, it is said, the well-known race of people called the Yus, who even now inhabit the mountainous regions of the Canton and Hunan provinces. It is not for this reason, however, that we have told the story here, but because we felt sure every reader would like to learn the secret of the dog that cured a sick girl and won her for his bride.

How Footbinding Started

IN THE VERY BEGINNING of all things, when the gods were creating the world, at last the time came to separate the earth from the heavens. This was hard work, and if it had not been for the coolness and skill of a young goddess all would have failed. This goddess was named Lu-o. She had been idly watching the growth of the planet, when, to her horror, she saw the newly made ball slipping slowly from its place. In another second it would have shot down into the bottomless pit. Quick as a flash Lu-o stopped it with her magic wand and held it firmly until the chief god came dashing up to the rescue.

But this was not all. When men and women were put on the earth Lu-o helped them greatly by setting an example of purity and kindness. Everyone loved her and pointed her out as the one who was always willing to do a good deed. After she had left the world and gone into the land of the gods, beautiful statues of her were set up in many temples to keep her image always before the eyes of sinful people. The greatest of these was in the capital city. Thus, when sorrowful women wished to offer up their prayers to some virtuous goddess they would go to a temple of Lu-o and pour out their hearts before her shrine.

At one time the wicked Chow-sin, last ruler of the Yins, went to pray in the city Temple. There his royal eyes were captivated by the sight of a wonderful face, the beauty of which was so great that he fell in love with it at once, telling his ministers that he wished he might take this goddess, who was no other than Lu-o, for one of his wives.

Now Lu-o was terribly angry that an earthly prince should dare to make such a remark about her. Then and there she determined to punish the Emperor. Calling her assistant spirits, she told them of Chow-sin's insult. Of all her servants the most cunning was one whom we shall call Fox Sprite, because he really belonged to the fox family. Lu-o ordered Fox Sprite to spare himself no trouble in making the wicked ruler suffer for his impudence.

For many days, try as he would, Chow-sin, the great Son of Heaven, could not forget the face he had seen in the temple.

"He is stark mad," laughed his courtiers behind his back, "to fall in love with a statue."

"I must find a woman just like her," said the Emperor, "and take her to wife."

"Why not, most Mighty One," suggested a favourite adviser, "send forth a command throughout the length and breadth of your Empire, that no maiden shall be taken in marriage until you have chosen yourself a wife whose beauty shall equal that of Lu-o?"

Chow-sin was pleased with this suggestion and doubtless would have followed it had not his Prime Minister begged him to postpone issuing the order. "Your Imperial Highness," began the official, "since you have been pleased once or twice to follow my counsel, I beg of you to give ear now to what I say."

"Speak, and your words shall have my best attention," replied Chow-sin, with a gracious wave of the hand.

"Know then, Great One, that in the southern part of your realm there dwells a viceroy whose bravery has made him famous in battle."

"Are you speaking of Su-nan?" questioned Chow-sin, frowning, for this Su-nan had once been a rebel.

"None other, mighty Son of Heaven. Famous is he as a soldier, but his name is now even greater in that he is the father of the most beautiful girl in all China. This lovely flower that has bloomed of late within his household is still unmarried. Why not order her father to bring her to the palace that you may wed her and place her in your royal dwelling?"

"And are you sure of this wondrous beauty you describe so prettily?" asked the ruler, a smile of pleasure lighting up his face.

"So sure that I will stake my head on your being satisfied."

"Enough! I command you at once to summon the viceroy and his daughter. Add the imperial seal to the message."

The Prime Minister smilingly departed to give the order. In his heart he was more than delighted that the Emperor had accepted his suggestion, for Su-nan, the viceroy, had long been his chief enemy, and he planned in this way to overthrow him. The viceroy, as he knew, was a man of iron. He would certainly not feel honoured at the thought of having his daughter enter the Imperial Palace as a secondary wife. Doubtless he would refuse to obey the order and would thus bring about his own immediate downfall.

Nor was the Prime Minister mistaken. When Su-nan received the imperial message his heart was hot with anger against his sovereign. To be robbed of his lovely Ta-ki, even by the throne, was, in his eyes, a terrible disgrace. Could he have been sure that she would be made Empress it might have been different, but with so many others sharing Chow-sin's favour, her promotion to first place in the Great One's household was by no means certain. Besides, she was Su-nan's favourite child, and the old man could not bear the thought of separation from her. Rather would he give up his life than let her go to this cruel ruler.

"No, you shall not do it," said he to Ta-ki, "not though I must die to save you."

The beautiful girl listened to her father's words, in tears. Throwing herself at his feet she thanked him for his mercy and promised to love him more fondly than ever. She told him that her vanity had not been flattered by what most girls might have thought an honour, that she would rather have the love of one good man like her father, than share with others the affections of a king.

After listening to his daughter, the viceroy sent a respectful answer to the palace, thanking the Emperor for his favour, but saying he could not give up Ta-ki. "She is unworthy of the honour you purpose doing her," he said, in conclusion, "for, having been the apple of her father's eye, she would not be happy to share even your most august favour with the many others you have chosen."

When the Emperor learned of Su-nan's reply he could hardly believe his ears. To have his command thus disobeyed was an unheard-of crime. Never before had a subject of the Middle Kingdom offered such an insult to a ruler. Boiling with rage, he ordered his prime minister to send forth an army that would bring the viceroy to his senses. "Tell him if he disobeys that he and his family, together with all they possess, shall be destroyed."

Delighted at the success of his plot against Su-nan, the Prime Minister sent a regiment of soldiers to bring the rebel to terms. In the meantime the friends of the daring viceroy had not been idle. Hearing of the danger threatening their ruler, who had become a general favourite, hundreds of men offered him their aid against the army of Chow-sin. Thus when the Emperor's banners were seen approaching and the war drums were heard rolling in the distance, the rebels, with a great shout, dashed forth to do battle for their leader. In the fight that took place the Imperial soldiers were forced to run.

When the Emperor heard of this defeat he was hot with anger. He called together his advisers and commanded that an army, double the size of the first one, should be sent to Su-nan's country to destroy the fields and villages of the people who had risen up against him. "Spare not one of them," he shouted, "for they are traitors to the Dragon Throne."

Once more the viceroy's friends resolved to support him, even to the death. Ta-ki, his daughter, went apart from the other members of the family, weeping most bitterly that she had brought such sorrow upon them. "Rather would I go into the palace and be the lowest among Chow-sin's women than to be the cause of all this grief," she cried, in desperation.

But her father soothed her, saying, "Be of good cheer, Ta-ki. The Emperor's army, though it be twice as large as mine, shall not overcome us. Right is on our side. The gods of battle will help those who fight for justice."

One week later a second battle was fought, and the struggle was so close that none could foresee the result. The Imperial army was commanded by the oldest nobles in the kingdom, those most skilled in warfare, while the viceroy's men were young and poorly drilled. Moreover, the members of the Dragon Army had been promised double pay if they should accomplish the wishes of their sovereign, while Su-nan's soldiers knew only too well that they would be put to the sword if they should be defeated.

Just as the clash of arms was at its highest, the sound of gongs was heard upon a distant hill. The government troops were amazed at seeing fresh companies marching to the rescue of their foe. With a wild cry of disappointment they turned and fled from the field. These unexpected reinforcements turned out to be women whom Ta-ki had persuaded to dress up as soldiers and go with her for the purpose of frightening the enemy. Thus for a second time was Su-nan victorious.

During the following year several battles occurred that counted for little, except that in each of them many of Su-nan's followers were killed. At last one of the viceroy's best friends came to him, saying, "Noble lord, it is useless to continue the struggle. I fear you must give up the fight. You have lost more than half your supporters; the remaining bowmen are either sick or wounded and can be of little use. The Emperor, moreover, is even now raising a new army from the distant provinces, and will soon send against us a force ten times as great as any we have yet seen. There being no hope of victory, further fighting would be folly. Lead, therefore, your daughter to the palace. Throw yourself upon the mercy of the throne. You must accept cheerfully the fate the gods have suffered you to bear."

Ta-ki, chancing to overhear this conversation, rushed in and begged her father to hold out no longer, but to deliver her up to the greed of the wicked Chow-sin.

With a sigh, the viceroy yielded to their wishes. The next day he despatched a messenger to the Emperor, promising to bring Ta-ki at once to the capital.

Now we must not forget Fox Sprite, the demon, who had been commanded by the good goddess Lu-o to bring a dreadful punishment upon the Emperor. Through all the years of strife between Chow-sin and the rebels, Fox Sprite had been waiting patiently for his chance. He knew well that some day, sooner or later, there would come an hour when Chow-sin would be at his mercy. When the time came, therefore, for Ta-ki to go to the palace, Fox Sprite felt that at last his chance had come. The beautiful maiden for whom Chow-sin had given up so many hundreds of his soldiers, would clearly have great power over the Emperor. She must be made to help in the punishment of her wicked husband. So Fox Sprite made himself invisible and travelled with the viceroy's party as it went from central China to the capital.

On the last night of their journey Su-nan and his daughter stopped for rest and food at a large inn. No sooner had the girl gone to her room for the night than Fox Sprite followed her. Then he made himself visible. At first she was frightened to see so strange a being in her room, but when Fox Sprite told her he was a servant of the great goddess, Lu-o, she was comforted, for she knew that Lu-o was the friend of women and children.

"But how can I help to punish the Emperor?" she faltered, when the sprite told her he wanted her assistance. "I am but a helpless girl," and here she began to cry.

"Dry your tears," he said soothingly. "It will be very easy. Only let me take your form for a little. When I am the Emperor's wife," laughing, "I shall find a way to punish him, for no one can give a man more pain that his wife can, if she desires to do so. You know, I am a servant of Lu-o and can do anything I wish."

"But the Emperor won't have a fox for a wife," she sobbed.

"Though I am still a fox I shall look like the beautiful Ta-ki. Make your heart easy. He will never know."

"Oh, I see," she smiled, "you will put your spirit into my body and you will look just like me, though you really won't be me. But what will become of the real me? Shall I have to be a fox and look like you?"

"No, not unless you want to. I will make you invisible, and you can be ready to go back into your own body when I have got rid of the Emperor."

"Very well," replied the girl, somewhat relieved by his explanation, "but try not to be too long about it, because I don't like the idea of somebody else walking about in my body."

So Fox Sprite caused his own spirit to enter the girl's body, and no one could have told by her outward appearance that any change had taken place. The beautiful girl was now in reality the sly Fox Sprite, but in one way only did she look like a fox. When the fox-spirit entered her body, her feet suddenly shrivelled up and became very similar in shape and size to the feet of the animal who had her in his power. When the fox noticed this, at first he was somewhat annoyed, but, feeling that no one else would know, he did not take the trouble to change the fox feet back to human form.

On the following morning, when the viceroy called his daughter for the last stage of their journey, he greeted Fox Sprite without suspecting that anything unusual had happened since he had last seen Ta-ki. So well did this crafty spirit perform his part that the father was completely deceived, by look, by voice, and by gesture.

The next day the travellers arrived at the capital and Su-nan presented himself before Chow-sin, the Emperor, leading Fox Sprite with him. Of course the crafty fox with all his magic powers was soon able to gain the mastery over the wicked ruler. The Great One pardoned Su-nan, although he had fully intended to put him to death as a rebel.

Now the chance for which Fox Sprite had been waiting had come. He began at once, causing the Emperor to do many deeds of violence. The people had already begun to dislike Chow-sin, and soon he became hateful in their sight. Many of the leading members of the court were put to death unjustly. Horrible tortures were devised for punishing those who did not find favour with the crown. At last there was open talk of a rebellion. Of course, all these things delighted the wily fox, for he saw that, sooner or later, the Son of Heaven would be turned out of the palace, and he knew that then his work for the goddess Lu-o would be finished.

Besides worming his way into the heart of the Emperor, the fox became a general favourite with the ladies of the palace. These women saw in Chow-sin's latest wife the most beautiful woman who had ever lived in the royal harem. One would think that this beauty might have caused them to hate Fox Sprite, but such was not the case. They admired the plumpness of Fox Sprite's body, the fairness of Fox Sprite's complexion, the fire in Fox Sprite's eyes, but most of all they wondered at the smallness of Fox Sprite's feet, for, you remember, the supposed Ta-ki now had fox's feet instead of those of human shape.

Thus small feet became the fashion among women. All the court ladies, old and young, beautiful and ugly, began thinking of plans for making their own feet as tiny as those of Fox Sprite. In this way they thought to increase their chances of finding favour with the Emperor.

Gradually people outside the palace began to hear of this absurd fashion. Mothers bound the feet of their little girls, in such a manner as to stop their growth. The bones of the toes were bent backwards and broken, so eager were the elders to have their daughters grow up into tiny-footed maidens. Thus, for several years of their girlhood the little ones were compelled to endure the most severe tortures. It was not long before the new fashion took firm root in China. It became almost impossible for parents to get husbands for their daughters unless the girls had suffered the severe pains of foot-binding. And even to this day we find that many of the people are still under the influence of Fox Sprite's magic, and believe that a tiny, misshapen foot is more beautiful than a natural one.

But let us return to the story of Fox Sprite and the wicked Emperor. For a number of years matters grew continually worse in the country. At last the people rose in a body against the ruler. A great battle was fought. The wicked Chow-sin was overthrown and put to death by means of those very instruments of torture he had used so often against his subjects. By this time it had become known to all the lords and noblemen that the Emperor's favourite had been the main cause of their ruler's wickedness; hence they demanded the death of Fox Sprite. But no one wished to kill so lovely a creature. Everyone appointed refused to do the deed.

Finally, a grey-headed member of the court allowed himself to be blindfolded. With a sharp sword he pierced the body of Fox Sprite to the heart. Those standing near covered their eyes with their hands, for they could not bear to see so wonderful a woman die. Suddenly, as they looked up, they saw a sight so strange that all were filled with amazement. Instead of falling to the ground, the graceful form swayed backward and forward for a moment, when all at once there seemed to spring from her side a huge mountain fox. The animal glanced around him, then, with a cry of fear, dashing past officials, courtiers and soldiers, he rushed through the gate of the enclosure.

"A fox!" cried the people, full of wonder.

At that moment Ta-ki fell in a swoon upon the floor. When they picked her up, thinking, of course, that she had died from the sword thrust, they could find no blood on her body, and, on looking more closely, they saw that there was not even the slightest wound.

"Marvel of marvels!" they all shouted. "The gods have shielded her!"

Just then Ta-ki opened her eyes and looked about her. "Where am I?" she asked, in faint voice. "Pray tell me what has happened."

Then they told her what they had seen, and at last it was plain to the beautiful woman that, after all these years, Fox Sprite had left her body. She was herself once more. For a long time she could not make the people believe her story; they all said that she must have lost her mind; that the gods had saved her life, but had punished her for her wickedness by taking away her reason.

But that night, when her maids were undressing her in the palace, they saw her feet, which had once more become their natural size, and then they knew she had been telling the truth.

How Ta-ki became the wife of a good nobleman who had long admired her great beauty is much too long a story to be told here. Of one thing, however, we are certain, that she lived long and was happy ever afterwards.

The Talking Fish

LONG, LONG BEFORE your great-grandfather was born there lived in the village of Everlasting Happiness two men called Li and Sing. Now, these two men were close friends, living together in the same house. Before settling down in the village of Everlasting Happiness they had ruled as high officials for more than twenty years. They had often treated the people very harshly, so that everybody, old and young, disliked and hated them. And yet, by robbing the wealthy merchants and by cheating the poor, these two evil companions had become rich, and it was in order to spend their ill-gotten gains in idle amusements that they sought out the village of Everlasting Happiness. "For here," said they, "we can surely find that joy which has been denied us in every other place. Here we shall no longer be scorned by men and reviled by women."

Consequently these two men bought for themselves the finest house in the village, furnished it in the most elegant manner, and decorated the walls with scrolls filled with wise sayings and pictures by famous artists. Outside there were lovely gardens filled with flowers and birds, and oh, ever so many trees with queer twisted branches growing in the shape of tigers and other wild animals.

Whenever they felt lonely Li and Sing invited rich people of the neighbourhood to come and dine with them, and after they had eaten, sometimes they would go out upon the little lake in the centre of their estate, rowing in an awkward flat-bottomed boat that had been built by the village carpenter.

One day, on such an occasion, when the sun had been beating down fiercely upon the clean-shaven heads of all those on the little barge, for you must know this was long before the day when hats were worn – at least, in the village of Everlasting Happiness – Mr. Li was suddenly seized with a giddy feeling, which rapidly grew worse and worse until he was in a burning fever.

"Snake's blood mixed with powdered deer-horn is the thing for him," said the wise-looking doctor who was called in, peering at Li carefully through his huge glasses, "Be sure," he continued, addressing Li's personal attendant, and, at the same time, snapping his long finger-nails nervously, "be sure, above all, not to leave him alone, for he is in danger of going raving mad at any moment, and I cannot say what he may do if he is not looked after carefully. A man in his condition has no more sense than a baby."

Now, although these words of the doctor's really made Mr. Li angry, he was too ill to reply, for all this time his head had been growing hotter and hotter, until at last a feverish sleep overtook him. No sooner had he closed his eyes than his faithful servant, half-famished, rushed out of the room to join his fellows at their mid-day meal.

Li awoke with a start. He had slept only ten minutes. "Water, water," he moaned, "bathe my head with cold water. I am half dead with pain!" But there was no reply, for the attendant was dining happily with his fellows.

"Air, air," groaned Mr. Li, tugging at the collar of his silk shirt. "I'm dying for water. I'm starving for air. This blazing heat will kill me. It is hotter than the Fire god himself ever dreamed of making it. Wang, Wang!" clapping his hands feebly and calling to his servant, "air and water, air and water!"

But still no Wang.

At last, with the strength that is said to come from despair, Mr. Li arose from his couch and staggered toward the doorway. Out he went into the paved courtyard, and then, after only a moment's hesitation, made his way across it into a narrow passage that led into the lake garden.

"What do they care for a man when he is sick?" he muttered. "My good friend Sing is doubtless even now enjoying his afternoon nap, with a servant standing by to fan him, and a block of ice near his head to cool the air. What does he care if I die of a raging fever? Doubtless he expects to inherit all my money. And my servants! That rascal Wang has been with me these ten years, living on me and growing lazier every season! What does he care if I pass away? Doubtless he is certain that Sing's servants will think of something for him to do, and he will have even less work than he has now. Water, water! I shall die if I don't soon find a place to soak myself!"

So saying, he arrived at the bank of a little brook that flowed in through a water gate at one side of the garden and emptied itself into the big fish-pond. Flinging himself down by a little stream Li bathed his hands and wrists in the cool water. How delightful! If only it were deep enough to cover his whole body, how gladly would he cast himself in and enjoy the bliss of its refreshing embrace!

For a long time he lay on the ground, rejoicing at his escape from the doctor's clutches. Then, as the fever began to rise again, he sprang up with a determined cry, "What am I waiting for? I will do it. There's no one to prevent me, and it will do me a world of good. I will cast myself head first into the fish-pond. It is not deep enough near the shore to drown me if I should be too weak to swim, and I am sure it will restore me to strength and health."

He hastened along the little stream, almost running in his eagerness to reach the deeper water of the pond. He was like some small Tom Brown who had escaped from the watchful eye of the master and run out to play in a forbidden spot.

Hark! Was that a servant calling? Had Wang discovered the absence of his employer? Would he sound the alarm, and would the whole place soon be alive with men searching for the fever-stricken patient?

With one last sigh of satisfaction Li flung himself, clothes and all, into the quiet waters of the fish-pond. Now Li had been brought up in Fukien province on the seashore, and was a skilful swimmer. He dived and splashed to his heart's content, then floated on the surface. "It takes me back to my boyhood," he cried, "why, oh why, is it not the fashion to swim? I'd love to live in the water all the time and yet some of my countrymen are even more afraid than a cat of getting their feet wet. As for me, I'd give anything to stay here for ever."

"You would, eh?" chuckled a hoarse voice just under him, and then there was a sort of wheezing sound, followed by a loud burst of laughter. Mr. Li jumped as if an arrow had struck him, but when he noticed the fat, ugly monster below, his fear turned into anger. "Look here, what do you mean by giving a fellow such a start! Don't you know what the Classics say about such rudeness?"

The giant fish laughed all the louder. "What time do you suppose I have for Classics? You make me laugh till I cry!"

"But you must answer my question," cried Mr. Li, more and more persistently, forgetting for the moment that he was not trying some poor culprit for a petty crime. "Why did you laugh? Speak out at once, fellow!"

"Well, since you are such a saucy piece," roared the other, "I will tell you. It was because you awkward creatures, who call yourselves men, the most highly civilized beings in the world, always think you understand a thing fully when you have only just found out how to do it."

"You are talking about the island dwarfs, the Japanese," interrupted Mr. Li, "We Chinese seldom undertake to do anything new."

"Just hear the man!" chuckled the fish. "Now, fancy your wishing to stay in the water for ever! What do you know about water? Why you're not even provided with the proper equipment for swimming. What would you do if you really lived here always?"

"What am I doing now?" spluttered Mr. Li, so angry that he sucked in a mouthful of water before he knew it.

"Floundering," retorted the other.

"Don't you see me swimming? Are those big eyes of yours made of glass?"

"Yes, I see you all right," guffawed the fish, "that's just it! I see you too well. Why you tumble about as awkwardly as a water buffalo wallowing in a mud puddle!"

Now, as Mr. Li had always considered himself an expert in water sports, he was, by this time, speechless with rage, and all he could do was to paddle feebly round and round with strokes just strong enough to keep himself from sinking.

"Then, too," continued the fish, more and more calm as the other lost his temper, "you have a very poor arrangement for breathing. If I am not mistaken, at the bottom of this pond you would find yourself worse off than I should be at the top of a palm tree. What would you do to keep yourself from starving? Do you think it would be convenient if you had to flop yourself out on to the land every time you wanted a bite to eat? And yet, being a man, I doubt seriously if you would be content to take the proper food for fishes. You have hardly a single feature that would make you contented if you were to join an under-water school. Look at your clothes, too, water-soaked and heavy. Do you think them suitable to protect you from cold and sickness? Nature forgot to give you any scales. Now I'm going to tell you a joke, so you must be sure to laugh. Fishes are like grocery shops – always judged by their scales. As you haven't a sign of a scale, how will people judge you? See the point, eh? Nature gave you a skin, but forgot the outer covering, except, perhaps at the ends of your fingers and your toes You surely see by this time why I consider your idea ridiculous?"

Sure enough, in spite of his recent severe attack of fever, Mr. Li had really cooled completely off. He had never understood before what great disadvantages there were connected with being a man. Why not make use of this chance acquaintance, find out from him how to get rid of that miserable possession he had called his manhood, and gain the delights that only a fish can have? "Then, are you indeed contented with your lot?" he asked finally. "Are there not moments when you would prefer to be a man?"

"I, a man!" thundered the other, lashing the water with his tail. "How dare you suggest such a disgraceful change! Can it be that you do not know my rank? Why, my fellow, you behold in me a favourite nephew of the king!"

"Then, may it please your lordship," said Mr. Li, softly, "I should be exceedingly grateful if you would speak a kind word for me to your master. Do you think it possible that he could change me in some manner into a fish and accept me as a subject?"

"Of course!" replied the other, "all things are possible to the king. Know you not that my sovereign is a loyal descendant of the great water dragon, and, as such, can never die, but lives on and on and on, for ever and ever and ever, like the ruling house of Japan?"

"Oh, oh!" gasped Mr. Li, "even the Son of Heaven, our most worshipful emperor, cannot boast of such long years. Yes, I would give my fortune to be a follower of your imperial master."

"Then follow me," laughed the other, starting off at a rate that made the water hiss and boil for ten feet around him.

Mr. Li struggled vainly to keep up. If he had thought himself a good swimmer, he now saw his mistake and every bit of remaining pride was torn to tatters. "Please wait a moment," he cried out politely, "I beg of you to remember that I am only a man!"

"Pardon me," replied the other, "it was stupid of me to forget, especially as I had just been talking about it."

Soon they reached a sheltered inlet at the farther side of the pond. There Mr. Li saw a gigantic carp idly floating about in a shallow pool, and then lazily flirting his huge tail or fluttering his fins proudly from side to side. Attendant courtiers darted hither and thither, ready to do the master's slightest bidding. One of them, splendidly attired in royal scarlet, announced, with a downward flip of the head, the approach of the King's nephew who was leading Mr. Li to an audience with his Majesty.

"Whom have you here, my lad?" began the ruler, as his nephew, hesitating for words to explain his strange request, moved his fins nervously backwards and forwards. "Strange company, it seems to me, you are keeping these days."

"Only a poor man, most royal sir," replied the other, "who beseeches your Highness to grant him your gracious favour."

"When man asks favour of a fish,
'Tis hard to penetrate his wish –
He often seeks a lordly dish
To serve upon his table,"

repeated the king, smiling. "And yet, nephew, you think this fellow is really peaceably inclined and is not coming among us as a spy?"

Before his friend could answer, Mr. Li had cast himself upon his knees in the shallow water, before the noble carp, and bowed thrice, until his face was daubed with mud from the bottom of the pool. "Indeed, your Majesty, I am only a poor mortal who seeks your kindly grace. If you would but consent to receive me into your school of fishes. I would for ever be your ardent admirer and your lowly slave."

"In sooth, the fellow talks as if in earnest," remarked the king, after a moment's reflection, "and though the request is, perhaps, the strangest to which I have ever listened, I really see no reason why I should not turn a fishly ear. But, have the goodness first to cease your bowing. You are stirring up enough mud to plaster the royal palace of a shark."

Poor Li, blushing at the monarch's reproof, waited patiently for the answer to his request.

"Very well, so be it," cried the king impulsively, "your wish is granted. Sir Trout," turning to one of his courtiers, "bring hither a fish-skin of proper size for this ambitious fellow."

No sooner said than done. The fish-skin was slipped over Mr. Li's head, and his whole body was soon tucked snugly away in the scaly coat. Only his arms remained uncovered. In the twinkling of an eye Li felt sharp pains shoot through every part of his body. His arms began to shrivel up and his hands changed little by little until they made an excellent pair of fins, just as good as those of the king himself. As for his legs and feet, they suddenly began to stick together until, wriggle as he would, Li could not separate them. "Ah, ha!" thought he, "my kicking days are over, for my toes are now turned into a first-class tail."

"Not so fast," laughed the king, as Li, after thanking the royal personage profusely, started out to try his new fins; "not so fast, my friend. Before you depart, perhaps I'd better give you a little friendly advice, else your new powers are likely to land you on the hook of some lucky fisherman, and you will find yourself served up as a prize of the pond."

"I will gladly listen to your lordly counsel, for the words of the Most High to his lowly slave are like pearls before sea slugs. However, as I was once a man myself I think I understand the simple tricks they use to catch us fish, and I am therefore in position to avoid trouble."

"Don't be so sure about it. 'A hungry carp often falls into danger,' as one of our sages so wisely remarked. There are two cautions I would impress upon you. One is, never, never, eat a dangling worm; no matter how tempting it looks there are sure to be horrible hooks inside. Secondly, always swim like lightning if you see a net, but in the opposite direction. Now, I will have you served your first meal out of the royal pantry, but after that, you must hunt for yourself, like every other self-respecting citizen of the watery world."

After Li had been fed with several slugs, followed by a juicy worm for dessert, and after again thanking the king and the king's nephew for their kindness, he started forth to test his tail and fins. It was no easy matter, at first, to move them properly. A single flirt of the tail, no more vigorous than those he had been used to giving with his legs, would send him whirling round and round in the water, for all the world like a living top; and when he wriggled his fins, ever so slightly, as he thought, he found himself sprawling on his back in a most ridiculous fashion for a dignified member of fishkind. It took several hours of constant practice to get the proper stroke, and then he found he could move about without being conscious of any effort. It was the easiest thing he had ever done in his life; and oh! the water was so cool and delightful! "Would that I might enjoy that endless life the poets write of!" he murmured blissfully.

Many hours passed by until at last Li was compelled to admit that, although he was not tired, he was certainly hungry. How to get something to eat? Oh! why had he not asked the friendly nephew a few simple questions? How easily his lordship might have told him the way to get a good breakfast! But alas! without such advice, it would be a whale's task to accomplish it. Hither and thither he swam, into the deep still water, and along the muddy shore; down, down to the pebbly bottom – always looking, looking for a tempting worm. He dived into the weeds and rushes, poked his nose among the lily pads. All for nothing! No fly or worm of any kind to gladden his eager eyes! Another hour passed slowly away, and all the time his hunger was growing greater and greater. Would the fish god, the mighty dragon, not grant him even one little morsel to satisfy his aching stomach, especially since, now that he was a fish, he had no way of tightening up his belt, as hungry soldiers do when they are on a forced march?

Just as Li was beginning to think he could not wriggle his tail an instant longer, and that soon, very soon, he would feel himself slipping, slipping, slipping down to the bottom of the pond to die – at that very moment, chancing to look up, he saw, oh joy! a delicious red worm dangling a few inches above his nose. The sight gave new strength to his weary fins and tail. Another minute, and he would have had the delicate morsel in his mouth, when alas! he chanced to recall the advice given him the day before by great King Carp. "No matter how tempting it looks, there are sure to be horrible hooks inside." For an instant Li hesitated. The worm floated a trifle nearer to his half-open mouth. How tempting! After all, what was a hook to a fish when he was dying? Why be a coward? Perhaps this worm was an exception to the rule, or perhaps, perhaps any thing – really a fish in such a plight as Mr. Li could not be expected to follow advice – even the advice of a real KING.

Pop! He had it in his mouth. Oh, soft morsel, worthy of a king's desire! Now he could laugh at words of wisdom, and eat whatever came before his eye. But ugh! What was that strange feeling that – Ouch! it was the fatal hook!

With one frantic jerk, and a hundred twists and turns, poor Li sought to pull away from the cruel barb that stuck so fast in the roof of his mouth. It was now too late to wish he had kept away from temptation. Better far to have starved at the bottom of the cool pond than to be jerked out by some miserable fisherman to the light and sunshine of the busy world. Nearer and nearer he approached the surface. The more he struggled the sharper grew the cruel barb. Then, with one final splash, he found himself dangling in mid-air, swinging helplessly at the end of a long line. With a chunk he fell into a flat-bottomed boat, directly on top of several smaller fish.

"Ah, a carp!" shouted a well-known voice gleefully; "the biggest fish I've caught these three moons. What good luck!"

It was the voice of old Chang, the fisherman, who had been supplying Mr. Li's table ever since that official's arrival in the village of Everlasting Happiness. Only a word of explanation, and he, Li, would be free once more to swim about where he willed. And then there should be no more barbs for him. An escaped fish fears the hook.

"I say, Chang," he began, gasping for breath, "really now, you must chuck me overboard at once, for, don't you see, I am Mr. Li, your old master. Come, hurry up about it. I'll excuse you this time for your mistake, for, of course, you had no way of knowing. Quick!"

But Chang, with a savage jerk, pulled the hook from Li's mouth, and looked idly towards the pile of glistening fish, gloating over his catch, and wondering how much money he could demand for it. He had heard nothing of Mr. Li's remarks, for Chang had been deaf since childhood.

"Quick, quick, I am dying for air," moaned poor Li, and then, with a groan, he remembered the fisherman's affliction.

By this time they had arrived at the shore, and Li, in company with his fellow victims, found himself suddenly thrown into a wicker basket. Oh, the horrors of that journey on land! Only a tiny bit of water remained in the closely-woven thing. It was all he could do to breathe.

Joy of joys! At the door of his own house he saw his good friend Sing just coming out. "Hey, Sing," he shouted, at the top of his voice, "help, help! This son of a turtle wants to murder me. He has me in here with these fish, and doesn't seem to know that I am Li, his master. Kindly order him to take me to the lake and throw me in, for it's cool there and I like the water life much better than that on land."

Li paused to hear Sing's reply, but there came not a single word.

"I beg your honour to have a look at my catch," said old Chang to Sing. "Here is the finest fish of the season. I have brought him here so that you and my honoured master, Mr. Li, may have a treat. Carp is his favourite delicacy."

"Very kind of you, my good Chang, I'm sure, but I fear poor Mr. Li will not eat fish for some time. He has a bad attack of fever."

"There's where you're wrong," shouted Li, from his basket, flopping about with all his might, to attract attention, "I'm going to die of a chill. Can't you recognise your old friend? Help me out of this trouble and you may have all my money for your pains."

"Hey, what's that!" questioned Sing, attracted, as usual, by the word money. "Shades of Confucius! It sounds as if the carp were talking."

"What, a talking fish," laughed Chang. "Why, master, I've lived nigh on to sixty year, and such a fish has never come under my sight. There are talking birds and talking beasts for that matter; but talking fish, who ever heard of such a wonder? No, I think your ears must have deceived you, but this carp will surely cause talk when I get him into the kitchen. I'm sure the cook has never seen his like. Oh, master! I hope you will be hungry when you sit down to this fish. What a pity Mr. Li couldn't help you to devour it!"

"Help to devour myself, eh?" grumbled poor Li, now almost dead for lack of water. "You must take me for a cannibal, or some other sort of savage."

Old Chang had now gone round the house to the servants' quarters, and, after calling out the cook, held up poor Li by the tail for the chef to inspect.

With a mighty jerk Li tore himself away and fell at the feet of his faithful cook. "Save me, save me!" he cried out in despair; "this miserable Chang is deaf and doesn't know that I am Mr. Li, his master. My fish voice is not strong enough for his hearing. Only take me back to the pond and set me free. You shall have a pension for life, wear good clothes and eat good food, all the rest of your days. Only hear me and obey! Listen, my dear cook, listen!"

"The thing seems to be talking," muttered the cook, "but such wonders cannot be. Only ignorant old women or foreigners would believe that a fish could talk." And seizing his former master by the tail, he swung him on to a table, picked up a knife, and began to whet it on a stone.

"Oh, oh!" screamed Li, "you will stick a knife into me! You will scrape off my beautiful shiny scales! You will whack off my lovely new fins! You will murder your old master!"

"Well, you won't talk much longer," growled the cook, "I'll show you a trick or two with the blade."

So saying, with a gigantic thrust, he plunged the knife deep into the body of the trembling victim.

With a shrill cry of horror and despair, Mr. Li awoke from the deep sleep into which he had fallen. His fever was gone, but he found himself trembling with fear at thought of the terrible death that had come to him in dreamland.

"Thanks be to Buddha, I am not a fish!" he cried out joyfully; "and now I shall be well enough to enjoy the feast to which Mr. Sing has bidden guests for tomorrow. But alas, now that I can eat the old fisherman's prize carp, it has changed back into myself.

"If only the good of our dreams came true,
I shouldn't mind dreaming the whole day through."

The Nodding Tiger

JUST OUTSIDE THE walls of a Chinese city there lived a young woodcutter named T'ang and his old mother, a woman of seventy. They were very poor and had a tiny one-room shanty, built of mud and grass, which they rented from a neighbour. Every day young T'ang rose bright and early and went up on the mountain near their house. There he spent the day cutting firewood to sell in the city near by. In the evening he would return home, take the wood to market, sell it, and bring back food for his mother and himself. Now, though these two people were poor, they were very happy, for the young man loved his mother dearly, and the old woman thought there was no one like her son in all the world. Their friends, however, felt sorry for them and said, "What a pity we have no grasshoppers here, so that the T'angs could have some food from heaven!"

One day young T'ang got up before daylight and started for the hills, carrying his axe on his shoulder. He bade his mother good-bye, telling her that he would be back early with a heavier load of wood than usual, for the morrow would be a holiday and they must eat good food. All day long Widow T'ang waited patiently, saying to herself over and over as she went about her simple work, "The good boy, the good boy, how he loves his old mother!"

In the afternoon she began watching for his return – but in vain. The sun was sinking lower and lower in the west, but still he did not come. At last the old woman was frightened. "My poor son!" she muttered. "Something has happened to him." Straining her feeble eyes, she looked along the mountain path. Nothing was to be seen there but a flock of sheep following the shepherd. "Woe is me!" moaned the woman. "My boy! my boy!" She took her crutch from its corner and limped off to a neighbour's house to tell him of her trouble and beg him to go and look for the missing boy.

Now this neighbour was kind-hearted, and willing to help old Mother T'ang, for he felt very sorry for her. "There are many wild beasts in the mountains," he said, shaking his head as he walked away with her, thinking to prepare the frightened woman for the worst, "and I fear that your son has been carried off by one of them." Widow T'ang gave a scream of horror and sank upon the ground. Her friend walked slowly up the mountain path, looking carefully for signs of a struggle. At last when he had gone half way up the slope he came to a little pile of torn clothing spattered with blood. The woodman's axe was lying by the side of the path, also his carrying pole and some rope. There could be no mistake: after making a brave fight, the poor youth had been carried off by a tiger.

Gathering up the torn garments, the man went sadly down the hill. He dreaded seeing the poor mother and telling her that her only boy was indeed gone for ever. At the foot of the mountain he found her still lying on the ground. When she looked up and saw what he was carrying, with a cry of despair she fainted away. She did not need to be told what had happened.

Friends bore her into the little house and gave her food, but they could not comfort her. "Alas!" she cried, "of what use is it to live? He was my only boy. Who will take care of me in my old age? Why have the gods treated me in this cruel way?"

She wept, tore her hair, and beat her chest, until people said she had gone mad. The longer she mourned, the more violent she became.

The next day, however, much to the surprise of her neighbours, she set out for the city, making her way along slowly by means of her crutch. It was a pitiful sight to see her, so old, so feeble, and so lonely. Everyone was sorry for her and pointed her out, saying, "See! the poor old soul has no one to help her!"

In the city she asked her way to the public hall. When she found the place she knelt at the front gate, calling out loudly and telling of her ill-fortune. Just at this moment the mandarin, or city judge, walked into the court room to try any cases which might be brought before him. He heard the old woman weeping and wailing outside, and bade one of the servants let her enter and tell him of her wrongs.

Now this was just what the Widow T'ang had come for. Calming herself, she hobbled into the great hall of trial.

"What is the matter, old woman? Why do you raise such an uproar in front of my yamen? Speak up quickly and tell me of your trouble."

"I am old and feeble," she began; "lame and almost blind. I have no money and no way of earning money. I have not one relative now in all the empire. I depended on my only son for a living. Every day he climbed the mountain, for he was a woodcutter, and every evening he came back home, bringing enough money for our food. But yesterday he went and did not return. A mountain tiger carried him off and ate him, and now, alas! there seems to be no help for it – I must die of hunger. My bleeding heart cries out for justice. I have come into this hall to-day, to beg your worship to see that the slayer of my son is punished. Surely the law says that none may shed blood without giving his own blood in payment."

"But, woman, are you mad?" cried the mandarin, laughing loudly. "Did you not say it was a tiger that killed your son? How can a tiger be brought to justice? Of a truth, you must have lost your senses."

The judge's questions were of no avail. The Widow T'ang kept up her clamour. She would not be turned away until she had gained her purpose. The hall echoed with the noise of her howling. The mandarin could stand it no longer. "Hold! woman," he cried, "stop your shrieking. I will do what you ask. Only go home and wait until I summon you to court. The slayer of your son shall be caught and punished."

The judge was, of course, only trying to get rid of the demented mother, thinking that if she were only once out of his sight, he could give orders not to let her into the hall again. The old woman, however, was too sharp for him. She saw through his plan and became more stubborn than ever.

"No, I cannot go," she answered, "until I have seen you sign the order for that tiger to be caught and brought into this judgment hall."

Now, as the judge was not really a bad man, he decided to humour the old woman in her strange plea. Turning to the assistants in the court room he asked which of them would be willing to go in search of the tiger. One of these men, named Li-neng, had been leaning against the wall, half asleep. He had been drinking heavily and so had not heard what had been going on in the room. One of his friends gave him a poke in the ribs just as the judge asked for volunteers.

Thinking the judge had called him by name, he stepped forward, knelt on the floor, saying, "I, Li-neng, can go and do the will of your worship."

"Very well, you will do," answered the judge. "Here is your order. Go forth and do your duty." So saying, he handed the warrant to Li-neng. "Now, old woman, are you satisfied?" he continued.

"Quite satisfied, your worship," she replied.

"Then go home and wait there until I send for you."

Mumbling a few words of thanks, the unhappy mother left the building.

When Li-neng went outside the court room, his friends crowded round him. "Drunken sot!" they laughed; "do you know what you have done?"

Li-neng shook his head. "Just a little business for the mandarin, isn't it? Quite easy."

"Call it easy, if you like. What! man, arrest a tiger, a man-eating tiger and bring him to the city! Better go and say good-bye to your father and mother. They will never see you again."

Li-neng slept off his drunkenness, and then saw that his friends were right. He had been very foolish. But surely the judge had meant the whole thing only as a joke! No such order had ever been written before! It was plain that the judge had hit on this plan simply to get rid of the wailing old woman. Li-neng took the warrant back to the judgment hall and told the mandarin that the tiger could not be found.

But the judge was in no mood for joking. "Can't be found? And why not? You agreed to arrest this tiger. Why is it that to-day you try to get out of your promise? I can by no means permit this, for I have given my word to satisfy the old woman in her cry for justice."

Li-neng knelt and knocked his head on the floor. "I was drunk," he cried, "when I gave my promise. I knew not what you were asking. I can catch a man, but not a tiger. I know nothing of such matters. Still, if you wish it, I can go into the hills and hire hunters to help me."

"Very well, it makes no difference how you catch him, as long as you bring him into court. If you fail in your duty, there is nothing left but to beat you until you succeed. I give you five days."

During the next few days Li-neng left no stone unturned in trying to find the guilty tiger. The best hunters in the country were employed. Night and day they searched the hills, hiding in mountain caves, watching and waiting, but finding nothing. It was all very trying for Li-neng, since he now feared the heavy hands of the judge more than the claws of the tiger. On the fifth day he had to report his failure. He received a thorough beating, fifty blows on the back. But that was not the worst of it. During the next six weeks, try as he would, he could find no traces of the missing animal. At the end of each five days, he got another beating for his pains. The poor fellow was in despair. Another month of such treatment would lay him on his deathbed. This he knew very well, and yet he had little hope. His friends shook their heads when they saw him. "He is drawing near the wood," they said to each other, meaning that he would soon be in his coffin. "Why don't you flee the country?" they asked him. "Follow the tiger's example. You see he has escaped completely. The judge would make no effort to catch you if you should go across the border into the next province."

Li-neng shook his head on hearing this advice. He had no desire to leave his family for ever, and he felt sure of being caught and put to death if he should try to run away.

One day after all the hunters had given up the search in disgust and gone back to their homes in the valley, Li-neng entered a mountain temple to pray. The tears rained down his cheeks as he knelt before the great fierce-looking idol. "Alas! I am a dead man!" he moaned between his prayers; "a dead man, for now there is no hope. Would that I had never touched a drop of wine!"

Just then he heard a slight rustling near by. Looking up, he saw a huge tiger standing at the temple gate. But Li-neng was no longer afraid of tigers. He knew there was only one way to save himself. "Ah," he said, looking the great cat straight in the eye, "you have come to eat me, have you? Well, I fear you would find my flesh a trifle tough, since I have been beaten with four hundred blows during these six weeks. You are the same fellow that carried off the woodman last month, aren't you? This woodman was an only son, the sole support of an old mother. Now this poor woman has reported you to the mandarin, who, in turn, has had a warrant drawn up for your arrest. I have been sent out to find you and lead you to trial. For some reason or other you have acted the coward, and remained in hiding. This has been the cause of my beating. Now I don't want to suffer any longer as a result of your murder. You must come with me to the city and answer the charge of killing the woodman."

All the time Li-neng was speaking, the tiger listened closely. When the man was silent, the animal made no effort to escape, but, on the contrary, seemed willing and ready to be captured. He bent his head forward and let Li-neng slip a strong chain over it. Then he followed the man quietly down the mountain, through the crowded streets of the city, into the court room. All along the way there was great excitement. "The man-slaying tiger has been caught," shouted the people. "He is being led to trial."

The crowd followed Li-neng into the hall of justice. When the judge walked in, everyone became as quiet as the grave. All were filled with wonder at the strange sight of a tiger being called before a judge.

The great animal did not seem to be afraid of those who were watching so curiously. He sat down in front of the mandarin, for all the world like a huge cat. The judge rapped on the table as a signal that all was ready for the trial.

"Tiger," said he, turning toward the prisoner, "did you eat the woodman whom you are charged with killing?"

The tiger gravely nodded his head.

"Yes, he killed my boy!" screamed the aged mother. "Kill him! Give him the death that he deserves!"

"A life for a life is the law of the land," continued the judge, paying no attention to the forlorn mother, but looking the accused directly in the eye. "Did you not know it? You have robbed a helpless old woman of her only son. There are no relatives to support her. She is crying for vengeance. You must be punished for your crime. The law must be enforced. However, I am not a cruel judge. If you can promise to take the place of this widow's son and support the woman in her old age, I am quite willing to spare you from a disgraceful death. What say you, will you accept my offer?"

The gaping people craned their necks to see what would happen, and once more they were surprised to see the savage beast nod his head in silent agreement.

"Very well, then, you are free to return to your mountain home; only, of course, you must remember your promise."

The chains were taken from the tiger's neck, and the great animal walked silently out of the yamen, down the street, and through the gate opening towards his beloved mountain cave.

Once more the old woman was very angry. As she hobbled from the room, she cast sour glances at the judge, muttering over and over again, "Who ever heard of a tiger taking the place of a son? A pretty game this is, to catch the brute, and then to set him free." There was nothing for her to do, however, but to return home, for the judge had given strict orders that on no account was she to appear before him again.

Almost broken-hearted she entered her desolate hovel at the foot of the mountain. Her neighbours shook their heads as they saw her. "She cannot live long," they said. "She has the look of death on her wrinkled face. Poor soul! she has nothing to live for, nothing to keep her from starving."

But they were mistaken. Next morning when the old woman went outside to get a breath of fresh air she found a newly killed deer in front of her door. Her tiger-son had begun to keep his promise, for she could see the marks of his claws on the dead animal's body. She took the carcass into the house and dressed it for the market. On the city streets next day she had no trouble in selling the flesh and skin for a handsome sum of money. All had heard of the tiger's first gift, and no one was anxious to drive a close bargain.

Laden with food, the happy woman went home rejoicing, with money enough to keep her for many a day. A week later the tiger came to her door with a roll of cloth and some money in his mouth. He dropped these new gifts at her feet and ran away without even waiting for her thank-you. The Widow T'ang now saw that the judge had acted wisely. She stopped grieving for her dead son and began to love in his stead the handsome animal that had come to take his place so willingly.

The tiger grew much attached to his foster-mother and often purred contentedly outside her door, waiting for her to come and stroke his soft fur. He no longer had the old desire to kill. The sight of blood was not nearly so tempting as it had been in his younger days. Year after year he brought the weekly offerings to his mistress until she was as well provided for as any other widow in the country.

At last in the course of nature the good old soul died. Kind friends laid her away in her last resting place at the foot of the great mountain. There was money enough left out of what she had saved to put up a handsome tombstone, on which this story was written just as you have read it here. The faithful tiger mourned long for his dear mistress. He lay on her grave, wailing like a child that had lost its mother. Long he listened for the voice he had loved so well, long he searched the mountain-slopes, returning each night to the empty cottage, but all in vain. She whom he loved was gone for ever.

One night he vanished from the mountain, and from that day to this no one in that province has ever seen him. Some who know this story say that he died of grief in a secret cave which he had long used as a hiding-place. Others add, with a wise shrug of the shoulders, that, like Shanwang, he was taken to the Western Heaven, there to be rewarded for his deeds of virtue and to live as a fairy for ever afterwards.

Ghostly Tales

Introduction

GHOSTS, SPIRITS and all things eerily supernatural have always held a firm grasp on the Chinese psyche. Traditionally it was believed that the spirits of the dead could be contacted through a medium and, with proper reward and respect, could help the living – indeed, during the Hungry Ghost Festival in early autumn, the spirits of the deceased are believed to come out from the Underworld into the realm of the living, who perform rituals and offerings to venerate, feed and redeem their dead relatives. However, generally, ghosts are deemed to be malevolent beings – which lends a chilling and gripping air to the many stories in which they feature.

Eerie tales can feature spirits of many forms and abodes – the story of 'The Haunted Pavilion' reveals that the voices plaguing the young student are in fact demons in the form of a black swine, red cock and a scorpion; while in the poignant classic story of 'The Soul of The Great Bell' a young maiden is forever trapped not in the netherworld but in the bell itself. Spirits sometimes arise in order to fulfil some lofty purpose – such as in 'The Punishment of Greed', but more often are malignant and self-serving, as in 'The Ghost Who Was Foiled'. Sometimes we never learn why they chase their terrified victims – see 'The Resuscitated Corpse' – but safe in our armchairs can enjoy the thrill of the ride.

The Haunted Pavilion

MANY YEARS AGO a student was walking along a road south of Anyang, heading towards that city. In those days it was common for students to travel the country, seeking knowledge from ancient sites and men of learning throughout China: 'wandering with sword and lute' as it was known.

On this particular night the student arrived at a village some twelve miles short of Anyang, and as night was closing in fast, he asked an old woman if there was an inn nearby. She replied, saying that the nearest inn was some miles distant, whereupon the student remarked that he had just passed a pavilion on the road and that he would rest there. Such pavilions were common in China at that time, used as resting places for weary travellers, and looked after by neighbouring villagers.

The old woman went white at the student's words, and told him he must on no account stay in the shelter, as it was cursed with demons, and no one who had stayed there had ever lived to tell the tale. But the student laughed off the dire warning, saying that he thought he could take care of himself, and brushing aside the protestations of the villagers, he set off for the pavilion.

Night fell, but the student did not sleep; instead he lit a lamp and read aloud to himself from one of his books. Time passed; for a long while nothing stirred, until, on the stroke of midnight, the student heard footsteps on the road outside. Peering out of the door, he saw a man in black. The man stopped and called the master of the pavilion.

"Here I am," came a voice from just behind him, causing the student to jump in surprise. "What do you want?"

"Who is in the pavilion?" the man in black asked.

"A scholar is in the pavilion, but he is reading his book and not yet asleep," the voice replied.

At this the man in black sighed, and turned towards the village, and the scholar returned to his reading. Some while later he again heard footsteps, and this time, as he peered of the door, he saw a man in a red hat stop on the road outside the pavilion.

"Master of the Pavilion!" the man cried.

"Here I am," came the voice from just behind him.

"Who is in the pavilion?" the man in the red hat asked.

"A scholar is in the pavilion, but he is reading his book and not yet asleep," the voice replied.

At this the man in the red hat sighed too and turned towards the village. Then the student waited for a few minutes, until he was sure there was no one else coming down the road. He crept out of the door, and standing on the road, called out, "Master of the Pavilion!"

"Here I am," came the voice from within.

"Who is in the pavilion?" the student asked.

"A scholar is in the pavilion, but he is reading his book and not yet asleep," the voice replied.

The scholar sighed, and then asked, "Who was the man in black?"

"That was the black swine of the North," the voice answered.

"And who was the man in the red hat?"

"That was the Red Cock of the West."

"And who are you?" the student asked.

"I am the Old Scorpion," came the reply. At this, the student slipped back into the pavilion, and stayed awake all night, reading his book undisturbed.

The next morning the villagers rushed to the pavilion to see if the student had survived the night, and were astonished to see him sitting on the veranda, strumming his lute. As they gathered round him, bombarding him with questions, the student held up his hand for silence.

"Follow me," he said, "and I will remove the curse from this building." Then he went back inside the pavilion, followed by the villagers. He pulled aside a rotting screen in one corner of the room, and there behind it was a huge black scorpion, many feet long, and ready to strike. With one sweep of his sword, the student split the creature from head to tail, and it fell lifeless to the floor.

Next he asked the villagers where they kept a black pig. "In the house north of the pavilion," they answered, and showed him the place. There was a huge black pig, its eyes glinting with demonic fury. Again the student drew his sword, and in moments the pig lay dead at his feet.

"Now, where do you keep a large red rooster?" he asked.

"In a shed to the west of the pavilion," they answered, and showed him the place. There was an enormous red cockerel, with a huge red comb, and long, sharp talons. With another swish of the student's sword, the bird was decapitated, and lay dead at his feet.

The scholar explained to the startled villagers how he had discovered the identities of the demons, and from that day on, no traveller's rest was ever against disturbed in the pavilion south of Anyang.

The Phantom Vessel

ONCE A SHIP LOADED with pleasure-seekers was sailing from North China to Shanghai. High winds and stormy weather had delayed her, and she was still one week from port when a great plague broke out on board. This plague was of the worst kind. It attacked passengers and sailors alike until there were so few left to sail the vessel that it seemed as if she would soon be left to the mercy of winds and waves.

On all sides lay the dead, and the groans of the dying were most terrible to hear. Of that great company of travellers only one, a little boy named Ying-lo, had escaped. At last the few sailors, who had been trying hard to save their ship, were obliged to lie down upon the deck, a prey to the dreadful sickness, and soon they too were dead.

Ying-lo now found himself alone on the sea. For some reason – he did not know why – the gods or the sea fairies had spared him, but as he looked about in terror at the friends and loved ones who had died, he almost wished that he might join them.

The sails flapped about like great broken wings, while the giant waves dashed higher above the deck, washing many of the bodies overboard and wetting the little boy to the skin. Shivering with cold, he gave himself up for lost and prayed to the gods, whom his mother had often told him about, to take him from this dreadful ship and let him escape the fatal illness.

As he lay there praying he heard a slight noise in the rigging just above his head. Looking up, he saw a ball of fire running along a yardarm near the top of the mast. The sight was so strange that he forgot his prayer and stared with open-mouthed wonder. To his astonishment, the ball grew brighter and brighter, and then suddenly began slipping down the mast, all the time increasing in size. The poor boy did not know what to do or to think. Were the gods, in answer to his prayer, sending fire to burn the vessel? If so, he would soon escape. Anything would be better than to be alone upon the sea.

Nearer and nearer came the fireball. At last, when it reached the deck, to Ying-lo's surprise, something very, very strange happened. Before he had time to feel alarmed, the light vanished, and a funny little man stood in front of him peering anxiously into the child's frightened face.

"Yes, you are the lad I'm looking for," he said at last, speaking in a piping voice that almost made Ying-lo smile. "You are Ying-lo, and you are the only one left of this wretched company." This he said, pointing towards the bodies lying here and there about the deck.

Although he saw that the old man meant him no harm, the child could say nothing, but waited in silence, wondering what would happen next.

By this time the vessel was tossing and pitching so violently that it seemed every minute as if it would upset and go down beneath the foaming waves, never to rise again. Not many miles distant on the right, some jagged rocks stuck out of the water, lifting their cruel heads as if waiting for the helpless ship.

The newcomer walked slowly towards the mast and tapped on it three times with an iron staff he had been using as a cane. Immediately the sails spread, the vessel righted itself and began to glide over the sea so fast that the gulls were soon left far behind, while the threatening rocks upon which the ship had been so nearly dashed seemed like specks in the distance.

"Do you remember me?" said the stranger, suddenly turning and coming up to Ying-lo, but his voice was lost in the whistling of the wind, and the boy knew only by the moving of his lips that the old man was talking. The greybeard bent over until his mouth was at Ying-lo's ear: "Did you ever see me before?"

With a puzzled look, at first the child shook his head. Then as he gazed more closely there seemed to be something that he recognized about the wrinkled face. "Yes, I think so, but I don't know when."

With a tap of his staff the fairy stopped the blowing of the wind, and then spoke once more to his small companion: "One year ago I passed through your village. I was dressed in rags, and was begging my way along the street, trying to find someone who would feel sorry for me. Alas! no one answered my cry for mercy. Not a crust was thrown into my bowl. All the people were deaf, and fierce dogs drove me from door to door. Finally when I was almost dying of hunger, I began to feel that here was a village without one good person in it. Just then you saw my suffering, ran into the house, and brought me out food. Your heartless mother saw you doing this and beat you cruelly. Do you remember now, my child?"

"Yes, I remember," he answered sadly, "and that mother is now lying dead. Alas! all, all are dead, my father and my brothers also. Not one is left of my family."

"Little did you know, my boy, to whom you were giving food that day. You took me for a lowly beggar, but, behold, it was not a poor man that you fed, for I am Iron Staff. You must have heard of me when they were telling of the fairies in the Western Heaven, and of their adventures here on earth."

"Yes, yes," answered Ying-lo, trembling half with fear and half with joy, "indeed I have heard of you many, many times, and all the people love you for your kind deeds of mercy."

"Alas! they did not show their love, my little one. Surely you know that if any one wishes to reward the fairies for their mercies, he must begin to do deeds of the same kind himself. No one but you in all your village had pity on me in my rags. If they had known that I was Iron Staff, everything would have been different; they would have given me a feast and begged for my protection.

"The only love that loves aright
Is that which loves in every plight.
The beggar in his sad array
Is moulded of the selfsame clay.

"Who knows a man by what he wears,
By what he says or by his prayers?
Hidden beneath that wrinkled skin
A fairy may reside within.
"Then treat with kindness and with love
The lowly man, the god above;
A friendly nod, a welcome smile –
For love is ever worth the while."

Ying-lo listened in wonder to Iron Staff's little poem, and when he had finished, the boy's face was glowing with the love of which the fairy had spoken. "My poor, poor father and mother!" he cried; "they knew nothing of these beautiful things you are telling me. They were brought up in poverty. As they were knocked about in childhood by those around them, so they learned to beat others who begged them for help. Is it strange that they did not have hearts full of pity for you when you looked like a beggar?"

"But what about you, my boy? You were not deaf when I asked you. Have you not been whipped and punished all your life? How then did you learn to look with love at those in tears?"

The child could not answer these questions, but only looked sorrowfully at Iron Staff. "Oh, can you not, good fairy, will you not restore my parents and brothers, and give them another chance to be good and useful people?"

"Listen, Ying-lo; it is impossible – unless you do two things first," he answered, stroking his beard gravely and leaning heavily upon his staff.

"What are they? What must I do to save my family? Anything you ask of me will not be too much to pay for your kindness."

"First you must tell me of some good deed done by these people for whose lives you are asking. Name only one, for that will be enough; but it is against our rules to help those who have done nothing."

Ying-lo was silent, and for a moment his face was clouded. "Yes, I know," he said finally, brightening. "They burned incense once at the temple. That was certainly a deed of virtue."

"But when was it, little one, that they did this?"

"When my big brother was sick, and they were praying for him to get well. The doctors could not save him with boiled turnip juice or with any other of the medicines they used, so my parents begged the gods."

"Selfish, selfish!" muttered Iron Staff. "If their eldest son had not been dying they would have spent no money at the temple. They tried in this way to buy back his health, for they were expecting him to support them in their old age."

Ying-lo's face fell. "You are right," he answered.

"Can you think of nothing else?"

"Yes, oh, yes, last year when the foreigner rode through our village and fell sick in front of our house, they took him in and cared for him."

"How long?" asked the other sharply.

"Until he died the next week."

"And what did they do with the mule he was riding, his bed, and the money in his bag? Did they try to restore them to his people?"

"No, they said they'd keep them to pay for the trouble." Ying-lo's face turned scarlet.

"But try again, dear boy! Is there not one little deed of goodness that was not selfish? Think once more."

For a long time Ying-lo did not reply. At length he spoke in a low voice; "I think of one, but I fear it amounts to nothing."

"No good, my child, is too small to be counted when the gods are weighing a man's heart."

"Last spring the birds were eating in my father's garden. My mother wanted to buy poison from the shop to destroy them, but my father said no, that the little things must live, and he for one was not in favour of killing them."

"At last, Ying-lo, you have named a real deed of mercy, and as he spared the tiny birds from poison, so shall his life and the lives of your mother and brothers be restored from the deadly plague.

"But remember there is one other thing that depends on you."

Ying-lo's eyes glistened gratefully. "Then if it rests with me, and I can do it, you have my promise. No sacrifice should be too great for a son to make for his loved ones even though his life itself is asked in payment."

"Very well, Ying-lo. What I require is that you carry out to the letter my instructions. Now it is time for me to keep my promise to you."

So saying, Iron Staff called on Ying-lo to point out the members of his family, and, approaching them one by one, with the end of his iron stick he touched their foreheads. In an instant each, without a word, arose. Looking round and recognising Ying-lo, they stood back, frightened at seeing him with the fairy. When the last had risen to his feet, Iron Staff beckoned all of them to listen. This they did willingly, too much terrified to speak, for they saw on all sides signs of the plague that had swept over the vessel, and they remembered the frightful agony they had suffered in dying. Each knew that he had been lifted by some magic power from darkness into light.

"My friends," began the fairy, "little did you think when less than a year ago you drove me from your door that soon you yourselves would be in need of mercy. To-day you have had a peep into the awful land of Yama. You have seen the horror of his tortures, have heard the screams of his slaves, and by another night you would have been carried before him to be judged. What power is it that has saved you from his clutches? As you look back through your wicked lives can you think of any reason why you deserved this rescue? No, there is no memory of goodness in your black hearts. Well, I shall tell you: it is this little boy, this Ying-lo, who many times has felt the weight of your wicked hands and has hidden in terror at your coming. To him alone you owe my help."

Father, mother, and brothers all gazed in turn, first at the fairy and then at the timid child whose eyes fell before their looks of gratitude.

"By reason of his goodness this child whom you have scorned is worthy of a place within the Western Heaven. In truth, I came this very day to lead him to that fairyland. For you, however, he wishes to make a sacrifice. With sorrow I am yielding to his wishes. His sacrifice will be that of giving up a place among the fairies and of continuing to live here on this earth with you. He will try to make a change within your household. If at any time you treat him badly and do not heed his wishes – mark you well my words – by the power of this magic staff which I shall place in his hands, he may enter at once into the land of the fairies, leaving you to die in your wickedness. This I command him to do, and he has promised to obey my slightest wish.

"This plague took you off suddenly and ended your wicked lives. Ying-lo has raised you from its grasp and his power can lift you from the bed of sin. No other hand than his can bear the rod which I am leaving. If one of you but touch it, instantly he will fall dead upon the ground.

"And now, my child, the time has come for me to leave you. First, however, I must show you what you are now able to do. Around you lie the corpses of sailors and passengers. Tap three times upon the mast and wish that they shall come to life," So saying he handed Ying-lo the iron staff.

Although the magic rod was heavy, the child lifted it as if it were a fairy's wand. Then, stepping forward to the mast, he rapped three times as he had been commanded. Immediately on all sides arose the bodies, once more full of life and strength.

"Now command the ship to take you back to your home port, for such sinful creatures as these are in no way fit to make a journey among strangers. They must first return and free their homes of sin."

Again rapping on the mast, the child willed the great vessel to take its homeward course. No sooner had he moved the staff than, like a bird wheeling in the heavens, the bark swung round and started on the return journey. Swifter than a flash of lightning flew the boat, for it was now become a fairy vessel. Before the sailors and the travellers could recover from their surprise, land was sighted and they saw that they were indeed entering the harbour.

Just as the ship was darting toward the shore the fairy suddenly, with a parting word to Ying-lo, changed into a flaming ball of fire which rolled along the deck and ascended the spars. Then, as it reached the top of the rigging, it floated off into the blue sky, and all on board, speechless with surprise, watched it until it vanished.

With a cry of thanksgiving, Ying-lo flung his arms about his parents and descended with them to the shore.

The Soul of the Great Bell

THE WATER-CLOCK MARKS the hour in the Ta-chung sz' – in the Tower of the Great Bell: now the mallet is lifted to smite the lips of the metal monster – the vast lips inscribed with Buddhist texts from the sacred Fa-hwa-King, from the chapters of the holy Ling-yen-King! Hear the great bell responding! – how mighty her voice, though tongueless! – KO-NGAI! All the little dragons on the high-tilted eaves of the green roofs shiver to the tips of their gilded tails under that deep wave of sound; all the porcelain gargoyles tremble on their carven perches; all the hundred little bells of the pagodas quiver with desire to speak. KO-NGAI! – all the green-and-gold tiles of the temple are vibrating; the wooden goldfish above them are writhing against the sky; the uplifted finger of Fo shakes high over the heads of the worshippers through the blue fog of incense! KO-NGAI! – What a thunder tone was that! All the lacquered goblins on the palace cornices wriggle their fire-colored tongues! And after each huge shock, how wondrous the multiple echo and the great golden moan and, at last, the sudden sibilant sobbing in the ears when the immense tone faints away in broken whispers of silver – as though a woman should whisper, "Hiai!" Even so the great bell hath sounded every day for well-nigh five hundred years – Ko-Ngai: first with stupendous clang, then with immeasurable moan of gold, then with silver murmuring of "Hiai!" And there is not a child in all the many-colored ways of the old Chinese city who does not know the story of the great bell, who cannot tell you why the great bell says Ko-Ngai and Hiai!

* * *

Now, this is the story of the great bell in the Ta-chung sz', as the same is related in the Pe-Hiao-Tou-Choue, written by the learned Yu-Pao-Tchen, of the City of Kwang-tchau-fu.

Nearly five hundred years ago the Celestially August, the Son of Heaven, Yong-Lo, of the "Illustrious," or Ming, dynasty, commanded the worthy official Kouan-Yu that he should have a bell made of such size that the sound thereof might be heard for one hundred li. And he further ordained that the voice of the bell should be strengthened with brass, and deepened with gold, and sweetened with silver; and that the face and the great lips of it should be graven with blessed sayings from the sacred books, and that it should be suspended in the centre of the imperial capital, to sound through all the many-colored ways of the City of Pe-king.

Therefore the worthy mandarin Kouan-Yu assembled the master-moulders and the renowned bellsmiths of the empire, and all men of great repute and cunning in foundry work; and they measured the materials for the alloy, and treated them skilfully, and prepared the moulds, the fires, the instruments, and the monstrous melting-pot for fusing the metal. And they labored exceedingly, like giants – neglecting only rest and sleep and the comforts of life; toiling both night and day in obedience to Kouan-Yu, and striving in all things to do the behest of the Son of Heaven.

But when the metal had been cast, and the earthen mould separated from the glowing casting, it was discovered that, despite their great labor and ceaseless care, the result was void of worth; for the metals had rebelled one against the other – the gold had scorned alliance with the brass, the silver would not mingle with the molten iron. Therefore the moulds had to be once more prepared, and the fires rekindled, and the metal remelted, and all the work tediously and toilsomely repeated. The Son of Heaven heard, and was angry, but spake nothing.

A second time the bell was cast, and the result was even worse. Still the metals obstinately refused to blend one with the other; and there was no uniformity in the bell, and the sides of it were cracked and fissured, and the lips of it were slagged and split asunder; so that all the labor had to be repeated even a third time, to the great dismay of Kouan-Yu. And when the Son of Heaven heard these things, he was angrier than before; and sent his messenger to Kouan-Yu with a letter, written upon lemon-colored silk, and sealed with the seal of the Dragon, containing these words:

"From the Mighty Yong-Lo, the Sublime Tait-Sung, the Celestial and August – whose reign is called 'Ming' – to Kouan-Yu the Fuh-yin: Twice thou hast betrayed the trust we have deigned graciously to place in thee; if thou fail a third time in fulfilling our command, thy head shall be severed from thy neck. Tremble, and obey!"

* * *

Now, Kouan-Yu had a daughter of dazzling loveliness, whose name – Ko-Ngai – was ever in the mouths of poets, and whose heart was even more beautiful than her face. Ko-Ngai loved her father with such love that she had refused a hundred worthy suitors rather than make his home desolate by her absence; and when she had seen the awful yellow missive, sealed with the Dragon-Seal, she fainted away with fear for her father's sake. And when her senses and her strength returned to her, she could not rest or sleep for thinking of her parent's danger, until she had secretly sold some of her jewels, and with the money so obtained had hastened to an astrologer, and paid him a great price to advise her by what means her father might be saved from the peril impending over him. So the astrologer made observations of the heavens, and marked the aspect of the Silver Stream (which we call the Milky Way), and examined the signs of the Zodiac – the Hwang-tao, or Yellow Road – and consulted the table of the Five Hin, or Principles of the Universe, and the mystical books of the alchemists. And after a long silence, he made answer to her, saying: "Gold and brass will never meet in wedlock, silver and iron never will embrace, until the flesh of a maiden be melted in the crucible; until the blood of a virgin be mixed with the metals in their fusion." So Ko-Ngai returned home sorrowful at heart; but she kept secret all that she had heard, and told no one what she had done.

* * *

At last came the awful day when the third and last effort to cast the great bell was to be made; and Ko-Ngai, together with her waiting-woman, accompanied her father to the foundry, and they took their places upon a platform overlooking the toiling of the moulders and the lava of liquefied metal. All the workmen wrought their tasks in silence; there was no sound heard but the muttering of the fires. And the muttering deepened into a roar like the roar of typhoons approaching, and the blood-red lake of metal slowly brightened like the vermilion of a sunrise, and the vermilion was transmuted into a radiant glow of gold, and the gold whitened blindingly, like the silver face of a full moon. Then the workers ceased to feed the raving flame, and all fixed their eyes upon the eyes of Kouan-Yu; and Kouan-Yu prepared to give the signal to cast.

But ere ever he lifted his finger, a cry caused him to turn his head; and all heard the voice of Ko-Ngai sounding sharply sweet as a bird's song above the great thunder of the fires, "For thy sake, O my Father!" And even as she cried, she leaped into the white flood of metal; and the lava of the furnace roared to receive her, and spattered monstrous flakes of flame to the roof, and burst over the verge of the earthen crater, and cast up a whirling fountain of many-colored fires, and subsided quakingly, with lightnings and with thunders and with mutterings.

Then the father of Ko-Ngai, wild with his grief, would have leaped in after her, but that strong men held him back and kept firm grasp upon him until he had fainted away and they could bear him like one dead to his home. And the serving-woman of Ko-Ngai, dizzy and speechless for pain, stood before the furnace, still holding in her hands a shoe, a tiny, dainty shoe, with embroidery of pearls and flowers – the shoe of her beautiful mistress that was. For she had sought to grasp Ko-Ngai by the foot as she leaped, but had only been able to clutch the shoe, and the pretty shoe came off in her hand; and she continued to stare at it like one gone mad.

But in spite of all these things, the command of the Celestial and August had to be obeyed, and the work of the moulders to be finished, hopeless as the result might be. Yet the glow of the metal seemed purer and whiter than before; and there was no sign of the beautiful body that had been entombed therein. So the ponderous casting was made; and lo! when the metal had become cool, it was found that the bell was beautiful to look upon, and perfect in form, and wonderful in color above all other bells. Nor was there any trace found of the body of Ko-Ngai; for it had been totally absorbed by the precious alloy, and blended with the well-blended brass and gold, with the intermingling of the silver and the iron. And when they sounded the bell, its tones were found to be deeper and mellower and mightier than the tones of any other bell – reaching even beyond the distance of one hundred li, like a pealing of summer thunder; and yet also like some vast voice uttering a name, a woman's name – the name of Ko-Ngai!

* * *

And still, between each mighty stroke there is a long low moaning heard; and ever the moaning ends with a sound of sobbing and of complaining, as though a weeping woman should murmur, "Hiai!" And still, when the people hear that great golden moan they keep silence; but when the sharp, sweet shuddering comes in the air, and the sobbing of "Hiai!" then, indeed, all the Chinese mothers in all the many-colored ways of Pe-king whisper to their little ones: "Listen! that is Ko-Ngai crying for her shoe! That is Ko-Ngai calling for her shoe!"

The Story of Ming-Y

DO YOU ASK me who she was, the beautiful Sie-Thao? For a thousand years and more the trees have been whispering above her bed of stone. And the syllables of her name come to the listener with the lisping of the leaves; with the quivering of many-fingered boughs; with the fluttering of lights and shadows; with the breath, sweet as a woman's presence, of numberless savage flowers – Sie-Thao. But, saving the whispering of her name, what the trees say cannot be understood; and they alone remember the years of Sie-Thao. Something about her you might, nevertheless, learn from any of those Kiang-kou-jin – those famous Chinese story-tellers, who nightly narrate to listening crowds, in consideration of a few tsien, the legends of the past. Something concerning her you may also find in the book entitled "Kin-Kou-Ki-Koan," which signifies in our tongue: "The Marvellous Happenings of Ancient and of Recent Times." And perhaps of all things therein written, the most marvellous is this memory of Sie-Thao:

Five hundred years ago, in the reign of the Emperor Houng-Wou, whose dynasty was Ming, there lived in the City of Genii, the city of Kwang-tchau-fu, a man celebrated for his learning and for his piety, named Tien-Pelou. This Tien-Pelou had one son, a beautiful boy, who for scholarship and for bodily grace and for polite accomplishments had no superior among the youths of his age. And his name was Ming-Y.

Now when the lad was in his eighteenth summer, it came to pass that Pelou, his father, was appointed Inspector of Public Instruction at the city of Tching-tou; and Ming-Y accompanied his parents thither. Near the city of Tching-tou lived a rich man of rank, a high commissioner of the government, whose name was Tchang, and who wanted to find a worthy teacher for his children. On hearing of the arrival of the new Inspector of Public Instruction, the noble Tchang visited him to obtain advice in this matter; and happening to meet and converse with Pelou's accomplished son, immediately engaged Ming-Y as a private tutor for his family.

Now as the house of this Lord Tchang was situated several miles from town, it was deemed best that Ming-Y should abide in the house of his employer. Accordingly the youth made ready all things necessary for his new sojourn; and his parents, bidding him farewell, counselled him wisely, and cited to him the words of Lao-tseu and of the ancient sages:

"By a beautiful face the world is filled with love; but Heaven may never be deceived thereby. Shouldst thou behold a woman coming from the East, look thou to the West; shouldst thou perceive a maiden approaching from the West, turn thine eyes to the East."

If Ming-Y did not heed this counsel in after days, it was only because of his youth and the thoughtlessness of a naturally joyous heart.

And he departed to abide in the house of Lord Tchang, while the autumn passed, and the winter also.

* * *

When the time of the second moon of spring was drawing near, and that happy day which the Chinese call Hoa-tchao, or, "The Birthday of a Hundred Flowers," a longing came upon Ming-Y to see his parents; and he opened his heart to the good Tchang, who not only gave him the permission he desired, but also pressed into his hand a silver gift of two ounces, thinking that the lad might wish to bring some little memento to his father and mother. For it is the Chinese custom, on the feast of Hoa-tchao, to make presents to friends and relations.

That day all the air was drowsy with blossom perfume, and vibrant with the droning of bees. It seemed to Ming-Y that the path he followed had not been trodden by any other for many long years; the grass was tall upon it; vast trees on either side interlocked their mighty and moss-grown arms above him, beshadowing the way; but the leafy obscurities quivered with bird-song, and the deep vistas of the wood were glorified by vapors of gold, and odorous with flower-breathings as a temple with incense. The dreamy joy of the day entered into the heart of Ming-Y; and he sat him down among the young blossoms, under the branches swaying against the violet sky, to drink in the perfume and the light, and to enjoy the great sweet silence. Even while thus reposing, a sound caused him to turn his eyes toward a shady place where wild peach-trees were in bloom; and he beheld a young woman, beautiful as the pinkening blossoms themselves, trying to hide among them. Though he looked for a moment only, Ming-Y could not avoid discerning the loveliness of her face, the golden purity of her complexion, and the brightness of her long eyes, that sparkled under a pair of brows as daintily curved as the wings of the silkworm butterfly outspread. Ming-Y at once turned his gaze away, and, rising quickly, proceeded on his journey. But so much embarrassed did he feel at the idea of those charming eyes peeping at him through the leaves, that he suffered the money he had been carrying in his sleeve to fall, without being aware of it. A few moments later he heard the patter of light feet running behind him, and a woman's voice calling him by name. Turning his face in great surprise, he saw a comely servant-maid, who said to him, "Sir, my mistress bade me pick up and return you this silver which you dropped upon the road." Ming-Y thanked the girl gracefully, and requested her to convey his compliments to her mistress. Then he proceeded on his way through the perfumed silence, athwart the shadows that dreamed along the forgotten path, dreaming himself also, and feeling his heart beating with strange quickness at the thought of the beautiful being that he had seen.

* * *

It was just such another day when Ming-Y, returning by the same path, paused once more at the spot where the gracious figure had momentarily appeared before him. But this time he was surprised to perceive, through a long vista of immense trees, a dwelling that had previously escaped his notice – a country residence, not large, yet elegant to an unusual degree. The bright blue tiles of its curved and serrated double roof, rising above the foliage, seemed to blend their color with the luminous azure of the day; the green-and-gold designs of its carven porticos were exquisite artistic mockeries of leaves and flowers bathed in sunshine. And at the summit of terrace-steps before it, guarded by great porcelain tortoises, Ming-Y saw standing the mistress of the mansion – the idol of his passionate fancy – accompanied by the same waiting-maid who had borne to her his message of gratitude. While Ming-Y looked, he perceived that their eyes were upon him; they smiled and conversed together as if speaking about him; and, shy though he was, the youth found courage to salute the fair one from a distance. To his astonishment, the young servant beckoned him to approach; and opening a rustic gate half veiled by trailing plants bearing crimson flowers, Ming-Y advanced along the verdant alley leading to the terrace, with mingled feelings of surprise and timid joy. As he drew near, the beautiful lady withdrew from sight; but the maid waited at the broad steps to receive him, and said as he ascended:

"Sir, my mistress understands you wish to thank her for the trifling service she recently bade me do you, and requests that you will enter the house, as she knows you already by repute, and desires to have the pleasure of bidding you good-day."

Ming-Y entered bashfully, his feet making no sound upon a matting elastically soft as forest moss, and found himself in a reception-chamber vast, cool, and fragrant with scent of blossoms freshly gathered. A delicious quiet pervaded the mansion; shadows of flying birds passed over the bands of light that fell through the half-blinds of bamboo; great butterflies, with pinions of fiery color, found their way in, to hover a moment about the painted vases, and pass out again into the mysterious woods. And noiselessly as they, the young mistress of the mansion entered by another door, and kindly greeted the boy, who lifted his hands to his breast and bowed low in salutation. She was taller than he had deemed her, and supplely-slender as a beauteous lily; her black hair was interwoven with the creamy blossoms of the chu-sha-kih; her robes of pale silk took shifting tints when she moved, as vapors change hue with the changing of the light.

"If I be not mistaken," she said, when both had seated themselves after having exchanged the customary formalities of politeness, "my honored visitor is none other than Tien-chou, surnamed Ming-Y, educator of the children of my respected relative, the High Commissioner Tchang. As the family of Lord Tchang is my family also, I cannot but consider the teacher of his children as one of my own kin."

"Lady," replied Ming-Y, not a little astonished, "may I dare to inquire the name of your honored family, and to ask the relation which you hold to my noble patron?"

"The name of my poor family," responded the comely lady, "is Ping – an ancient family of the city of Tching-tou. I am the daughter of a certain Sie of Moun-hao; Sie is my name, likewise; and I was married to a young man of the Ping family, whose name was Khang. By this marriage I became related to your excellent patron; but my husband died soon after our wedding, and I have chosen this solitary place to reside in during the period of my widowhood."

There was a drowsy music in her voice, as of the melody of brooks, the murmurings of spring; and such a strange grace in the manner of her speech as Ming-Y had never heard before. Yet, on learning that she was a widow, the youth would not have presumed to remain long in her presence without a formal invitation; and after having sipped the cup of rich tea presented to him, he arose to depart. Sie would not suffer him to go so quickly.

"Nay, friend," she said; "stay yet a little while in my house, I pray you; for, should your honored patron ever learn that you had been here, and that I had not treated you as a respected guest, and regaled you even as I would him, I know that he would be greatly angered. Remain at least to supper."

So Ming-Y remained, rejoicing secretly in his heart, for Sie seemed to him the fairest and sweetest being he had ever known, and he felt that he loved her even more than his father and his mother. And while they talked the long shadows of the evening slowly blended into one violet darkness; the great citron-light of the sunset faded out; and those starry beings that are called the Three Councillors, who preside over life and death and the destinies of men, opened their cold bright eyes in the northern sky. Within the mansion of Sie the painted lanterns were lighted; the table was laid for the evening repast; and Ming-Y took his place at it, feeling little inclination to eat, and thinking only of the charming face before him. Observing that he scarcely tasted the dainties laid upon his plate, Sie pressed her young guest to partake of wine; and they drank several cups together. It was a purple wine, so cool that the cup into which it was poured became covered with vapory dew; yet it seemed to warm the veins with strange fire. To Ming-Y, as he drank, all things became more luminous as by enchantment; the walls of the chamber appeared to recede, and the roof to heighten; the lamps glowed like stars in their chains, and the voice of Sie floated to the boy's ears like some far melody heard through the spaces of a drowsy night. His heart swelled; his tongue loosened; and words flitted from his lips that he had fancied he could never dare to utter. Yet Sie sought not to restrain him; her lips gave no smile; but her long bright eyes seemed to laugh with pleasure at his words of praise, and to return his gaze of passionate admiration with affectionate interest.

"I have heard," she said, "of your rare talent, and of your many elegant accomplishments. I know how to sing a little, although I cannot claim to possess any musical learning; and now that I have the honor of finding myself in the society of a musical professor, I will venture to lay modesty aside, and beg you to sing a few songs with me. I should deem it no small gratification if you would condescend to examine my musical compositions."

"The honor and the gratification, dear lady," replied Ming-Y, "will be mine; and I feel helpless to express the gratitude which the offer of so rare a favor deserves."

The serving-maid, obedient to the summons of a little silver gong, brought in the music and retired. Ming-Y took the manuscripts, and began to examine them with eager delight. The paper upon which they were written had a pale yellow tint, and was light as a fabric of gossamer; but the characters were antiquely beautiful, as though they had been traced by the brush of Hei-song Che-Tchoo himself – that divine Genius of Ink, who is no bigger than a fly; and the signatures attached to the compositions were the signatures of Youen-tchin, Kao-pien, and Thou-mou – mighty poets and musicians of the dynasty of Thang! Ming-Y could not repress a scream of delight at the sight of treasures so inestimable and so unique; scarcely could he summon resolution enough to permit them to leave his hands even for a moment. "O Lady!" he cried, "these are veritably priceless things, surpassing in worth the treasures of all kings. This indeed is the handwriting of those great masters who sang five hundred years before our birth. How marvellously it has been preserved! Is not this the wondrous ink of which it was written: Po-nien-jou-chi, i-tien-jou-ki: 'After centuries I remain firm as stone, and the letters that I make like lacquer'? And how divine the charm of this composition! The song of Kao-pien, prince of poets, and Governor of Sze-tchouen five hundred years ago!"

"Kao-pien! darling Kao-pien!" murmured Sie, with a singular light in her eyes. "Kao-pien is also my favorite. Dear Ming-Y, let us chant his verses together, to the melody of old, the music of those grand years when men were nobler and wiser than to-day."

And their voices rose through the perfumed night like the voices of the wonder-birds – of the Fung-hoang – blending together in liquid sweetness. Yet a moment, and Ming-Y, overcome by the witchery of his companion's voice, could only listen in speechless ecstasy, while the lights of the chamber swam dim before his sight, and tears of pleasure trickled down his cheeks.

So the ninth hour passed; and they continued to converse, and to drink the cool purple wine, and to sing the songs of the years of Thang, until far into the night. More than once Ming-Y thought of departing; but each time Sie would begin, in that silver-sweet voice of hers, so wondrous a story of the great poets of the past, and of the women whom they loved, that he became as one entranced; or she would sing for him a song so strange that all his senses seemed to die except that of hearing. And at last, as she paused to pledge him in a cup of wine, Ming-Y could not restrain himself from putting his arm about her round neck and drawing her dainty head closer to him, and kissing the lips that were so much ruddier and sweeter than the wine. Then their lips separated no more; – the night grew old, and they knew it not.

* * *

The birds awakened, the flowers opened their eyes to the rising sun, and Ming-Y found himself at last compelled to bid his lovely enchantress farewell. Sie, accompanying him to the terrace, kissed him fondly and said, "Dear boy, come hither as often as you are able – as often as your heart whispers you to come. I know that you are not of those without faith and truth, who betray secrets; yet, being so young, you might also be sometimes thoughtless; and I pray you never to forget that only the stars have been the witnesses of our love. Speak of it to no living person, dearest; and take with you this little souvenir of our happy night."

And she presented him with an exquisite and curious little thing – a paper-weight in likeness of a couchant lion, wrought from a jade-stone yellow as that created by a rainbow in honor of Kong-fu-tze. Tenderly the boy kissed the gift and the beautiful hand that gave it. "May the Spirits punish me," he vowed, "if ever I knowingly give you cause to reproach me, sweetheart!" And they separated with mutual vows.

That morning, on returning to the house of Lord Tchang, Ming-Y told the first falsehood which had ever passed his lips. He averred that his mother had requested him thenceforward to pass his nights at home, now that the weather had become so pleasant; for, though the way was somewhat long, he was strong and active, and needed both air and healthy exercise. Tchang believed all Ming-Y said, and offered no objection. Accordingly the lad found himself enabled to pass all his evenings at the house of the beautiful Sie. Each night they devoted to the same pleasures which had made their first acquaintance so charming: they sang and conversed by turns; they played at chess – the learned game invented by Wu-Wang, which is an imitation of war; they composed pieces of eighty rhymes upon the flowers, the trees, the clouds, the streams, the birds, the bees. But in all accomplishments Sie far excelled her young sweetheart. Whenever they played at chess, it was always Ming-Y's general, Ming-Y's tsiang, who was surrounded and vanquished; when they composed verses, Sie's poems were ever superior to his in harmony of word-coloring, in elegance of form, in classic loftiness of thought. And the themes they selected were always the most difficult – those of the poets of the Thang dynasty; the songs they sang were also the songs of five hundred years before – the songs of Youen-tchin, of Thou-mou, of Kao-pien above all, high poet and ruler of the province of Sze-tchouen.

So the summer waxed and waned upon their love, and the luminous autumn came, with its vapors of phantom gold, its shadows of magical purple.

* * *

Then it unexpectedly happened that the father of Ming-Y, meeting his son's employer at Tching-tou, was asked by him: "Why must your boy continue to travel every evening to the city, now that the winter is approaching? The way is long, and when he returns in the morning he looks fordone with weariness. Why not permit him to slumber in my house during the season of snow?" And the father of Ming-Y, greatly astonished, responded: "Sir, my son has not visited the city, nor has he been to our house all this summer. I fear that he must have acquired wicked habits, and that he passes his nights in evil company – perhaps in gaming, or in drinking with the women of the flower-boats." But the High Commissioner returned: "Nay! that is not to be thought of. I have never found any evil in the boy, and there are no taverns nor flower-boats nor any places of dissipation in our neighborhood. No doubt Ming-Y has found some amiable youth of his own age with whom to spend his evenings, and only told me an untruth for fear that I would not otherwise permit him to leave my residence. I beg that you will say nothing to him until I shall have sought to discover this mystery; and this very evening I shall send my servant to follow after him, and to watch whither he goes."

Pelou readily assented to this proposal, and promising to visit Tchang the following morning, returned to his home. In the evening, when Ming-Y left the house of Tchang, a servant followed him unobserved at a distance. But on reaching the most obscure portion of the road, the boy disappeared from sight as suddenly as though the earth had swallowed him. After having long sought after him in vain, the domestic returned in great bewilderment to the house, and related what had taken place. Tchang immediately sent a messenger to Pelou.

In the mean time Ming-Y, entering the chamber of his beloved, was surprised and deeply pained to find her in tears. "Sweetheart," she sobbed, wreathing her arms around his neck, "we are about to be separated forever, because of reasons which I cannot tell you. From the very first I knew this must come to pass; and nevertheless it seemed to me for the moment so cruelly sudden a loss, so unexpected a misfortune, that I could not prevent myself from weeping! After this night we shall never see each other again, beloved, and I know that you will not be able to forget me while you live; but I know also that you will become a great scholar, and that honors and riches will be showered upon you, and that some beautiful and loving woman will console you for my loss. And now let us speak no more of grief; but let us pass this last evening joyously, so that your recollection of me may not be a painful one, and that you may remember my laughter rather than my tears."

She brushed the bright drops away, and brought wine and music and the melodious kin of seven silken strings, and would not suffer Ming-Y to speak for one moment of the coming separation. And she sang him an ancient song about the calmness of summer lakes reflecting the blue of heaven only, and the calmness of the heart also, before the clouds of care and of grief and of weariness darken its little world. Soon they forgot their sorrow in the joy of song and wine; and those last hours seemed to Ming-Y more celestial than even the hours of their first bliss.

But when the yellow beauty of morning came their sadness returned, and they wept. Once more Sie accompanied her lover to the terrace-steps; and as she kissed him farewell, she pressed into his hand a parting gift – a little brush-case of agate, wonderfully chiselled, and worthy the table of a great poet. And they separated forever, shedding many tears.

* * *

Still Ming-Y could not believe it was an eternal parting. "No!" he thought, "I shall visit her tomorrow; for I cannot now live without her, and I feel assured that she cannot refuse to receive me." Such were the thoughts that filled his mind as he reached the house of Tchang, to find his father and his patron standing on the porch awaiting him. Ere he could speak a word, Pelou demanded: "Son, in what place have you been passing your nights?"

Seeing that his falsehood had been discovered, Ming-Y dared not make any reply, and remained abashed and silent, with bowed head, in the presence of his father. Then Pelou, striking the boy violently with his staff, commanded him to divulge the secret; and at last, partly through fear of his parent, and partly through fear of the law which ordains that "the son refusing to obey his father shall be punished with one hundred blows of the bamboo," Ming-Y faltered out the history of his love.

Tchang changed color at the boy's tale. "Child," exclaimed the High Commissioner, "I have no relative of the name of Ping; I have never heard of the woman you describe; I have never heard even of the house which you speak of. But I know also that you cannot dare to lie to Pelou, your honored father; there is some strange delusion in all this affair."

Then Ming-Y produced the gifts that Sie had given him – the lion of yellow jade, the brush-case of carven agate, also some original compositions made by the beautiful lady herself. The astonishment of Tchang was now shared by Pelou. Both observed that the brush-case of agate and the lion of jade bore the appearance of objects that had lain buried in the earth for centuries, and were of a workmanship beyond the power of living man to imitate; while the compositions proved to be veritable master-pieces of poetry, written in the style of the poets of the dynasty of Thang.

"Friend Pelou," cried the High Commissioner, "let us immediately accompany the boy to the place where he obtained these miraculous things, and apply the testimony of our senses to this mystery. The boy is no doubt telling the truth; yet his story passes my understanding." And all three proceeded toward the place of the habitation of Sie.

* * *

But when they had arrived at the shadiest part of the road, where the perfumes were most sweet and the mosses were greenest, and the fruits of the wild peach flushed most pinkly, Ming-Y, gazing through the groves, uttered a cry of dismay. Where the azure-tiled roof had risen against the sky, there was now only the blue emptiness of air; where the green-and-gold facade had been, there was visible only the flickering of leaves under the aureate autumn light; and where the broad terrace had extended, could be discerned only a ruin – a tomb so ancient, so deeply gnawed by moss, that the name graven upon it was no longer decipherable. The home of Sie had disappeared!

All suddenly the High Commissioner smote his forehead with his hand, and turning to Pelou, recited the well-known verse of the ancient poet Tching-Kou:

"Surely the peach-flowers blossom over the tomb of SIE-THAO."

"Friend Pelou," continued Tchang, "the beauty who bewitched your son was no other than she whose tomb stands there in ruin before us! Did she not say she was wedded to Ping-Khang? There is no family of that name, but Ping-Khang is indeed the name of a broad alley in the city near. There was a dark riddle in all that she said. She called herself Sie of Moun-Hiao: there is no person of that name; there is no street of that name; but the Chinese characters Moun and hiao, placed together, form the character 'Kiao'. Listen! The alley Ping-Khang, situated in the street Kiao, was the place where dwelt the great courtesans of the dynasty of Thang! Did she not sing the songs of Kao-pien? And upon the brush-case and the paper-weight she gave your son, are there not characters which read, 'Pure object of art belonging to Kao, of the city of Pho-hai'? That city no longer exists; but the memory of Kao-pien remains, for he was governor of the province of Sze-tchouen, and a mighty poet. And when he dwelt in the land of Chou, was not his favorite the beautiful wanton Sie – Sie-Thao, unmatched for grace among all the women of her day? It was he who made her a gift of those manuscripts of song; it was he who gave her those objects of rare art.

Sie-Thao died not as other women die. Her limbs may have crumbled to dust; yet something of her still lives in this deep wood – her Shadow still haunts this shadowy place."

Tchang ceased to speak. A vague fear fell upon the three. The thin mists of the morning made dim the distances of green, and deepened the ghostly beauty of the woods. A faint breeze passed by, leaving a trail of blossom-scent – a last odor of dying flowers – thin as that which clings to the silk of a forgotten robe; and, as it passed, the trees seemed to whisper across the silence, "Sie-Thao."

* * *

Fearing greatly for his son, Pelou sent the lad away at once to the city of Kwang-tchau-fu. And there, in after years, Ming-Y obtained high dignities and honors by reason of his talents and his learning; and he married the daughter of an illustrious house, by whom he became the father of sons and daughters famous for their virtues and their accomplishments. Never could he forget Sie-Thao; and yet it is said that he never spoke of her – not even when his children begged him to tell them the story of two beautiful objects that always lay upon his writing-table: a lion of yellow jade, and a brush-case of carven agate.

The Legend of Tchi-Niu

IN THE QUAINT commentary accompanying the text of that holy book of Lao-tseu called Kan-ing-p'ien may be found a little story so old that the name of the one who first told it has been forgotten for a thousand years, yet so beautiful that it lives still in the memory of four hundred millions of people, like a prayer that, once learned, is forever remembered. The Chinese writer makes no mention of any city nor of any province, although even in the relation of the most ancient traditions such an omission is rare; we are only told that the name of the hero of the legend was Tong-yong, and that he lived in the years of the great dynasty of Han, some twenty centuries ago.

* * *

Tong-Yong's mother had died while he was yet an infant; and when he became a youth of nineteen years his father also passed away, leaving him utterly alone in the world, and without resources of any sort; for, being a very poor man, Tong's father had put himself to great straits to educate the lad, and had not been able to lay by even one copper coin of his earnings. And Tong lamented greatly to find himself so destitute that he could not honor the memory of that good father by having the customary rites of burial performed, and a carven tomb erected upon a propitious site. The poor only are friends of the poor; and among all those whom Tong knew; there was no one able to assist him in defraying the expenses of the funeral. In one way only could the youth obtain money – by selling himself as a slave to some rich cultivator; and this he at last decided to do. In vain his friends did their utmost to dissuade him; and to no purpose did they attempt to delay the accomplishment of his sacrifice by beguiling promises of future aid. Tong only replied that he would sell his freedom a hundred times, if it were possible, rather than suffer his father's memory to remain unhonored even for a brief season. And furthermore, confiding in his youth and strength, he determined to put a high price upon his servitude – a price which would enable him to build a handsome tomb, but which it would be well-nigh impossible for him ever to repay.

* * *

Accordingly he repaired to the broad public place where slaves and debtors were exposed for sale, and seated himself upon a bench of stone, having affixed to his shoulders a placard inscribed with the terms of his servitude and the list of his qualifications as a laborer. Many who read the characters upon the placard smiled disdainfully at the price asked, and passed on without a word; others lingered only to question him out of simple curiosity; some commended him with hollow praise; some openly mocked his unselfishness, and laughed at his childish piety. Thus many hours wearily passed, and Tong had almost despaired of finding a master, when there rode up a high official of the province – a grave and handsome man, lord of a thousand slaves, and owner of vast estates. Reining in his Tartar horse, the official halted to read the placard and to consider the value of the slave. He did not smile, or advise, or ask any questions; but having observed the price asked, and the fine strong limbs of the youth, purchased him without further ado, merely ordering his attendant to pay the sum and to see that the necessary papers were made out.

* * *

Thus Tong found himself enabled to fulfil the wish of his heart, and to have a monument built which, although of small size, was destined to delight the eyes of all who beheld it, being designed by cunning artists and executed by skilful sculptors. And while it was yet designed only, the pious rites were performed, the silver coin was placed in the mouth of the dead, the white lanterns were hung at the door, the holy prayers were recited, and paper shapes of all things the departed might need in the land of the Genii were consumed in consecrated fire. And after the geomancers and the necromancers had chosen a burial-spot which no unlucky star could shine upon, a place of rest which no demon or dragon might ever disturb, the beautiful chih was built. Then was the phantom money strewn along the way; the funeral procession departed from the dwelling of the dead, and with prayers and lamentation the mortal remains of Tong's good father were borne to the tomb.

Then Tong entered as a slave into the service of his purchaser, who allotted him a little hut to dwell in; and thither Tong carried with him those wooden tablets, bearing the ancestral names, before which filial piety must daily burn the incense of prayer, and perform the tender duties of family worship.

* * *

Thrice had spring perfumed the breast of the land with flowers, and thrice had been celebrated that festival of the dead which is called Siu-fan-ti, and thrice had Tong swept and garnished his father's tomb and presented his fivefold offering of fruits and meats. The period of mourning had passed, yet he had not ceased to mourn for his parent. The years revolved with their moons, bringing him no hour of joy, no day of happy rest; yet he never lamented his servitude, or failed to perform the rites of ancestral worship – until at last the fever of the rice-fields laid strong hold upon him, and he could not arise from his couch; and his fellow-laborers thought him destined to die. There was no one to wait upon him, no one to care for his needs, inasmuch as slaves and servants were wholly busied with the duties of the household or the labor of the fields – all departing to toil at sunrise and returning weary only after the sundown.

Now, while the sick youth slumbered the fitful slumber of exhaustion one sultry noon, he dreamed that a strange and beautiful woman stood by him, and bent above him and touched his forehead with the long, fine fingers of her shapely hand. And at her cool touch a weird sweet shock passed through him, and all his veins tingled as if thrilled by new life. Opening his eyes in wonder, he saw verily bending over him the charming being of whom he had dreamed, and he knew that her lithe hand really caressed his throbbing forehead. But the flame of the fever was gone, a delicious coolness now penetrated every fibre of his body, and the thrill of which he had dreamed still tingled in his blood like a great joy. Even at the same moment the eyes of the gentle visitor met his own, and he saw they were singularly beautiful, and shone like splendid black jewels under brows curved like the wings of the swallow. Yet their calm gaze seemed to pass through him as light through crystal; and a vague awe came upon him, so that the question which had risen to his lips found no utterance. Then she, still caressing him, smiled and said: "I have come to restore thy strength and to be thy wife. Arise and worship with me."

Her clear voice had tones melodious as a bird's song; but in her gaze there was an imperious power which Tong felt he dare not resist. Rising from his couch, he was astounded to find his strength wholly restored; but the cool, slender hand which held his own led him away so swiftly that he had little time for amazement. He would have given years of existence for courage to speak of his misery, to declare his utter inability to maintain a wife; but something irresistible in the long dark eyes of his companion forbade him to speak; and as though his inmost thought had been discerned by that wondrous gaze, she said to him, in the same clear voice, "I will provide." Then shame made him blush at the thought of his wretched aspect and tattered apparel; but he observed that she also was poorly attired, like a woman of the people – wearing no ornament of any sort, nor even shoes upon her feet. And before he had yet spoken to her, they came before the ancestral tablets; and there she knelt with him and prayed, and pledged him in a cup of wine – brought he knew not from whence – and together they worshipped Heaven and Earth. Thus she became his wife.

* * *

A mysterious marriage it seemed, for neither on that day nor at any future time could Tong venture to ask his wife the name of her family, or of the place whence she came, and he could not answer any of the curious questions which his fellow-laborers put to him concerning her; and she, moreover, never uttered a word about herself, except to say that her name was Tchi. But although Tong had such awe of her that while her eyes were upon him he was as one having no will of his own, he loved her unspeakably; and the thought of his serfdom ceased to weigh upon him from the hour of his marriage. As through magic the little dwelling had become transformed: its misery was masked with charming paper devices – with dainty decorations created out of nothing by that pretty jugglery of which woman only knows the secret.

Each morning at dawn the young husband found a well-prepared and ample repast awaiting him, and each evening also upon his return; but the wife all day sat at her loom, weaving silk after a fashion unlike anything which had ever been seen before in that province. For as she wove, the silk flowed from the loom like a slow current of glossy gold, bearing upon its undulations strange forms of violet and crimson and jewel-green: shapes of ghostly horsemen riding upon horses, and of phantom chariots dragon-drawn, and of standards of trailing cloud. In every dragon's beard glimmered the mystic pearl; in every rider's helmet sparkled the gem of rank. And each day Tchi would weave a great piece of such figured silk; and the fame of her weaving spread abroad. From far and near people thronged to see the marvellous work; and the silk-merchants of great cities heard of it, and they sent messengers to Tchi, asking her that she should weave for them and teach them her secret. Then she wove for them, as they desired, in return for the silver cubes which they brought her; but when they prayed her to teach them, she laughed and said, "Assuredly I could never teach you, for no one among you has fingers like mine." And indeed no man could discern her fingers when she wove, any more than he might behold the wings of a bee vibrating in swift flight.

* * *

The seasons passed, and Tong never knew want, so well did his beautiful wife fulfil her promise – "I will provide"; and the cubes of bright silver brought by the silk-merchants were piled up higher and higher in the great carven chest which Tchi had bought for the storage of the household goods.

One morning, at last, when Tong, having finished his repast, was about to depart to the fields, Tchi unexpectedly bade him remain; and opening the great chest, she took out of it and gave him a document written in the official characters called li-shu. And Tong, looking at it, cried out and leaped in his joy, for it was the certificate of his manumission. Tchi had secretly purchased her husband's freedom with the price of her wondrous silks!

"Thou shalt labor no more for any master," she said, "but for thine own sake only. And I have also bought this dwelling, with all which is therein, and the tea-fields to the south, and the mulberry groves hard by, all of which are thine."

Then Tong, beside himself for gratefulness, would have prostrated himself in worship before her, but that she would not suffer it.

* * *

Thus he was made free; and prosperity came to him with his freedom; and whatsoever he gave to the sacred earth was returned to him centupled; and his servants loved him and blessed the beautiful Tchi, so silent and yet so kindly to all about her. But the silk-loom soon remained untouched, for Tchi gave birth to a son, a boy so beautiful that Tong wept with delight when he looked upon him. And thereafter the wife devoted herself wholly to the care of the child.

Now it soon became manifest that the boy was not less wonderful than his wonderful mother. In the third month of his age he could speak; in the seventh month he could repeat by heart the proverbs of the sages, and recite the holy prayers; before the eleventh month he could use the writing-brush with skill, and copy in shapely characters the precepts of Lao-tseu. And the priests of the temples came to behold him and to converse with him, and they marvelled at the charm of the child and the wisdom of what he said; and they blessed Tong, saying: "Surely this son of thine is a gift from the Master of Heaven, a sign that the immortals love thee. May thine eyes behold a hundred happy summers!"

* * *

It was in the Period of the Eleventh Moon: the flowers had passed away, the perfume of the summer had flown, the winds were growing chill, and in Tong's home the evening fires were lighted. Long the husband and wife sat in the mellow glow – he speaking much of his hopes and joys, and of his son that was to be so grand a man, and of many paternal projects; while she, speaking little, listened to his words, and often turned her wonderful eyes upon him with an answering smile. Never had she seemed so beautiful before; and Tong, watching her face, marked not how the night waned, nor how the fire sank low, nor how the wind sang in the leafless trees without.

All suddenly Tchi arose without speaking, and took his hand in hers and led him, gently as on that strange wedding-morning, to the cradle where their boy slumbered, faintly smiling in his dreams. And in that moment there came upon Tong the same strange fear that he knew when Tchi's eyes had first met his own – the vague fear that love and trust had calmed, but never wholly cast out, like unto the fear of the gods. And all unknowingly, like one yielding to the pressure of mighty invisible hands, he bowed himself low before her, kneeling as to a divinity. Now, when he lifted his eyes again to her face, he closed them forthwith in awe; for she towered before him taller than any mortal woman, and there was a glow about her as of sunbeams, and the light of her limbs shone through her garments. But her sweet voice came to him with all the tenderness of other hours, saying: "Lo! my beloved, the moment has come in which I must forsake thee; for I was never of mortal born, and the Invisible may incarnate themselves for a time only. Yet I leave with thee the pledge of our love – this fair son, who shall ever be to thee as faithful and as fond as thou thyself hast been. Know, my beloved, that I was sent to thee even by the Master of Heaven, in reward of thy filial piety, and that I must now return to the glory of His house: I AM THE GODDESS XXHI-NIU."

Even as she ceased to speak, the great glow faded; and Tong, re-opening his eyes, knew that she had passed away forever – mysteriously as pass the winds of heaven, irrevocably as the light of a flame blown out. Yet all the doors were barred, all the windows unopened. Still the child slept, smiling in his sleep. Outside, the darkness was breaking; the sky was brightening swiftly; the night was past. With splendid majesty the East threw open high gates of gold for the coming of the sun; and, illuminated by the glory of his coming, the vapors of morning wrought themselves into marvellous shapes of shifting color – into forms weirdly beautiful as the silken dreams woven in the loom of Tchi-Niu.

The Return of Yen-Tchin-King

IN THE THIRTY-EIGHTH CHAPTER of the holy book, Kan-ing-p'ien, wherein the Recompense of Immortality is considered, may be found the legend of Yen-Tchin-King. A thousand years have passed since the passing of the good Tchin-King; for it was in the period of the greatness of Thang that he lived and died.

Now, in those days when Yen-Tchin-King was Supreme Judge of one of the Six August Tribunals, one Li-hi-lie, a soldier mighty for evil, lifted the black banner of revolt, and drew after him, as a tide of destruction, the millions of the northern provinces. And learning of these things, and knowing also that Hi-lie was the most ferocious of men, who respected nothing on earth save fearlessness, the Son of Heaven commanded Tchin-King that he should visit Hi-lie and strive to recall the rebel to duty, and read unto the people who followed after him in revolt the Emperor's letter of reproof and warning. For Tchin-King was famed throughout the provinces for his wisdom, his rectitude, and his fearlessness; and the Son of Heaven believed that if Hi-lie would listen to the words of any living man steadfast in loyalty and virtue, he would listen to the words of Tchin-King. So

Tchin-King arrayed himself in his robes of office, and set his house in order; and, having embraced his wife and his children, mounted his horse and rode away alone to the roaring camp of the rebels, bearing the Emperor's letter in his bosom. "I shall return; fear not!" were his last words to the gray servant who watched him from the terrace as he rode.

* * *

And Tchin-King at last descended from his horse, and entered into the rebel camp, and, passing through that huge gathering of war, stood in the presence of Hi-lie. High sat the rebel among his chiefs, encircled by the wave-lightning of swords and the thunders of ten thousand gongs: above him undulated the silken folds of the Black Dragon, while a vast fire rose bickering before him. Also Tchin-King saw that the tongues of that fire were licking human bones, and that skulls of men lay blackening among the ashes. Yet he was not afraid to look upon the fire, nor into the eyes of Hi-lie; but drawing from his bosom the roll of perfumed yellow silk upon which the words of the Emperor were written, and kissing it, he made ready to read, while the multitude became silent. Then, in a strong, clear voice he began:

"The words of the Celestial and August, the Son of Heaven, the Divine Ko-Tsu-Tchin-Yao-ti, unto the rebel Li-Hi-lie and those that follow him."

And a roar went up like the roar of the sea – a roar of rage, and the hideous battle-moan, like the moan of a forest in storm – "Hoo! hoo-oo-oo-oo!" – and the sword-lightnings brake loose, and the thunder of the gongs moved the ground beneath the messenger's feet. But Hi-lie waved his gilded wand, and again there was silence. "Nay!" spake the rebel chief; "let the dog bark!" So Tchin-King spake on:

"Knowest thou not, O most rash and foolish of men, that thou leadest the people only into the mouth of the Dragon of Destruction? Knowest thou not, also, that the people of my kingdom are the first-born of the Master of Heaven? So it hath been written that he who doth needlessly subject the people to wounds and death shall not be suffered by Heaven to live! Thou who wouldst subvert those laws founded by the wise – those laws in obedience to which may happiness and prosperity alone be found – thou art committing the greatest of all crimes – the crime that is never forgiven!

"O my people, think not that I your Emperor, I your Father, seek your destruction. I desire only your happiness, your prosperity, your greatness; let not your folly provoke the severity of your Celestial Parent. Follow not after madness and blind rage; hearken rather to the wise words of my messenger."

"Hoo! hoo-oo-oo-oo-oo!" roared the people, gathering fury. "Hoo! hoo-oo-oo-oo!" – till the mountains rolled back the cry like the rolling of a typhoon; and once more the pealing of the gongs paralyzed voice and hearing. Then Tchin-King, looking at Hi-lie, saw that he laughed, and that the words of the letter would not again be listened to. Therefore he read on to the end without looking about him, resolved to perform his mission in so far as lay in his power. And having read all, he would have given the letter to Hi-lie; but Hi-lie would not extend his hand to take it. Therefore Tchin-King replaced it in his bosom, and folding his arms, looked Hi-lie calmly in the face, and waited. Again Hi-lie waved his gilded wand; and the roaring ceased, and the booming of the gongs, until nothing save the fluttering of the Dragon-banner could be heard. Then spake Hi-lie, with an evil smile:

"Tchin-King, O son of a dog! if thou dost not now take the oath of fealty, and bow thyself before me, and salute me with the salutation of Emperors – even with the luh-kao, the triple prostration – into that fire thou shalt be thrown."

But Tchin-King, turning his back upon the usurper, bowed himself a moment in worship to Heaven and Earth; and then rising suddenly, ere any man could lay hand upon him, he leaped into the towering flame, and stood there, with folded arms, like a God.

Then Hi-lie leaped to his feet in amazement, and shouted to his men; and they snatched Tchin-King from the fire, and wrung the flames from his robes with their naked hands, and extolled him, and praised him to his face. And even Hi-lie himself descended from his seat, and spoke fair words to him, saying: "O Tchin-King, I see thou art indeed a brave man and true, and worthy of all honor; be seated among us, I pray thee, and partake of whatever it is in our power to bestow!"

But Tchin-King, looking upon him unswervingly, replied in a voice clear as the voice of a great bell:

"Never, O Hi-lie, shall I accept aught from thy hand, save death, so long as thou shalt continue in the path of wrath and folly. And never shall it be said that Tchin-King sat him down among rebels and traitors, among murderers and robbers."

Then Hi-lie in sudden fury, smote him with his sword; and Tchin-King fell to the earth and died, striving even in his death to bow his head toward the South – toward the place of the Emperor's palace – toward the presence of his beloved Master.

* * *

Even at the same hour the Son of Heaven, alone in the inner chamber of his palace, became aware of a Shape prostrate before his feet; and when he spake, the Shape arose and stood before him, and he saw that it was Tchin-King. And the Emperor would have questioned him; yet ere he could question, the familiar voice spake, saying:

"Son of Heaven, the mission confided to me I have performed; and thy command hath been accomplished to the extent of thy humble servant's feeble power. But even now must I depart, that I may enter the service of another Master."

And looking, the Emperor perceived that the Golden Tigers upon the wall were visible through the form of Tchin-King; and a strange coldness, like a winter wind, passed through the chamber; and the figure faded out. Then the Emperor knew that the Master of whom his faithful servant had spoken was none other than the Master of Heaven.

Also at the same hour the gray servant of Tchin-King's house beheld him passing through the apartments, smiling as he was wont to smile when he saw that all things were as he desired. "Is it well with thee, my lord?" questioned the aged man. And a voice answered him: "It is well"; but the presence of Tchin-King had passed away before the answer came.

* * *

So the armies of the Son of Heaven strove with the rebels. But the land was soaked with blood and blackened with fire; and the corpses of whole populations were carried by the rivers to feed the fishes of the sea; and still the war prevailed through many a long red year. Then came to aid the Son of Heaven the hordes that dwell in the desolations of the West and North – horsemen born, a nation of wild archers, each mighty to bend a two-hundred-pound bow until the ears should meet. And as a whirlwind they came against rebellion, raining raven-feathered arrows in a storm of death; and they prevailed against Hi-lie and his people. Then those that survived destruction and defeat submitted, and promised allegiance; and once more was the law of righteousness restored. But Tchin-King had been dead for many summers.

And the Son of Heaven sent word to his victorious generals that they should bring back with them the bones of his faithful servant, to be laid with honor in a mausoleum erected by imperial decree. So the generals of the Celestial and August sought after the nameless grave and found it, and had the earth taken up, and made ready to remove the coffin.

But the coffin crumbled into dust before their eyes; for the worms had gnawed it, and the hungry earth had devoured its substance, leaving only a phantom shell that vanished at touch of the light. And lo! as it vanished, all beheld lying there the perfect form and features of the good Tchin-King. Corruption had not touched him, nor had the worms disturbed his rest, nor had the bloom of life departed from his face. And he seemed to dream only – comely to see as upon the morning of his bridal, and smiling as the holy images smile, with eyelids closed, in the twilight of the great pagodas.

Then spoke a priest, standing by the grave: "O my children, this is indeed a Sign from the Master of Heaven; in such wise do the Powers Celestial preserve them that are chosen to be numbered with the Immortals. Death may not prevail over them, neither may corruption come nigh them. Verily the blessed Tchin-King hath taken his place among the divinities of Heaven!"

Then they bore Tchin-King back to his native place, and laid him with highest honors in the mausoleum which the Emperor had commanded; and there he sleeps, incorruptible forever, arrayed in his robes of state. Upon his tomb are sculptured the emblems of his greatness and his wisdom and his virtue, and the signs of his office, and the Four Precious Things: and the monsters which are holy symbols mount giant guard in stone about it; and the weird Dogs of Fo keep watch before it, as before the temples of the gods.

The Tale of the Porcelain-God

WHO FIRST of men discovered the secret of the Kao-ling, of the Pe-tun-tse – the bones and the flesh, the skeleton and the skin, of the beauteous Vase? Who first discovered the virtue of the curd-white clay? Who first prepared the ice-pure bricks of tun: the gathered-hoariness of mountains that have died for age; blanched dust of the rocky bones and the stony flesh of sun-seeking Giants that have ceased to be? Unto whom was it first given to discover the divine art of porcelain?

Unto Pu, once a man, now a god, before whose snowy statues bow the myriad populations enrolled in the guilds of the potteries. But the place of his birth we know not; perhaps the tradition of it may have been effaced from remembrance by that awful war which in our own day consumed the lives of twenty millions of the Black-haired Race, and obliterated from the face of the world even the wonderful City of Porcelain itself – the City of King-te-chin, that of old shone like a jewel of fire in the blue mountain-girdle of Feou-liang.

Before his time indeed the Spirit of the Furnace had being; had issued from the Infinite Vitality; had become manifest as an emanation of the Supreme Tao. For Hoang-ti, nearly five thousand years ago, taught men to make good vessels of baked clay; and in his time all potters had learned to know the God of Oven-fires, and turned their wheels to the murmuring of prayer. But Hoang-ti had been gathered unto his fathers for thrice ten hundred years before that man was born destined by the Master of Heaven to become the Porcelain-God.

And his divine ghost, ever hovering above the smoking and the toiling of the potteries, still gives power to the thought of the shaper, grace to the genius of the designer, luminosity to the touch of the enamellist. For by his heaven-taught wisdom was the art of porcelain created; by his inspiration were accomplished all the miracles of Thao-yu, maker of the Kia-yu-ki, and all the marvels made by those who followed after him;

All the azure porcelains called You-kouo-thien-tsing; brilliant as a mirror, thin as paper of rice, sonorous as the melodious stone Khing, and colored, in obedience to the mandate of the Emperor Chi-tsong, "blue as the sky is after rain, when viewed through the rifts of the clouds." These were, indeed, the first of all porcelains, likewise called Tchai-yao, which no man, howsoever wicked, could find courage to break, for they charmed the eye like jewels of price;

And the Jou-yao, second in rank among all porcelains, sometimes mocking the aspect and the sonority of bronze, sometimes blue as summer waters, and deluding the sight with mucid appearance of thickly floating spawn of fish;

And the Kouan-yao, which are the Porcelains of Magistrates, and third in rank of merit among all wondrous porcelains, colored with colors of the morning – skyey blueness, with the rose of a great dawn blushing and bursting through it, and long-limbed marsh-birds flying against the glow;

Also the Ko-yao – fourth in rank among perfect porcelains – of fair, faint, changing colors, like the body of a living fish, or made in the likeness of opal substance, milk mixed with fire; the work of Sing-I, elder of the immortal brothers Tchang;

Also the Ting-yao – fifth in rank among all perfect porcelains – white as the mourning garments of a spouse bereaved, and beautiful with a trickling as of tears – the porcelains sung of by the poet Son-tong-po;

Also the porcelains called Pi-se-yao, whose colors are called "hidden," being alternately invisible and visible, like the tints of ice beneath the sun – the porcelains celebrated by the far-famed singer Sin-in;

Also the wondrous Chu-yao – the pallid porcelains that utter a mournful cry when smitten – the porcelains chanted of by the mighty chanter, Thou-chao-ling;

Also the porcelains called Thsin-yao, white or blue, surface-wrinkled as the face of water by the fluttering of many fins.... And ye can see the fish!

Also the vases called Tsi-hong-khi, red as sunset after a rain; and the T'o-t'ai-khi, fragile as the wings of the silkworm-moth, lighter than the shell of an egg;

Also the Kia-tsing – fair cups pearl-white when empty, yet, by some incomprehensible witchcraft of construction, seeming to swarm with purple fish the moment they are filled with water;

Also the porcelains called Yao-pien, whose tints are transmuted by the alchemy of fire; for they enter blood-crimson into the heat, and change there to lizard-green, and at last come forth azure as the cheek of the sky;

Also the Ki-tcheou-yao, which are all violet as a summer's night; and the Hing-yao that sparkle with the sparklings of mingled silver and snow;

Also the Sieouen-yao – some ruddy as iron in the furnace, some diaphanous and ruby-red, some granulated and yellow as the rind of an orange, some softly flushed as the skin of a peach;

Also the Tsoui-khi-yao, crackled and green as ancient ice is; and the Tchou-fou-yao, which are the Porcelains of Emperors, with dragons wriggling and snarling in gold; and those yao that are pink-ribbed and have their angles serrated as the claws of crabs are;

Also the Ou-ni-yao, black as the pupil of the eye, and as lustrous; and the Hou-tien-yao, darkly yellow as the faces of men of India; and the Ou-kong-yao, whose color is the dead-gold of autumn-leaves;

Also the Long-kang-yao, green as the seedling of a pea, but bearing also paintings of sun-silvered cloud, and of the Dragons of Heaven;

Also the Tching-hoa-yao – pictured with the amber bloom of grapes and the verdure of vine-leaves and the blossoming of poppies, or decorated in relief with figures of fighting crickets;

Also the Khang-hi-nien-ts'ang-yao, celestial azure sown with star-dust of gold; and the Khien-long-nien-thang-yao, splendid in sable and silver as a fervid night that is flashed with lightnings.

Not indeed the Long-Ouang-yao – painted with the lascivious Pi-hi, with the obscene Nan-niu-sse-sie, with the shameful Tchun-hoa, or "Pictures of Spring"; abominations created by command of the wicked Emperor Moutsong, though the Spirit of the Furnace hid his face and fled away;

But all other vases of startling form and substance, magically articulated, and ornamented with figures in relief, in cameo, in transparency – the vases with orifices belled like the cups of flowers, or cleft like the bills of birds, or fanged like the jaws of serpents, or pink-lipped as the mouth of a girl; the vases flesh-colored and purple-veined and dimpled, with ears and with earrings; the vases in likeness of mushrooms, of lotos-flowers, of lizards, of horse-footed dragons woman-faced; the vases strangely translucid, that simulate the white glimmering of grains of prepared rice, that counterfeit the vapory lace-work of frost, that imitate the efflorescences of coral;

Also the statues in porcelain of divinities: the Genius of the Hearth; the Long-pinn who are the Twelve Deities of Ink; the blessed Lao-tseu, born with silver hair; Kong-fu-tse, grasping the scroll of written wisdom; Kouan-in, sweetest Goddess of Mercy, standing snowy-footed upon the heart of her golden lily; Chi-nong, the god who taught men how to cook; Fo, with long eyes closed in meditation, and lips smiling the mysterious smile of Supreme Beatitude; Cheou-lao, god of Longevity, bestriding his aerial steed, the white-winged stork; Pou-t'ai, Lord of Contentment and of Wealth, obese and dreamy; and that fairest Goddess of Talent, from whose beneficent hands eternally streams the iridescent rain of pearls.

* * *

And though many a secret of that matchless art that Pu bequeathed unto men may indeed have been forgotten and lost forever, the story of the Porcelain-God is remembered; and I doubt not that any of the aged Jeou-yen-liao-kong, any one of the old blind men of the great potteries, who sit all day grinding colors in the sun, could tell you Pu was once a humble Chinese workman, who grew to be a great artist by dint of tireless study and patience and by the inspiration of Heaven. So famed he became that some deemed him an alchemist, who possessed the secret called White-and-Yellow, by which stones might be turned into gold; and others thought him a magician, having the ghastly power of murdering men with horror of nightmare, by hiding charmed effigies of them under the tiles of their own roofs; and others, again, averred that he was an astrologer who had discovered the mystery of those Five Hing which influence all things – those Powers that move even in the currents of the star-drift, in the milky Tien-ho, or River of the Sky. Thus, at least, the ignorant spoke of him; but even those who stood about the Son of Heaven, those whose hearts had been strengthened by the acquisition of wisdom, wildly praised the marvels of his handicraft, and asked each other if there might be any imaginable form of beauty which Pu could not evoke from that beauteous substance so docile to the touch of his cunning hand.

And one day it came to pass that Pu sent a priceless gift to the Celestial and August: a vase imitating the substance of ore-rock, all aflame with pyritic scintillation – a shape of glittering splendor with chameleons sprawling over it; chameleons of porcelain that shifted color as often as the beholder changed his position. And the Emperor, wondering exceedingly at the splendor of the work, questioned the princes and the mandarins concerning him that made it. And the princes and the mandarins answered that he was a workman named Pu, and that he was without equal among potters, knowing secrets that seemed to have been inspired either by gods or by demons. Whereupon the Son of Heaven sent his officers to Pu with a noble gift, and summoned him unto his presence.

So the humble artisan entered before the Emperor, and having performed the supreme prostration – thrice kneeling, and thrice nine times touching the ground with his forehead – awaited the command of the August.

And the Emperor spake to him, saying: "Son, thy gracious gift hath found high favor in our sight; and for the charm of that offering we have bestowed upon thee a reward of five thousand silver liang. But thrice that sum shall be awarded thee so soon as thou shalt have fulfilled our behest. Hearken, therefore, O matchless artificer! it is now our will that thou make for us a vase having the tint and the aspect of living flesh, but – mark well our desire! – of flesh made to creep by the utterance of such words as poets utter – flesh moved by an Idea, flesh horripilated by a Thought! Obey, and answer not! We have spoken."

* * *

Now Pu was the most cunning of all the P'ei-se-kong – the men who marry colors together; of all the Hoa-yang-kong, who draw the shapes of vase-decoration; of all the Hoei-sse-kong, who paint in enamel; of all the T'ien-thsai-kong, who brighten color; of all the Chao-lou-kong, who watch the furnace-fires and the porcelain-ovens. But he went away sorrowing from the Palace of the Son of Heaven, notwithstanding the gift of five thousand silver liang which had been given to him. For he thought to himself: "Surely the mystery of the comeliness of flesh, and the mystery of that by which it is moved, are the secrets of the Supreme Tao. How shall man lend the aspect of sentient life to dead clay? Who save the Infinite can give soul?"

Now Pu had discovered those witchcrafts of color, those surprises of grace, that make the art of the ceramist. He had found the secret of the feng-hong, the wizard flush of the Rose; of the hoa-hong, the delicious incarnadine; of the mountain-green called chan-lou; of the pale soft yellow termed hiao-hoang-yeou; and of the hoang-kin, which is the blazing beauty of gold. He had found those eel-tints, those serpent-greens, those pansy-violets, those furnace-crimsons, those carminates and lilacs, subtle as spirit-flame, which our enamellists of the Occident long sought without success to reproduce. But he trembled at the task assigned him, as he returned to the toil of his studio, saying: "How shall any miserable man render in clay the quivering of flesh to an Idea – the inexplicable horripilation of a Thought? Shall a man venture to mock the magic of that Eternal Moulder by whose infinite power a million suns are shapen more readily than one small jar might be rounded upon my wheel?"

* * *

Yet the command of the Celestial and August might never be disobeyed; and the patient workman strove with all his power to fulfil the Son of Heaven's desire. But vainly for days, for weeks, for months, for season after season, did he strive; vainly also he prayed unto the gods to aid him; vainly he besought the Spirit of the Furnace, crying: "O thou Spirit of Fire, hear me, heed me, help me! how shall I – a miserable man, unable to breathe into clay a living soul – how shall I render in this inanimate substance the aspect of flesh made to creep by the utterance of a Word, sentient to the horripilation of a Thought?"

For the Spirit of the Furnace made strange answer to him with whispering of fire: "Vast thy faith, weird thy prayer! Has Thought feet, that man may perceive the trace of its passing? Canst thou measure me the blast of the Wind?"

* * *

Nevertheless, with purpose unmoved, nine-and-forty times did Pu seek to fulfil the Emperor's command; nine-and-forty times he strove to obey the behest of the Son of Heaven. Vainly, alas! did he consume his substance; vainly did he expend his strength; vainly did he exhaust his knowledge: success smiled not upon him; and Evil visited his home, and Poverty sat in his dwelling, and Misery shivered at his hearth.

Sometimes, when the hour of trial came, it was found that the colors had become strangely transmuted in the firing, or had faded into ashen pallor, or had darkened into the fuliginous hue of forest-mould. And Pu, beholding these misfortunes, made wail to the Spirit of the Furnace, praying: "O thou Spirit of Fire, how shall I render the likeness of lustrous flesh, the warm glow of living color, unless thou aid me?"

And the Spirit of the Furnace mysteriously answered him with murmuring of fire: "Canst thou learn the art of that Infinite Enameller who hath made beautiful the Arch of Heaven, whose brush is Light; whose paints are the Colors of the Evening?"

Sometimes, again, even when the tints had not changed, after the pricked and labored surface had seemed about to quicken in the heat, to assume the vibratility of living skin – even at the last hour all the labor of the workers proved to have been wasted; for the fickle substance rebelled against their efforts, producing only crinklings grotesque as those upon the rind of a withered fruit, or granulations like those upon the skin of a dead bird from which the feathers have been rudely plucked. And Pu wept, and cried out unto the Spirit of the Furnace: "O thou Spirit of Flame, how shall I be able to imitate the thrill of flesh touched by a Thought, unless thou wilt vouchsafe to lend me thine aid?"

And the Spirit of the Furnace mysteriously answered him with muttering of fire: "Canst thou give ghost unto a stone? Canst thou thrill with a Thought the entrails of the granite hills?"

Sometimes it was found that all the work indeed had not failed; for the color seemed good, and all faultless the matter of the vase appeared to be, having neither crack nor wrinkling nor crinkling; but the pliant softness of warm skin did not meet the eye; the flesh-tinted surface offered only the harsh aspect and hard glimmer of metal. All their exquisite toil to mock the pulpiness of sentient substance had left no trace; had been brought to nought by the breath of the furnace. And Pu, in his despair, shrieked to the Spirit of the Furnace: "O thou merciless divinity! O thou most pitiless god! – thou whom I have worshipped with ten thousand sacrifices! – for what fault hast thou abandoned me? for what error hast thou forsaken me? How may I, most wretched of men! ever render the aspect of flesh made to creep with the utterance of a Word, sentient to the titillation of a Thought, if thou wilt not aid me?"

And the Spirit of the Furnace made answer unto him with roaring of fire: "Canst thou divide a Soul? Nay!... Thy life for the life of thy work! – thy soul for the soul of thy Vase!"

And hearing these words Pu arose with a terrible resolve swelling at his heart, and made ready for the last and fiftieth time to fashion his work for the oven.

One hundred times did he sift the clay and the quartz, the kao-ling and the tun; one hundred times did he purify them in clearest water; one hundred times with tireless hands did he knead the creamy paste, mingling it at last with colors known only to himself. Then was the vase shapen and reshapen, and touched and retouched by the hands of Pu, until its blandness seemed to live, until it appeared to quiver and to palpitate, as with vitality from within, as with the quiver of rounded muscle undulating beneath the integument. For the hues of life were upon it and infiltrated throughout its innermost substance, imitating the carnation of blood-bright tissue, and the reticulated purple of the veins; and over all was laid the envelope of sun-colored Pe-kia-ho, the lucid and glossy enamel, half diaphanous, even like the substance that it counterfeited – the polished skin of a woman. Never since the making of the world had any work comparable to this been wrought by the skill of man.

Then Pu bade those who aided him that they should feed the furnace well with wood of tcha; but he told his resolve unto none. Yet after the oven began to glow, and he saw the work of his hands blossoming and blushing in the heat, he bowed himself before the Spirit of Flame, and murmured: "O thou Spirit and Master of Fire, I know the truth of thy words! I know that a Soul may never be divided! Therefore my life for the life of my work! – my soul for the soul of my Vase!"

And for nine days and for eight nights the furnaces were fed unceasingly with wood of tcha; for nine days and for eight nights men watched the wondrous vase crystallizing into being, rose-lighted by the breath of the flame. Now upon the coming of the ninth night, Pu bade all his weary comrades retire to, rest, for that the work was well-nigh done, and the success assured. "If you find me not here at sunrise," he said, "fear not to take forth the vase; for I know that the task will have been accomplished according to the command of the August." So they departed.

But in that same ninth night Pu entered the flame, and yielded up his ghost in the embrace of the Spirit of the Furnace, giving his life for the life of his work – his soul for the soul of his Vase.

And when the workmen came upon the tenth morning to take forth the porcelain marvel, even the bones of Pu had ceased to be; but lo! the Vase lived as they looked upon it: seeming to be flesh moved by the utterance of a Word, creeping to the titillation of a Thought. And whenever tapped by the finger it uttered a voice and a name – the voice of its maker, the name of its creator: PU.

* * *

And the son of Heaven, hearing of these things, and viewing the miracle of the vase, said unto those about him: "Verily, the Impossible hath been wrought by the strength of faith, by the force of obedience! Yet never was it our desire that so cruel a sacrifice should have been; we sought only to know whether the skill of the matchless artificer came from the Divinities or from the Demons – from heaven or from hell. Now, indeed, we discern that Pu hath taken his place among the gods." And the Emperor mourned exceedingly for his faithful servant. But he ordained that godlike honors should be paid unto the spirit of the marvellous artist, and that his memory should be revered forevermore, and that fair statues of him should be set up in all the cities of the Celestial Empire, and above all the toiling of the potteries, that the multitude of workers might unceasingly call upon his name and invoke his benediction upon their labors.

The Beautiful Daughter Of Liu-Kung

IN ONE OF the central provinces of this long-lived Empire of China, there lived in very early times a man of the name of Chan. He was a person of a bright, active nature which made him enjoy life, and caused him to be popular amongst his companions and a favourite with everyone who knew him. But he was also a scholar, well-versed in the literature of his country, and he spent every moment that he could spare in the study of the great writings of the famous men of former days.

In order that he might be interrupted as little as possible in his pursuit of learning, he engaged a room in a famous monastery some miles away from his own home. The only inhabitants of this monastery were a dozen or so of Buddhist priests, who, except when they were engaged in the daily services of the temple, lived a quiet, humdrum, lazy kind of existence which harmonized well with the solitude and the majestic stillness of the mountain scenery by which they were surrounded.

This monastery was indeed one of the most beautiful in China. It was situated on the slope of a hill, looking down upon a lovely valley, where the natural solitude was as complete as the most devoted hermit could desire. The only means of getting to it were the narrow hill footpaths along which the worshippers from the great city and the scattered villages wound in and out on festal days, when they came trooping to the temple to make their offerings to the famous God enshrined within.

Chan was a diligent student, and rarely indulged in recreation of any kind. Occasionally, when his mind became oppressed with excessive study he would go for a quiet walk along the hillside; but these occasions were few and far between, for he made up for every hour he spent away from his beloved books by still closer application to them in the hours that followed.

One day he was strolling in an aimless kind of way on the hillside, when suddenly a party of hunters from the neighbouring city of Eternal Spring came dashing into view. They were a merry group and full of excitement, for they had just sighted a fox which Chan had seen a moment before flying away at its highest speed in mortal dread of its pursuers.

Prominent amongst the hunters was a young girl, who was mounted on a fiery little steed, so full of spirit and so eager to follow in the mad chase after the prey, that its rider seemed to have some difficulty in restraining it. The girl herself was a perfect picture. Her face was the loveliest that Chan had ever looked upon, and her figure, which her trim hunting dress showed off to the utmost advantage, was graceful in the extreme. As she swept by him with her face flushed with excitement and her features all aglow with health, Chan felt at once that he had lost his heart and that he was deeply and profoundly in love with her.

On making enquiries, he found that she was named Willow, that she was the daughter of the chief mandarin of the town in which she lived, and that she was intensely fond of the chase and delighted in galloping over the hills and valleys in the pursuit of the wild animals to be found there. So powerfully had Chan's mind been affected by what he had seen of Willow, that he had already begun to entertain serious thoughts of making her his wife; but while his mind was full of this delightful prospect he was plunged into the deepest grief by hearing that she had suddenly died. For some days he was so stricken with sorrow that he lost all interest in life, and could do nothing but dwell on the memory of her whom he had come to love with all the devotion of his heart.

A few weeks after the news of her death, the quiet of the retreat was one day broken by a huge procession which wound its way along the mountain path leading to the monastery doors. On looking out, Chan saw that many of the men in this procession were dressed in sackcloth, and that in front of it was a band of musicians producing weird, shrill notes on their various instruments.

By these signs Chan knew that what he saw was a funeral, and he expected to see the long line of mourners pass on to some spot on the hillside where the dead would be buried. Instead of that, however, they entered through the great gates of the monastery, and the coffin, the red pall of which told him that it contained the body of a woman, was carried into an inner room of the building and laid on trestles that had been made ready for it.

After the mourners had dispersed, Chan asked one of the priests the name of the woman who had died, and how it was that the coffin was laid within the precincts of the temple instead of in the house of the deceased, where it could be looked after by her relatives and where the customary sacrifices to the spirit of the dead could be offered more conveniently than in the monastery.

The bonze replied that this was a peculiar case, calling for special treatment.

"The father of the poor young girl who died so suddenly," he said, "was the mandarin of the neighbouring city of Eternal Spring. Just after the death of his daughter an order came from the Emperor transferring him to another district, a thousand miles from here.

"The command was very urgent that he should proceed without delay to take up his post in the far-off province, and that he was to allow nothing to hinder him from doing so. He could not carry his daughter's body with him on so long a journey, and no time was permitted him to take the coffin to his home, where she might be buried amongst her own kindred. It was equally impossible to deposit the coffin in the yamen he was about to leave, for the new mandarin who was soon to arrive would certainly object to have the body of a stranger in such close proximity to his family. It might bring him bad luck, and his career as an official might end in disaster.

"Permission was therefore asked from our abbot to allow the coffin to be placed in one of our vacant rooms, until the father some day in the future can come and bear the body of his beloved daughter to the home of his ancestors, there to be laid at rest amongst his own people.

"This request was readily granted, for whilst he was in office the mandarin showed us many favours, and his daughter was a beautiful girl who was beloved by everyone; and so we were only too glad to do anything in our power to help in this unhappy matter."

Chan was profoundly moved when he realized that the woman whom he had loved as his own life lay dead within a chamber only a few steps away from his own. His passion, instead of being crushed out of his heart by the thought that she was utterly beyond his reach, and by no possibility could ever be more to him than a memory, seemed to grow in intensity as he became conscious that it was an absolutely hopeless one.

On that very same evening, about midnight, when silence rested on the monastery, and the priests were all wrapped in slumber, Chan, with a lighted taper in his hand, stole with noiseless footsteps along the dark passages into the chamber of death where his beloved lay. Kneeling beside the coffin with a heart full of emotion, in trembling accents he called upon Willow to listen to the story of his passion.

He spoke to her just as though she were standing face to face with him, and he told her how he had fallen in love with her on the day on which he had caught a glimpse of her as she galloped in pursuit of the fox that had fled through the valley from the hunters. He had planned, he told her, to make her his wife, and he described, in tones through which the tears could be heard to run, how heart-broken he was when he heard of her death.

"I want to see you," he continued, "for I feel that I cannot live without you. You are near to me, and yet oh! how far away. Can you not come from the Land of Shadows, where you are now, and comfort me by one vision of your fair face, and one sound of the voice that would fill my soul with the sweetest music?"

For many months the comfort of Chan's life was this nightly visit to the chamber where his dead love lay. Not a single night passed without his going to tell her of the unalterable and undying affection that filled his heart; and whilst the temple lay shrouded in darkness, and the only sounds that broke the stillness were those inexplicable ones in which natufe seems to indulge when man is removed by sleep from the scene, Chan was uttering those love notes which had lain deeply hidden within his soul, but which now in the utter desolation of his heart burst forth to ease his pain by their mere expression.

One night as he was sitting poring over his books, he happened to turn round, and was startled to see the figure of a young girl standing just inside the door of his room. It seemed perfectly human, and yet it was so ethereal that it had the appearance of a spirit of the other world. As he looked at the girl with a wondering gaze, a smile lit up her beautiful features, and he then discovered to his great joy that she was none other than Willow, his lost love whom he had despaired of ever seeing again.

With her face wreathed in smiles, she sat down beside him and said in a timid, modest way:

"I am here tonight in response to the great love which has never faltered since the day I died. That is the magnet which has had the power of drawing me from the Land of Shadows. I felt it there, and many speak about it in that sunless country. Even Yam-lo, the lord of the spirits of that dreary world, has been moved by your unchanging devotion; so much so that he has given me permission to come and see you, in order that I might tell you how deeply my heart is moved by the profound affection that you have exhibited for me all these months during which you never had any expectation of its being returned."

For many months this sweet intercourse between Chan and his beloved Willow was carried on, and no one in the whole monastery knew anything of it. The interviews always took place about midnight, and Willow, who seemed to pass with freedom through closed doors or the stoutest walls, invariably vanished during the small hours of the morning.

One evening whilst they were conversing on topics agreeable to them both, Willow unburdened her heart to Chan, and told him how unhappy she was in the world of spirits.

"You know," she said, "that before I died I was not married, and so I am only a wandering spirit with no place where I can rest, and no friends to whom I can betake myself. I travel here and there and everywhere, feeling that no one cares for me, and that there are no ties to bind me to any particular place or thing. For a young girl like me, this is a very sad and sorrowful state of things.

"There is another thing that adds to my sorrow in the Land of Shadows," she went on to say, with a mournful look on her lovely countenance. "I was very fond of hunting when I was in my father's home, and many a wild animal was slain in the hunting expeditions in which I took an active part. This has all told against me in the world in which I am now living, and for the share I took in destroying life I have to suffer by many pains and penalties which are hard for me to endure.

"My sin has been great," she said, "and so I wish to make special offerings in this temple to the Goddess of Mercy and implore her to send down to the other world a good report of me to Yam-lo, and intercede with him to forgive the sins of which I have been guilty. If you will do this for me, I promise that after I have been born again into the world I will never forget you, and if you like to wait for me I shall willingly become your wife and serve you with the deepest devotion of which my heart is capable, as long as Heaven will permit you and me to live together as husband and wife."

From this time, much to the astonishment of the priests in the monastery, Chan began to show unwonted enthusiasm for the service of the Goddess, and would sometimes spend hours before her image and repeat long prayers to her. This was all the more remarkable, as the scholar had rarely if ever shown any desire to have anything to do with the numerous gods which were enshrined in various parts of the temple.

After some months of this daily appeal to the Goddess of Mercy, Willow informed him that his prayers had been so far successful that the misery of her lot in the Land of Shadows had been greatly mitigated. The pleadings of the Goddess with Yam-lo had so influenced his heart towards Willow that she believed her great sin in the destruction of animal life had been forgiven, and there were signs that the dread ruler of the Underworld was looking upon her with kindness.

Chan was delighted with this news, and his prayers and offerings became still more frequent and more fervent. He little dreamed that his devotion to the Goddess would be the means of his speedy separation from Willow, but so it was. One evening she came as usual to see him, but instead of entering with smiling face and laughter in her eyes, she was weeping bitterly as though she were in the direst sorrow.

Chan was in the greatest distress when he saw this and asked her to explain the reason for her grief. "The reason for my tears," she said, "is because after this evening I shall not see you again. Your petitions to the Goddess have had such a powerful effect upon her mind that she has used all her influence with Yam-lo to induce him to set me free from the misery of the Land of Shadows, and so I am to leave that sunless country and to be born again into life in this upper world."

As she uttered these words her tears began to flow once more and her whole frame was convulsed with sobbing.

"I am glad," she said, "that I am to be born once more and live amongst men, but I cannot bear the thought of having to be separated for so long from you. Let us not grieve too much, however. It is our fate, and we may not rebel against it. Yam-lo has been kinder to me than he has ever been to any one in the past, for he has revealed to me the family into which I am to be born and the place where they live, so if you come to me in eighteen years you will find me waiting for you. Your love has been so great that it has entered into my very soul, and there is nothing that can ever efface it from my heart. A thousand re-births may take place, but never shall I love any one as I love you."

Chan professed that he was greatly comforted by this confession of her love, but all the same he felt in despair when he thought of the future.

"When next I shall see you," he said with a sigh, "I shall be getting so old that you, a young girl in the first flush of womanhood, will not care to look at me. My hair will have turned grey and my face will be marked with wrinkles, and in the re-birth you will have forgotten all that took place in the Land of Shadows, and the memory of me will have vanished from your heart for ever."

Willow looked with loving but sorrowful eyes upon her lover as he was expressing his concern about the future, but quickly assured him that nothing in the world would ever cause her to cease to remember him with the tenderest affection.

"In order to comfort you," she said, "let me tell you of two things that the dread Yam-lo, out of consideration for your love for me, has granted me – two things which he has never bestowed upon any other mortal who has come within the region of his rule. The first is, he has allowed me to inspect the book of Life and Death, in which is recorded the history of every human being, with the times of their re-births and the places in which they are to be born. I want you this very minute to write down the secret which has been revealed to me as to my new name and family and the place where I shall reside, so that you will have no difficulty in finding me, when eighteen years hence you shall come to claim me as your wife.

"The next is a gift so precious that I have no words in which to express my gratitude for its having been bestowed upon me. It is this. I am given the privilege of not forgetting what has taken place during my stay in the Land of Shadows, and so when I am re-born into another part of

China, with a new father and mother, I shall hold within my memory my recollection of you. The years will pass quickly, for I shall be looking for you, and this day eighteen years hence will be the happiest in my life, for it will bring you to me never more to be separated from me.

"But I must hasten on," she hurriedly exclaimed, "for the footsteps of fate are moving steadily towards me. In a few minutes the gates of Hades will have closed against me, and Willow will have vanished, and I shall be a babe once more with my new life before me. See, but a minute more is left me, and I seem to have so much to say. Farewell! Never forget me! I shall ever remember you, but my time is come!"

As she uttered these words, a smile of ineffable sweetness flashed across, her beautiful face, and she was gone.

Chan was inexpressibly sad at the loss he had sustained by the re-birth of Willow, and in order to drive away his sorrow he threw his heart and soul into his studies. His books became his constant companions, and he tried to find in them a solace for the loneliness which had come upon him since the visits of Willow had ceased. He also became a diligent worshipper of the idols, and especially of the Goddess of Mercy, who had played such an important part in the history of his beloved Willow.

The years went slowly by, and Chan began to feel that he was growing old. His hair became dashed with silver threads, and wrinkles appeared in his forehead and under his eyes. The strain of waiting for the one woman who had taken complete possession of his heart had been too much for him. As the time drew near, too, when he should go to meet her, a great and nervous dread began to fill him with anxiety. Would she recognize him? And would she, a young girl of eighteen, be content to accept as a husband a man so advanced in years as he now was? These questions were constantly flashing through his brain.

At last only a few months remained before he was to set out on his journey to the distant province where Yam-lo had decided that Willow was to begin her new life on earth.

He was sitting one evening in his study, brooding over the great problem that would be solved before long, when a man dressed in black silently entered the room. Looking on Chan with a kindly smile which seemed to find its way instantly to his heart, he informed him that he was a fairy from the Western Heaven and that he had been specially deputed by the rulers there to render him all the assistance in his power at this particular crisis, when they knew his heart was so full of anxiety.

"We have all heard in that far-off fairyland," he continued, "of the devotion you have shown to Willow, and how during all the years which have intervened since you saw her last you have never faltered in your love for her. Such affection is rare among mortals, and the dwellers in fairyland would like to help in bringing together two such loving hearts; for let me assure you that however strong your feeling for the one whom you are so anxious to see again, she on her part is just as deeply in love with you, and is now counting the days until she will be able to see you and until you need never again be parted from each other. In order to assist in this happy consummation, I want you to take a short trip with me. It will only take a few hours, and you will then find that something has happened to remove all your fears as to how you will be received by Willow."

The fairy man then led Chan to the door, and gave a wave of his hand in the direction of the sky. Instantly the sound of the fluttering and swish of wings was heard, and in a moment a splendid eagle landed gracefully at their feet. Taking their seats upon its back, they found themselves flashing at lightning speed away through the darkness of the night. Higher and higher they rose, till they had pierced the heavy masses of clouds which hung hovering in the sky. Swift as an arrow the eagle still cleft its way upward until the clouds had vanished to an infinite distance below them; and still onward they were borne in the mighty stillness of an expanse where no human being had ever travelled before.

Chan felt his heart throb with a nervousness which he could not control. What if the bird should tire, he thought, and he should be dropped into the fathomless abyss below? Life's journey would then come to a tragic end. Where, too, was he being carried and how should he be ever able to return to his far-off home on the earth? He was becoming more and more agitated, when the fairy took hold of his hand and in a voice which at once stilled his fears, assured him that there was not the least danger in this journey through the air.

"We are as safe here," he assured him, "as though we were standing upon a mountain whose roots lie miles below the surface of the earth. And see," he continued, pointing to something in the distance, "we shall arrive at our destination in the course of a few seconds."

True enough, he had hardly finished speaking when a land, fairer than Chan had ever seen on earth or pictured in imagination, loomed up suddenly in front of them; and before he could gather together his astonished thoughts, the eagle had landed them on its shores, and with outspread wings was soaring into the mystery of the unknown beyond.

The fairy now led Chan along a road surrounded by the most bewildering beauty. Rare flowers, graceful trees, and birds which made the groves resound with the sweetest music, were objects that kept his mind in one continual state of delight. Before long they arrived in front of a magnificent palace, so grand and vast that Chan felt afraid to enter within its portals, or even tread the avenue leading up to it.

Once more his companion relieved Chan's anxiety by assuring him that he was an expected guest, and that the Queen of this fairy country had sent him to earth specially to invite him to come and visit her, in order that she might bestow upon him a blessing which would enrich the whole of his life and would enable him to spend many happy years with her whom he had loved with such devotion.

Chan was ushered into a large reception hall, where he was met by a very stately lady, with a face full of benevolence, whom he at once recognized, from the images he had often worshipped, as the Goddess of Mercy. He was startled when he discovered in what august presence he was standing, and began to tremble with excitement as he realized that here in actual life was the famous personage whose image was worshipped by the millions of China, and whose influence spread even into the Land of Shadows.

Seeing Chan's humility and evident terror of her, the Goddess spoke to him in a gentle, loving voice, and told him to have no fear, for she had summoned him to her presence not to rebuke but to comfort him.

"I know your story," she said, "and I think it is a beautiful one. Before I was raised to the high position I now occupy I was at one time a woman like Willow, and I can sympathize with her in her devotion to you because of the wonderful love you have shown her from the first moment that you saw her.

"I know, too, your anxiety about your age, and your fear lest when Willow sees you with the marks of advancing years upon you, her love may die out and you will be left with your heart broken and in despair.I have foreseen this difficulty, and I am going to have it removed.

"The fairy who brought you here," she continued, "will now take you round the palace grounds, and if you will carry out my wishes, the fears which have been troubling you for years shall entirely vanish. You will then meet Willow with a heart as light as that of any man in the flush of youth, who awaits the coming of the bridal chair which bears his future wife to his home."

Chan at once, without any hesitation, followed his guide through the spacious grounds which surrounded the palace, and was finally led to the edge of a beautiful little lake embowered amongst trees and ferns, and rare and fragrant flowers. It was the most exquisite scene on which his vision had ever rested.

With a kindly look at his companion, the fairy said, "This beautiful piece of water goes by the name of the 'Fountain of Eternal Youth', and it is the Queen's express desire that you should bathe in it."

Quickly undressing, Chan plunged into the pool and for a moment sank beneath the surface of the waters. Emerging quickly from them, a delightful feeling of new-born strength seemed to be creeping in at every pore of his body. The sense of advancing age passed away, and the years of youth appeared to come back to him again. He felt as though he were a young man once more; for the weary doubts, which for some years past had made his footsteps lag, had gone with his first plunge into those fragrant waters.

By-and-by he came out of this "Fountain of Eternal Youth" with the visions and ambitions of his young manhood rushing through his brain. His powers, which seemed of late to have become dull and sluggish, had recovered the impetus which in earlier years had carried him so successfully through many a severe examination. His thoughts, too, about Willow had so completely changed that instead of dreading the day when he should stand before her, his one passionate desire now was to start upon his journey to keep his appointment with her.

Chan and the fairy then proceeded to the edge of the vast and boundless expanse which bordered the palace of the Goddess, and found a magnificent dragon waiting to convey them back to earth. No sooner had they taken their seats on its back than it fled with the swiftness of the wind through the untrodden spaces of the air, until at length the mountains came looming out of the dim and shadowy distance, and with a rush Chan found himself safely landed at the door of the temple from which he had taken his departure for his amazing journey to the Western Heaven.

Whilst these wonderful things were taking place, Willow – or rather Precious Pearl, as she had been named by her new parents, who of course had no knowledge of her previous history – had grown up to be a most beautiful and fascinating woman.

During all these years she had never ceased to look forward with an anxious heart to the day when she would once more meet the man to whom she had betrothed herself eighteen years ago. Latterly she had begun to count the days that must still elapse before she could see him again. She never forgot the night in the temple when she bade him "Good-bye" just before she was reborn into this world. The day and the hour had been stamped upon her memory, and since then the years had seemed to travel with halting, leaden feet, as though they were loth to move on. But now only a few months remained, and no doubt ever entered her brain that Chan would fail her.

Just about this time her mother had an offer of marriage for her from a very wealthy and distinguished family, and contrary to the usual custom of mothers in China she asked her daughter what she thought of the proposal. Pearl was distressed beyond measure, and prayed and entreated her mother on no account to broach the subject to her again, as she could never entertain any proposition of the kind.

Amazed at such a statement, her mother begged her to explain her reason for such strange views. "Girls at your age," she said, "are usually betrothed and are thinking of having homes of their own. This is the universal custom throughout the Empire, and therefore there must be some serious reason why you will not allow me to make arrangements for your being allied to some respectable family."

Pearl had been feeling that the time was drawing near when she would have to divulge the secret of her love affair, and she considered that now was the best opportunity for doing so. To the astonishment therefore of her mother, who believed that she was romancing, she told her the whole story of the past; how Chan had fallen in love with her, and how after she had died and had come under the control of Yam-lo in the Land of Shadows, that dread lord had permitted her spirit to visit her lover in the temple where her body had been laid until a lucky resting-place could be found for it on the hillside. She also explained how it had been agreed between them that she was to wait for him until after the lapse of eighteen years, when she would be old enough to become his wife. "In a few months the time will be up," she concluded, "and so I beseech you not to speak of my being betrothed to any one else, for I feel that if I am compelled to marry any other than Chan I shall die."

The mother was thunderstruck at this wonderful story which her daughter told her. She could only imagine that Pearl had in some way or another been bewitched, and was under a fatal delusion that she was in love with some hero of romance, to whom she believed she was betrothed. Still, her daughter had always been most loving and devoted to her, and had shown more brightness and ability than Chinese girls of her age usually possessed. Her mother did not like, therefore, to reprove her for what she considered her ridiculous ideas, so she determined to try another plan to cure her of her folly.

"What age was this man Chan," she asked, "when you entered into this engagement with him?"

"He was just thirty," Pearl replied. "He was of very good family and a scholar, and had distinguished himself for his proficiency in the ancient literature of China."

"Oh! then he must be nearly fifty now. A fine mate he would make for you, a young girl of only eighteen! But who knows how he may have changed since last you saw him? His hair must be turning grey, and his teeth may have fallen out; and for anything you know he may have been dead and buried so long ago that by this time they have taken up his bones, and nothing is left of him but what the funeral urn may contain of his ashes."

"Oh! I do pray that nothing of that kind has happened to him," cried Pearl, in a tone of voice which showed the anguish she was suffering. "Let us leave the question for a few months, and then when he comes for me, as I know he will, you will find by personal knowledge what a splendid man he is, and how entirely worthy he is of being your son-in-law."

On the day which had been appointed under such romantic circumstances eighteen years before, Chan arrived in the town, and after taking a room in an inn and making certain enquiries, he made his way to the home where he believed that Willow resided. On his arrival, however, he was roughly told by the servant that no such person as Willow lived there, and that they did not like strangers coming about the house. Indeed he was given plainly to understand that the sooner he left, the better everyone would be pleased. This treatment was of course part of a scheme devised by Pearl's parents to frustrate any plans that Chan might have formed for seeing her. They were determined not to give their daughter to a man so old as he must be, and therefore they decided that an interview between the two must be prevented at all hazards.

Chan was greatly distressed at the rebuff which he had received. Had Willow after all made a mistake eighteen years ago when she gave him the name of this town as the place where her new home was to be? He had carefully written it down at her dictation, and it had been burned into his brain all the years since. No, there could be no mistake on that point. If there were any, then it was one that had been made purposely by Yam-lo in order to deceive them both. That idea, however, was unthinkable, and so there must be something else to account for his not finding Willow as he had expected. He at once made enquiries at the inn at which he was staying, and found that there was a daughter at the very house to which he had gone, and that in almost every particular the description he was given of her corresponded with his beloved Willow.

In the meantime, poor Pearl was in a state of the greatest anxiety. The eventful day on which she was to meet her lover had opened for her with keen expectation of meeting him after their long and romantic separation. She had never for one moment doubted that he would keep his engagement with her. An instinct which she could not explain made her feel certain that he was still alive, and that nothing in the world would prevent him from meeting her, as had been agreed upon between them at that eventful parting in the temple eighteen years before.

As the day wore on, however, and there were no signs of Chan, Pearl's distress became exceedingly pitiful; and when night came and her mother declared that nothing had been seen of him, she was so stricken with despair that she lost all consciousness, and had to be carried to bed, where she lay in a kind of trance from which, for some time, it seemed impossible to arouse her.

When at last she did regain consciousness, her mother tried to comfort her by saying that perhaps Chan was dead, or that he had forgotten her in the long course of years, and that therefore she must not grieve too much. "You are a young girl," she said, "and you have a long life before you. Chan is an old man by this time; no doubt he has long ago married, and the home ties which he has formed have caused him to forget you. But you need not be broken-hearted on that account. There are many other men who will be more suitable for you than he could possibly be. By-and-by we shall arrange a marriage for you, and then life will appear to you very different from what it does now."

Instead of being comforted, however, Pearl was only the more distressed by her mother's words. Her love, which had begun in the Land of Shadows, and which had been growing in her heart for the last eighteen years, was not one to be easily put aside by such plausible arguments as those she had just listened to. The result was that she had a relapse, and for several days her life was in great danger.

The father and mother, fearing now that their daughter would die, determined, as there seemed no other remedy, to bring Chan to their home, and see whether his presence would not deliver Pearl from the danger in which the doctor declared she undoubtedly was.

The father accordingly went to the inn where he knew Chan was staying, and to his immense surprise he found him to be a young man of about twenty-five, highly polished in manner, and possessed of unusual intelligence. For some time he utterly refused to believe that this handsome young fellow was really the man with whom Pearl was so deeply in love, and it was not until Chan had told him the romantic story of his life that he could at all believe that he was not being imposed upon. Eventually, however, he was so taken with Chan that he became determined to do all in his power to bring about his marriage with his daughter.

"Come with me at once," he said, "and see if your presence will not do more than the cleverest doctors in the town have been able to accomplish. Pearl has been so distressed at not seeing you that she is now seriously ill, and we have been afraid that she would die of a broken heart."

When they arrived at the house Chan was taken into the sick-room, and the girl gazed into his face with a look of wonderment. "I do not seem to recognize you," she said in a feeble voice. "You are much younger than Chan, and although there is something about you that reminds me of him, I cannot realize that you are the same person with whom my spirit eighteen years ago held fellowship in the monastery where my body lay unburied."

Chan proceeded to explain the mystery. "For years," he said, "my mind was troubled about the difference between our ages. I was afraid that when you saw me with grey hairs and with wrinkles on my face, your love would receive a shock, and you might regret that you had ever pledged yourself to me. Although you had vanished from my sight, my prayers still continued to be offered to the Goddess of Mercy. She had heard them for you, you remember, when you were in the Land of Shadows, and through her intercession Yam-lo had forgiven your sins, and had made life easier for you in that gloomy country.

"I still continued to pray to her, hoping in some vague way that she would intervene to bring about the desire of my heart, and that when in due time I should meet you again, every obstacle to our mutual love would be for ever removed.

"One day a fairy came into the very room where your spirit had often conversed with me. He carried me away with him to the Western Heaven and brought me into the very presence of the Goddess of Mercy. She gave directions for me to bathe in the 'Fountain of Eternal Youth', and I became young again. That is why you see me now with a young face and a young nature, but my heart in its love for you has never changed, and never will as long as life lasts."

As he was telling this entrancing story, a look of devoted love spread over the beautiful countenance of Pearl. She gradually became instinct with life, and before he had finished speaking, the lassitude and exhaustion which had seemed to threaten her very life entirely disappeared. A rosy look came over her face, and her coal-black eyes flashed with hidden fires.

"Now I know," she cried, "that you are Chan. You are so changed that when I first caught sight of you my heart sank within me, for I had pictured an older man, and I could not at once realize that you were the same Chan who showed such unbounded love for me in the years gone by.

"It was not that I should have loved you less even though you had really been older. My heart would never have changed. It was only my doubt as to your reality that made me hesitate, but now my happiness is indeed great; for since through the goodness of the Goddess you have recovered your youth, I need not fear that the difference between our years may in the near future bring to us an eternal separation."

In a few days Pearl was once more herself again. Her parents, delighted with the romantic turn that things had taken and highly pleased with Chan himself, arranged for the betrothal of their daughter to him; and in the course of a few months, the loving couple were united in marriage. And so, after years of waiting, the happy consummation was accomplished, which Heaven and the Goddess of Mercy and even the dread Ruler of the Land of Shadows had each taken a share in bringing about; and for many and many a long year the story of Chan and his wife was spread abroad throughout the region in which they lived.

The Tragedy Of The Yin Family

IN A CERTAIN district in one of the central provinces of China, there lived a man of the name of Yin. He was possessed of considerable property, with a great ambition to become distinguished in life. The one desire of his heart, which seemed to master every other, was that his family should become an aristocratic one.

So far as he knew, none of his immediate predecessors had ever been a conspicuous scholar, or had gained any honour in the great triennial examinations. The result was that his family was a plebeian one, from which no mandarin had ever sprung. In what way, then, could he secure that the fame and dignities, which had come to some of the clans in the region in which he lived, should descend upon his home and upon his grandsons?

He was a rich man, it is true, but he was entirely illiterate, and all his money had been made in trade. As a lad his education had been neglected, for his early life had been spent in the mere struggle for existence. He had been more than successful, but the honours of the student never could be his, and never could he act as one of the officials of the Empire. It occurred to him, however, that though it was impossible that he himself should ever be classed amongst the great scholars of China, his sons and grandsons might be so honoured. In that case the glory of their success would be reflected upon him, and men would talk of him as the head of a family which had become distinguished for scholarship and high dignities in the State.

He finally came to the conclusion that the most effectual way of accomplishing this was to secure a lucky burying-ground in which he could lay the bodies of his father and his grandfather, who had departed this life some years before. The universal belief that in some mysterious way the dead have the power of showering down wealth and honours and prosperity upon the surviving members of their families, was held most tenaciously by Mr. Yin. This belief pointed out to him how he could emerge from the common and dreary road along which his ancestors had travelled, into the one where royal favours and official distinction would mark out his posterity in the future.

As he had retired from business, he was able to spend nearly the whole of his time in searching the country for the spots where certain unseen forces are supposed to collect with such dominant and overmastering power that the body of any person laid to rest amongst them will be found to dispense untold riches and dignities upon his nearest relatives. Accordingly, attended by a professor of the art, whose study of this intricate science enable him to detect at a glance the places which fulfilled the required conditions, Yin made frequent excursions in the regions around his home.

The valleys through which the streams ran, and where the sound of the running waters could be heard day and night as they sang their way to the sea, were all explored. Wherever water and hills were to be found in a happy conjunction, there these two men were to be seen peering over the ground, and with the aid of a compass which the professor carried with him in a cloth bag, marking whether the lines upon which they ran indicated that the mysterious Dragon had his residence beneath.

Innumerable places were carefully examined, and whilst some of them would have been admirably suited for a person of ordinary ambition, they did not satisfy the large expectations for the future which were cherished by Mr. Yin. The rising knolls and winding streams and far-off views of hills lying in the mist-like distance, showed perhaps that moderate prosperity would be the lot of those whose kindred might be buried there; but there were no signs of preeminence in scholarship, or of mandarins riding on horseback or in sedan-chairs, with great retinues attending them, as they proceeded in haughty dignity through the streets of the city in which they lived as rulers. Such places were therefore rejected as unsuitable.

Days and months went by in this search for a spot with which the fortunes of the Yin family were to be linked for many generations yet to come; but every place failed in someone or two particulars which would have marred the splendid prospect that ambition had pictured before the vision of this wealthy man.

At last, as they were sauntering along one day with eyes keen and alert, they stayed for a moment to rest on the top of a low hill which they had just ascended. Hardly had they cast a rapid glance over the beautiful scenery that lay stretched out before them, before the professor, with flashing eyes and unusual enthusiasm, exclaimed with excitement in his voice, "See! this is the very place we have been looking for all these days!

"No more suitable spot could have been found in the whole of China than this. We stand, as it were, in the centre of a great amphitheatre in which have been gathered the finest forces of Fung-Shuy. Behind us the hill rises in a graceful semi-circular form to shield the spot, where the dead shall lie buried, from the northern blasts, and from the fierce and malignant spirits that come flying on the wings of the great gales which blow with the touch of the ice and snow in them.

"On the plain in front of us, scattered over its surface, are gentle risings showing where the Dragon lies reposing, waiting to dispense its favours to all who come within its magic influence. And then, behold how the river winds in and out, seemingly unwilling to leave a place where unseen influences are at work to enrich the homes and gladden the hearts of the men and women of this region. See how it flows out with a hasty rush towards the sea beyond, and how it threads its way round yonder cape and is lost to view. Then mark again how it would seem as though some force it could not control had swung it round in its course, for it winds back upon the plain with gleaming eyes and joyous looks as if it were glad to return once more towards the distant mountains from whence it took its rise.

"The meaning of all this is," he continued, "that the prosperity, which the Dragon will bestow upon the living through the ministry of the dead lying within its domain, shall not soon pass away, but like the river that we see meandering before us, shall stay and comfort for many a long year those to whom it has been granted.

"That riches will come is certain, and official rank, and honours as well; for cast your eyes upon yonder ridge gleaming in the morning sun, and note the figure which rises up distinct and well-defined from its summit. It is simply a rock, it is true, but mark well its contour and you will note how the outline grows upon your vision until it assumes the form of a mandarin in full official robes standing with his face towards us.

"I would strongly advise you," concluded the professor, "to secure this plot of land on which we stand, whatever it may cost you, for every ambition that has ever filled your soul shall in time be satisfied by the wealth and honours which not only the Dragon but all his attendant spirits shall combine to pour into your home."

Yin was entranced with the prospect which was pictured before him in such glowing language by the man at his side, and he heartily agreed with the proposal that he should stay his search and purchase the ground on which they were standing as a cemetery for his family.

Just at this moment a man came sauntering along to see what these two strangers were doing in this out-of-the-way place, to which no road ran and from which no by-paths led to the villages beyond.

"Can you tell me, my man," asked Yin, "to whom this piece of land belongs?"

"Yes, I can easily do that," he replied. "Do you see that dilapidated-looking cottage down by the riverside? Well, it is occupied by a man named Lin, together with his wife and a daughter about nineteen years of age. They are exceedingly poor, as you can see by their house. The only property Lin possesses is this plot of ground, which has come down to him from his forefathers, and which he hopes one day to dispose of to some well-to-do person as a burying-ground that may bring him good luck."

"I am very willing to buy the land, if I can only get it at a reasonable price," replied Yin, "and I shall be glad if you will consent to act as middleman and negotiate the matter for me. You might go at once and see Lin, and find out what are the terms upon which he is willing to transfer the property to me."

On the morrow the middle-man returned and reported to Yin that Lin would on no consideration consent to let him have the ground. "The fact is," he continued, "that Lin has a settled purpose in his mind with which this particular plot of land has a good deal to do. He and his wife are getting on in years, and when the daughter is married off he is afraid that his branch of the family will become extinct; so he plans to get a husband for her who will come into the home and act the part of a son as well as that of son-in-law."

So determined, however, was Yin to gain possession of this particular piece of land that after considerable negotiations during which it seemed as though the old father would never be moved from his settled purpose, it was finally agreed that his daughter should be married to Yin's eldest son, Shung, and that her father and mother should remove to rooms in Yin's family mansion, where they should be maintained by him in ease and comfort as long as they lived. Had Yin been a large-hearted and generous person, this plan would have been an ideal one, but seeing that he was by nature a stingy, money-grubbing individual, it was attended with the most tragic results.

No sooner had the deeds of the coveted plot of ground been passed over to him than Yin had the body of his father, who had been buried in a place far removed from the influence of the Dragon, transferred to this new location, where he would be in touch with the higher spirits of the Underworld. Here, also, he could catch the eye of the mandarin, who day and night would have his face turned towards him, and who from the very fact of the sympathy that would grow up between them, must in time give him the mysterious power of turning his grandsons, and their sons after them, into scholars, who would obtain high positions in the service of the State.

In the meanwhile preparations were being made for the marriage of the young maiden of low degree to a man in a much higher social position than she could ever have aspired to in the ordinary course of events. Pearl was a sweet, comely-looking damsel, who would have made a model wife to one of her own station in life, but who was utterly unsuited for the new dignity which would be thrust upon her as soon as she crossed the threshold of the wealthy family of Yin. She was simply a peasant girl, without education and without refinement. Her days had been passed amidst scenes of poverty, and though she was a thoroughly good girl, with the high ideals that the commonest people in China everywhere have, her proper position was after all amongst the kind of people with whom she had lived all her life.

Her father and mother had indeed all along been doubtful about the propriety of marrying their daughter into a family so much above them as the Yins, and for a long time they had stood out against all the arguments in favour of it. Finally, overborne by the impetuosity of Yin, and dazzled with the prospects which such an alliance offered not only to the girl herself but also to themselves by the agreement to keep them in comfort for the rest of their lives, they had given an unwilling consent.

In order that Pearl should suffer as little disgrace as possible when she appeared amongst her new relations, her father sold all his available belongings in order to procure suitable wedding-garments for her. His idea, however, of the fitness of things had been gathered from the humble surroundings in which he had lived all his days, and the silks and satins and expensive jewellery that adorn the brides of the wealthy had never come within the vision of his dreams. Still Pearl was a pretty girl, and with her piercing black eyes which always seemed to be suffused with laughter, and with a smile which looked like a flash from a summer sky, she needed but little adornment, and would have won the heart of any man who had the soul to appreciate a true woman when he saw one.

At last the day came, hurried on by the eager desire of Yin to have the whole thing settled, when the humble home was to be given up and its inmates transferred to the rich house that lay just over a neighbouring hill.

A magnificent bridal chair, whose brilliant crimson colour made it a conspicuous object on the grey landscape, wound its way towards the cottage where the bride was attired all ready to step into it the moment it appeared at the door.

In front of it there marched a band, making the country-side resound with weird notes which seemed to fly on the air with defiance in their tones, and to send their echoes mounting to the tops of the hills and piercing down into the silent valleys. There were also crowds of retainers and dependants of the wealthy man. These were dressed in semi-official robes, and flocked along with smiling faces and joyous shouts. The occasion was a festal one, and visions of rare dishes and of generous feasting, kept up for several days, filled the minds of the happy procession as it went to meet the bride.

The return of the party was still more boisterous in its merriment. The members of the band seemed inspired by the occasion and sent forth lusty strains, whilst the instruments, as if aware how much depended upon them, responded to the efforts of the performers and filled the air with joyful notes.

A distinguished company had assembled to receive the bride, as she was led by her husband from the crimson chair and advanced with timid steps and faltering heart into the room that had been prepared for her reception. As she entered the house something in the air struck a chill into her heart and caused the hopes of happiness, which she had been cherishing, to die an almost instant death.

Shung, her husband, was a man of ignoble mind, and had always objected to marrying a woman so far beneath him. The sight of his bride, with her rustic air, and the ill-made commonplace-looking clothes in which she was dressed, made his face burn with shame, for he knew that a sneer was lurking on the face of everyone who had gathered to have a look at her.

A profound feeling of hatred entered his narrow soul, and as the days went by the one purpose of his life was to humiliate this sweet-tempered woman, who had been sacrificed simply to further the ambitious schemes of her designing father-in-law, Mr. Yin. For a few weeks he simply ignored her, but by degrees he treated her so cruelly that many a time she had serious thoughts of putting an end to her life. It soon turned out that a systematic attempt was being made by both father and son to get rid of the whole family.

The old father and mother, whom Yin had agreed to provide for during the rest of their lives, found things so intolerable that they voluntarily left the miserable quarters assigned to them and returned to their empty cottage. Every stick of furniture had been sold in order to buy their daughter's wedding garments, so that when they reached their old home they found absolutely nothing in it. With a few bundles of straw they made up a bed on the floor, but there was no food to eat, and not a single thing to comfort them in this their hour of darkest misery.

Sorrow for their daughter, and disappointment and anguish of heart at the thought of how they had been tricked and cheated by Mr. Yin in order that he might gain possession of their bit of land, so told upon their spirits that they both fell ill of a low fever, which laid them prostrate on their bed of straw. As they lived remote from other people, for some time no one knew that they were sick. Days went by without anyone visiting them, and when at last one kindly-hearted farmer came to make enquiries, he found to his horror that both husband and wife lay dead, side by side, in their miserable cabin.

The news of their death produced the greatest pleasure in the mind of the wretched man who was really the cause of it. He was now freed from the compact compelling him to provide for them during their life, and so there would be an actual saving of the money which he would have had to spend in providing them with food and clothing. A cruel, wintry smile lingered on his hard face for several days after the poor old couple had been lain to rest on the hillside near their cottage, and this was the only look of mourning his features ever assumed.

From this time Pearl's life became more and more of a burden to her. Love, the one element which would have filled her heart with happiness, was the one thing that was never offered her. Instead of affection there were cruel, cutting words and scornful looks and heavy blows – all these were plentifully bestowed upon her by the soulless man who was called her husband.

At length, to show his utter contempt and abhorrence of her, he arranged with the connivance of his father to bring a concubine into his home. This lady came from a comparatively good family, and was induced to take this secondary position because of the large sum of money that was paid to her father for her. The misery of Pearl was only intensified by her appearance on the scene. Following the lead of her husband, and jealous of the higher position in the family that the law gave her rival, she took every means that a spiteful woman could devise to make her life still more miserable.

The death of her parents had filled Pearl's heart with such intense grief and sorrow that life had lost all its charm for her. She saw, moreover, from the sordid rejoicing that was openly made at their tragic end, that the Yins would never be satisfied until she too had followed them into the Land of Shadows. She would therefore anticipate the cruel purposes of her husband and his father, and so deliver herself from a persecution that would only cease with her death. So one midnight, when all the rest of the family were asleep, and nothing was heard outside but the moaning of the wind which seemed as though it was preparing to sing a requiem over her, she put an end to all her earthly troubles by hanging herself in her own room.

When the body was found next day, suspended from a hook in one of the beams, a great cry of delight was uttered by Yin and his son. Without any violence on their part they had been set free from their alliance with this low-class family, and at a very small cost they had obtained firm possession of the land which was to enrich and ennoble their descendants.

And so whilst the poor girl lay dead, driven to an untimely end by spirits more fierce and malignant than any that were supposed to be flying with hatred in their hearts in the air around, smiles and laughter and noisy congratulations were indulged in by the living ghouls whose persecution had made this sweet-tempered woman's life unbearable.

But retribution was at hand. Heaven moves slowly in the punishment of the wicked, but its footsteps are sure and they travel irresistibly along the road that leads to vengeance on the wrongdoer.

One dark night, when the sky was overcast and neither moon nor stars were to be seen, and a storm of unusual violence was filling the air with a tumult of fierce and angry meanings, a weird and gruesome scene was enacted at the grave where the father of Yin had been buried. Hideous sounds of wailing and shrieking could be heard, as though all the demons of the infernal regions had assembled there to hold a night of carnival. Louder than the storm, the cries penetrated through the shrillest blasts, and people in their homes far away were wakened out of their sleep by the unearthly yells which froze their blood with terror. At last a thunderbolt rolled from the darkened heavens, louder than ever mortal man had heard. The lightnings flashed, and concentrating all their force upon the grave just where the coffin lay, they tore up a huge chasm in the earth, and gripping the coffin within their fiery fingers, they tossed it with disdain upon a hillside a mile away.

After a long search, Yin discovered it next day in the lonely spot where it had been cast, and was returning to make arrangements for its interment, when in a lonely part of the road two unearthly figures suddenly rose up before him. These, to his horror, he recognized as the spirits of Pearl's father and mother who had practically been done to death by him, and whom Yam-lo had allowed to revisit the earth in order to plague the man who was the author of their destruction. So terrified was Yin at their wild and threatening aspect, that he fell to the ground in a swoon, and thus he was found, hours afterwards, by his son, who had come out in search of him.

For several days he was tended with the greatest care, and the most famous physicians were called in to prescribe for him. He never rallied, however, and there was always a vague and haunted look in his eyes, as though he saw some terrible vision which frightened away his reasoning powers and prevented him from regaining consciousness. In this condition he died, without a look of recognition for those he loved, and without a word of explanation as to the cause of this tragic conclusion of a life that was still in its prime.

The eldest son was now master of his father's wealth; but instead of learning a lesson from the terrible judgment which had fallen on his home because of the injustice and wrong that had been committed on an innocent family, he only became more hard-hearted in his treatment of those who were within his power. He never dreamed of making any reparation for the acts of cruelty by which he had driven his wife to hang herself in order to escape his tyranny. But the steps of Fate were still moving on towards him. Leaden-footed they might be and slow, but with unerring certainty they were travelling steadily on to carry out the vengeance of the gods.

By-and-by the room in which Pearl had died became haunted. Her spectral figure could be seen in the gloaming, flitting about and peering out of the door with a look of agony on her face. Sometimes she would be seen in the early dawn, restless and agitated, as though she had been wandering up and down the whole night; and again she would flit about in the moonlight and creep into the shadow of the houses, but always with a ghost of the old look that had made her face so winning and so charming when she was alive.

When it was realized that it was her spirit which was haunting the house, the greatest alarm and terror were evinced by everyone in it. There is nothing more terrible than the appearance of the spirits of those who have been wronged, for they always come with some vengeful purpose. No matter how loving the persons themselves may have been in life, with death their whole nature changes and they are filled with the most passionate desire to inflict injury and especially death upon the object of their hatred.

The course of ill-usage which her husband Shung had cruelly adopted in order to drive Pearl to commit suicide was known to everyone, and that she should now appear to wreak vengeance on him was not considered at all wonderful; but still everyone was mortally afraid lest they should become involved in the punishment that was sure to be meted out.

As the ghost continued to linger about and showed no signs of disappearing, Shung was at last seized with apprehension lest some calamity was about to fall upon his house. In order to protect himself from any unexpected attack from the spirit that wandered and fluttered about in the darkest and most retired rooms in his home, he provided himself with a sword which he had ground down to a very sharp edge and which he carried in his hand ready uplifted to lunge at Pearl should she dare to attack him.

One evening, unaware that his concubine was sitting in a certain room on which the shadows had thickly fallen, he was entering it for some purpose, when the spirit of his late wife gripped his hand with an overmastering force which he felt himself unable to resist, and forced him to strike repeated blows against the poor defenceless woman. Not more than a dozen of these had been given before she was lying senseless on the ground, breathing out her life from the gaping wounds through which her life-blood was flowing in streams.

When the grip of the ghost had relaxed its hold upon him and he felt himself free to look at what he had done, Shung was horrified beyond measure as he gazed with staring eyes upon the dreadful sight before him, and realized the judgment that had come upon him for the wrongs he had done to Pearl and her family.

As soon as the news of the murder of the woman was carried to her father, he entered a complaint before the nearest mandarin, who issued a warrant for Shung's apprehension. At his trial he attempted to defend himself by declaring that it was not he who had killed his concubine, but an evil spirit which had caught hold of his arm and had directed the blows that had caused her death.

The magistrate smiled at this extraordinary defence, and said that Shung must consider him a great fool if he thought for a moment that he would be willing to accept such a ridiculous excuse for the dreadful crime he had committed.

As Shung was a wealthy man and had the means of bribing the under-officials in the yamen, his case was remanded in order to see how much money could be squeezed out of him before the final sentence was given. The murder – apparently without reason or provocation – of a woman who had been a member of a prominent family in society, produced a widespread feeling of indignation, and public opinion was strong in condemnation of Shung. Everyone felt that there ought to be exemplary punishment in his case; otherwise any man who had only money enough might be able to defy all the great principles established by Heaven for the government of society and for the prevention of crime.

In order to make it easy for Shung whilst he was in prison, his mother had to spend large sums in bribing everyone connected with the yamen. Never before had such an opportunity for reaping a golden harvest been presented to the avaricious minions entrusted by the Emperor with the administration of justice amongst his subjects. In her anxiety for her son the poor woman sold field after field to find funds wherewith to meet the demands of these greedy officials. Dark hints had simply to be thrown out by some of these that Shung was in danger of his life, and fresh sales would be made to bribe the mandarin to be lenient in his judgment of him.

At length the property had all been disposed of, and when it was known that no further money could be obtained, sentence was given that Shung should be imprisoned for life. This was a cruel blow to his mother, who had all along hoped that he might be released. Full of sorrow and absolutely penniless in a few weeks she died of a broken heart, whilst the son, seeing nothing but a hopeless imprisonment before him, committed suicide and thus ended his worthless life.

This tragic extinction of a family, which only a short year before was in the highest state of prosperity, was accepted by everyone who heard the story as a just and righteous punishment from Heaven. For Heaven is so careful of human life that any one who destroys it comes under the inevitable law that he too shall in his turn be crushed under the wheels of avenging justice.

The Ghost Who Was Foiled

THERE ARE GHOSTS of many kinds, but the ghosts of those who have hung themselves are the worst. Such ghosts are always coaxing other living people to hang themselves from the beams of the roof. If they succeed in persuading someone to hang himself, then the road to the Nether World is open to them, and they can once more enter into the wheel of transformation. The following story of such a ghost is told by persons worthy of belief.

Once upon a time there lived a man in Tsing Tschoufu who had passed his military examination, and had been ordered to Tsinanfu to report for duty. It was at the season of rains. So it happened that evening came on before he could reach the town-inn where he had expected to pass the night. Just as the sun was setting he reached a small village and asked for a night's lodging. But there were only poor families in the village who had no room for him in their huts. So they directed him to an old temple which stood outside the village, and said he could spend the night there.

The images of the gods in the temple were all decayed, so that one could not distinguish one from the other. Thick spider-webs covered the entrance, and the dust lay inches high everywhere. So the soldier went out into the open, where he found an old flight of steps. He spread out his knapsack on a stone step, tied his horse to an old tree, took his flask from his pocket and drank – for it had been a hot day. There had been a heavy rain, but it had just cleared again. The new moon was on the decline. The soldier closed his eyes and tried to sleep.

Suddenly he heard a rustling sound in the temple, and a cool wind passed over his face and made him shudder. And he saw a woman come out of the temple, dressed in an old dirty red gown, and with a face as white as a chalk wall. She stole past quietly as though she were afraid of being seen. The soldier knew no fear. So he pretended to be asleep and did not move, but watched her with half-shut eyes. And he saw her draw a rope from her sleeve and disappear. Then he knew that she was the ghost of one who had hung herself. He got up softly and followed her, and, sure enough, she went into the village.

When she came to a certain house she slipped into the court through a crack in the door. The soldier leaped over the wall after her. It was a house with three rooms. In the rear room a lamp was burning dimly. The soldier looked through the window into the room, and there was a young woman of about twenty sitting on the bed, sighing deeply, and her kerchief was wet through with tears. Beside her lay a little child, asleep. The woman looked up toward the beam of the ceiling. One moment she would weep and the next she would stroke the child. When the soldier looked more closely, there was the ghost sitting up on the beam. She had passed the rope around her neck and was hanging herself in dumb show. And whenever she beckoned with her hand the woman looked up toward her. This went on for some time.

Finally the woman said: "You say it would be best for me to die. Very well, then, I will die; but I cannot part from my child!"

And once more she burst into tears. But the ghost merely laughed and coaxed her again.

So the woman said determinedly: "It is enough. I will die!"

With these words she opened her chest of clothes, put on new garments, and painted her face before the mirror. Then she drew up a bench and climbed up on it. She undid her girdle and knotted it to the beam. She had already stretched forth her neck and was about to leap from the bench, when the child suddenly awoke and began to cry. The woman climbed down again and soothed and quieted her child, and while she was petting it she wept, so that the tears fell from her eyes like a string of pearls. The ghost frowned and hissed, for it feared to lose its prey. In a short time the child had fallen asleep again, and the woman once more began to look aloft. Then she rose, again climbed on the bench, and was about to lay the noose about her neck when the soldier began to call out loudly and drum on the window-pane. Then he broke it and climbed into the room. The woman fell to the ground and the ghost disappeared. The soldier recalled the woman to consciousness, and then he saw something hanging down from the beam, like a cord without an end. Knowing that it belonged to the ghost of the hanged woman he took and kept it.

Then he said to the woman: "Take good care of your child! You have but one life to lose in this world!"

And with that he went out.

Then it occurred to him that his horse and his baggage were still in the temple. And he went there to get them. When he came out of the village there was the ghost, waiting for him in the road.

The ghost bowed and said: "I have been looking for a substitute for many years, and to-day, when it seemed as though I should really get one, you came along and spoiled my chances. So there is nothing more for me to do. Yet there is something which I left behind me in my hurry. You surely must have found it, and I will ask you to return it to me. If I only have this one thing, my not having found a substitute will not worry me."

Then the soldier showed her the rope and said with a laugh: "Is this the thing you mean? Why, if I were to give it back to you then someone is sure to hang themselves. And that I could not allow."

With these words he wound the rope around his arm, drove her off and said: "Now be off with you!"

But then the ghost grew angry. Her face turned greenish-black, her hair fell in wild disorder down her neck, her eyes grew bloodshot, and her tongue hung far out of her mouth. She stretched forth both hands and tried to seize the soldier, but he struck out at her with his clenched fist. By mistake he hit himself in the nose and it began to bleed. Then he sprinkled a few drops of blood in her direction and, since the ghosts cannot endure human blood, she ceased her attack, moved off a few paces and began to abuse him. This she did for some time, until the cock in the village began to crow. Then the ghost disappeared.

In the meantime the farmer-folk of the village had come to thank the soldier. It seems that after he had left the woman her husband had come home, and asked his wife what had happened. And then for the first time he had learned what had occurred. So they all set out together along the road in order to look for the soldier outside the village. When they found him he was still beating the air with his fists and talking wildly. So they called out to him and he told them what had taken place. The rope could still be seen on his bare arm; yet it had grown fast to it, and surrounded it in the shape of a red ring of flesh.

The day was just dawning, so the soldier swung himself into his saddle and rode away.

The Punishment of Greed

ONCE UPON A TIME there lived a man south of the Yangtze-kiang. He had taken a position as a teacher in Sutschoufu, on the border of Shantung. But when he got there he found that the schoolhouse had not yet been completed. Yet a two-story building in the neighborhood had been rented, in which the teacher was to live and hold school in the meantime. This house stood outside the village, not far from the river bank. A broad plain, overgrown with tangled brush, stretched out from it on every side. The teacher was pleased with the view.

Well, one evening he was standing in the door of his house watching the sun go down. The smoke that rose from the village chimneys gradually merged with the twilight shadows. All the noises of the day had died away. Suddenly, off in the distance, along the river bank, he beheld a fiery gleam. He hurried away at once in order to see what it might be. And there, on the bank, he found a wooden coffin, from which came the radiance he had noticed. Thought the teacher to himself: "The jewels with which they adorn the dead on their journey shine by night. Perhaps there are gems in the coffin!" And greed awoke in his heart, and he forgot that a coffin is a resting-place of the dead and should be respected. He took up a large stone, broke the cover of the coffin, and bent over to look more closely. And there in the coffin lay a youth. His face was as white as paper, he wore a mourning turban[1] on his head, his body was wrapped in hempen garments, and he wore straw sandals on his feet. The teacher was greatly frightened and turned to go away. But the corpse had already raised itself to a sitting posture. Then the teacher's fear got the better of him, and he began to run. And the corpse climbed out of its coffin and ran after him. Fortunately the house was not far away. The teacher ran as fast as he could, flew up the steps and locked the door after him. Gradually he caught his breath again. Outside there was not a sound to be heard. So he thought that perhaps the corpse had not followed him all the way. He opened the window and peered down. The corpse was leaning against the wall of the house. Suddenly it saw that the window had been opened, and with one leap it bounded up and in through it. Overcome by terror, the teacher fell down the stairs of the house, and rolled unconscious to the bottom of the flight. And when he did so the corpse fell down on the floor of the room above.

At the time the school children had all long since gone home. And the owner of the house lived in another dwelling, so that no one knew anything about what had happened. On the following morning the children came to school as usual. They found the door locked, and when they called no one answered. Then they broke down the door and found their teacher lying unconscious on the ground. They sprinkled him with ginger, but it took a long time before he woke from his coma. When they asked he told them all that had occurred. Then they all went upstairs and took away the corpse. It was taken outside the village limits and burned, and the bones which remained were once more laid in the coffin. But the teacher said, with a sigh: "Because of a moment's greed, I nearly lost my life!" He resigned his position, returned home and never, through all the days of his life, did he speak of gain again.

Footnotes for 'The Punishment of Greed'

1. The corpse wears a mourning turban and is dressed in mourning. According to local tradition, young people who die before their parents, are laid in their coffins clad in mourning, so that even in death they may do their duty and be able to mourn their parents when the latter shall have died.

The Night on the Battlefield

ONCE UPON A TIME there was a merchant, who was wandering toward Shantung with his wares, along the road from the South. At about the second watch of the night, a heavy storm blew up from the North. And he chanced to see an inn at one side of the road, whose lights were just being lit. He went in to get something to drink and order lodgings for the night, but the folk at the inn raised objections. Yet an old man among them took pity on his unhappy situation and said: "We have just prepared a meal for warriors who have come a long distance, and we have no wine left to serve you. But there is a little side room here which is still free, and there you may stay overnight." With these words he led him into it. But the merchant could not sleep because of his hunger and thirst. Outside he could hear the noise of men and horses. And since all these proceedings did not seem quite natural to him, he got up and looked through a crack in the door. And he saw that the whole inn was filled with soldiers, who were sitting on the ground, eating and drinking, and talking about campaigns of which he had never heard. After a time they began calling to each other: "The general is coming!" And far off in the distance could be heard the cries of his bodyguard. All the soldiers hurried out to receive him. Then the merchant saw a procession with many paper lanterns, and riding in their midst a man of martial appearance with a long beard. He dismounted, entered the inn, and took his place at the head of the board. The soldiers mounted guard at the door, awaiting his commands, and the inn-keeper served food and drink, to which the general did full justice.

When he had finished his officers entered, and he said to them: "You have now been underway for some time. Go back to your men. I shall rest a little myself. It will be time enough to beat the assembly when the order to advance is given."

The officers received his commands and withdrew. Then the general called out: "Send Asti in!" and a young officer entered from the left side of the house. The people of the inn locked the gates and withdrew for the night, while Asti conducted the long-haired general to a door at the left, through a crack of which shone the light of a lamp. The merchant stole from his room and looked through the crack in the door. Within the room was a bed of bamboo, without covers or pillows. The lamp stood on the ground. The long-bearded general took hold of his head. It came off and he placed it on the bed. Then Asti took hold of his arms. These also came off and were carefully placed beside the head. Then the old general threw himself down on the bed crosswise, and Asti took hold of his body, which came apart below the thighs, and the two legs fell to the ground. Then the lamp went out. Overcome by terror the merchant hurried back to his room as fast as he could, holding his sleeves before his eyes, and laid down on his bed, where he tossed about sleepless all night.

At last he heard a cock crow in the distance. He was shivering. He took his sleeves from his face and saw that dawn was stealing along the sky. And when he looked about him, there he was lying in the middle of a thick clump of brush. Round about him was a wilderness, not a house, not even a grave was to be seen anywhere. In spite of being chilled, he ran about three miles till he came to the nearest inn. The inn-keeper opened the door and asked him with astonishment where he came from at that early hour. So the merchant told him his experiences and inquired as to the sort of place at which he had spent the night. The inn-keeper shook his head: "The whole neighborhood is covered with old battlefields," was his reply, "and all sorts of supernatural things take place on them after dark."

The Constable

IN A CITY in the neighborhood of Kaiutschou there once lived a constable by the name of Dung. One day when he returned from a hunt after thieves the twilight had already begun to fall. So before he waded through the stream that flowed through the city he sat down on the bank, lit a pipe and took off his shoes. When he looked up, he suddenly saw a man in a red hat dressed as a constable crouching beside him.

Astonished, he inquired: "Who are you? Your clothes indicate that you are a member of our profession, but I have never yet seen you among the men of our local force. Tell me, pray, whence you come?"

The other answered: "I am weary, having come a long journey, and would like to enjoy a pipeful of tobacco in your company. I am sure you will not object to that."

Dung handed him a pipe and tobacco.

But the other constable said: "I do not need them. Just you keep on smoking. It is enough for me to enjoy the odor."

So they chatted awhile together, and together waded through the stream. And gradually they became quite confidential and the stranger said: "I will be quite frank with you. I am the head constable of the Nether World, and am subject to the Lord of the Great Mountain. You yourself are a constable of reputation here in the upper world. And, because of my skill, I have standing in the world below. Since we are so well suited to each other, I should like to enter into a bond of brotherhood with you."

Dung was agreeable and asked: "But what really brings you here?"

Said the other: "In your district there lives a certain Wang, who was formerly superintendent of the granaries, and at that time caused the death of an officer. This man has now accused him in the Nether World. The King of the Nether World cannot come to a decision in the case, and therefore has asked the Lord of the Great Mountain to settle it. The Lord of the Great Mountain has ordered that Wang's property and life be shortened. First his property is to be sequestered here in the upper world, and then his soul is to be dragged to the nether one. I have been sent out by the Judge of the Dead to fetch him. Yet the established custom is, when someone is sent for, that the constable has first to report to the god of the city. The god of the city then issues a summons, and sends one of his own spirit constables to seize the soul and deliver it over to me. Only then may I take it away with me."

Dung asked him further particulars; but the other merely said: "Later on you will see it all for yourself."

When they reached the city Dung invited his colleague to stay at his home, and entertained him with wine and food. But the other only talked and touched neither the goblet nor the chop-sticks.

Said Dung: "In my haste I could not find any better meal for you. I am afraid it is not good enough."

But his guest replied: "Oh no, I am already surfeited and satisfied! We spirits feed only on odors; in which respect we differ from men."

It was late at night before he set out to visit the temple of the city god.

No sooner did morning dawn than he reappeared to take farewell and said: "Now all is in order: I am off! In two years' time you will go to Taianfu, the city near the Great Mountain, and there we will meet again."

Dung began to feel ill at ease. A few days later, in fact, came the news that Wang had died. The district mandarin journeyed to the dead man's natal village in order to express his sympathy. Among his followers was Dung. The inn-keeper there was a tenant of Wang's.

Dung asked him: "Did anything out of the ordinary happen when Sir Wang died?"

"It was all very strange," answered the inn-keeper, "and my mother who had been very busy in his house, came home and fell into a violent fever. She was unconscious for a day and a night, and could hardly breathe. She came to on the very day when the news of Sir Wang's death was made public, and said: 'I have been to the Nether World and I met him there. He had chains about his neck and several devils were dragging him along. I asked him what he had done, but he said: "I have no time to tell you now. When you return ask my wife and she will tell you all!"' And yesterday my mother went there and asked her. And Wang's wife told her with tears: 'My master was an official, but for a long time he did not make any head-way. He was superintendent of the granaries in Nanking, and in the same city was a high officer, with whom my master became very intimate. He always came to visit at our house and he and my master would talk and drink together. One day my master said to him: "We administrative mandarins have a large salary and a good income besides. You are an officer, and have even reached the second step in rank, yet your salary is so small that you cannot possibly make it do. Have you any other income aside from it?"

The officer replied: "We are such good friends that I know I can speak openly to you. We officers are compelled to find some additional sources of revenue in order that our pockets may not be altogether empty. When we pay our men we make a small percentage of gains on the exchange; and we also carry more soldiers on our rosters than there actually are present. If we had to live on our salaries we would die of hunger!"

"'When my husband heard him say this he could not rid himself of the idea that by disclosing these criminal proceedings the State would be indebted to him, and that it would surely aid his plans for advancement. On the other hand, he reflected that it would not be right to abuse his friend's confidence. With these ideas in his mind he retired to his inner rooms. In the courtyard stood a round pavilion. Lost in heavy thought, he crossed his hands behind his back, and for a long time walked round and round the pavilion. Finally he said with a sigh: "Charity begins at home; I will sacrifice my friend!" Then he drew up his report, in which the officer was indicted. An imperial order was issued, the matter was investigated, and the officer was condemned to death. My husband, however, was at once increased in rank, and from that time on advanced rapidly. And with the exception of myself no one ever knew anything of the matter.' When my mother told them of her encounter with Wang in the Nether World, the whole family burst into loud weeping. Four tents full of Buddhist and Taoist priests were sent for, who fasted and read masses for thirty-five days in order that Wang might be delivered. Whole mountains of paper money, silk and straw figures were burned, and the ceremonies have not as yet come to an end."

When Dung heard this he was very much frightened.

Two years later he received an order to journey to Taianfu in order to arrest some robbers there. He thought to himself: "My friend, the spirit, must be very powerful indeed, to have known about this trip so far in advance. I must inquire for him. Perhaps I will see him again."

When he reached Taianfu he sought out an inn.

The inn-keeper received him with the words: "Are you Master Dung, and have you come from the bay of Kaiutschou?"

"I am the man," answered Dung, alarmed, "how do you happen to know me?"

The inn-keeper replied: "The constable of the temple of the Great Mountain appeared to me last night and said: 'Tomorrow a man by the name of Dung who is a good friend of mine is coming from the bay of Kaiutschou!' And then he described your appearance and your clothes to me exactly, and told me to make careful note of them, and when you came to treat you with the greatest consideration, and to take no pay from you, since he would repay me lavishly. So when I saw you coming everything was exactly as my dreams had foretold, and I knew you at once. I have already prepared a quiet room for you, and beg that you will condescend to make yourself at ease."

Joyfully Dung followed him, and the inn-keeper waited on him with the greatest consideration, and saw that he had great plenty to eat and to drink.

At midnight the spirit arrived. Without having opened the door, he stood by Dung's bedside, gave him his hand, and asked how things had gone with him since he had last seen him.

Dung answered all his questions and thanked him into the bargain for appearing to the inn-keeper in a dream.

He continued to live for some days at the inn. During the day he went walking on the Great Mountain and at night his friend came to visit him and talked with him, and at the same time asked him what had happened to Sir Wang.

"His sentence has already been spoken," answered the other. "This man pretended to be conscientious, and traitorously brought about the death of his friend. Of all sins there is no greater sin than this. As a punishment he will be sent forth again into the world as an animal." Then he added: "When you reach home you must take constant care of your health. Fate has allowed you seventy-eight years of mortal life. When your time is up I will come to fetch you myself. Then I will see that you obtain a place as constable in the Nether World, where we can always be together."

When he had said this, he disappeared.

The Dangerous Reward

ONCE UPON A TIME a man named Hu-Wu-Bau, who lived near the Great Mountain, went walking there one day. And there, under a tree, he met a messenger in a red robe who called out to him: "The Lord of the Great Mountain would like to see you!" The man was much frightened, but dared offer no objection. The messenger bade him shut his eyes, and when he was allowed to open them again after a short time, he found himself standing before a lofty palace. He entered it to see the god. The latter had a meal prepared for him and said: "I only sent for you to-day because I had heard you intended traveling to the West. And in that case I should like to give you a letter to take to my daughter."

"But where is your daughter?" asked the man.

"She is married to the river-god," was the reply. "All you need to do is to take along the letter lying there. When you reach the middle of the Yellow River, beat against the side of the ship and call out: 'Greencoat!' Then someone will appear and take the letter from you."

And with these words he handed Hu-Wu-Bau the letter, and he was taken back again to the upper world.

When he came to the Yellow River on his journey, he did what the Lord of the Great Mountain had told him, and cried: "Greencoat!" And sure enough, a girl in green garments rose from the water, took him by the hand and told him to close his eyes. Then she led him into the palace of the river-god and he delivered the letter. The river-god entertained him splendidly, and thanked him as best he knew how. At parting he said: "I am grateful that you have made this long journey to see me. I have nothing to give you, however, save this pair of green silk shoes. While you are wearing them you can keep on walking as long as you like and never grow weary. And they will give you the second sight, so that you will be able to see the spirits and gods."

The man thanked him for the gift and returned to his ship. He continued on his journey to the West, and after a year had passed, came back again. When he reached the Great Mountain, he thought it would be fit and proper to report to the god. So he once more knocked against the tree and gave his name. In a moment the red-clad messenger appeared and led him to the Lord of the Mountain. So he reported that he had delivered the letter to the river-god, and how all things were there, and the Lord of the Mountain thanked him. During the meal which the god had prepared for him, he withdrew for a few moments to a quiet spot. Suddenly he saw his deceased father, bound and loaded with chains, who together with several hundred other criminals, was doing menial labor.

Moved to tears, he asked: "O my father, why are you here?"

His father replied: "During my life on earth I happened to tread on bread, hence I was condemned to hard labor at this spot. I have passed two years in this manner, yet their bitterness has been unspeakable. Since you are acquainted with the Lord of the Mountain, you might plead for me, and beg him to excuse me from this task and make me the field-god in our village."

His son promised to do so, and went back and pleaded with the Lord of the Mountain as he had agreed. The latter seemed inclined to listen to his prayer, yet said warningly: "The quick and the dead tread different paths. It is not well for the dead and the living to abide near one another permanently."

The man returned home. Yet, in about a year's time nearly all his children had died. In the terror of his heart he turned to the Lord of the Great Mountain. He beat on the tree; the red-coat came and led him into the palace. There he told of his misfortune and begged the god to protect him. The Lord of the Mountain smiled: "Did I not tell you in the start that the quick and the dead tread different paths, and that it is not well if they abide near each other permanently? Now you see what has happened!" Yet he sent his messenger to fetch the man's father. The father came and the god spake to him as follows: "I forgave you your offense and sent you back to your home as a field-god. It was your duty to bring happiness to your family. Instead, nearly all of your grand-children have died off. Why is this?"

And the father said: "I had been away from home so long that I was overjoyed to return. Besides I had meat and drink in overflowing measure. So I thought of my little grand-children and called them to me."

Then the Lord of the Great Mountain appointed another field-god for that village, and also gave the father another place. And from that time no further misfortune happened to the family of Hu-Wu-Bau.

His Father's Ghost

A MAN NAMED T'ien Tzu-ch'eng, of Chiang-ning, was crossing the Tung-t'ing lake, when the boat was capsized, and he was drowned. His son, Liang-ssu, who, towards the close of the Ming dynasty, took the highest degree, was then a baby in arms; and his wife, hearing the bad news, swallowed poison forthwith, and left the child to the care of his grandmother. When Liang-ssu grew up, he was appointed magistrate in Hu-pei, where he remained about a year. He was then transferred to Hu-nan, on military service; but, on reaching the Tung-t'ing lake, his feelings overpowered him, and he returned to plead inability as an excuse for not taking up his post. Accordingly, he was degraded to the rank of Assistant-Magistrate, which he at first declined, but was finally compelled to accept; and thenceforward gave himself up to roaming about on the lakes and streams of the surrounding country, without paying much attention to his official duties.

One night he had anchored his boat alongside the bank of a river, when suddenly the cadence of a sweetly-played flageolet broke upon his ear; so he strolled along by the light of the moon in the direction of the music, until, after a few minutes' walking, he reached a cottage standing by itself, with a few citron-trees round it, and brilliantly-lighted inside. Approaching a window, he peeped in, and saw three persons sitting at a table, engaged in drinking. In the place of honour was a graduate of about thirty years of age; an old man played the host, and at the side sat a much younger man playing on the flageolet. When he had finished, the old man clapped his hands in admiration; but the graduate turned away with a sigh, as if he had not heard a note. "Come now, Mr. Lu," cried the old man, addressing the latter, "kindly favour us with one of your songs, which, I know, must be worth hearing." The graduate then began to sing as follows:

"Over the river the wind blows cold on lonely me:
Each flow'ret trampled under foot, all verdure gone.
At home a thousand li away, I cannot be;
So towards the Bridge my spirit nightly wanders on."

The above was given in such melancholy tones that the old man smiled and said, "Mr. Lu, these must be experiences of your own," and, immediately filling a goblet, added, "I can do nothing like that; but if you will let me, I will give you a song to help us on with our wine." He then sung a verse from "Li T'ai-poh," and put them all in a lively humour again; after which the young man said he would just go outside and see how high the moon was, which he did, and observing Liang-ssu outside, clapped his hands, and cried out to his companions, "There is a man at the window, who has seen all we have been doing." He then led Liang-ssu in; whereupon the other two rose, and begged him to be seated, and to join them in their wine. The wine, however, was cold, and he therefore declined; but the young man at once perceived his reason, and proceeded to warm some for him. Liang-ssu now ordered his servant to go and buy some more, but this his host would not permit him to do. They next inquired Liang-ssu's name, and whence he came, and then the old man said, "Why, then, you are the father and mother of the district in which I live. My name is River: I am an old resident here. This young man is a Mr. Tu, of Kiang-si; and this gentleman," added he, pointing to the graduate, "is Mr. Rushten, a fellow-provincial of yours." Mr. Rushten looked at Liang-ssu in rather a contemptuous way, and without taking much notice of him; whereupon Liang-ssu asked him whereabouts he lived in Chiang-ning, observing that it was strange he himself should never have heard of such an accomplished gentleman. "Alas!" replied Rushten, "it is many a long day since I left my home, and I know nothing even of my own family. Alas, indeed!" These words were uttered in so mournful a tone of voice that the old man broke in with, "Come, come, now! talking like this, instead of drinking when we're all so jolly together; this will never do." He then drained a bumper himself, and said, "I propose a game of forfeits. We'll throw with three dice; and whoever throws so that the spots on one die equal those on the other two shall give us a verse with a corresponding classical allusion in it." He then threw himself, and turned up an ace, a two, and a three; whereupon he sang the following lines:

"An ace and a deuce on one side, just equal a three on the other:
For Fan a chicken was boiled, though three years had passed, by Chang's mother.
Thus friends love to meet!"

Then the young musician threw, and turned up two twos and a four; whereupon he exclaimed, "Don't laugh at the feeble allusion of an unlearned fellow like me:

'Two deuces are equal to a four:
Four men united their valour in the old city.
Thus brothers love to meet!'"

Mr. Rushten followed with two aces and a two, and recited these lines:

"Two aces are equal to a two:
Lu-hsiang stretched out his two arms and embraced his father.
Thus father and son love to meet!"

Liang then threw, and turned up the same as Mr. Rushten; whereupon he said:

"Two aces are equal to a two:
Mao-jung regaled Lin-tsung with two baskets.
Thus host and guest love to meet!"

When the *partie* was over Liang-ssu rose to go, but Mr. Rushten said, "Dear me! why are you in such a hurry; we haven't had a moment to speak of the old place. Please stay: I was just going to ask you a few questions." So Liang-ssu sat down again, and Mr. Rushten proceeded. "I had an old friend," said he, "who was drowned in the Tung-t'ing lake. He bore the same name as yourself; was he a relative?" "He was my father," replied Liang-ssu; "how did you know him?" "We were friends as boys together; and when he was drowned, I recovered and buried his body by the river-side." Liang-ssu here burst into tears, and thanked Mr. Rushten very warmly, begging him to point out his father's grave. "Come again tomorrow," said Mr. Rushten, "and I will shew it to you. You could easily find it yourself. It is close by here, and has ten stalks of water-rush growing on it." Liang-ssu now took his leave, and went back to his boat, but he could not sleep for thinking of what Mr. Rushten had told him; and at length, without waiting for the dawn, he set out to look for the grave. To his great astonishment, the house where he had spent the previous evening had disappeared; but hunting about in the direction indicated by Mr. Rushten, he found a grave with ten water-rushes growing on it, precisely as Mr. Rushten had described. It then flashed across him that Mr. Rushten's name had a special meaning, and that he had been holding converse with none other than the disembodied spirit of his own father. And, on inquiring of the people of the place, he learnt that twenty years before a benevolent old gentleman, named Kao, had been in the habit of collecting the bodies of persons found drowned, and burying them in that spot. Liang then opened the grave, and carried off his father's remains to his own home, where his grandmother, to whom he described Mr. Rushten's appearance, confirmed the suspicion he himself had formed. It also turned out that the young musician was a cousin of his, who had been drowned when nineteen years of age; and then he recollected that the boy's father had subsequently gone to Kiang-si, and that his mother had died there, and had been buried at the Bamboo Bridge, to which Mr. Rushten had alluded in his song. But he did not know who the old man was.

The Resuscitated Corpse

A CERTAIN old man lived at Ts'ai-tien, in the Yang-hsin district. The village was some miles from the district city, and he and his son kept a roadside inn where travellers could pass the night.

One day, as it was getting dusk, four strangers presented themselves and asked for a night's lodging; to which the landlord replied that every bed was already occupied. The four men declared it was impossible for them to go back, and urged him to take them in somehow; and at length the landlord said he could give them a place to sleep in if they were not too particular – which the strangers immediately assured him they were not.

The fact was that the old man's daughter-in-law had just died, and that her body was lying in the women's quarters, waiting for the coffin, which his son had gone away to buy. So the landlord led them round thither, and walking in, placed a lamp on the table. At the further end of the room lay the corpse, decked out with paper robes, etc., in the usual way; and in the foremost section were sleeping-couches for four people.

The travellers were tired, and, throwing themselves on the beds, were soon snoring loudly, with the exception of one of them, who was not quite off when suddenly he heard a creaking of the trestles on which the dead body was laid out, and, opening his eyes, he saw by the light of the lamp in front of the corpse that the girl was raising the coverings from her and preparing to get down. In another moment she was on the floor and advancing towards the sleepers. Her face was of a light yellow hue, and she had a silk kerchief round her head; and when she reached the beds she blew on the other three travellers, whereupon the fourth, in a great fright, stealthily drew up the bed-clothes over his face, and held his breath to listen. He heard her breathe on him as she had done on the others, and then heard her go back again and get under the paper robes, which rustled distinctly as she did so.

He now put out his head to take a peep, and saw that she was lying down as before; whereupon, not daring to make any noise, he stretched forth his foot and kicked his companions, who, however, shewed no signs of moving. He now determined to put on his clothes and make a bolt for it; but he had hardly begun to do so before he heard the creaking sound again, which sent him back under the bed-clothes as fast as he could go. Again the girl came to him, and breathing several times on him, went away to lie down as before, as he could tell by the noise of the trestles. He then put his hand very gently out of bed, and, seizing his trousers, got quickly into them, jumped up with a bound, and rushed out of the place as fast as his legs would carry him. The corpse, too, jumped up; but by this time the traveller had already drawn the bolt, and was outside the door, running along and shrieking at the top of his voice, with the corpse following close behind. No one seemed to hear him, and he was afraid to knock at the door of the inn for fear they should not let him in in time; so he made for the highway to the city, and after awhile he saw a monastery by the roadside, and, hearing the "wooden fish", he ran up and thumped with all his might at the gate. The priest, however, did not know what to make of it, and would not open to him; and as the corpse was only a few yards off, he could do nothing but run behind a tree which stood close by, and there shelter himself, dodging to the right as the corpse dodged to the left, and so on. This infuriated the dead girl to madness; and at length, as tired and panting they stood watching each other on opposite sides of the tree, the corpse made a rush forward with one arm on each side in the hope of thus grabbing its victim. The traveller, however, fell backwards and escaped, while the corpse remained rigidly embracing the tree.

By-and-by the priest, who had been listening from the inside, hearing no sounds for some time, came out and found the traveller lying senseless on the ground; whereupon he had him carried into the monastery, and by morning they had got him round again. After giving him a little broth to drink, he related the whole story; and then in the early dawn they went out to examine the tree, where they found the girl fixed tightly to the tree. The news being sent to the magistrate, that functionary attended at once in person, and gave orders to remove the body; but this they were at first unable to do, the girl's fingers having penetrated into the bark so far that her nails were not to be seen.

At length they got her away, and then a messenger was despatched to the inn, already in a state of great commotion over the three travellers, who had been found dead in their beds. The old man accordingly sent to fetch his daughter-in-law; and the surviving traveller petitioned the magistrate, saying, "Four of us left home, but only one will go back. Give me something that I may show to my fellow-townsmen." So the magistrate gave him a certificate and sent him home again.

A Supernatural Wife

A CERTAIN Mr. Chao, of Ch'ang-shan, lodged in a family of the name of T'ai. He was very badly off, and, falling sick, was brought almost to death's door. One day they moved him into the verandah, that it might be cooler for him; and, when he awoke from a nap, lo! a beautiful girl was standing by his side. "I am come to be your wife," said the girl, in answer to his question as to who she was; to which he replied that a poor fellow like himself did not look for such luck as that; adding that, being then on his death-bed, he would not have much occasion for the services of a wife. The girl said she could cure him; but he told her he very much doubted that; "And even," continued he, "should you have any good prescription, I have not the means of getting it made up." "I don't want medicine to cure you with," rejoined the girl, proceeding at once to rub his back and sides with her hand, which seemed to him like a ball of fire.

He soon began to feel much better, and asked the young lady what her name was, in order, as he said, that he might remember her in his prayers. "I am a spirit," replied she; "and you, when alive under the Han dynasty as Ch'u Sui-liang, were a benefactor of my family. Your kindness being engraven on my heart, I have at length succeeded in my search for you, and am able in some measure to requite you." Chao was dreadfully ashamed of his poverty-stricken state, and afraid that his dirty room would spoil the young lady's dress; but she made him show her in, and accordingly he took her into his apartment, where there were neither chairs to sit upon, nor signs of anything to eat, saying, "You might, indeed, be able to put up with all this; but you see my larder is empty, and I have absolutely no means of supporting a wife." "Don't be alarmed about that," cried she; and in another moment he saw a couch covered with costly robes, the walls papered with a silver-flecked paper, and chairs and tables appear, the latter laden with all kinds of wine and exquisite viands.

They then began to enjoy themselves, and lived together as husband and wife, many people coming to witness these strange things, and being all cordially received by the young lady, who in her turn always accompanied Mr. Chao when he went out to dinner anywhere.

One day there was an unprincipled young graduate among the company, which she seemed immediately to become aware of; and, after calling him several bad names, she struck him on the side of the head, causing his head to fly out of the window while his body remained inside; and there he was, stuck fast, unable to move either way, until the others interceded for him and he was released. After some time visitors became too numerous, and if she refused to see them they turned their anger against her husband. At length, as they were sitting together drinking with some friends at the Tuan-yang festival, a white rabbit ran in, whereupon the girl jumped up and said, "The doctor has come for me;" then, turning to the rabbit, she added, "You go on: I'll follow you." So the rabbit went away, and then she ordered them to get a ladder and place it against a high tree in the back yard, the top of the ladder overtopping the tree. The young lady went up first and Chao close behind her; after which she called out to anybody who wished to join them to make haste up. None ventured to do so with the exception of a serving-boy belonging to the house, who followed after Chao; and thus they went up, up, up, up, until they disappeared in the clouds and were seen no more. However, when the bystanders came to look at the ladder, they found it was only an old door-frame with the panels knocked out; and when they went into Mr. Chao's room, it was the same old, dirty, unfurnished room as before. So they determined to find out all about it from the serving-boy when he came back; but this he never did.

The Dead Priest

A CERTAIN Taoist priest, overtaken in his wanderings by the shades of evening, sought refuge in a small Buddhist monastery. The monk's apartment was, however, locked; so he threw his mat down in the vestibule of the shrine, and seated himself upon it. In the middle of the night, when all was still, he heard a sound of someone opening the door behind him; and looking round, he saw a Buddhist priest, covered with blood from head to foot, who did not seem to notice that anybody else was present. Accordingly, he himself pretended not to be aware of what was going on; and then he saw the other priest enter the shrine, mount the altar, and remain there some time embracing Buddha's head, and laughing by turns.

When morning came, he found the monk's room still locked; and, suspecting something was wrong, he walked to a neighbouring village, where he told the people what he had seen. Thereupon the villagers went back with him, and broke open the door, and there before them lay the priest weltering in his blood, having evidently been killed by robbers, who had stripped the place bare. Anxious now to find out what had made the disembodied spirit of the priest laugh in the way it had been seen to do, they proceeded to inspect the head of the Buddha on the altar; and, at the back of it, they noticed a small mark, scraping through which they discovered a sum of over thirty ounces of silver. This sum was forthwith used for defraying the funeral expenses of the murdered man.

The Disembodied Friend

MR. CH'EN, M.A., of Shun-t'ien Fu, when a boy of sixteen, went to school at a Buddhist temple. There were a great many scholars besides himself, and, among others, one named Ch'u, who said he came from Shantung. This Ch'u was a very hard-working fellow; he never seemed to be idle, and actually slept in the school-room, not going home at all. Ch'en became much attached to him, and one day asked him why he never went away. "Well, you see," replied Ch'u, "my people are very poor, and can hardly afford to pay for my schooling; but, by dint of working half the night, two of my days are equal to three of anybody else's." Thereupon Ch'en said he would bring his own bed to the school, and that they would sleep there together; to which Ch'u replied that the teaching they got wasn't worth much, and that they would do better by putting themselves under a certain old scholar named Lu. This they were easily able to do, as the arrangement at the temple was monthly, and at the end of each month anyone was free to go or to come.

So off they went to this Mr. Lu, a man of considerable literary attainments, who had found himself in Shun-t'ien Fu without a cash in his pocket, and was accordingly obliged to take pupils. He was delighted at getting two additions to his number and, Ch'u showing himself an apt scholar, the two soon became very great friends, sleeping in the same room and eating at the same table.

At the end of the month Ch'u asked for leave of absence, and, to the astonishment of all, ten days elapsed without anything being heard of him. It then chanced that Ch'en went to the T'ien-ning temple, and there he saw Ch'u under one of the verandahs, occupied in cutting wood for lucifer-matches. The latter was much disconcerted by the arrival of Ch'en, who asked him why he had given up his studies; so the latter took him aside, and explained that he was so poor as to be obliged to work half a month to scrape together funds enough for his next month's schooling. "You come along back with me," cried Ch'en, on hearing this, "I will arrange for the payment," which Ch'u immediately consented to do on condition that Ch'en would keep the whole thing a profound secret.

Now Ch'en's father was a wealthy tradesman, and from his till Ch'en abstracted money wherewith to pay for Ch'u; and by-and-by, when his father found him out, he confessed why he had done so. Thereupon Ch'en's father called him a fool, and would not let him resume his studies; at which Ch'u was much hurt, and would have left the school too, but that old Mr. Lu discovered what had taken place, and gave him the money to return to Ch'en's father, keeping him still at the school, and treating him quite like his own son. So Ch'en studied no more, but whenever he met Ch'u he always asked him to join in some refreshment at a restaurant, Ch'u invariably refusing, but yielding at length to his entreaties, being himself loth to break off their old acquaintanceship.

Thus two years passed away, when Ch'en's father died, and Ch'en went back to his books under the guidance of old Mr. Lu, who was very glad to see such determination. Of course Ch'en was now far behind Ch'u; and in about six months Lu's son arrived, having begged his way in search of his father, so Mr. Lu gave up his school and returned home with a purse which his pupils had made up for him, Ch'u adding nothing thereto but his tears. At parting, Mr. Lu advised Ch'en to take Ch'u as his tutor, and this he did, establishing him comfortably in the house with him. The examination was very shortly to commence, and Ch'en felt convinced that he should not get through; but Ch'u said he thought he should be able to manage the matter for him. On the appointed day he introduced Ch'en to a gentleman who he said was a cousin of his, named Liu, and asked Ch'en to accompany this cousin, which Ch'en was just proceeding to do when Ch'u pulled him back from behind, and he would have fallen down but that the cousin pulled him up again, and then, after having scrutinized his appearance, carried him off to his own house. There being no ladies there, Ch'en was put into the inner apartments; and a few days afterwards Liu said to him, "A great many people will be at the gardens to-day; let us go and amuse ourselves awhile, and afterwards I will send you home again." He then gave orders that a servant should proceed on ahead with tea and wine, and by-and-by they themselves went, and were soon in the thick of the fete. Crossing over a bridge, they saw beneath an old willow tree a little painted skiff, and were soon on board, engaged in freely passing round the wine. However, finding this a little dull, Liu bade his servant go and see if Miss Li, the famous singing-girl, was at home; and in a few minutes the servant returned bringing Miss Li with him. Ch'en had met her before, and so they at once exchanged greetings, while Liu begged her to be good enough to favour them with a song. Miss Li, who seemed labouring under a fit of melancholy, forthwith began a funeral dirge; at which Ch'en was not much pleased, and observed that such a theme was hardly suitable to the occasion. With a forced smile, Miss Li changed her key, and gave them a love-song; whereupon Ch'en seized her hand, and said, "There's that song of the Huan-sha river, which you sang once before; I have read it over several times, but have quite forgotten the words." Then Miss Li began:

"Eyes overflowing with tears, she sits gazing into her glass,
Lifting the bamboo screen, one of her comrades approaches;
She bends her head and seems intent on her bow-like slippers,
And forces her eyebrows to arch themselves into a smile.
With her scarlet sleeve she wipes the tears from her perfumed cheek,
In fear and trembling lest they should guess the thoughts that o'erwhelm her."

Ch'en repeated this over several times, until at length the skiff stopped, and they passed through a long verandah, where a great many verses had been inscribed on the walls, to which Ch'en at once proceeded to add a stanza of his own. Evening was now coming on, and Liu remarked that the candidates would be just about leaving the examination-hall; so he escorted him back to his own home, and there left him. The room was dark, and there was no one with him; but by-and-by the servants ushered in someone whom at first he took to be Ch'u. However, he soon saw that it was not Ch'u, and in another moment the stranger had fallen against him and knocked him down. "Master's fainted!" cried the servants, as they ran to pick him up; and then Ch'en discovered that the one who had fallen down was really no other than himself.

On getting up, he saw Ch'u standing by his side; and when they had sent away the servants the latter said, "Don't be alarmed: I am nothing more than a disembodied spirit. My time for re-appearing on earth is long overdue, but I could not forget your great kindness to me, and accordingly I have remained under this form in order to assist in the accomplishment of your wishes. The three bouts are over, and your ambition will be gratified." Ch'en then inquired if Ch'u could assist him in like manner for his doctor's degree; to which the latter replied, "Alas! the luck descending to you from your ancestors is not equal to that. They were a niggardly lot, and unfit for the posthumous honours you would thus confer on them." Ch'en next asked him whither he was going; and Ch'u replied that he hoped, through the agency of his cousin, who was a clerk in Purgatory, to be born again in old Mr. Lu's family.

They then bade each other adieu; and, when morning came, Ch'en set off to call on Miss Li, the singing-girl; but on reaching her house he found that she had been dead some days. He walked on to the gardens, and there he saw traces of verses that had been written on the walls, and evidently rubbed out, so as to be hardly decipherable. In a moment it flashed across him that the verses and their composers belonged to the other world. Towards evening Ch'u re-appeared in high spirits, saying that he had succeeded in his design, and had come to wish Ch'en a long farewell. Holding out his open palms, he requested Ch'en to write the word Ch'u on each; and then, after refusing to take a parting cup, he went away, telling Ch'en that the examination-list would soon be out, and that they would meet again before long. Ch'en brushed away his tears and escorted him to the door, where a man, who had been waiting for him, laid his hand on Ch'u's head and pressed it downwards until Ch'u was perfectly flat. The man then put him in a sack and carried him off on his back.

A few days afterwards the list came out, and, to his great joy, Ch'en found his name among the successful candidates; whereupon he immediately started off to visit his old tutor, Mr. Lu. Now Mr. Lu's wife had had no children for ten years, being about fifty years of age, when suddenly she gave birth to a son, who was born with both fists doubled up so that no one could open them. On his arrival Ch'en begged to see the child, and declared that inside its hands would be found written the word Ch'u. Old Mr. Lu laughed at this; but no sooner had the child set eyes on Ch'en than both its fists opened spontaneously, and there was the word as Ch'en had said. The story was soon told, and Ch'en went home, after making a handsome present to the family; and later on, when Mr. Lu went up for his doctor's degree and stayed at Ch'en's house, his son was thirteen years old, and had already matriculated as a candidate

Parables & Fairy Tales

Introduction

THE TALES THAT FOLLOW demonstrate the mixture of beliefs and religions that were a part of ancient China. In many of the stories the immortal Gods and human beings interact, not exactly as equals, but not within the rigid hierarchy one might expect; it is perfectly feasible, even customary, for the daughter of a God to marry a human, and for such marriages to be successful. Often, we are also transported into a world of spirits and demons.

The image which we perhaps associate most with Chinese myth is that of the dragon. The Chinese dragon breathes cloud, not fire, and is a creature of awesome beauty. Although quick to anger and terrible in its fury, the dragon was mostly a force for good, representing the male principle, the yang, just as the phoenix represents the female, the yin.

Most of the tales told here do not have such a formal meaning. Some might be parables illustrating foolishness or steadfastness, wisdom or filial piety, while others may have more nebulous morals or lack any ethical instruction, being fairy tales that revel in the romance and whimsy of storytelling (see the magical adventure of 'How Molo Stole the Lovely Rose Red' or the enchanted characters of 'The Flower Elves'). Some are clearly Chinese versions of classic fairy tales such as 'Little Red Riding Hood' (see 'The Panther'). Above all they are for entertainment and enjoyment, telling of a mythical time when Gods and dragons walked the earth, and when human destiny was determined by magic spirits.

Bamboo and the Turtle

A PARTY OF visitors had been seeing the sights at Hsi Ling. They had just passed down the Holy Way between the huge stone animals when Bamboo, a little boy of twelve, son of a keeper, rushed out from his father's house to see the mandarins go by. Such a parade of great men he had never seen before, even on the feast days. There were ten sedan chairs, with bearers dressed in flaming colours, ten long-handled, red umbrellas, each carried far in front of its proud owner, and a long line of horsemen.

When this gay procession had filed past, Bamboo was almost ready to cry because he could not run after the sightseers as they went from temple to temple and from tomb to tomb. But, alas! his father had ordered him never to follow tourists. "If you do, they will take you for a beggar, Bamboo," he had said shrewdly, "and if you're a beggar, then your daddy's one too. Now they don't want any beggars around the royal tombs." So Bamboo had never known the pleasure of pursuing the rich. Many times he had turned back to the little mud house, almost broken-hearted at seeing his playmates running, full of glee, after the great men's chairs.

On the day when this story opens, just as the last horseman had passed out of sight among the cedars, Bamboo chanced to look up toward one of the smaller temple buildings of which his father was the keeper. It was the house through which the visitors had just been shown. Could his eyes be deceiving him? No, the great iron doors had been forgotten in the hurry of the moment, and there they stood wide open, as if inviting him to enter.

In great excitement he scurried toward the temple. How often he had pressed his head against the bars and looked into the dark room, wishing and hoping that some day he might go in. And yet, not once had he been granted this favour. Almost every day since babyhood he had gazed at the high stone shaft, or tablet, covered with Chinese writing, that stood in the centre of the lofty room, reaching almost to the roof. But with still greater surprise his eyes had feasted on the giant turtle underneath, on whose back the column rested. There are many such tablets to be seen in China, many such turtles patiently bearing their loads of stone, but this was the only sight of the kind that Bamboo had seen. He had never been outside the Hsi Ling forest, and, of course, knew very little of the great world beyond.

It is no wonder then that the turtle and the tablet had always astonished him. He had asked his father to explain the mystery. "Why do they have a turtle? Why not a lion or an elephant?" For he had seen stone figures of these animals in the park and had thought them much better able than his friend, the turtle, to carry loads on their backs. "Why it's just the custom," his father had replied – the answer always given when Bamboo asked a question, "just the custom." The boy had tried to imagine it all for himself, but had never been quite sure that he was right, and now, joy of all joys, he was about to enter the very turtle-room itself. Surely, once inside, he could find some answer to this puzzle of his childhood.

Breathless, he dashed through the doorway, fearing every minute that someone would notice the open gates and close them before he could enter. Just in front of the giant turtle he fell in a little heap on the floor, which was covered inch-deep with dust. His face was streaked, his clothes were a sight to behold; but Bamboo cared nothing for such trifles. He lay there for a few moments, not daring to move. Then, hearing a noise outside, he crawled under the ugly stone beast and crouched in his narrow hiding-place, as still as a mouse.

"There, there!" said a deep voice. "See what you are doing, stirring up such a dust! Why, you will strangle me if you are not careful."

It was the turtle speaking, and yet Bamboo's father had often told him that it was not alive. The boy lay trembling for a minute, too much frightened to get up and run.

"No use in shaking so, my lad," the voice continued, a little more kindly. "I suppose all boys are alike – good for nothing but kicking up a dust." He finished this sentence with a hoarse chuckle, and the boy, seeing that he was laughing, looked up with wonder at the strange creature.

"I meant no harm in coming," said the child finally. "I only wanted to look at you more closely."

"Oh, that was it, hey? Well, that is strange. All the others come and stare at the tablet on my back. Sometimes they read aloud the nonsense written there about dead emperors and their titles, but they never so much as look at me, at me whose father was one of the great four who made the world."

Bamboo's eyes shone with wonder. "What! your father helped make the world?" he gasped.

"Well, not my father exactly, but one of my grandfathers, and it amounts to the same thing, doesn't it. But, hark! I hear a voice. The keeper is coming back. Run up and close those doors, so he won't notice that they have not been locked. Then you may hide in the corner there until he has passed. I have something more to tell you."

Bamboo did as he was told. It took all his strength to swing the heavy doors into place. He felt very important to think that he was doing something for the grandson of a maker of the world, and it would have broken his heart if this visit had been ended just as it was beginning.

Sure enough, his father and the other keepers passed on, never dreaming that the heavy locks were not fastened as usual. They were talking about the great men who had just gone. They seemed very happy and were jingling some coins in their hands.

"Now, my boy," said the stone turtle when the sound of voices had died away and Bamboo had come out from his corner, "maybe you think I'm proud of my job. Here I've been holding up this chunk for a hundred years, I who am fond of travel. During all this time night and day, I have been trying to think of some way to give up my position. Perhaps it's honourable, but, you may well imagine, it's not very pleasant."

"I should think you would have the backache," ventured Bamboo timidly.

"Backache! well, I think so; back, neck, legs, eyes, everything I have is aching, aching for freedom. But, you see, even if I had kicked up my heels and overthrown this monument, I had no way of getting through those iron bars," and he nodded toward the gate.

"Yes, I understand," agreed Bamboo, beginning to feel sorry for his old friend.

"But, now that you are here, I have a plan, and a good one it is, too, I think. The watchmen have forgotten to lock the gate. What is to prevent my getting my freedom this very night? You open the gate, I walk out, and no one the wiser."

"But my father will lose his head if they find that he has failed to do his duty and you have escaped."

"Oh, no; not at all. You can slip his keys tonight, lock the gates after I am gone, and no one will know just what has happened. Why it will make this building famous. It won't hurt your father, but will do him good. So many travellers will be anxious to see the spot from which I vanished. I am too heavy for a thief to carry off, and they will be sure that it is another miracle of the gods. Oh, I shall have a good time out in the big world."

Just here Bamboo began to cry.

"Now what is the silly boy blubbering about?" sneered the turtle. "Is he nothing but a cry-baby?"

"No, but I don't want you to go."

"Don't want me to go, eh? Just like all the others. You're a fine fellow! What reason have you for wanting to see me weighed down here all the rest of my life with a mountain on my back? Why, I thought you were sorry for me, and it turns out that you are as mean as anybody else."

"It is so lonely here, and I have no playmates. You are the only friend I have."

The tortoise laughed loudly. "Ho, ho! so it's because I make you a good playmate, eh? Now, if that's your reason, that's another story altogether. What do you say to going with me then? I, too, need a friend, and if you help me to escape, why, you are the very friend for me."

"But how shall you get the tablet off your back?" questioned Bamboo doubtfully. "It's very heavy."

"That's easy, just walk out of the door. The tablet is too tall to go through. It will slide off and sit on the floor instead of on my shell."

Bamboo, wild with delight at the thought of going on a journey with the turtle, promised to obey the other's commands. After supper, when all were asleep in the little house of the keeper, he slipped from his bed, took down the heavy key from its peg, and ran pell-mell to the temple.

"Well, you didn't forget me, did you?" asked the turtle when Bamboo swung the iron gates open.

"Oh, no, I would not break a promise. Are you ready?"

"Yes, quite ready." So saying, the turtle took a step. The tablet swayed backward and forward, but did not fall. On walked the turtle until finally he stuck his ugly head through the doorway. "Oh, how good it looks outside," he said. "How pleasant the fresh air feels! Is that the moon rising over yonder? It's the first time I've seen it for an age. My word! just look at the trees! How they have grown since they set that tombstone on my back! There's a regular forest outside now."

Bamboo was delighted when he saw the turtle's glee at escaping. "Be careful," he cried, "not to let the tablet fall hard enough to break it."

Even as he spoke, the awkward beast waddled through the door. The upper end of the monument struck against the wall, toppled off, and fell with a great crash to the floor. Bamboo shivered with fear. Would his father come and find out what had happened?

"Don't be afraid, my boy. No one will come at this hour of the night to spy on us."

Bamboo quickly locked the gates, ran back to the house, and hung the key on its peg. He took a long look at his sleeping parents, and then returned to his friend. After all, he would not be gone long and his father would surely forgive him.

Soon the comrades were walking down the broad road, very slowly, for the tortoise is not swift of foot and Bamboo's legs were none too long.

"Where are you going?" said the boy at last, after he had begun to feel more at home with the turtle.

"Going? Where should you think I would want to go after my century in prison? Why, back to the first home of my father, back to the very spot where the great god, P'anku, and his three helpers hewed out the world."

"And is it far?" faltered the boy, beginning to feel just the least bit tired.

"At this rate, yes, but, bless my life, you didn't think we could travel all the way at this snail's pace, I hope. Jump on my back, and I'll show you how to go. Before morning we shall be at the end of the world, or rather, the beginning."

"Where is the beginning of the world?" asked Bamboo. "I have never studied geography."

"We must cross China, then Thibet, and at last in the mountains just beyond we shall reach the spot which P'anku made the centre of his labour."

At that moment Bamboo felt himself being lifted from the ground. At first he thought he would slip off the turtle's rounded shell, and he cried out in fright.

"Never fear," said his friend. "Only sit quietly, and there will be no danger."

They had now risen far into the air, and Bamboo could look down over the great forest of Hsi Ling all bathed in moonlight. There were the broad white roads leading up to the royal tombs, the beautiful temples, the buildings where oxen and sheep were prepared for sacrifice, the lofty towers, and the high tree-covered hills under which the emperors were buried. Until that night Bamboo had not known the size of this royal graveyard. Could it be that the turtle would carry him beyond the forest? Even as he asked himself this question he saw that they had reached a mountain, and the turtle was ascending higher, still higher, to cross the mighty wall of stone.

Bamboo grew dizzy as the turtle rose farther into the sky. He felt as he sometimes did when he played whirling games with his little friends, and got so dizzy that he tumbled over upon the ground. However, this time he knew that he must keep his head and not fall, for it must have been almost a mile to the ground below him. At last they had passed over the mountain and were flying above a great plain. Far below Bamboo could see sleeping villages and little streams of water that looked like silver in the moonlight. Now, directly beneath them was a city. A few feeble lights could be seen in the dark narrow streets, and Bamboo thought he could hear the faint cries of peddlers crying their midnight wares.

"That's the capital of Shan-shi just below us," said the turtle, breaking his long silence. "It is almost two hundred miles from here to your father's house, and we have taken less than half an hour. Beyond that is the Province of the Western Valleys. In one hour we shall be above Thibet."

On they whizzed at lightning speed. If it had not been hot summer time Bamboo would have been almost frozen. As it was, his hands and feet were cold and stiff. The turtle, as if knowing how chilly he was, flew nearer to the ground where it was warmer. How pleasant for Bamboo! He was so tired that he could keep his eyes open no longer and he was soon soaring in the land of dreams.

When he waked up it was morning. He was lying on the ground in a wild, rocky region. Not far away burned a great wood fire, and the turtle was watching some food that was cooking in a pot.

"Ho, ho, my lad! so you have at last waked up after your long ride. You see we are a little early. No matter if the dragon does think he can fly faster, I beat him, didn't I? Why, even the phoenix laughs at me and says I am slow, but the phoenix has not come yet either. Yes, I have clearly broken the record for speed, and I had a load to carry too, which neither of the others had, I am sure."

"Where are we?" questioned Bamboo.

"In the land of the beginning," said the other wisely. "We flew over Thibet, and then went northwest for two hours. If you haven't studied geography you won't know the name of the country. But, here we are, and that is enough, isn't it, enough for any one? And to-day is the yearly feast-day in honour of the making of the world. It was very fortunate for me that the gates were left open yesterday. I am afraid my old friends, the dragon and the phoenix, have almost forgotten what I look like. It is so long since they saw me. Lucky beasts they are, not to be loaded down under an emperor's tablet. Hello! I hear the dragon coming now, if I am not mistaken. Yes, here he is. How glad I am to see him!"

Bamboo heard a great noise like the whirr of enormous wings, and then, looking up, saw a huge dragon just in front of him. He knew it was a dragon from the pictures he had seen and the carvings in the temples.

The dragon and the turtle had no sooner greeted each other, both very happy at the meeting, than they were joined by a queer-looking bird, unlike any that Bamboo had ever seen, but which he knew was the phœnix. This phœnix looked somewhat like a wild swan, but it had the bill of a cock, the neck of a snake, the tail of a fish and the stripes of a dragon. Its feathers were of five colours.

When the three friends had chatted merrily for a few minutes, the turtle told them how Bamboo had helped him to escape from the temple.

"A clever boy," said the dragon, patting Bamboo gently on the back.

"Yes, yes, a clever boy indeed," echoed the phœnix.

"Ah," sighed the turtle, "if only the good god, P'anku, were here, shouldn't we be happy! But, I fear he will never come to this meeting-place. No doubt he is off in some distant spot, cutting out another world. If I could only see him once more, I feel that I should die in peace."

"Just listen!" laughed the dragon. "As if one of us could die! Why, you talk like a mere mortal."

All day long the three friends chatted, feasted, and had a good time looking round at the places where they had lived so happily when P'anku had been cutting out the world. They were good to Bamboo also and showed him many wonderful things of which he had never dreamed.

"You are not half so mean-looking and so fierce as they paint you on the flags," said Bamboo in a friendly voice to the dragon just as they were about to separate.

The three friends laughed heartily.

"Oh, no, he's a very decent sort of fellow, even if he is covered with fish-scales," joked the phœnix.

Just before they bade each other good-bye, the phœnix gave Bamboo a long scarlet tail-feather for a keepsake, and the dragon gave him a large scale which turned to gold as soon as the boy took it into his hand.

"Come, come, we must hurry," said the turtle. "I am afraid your father will think you are lost." So Bamboo, after having spent the happiest day of his life, mounted the turtle's back, and they rose once more above the clouds. Back they flew even faster than they had come. Bamboo had so many things to talk about that he did not once think of going to sleep, for he had really seen the dragon and the phœnix, and if he never were to see anything else in his life, he would always be happy.

Suddenly the turtle stopped short in his swift flight, and Bamboo felt himself slipping. Too late he screamed for help, too late he tried to save himself. Down, down from that dizzy height he tumbled, turning, twisting, thinking of the awful death that was surely coming. Swish! he shot through the tree tops trying vainly to clutch the friendly branches. Then with a loud scream he struck the ground, and his long journey was ended.

"Come out from under that turtle, boy! What are you doing inside the temple in the dirt? Don't you know this is not the proper place for you?"

Bamboo rubbed his eyes. Though only half awake, he knew it was his father's voice.

"But didn't it kill me?" he said as his father pulled him out by the heel from under the great stone turtle.

"What killed you, foolish boy? What can you be talking about? But I'll half-kill you if you don't hurry out of this and come to your supper. Really I believe you are getting too lazy to eat. The idea of sleeping the whole afternoon under that turtle's belly!"

Bamboo, not yet fully awake, stumbled out of the tablet room, and his father locked the iron doors.

The Mad Goose and the Tiger Forest

HU-LIN WAS a little slave girl. She had been sold by her father when she was scarcely more than a baby, and had lived for five years with a number of other children in a wretched houseboat. Her cruel master treated her very badly. He made her go out upon the street, with the other girls he had bought, to beg for a living. This kind of life was especially hard for Hu-lin. She longed to play in the fields, above which the huge kites were sailing in the air like giant birds. She liked to see the crows and magpies flying hither and thither. It was great fun to watch them build their stick nests in the tall poplars. But if her master ever caught her idling her time away in this manner he beat her most cruelly and gave her nothing to eat for a whole day. In fact he was so wicked and cruel that all the children called him Black Heart.

Early one morning when Hu-lin was feeling very sad about the way she was treated, she resolved to run away, but, alas! she had not gone more than a hundred yards from the houseboat when she saw Black Heart following her. He caught her, scolded her most dreadfully, and gave her such a beating that she felt too faint to stir.

For several hours she lay on the ground without moving a muscle, moaning as if her heart would break. "Ah! if only someone would save me!" she thought, "how good I would be all the rest of my days!"

Now, not far from the river there lived an old man in a tumble-down shanty. The only companion he had was a goose that watched the gate for him at night and screamed out loudly if any stranger dared to prowl about the place. Hu-lin and this goose were close friends, and the slave girl often stopped to chat with the wise fowl as she was passing the old man's cottage. In this way she had learned that the bird's owner was a miser who kept a great deal of money hidden in his yard. Ch'ang, the goose, had an unusually long neck, and was thus able to pry into most of his master's affairs. As the fowl had no member of his own family to talk with, he told all he knew to Hu-lin.

On the very morning when Black Heart gave Hu-lin a beating for trying to run away, Ch'ang made a startling discovery. His lord and master was not really an old miser, but a young man in disguise. Ch'ang, feeling hungry, had slipped into the house at daybreak to see if any scraps had been left from the last evening's meal. The bedroom door had blown open in the night, and there lay a young man sound asleep, instead of the greybeard whom the gander called his master. Then, before his very eyes, the youth changed suddenly into his former shape and was an old man again.

In his excitement, forgetting all about his empty stomach, the terror-stricken goose rushed out into the yard to think over the mystery, but the longer he puzzled, the more strange it all seemed. Then he thought of Hu-lin, and wished that she would come by, that he might ask her opinion. He had a high regard for the slave girl's knowledge and believed that she would understand fully what had taken place.

Ch'ang went to the gate. As usual, it was locked, and there was nothing for him to do but wait for his master to rise. Two hours later the miser walked out into the yard. He seemed in good spirits, and he gave Ch'ang more to eat than usual. After taking his morning smoke on the street in front of the house, he strolled around it leaving the front gate ajar.

This was precisely what the gander had been expecting. Slipping quietly into the road, he turned towards the river where he could see the houseboats lined up at the wharf. On the sand near by lay a well-known form.

"Hu-lin," he called as he drew near, "wake up, for I have something to tell you."

"I am not asleep," she answered, turning her tear-stained face towards her friend.

"Why, what's the matter? You've been crying again. Has old Black Heart been beating you?"

"Hush! he's taking a nap in the boat. Don't let him hear you."

"It's not likely he would understand goose-talk if he did," replied Ch'ang, smiling. "However, I suppose it's always best to be on the safe side, so I'll whisper what I have to say."

Putting his bill close to her ear, he told Hu-lin of his recent discovery, and ended by asking her to tell him what it all meant.

The child forgot her own misery at hearing his wonderful story. "Are you quite sure there was not some friend of the miser's spending the night with him?" she asked gravely.

"Yes, yes, perfectly sure, for he has no friends," replied the gander. "Besides, I was in the house just before he locked up for the night, and I saw neither hair nor hide of any other person."

"Then he must be a fairy in disguise!" announced Hu-lin wisely.

"A fairy! what's that?" questioned Ch'ang, more and more excited.

"Why, you old goose, don't you know what a fairy is?" And Hu-lin laughed outright. By this time she had forgotten her own troubles and was becoming more and more amused at what she had heard. "Hark!" she said in a low tone, and speaking very slowly, "a fairy is – – " Here she lowered her voice to a whisper.

The gander nodded violently as she went on with her explanation, and when she had finished, was speechless with amazement, for a few moments. "Well," he said finally, "if my master is that kind of man, suppose you slip away quietly and come with me, for, if a fairy is what you say he is, he can save you from all your troubles and make me happy for the rest of my days."

"I wonder if I dare?" she answered, looking round fearfully towards the houseboat, from the open scuttle of which came the sound of deep snoring.

"Yes, yes, of course!" coaxed Ch'ang. "He gave you such a beating that he won't be afraid of your taking to your heels again very soon."

Hurriedly they went to the miser's compound. Hu-lin's heart was beating fast as she tried to decide what to say when she should actually stand before the fairy. The gate was still partly open and the two friends entered boldly.

"Come this way," said Ch'ang. "He must be in the back-yard digging in his garden."

But when they reached the vegetable patch there was no one to be seen.

"This is very strange," whispered the gander. "I don't understand it, for I have never known him to grow tired of work so early. Surely he cannot have gone in to rest."

Led by her friend, Hu-lin entered the house on tiptoe. The door of the miser's bedroom stood wide open, and they saw that there was no one either in that room or any other room of the miserable cottage.

"Come! let's see what kind of bed he sleeps on," said Hu-lin, filled with curiosity. "I have never been in a fairy's room. It must be different from other people's rooms."

"No, no! just a plain brick bed, like all the rest," answered Ch'ang, as they crossed the threshold.

"Does he have a fire in cold weather?" asked Hu-lin, stooping to examine the small fire hole in the bricks.

"Oh, yes, a hot fire every night, and even in spring when other people have stopped having fires, the brick bed is hot every night."

"Well, that's rather strange for a miser, don't you think?" said the girl. "It costs more to keep a fire going than it does to feed a man."

"Yes, that's true," agreed Ch'ang, pruning his feathers. "I hadn't thought of that. It is strange, very. Hu-lin, you're a wise child. Where did you learn so much?"

At that moment the gander turned pale at hearing the gate slam loudly and the bar thrown into place.

"Good gracious! what ever shall we do?" asked Hu-lin. "What will he say if he finds us here?"

"No telling," said the other, trembling, "but, my dear little friend, we are certainly caught, for we can't get away without his seeing us."

"Yes, and I've already had one beating to-day! And such a hard one that I don't believe I could live through another," sighed the child, as the tears began to flow.

"There, there, little girl, don't worry! Let's hide in this dark corner behind the baskets," suggested the gander, just as the master's step was heard at the front door.

Soon the frightened companions were crouching on the ground, trying to hide. Much to their relief, however, the miser did not go into his bedroom, and they soon heard him hard at work in the garden. All that day the two remained in their hiding place, afraid to show themselves outside the door.

"I can't imagine what he would say if he found out that his watch-goose had brought a stranger into the house," said Ch'ang.

"Perhaps he would think we were trying to steal some of the money he has hidden away," she answered, laughing, for as Hu-lin became used to her cramped quarters she grew less frightened. At any rate she was not nearly so much afraid of the miser as she had thought she was. "Besides," she reflected, "he can't be so bad as old Black Heart."

Thus the day wore on and darkness fell over the land. By this time girl and goose were fast asleep in one corner of the miser's room and knew nothing more of what was happening.

When the first light of a new day filtered through the paper-covered window above the miser's bed, Hu-lin awoke with a start, and at first she could not think where she was. Ch'ang was staring at her with wide-open frightened eyes that seemed to be asking, "What can it all mean? It is more than my goose brain can think out."

For on the bed, instead of the miser, there lay a young man whose hair was a black as a raven's wing. A faint smile lightened up his handsome face, as if he was enjoying some delightful dream. A cry of wonder escaped Hu-lin's lips before she could hold it back. The sleeper's eyes opened instantly and were fixed upon her. The girl was so frightened that she could not move, and the gander trembled violently as he saw the change that had come over his master.

The young man was even more surprised than his guests, and for two minutes he was speechless. "What does this mean?" he asked, finally, looking at Ch'ang. "What are you doing in my bedroom and who is this child who seems so frightened?"

"Forgive me, kind sir, but what have you done to my master?" asked the gander, giving question for question.

"Am I not your master, you mad creature?" said the man, laughing. "You are more stupid than ever this morning."

"My master was old and ugly, but you are still young and handsome," replied Ch'ang in a tone of flattery.

"What," shouted the other, "you say I am still young?"

"Why, yes. Ask Hu-lin, if you don't believe me."

The man turned towards the little girl.

"Yes, indeed you are, sir," she replied in answer to his look. "Never have I seen a man so beautiful."

"At last! at last!" he cried, laughing joyfully, "I am free, free, free from all my troubles, but how it has come about is more than I can say!"

For a few minutes he stood in a deep study, snapping his long fingers as if trying to solve some hard problem. At last a smile lighted up his face. "Ch'ang," he asked, "what was it you called your guest when you spoke of her a minute ago?"

"I am Hu-lin," said the child simply, "Hu-lin, the slave girl."

He clapped his hands. "That's right! That's right!" he cried. "I see it all now; it is as plain as day." Then, noticing the look of wonder on her face, "It is to you that I owe my freedom from a wicked fairy, and if you like, I'll tell you the story of my misfortune."

"Pray do, kind sir," she replied eagerly. "I told Ch'ang that you were a fairy, and I should like to know if I was right."

"Well, you see," he began, "my father is a rich man who lives in a distant county. When I was a boy he gave me everything I wished. I was so humoured and petted from earliest childhood that at last I began to think there was nothing at all in the world I could not have for the asking, and nothing that I must not do if I wished to.

"My teacher often scolded me for having such notions. He told me there was a proverb: 'Men die for gain, birds perish to get food.' He thought such men were very foolish. He told me that money would go a long way towards making a man happy, but he always ended by saying that the gods were more powerful than men. He said I must always be careful not to make the evil spirits angry. Sometimes I laughed in his face, telling him that I was rich and could buy the favour of gods and fairies. The good man would shake his head, saying, 'Take care, my boy, or you will be sorry for these rash speeches.'"

"One day, after he had been giving me a long lecture of this sort, we were walking in the garden of my father's compound. I was even more daring than usual and told him that I cared nothing for the rules other people followed. 'You say,' said I, 'that this well here in my father's yard is ruled by a spirit, and that if I were to anger him by jumping over it, he would be vexed and give me trouble.' 'Yes,' said he, 'that is exactly what I said, and I repeat it. Beware, young man, beware of idle boasting and of breaking the law.' 'What do I care for a spirit that lives on my father's land?' I answered with a sneer. 'I don't believe there is a spirit in this well. If there is, it is only another of my father's slaves.'

"So saying, and before my tutor could stop me, I leaped across the mouth of the well. No sooner had I touched the ground than I felt a strange shrinking of my body. My strength left me in the twinkling of an eye, my bones shortened, my skin grew yellow and wrinkled. I looked at my pigtail and found that the hair had suddenly grown thin and white. In every way I had been changed completely into an old man.

"My teacher stared at me in amazement, and when I asked him what it all meant my voice was as shrill as that of early childhood. 'Alas! my dear pupil,' he replied, 'now you will believe what I told you. The spirit of the well is angry at your wicked conduct and has punished you. You have been told a hundred times that it is wrong to leap over a well; yet you did this very thing,' 'But is there nothing that can be done,' I cried; 'is there no way of restoring my lost youth?' He looked at me sadly and shook his head.

"When my father learned of my sad condition he was terribly upset. He did everything that could be done to find some way for me to regain my youth. He had incense burned at a dozen temples and he himself offered up prayers to various gods. I was his only son, and he could not be happy without me. At last, when everything else had been done, my worthy teacher thought of asking a fortune-teller who had become famous in the city. After inquiring about everything that had led up to my sad plight, the wise man said that the spirit of the well, as a punishment, had changed me into a miser. He said that only when I was sleeping would I be in my natural state, and even then if any one chanced to enter my room or catch a glimpse of my face, I would be at once changed back into a greybeard."

"I saw you yesterday morning," shouted the gander. "You were young and handsome, and then before my very eyes you were changed back into an old man!"

"To continue my story," said the young man, "the fortune-teller at last announced that there was only one chance for my recovery and that a very small one. If at any time, while I was in my rightful shape, that is, as you see me now, a mad goose should come in, leading a tiger-forest out of slavery, the charm would be broken, and the evil spirit would no longer have control over me. When the fortune-teller's answer was brought to my father, he gave up hope, and so did I, for no one understood the meaning of such a senseless riddle.

"That night I left my native city, resolved not to disgrace my people any longer by living with them. I came to this place, bought this house with some money my father had given me, and at once began living the life of a miser. Nothing satisfied my greed for money. Everything must be turned into cash. For five years I have been storing away money, and, at the same time, starving myself, body and soul.

"Soon after my arrival here, remembering the fortune-teller's riddle, I decided that I would keep a goose to serve as night watch-man instead of a dog. In this way I made a start at working out the riddle."

"But I am not a mad goose," hissed the gander angrily. "If it had not been for me you would still be a wrinkled miser."

"Quite right, dear Ch'ang, quite right," said the young man soothingly; "you were not mad; so I gave you the name Ch'ang, which means mad, and thus made a mad goose of you."

"Oh, I see," said Hu-lin and Ch'ang together. "How clever!"

"So, you see, I had part of my cure here in my back-yard all the time; but though I thought as hard as I could, I could think of no way of securing that Ch'ang should lead a tiger-forest into my room while I was sleeping. The thing seemed absurd, and I soon gave up trying to study it out. To-day by accident it has really come to pass."

"So I am the tiger-forest, am I?" laughed Hu-lin.

"Yes, indeed, you are, my dear child, a pretty little tiger-forest, for Hu means tiger, and lin is surely good Chinese for a grove of trees. Then, too, you told me you were a slave girl. Hence, Ch'ang led you out of slavery."

"Oh, I am so glad!" said Hu-lin, forgetting her own poverty, "so glad that you don't have to be a horrible old miser any longer."

Just at that moment there was a loud banging on the front gate.

"Who can be knocking in that fashion?" asked the young man in astonishment.

"Alas! it must be Black Heart, my master," said Hu-lin, beginning to cry.

"Don't be frightened," said the youth, soothingly stroking the child's head. "You have saved me, and I shall certainly do as much for you. If this Mr. Black Heart doesn't agree to a fair proposal he shall have a black eye to remember his visit by."

It did not take long for the grateful young man to buy Hu-lin's liberty, especially as he offered as much for her freedom as her master had expected to get when she was fourteen or fifteen years of age.

When Hu-lin was told of the bargain she was wild with delight. She bowed low before her new master and then, kneeling, touched her head nine times on the floor. Rising, she cried out, "Oh, how happy I am, for now I shall be yours for ever and ever and ever, and good old Ch'ang shall be my playmate."

"Yes, indeed," he assured her, "and when you are a little older I shall make you my wife. At present you will go with me to my father's house and become my little betrothed."

"And I shall never again have to beg for crusts on the street?" she asked him, her eyes full of wonder.

"No! never!" he answered, laughing, "and you need never fear another beating."

The Princess Kwan-Yin

ONCE UPON A time in China there lived a certain king who had three daughters. The fairest and best of these was Kwan-yin, the youngest. The old king was justly proud of this daughter, for of all the women who had ever lived in the palace she was by far the most attractive. It did not take him long, therefore, to decide that she should be the heir to his throne, and her husband ruler of his kingdom. But, strange to say, Kwan-yin was not pleased at this good fortune. She cared little for the pomp and splendour of court life. She foresaw no pleasure for herself in ruling as a queen, but even feared that in so high a station she might feel out of place and unhappy.

Every day she went to her room to read and study. As a result of this daily labour she soon went far beyond her sisters along the paths of knowledge, and her name was known in the farthest corner of the kingdom as "Kwan-yin, the wise princess." Besides being very fond of books, Kwan-yin was thoughtful of her friends. She was careful about her behaviour both in public and in private. Her warm heart was open at all times to the cries of those in trouble. She was kind to the poor and suffering. She won the love of the lower classes, and was to them a sort of goddess to whom they could appeal whenever they were hungry and in need. Some people even believed that she was a fairy who had come to earth from her home within the Western Heaven, while others said that once, long years before, she had lived in the world as a prince instead of a princess. However this may be, one thing is certain – Kwan-yin was pure and good, and well deserved the praises that were showered upon her.

One day the king called this favourite daughter to the royal bedside, for he felt that the hour of death was drawing near. Kwan-yin kowtowed before her royal father, kneeling and touching her forehead on the floor in sign of deepest reverence. The old man bade her rise and come closer. Taking her hand tenderly in his own, he said, "Daughter, you know well how I love you. Your modesty and virtue, your talent and your love of knowledge, have made you first in my heart. As you know already, I chose you as heir to my kingdom long ago. I promised that your husband should be made ruler in my stead. The time is almost ripe for me to ascend upon the dragon and become a guest on high. It is necessary that you be given at once in marriage."

"But, most exalted father," faltered the princess, "I am not ready to be married."

"Not ready, child! Why, are you not eighteen? Are not the daughters of our nation often wedded long before they reach that age? Because of your desire for learning I have spared you thus far from any thought of a husband, but now we can wait no longer."

"Royal father, hear your child, and do not compel her to give up her dearest pleasures. Let her go into a quiet convent where she may lead a life of study!"

The king sighed deeply at hearing these words. He loved his daughter and did not wish to wound her. "Kwan-yin," he continued, "do you wish to pass by the green spring of youth, to give up this mighty kingdom? Do you wish to enter the doors of a convent where women say farewell to life and all its pleasures? No! your father will not permit this. It grieves me sorely to disappoint you, but one month from this very day you shall be married. I have chosen for your royal partner a man of many noble parts. You know him by name already, although you have not seen him. Remember that, of the hundred virtues filial conduct is the chief, and that you owe more to me than to all else on earth."

Kwan-yin turned pale. Trembling, she would have sunk to the floor, but her mother and sisters supported her, and by their tender care brought her back to consciousness.

Every day of the month that followed, Kwan-yin's relatives begged her to give up what they called her foolish notion. Her sisters had long since given up hope of becoming queen. They were amazed at her stupidity. The very thought of any one's choosing a convent instead of a throne was to them a sure sign of madness. Over and over again they asked her reason for making so strange a choice. To every question, she shook her head, replying, "A voice from the heavens speaks to me, and I must obey it."

On the eve of the wedding day Kwan-yin slipped out of the palace, and, after a weary journey, arrived at a convent called, "The Cloister of the White Sparrow." She was dressed as a poor maiden. She said she wished to become a nun. The abbess, not knowing who she was, did not receive her kindly. Indeed, she told Kwan-yin that they could not receive her into the sisterhood, that the building was full. Finally, after Kwan-yin had shed many tears, the abbess let her enter, but only as a sort of servant, who might be cast out for the slightest fault.

Now that Kwan-yin found herself in the life which she had long dreamt of leading, she tried to be satisfied. But the nuns seemed to wish to make her stay among them most miserable. They gave her the hardest tasks to do, and it was seldom that she had a minute to rest. All day long she was busy, carrying water from a well at the foot of the convent hill or gathering wood from a neighbouring forest. At night when her back was almost breaking, she was given many extra tasks, enough to have crushed the spirit of any other woman than this brave daughter of a king. Forgetting her grief, and trying to hide the lines of pain that sometimes wrinkled her fair forehead, she tried to make these hard-hearted women love her. In return for their rough words, she spoke to them kindly, and never did she give way to anger.

One day while poor Kwan-yin was picking up brushwood in the forest she heard a tiger making his way through the bushes. Having no means of defending herself, she breathed a silent prayer to the gods for help, and calmly awaited the coming of the great beast. To her surprise, when the bloodthirsty animal appeared, instead of bounding up to tear her in pieces, he began to make a soft purring noise. He did not try to hurt Kwan-yin, but rubbed against her in a friendly manner, and let her pat him on the head.

The next day the princess went back to the same spot. There she found no fewer than a dozen savage beasts working under the command of the friendly tiger, gathering wood for her. In a short time enough brush and firewood had been piled up to last the convent for six months. Thus, even the wild animals of the forest were better able to judge of her goodness than the women of the sisterhood.

At another time when Kwan-yin was toiling up the hill for the twentieth time, carrying two great pails of water on a pole, an enormous dragon faced her in the road. Now, in China, the dragon is sacred, and Kwan-yin was not at all frightened, for she knew that she had done no wrong.

The animal looked at her for a moment, switched its horrid tail, and shot out fire from its nostrils. Then, dashing the burden from the startled maiden's shoulder, it vanished. Full of fear, Kwan-yin hurried up the hill to the nunnery. As she drew near the inner court, she was amazed to see in the centre of the open space a new building of solid stone. It had sprung up by magic since her last journey down the hill. On going forward, she saw that there were four arched doorways to the fairy house. Above the door facing west was a tablet with these words written on it: "In honour of Kwan-yin, the faithful princess." Inside was a well of the purest water, while, for drawing this water, there a strange machine, the like of which neither Kwan-yin nor the nuns had ever seen.

The sisters knew that this magic well was a monument to Kwan-yin's goodness. For a few days they treated her much better. "Since the gods have dug a well at our very gate," they said, "this girl will no longer need to bear water from the foot of the hill. For what strange reason, however, did the gods write this beggar's name on the stone?"

Kwan-yin heard their unkind remarks in silence. She could have explained the meaning of the dragon's gift, but she chose to let her companions remain in ignorance. At last the selfish nuns began to grow careless again, and treated her even worse than before. They could not bear to see the poor girl enjoy a moment's idleness.

"This is a place for work," they told her. "All of us have laboured hard to win our present station. You must do likewise." So they robbed her of every chance for study and prayer, and gave her no credit for the magic well.

One night the sisters were awakened from their sleep by strange noises, and soon they heard outside the walls of the compound the blare of a trumpet. A great army had been sent by Kwan-yin's father to attack the convent, for his spies had at last been able to trace the runaway princess to this holy retreat.

"Oh, who has brought this woe upon us?" exclaimed all the women, looking at each other in great fear. "Who has done this great evil? There is one among us who has sinned most terribly, and now the gods are about to destroy us." They gazed at one another, but no one thought of Kwan-yin, for they did not believe her of enough importance to attract the anger of heaven, even though she might have done the most shocking of deeds. Then, too, she had been so meek and lowly while in their holy order that they did not once dream of charging her with any crime.

The threatening sounds outside grew louder and louder. All at once a fearful cry arose among the women: "They are about to burn our sacred dwelling." Smoke was rising just beyond the enclosure where the soldiers were kindling a great fire, the heat of which would soon be great enough to make the convent walls crumble into dust.

Suddenly a voice was heard above the tumult of the weeping sisters: "Alas! I am the cause of all this trouble."

The nuns, turning in amazement, saw that it was Kwan-yin who was speaking. "You?" they exclaimed, astounded.

"Yes, I, for I am indeed the daughter of a king. My father did not wish me to take the vows of this holy order. I fled from the palace. He has sent his army here to burn these buildings and to drag me back a prisoner."

"Then, see what you have brought upon us, miserable girl!" exclaimed the abbess. "See how you have repaid our kindness! Our buildings will be burned above our heads! How wretched you have made us! May heaven's curses rest upon you!"

"No, no!" exclaimed Kwan-yin, springing up, and trying to keep the abbess from speaking these frightful words. "You have no right to say that, for I am innocent of evil. But, wait! You shall soon see whose prayers the gods will answer, yours or mine!" So saying, she pressed her forehead to the floor, praying the almighty powers to save the convent and the sisters.

Outside the crackling of the greedy flames could already be heard. The fire king would soon destroy every building on that hill-top. Mad with terror, the sisters prepared to leave the compound and give up all their belongings to the cruel flames and still more cruel soldiers. Kwan-yin alone remained in the room, praying earnestly for help.

Suddenly a soft breeze sprang up from the neighbouring forest, dark clouds gathered overhead, and, although it was the dry season a drenching shower descended on the flames. Within five minutes the fire was put out and the convent was saved. Just as the shivering nuns were thanking Kwan-yin for the divine help she had brought them, two soldiers who had scaled the outer wall of the compound came in and roughly asked for the princess.

The trembling girl, knowing that these men were obeying her father's orders, poured out a prayer to the gods, and straightway made herself known. They dragged her from the presence of the nuns who had just begun to love her. Thus disgraced before her father's army, she was taken to the capital.

On the morrow, she was led before the old king. The father gazed sadly at his daughter, and then the stern look of a judge hardened his face as he beckoned the guards to bring her forward.

From a neighbouring room came the sounds of sweet music. A feast was being served there amid great splendour. The loud laughter of the guests reached the ears of the young girl as she bowed in disgrace before her father's throne. She knew that this feast had been prepared for her, and that her father was willing to give her one more chance.

"Girl," said the king, at last regaining his voice, "in leaving the royal palace on the eve of your wedding day, not only did you insult your father, but your king. For this act you deserve to die. However, because of the excellent record you had made for yourself before you ran away, I have decided to give you one more chance to redeem yourself. Refuse me, and the penalty is death: obey me, and all may yet be well – the kingdom that you spurned is still yours for the asking. All that I require is your marriage to the man whom I have chosen."

"And when, most august King, would you have me decide?" asked Kwan-yin earnestly.

"This very day, this very hour, this very moment," he answered sternly. "What! would you hesitate between love upon a throne and death? Speak, my daughter, tell me that you love me and will do my bidding!"

It was now all that Kwan-yin could do to keep from throwing herself at her father's feet and yielding to his wishes, not because he offered her a kingdom, but because she loved him and would gladly have made him happy. But her strong will kept her from relenting. No power on earth could have stayed her from doing what she thought her duty.

"Beloved father," she answered sadly, and her voice was full of tenderness, "it is not a question of my love for you – of that there is no question, for all my life I have shown it in every action. Believe me, if I were free to do your bidding, gladly would I make you happy, but a voice from the gods has spoken, has commanded that I remain a virgin, that I devote my life to deeds of mercy. When heaven itself has commanded, what can even a princess do but listen to that power which rules the earth?"

The old king was far from satisfied with Kwan-yin's answer. He grew furious, his thin wrinkled skin turned purple as the hot blood rose to his head. "Then you refuse to do my bidding! Take her, men! Give to her the death that is due to a traitor to the king!" As they bore Kwan-yin away from his presence the white-haired monarch fell, swooning, from his chair.

That night, when Kwan-yin was put to death, she descended into the lower world of torture. No sooner had she set foot in that dark country of the dead than the vast region of endless punishment suddenly blossomed forth and became like the gardens of Paradise. Pure white lilies sprang up on every side, and the odour of a million flowers filled all the rooms and corridors. King Yama, ruler of the dominion, rushed forth to learn the cause of this wonderful change. No sooner did his eyes rest upon the fair young face of Kwan-yin than he saw in her the emblem of a purity which deserved no home but heaven.

"Beautiful virgin, doer of many mercies," he began, after addressing her by her title, "I beg you in the name of justice to depart from this bloody kingdom. It is not right that the fairest flower of heaven should enter and shed her fragrance in these halls. Guilt must suffer here, and sin find no reward. Depart thou, then, from my dominion. The peach of immortal life shall be bestowed upon you, and heaven alone shall be your dwelling place."

Thus Kwan-yin became the Goddess of Mercy; thus she entered into that glad abode, surpassing all earthly kings and queens. And ever since that time, on account of her exceeding goodness, thousands of poor people breathe out to her each year their prayers for mercy. There is no fear in their gaze as they look at her beautiful image, for their eyes are filled with tears of love.

The Two Jugglers

ONE BEAUTIFUL spring day two men strolled into the public square of a well-known Chinese city. They were plainly dressed and looked like ordinary countrymen who had come in to see the sights. Judging by their faces, they were father and son. The elder, a wrinkled man of perhaps fifty, wore a scant grey beard. The younger had a small box on his shoulder.

At the hour when these strangers entered the public square, a large crowd had gathered, for it was a feast day, and everyone was bent on having a good time. All the people seemed very happy. Some, seated in little open-air booths, were eating, drinking, and smoking. Others were buying odds and ends from the street-vendors, tossing coins, and playing various games of chance.

The two men walked about aimlessly. They seemed to have no friends among the pleasure-seekers. At last, however, as they stood reading a public notice posted at the entrance of the town-hall or yamen, a bystander asked them who they were.

"Oh, we are jugglers from a distant province," said the elder, smiling and pointing towards the box. "We can do many tricks for the amusement of the people."

Soon it was spread about among the crowd that two famous jugglers had just arrived from the capital, and that they were able to perform many wonderful deeds. Now it happened that the mandarin or mayor of the city, at that very moment was entertaining a number of guests in the yamen. They had just finished eating, and the host was wondering what he should do to amuse his friends, when a servant told him of the jugglers.

"Ask them what they can do," said the mandarin eagerly. "I will pay them well if they can really amuse us, but I want something more than the old tricks of knife-throwing and balancing. They must show us something new."

The servant went outside and spoke to the jugglers: "The great man bids you tell him what you can do. If you can amuse his visitors he will bring them out to the private grand stand, and let you perform before them and the people who are gathered together."

"Tell your honourable master," said the elder, whom we shall call Chang, "that, try us as he will, he will not be disappointed. Tell him that we come from the unknown land of dreams and visions, that we can turn rocks into mountains, rivers into oceans, mice into elephants, in short, that there is nothing in magic too difficult for us to do."

The official was delighted when he heard the report of his servant. "Now we may have a little fun," he said to his guests, "for there are jugglers outside who will perform their wonderful tricks before us."

The guests filed out on to the grand stand at one side of the public square. The mandarin commanded that a rope should be stretched across so as to leave an open space in full view of the crowd, where the two Changs might give their exhibition.

For a time the two strangers entertained the people with some of the simpler tricks, such as spinning plates in the air, tossing bowls up and catching them on chopsticks, making flowers grow from empty pots, and transforming one object into another. At last, however, the mandarin cried out: "These tricks are very good of their kind, but how about those idle boasts of changing rivers into oceans and mice into elephants? Did you not say that you came from the land of dreams? These tricks you have done are stale and shopworn. Have you nothing new with which to regale my guests on this holiday?"

"Most certainly, your excellency. But surely you would not have a labourer do more than his employer requires? Would that not be quite contrary to the teachings of our fathers? Be assured, sir, anything that you demand I can do for you. Only say the word."

The mandarin laughed outright at this boasting language. "Take care, my man! Do not go too far with your promises. There are too many impostors around for me to believe every stranger. Hark you! no lying, for if you lie in the presence of my guests, I shall take great pleasure in having you beaten."

"My words are quite true, your excellency," repeated Chang earnestly. "What have we to gain by deceit, we who have performed our miracles before the countless hosts of yonder Western Heaven?"

"Ha, ha! hear the braggarts!" shouted the guests. "What shall we command them to do?"

For a moment they consulted together, whispering and laughing.

"I have it," cried the host finally. "Our feast was short of fruit, since this is the off season. Suppose we let this fellow supply us. Here, fellow, produce us a peach, and be quick about it. We have no time for fooling."

"What, masters, a peach?" exclaimed the elder Chang in mock dismay. "Surely at this season you do not expect a peach."

"Caught at his own game," laughed the guests, and the people began to hoot derisively.

"But, father, you promised to do anything he required," urged the son. "If he asks even a peach, how can you refuse and at the same time save your face?"

"Hear the boy talk," mumbled the father, "and yet, perhaps he's right. Very well, masters," turning to the crowd, "if it's a peach you want, why, a peach you shall have, even though I must send into the garden of the Western Heaven for the fruit."

The people became silent and the mandarin's guests forgot to laugh. The old man, still muttering, opened the box from which he had been taking the magic bowls, plates, and other articles. "To think of people wanting peaches at this season! What is the world coming to?"

After fumbling in the box for some moments he drew out a skein of golden thread, fine spun and as light as gossamer. No sooner had he unwound a portion of this thread than a sudden gust of wind carried it up into the air above the heads of the onlookers. Faster and faster the old man paid out the magic coil, higher and higher the free end rose into the heavens, until, strain his eyes as he would, no one present could see into what far-region it had vanished.

"Wonderful, wonderful!" shouted the people with one voice, "the old man is a fairy."

For a moment they forgot all about the mandarin, the jugglers, and the peach, so amazed were they at beholding the flight of the magic thread.

At last the old man seemed satisfied with the distance to which his cord had sailed, and, with a bow to the spectators, he tied the end to a large wooden pillar which helped to support the roof of the grand stand. For a moment the structure trembled and swayed as if it too would be carried off into the blue ether, the guests turned pale and clutched their chairs for support, but not even the mandarin dared to speak, so sure were they now that they were in the presence of fairies.

"Everything is ready for the journey," said old Chang calmly.

"What! shall you leave us?" asked the mayor, finding his voice again.

"I? Oh, no, my old bones are not spry enough for quick climbing. My son here will bring us the magic peach. He is handsome and active enough to enter that heavenly garden. Graceful, oh graceful is that peach tree – of course, you remember the line from the poem – and a graceful man must pluck the fruit."

The mandarin was still more surprised at the juggler's knowledge of a famous poem from the classics. It made him and his friends all the more certain that the newcomers were indeed fairies.

The young man at a sign from his father tightened his belt and the bands about his ankles, and then, with a graceful gesture to the astonished people, sprang upon the magic string, balanced himself for a moment on the steep incline, and then ran as nimbly up as a sailor would have mounted a rope ladder. Higher and higher he climbed till he seemed no bigger than a lark ascending into the blue sky, and then, like some tiny speck, far, far away, on the western horizon.

The people gazed in open-mouthed wonder. They were struck dumb and filled with some nameless fear; they hardly dared to look at the enchanter who stood calmly in their midst, smoking his long-stemmed pipe.

The mandarin, ashamed of having laughed at and threatened this man who was clearly a fairy, did not know what to say. He snapped his long finger nails and looked at his guests in mute astonishment. The visitors silently drank their tea, and the crowd of sightseers craned their necks in a vain effort to catch sight of the vanished fairy. Only one in all that assembly, a bright-eyed little boy of eight, dared to break the silence, and he caused a hearty burst of merriment by crying out, "Oh, daddy, will the bad young man fly off into the sky and leave his poor father all alone?"

The greybeard laughed loudly with the others, and tossed the lad a copper. "Ah, the good boy," he said smiling, "he has been well trained to love his father; no fear of foreign ways spoiling his filial piety."

After a few moments of waiting, old Chang laid aside his pipe and fixed his eyes once more on the western sky. "It is coming," he said quietly. "The peach will soon be here."

Suddenly he held out his hand as if to catch some falling object, but, look as they would, the people could see nothing. Swish! thud! it came like a streak of light, and, lo, there in the magician's fingers was a peach, the most beautiful specimen the people had ever seen, large and rosy. "Straight from the garden of the gods," said Chang, handing the fruit to the mandarin, "a peach in the Second Moon, and the snow hardly off the ground."

Trembling with excitement, the official took the peach and cut it open. It was large enough for all his guests to have a taste, and such a taste it was! They smacked their lips and wished for more, secretly thinking that never again would ordinary fruit be worth the eating.

But all this time the old juggler, magician, fairy or whatever you choose to call him, was looking anxiously into the sky. The result of this trick was more than he had bargained for. True, he had been able to produce the magic peach which the mandarin had called for, but his son, where was his son? He shaded his eyes and looked far up into the blue heavens, and so did the people, but no one could catch a glimpse of the departed youth.

"Oh, my son, my son," cried the old man in despair, "how cruel is the fate that has robbed me of you, the only prop of my declining years! Oh, my boy, my boy, would that I had not sent you on so perilous a journey! Who now will look after my grave when I am gone?"

Suddenly the silken cord on which the young man had sped so daringly into the sky, gave a quick jerk which almost toppled over the post to which it was tied, and there, before the very eyes of the people, it fell from the lofty height, a silken pile on the ground in front of them.

The greybeard uttered a loud cry and covered his face with his hands. "Alas! the whole story is plain enough," he sobbed. "My boy was caught in the act of plucking the magic peach from the garden of the gods, and they have thrown him into prison. Woe is me! Ah! woe is me!"

The mandarin and his friends were deeply touched by the old man's grief, and tried in vain to comfort him. "Perhaps he will return," they said. "Have courage!"

"Yes, but in what a shape?" replied the magician. "See! even now they are restoring him to his father."

The people looked, and they saw twirling and twisting through the air the young man's arm. It fell upon the ground in front of them at the fairy's feet. Next came the head, a leg, the body. One by one before the gasping, shuddering people, the parts of the unfortunate young man were restored to his father.

After the first outburst of wild, frantic grief the old man by a great effort gained control of his feelings, and began to gather up these parts, putting them tenderly into the wooden box.

By this time many of the spectators were weeping at the sight of the father's affliction. "Come," said the mandarin at last, deeply moved, "let us present the old man with sufficient money to give his boy a decent burial."

All present agreed willingly, for there is no sight in China that causes greater pity than that of an aged parent robbed by death of an only son. The copper cash fell in a shower at the juggler's feet, and soon tears of gratitude were mingled with those of sorrow. He gathered up the money and tied it in a large black cloth. Then a wonderful change came over his face. He seemed all of a sudden to forget his grief. Turning to the box, he raised the lid. The people heard him say: "Come, my son; the crowd is waiting for you to thank them. Hurry up! They have been very kind to us."

In an instant the box was thrown open with a bang, and before the mandarin and his friends, before the eyes of all the sightseers the young man, strong and whole once more, stepped forth and bowed, clasping his hands and giving the national salute.

For a moment all were silent. Then, as the wonder of the whole thing dawned upon them, the people broke forth into a tumult of shouts, laughter, and compliments. "The fairies have surely come to visit us!" they shouted. "The city will be blessed with good fortune! Perhaps it is Fairy Old Boy himself who is among us!"

The mandarin rose and addressed the jugglers, thanking them in the name of the city for their visit and for the taste they had given to him and his guests of the peach from the heavenly orchard.

Even as he spoke, the magic box opened again; the two fairies disappeared inside, the lid closed, and the chest rose from the ground above the heads of the people. For a moment it floated round in a circle like some homing pigeon trying to find its bearings before starting on a return journey. Then, with a sudden burst of speed, it shot off into the heavens and vanished from the sight of those below, and not a thing remained as proof of the strange visitors except the magic peach seed that lay beside the teacups on the mandarin's table.

According to the most ancient writings there is now nothing left to tell of this story. It has been declared, however, by later scholars that the official and his friends who had eaten the magic peach, at once began to feel a change in their lives. While, before the coming of the fairies, they had lived unfairly, accepting bribes and taking part in many shameful practices, now, after tasting of the heavenly fruit, they began to grow better. The people soon began to honour and love them, saying, "Surely these great men are not like others of their kind, for these men are just and honest in their dealings with us. They seem not to be ruling for their own reward!"

However this may be, we do know that before many years their city became the centre of the greatest peach-growing section of China, and even yet when strangers walk in the orchards and look up admiringly at the beautiful sweet-smelling fruit, the natives sometimes ask proudly, "And have you never heard about the wonderful peach which was the beginning of all our orchards, the magic peach the fairies brought us from the Western Heaven?"

The Wooden Tablet

"YES, MY BOY, whatever happens, be sure to save that tablet. It is the only thing we have left worth keeping."

K'ang-p'u's father was just setting out for the city, to be gone all day. He had been telling K'ang-p'u about some work in the little garden, for the boy was a strong and willing helper.

"All right, father, I'll do what you tell me; but suppose the foreign soldiers should come while you are gone? I heard that they were over at T'ang Shu yesterday and burned the village. If they should come here, what must I do?"

Mr. Lin laughed heartily. "Why, there's nothing here for them to burn, if it comes to that! – a mud house, a grass roof, and a pile of ragged bedding. Surely they won't bother my little hut. It's loot they're after – money – or something they can sell."

"But, father," persisted the boy, "haven't you forgotten? Surely you wouldn't wish them to burn your father's tablet?"

"Quite right; for the moment I did forget. Yes, yes, my boy, whatever happens be sure to save the tablet. It is the only thing we have worth keeping."

With that, Mr. Lin went out at the gate, leaving K'ang-p'u standing all alone. The little fellow was scarcely twelve years old. He had a bright, sunny face and a happy heart. Being left by himself did not mean tears and idleness for him.

He went into the poor little house and stood for a moment looking earnestly at the wooden tablet. It was on a shelf in the one-roomed shanty, an oblong piece of wood about twelve inches high, enclosed in a wooden case. Through the carved screen work in the front, K'ang-p'u could see his grandfather's name written in Chinese characters on the tablet. Ever since babyhood K'ang-p'u had been taught to look at this piece of wood with a feeling of reverence.

"Your grandfather's spirit is inside," his father had said one day. "You must worship his spirit, for he was a good man, far better than your dad. If I had obeyed him in all things, I, his only son, should not now be living in this miserable hut."

"But didn't he live here, too?" asked K'ang-p'u in surprise.

"Oh, no, we lived in a big house over yonder in another village; in a big house with a high stone wall."

The little fellow had gasped with surprise at hearing this, for there was not such a thing as a stone wall in his village, and he felt that his grandfather must have been a rich man. He had not asked any more questions, but from that day on he had been rather afraid of the carved wooden box in which his grandfather's spirit was supposed to live.

So, on this day when his father left him alone, the boy stood looking at the tablet, wondering how a big man's spirit could squeeze into such a small space. He put out his finger cautiously and touched the bottom of the box, then drew back, half-frightened at his own daring. No bad results followed. It seemed just like any other piece of wood. Somewhat puzzled, he walked out of the house into the little garden. His father had told him to re-set some young cabbages. This was work which K'ang-p'u had done many times before. First, he gathered a basket of chicken feathers, for his father had told him that a few feathers placed at the roots of the young plant would do more to make it strong and healthy than anything else that could be used.

All day K'ang-p'u worked steadily in the garden. He was just beginning to feel tired, when he heard a woman screaming in the distance. He dropped his basket and rushed to the gate. Down the road at the far side of the village he saw a crowd of women and children running hither and thither, and – yes! there were the soldiers – the dreaded foreign soldiers! They were burning the houses; they were stealing whatever they could find.

Now, most boys would have been frightened – would have taken to their heels without thought of consequences. K'ang-p'u, however, though like other lads afraid of soldiers, was too brave to run without first doing his duty. He decided to stand his ground until he was sure the foreigners were coming his way. Perhaps they would grow tired of their cruel sport and leave the little house unharmed. He watched with wide-open eyes the work of pillage. Alas! these men did not seem to tire of their amusement. One after another the houses were entered and robbed. Women were screaming and children crying. Nearly all the village men were away in a distant market town, for none of them had expected an attack.

Nearer and nearer came the robbers. At last they were next door to K'ang-p'u's hut, and he knew the time had come for him to do his duty. Seizing the basket of chicken feathers, he rushed into the house, snatched the precious tablet from the shelf, and hid it in the bottom of the basket. Then, without stopping to say good-bye to the spot which he had known all his life, he rushed out of the gate and down the narrow street.

"Kill the kid!" shouted a soldier, whom K'ang-p'u nearly ran against in his hurry. "Put down the basket, boy! No stealing here."

"Yes, kill him!" shouted another with a loud laugh; "he'd make a good bit of bacon."

But no one touched him, and K'ang-p'u, still holding tightly to his burden, was soon far out on the winding road among the cornfields. If they should follow, he thought of hiding among the giant cornstalks. His legs were tired now, and he sat down under a stone memorial arch near some crossroads to rest.

Where was he going, and what should he do? These were the questions that filled the boy's whirling little brain. First, he must find out if the soldiers were really destroying all the houses in his village. Perhaps some of them would not be burned and he could return at night to join his father.

After several failures he managed to climb one of the stone pillars and from the arch above he could get a good view of the surrounding country. Over to the west was his village. His heart beat fast when he saw that a great cloud of smoke was rising from the houses. Clearly, the thieves were making quick work of the place, and soon there would be nothing left but piles of mud, brick, ashes and other rubbish.

Night came on. K'ang-p'u clambered down from his stone perch. He was beginning to feel hungry, and yet he dared not turn back towards home. And besides, would not all the other villagers be hungry, too? He lay down at the foot of the stone monument, placing the basket within reach at one side. Soon he fell fast asleep.

How long he had been sleeping he never knew; but it was not yet day when he awoke with a start and looked round him in the moonlight. Someone had called him distinctly by name. At first, he thought it must have been his father's voice; and then as he grew wider and wider awake he knew this could not be, for the voice sounded like that of an old man. K'ang-p'u looked round in amazement, first at the stone columns, then at the arch above. No one was to be seen. Had he been dreaming?

Just as he lay back to sleep once more, the voice sounded again very faintly, "K'ang-p'u! K'ang-p'u! why don't you let me out? I can't breathe under all these feathers."

Quick as a flash he knew what was the matter. Burying his hand in the basket, he seized the wooden tablet, drew it from its hiding-place, and stood it up on the stone base. Wonder of wonders! There before his very eyes he saw a tiny fellow, not six inches high, sitting on top of the wooden upright and dangling his legs over the front of the tablet. The dwarf had a long grey beard, and K'ang-p'u, without looking twice, knew that this was the spirit of his dead grandfather come to life and clothed with flesh and blood.

"Ho, ho!" said the small man, laughing, "so you thought you'd bury your old grandfather in feathers, did you? A soft enough grave, but rather smelly."

"But, sir," cried K'ang-p'u, "I had to do it, to save you from the soldiers! They were just about to burn our house and you in it."

"There, there, my boy! don't be uneasy. I am not scolding you. You did the best you could for your old gran'ther. If you had been like most lads, you would have taken to your heels and left me to those sea-devils who were sacking the village. There is no doubt about it: you saved me from a second death much more terrible than the first one."

K'ang-p'u shuddered, for he knew that his grandfather had been killed in battle. He had heard his father tell the story many times.

"Now, what do you propose doing about it?" asked the old man finally, looking straight into the boy's face.

"Doing about it, sir? Why, really, I don't know. I thought that perhaps in the morning the soldiers would be gone and I could carry you back. Surely my father will be looking for me."

"What! looking for you in the ashes? And what could he do if he did find you? Your house is burned, your chickens carried away and your cabbages trampled underfoot. A sorry home he will return to. You would be just one more mouth to feed. No! that plan will never do. If your father thinks you are dead, he will go off to another province to get work. That would save him from starvation."

"But what am I to do?" wailed poor K'ang-p'u. "I don't want him to leave me all alone!"

"All alone! What! don't you count your old grand-daddy? Surely you are not a very polite youngster, even if you did save me from burning to death."

"Count you?" repeated the boy, surprised. "Why, surely you can't help me to earn a living?"

"Why not, boy? Is this an age when old men are good for nothing?"

"But, sir, you are only the spirit of my grandfather, and spirits cannot work!"

"Ha, ha! just hear the child. Why, look you, I will show you what spirits can do, provided you will do exactly what I tell you."

Of course, K'ang-p'u promised, for he was always obedient; and was not this little man who spoke so strangely, the spirit of his grandfather? And is not every lad in China taught to honour his ancestors?

"Now, listen, my boy. First, let me say that if you had not been kind, brave and filial, I should not take the trouble to help you out of your misfortune. As it is, there is nothing else for me to do. I cast your father off because he was disobedient. He has lived in a dirty hovel ever since. Doubtless, he has been sorry for his misdeeds, for I see that although he was disgraced by being sent away from the family home, he has taught you to honour and love me. Most boys would have snatched up a blanket or a piece of bread before running from the enemy, but you thought only of my tablet. You saved me and went to bed hungry. For this bravery, I shall give back to you the home of your ancestors."

"But I can't live in it," said K'ang-p'u, full of wonder, "if you will not let my father come back to it. If he goes away he will have a very hard time: he will be lonely without me, and may die; and then I would not be able to take care of his grave, or to burn incense there at the proper season!"

"Quite right, K'ang-p'u. I see you love your father as well as your grandfather's tablet. Very well; you shall have your way. I daresay your father is sorry by this time that he treated me so badly."

"Indeed, he must be," said the boy earnestly, "for I have seen him kneel before your tablet many times and burn incense there on the proper days. I know he is very sorry."

"Very well; go to sleep again. Let us wait until morning and then I shall see what I can do for you. This moonlight is not bright enough for my old eyes. I shall have to wait for morning."

As he spoke these last words, the little man began to grow smaller and smaller before the eyes of his grandson, until at last he had altogether disappeared.

At first, K'ang-p'u was too much excited to close his eyes. He remained for a time looking up into the starry sky and wondering if what he had heard would really come true, or whether he could have dreamt the whole story of his grandfather's coming to life again. Could it really be that the old family property would be given back to his father? He remembered now that he had once heard his father speak of having lived in a large house on a beautiful compound. It was just before K'ang-p'u's mother had been carried away by the fever. As she had lain tossing upon the rude stone bed, with none of those comforts which are so necessary for the sick, K'ang-p'u remembered that his father had said to her: "What a shame that we are not living in my father's house! There you might have had every luxury. It is all my fault; I disobeyed my father."

Soon after that his mother had died, but K'ang-p'u had remembered those words ever since, and had often wished that he could hear more about this house where his father had spent his boyhood. Could it be possible that they would soon be living in it? No, surely there must be some mistake: the night fairies of his dreams had been deceiving him. With a sigh he closed his eyes and once more fell asleep.

* * *

When K'ang-p'u next awoke, the sun was shining full in his face. He looked around him, sleepily rubbing his eyes and trying to remember all that had happened. Suddenly he thought of the tablet and of his grandfather's appearance at midnight. But, strange to say, the basket had disappeared with all its contents. The tablet was nowhere to be seen, and even the stone arch under which he had gone to sleep had completely vanished. Alas! his grandfather's tablet – how poorly he had guarded it! What terrible thing would happen now that it was gone!

K'ang-p'u stood up and looked round him in trembling surprise. What could have taken place while he was sleeping? At first, he did not know what to do. Fortunately, the path through the corn was still there, and he decided to return to the village and see if he could find any trace of his father. His talk with the old man must have been only an idle dream, and some thief must have carried off the basket. If only the stone arch had not vanished K'ang-p'u would not have been so perplexed.

He hurried along the narrow road, trying to forget the empty stomach which was beginning to cry for food. If the soldiers were still in the village, surely they would not hurt an empty-handed little boy. More than likely they had gone the day before. If he could only find his father! Now he crossed the little brook where the women came to rub their clothes upon the rocks. There was the big mulberry tree where the boys used to gather leaves for their silkworms. Another turn of the road and he would see the village.

When K'ang-p'u passed round the corner and looked for the ruins of the village hovels, an amazing sight met his gaze. There, rising directly before him, was a great stone wall, like those he had seen round the rich people's houses when his father had taken him to the city. The great gate stood wide open, and the keeper, rushing out, exclaimed:

"Ah! the little master has come!"

Completely bewildered, the boy followed the servant through the gateway, passed through several wide courts, and then into a garden where flowers and strangely-twisted trees were growing.

This, then, was the house which his grandfather had promised him – the home of his ancestors. Ah! how beautiful! how beautiful! Many men and women servants bowed low as he passed, saluting with great respect and crying out:

"Yes, it is really the little master! He has come back to his own!"

K'ang-p'u, seeing how well dressed the servants were, felt much ashamed of his own ragged garments, and put up his hands to hide a torn place. What was his amazement to find that he was no longer clad in soiled, ragged clothes, that he was dressed in the handsomest embroidered silk. From head to foot he was fitted out like the young Prince his father had pointed out to him one day in the city.

Then they entered a magnificent reception-hall on the other side of the garden. K'ang-p'u could not keep back his tears, for there stood his father waiting to meet him.

"My boy! my boy!" cried the father, "you have come back to me. I feared you had been stolen away for ever."

"Oh, no!" said K'ang-p'u, "you have not lost me, but I have lost the tablet. A thief came and took it last night while I was sleeping."

"Lost the tablet! A thief! Why, no, my son, you are mistaken! There it is, just before you."

K'ang-p'u looked, and saw standing on a handsome carved table the very thing he had mourned as lost. As he stared in surprise he almost expected to see the tiny figure swinging its legs over the top, and to hear the high-pitched voice of his grandfather.

"Yes, it is really the lost tablet!" he cried joyfully. "How glad I am it is back in its rightful place once more."

Then father and son fell upon their knees before the wooden emblem, and bowed reverently nine times to the floor, thanking the spirit for all it had done for them. When they arose their hearts were full of a new happiness.

The Golden Nugget

ONCE UPON A TIME many, many years ago, there lived in China two friends named Ki-wu and Pao-shu. These two young men, like Damon and Pythias, loved each other and were always together. No cross words passed between them; no unkind thoughts marred their friendship. Many an interesting tale might be told of their unselfishness, and of how the good fairies gave them the true reward of virtue. One story alone, however, will be enough to show how strong was their affection and their goodness.

It was a bright beautiful day in early spring when Ki-wu and Pao-shu set out for a stroll together, for they were tired of the city and its noises.

"Let us go into the heart of the pine forest," said Ki-wu lightly. "There we can forget the cares that worry us; there we can breathe the sweetness of the flowers and lie on the moss-covered ground."

"Good!" said Pao-shu, "I, too, am tired. The forest is the place for rest."

Happy as two lovers on a holiday, they passed along the winding road, their eyes turned in longing toward the distant tree-tops. Their hearts beat fast in youthful pleasure as they drew nearer and nearer to the woods.

"For thirty days I have worked over my books," sighed Ki-wu. "For thirty days I have not had a rest. My head is stuffed so full of wisdom, that I am afraid it will burst. Oh, for a breath of the pure air blowing through the greenwood."

"And I," added Pao-shu sadly, "have worked like a slave at my counter and found it just as dull as you have found your books. My master treats me badly. It seems good, indeed, to get beyond his reach."

Now they came to the border of the grove, crossed a little stream, and plunged headlong among the trees and shrubs. For many an hour they rambled on, talking and laughing merrily; when suddenly on passing round a clump of flower-covered bushes, they saw shining in the pathway directly in front of them a lump of gold.

"See!" said both, speaking at the same time, and pointing toward the treasure.

Ki-wu, stooping, picked up the nugget. It was nearly as large as a lemon, and was very pretty. "It is yours, my dear friend," said he, at the same time handing it to Pao-shu; "yours because you saw it first."

"No, no," answered Pao-shu, "you are wrong, my brother, for you were first to speak. Now, you can never say hereafter that the good fairies have not rewarded you for all your faithful hours of study."

"Repaid me for my study! Why, that is impossible. Are not the wise men always saying that study brings its own reward? No, the gold is yours: I insist upon it. Think of your weeks of hard labour – of the masters that have ground you to the bone! Here is something far better. Take it," laughing. "May it be the nest egg by means of which you may hatch out a great fortune."

Thus they joked for some minutes, each refusing to take the treasure for himself; each insisting that it belonged to the other. At last, the chunk of gold was dropped in the very spot where they had first spied it, and the two comrades went away, each happy because he loved his friend better than anything else in the world. Thus they turned their backs on any chance of quarrelling.

"It was not for gold that we left the city," exclaimed Ki-wu warmly.

"No," replied his friend, "One day in this forest is worth a thousand nuggets."

"Let us go to the spring and sit down on the rocks," suggested Ki-wu. "It is the coolest spot in the whole grove."

When they reached the spring they were sorry to find the place already occupied. A countryman was stretched at full length on the ground.

"Wake up, fellow!" cried Pao-shu, "there is money for you near by. Up yonder path a golden apple is waiting for some man to go and pick it up."

Then they described to the unwelcome stranger the exact spot where the treasure was, and were delighted to see him set out in eager search.

For an hour they enjoyed each other's company, talking of all the hopes and ambitions of their future, and listening to the music of the birds that hopped about on the branches overhead.

At last they were startled by the angry voice of the man who had gone after the nugget. "What trick is this you have played on me, masters? Why do you make a poor man like me run his legs off for nothing on a hot day?"

"What do you mean, fellow?" asked Ki-wu, astonished. "Did you not find the fruit we told you about?"

"No," he answered, in a tone of half-hidden rage, "but in its place a monster snake, which I cut in two with my blade. Now, the gods will bring me bad luck for killing something in the woods. If you thought you could drive me from this place by such a trick, you'll soon find you were mistaken, for I was first upon this spot and you have no right to give me orders."

"Stop your chatter, bumpkin, and take this copper for your trouble. We thought we were doing you a favour. If you are blind, there's no one but yourself to blame. Come, Pao-shu, let us go back and have a look at this wonderful snake that has been hiding in a chunk of gold."

Laughing merrily, the two companions left the countryman and turned back in search of the nugget.

"If I am not mistaken," said the student, "the gold lies beyond that fallen tree."

"Quite true; we shall soon see the dead snake."

Quickly they crossed the remaining stretch of pathway, with their eyes fixed intently on the ground. Arriving at the spot where they had left the shining treasure, what was their surprise to see, not the lump of gold, not the dead snake described by the idler, but, instead, two beautiful golden nuggets, each larger than the one they had seen at first.

Each friend picked up one of these treasures and handed it joyfully to his companion.

"At last the fairies have rewarded you for your unselfishness!" said Ki-wu.

"Yes," answered Pao-shu, "by granting me a chance to give you your deserts."

The Man Who Would Not Scold

OLD WANG LIVED in a village near Nanking. He cared for nothing in the world but to eat good food and plenty of it. Now, though this Wang was by no means a poor man, it made him very sad to spend money, and so people called him in sport, the Miser King, for Wang is the Chinese word for king. His greatest pleasure was to eat at someone else's table when he knew that the food would cost him nothing, and you may be sure that at such times he always licked his chopsticks clean. But when he was spending his own money, he tightened his belt and drank a great deal of water, eating very little but scraps such as his friends would have thrown to the dogs. Thus people laughed at him and said:

"When Wang an invitation gets,
He chews and chews until he sweats,
But, when his own food he must eat.
The tears flow down and wet his feet."

One day while Wang was lying half asleep on the bank of a stream that flowed near his house he began to feel hungry. He had been in that spot all day without tasting anything. At last he saw a flock of ducks swimming in the river. He knew that they belonged to a rich man named Lin who lived in the village. They were fat ducks, so plump and tempting that it made him hungry to look at them. "Oh, for a boiled duck!" he said to himself with a sigh. "Why is it that the gods have not given me a taste of duck during the past year? What have I done to be thus denied?"

Then the thought flashed into his mind: "Here am I asking why the gods have not given me ducks to eat. Who knows but that they have sent this flock thinking I would have sense enough to grab one? Friend Lin, many thanks for your kindness. I think I shall accept your offer and take one of these fowls for my dinner." Of course Mr. Lin was nowhere near to hear old Wang thanking him.

By this time the flock had come to shore. The miser picked himself up lazily from the ground, and, after tiring himself out, he at last managed to pick one of the ducks up, too. He took it home joyfully, hiding it under his ragged garment. Once in his own yard, he lost no time in killing and preparing it for dinner. He ate it, laughing to himself all the time at his own slyness, and wondering what his friend Lin would think if he chanced to count his ducks that night. "No doubt he will believe it was a giant hawk that carried off that bird," he said, chuckling. "My word! but didn't I do a great trick? I think I will repeat the dose tomorrow. The first duck is well lodged in my stomach, and I am ready to take an oath that all the others will find a bed in the same boarding-house before many weeks are past. It would be a pity to leave the first one to pine away in lonely grief. I could never be so cruel."

So old Wang went to bed happy. For several hours he snored away noisily, dreaming that a certain rich man had promised him good food all the rest of his life, and that he would never be forced to do another stroke of work. At midnight, however, he was wakened from his sleep by an unpleasant itching. His whole body seemed to be on fire, and the pain was more than he could bear. He got up and paced the floor. There was no oil in the house for his lamp, and he had to wait until morning to see what was the matter. At early dawn he stepped outside his shanty. Lo, and behold! he found little red spots all over his body. Before his very eyes he saw tiny duck feathers sprouting from these spots. As the morning went by, the feathers grew larger and larger, until his whole body was covered with them from head to foot. Only his face and hands were free of the strange growth.

With a cry of horror, Wang began to pull the feathers out by handfuls, flinging them in the dirt and stamping on them. "The gods have fooled me!" he yelled. "They made me take the duck and eat it, and now they are punishing me for stealing." But the faster he jerked the feathers out, the faster they grew in again, longer and more glossy than before. Then, too, the pain was so great that he could scarcely keep from rolling on the ground. At last completely worn out by his useless labour, and moaning with despair, he took to his bed. "Am I to be changed into a bird?" he groaned. "May the gods have mercy on me!"

He tossed about on his bed: he could not sleep; his heart was sick with fear. Finally he fell into a troubled sleep, and, sleeping, had a dream. A fairy came to his bedside; it was Fairy Old Boy, the friend of the people. "Ah, my poor Wang," said the fairy, "all this trouble you have brought upon yourself by your shiftless, lazy habits. When others work, why do you lie down and sleep your time away? Why don't you get up and shake your lazy legs? There is no place in the world for such a man as you except the pig-sty."

"I know you are telling the truth," wailed Wang, "but how, oh, how can I ever work with all these feathers sticking out of me? They will kill me! They will kill me!"

"Hear the man!" laughed Old Boy. "Now, if you were a hopeful, happy fellow, you would say, 'What a stroke of luck! No need to buy garments. The gods have given me a suit of clothes that will never wear out.' You are a pretty fellow to be complaining, aren't you?"

After joking in this way for a little while, the good fairy changed his tone of voice and said, "Now, Wang, are you really sorry for the way you have lived, sorry for your years of idleness, sorry because you disgraced your old Father and Mother? I hear your parents died of hunger because you would not help them."

Wang, seeing that Old Boy knew all about his past life, and, feeling his pain growing worse and worse every minute, cried out at last: "Yes! Yes! I will do anything you say. Only, I pray you, free me of these feathers!"

"I wouldn't have your feathers," said Old Boy, "and I cannot free you of them. You will have to do the whole thing yourself. What you need is to hear a good scolding. Go and get Mr. Lin, the owner of the stolen duck, to scold freely. The harder he scolds, the sooner will your feathers drop out."

Now, of course, some readers will laugh and say, "But this was only a silly dream, and meant nothing." Mr. Wang, however, did not think in this way. He woke up very happy. He would go to Mr. Lin, confess everything and take the scolding. Then he would be free of his feathers and would go to work. Truly he had led a lazy life. What the good Fairy Old Boy had said about his father and mother had hurt him very badly, for he knew that every word was true. From this day on, he would not be lazy; he would take a wife and become the father of a family.

Miser Wang meant all right when he started out from his shanty. From his little hoard of money he took enough cash to pay Mr. Lin for the stolen duck. He would do everything the fairy had told him and even more. But this doing more was just where he got into trouble. As he walked along the road jingling the string of cash, and thinking that he must soon give it up to his neighbour, he grew very sad. He loved every copper of his money and he disliked to part with it. After all, Old Boy had not told him he must confess to the owner of the duck; he had said he must go to Lin and get Lin to give a good scolding. "Old Boy did not say that Lin must scold me," thought the miser. "All that I need do is to get him to scold, and then my feathers will drop off and I shall be happy. Why not tell him that old Sen stole his duck, and get him to give Sen a scolding? That will surely do just as well, and I shall save my money as well as my face. Besides, if I tell Lin that I am a thief, perhaps he will send for a policeman and they will haul me off to prison. Surely going to jail would be as bad as wearing feathers. Ha, ha! This will be a good joke on Sen, Lin, and the whole lot of them. I shall fool Fairy Old Boy too. Really he had no right to speak of my father and mother in the way he did. After all, they died of fever, and I was no doctor to cure them. How could he say it was my fault?"

The longer Wang talked to himself, the surer he became that it was useless to tell Lin that he had stolen the duck. By the time he had reached the duck man's house he had fully made up his mind to deceive him. Mr. Lin invited him to come in and sit down. He was a plain-spoken, honest kind of man, this Lin. Everybody liked him, for he never spoke ill of any man and he always had something good to say of his neighbours.

"Well, what's your business, friend Wang? You have come out bright and early, and it's a long walk from your place to mine."

"Oh, I had something important I wanted to talk to you about," began Wang slyly. "That's a fine flock of ducks you have over in the meadow."

"Yes," said Mr. Lin smiling, "a fine flock indeed." But he said nothing of the stolen fowl.

"How many have you?" questioned Wang more boldly.

"I counted them yesterday morning and there were fifteen."

"But did you count them again last night?"

"Yes, I did," answered Lin slowly.

"And there were only fourteen then?"

"Quite right, friend Wang, one of them was missing; but one duck is of little importance. Why do you speak of it?"

"What, no importance! losing a duck? How can you say so? A duck's a duck, isn't it, and surely you would like to know how you lost it?"

"A hawk most likely."

"No, it wasn't a hawk, but if you would go and look in old Sen's duck yard, you would likely find feathers."

"Nothing more natural, I am sure, in a duck yard."

"Yes, but your duck's feathers," persisted Wang.

"What! you think old Sen is a thief, do you, and that he has been stealing from me?"

"Exactly! you have it now."

"Well, well, that is too bad! I am sorry the old fellow is having such a hard time. He is a good worker and deserves better luck. I should willingly have given him the duck if he had only asked for it. Too bad that he had to steal it."

Wang waited to see how Mr. Lin planned to punish the thief, feeling sure that the least he could do, would be to go and give him a good scolding.

But nothing of the kind happened. Instead of growing angry, Mr. Lin seemed to be sorry for Sen, sorry that he was poor, sorry that he was willing to steal.

"Aren't you even going to give him a scolding?" asked Wang in disgust. "Better go to his house with me and give him a good raking over the coals."

"What use, what use? Hurt a neighbour's feelings just for a duck? That would be foolish indeed."

By this time the Miser King had begun to feel an itching all over his body. The feathers had begun hurting again, and he was frightened once more. He became excited and threw himself on the floor in front of Mr. Lin.

"Hey! what's the matter, man?" cried Lin, thinking Wang was in a fit. "What's the matter? Are you ill?"

"Yes, very ill," wailed Wang. "Mr. Lin, I'm a bad man, and I may as well own it at once and be done with it. There is no use trying to dodge the truth or hide a fault. I stole your duck last night, and to-day I came sneaking over here and tried to put the thing off on old Sen."

"Yes, I knew it," answered Lin. "I saw you carrying the duck off under your garment. Why did you come to see me at all if you thought I did not know you were guilty?"

"Only wait, and I'll tell you everything," said Wang, bowing still lower. "After I had boiled your duck and eaten it, I went to bed. Pretty soon I felt an itching all over my body. I could not sleep and in the morning I found that I had a thick growth of duck's feathers from head to foot. The more I pulled them out, the thicker they grew in. I could hardly keep from screaming. I took to my bed, and after I had tossed about for hours a fairy came and told me that I could never get rid of my trouble unless I got you to give me a thorough scolding. Here is the money for your duck. Now for the love of mercy, scold, and do it quickly, for I can't stand the pain much longer."

Wang was grovelling in the dirt at Lin's feet, but Lin answered him only with a loud laugh which finally burst into a roar. "Duck feathers! ha! ha! ha! and all over your body? Why, that's too good a story to believe! You'll be wanting to live in the water next. Ha! Ha! Ha!"

"Scold me! scold me!" begged Wang, "for the love of the gods scold me!"

But Lin only laughed the louder. "Pray let me see this wonderful growth of feathers first, and then we'll talk about the scolding."

Wang willingly opened his garment and showed the doubting Lin that he had been really speaking the truth.

"They must be warm," said Lin, laughing. "Winter is soon coming and you are not over fond of work. Won't they save you the trouble of wearing clothing?"

"But they make me itch so I can scarcely stand it! I feel like screaming out, the pain is so great," and again Wang got down and began to kowtow to the other; that is, he knelt and bumped his forehead against the ground.

"Be calm, my friend, and give me time to think of some good scold-words," said Lin at last. "I am not in the habit of using strong language, and very seldom lose my temper. Really you must give me time to think of what to say."

By this time Wang was in such pain that he lost all power over himself. He seized Mr. Lin by the legs crying out, "Scold me! scold me!"

Mr. Lin was now out of patience with his visitor. Besides Wang was holding him so tightly that it really felt as if Lin were being pinched by some gigantic crawfish. Suddenly Lin could hold his tongue no longer: "You lazy hound! you whelp! you turtle! you lazy, good-for-nothing creature! I wish you would hurry up and roll out of this!"

Now, in China, this is very strong language, and, with a cry of joy, Wang leaped from the ground, for he knew that Lin had scolded him. No sooner had the first hasty words been spoken than the feathers began falling from the lazy man's body, and, at last, the dreadful itching had entirely stopped. On the floor in front of Lin lay a great pile of feathers, and Wang freed from his trouble, pointed to them and said, "Thank you kindly, my dear friend, for the pretty names you have called me. You have saved my life, and, although I have paid for the duck, I wish to add to the bargain by making you a present of these handsome feathers. They will, in a measure, repay you for your splendid set of scold-words. I have learned my lesson well, I hope, and I shall go out from here a better man. Fairy Old Boy told me that I was lazy. You agree with the fairy. From this day, however, you shall see that I can bend my back like a good fellow. Good-bye, and, many thanks for your kindness."

So saying, with many low bows and polite words, Wang left the duck owner's house, a happier and a wiser man.

Lu-San, Daughter of Heaven

LU-SAN WENT to bed without any supper, but her little heart was hungry for something more than food. She nestled up close beside her sleeping brothers, but even in their slumber they seemed to deny her that love which she craved. The gentle lapping of the water against the sides of the houseboat, music which had so often lulled her into dreamland, could not quiet her now. Scorned and treated badly by the entire family, her short life had been full of grief and shame.

Lu-san's father was a fisherman. His life had been one long fight against poverty. He was ignorant and wicked. He had no more feeling of love for his wife and five children than for the street dogs of his native city. Over and over he had threatened to drown them one and all, and had been prevented from doing so only by fear of the new mandarin. His wife did not try to stop her husband when he sometimes beat the children until they fell half dead upon the deck. In fact, she herself was cruel to them, and often gave the last blow to Lu-san, her only daughter. Not on one day in the little girl's memory had she escaped this daily whipping, not once had her parents pitied her.

On the night with which this story opens, not knowing that Lu-san was listening, her father and mother were planning how to get rid of her.

"The mandarin cares only about boys," said he roughly. "A man might kill a dozen girls and he wouldn't say a word."

"Lu-san's no good anyway," added the mother. "Our boat is small, and she's always in the wrong place."

"Yes, and it takes as much to feed her as if she were a boy. If you say so, I'll do it this very night."

"All right," she answered, "but you'd better wait till the moon has set."

"Very well, wife, we'll let the moon go down first, and then the girl."

No wonder Lu-san's little heart beat fast with terror, for there could be no doubt as to the meaning of her parents' words.

At last when she heard them snoring and knew they were both sound asleep, she got up silently, dressed herself, and climbed the ladder leading to the deck. Only one thought was in her heart, to save herself by instant flight. There were no extra clothes, not a bite of food to take with her. Besides the rags on her back there was only one thing she could call her own, a tiny soapstone image of the goddess Kwan-yin, which she had found one day while walking in the sand. This was the only treasure and plaything of her childhood, and if she had not watched carefully, her mother would have taken even this away from her. Oh, how she had nursed this idol, and how closely she had listened to the stories an old priest had told about Kwan-yin the Goddess of Mercy, the best friend of women and children, to whom they might always pray in time of trouble.

It was very dark when Lu-san raised the trapdoor leading to the outer air, and looked out into the night. The moon had just gone down, and frogs were croaking along the shore. Slowly and carefully she pushed against the door, for she was afraid that the wind coming in suddenly might awaken the sleepers or, worse still, cause her to let the trap fall with a bang. At last, however, she stood on the deck, alone and ready to go out into the big world. As she stepped to the side of the boat the black water did not make her feel afraid, and she went ashore without the slightest tremble.

Now she ran quickly along the bank, shrinking back into the shadows whenever she heard the noise of footsteps, and thus hiding from the passers-by. Only once did her heart quake, full of fear. A huge boat dog ran out at her barking furiously. The snarling beast, however, was not dangerous, and when he saw this trembling little girl of ten he sniffed in disgust at having noticed any one so small, and returned to watch his gate.

Lu-san had made no plans. She thought that if she could escape the death her parents had talked about, they would be delighted at her leaving them and would not look for her. It was not, then, her own people that she feared as she passed the rows of dark houses lining the shore. She had often heard her father tell of the dreadful deeds done in many of these houseboats. The darkest memory of her childhood was of the night when he had almost decided to sell her as a slave to the owner of a boat like these she was now passing. Her mother had suggested that they should wait until Lu-san was a little older, for she would then be worth more money. So her father had not sold her. Lately, perhaps, he had tried and failed.

That was why she hated the river dwellers and was eager to get past their houses. On and on she sped as fast as her little legs could carry her. She would flee far away from the dark water, for she loved the bright sunshine and the land.

As Lu-san ran past the last houseboat she breathed a sigh of relief and a minute later fell in a little heap upon the sand. Not until now had she noticed how lonely it was. Over there was the great city with its thousands of sleepers. Not one of them was her friend. She knew nothing of friendship, for she had had no playmates. Beyond lay the open fields, the sleeping villages, the unknown world. Ah, how tired she was! How far she had run! Soon, holding the precious image tightly in her little hand and whispering a childish prayer to Kwan-yin, she fell asleep.

When Lu-san awoke, a cold chill ran through her body, for bending over her stood a strange person. Soon she saw to her wonder that it was a woman dressed in beautiful clothes like those worn by a princess. The child had never seen such perfect features or so fair a face. At first, conscious of her own filthy rags, she shrank back fearfully, wondering what would happen if this beautiful being should chance to touch her and thus soil those slender white fingers. As the child lay there trembling on the ground, she felt as if she would like to spring into the fairy creature's arms and beg for mercy. Only the fear that the lovely one would vanish kept her from so doing. Finally, unable to hold back any longer, the little girl, bending forward, stretched out her hand to the woman, saying, "Oh, you are so beautiful! Take this, for it must be you who lost it in the sand."

The princess took the soapstone figure, eyed it curiously, and then with a start of surprise said, "And do you know, my little creature, to whom you are thus giving your treasure?"

"No," answered the child simply, "but it is the only thing I have in all the world, and you are so lovely that I know it belongs to you. I found it on the river bank."

Then a strange thing happened. The graceful, queenly woman bent over, and held out her arms to the ragged, dirty child. With a cry of joy the little one sprang forward; she had found the love for which she had been looking so long.

"My precious child, this little stone which you have kept so lovingly, and which without a thought of self you have given to me – do you know of whom it is the image?"

"Yes," answered Lu-san, the colour coming to her cheeks again as she snuggled up contentedly in her new friend's warm embrace, "it is the dear goddess Kwan-yin, she who makes the children happy."

"And has this gracious goddess brought sunshine into your life, my pretty one?" said the other, a slight flush covering her fair cheeks at the poor child's innocent words.

"Oh, yes indeed; if it had not been for her I should not have escaped tonight. My father would have killed me, but the good lady of heaven listened to my prayer and bade me stay awake. She told me to wait until he was sleeping, then to arise and leave the houseboat."

"And where are you going, Lu-san, now that you have left your father? Are you not afraid to be alone here at night on the bank of this great river?"

"No, oh no! for the blessed mother will shield me. She has heard my prayers, and I know she will show me where to go."

The lady clasped Lu-san still more tightly, and something glistened in her radiant eye. A tear-drop rolled down her cheek and fell upon the child's head, but Lu-san did not see it, for she had fallen fast asleep in her protector's arms.

When Lu-san awoke, she was lying all alone on her bed in the houseboat, but, strange to say, she was not frightened at finding herself once more near her parents. A ray of sunlight came in, lighting up the child's face and telling her that a new day had dawned. At last she heard the sound of low voices, but she did not know who were the speakers. Then as the tones grew louder she knew that her parents were talking. Their speech, however, seemed to be less harsh than usual, as if they were near the bed of some sleeper whom they did not wish to wake.

"Why," said her father, "when I bent over to lift her from the bed, there was a strange light about her face. I touched her on the arm, and at once my hand hung limp as if it had been shot. Then I heard a voice whispering in my ears, 'What! would you lay your wicked hands on one who made the tears of Kwan-yin flow? Do you not know that when she cries the gods themselves are weeping?'"

"I too heard that voice," said the mother, her voice trembling; "I heard it, and it seemed as if a hundred wicked imps pricked me with spears, at every prick repeating these terrible words, 'And would you kill a daughter of the gods?'"

"It is strange," he added, "to think how we had begun to hate this child, when all the time she belonged to another world than ours. How wicked we must be since we could not see her goodness."

"Yes, and no doubt for every time we have struck her, a thousand blows will be given us by Yama, for our insults to the gods."

Lu-san waited no longer, but rose to dress herself. Her heart was burning with love for everything around her. She would tell her parents that she forgave them, tell them how she loved them still in spite of all their wickedness. To her surprise the ragged clothes were nowhere to be seen. In place of them she found on one side of the bed the most beautiful garments. The softest of silks, bright with flowers – so lovely that she fancied they must have been taken from the garden of the gods – were ready to slip on her little body. As she dressed herself she saw with surprise that her fingers were shapely, that her skin was soft and smooth. Only the day before, her hands had been rough and cracked by hard work and the cold of winter. More and more amazed, she stooped to put on her shoes. Instead of the worn-out soiled shoes of yesterday, the prettiest little satin slippers were there all ready for her tiny feet.

Finally she climbed the rude ladder, and lo, everything she touched seemed to be changed as if by magic, like her gown. The narrow rounds of the ladder had become broad steps of polished wood, and it seemed as if she was mounting the polished stairway of some fairy-built pagoda. When she reached the deck everything was changed. The ragged patchwork which had served so long as a sail had become a beautiful sheet of canvas that rolled and floated proudly in the river breeze. Below were the dirty fishing smacks which Lu-san was used to, but here was a stately ship, larger and fairer than any she had ever dreamed of, a ship which had sprung into being as if at the touch of her feet.

After searching several minutes for her parents she found them trembling in a corner, with a look of great fear on their faces. They were clad in rags, as usual, and in no way changed except that their savage faces seemed to have become a trifle softened. Lu-san drew near the wretched group and bowed low before them.

Her mother tried to speak; her lips moved, but made no sound: she had been struck dumb with fear.

"A goddess, a goddess!" murmured the father, bending forward three times and knocking his head on the deck. As for the brothers, they hid their faces in their hands as if dazzled by a sudden burst of sunlight.

For a moment Lu-san paused. Then, stretching out her hand, she touched her father on the shoulder. "Do you not know me, father? It is Lu-san, your little daughter."

The man looked at her in wonder. His whole body shook, his lips trembled, his hard brutish face had on it a strange light. Suddenly he bent far over and touched his forehead to her feet. Mother and sons followed his example. Then all gazed at her as if waiting for her command.

"Speak, father," said Lu-san. "Tell me that you love me, say that you will not kill your child."

"Daughter of the gods, and not of mine," he mumbled, and then paused as if afraid to continue.

"What is it, father? Have no fear."

"First, tell me that you forgive me."

The child put her left hand upon her father's forehead and held the right above the heads of the others, "As the Goddess of Mercy has given me her favour, so I in her name bestow on you the love of heaven. Live in peace, my parents. Brothers, speak no angry words. Oh, my dear ones, let joy be yours for ever. When only love shall rule your lives, this ship is yours and all that is in it."

Thus did Lu-san change her loved ones. The miserable family which had lived in poverty now found itself enjoying peace and happiness. At first they did not know how to live as Lu-san had directed. The father sometimes lost his temper and the mother spoke spiteful words; but as they grew in wisdom and courage they soon began to see that only love must rule.

All this time the great boat was moving up and down the river. Its company of sailors obeyed Lu-san's slightest wish. When their nets were cast overboard they were always drawn back full of the largest, choicest fish. These fish were sold at the city markets, and soon people began to say that Lu-san was the richest person in the whole country.

One beautiful day during the Second Moon, the family had just returned from the temple. It was Kwan-yin's birthday, and, led by Lu-san, they had gone gladly to do the goddess honour. They had just mounted to the vessel's deck when Lu-san's father, who had been looking off towards the west, suddenly called the family to his side. "See!" he exclaimed. "What kind of bird is that yonder in the sky?"

As they looked, they saw that the strange object was coming nearer and nearer, and directly towards the ship. Everyone was excited except Lu-san. She was calm, as if waiting for something she had long expected.

"It is a flight of doves," cried the father in astonishment, "and they seem to be drawing something through the air."

At last, as the birds flew right over the vessel, the surprised onlookers saw that floating beneath their wings was a wonderful chair, all white and gold, more dazzling even than the one they had dreamed the Emperor himself sat in on the Dragon Throne. Around each snow-white neck was fastened a long streamer of pure gold, and these silken ribbons were tied to the chair in such a manner as to hold it floating wherever its light-winged coursers chose to fly.

Down, down, over the magic vessel came the empty chair, and as it descended, a shower of pure white lilies fell about the feet of Lu-san, until she, the queen of all the flowers, was almost buried. The doves hovered above her head for an instant, and then gently lowered their burden until it was just in front of her.

With a farewell wave to her father and mother, Lu-san stepped into the fairy car. As the birds began to rise, a voice from the clouds spoke in tones of softest music: "Thus Kwan-yin, Mother of Mercies, rewards Lu-san, daughter of the earth. Out of the dust spring the flowers; out of the soil comes goodness. Lu-san! that tear which you drew from Kwan-yin's eye fell upon the dry ground and softened it; it touched the hearts of those who loved you not. Daughter of earth no longer, rise into the Western Heaven, there to take your place among the fairies, there to be a star within the azure realms above."

As Lu-san's doves disappeared in the distant skies, a rosy light surrounded her flying car. It seemed to those who gazed in wonder that heaven's gates were opening to receive her. At last when she was gone beyond their sight, suddenly it grew dark upon the earth, and the eyes of all that looked were wet with tears.

The Fairy Bonze

IN A CERTAIN well-known and populous city in one of the north-western provinces of China, there once resided a man of the name of Meng. Everyone knew about him. His fame had spread not only throughout the town, but also far away into the country beyond; for of all the merchants who carried on business in this great commercial centre he was the wealthiest and the most enterprising.

He had begun life as a poor lad; but through great strength of purpose and positive genius for business, he had steadily risen step by step, until by the time our story opens, he had become exceedingly wealthy and was the acknowledged leader in all the great undertakings for which the city was famous.

Meng had always gained the admiration and affection of everyone who became acquainted with him. He was of an artless, open-hearted disposition which won men to him, and his reputation for generosity made his name fragrant throughout the entire region in which he lived.

Forty years ago he had come to the city in search of employment. His father was a farmer in one of the outlying country districts; but Meng, discontented with the dulness of the life and with the strain and trouble brought upon his home by bad seasons, started out for the great town to make his fortune.

All that he possessed he carried on his person. His stock-in-trade consisted simply of a stout bamboo pole and a good strong rope, the usual signs of a porter; but his willingness to oblige, and the hearty, pleasant way in which he performed his arduous duties, gained him the goodwill of all who employed him. Before many months had passed he was in constant demand, and was slowly saving up money that was to enable him to rise from the position of a coolie and to enter some business which would give him a more honourable place in society.

He had a shrewd and common-sense mind which enabled him to take advantage of any trade-opening that presented itself, and as he had a genial and happy disposition, everyone who had had any business relations with him was glad to do all in his power to give him a lift in the upward road along which he had made up his mind to travel. The result was that before many years had passed away he had established himself in a very lucrative line of business which brought a steady flow of wealth into his coffers.

In time he opened branches in distant cities, and his fame reached the far-off provinces in the East, where the merchant-princes who had dealings with him counted him as one of the most trustworthy of their clients, to whom they were glad to give as much credit as he might desire.

There was one delightful feature about Meng, and that was the intense sympathy he had for his fellow-creatures. He had a heart of gold that no prosperity could spoil; no one who ever applied to him for relief was sent away empty-handed. The struggling shopkeeper made his humble appeal when fate seemed determined to crush him, and the substantial loan that Meng made to him without hesitation kept him from closing his shutters and once more set him on his feet to commence the struggle again. The widow who had been left in absolute poverty had but to state her case, when with a countenance beaming with compassion and with eyes moist at her piteous story, Meng would make such arrangements for her and her children that the terror of starvation was lifted from her heart, and she left his presence with a smiling face and with heart-felt words of praise for the man who by his generosity had given her a new glimpse of life.

The character of Meng's mind may well be discovered from the manner in which he distributed a considerable portion of his riches amongst those who had been born under an unlucky star, and upon whom an unhappy fate had pressed heavily in the distribution of this world's goods and favours.

The generous men in China are not the rich. It is true that occasionally one does hear of a munificent donation having been made by some millionaire, but the public is never deceived by these unusual outbursts of generosity. There is a selfish motive at the back of nearly every one of them, for the hope of the donors is that by gaining the favour of the mandarins they may obtain some high official position which will enable them to recoup themselves most handsomely for any sums they may have expended in charity.

Meng's deeds, however, were always purely unselfish, and no idea of reward ever entered his head. He was moved solely by a sincere desire to alleviate human suffering. The look of gladness that flashed over the faces of those whom he assisted, their gleaming eyes, and the words of gratitude that burst from their lips, were to him the sweetest payment that could possibly be made to him in return for the sums he had given away.

That Meng's fame had travelled far was shown by an occurrence which was destined to have a considerable influence on the fortunes of his only son, Chin, in whom his whole soul was bound up.

One day he received a letter from the head of a most aristocratic family in a distant city, begging that he would consent to an alliance with him. This man wrote that he had a daughter, who was declared by all who saw her to be possessed of no ordinary beauty, and he wished to have her betrothed to Meng's son. Meng's reputation for goodness and for love to his fellow-men had reached his ears, and he was anxious that their families should be united by the marriage of two young people.

The rich merchant, whose heart always retained its child-like spirit, was delighted with this proposal, which had come to him spontaneously, and not through the intrigues of a middle-woman. He was also touched by the apparently generous spirit of the writer, so he at once responded to the appeal. After some little correspondence, the betrothal was drawn up in due form, and the young couple were bound to each other by legal ties which no court in the Empire would ever dream of unloosing.

Just at this juncture, when the tide in Meng's affairs seemed at its highest, there appeared at his doors one day a venerable-looking bonze, who asked to be received as a guest for a few days, as he was on a pilgrimage to a famous shrine and was tired out with the long journey that he had already made.

Meng, who was a very devout and religious man, gave the old priest a most hearty welcome. He placed one of the best rooms in the house at his disposal, and treated him with all the generous hospitality which he was accustomed to bestow upon men of his profession, who in travelling from one monastery to another had very often stayed with him for a night or two before proceeding further on their way.

Now, this priest had such pleasing manners, and was so refined and cultivated, that he completely captured the hearts of all the household, so much so that Meng insisted upon his prolonging his stay. The result was that months went by and the bonze still remained with him as his guest.

Everyone in the house seemed to be attracted by this stranger, so winning were his ways, and so full of quiet power were his whole bearing and character. He was affable and pleasant with all, but he seemed to take most pleasure in the company of Chin, over whom he soon came to exercise a very powerful influence.

Their habit was to wander about on the hillside, when the priest would entertain his young friend with stories of the wonderful things he had seen and the striking adventures he had met with. His whole aim, however, seemed to be not so much to amuse Chin as to elevate his mind with lofty and noble sentiments, which were instilled into him on every possible occasion.

It was also their custom to retire every morning to some outhouses at the extremity of the large garden attached to the dwelling-house, where undisturbed they could converse together upon the many questions upon which the bonze was ready to discourse. One thing, however, struck Chin as very singular, and this was that the bonze made him collect certain curiously-shaped tiles, and bury them in the earthen floors of these little-used buildings. Chin would have rebelled against what he considered a child-like proceeding, but he was restrained by the profound love and veneration he felt for his companion.

At length the day came when the bonze announced that he must proceed upon his journey. He had already, he declared, stayed much longer than he had originally intended, and now the imperative call of duty made it necessary that he should not linger in the house where he had been so royally treated.

Seeing that he was determined in his purpose, Meng wanted to press upon him a considerable sum of money to provide for any expenses to which he might be put in the future. This, however, the bonze absolutely refused to accept, declaring that his wants were few, and that he would have no difficulty in meeting them by the donations he would receive from the different temples he might pass on his way to his destination.

Little did Meng dream that the guest from whom he was parting with so heavy a heart was a fairy in disguise. Yet such was the case. The rulers of the far-off Western Heaven, who had been greatly moved by Meng's noble and generous life in succouring the distressed and the forlorn, had sent the bonze to make arrangements to meet a certain calamitous crisis which was soon to take place in the home of the wealthy merchant.

A few months after the good bonze had left them, a series of disasters fell with crushing effect upon the house of Meng. Several firms which owed him very large sums of money suddenly failed, and he found himself in such financial difficulties that it was utterly impossible for him to pay his debts.

In consequence, Meng was utterly ruined, and after paying out all that he possessed, even to the uttermost cash, found himself absolutely penniless. This so wrought upon his mind that he became seriously ill, and after a few days of intense agony, his spirit vanished into the Land of Shadows, and his wife and son were left desolate and bereaved.

After a time Chin bethought himself of the wealthy and distinguished man who had been so anxious to recognize him as a son-in-law, and after consultation with his mother, who was completely broken-hearted, he set off for the distant city in which his proposed father-in-law lived. Chin hoped that the latter's heart would be moved by the disasters which had befallen his father, and that he would be willing to extend him a helping hand in his hour of dire sorrow, when even Heaven itself seemed to have abandoned him and to have heaped upon his head calamities such as do not often occur to the vilest of men.

Weary and worn with the long journey, which he had been compelled to make on foot, he arrived one day about noon at the gates which led into the spacious courtyard of the palatial mansion in which his father-in-law lived. The doors, however, were shut and barred, as though some enemy was expected to storm them and carry off the property within.

Chin called loudly to the porter to open them for him, but to his amazement he was told that orders had been received from the master of the house that he was not to be admitted on any terms whatsoever.

"But are you aware who I am?" he asked. "Do you not know that the man who owns this building is my father-in-law, and that his daughter is my promised wife? It ill becomes you therefore to keep me standing here, when I should be received with all the honours that a son-in-law can claim."

"But I have been specially warned against you," replied the surly gatekeeper. "You talk of being a son-in-law, but you are greatly mistaken if you imagine that any such kinship is going to be recognized in this house. News has reached my master of the utter failure of your father's business, and of his death, and he declares that he does not wish to be mixed up in any way with doubtful characters or with men who have become bankrupt."

Chin, who was imbued with the fine and generous spirit of his father, was so horrified at these words that he fled from the gate, determined to suffer any indignity rather than accept a favour from a man of such an ignoble disposition as his father-in-law apparently possessed.

He was crossing the road with his heart completely cast down, and in absolute despair as to how he was ever to get back to his home again, when a woman in one of the low cottages by the roadside, beckoned him to come in and sit down.

"You seem to be in distress, sir," she said, "and to be worn out with fatigue, as though you had just finished a long journey. My children and I are just about to sit down to our midday meal, and we shall be so pleased if you will come and partake of it with us. I have just been watching you as you stood at the gate of that wealthy man's house, and I saw how roughly you were treated. Never mind," she continued, "Heaven knows how you have been wronged, and in time you will be avenged for all the injury you have suffered."

Comforted and gladdened by these kindly words and by the motherly reception given him by this poor woman, Chin started out on his return journey, and after much suffering finally reached his home. Here he found his mother in the direst poverty, and with a heart still full of the deepest woe because of the death of her noble-minded husband.

Almost immediately after Chin had been refused admission to the house of his father-in-law, the latter's daughter, Water-Lily, became aware of the insulting way in which he had been treated. She was grieved beyond measure, and with tears in her eyes and her voice full of sorrow, she besought her mother to appeal to her father on her behalf, and to induce him to give up his purpose of arranging a marriage for her with a wealthy man in the neighbourhood.

"My father may plan another husband for me," she said, "but I shall never consent to be married to anyone but Chin. All the rites and ceremonies have been gone through which bind me to him as long as I live, and to cast him off now because calamity has fallen upon his home is but to invite the vengeance of the Gods, who will surely visit us with some great sorrow if we endeavour to act in a way contrary to their laws."

The piteous appeals of Water-Lily had no effect upon her father, who hurried on the arrangements for his daughter's wedding to the new suitor, anxious to marry her off in order to prevent the unfortunate Chin from appearing again to claim her as his wife.

She, however, was just as determined as her father, and when she realized that all her entreaties and prayers had produced not the slightest effect upon him, and that in the course of a few days the crimson bridal chair would appear at the door to carry her away to the home of her new husband, she determined to adopt heroic methods to prevent the accomplishment of such a tragedy.

Next morning, as dawn began to break, the side-gate of the rich man's house was stealthily opened, and a degraded-looking beggar-woman stepped out into the dull grey streets, and proceeded rapidly towards the open country beyond.

She was as miserable a specimen of the whining, cringing beggar as could have been met with in any of the beggar-camps where these unhappy outcasts of society live. She was dressed in rags which seemed to be held together only by some invisible force. Her hair was tied up in disjointed knots, and looked as if no comb had ever tried to bring it into order. Her face was black with grime, and a large, dirty patch was plastered over one of her ears in such a way that its shape was completely hidden from the gaze of those who took the trouble to cast a passing glance upon her.

Altogether she was a most unattractive object; and yet she was the most lovely woman in all that region, for she was none other than Water-Lily, the acknowledged beauty of the town, who had adopted this disguise in order to escape from the fate which her father had planned for her.

For several weary months she travelled on, suffering the greatest hardships, and passing through adventures, which, if some gifted writer had collected them into a volume, would have thrilled many a reader with admiration for this brave young maiden. Though reared and nurtured in a home where every luxury was supplied her, yet she endured the degradation and privations of a beggar's life rather than be forced to be untrue to the man whom she believed Heaven had given her as a mate.

One evening, as the shadows were falling thickly on the outer courtyard of the desolate house where Chin lived, a pitiful-looking beggar-woman stood timidly at the front door, gazing with wistful looks into the room which faced the street. Not a sound did she utter, not a single word escaped her lips to indicate that she had come there to obtain charity.

In a few minutes Chin's mother came out from a room beyond. When she saw this ragged, forlorn creature standing silently as though she were afraid that some word of scorn and reproach would be hurled at her, she was filled with a great and overmastering pity, and stepping up to her she began to comfort her in loving, gentle language.

To her astonishment this draggled, uncleanly object became violently affected by the tender, motherly way in which she was addressed. Great tear-drops trickled down her grimy face, leaving a narrow, snow-like line in their wake. Presently she was convulsed with sobs that shook her whole body, whilst she wrung her hands as though some great sorrow was gripping her heart.

Mrs. Meng was deeply affected by the sight of this unhappy woman, and whilst she was gazing at her with a look of profound sympathy, the broad patch which had concealed and at the same time disfigured the beggar's countenance, suddenly dropped to the ground.

The effect of this was most startling, for a pair of as beautiful black eyes as ever danced in a woman's head were now revealed to Mrs. Meng's astonished gaze. Looking at the stranger more intently, she saw that her features were exquisitely perfect, and had the grace and the poetry which the great painters of China have attributed to the celebrated beauties of the Empire.

"Tell me who you are," she cried, as she laid her hand tenderly and affectionately on her shoulder, "for that you are a common beggar-woman I can never believe. You must be the daughter of some great house, and have come here in this disguise in order to escape some great evil.

"Confide in me," she continued, "and everything that one woman can do for another, I am willing to do for you. But come in, dear child, and let us talk together and devise some plan by which I can really help you, for I feel my heart drawn towards you in a way I have never felt for any stranger before."

Mrs. Meng then led her into her bedroom, where Water-Lily threw off the outer garments in which she had appeared to the public as a beggar, and telling her wonderful story to Chin's mother, she revealed herself as her daughter-in-law.

But though her romantic arrival into this gloomy and distressed home brought with it a sudden gleam of happiness, the great question as to how they were to live had still to be solved. They were absolutely without means, and they could only hope to meet their meagre expenses by the sale of the house in which they were living.

At last this plan was discussed, and it was decided that the unused buildings, in which Chin and the Buddhist priest had been accustomed to spend a part of every day together, should be first of all disposed of.

In order to have some idea as to how much these outhouses were worth, Chin went to see what condition they were in, so that he might fix a price for them. As they had not been used for some time, the grass had grown rank about them, and they had a dilapidated and forlorn air which made Chin fear that their market value would not be very great.

Entering in by an open door, which a creeping vine, with the luxuriance of nature, was trying to block up, Chin looked round with a feeling of disappointment sending a chill into his very heart.

The air of the place was damp and musty. The white mould could be seen gleaming on the walls, as if it wished to give a little colour to the sombre surroundings. Great cobwebs flung their streaming banners from the beams and rafters overhead, whilst smaller ones, with delicate lace-like tracery, tried to beautify the corners of the windows, through which the light from the outside world struggled to enter the gloomy room.

Throwing the windows wide open to let in as much sunshine as was possible, Chin soon became convinced that the market value of this particular part of his property would be very small, and that unless he carried out extensive repairs, it would be impossible to induce any one to entertain the idea of buying it.

While he was musing over the problem that lay before him, his eye caught a silvery gleam from a part of the earthen floor, where the surface had evidently been scratched away by some animal that had wandered in.

Looking down intently at the white, shining thing which had caught his attention, Chin perceived that it was one of the tiles that the bonze had made him bury in the earth, and when he picked it up, he discovered to his amazement that in some mysterious manner it had been transformed into silver! Digging further into the earth, he found that the same process had taken place with every tile that had been hidden away beneath the floor of this old and apparently useless building.

After some days occupied in transporting his treasure to a safe place in his dwelling-house, Chin realized by a rough calculation that he was now the possessor of several millions' worth of dollars, and that from being one of the poorest men in the town he had become a millionaire with enormous wealth at his command.

Thus did the Gods show their appreciation of the noble life of Mr. Meng, and of his loving sympathy for the poor and the distressed, by raising his fallen house to a higher pinnacle of prosperity than it had ever attained even during his lifetime.

The Mysterious Buddhist Robe

THE SHORT VISIT which the Emperor Li Shih-ming paid to the Land of Shadows had produced a profound impression on his mind. The pain and misery that men had to endure there, because of the evils they had committed in this life by their own voluntary action, had been brought before him in a most vivid manner. He had seen with his own eyes what he had always been unwilling to believe – namely, that wrong-doing is in every case followed by penalties, which have to be paid either in this world or the next.

He was now convinced that the doctrine of the sages on this point was true, for he had witnessed the horrors that criminals who had practically escaped punishment in this life had to suffer when they came under the jurisdiction of Yam-lo.

What distressed him most of all, however, was the grim thought which clung to him and refused to be silenced, that a large number of those in the Land of Shadows who were suffering from hunger and nakedness, were there as the result of his own cruelty and injustice, and that the cries of these men and women would reach to Heaven, and in due time bring down vengeance on himself.

With this fear of coming judgment there was at the same time mingled in his mind an element of compassion, for he was really sorry for the poor wretches whom he had seen in the "City of the Wronged Ones," and whose reproaches and threats of divine vengeance had entered into his very soul.

He therefore determined to institute a magnificent service for those spirits of the dead, who through the injustice of rulers, or the impotence of law, or private revenge, had lost their lives and were suffering untold hardships in the other world. He would have prayers said for their souls, that would flood their lives with plenty, and in course of time would open up the way for their being reborn into the world of men.

In this way he would propitiate those whom he had injured, and at the same time accumulate such an amount of merit for his benevolence, that the gods would make it easy for him when his time of reckoning came, and the accounts of his life were made up and balanced.

As this ceremony was to be one such as had never before been held at any period of Chinese history, he was anxious that the man who should be the leader and conductor of it should not be one of the men of indifferent lives who are usually found in the Buddhist temples and monasteries. He must be a man of sterling character, and of a life so pure and holy that no stain could be found upon it to detract from the saintly reputation he had acquired.

His Majesty accordingly sent out edicts to all the Viceroys in the Empire, commanding them to issue proclamations throughout the length and breadth of the country, telling the people of the great religious service which he was going to hold in the capital for the unhappy spirits in the Land of Shadows. In these edicts he ordered that search should be made for a priest of unblemished character – one who had proved his love for his fellow-men by great acts of sympathy for them. This man was to be invited to present himself before the Emperor, to take charge of the high and splendid service which had been designed by the Sovereign himself.

The tidings of this noble conception of Li Shih-ming spread with wonderful rapidity throughout his dominions, and even reached the far-off Western Heaven, where the mysterious beings who inhabit that happy land are ever on the alert to welcome any movement for the relief of human suffering. The Goddess of Mercy considered the occasion of such importance that she determined to take her share of responsibility for this distinguished service, by providing suitable vestments in which the leader of the great ceremony should be attired.

So it came to pass that while men's minds were excited about the proposed celebration for the dead, two priests suddenly appeared in the streets of the capital. No one had ever seen such old-fashioned and weird-looking specimens of manhood before. They were mean and insignificant in appearance, and the distinctive robes in which they were dressed were so travel-stained and unclean that it was evident they had not been washed for many a long day.

Men looked at them with astonishment as they passed along the road, for there was something so strange about them that they seemed to have come down from a far-off distant age, and to have suddenly burst into a civilization which had long out-grown the type from which they were descended. But by-and-by their curious old-world appearance was forgotten in amazement at the articles they carried with them. These were carefully wrapped in several folds of cloth to keep them from being soiled, though the two priests were perfectly willing to unfold the wrappers, and exhibit them to anyone who wished to examine them.

The precious things which were preserved with such jealous care were a hat and robe such as an abbot might wear on some great occasion when the Buddhist Church was using its most elaborate ceremonial to perform some function of unusual dignity and importance. There was also a crosier, beautifully wrought with precious stones, which was well worthy of being held in the hand of the highest functionary of the Church in any of its most sacred and solemn services. The remarkable thing about the hat and robe was their exquisite beauty. The richness of the embroidered work, the quaint designs, the harmonious blending of colours, and the subtle exhibition of the genius of the mind which had fashioned and perfected them, arrested the attention of even the lowest class in the crowds of people who gathered round the two priests to gaze upon the hat and robe, with awe and admiration in their faces.

Some instinct that flashed through the minds of the wondering spectators told them that these rare and fairy-like vestments were no ordinary products manufactured in any of the looms throughout the wide domains of the Empire. No human mind or hand had ever designed or worked out the various hues and shades of such marvellous colours as those which flashed before their eyes, and which possessed a delicacy and beauty such as none of the great artists of the past had ever been able to produce.

The priests from the various temples and monasteries of the capital soon heard the reports that spread through the city about the marvellous hat and robe, and flocked in large numbers to see these wonderful things, which the two curious-looking men were displaying to all who cared to gaze upon them.

"Do you wish to dispose of these things?" asked one of the city priests.

"If any one can pay the price at which alone we are prepared to sell, we shall be willing to part with them to him," was the reply.

"And what may the price be?" anxiously enquired the priest.

"The hat and robe will cost four thousand taels, and the crosier, which is of the rarest materials and manufacture, will be sold for the same amount."

At this a great laugh resounded through the crowd. In those days eight thousand taels was a huge fortune which only one or two of the wealthiest men of the State could have afforded to give. The boisterous mirth, however, which convulsed the crowd when they heard the fabulous sums asked by these strangers for their articles, soon became hushed when the latter proceeded to explain that the sums demanded were purposely prohibitive, in order that the sacred vestments should not fall into the hands of anyone who was unworthy to possess them.

"You are all aware," said one of the strangers, "that His Majesty the Emperor, recognizing that the service for the dead which he is about to hold is one of momentous importance, not only to the spirits suffering in the Land of Shadows, but also to the prosperity and welfare of the Chinese Empire, has already issued edicts to secure the presence of some saintly and godly priest, who shall be worthy to superintend the prayers that will be said for the men and women who are leading dreary lives in the land over which Yam-lo rules."

The story of these two men spread with great rapidity throughout the homes of all classes in the metropolis, and when it was understood that they had no desire to make money by the rare and beautiful articles which they readily displayed to the crowds that followed them whenever they appeared on the streets, they began to be surrounded with a kind of halo of romance. Men whispered to each other that these were no common denizens of the earth, but fairies in disguise, who had come as messengers from the Goddess of Mercy. The garments which they had with them were such as no mortal eyes had ever beheld, and were clearly intended for use only at some special ceremony of exceptional importance such as that which the Emperor was planning to have carried out.

At length rumours reached the palace of the strange scenes which were daily taking place in the streets of the capital, and Li Shih-ming sent officers to command the two strange priests to appear in his presence.

When they were brought before him, and he saw the wonderful robe embroidered in delicate hues and colours such as no workman had ever been known to design before, and grasped the crosier which sparkled and flashed with the brilliancy of the precious stones adorning it, the Emperor felt that the invisible gods had approved of his design for the solemn service for the dead and had prepared vestments for the High Priest which would be worthy of the exalted position he would occupy in the great ceremony.

"I hear that you want eight thousand taels for these articles," said the Emperor to the two men, who stood respectfully before him.

"We are not anxious, your Majesty," replied one of the strangers, "about the price. That is to us of very little importance. We have mentioned this large sum simply to prevent any man of unworthy mind from becoming their possessor.

"There is a peculiarity about that robe," he continued. "Any person of pure and upright heart who wears it will be preserved from every kind of disaster that can possibly assail him in this world. No sorrow can touch him, and the schemes of the most malignant of evil spirits will have no influence upon him. On the other hand, any man who is under the dominion of any base passion, if he dares to put on that mystic robe, will find himself involved in all kinds of calamities and sorrows, which will never leave him until he has put it off and laid it aside for ever.

"What we are really here for," he concluded, "is to endeavour to assist your Majesty in the discovery of a priest of noble and blameless life who will be worthy of presiding at the service you are about to hold for the unhappy spirits in the Land of Shadows. When we have found him we shall consider that our mission has been fulfilled, and we can then return and report the success we have achieved."

At this moment despatches from high officials throughout the country were presented to the Emperor, all recommending Sam-Chaong as the only man in the dominions who was fit to act as High Priest in the proposed great service. As Sam-Chaong happened to be then in the capital, he was sent for and, being approved of by His Majesty, was at once appointed to the sacred office, which he alone of the myriads of priests in China seemed to be worthy of occupying.

The two strangers, who had been noting the proceedings with anxious and watchful eyes, expressed their delight at the decision that had been arrived at. Stepping up to Sam-Chaong with the most reverential attitude, they presented him with the costly vestments which had excited the wonder and admiration of everyone who had seen them. Refusing to receive any remuneration for them, they bowed gracefully to the Emperor and retired. As the door of the audience-chamber closed upon them they vanished from human sight, and no trace of them could anywhere be found.

On the great day appointed by the Emperor, such a gathering was assembled as China in all the long history of the past had never before witnessed. Abbots from far-off distant monasteries were there, dressed in their finest vestments. Aged priests, with faces wrinkled by the passage of years, and young bonzes in their slate-coloured gowns, had travelled over the hills and mountains of the North to be present, and took up their positions in the great building. Men of note, too, who had made themselves famous by their devoted zeal for the ceremonies of the Buddhist Church and by their munificent gifts to the temples and shrines, had come with great retinues of their clansmen to add to the splendour and dignity of the occasion.

But the chief glory and attraction of the day to the assembled crowds was the Emperor, Li Shih-Ming. Never had he been seen in such pomp and circumstance as on this occasion. Close round him stood the princes of the royal family, the great officers of state and the members of the Cabinet in their rich and picturesque dresses. Immediately beyond were earls and dukes, viceroys of provinces and great captains and commanders, whose fame for mighty deeds of valour in the border warfare had spread through every city and town and hamlet in the Empire.

There were also present some of the most famous scholars of China, who, though not members of the Buddhist Church, yet felt that they could not refuse the invitation which the Emperor had extended to them.

In short, the very flower of the Empire was gathered together to carry out the benevolent purpose of rescuing the spirits of the dead from an intolerable state of misery which only the living had the power of alleviating.

The supreme moment, however, was when Sam-Chaong and more than a hundred of the priests most distinguished for learning and piety in the whole of the church, marched in solemn procession, chanting a litany, and took their places on the raised platform from which they were to conduct the service for the dead.

During the ceremony, much to his amazement, Li Shih-Ming saw the two men who had bestowed the fairy vestments on Sam-Chaong, standing one on each side of him; but though they joined heartily in the proceedings, he could not help noticing that a look of dissatisfaction and occasionally of something which seemed like contempt, rested like a shadow on their faces.

At the close of the service he commanded them to appear before him, and expressed his surprise at their conduct, when they explained that the discontent they had shown was entirely due to a feeling that the ritual which had been used that day was one entirely inadequate to the occasion. It was so wanting in dignity and loftiness of conception, they said, that though some ease might be brought to the spirits suffering in the Land of Shadows from the service which had been performed, it would utterly fail in the most important particular of all – namely, their deliverance from Hades, and their rebirth into the land of the living.

That this was also a matter which had given the Goddess of Mercy a vast amount of concern was soon made evident to the Emperor, for in the midst of this conversation there suddenly sounded, throughout the great hall in which the vast congregation still lingered, a voice saying: "Send Sam-Chaong to the Western Heaven to obtain the ritual which shall there be given him and which shall be worthy of being chanted by a nation."

This command from the invisible Goddess produced such an impression upon the Emperor that he made immediate preparations for the departure of Sam-Chaong on his momentous journey; and in a few days, supplied with everything necessary for so toilsome an undertaking, the famous priest started on what seemed a wild and visionary enterprise in pursuit of an object which anyone with less faith than himself would have deemed beyond the power of any human being to accomplish.

In order to afford him protection by the way and to act as his body-servants, the Emperor appointed two men to accompany Sam-Chaong on the long journey which he had undertaken at the command of the Goddess of Mercy. His Majesty would indeed have given him a whole regiment of soldiers, if he had been willing to accept them; but he absolutely refused to take more than just two men. He relied chiefly on the fairy robe which he had received, for that secured him from all danger from any foes whom he might meet on the road. Moreover, his mission, as he assured the Emperor, was one of peace and good-will, and it would not harmonize either with his own wishes or with those of the Goddess for him to be in a position to avenge his wrongs by the destruction of human life.

Before many days had elapsed Sam-Chaong began to realize the perilous nature of the service he had been called upon to perform. One afternoon, the travellers were jogging leisurely along in a wild and unsettled district, when suddenly two fierce-looking hobgoblins swooped down upon them, and almost before a word could be said had swallowed up both his poor followers. They were proceeding to do the same with Sam-Chaong when a fairy appeared upon the scene, and sent them flying with screams of terror to the caverns in the neighbouring hills where their homes seemed to be.

For a moment or two, Sam-Chaong was in extreme distress. He had just escaped an imminent peril; he was absolutely alone in an apparently uninhabited region; and the shadows of night were already darkening everything around. He was wondering where he would spend the night, when a man appeared upon the scene and invited him to come home with him to a mountain village on the spur of the hills which rose abruptly some distance away in front of them.

Although an entire stranger, who had never even heard Sam-Chaong's name, this man treated his guest right royally and gave him the very best that his house contained. Deeply impressed with the generous treatment he had received, Sam-Chaong determined that he would repay his host's generosity by performing an act which would be highly gratifying both to him and to all the members of his household.

Arranging a temporary altar in front of the image of the household god, who happened to be the Goddess of Mercy, he chanted the service for the dead before it with such acceptance that the spirit of the father of his host, who had been confined in the Land of Shadows, was released from that sunless land and was allowed to be reborn and take his place amongst the living. Moreover, that very night, the father appeared before his son in a vision, and told him that in consequence of the intercession of Sam-Chaong, whose reputation for piety was widely known in the dominions of Yam-lo, he had been allowed to leave that dismal country and had just been born into a family in the province of Shensi.

The son was rejoiced beyond measure at this wonderful news, and in order to show his gratitude for this generous action, he volunteered to accompany Sam-Chaong right to the very frontiers of China and to share with him any dangers and hardships he might have to endure by the way.

After many weary days of travelling this part of the journey was at last accomplished, and they were about to separate at the foot of a considerable hill which lay on the border line between China and the country of the barbarians beyond, when a loud and striking voice was heard exclaiming, "The priest has come! The priest has come!"

Sam-Chaong asked his companion the meaning of these words and to what priest they referred.

"There is a tradition in this region," replied the man, "that five hundred years ago, a certain fairy, inflamed with pride, dared to raise himself in rebellion against the Goddess of Mercy in the Western Heaven. To punish him she turned him into a monkey, and confined him in a cave near the top of this hill. There she condemned him to remain until Sam-Chaong should pass this way, when he could earn forgiveness by leading the priest into the presence of the Goddess who had commanded him to appear before her."

Ascending the hill in the direction of the spot from whence the cry "The priest has come!" kept ringing through the air, they came upon a natural cavern, the mouth of which was covered by a huge boulder, nicely poised in such a position that all exit from it was rendered an impossibility. Peering through the crevices at the side, they could distinctly see the figure of a monkey raising its face with an eager look of expectation in the direction of Sam-Chaong and his companion.

"Let me out," it cried, "and I will faithfully lead you to the Western Heaven, and never leave you until you find yourself standing in the presence of the Goddess of Mercy."

"But how am I to get you out?" asked Sam-Chaong. "The boulder that shuts you in is too large for human hands to move, and so, though I pity you in your misfortune and greatly desire your help to guide me along the unknown paths that lie before me, I fear that the task of setting you free must fall to other hands than mine."

"Deliverance is more easy than you imagine," replied the monkey. "Cast your eye along the edge of this vast rock, which the Goddess with but a simple touch of one of her fingers moved into its place five hundred years ago, as though it had been the airiest down that ever floated in a summer's breeze, and you will see something yellow standing out in marked contrast to the black lichen-covered stone. That is the sign-manual of the Goddess. She printed it on the rock when she condemned me centuries ago to be enclosed within this narrow cell until you should come and release me. Your hand alone can remove that mystic symbol and save me from the penalty of a living death."

Following the directions of the monkey, Sam-Chaong carefully scraped away the yellow-coloured tracings which he tried in vain to decipher; and when the last faint scrap had been finally removed, the huge, gigantic boulder silently moved aside with a gentle, easy motion and tilted itself to one side until the prisoner had emerged, when once more it slid gracefully back into its old position.

Under the guidance of the monkey, who had assumed the appearance of a strong and vigorous young athlete, Sam-Chaong proceeded on his journey – over mountains so high that they seemed to touch the very heavens, and through valleys which lay at their foot in perpetual shadow, except only at noon-tide when the sun stood directly overhead. Then again they travelled across deserts whose restless, storm-tossed, sandy billows left no traces of human footsteps, and where death seemed, like some cunning foe, to be lying in wait to destroy their lives.

It was here that Sam-Chaong realized the protecting care of the Goddess in providing such a valuable companion as the monkey proved himself to be. He might have been born in these sandy wastes, so familiar was he with their moods. There was something in the air, and in the colours of the sky at dawn and at sunset, that told him what was going to happen, and he could say almost to a certainty whether any storm was coming to turn these silent deserts into storm-tossed oceans of sand, which more ruthless even than the sea, would engulf all living things within their pitiless depths. He knew, moreover, where the hidden springs of water lay concealed beneath the glare and glitter that pained the eyes simply to look upon them; and without a solitary landmark in the boundless expanse, by unerring instinct, he would travel straight to the very spot where the spring bubbled up from the great fountains below.

Having crossed these howling wildernesses, where Sam-Chaong must have perished had he travelled alone, they came to a region inhabited by a pastoral people, but abounding in bands of robbers. Monkey was a daring fellow and was never afraid to meet any foe in fair fight; yet for the sake of Sam-Chaong, whose loving disposition had been insensibly taming his wild and fiery nature, he tried as far as possible to avoid a collision with any evil characters, whether men or spirits, who might be inclined to have a passage of arms with them.

One day they had passed over a great plain, where herds of sheep could be seen in all directions browsing under the watchful care of their shepherds, and they had come to the base of the foot-hills leading to a mountainous country beyond, when the profound meditation in which Sam-Chaong was usually absorbed was suddenly interrupted by a startled cry from Monkey.

Drawing close up to him, he said in a low voice, "Do you see those six men who are descending the hill and coming in our direction? They look like simple-minded farmers, and yet they are all devils who have put on the guise of men in order to be able to take us unawares. Their real object is to kill you, and thus frustrate the gracious purpose of the Goddess, who wishes to deliver the souls in the Land of Shadows from the torments they are enduring there.

"I know them well," he went on; "they are fierce and malignant spirits and very bold, for rarely have they ever been put to flight in any conflict in which they have been engaged. They little dream, however, who it is you have by your side. If they did they would come on more warily, for though I am single-handed they would be chary of coming to issues with me.

"But I am glad," he continued, "that they have not yet discovered who I am, for my soul has long desired just such a day as this, when in a battle that shall be worthy of the gods, my fame shall spread throughout the Western Heaven and even into the wide domains of the Land of Shadows."

With a cry of gladness, as though some wondrous good-fortune had befallen him, he bounded along the road to meet the coming foe, and in contemptuous tones challenged them to mortal combat.

No sooner did they discover who it was that dared to champion Sam-Chaong with such bold and haughty front, than with hideous yells and screams they rushed tumultuously upon him, hoping by a combined attack to confuse him and to make him fly in terror before them.

In this however they had reckoned without their host. With a daring quite as great as theirs, but with a skill far superior to that of the six infuriated demons, Monkey seized a javelin which came gleaming through the air just at the precise moment that he needed it, and hurled it at one of his opponents with such fatal effect that he lay sprawling on the ground, and with a cry that might have come from a lost spirit breathed his last.

And now the battle became a mighty one indeed. Arrows shot from invisible bows flew quicker than flashes of light against this single mighty fighter, but they glanced off a magic shield which fairy arts had interposed in front of him. Weapons such as mortal hands had never wielded in any of the great battles of the world were now brought into play; but never for a moment did Monkey lose his head. With marvellous intrepidity he warded them off, and striking back with one tremendous lunge, he laid another of the demons dead at his feet.

Dismay began to raise the coward in the minds of those who were left, and losing heart they turned to those subtle and cunning devices that had never before failed in their attacks on mankind. Their great endeavour now was to inveigle Monkey into a position where certain destruction would be sure to follow. Three-pronged spears were hurled against him with deadly precision, and had he not at that precise moment leaped high into the air no power on earth could have saved him.

It was at this tremendous crisis in the fight that Monkey won his greatest success. Leaping lightly to the ground whilst the backs of his foes were still turned towards him, he was able with the double-edged sword which he held in each of his hands to despatch three more of his enemies. The last remaining foe was so utterly cowed when he beheld his comrades lying dead upon the road that he took to flight, and soon all that was to be seen of him was a black speck slowly vanishing on the distant horizon.

Thus ended the great battle in which Monkey secured such a signal victory over the wild demons of the frozen North, and Sam-Chaong drew near to gaze upon the mangled bodies of the fierce spirits who but a moment ago were fighting so desperately for their very lives.

Now, Sam-Chaong was a man who naturally had the tenderest heart for every living thing; and so, as he looked, a cloud of sadness spread over his countenance and he sighed as he thought of the destruction of life which he had just witnessed. It was true that the demons had come with the one settled purpose of killing him, and there was no reason therefore why he should regret their death. But life to him was always precious, no matter in what form it might be enshrined. Life was the special gift of Heaven, and could not be wilfully destroyed without committing a crime against the gods.

So absorbed did Sam-Chaong become in this thought, and so sombre were the feelings filling his heart, that he entirely forgot to thank the hero by his side who had risked his life for him, and but for whose prowess he would have fallen a victim to the deadly hatred of these enemies of mankind. Feelings of resentment began to spring up in the mind of Monkey as he saw that Sam-Chaong seemed to feel more pity for the dead demons than gratitude for the heroic efforts which had saved him from a cruel death.

"Are you dissatisfied with the services I have rendered to you to-day?" he asked him abruptly.

"My heart is deeply moved by what you have done for me," replied Sam-Chaong. "My only regret is that you could not have delivered me without causing the death of these poor wretched demons, and thus depriving them of the gift of life, a thing as dear to them as it is to you or me."

Now Monkey, who was of a fierce and hasty temper, could not brook such meagre praise as this, and so in passionate and indignant language he declared that no longer would he be content to serve so craven a master, who, though beloved of the Goddess, was not a man for whom he would care to risk his life again.

With these words he vaulted into the air, and soared away into the distance, on and on through countless leagues of never-ending sky, until he came to the verge of a wide-spreading ocean. Plunging into this as though it had been the home in which he had always lived, he made his way by paths with which he seemed familiar, until he reached the palace of the Dragon Prince of the Sea, who received him with the utmost cordiality and gave him an invitation to remain with him as his guest as long as he pleased.

For some time he entertained himself with the many marvellous sights which are hidden away beneath the waters of the great ocean and which have a life and imagery of their own, stranger and more mysterious perhaps than those on which men are accustomed to look. But in time he became restless and dissatisfied with himself. The unpleasant thought crept slowly into his heart that in a moment of passion he had basely deserted Sam-Chaong and had left him helpless in a strange and unknown region; and worse still that he had been unfaithful to the trust which the Goddess had committed to him. He became uncomfortably conscious, too, that though he had fled to the depths of the ocean he could never get beyond the reach of her power, and that whenever she wished to imprison him in the mountain cavern where he had eaten out his heart for five hundred years, she could do so with one imperious word of command.

In this mood of repentance for his past errors, he happened to cast his eye upon a scroll which hung in one of the rooms of the palace. As he read the story on it his heart smote him, and from that moment he determined to hasten back to the post from which he had fled.

The words on the scroll were written in letters of gold and told how on a certain occasion in the history of the past the fairies determined to assist the fortunes of a young man named Chang-lung, who had gained their admiration because of the nobility of character which he had exhibited in his ordinary conduct in life. He belonged to an extremely poor family, and so without some such aid as they could give him, he could never attain to that eminence in the State which would enable him to be of service to his country. But he must first be tested to see whether he had the force of character necessary to bear the strain which greatness would put upon him. Accordingly one of the most experienced amongst their number was despatched to make the trial.

Assuming the guise of an old countryman in poor and worn-out clothing, the fairy sat down on a bridge over a stream close to the village where the favourite of the gods lived. By-and-by Chang-lung came walking briskly along. Just as he came up to the disguised fairy, the latter let one of his shoes drop into the water below. With an air of apparent distress, he begged the young man to wade into the stream and pick it up for him.

Cheerfully smiling, Chang-lung at once jumped into the water. In a moment he had returned with the shoe and was handing it to the old man, when the latter requested him to put it on his foot for him. This was asking him to do a most menial act, which most men would have scornfully resented; but Chang-lung, pitying the decrepit-looking old stranger, immediately knelt on the ground and carefully fastened the dripping shoe on to his foot.

Whilst he was in the act of doing this, the fairy, as if by accident, skilfully managed to let the other shoe slip from his foot over the edge of the bridge into the running stream. Apologizing for his stupidity, and excusing himself on the ground that he was an old man and that his fingers were not as nimble as they used to be, he begged Chang-lung to repeat his kindness and do him the favour of picking up the second shoe and restoring it to him.

With the same cheery manner, as though he were not being asked to perform a servile task, Chang-lung once more stepped into the shallow brook and bringing back the shoe, proceeded without any hesitation to repeat the process of putting it on the old man's foot.

The fairy was now perfectly satisfied. Thanking Chang-lung for his kindness, he presented him with a book, which he took out of one of the sleeves of his jacket, and urging him to study it with all diligence, vanished out of his sight. The meeting that day on the country bridge had an important influence on the destiny of Chang-lung, who in time rose to great eminence and finally became Prime Minister of China.

As Monkey studied the golden words before him, he contrasted his own conduct with that of Chang-lung, and, pricked to the heart by a consciousness of his wrong, he started at once, without even bidding farewell to the Dragon Prince of the Sea, to return to the service of Sam-Chaong.

He was just emerging from the ocean, when who should be standing waiting for him on the yellow sands of the shore but the Goddess of Mercy herself, who had come all the way from her distant home to warn him of the consequences that would happen to him were he ever again to fail in the duty she had assigned him of leading Sam-Chaong to the Western Heaven.

Terrified beyond measure at the awful doom which threatened him, and at the same time truly repentant for the wrong he had committed, Monkey bounded up far above the highest mountains which rear their peaks to the sky, and fled with incredible speed until he stood once more by the side of Sam-Chaong.

No reproof fell from the latter's lips as the truant returned to his post. A tender gracious smile was the only sign of displeasure that he evinced.

"I am truly glad to have you come back to me," he said, "for I was lost without your guidance in this unknown world in which I am travelling. I may tell you, however, that since you left me the Goddess appeared to me and comforted me with the assurance that you would ere long resume your duties and be my friend, as you have so nobly been in the past. She was very distressed at my forlorn condition and was so determined that nothing of the kind should happen again in the future, that she graciously presented me with a mystic cap wrought and embroidered by the fairy hands of the maidens in her own palace.

"'Guard this well,' she said, 'and treasure it as your very life, for it will secure you the services of one who for five hundred years was kept in confinement in order that he might be ready to escort you on the way to the Western Heaven. He is the one man who has the daring and the courage to meet the foes who will endeavour to destroy you on your journey, but he is as full of passion as the storm when it is blowing in its fury. Should he ever desert you again, you have but to place this cap on your head, and he will be wrung with such awful and intolerable agonies that though he were a thousand miles away he would hurry back with all the speed he could command to have you take it off again, so that he might be relieved from the fearful pains racking his body.'"

After numerous adventures too long to relate, Sam-Chaong reached the borders of an immense lake, many miles in extent, spanned by a bridge of only a single foot in width. With fear and trembling, as men tremble on the brink of eternity, and often with terror in his eyes and a quivering in his heart as he looked at the narrow foothold on which he was treading, he finally crossed in safety, when he found to his astonishment that the pulsations of a new life had already begun to beat strongly within him. Beyond a narrow strip of land, which bounded the great expanse of water over which he had just passed, was a wide flowing river, and on its bank was a boat with a ferryman in it ready to row him over.

When they had reached the middle of the stream, Sam-Chaong saw a man struggling in the water as if for dear life. Moved with pity he urged upon the boatman to go to his rescue and deliver him from drowning. He was sternly told, however, to keep silence. "The figure you see there," said the boatman, "is yourself – or rather, it is but the shell of your old self, in which you worked out your redemption in the world beyond, and which you could never use in the new life upon which you have entered."

On the opposite bank of the river stood the Goddess of Mercy, who with smiling face welcomed him into the ranks of the fairies.

Since then, it is believed by those whose vision reaches further than the grey and common scenes of earthly life, Sam-Chaong has frequently appeared on earth, in various disguises, when in some great emergency more than human power was required to deliver men from destruction. There is one thing certain at least – these gifted people declare – and that is that in the guise of a priest Sam-Chaong did once more revisit this world and delivered to the Buddhist Church the new ritual which the Goddess of Mercy had prepared for it, and which is used to-day in its services throughout the East.

The Vengeance Of The Goddess

IN A CERTAIN TEMPLE in the northern part of the Empire, there once lived a famous priest named Hien-Chung, whose reputation had spread far and wide, not merely for the sanctity of his life, but also for the supernatural powers which he was known to possess, and which he had exhibited on several remarkable occasions. Men would have marvelled less about him had they known that the man dressed in the long slate-coloured robe, with shaven head, and saintly-looking face, over which no one had ever seen a smile flicker, was in reality a pilgrim on his way to the Western Heaven, which he hoped to reach in time, and to become a fairy there.

One night Hien-Chung lay asleep in a room opening out of the main hall in which the great image of the Goddess of Mercy, with her benevolent, gracious face, sat enshrined amidst the darkness that lay thickly over the temple. All at once, there stood before him a most striking and stately-looking figure. The man had a royal look about him, as though he had been accustomed to rule. On his head there was a crown, and his dress was such as no mere subject would ever be allowed to wear.

Hien-Chung gazed at him in wonder, and was at first inclined to believe that he was some evil spirit who had assumed this clever disguise in order to deceive him. As this thought flashed through his mind, the man began to weep. It was pitiable indeed to see this kingly person affected with such oppressive grief that the tears streamed down his cheeks, and with the tenderness that was distinctive of him Hien-Chung expressed his deep sympathy for a sorrow so profound.

"Three years ago," said his visitor, "I was the ruler of this 'Kingdom of the Black Flower'. I was indeed the founder of my dynasty, for I carved my own fortune with my sword, and made this little state into a kingdom. For a long time I was very happy, and my people were most devoted in their allegiance to me. I little dreamed of the sorrows that were coming on me, and the disasters which awaited me in the near future.

"Five years ago my kingdom was visited with a very severe drought. The rains ceased to fall; the streams which used to fall down the mountain-sides and irrigate the plains dried up; and the wells lost the fountains which used to fill them with water. Everywhere the crops failed, and the green herbage on which the cattle browsed was slowly blasted by the burning rays of the sun.

"The common people suffered in their homes from want of food, and many of the very poorest actually died of starvation. This was a source of great sorrow to me, and every day my prayers went up to Heaven, that it would send down rain upon the dried-up land and so deliver my people from death. I knew that this calamity had fallen on my kingdom because of some wrong that I had done, and so my heart was torn with remorse.

"One day while my mind was full of anxiety, a man suddenly appeared at my palace and begged my ministers to be allowed to have an audience with me. He said that it was of the utmost importance that he should see me, for he had come to propose a plan for the deliverance of my country.

"I gave orders that he should instantly be brought into my presence, when I asked him if he had the power to cause the rain to descend upon the parched land.

"'Yes,' he replied, 'I have, and if you will step with me now to the front of your palace I will prove to you that I have the ability to do this, and even more.'

"Striding out to a balcony which overlooked the capital, and from which one could catch a view of the hills in the distance, the stranger lifted up his right hand towards the heavens and uttered certain words which I was unable to understand.

"Instantly, and as if by magic, a subtle change crept through the atmosphere. The sky became darkened, and dense masses of clouds rolled up and blotted out the sun. The thunder began to mutter, and vivid flashes of lightning darted from one end of the heavens to the other, and before an hour had elapsed the rain was descending in torrents all over the land, and the great drought was at an end.

"My gratitude to this mysterious stranger for the great deliverance he had wrought for my kingdom was so great that there was no favour which I was not willing to bestow upon him. I gave him rooms in the palace, and treated him as though he were my equal. I had the truest and the tenderest affection for him, and he seemed to be equally devoted to me.

"One morning we were walking hand in hand in the royal gardens. The peach blossoms were just out, and we were enjoying their perfume and wandering up and down amongst the trees which sent forth such exquisite fragrance.

"As we sauntered on, we came by-and-by upon a well which was hidden from sight by a cluster of oleander trees. We stayed for a moment to peer down its depths and to catch a sight of the dark waters lying deep within it. Whilst I was gazing down, my friend gave me a sudden push and I was precipitated head first into the water at the bottom. The moment I disappeared, he took a broad slab of stone and completely covered the mouth of the well. Over it he spread a thick layer of earth, and in this he planted a banana root, which, under the influence of the magic powers he possessed, in the course of a few hours had developed into a full-grown tree. I have lain dead in the well now for three years, and during all that time no one has arisen to avenge my wrong or to bring me deliverance."

"But have your ministers of State made no efforts during all these three years to discover their lost king?" asked Hien-Chung. "And what about your wife and family? Have they tamely submitted to have you disappear without raising an outcry that would resound throughout the whole kingdom? It seems to me inexplicable that a king should vanish from his palace and that no hue and cry should be raised throughout the length and breadth of the land until the mystery should be solved and his cruel murder fully avenged."

"It is here," replied the spirit of the dead king, "that my enemy has shown his greatest cunning. The reason why men never suspect that any treason has been committed is because by his enchantments he has transformed his own appearance so as to become the exact counterpart of myself. The man who called down the rain and saved my country from drought and famine has simply disappeared, so men think, and I the King still rule as of old in my kingdom. Not the slightest suspicion as to the true state of things has ever entered the brain of anyone in the nation, and so the usurper is absolutely safe in the position he occupies to-day."

"But have you never appealed to Yam-lo, the ruler of the Land of Shadows?", asked Hien-Chung. "He is the great redresser of the wrongs and crimes of earth, and now that you are a spirit and immediately within his jurisdiction, you should lay your complaint before him and pray him to avenge the sufferings you have been called upon to endure."

"You do not understand," the spirit hastily replied. "The one who has wrought such ruin in my life is an evil spirit. He has nothing in common with men, but has been let loose from the region where evil spirits are confined to punish me for some wrong that I have committed in the past. He therefore knows the ways of the infernal regions, and is hand in glove with the rulers there, and even with Yam-lo himself. He is, moreover, on the most friendly terms with the tutelary God of my capital, and so no complaint of mine would ever be listened to for a moment by any of the powers who rule in the land of the dead.

"There is another very strong reason, too, why any appeal that I might make for justice would be disregarded. My soul has not yet been loosed from my body, but is still confined within it in the well. The courts of the Underworld would never recognize me, because I still belong to this life, over which they have no control.

"Only to-day," he continued, "a friendly spirit whispered in my ear that my confinement in the well was drawing to a close, and that the three years I had been adjudged to stay there would soon be up. He strongly advised me to apply to you, for you are endowed, he said, with powers superior to those possessed by my enemy, and if you are only pleased to exercise them I shall speedily be delivered from his evil influence."

Now the Goddess of Mercy had sent Hien-Chung a number of familiar spirits to be a protection to him in time of need. Next morning, accordingly, he summoned the cleverest of these, whose name was Hing, in order to consult with him as to how the king might be delivered from the bondage in which he had been held for the three years.

"The first thing we have to do," said Hing, "is to get the heir to the Throne on our side. He has often been suspicious at certain things in the conduct of his supposed father, one of which is that for three years he has never been allowed to see his mother. All that is needed now is to get some tangible evidence to convince him that there is some mystery in the palace, and we shall gain him as our ally.

"I have been fortunate," he continued, "in obtaining one thing which we shall find very useful in inducing the Prince to listen to what we have to say to him about his father. You may not know it, but about the time when the King was thrown into the well, the seal of the kingdom mysteriously disappeared and a new one had to be cut.

"Knowing that you were going to summon me to discuss this case, I went down into the well at dawn this morning, and found the missing seal on the body of the King. Here it is, and now we must lay our plans to work on the mind of the son for the deliverance of the father. Tomorrow I hear that the Prince is going out hunting on the neighbouring hills. In one of the valleys there is a temple to the Goddess of Mercy, and if you will take this seal and await his coming there, I promise you that I will find means to entice him to the shrine."

Next morning the heir to the Throne of the "Kingdom of the Black Flower" set out with a noisy retinue to have a day's hunting on the well-wooded hills overlooking the capital. They had scarcely reached the hunting grounds when great excitement was caused by the sudden appearance of a remarkable-looking hare. It was decidedly larger than an ordinary hare, but the curious feature about it was its colour, which was as white as the driven snow.

No sooner had the hounds caught sight of it, than with loud barkings and bayings they dashed madly in pursuit. The hare, however, did not seem to show any terror, but with graceful bounds that carried it rapidly over the ground, it easily out-distanced the fleetest of its pursuers. It appeared, indeed, as though it were thoroughly enjoying the facility with which it could outrun the dogs, while the latter grew more and more excited as they always saw the quarry before them and yet could never get near enough to lay hold upon it.

Another extraordinary thing was that this hare did not seem anxious to escape. It took no advantage of undergrowth or of clumps of trees to hide the direction in which it was going. It managed also to keep constantly in view of the whole field; and when it had to make sudden turns in the natural windings of the road which led to a valley in the distance, where there stood a famous temple, it hesitated for a moment and allowed the baying hounds to come perilously near, before it darted off with the speed of lightning and left the dogs far behind it.

Little did the hunters dream that the beautiful animal which was giving them such an exciting chase was none other than the fairy Hing, who had assumed this disguise in order to bring the Prince to the lonely temple in the secluded valley, where, beyond the possibility of being spied upon by his father's murderer, the story of treachery could be told, and means be devised for his restoration to the throne.

Having arrived close to the temple, the mysterious hare vanished as suddenly as it had appeared, and not a trace was left to enable the dogs, which careered wildly round and round, to pick up the scent.

The Prince, who was a devoted disciple of the Goddess of Mercy, now dismounted and entered the temple, where he proceeded to burn incense before her shrine and in muttered tones to beseech her to send down blessings upon him.

After a time, he became considerably surprised to find that the presiding priest of the temple, instead of coming forward to attend upon him and to show him the courtesies due to his high position, remained standing in a corner where the shadows were darkest, his eyes cast upon the ground and with a most serious look overspreading his countenance.

Accordingly, when he had finished his devotions to the Goddess, the Prince approached the priest, and asked him in a kindly manner if anything was distressing him.

"Yes," replied Hien-Chung, "there is, and it is a subject which materially affects your Royal Highness. If you will step for a moment into my private room, I shall endeavour to explain to you the matter which has filled my mind with the greatest possible anxiety."

When they entered the abbot's room, Hien-Chung handed the Prince a small box and asked him to open it and examine the article it contained.

Great was the Prince's amazement when he took it out and cast a hurried glance over it. A look of excitement passed over his face and he cried out, "Why, this is the great seal of the kingdom which was lost three years ago, and of which no trace could ever be found! May I ask how it came into your possession and what reason you can give for not having restored it to the King, who has long wished to discover it?"

"The answer to that is a long one, your Highness, and to satisfy you, I must go somewhat into detail."

Hien-Chung then told the Prince of the midnight visit his father had made him, and the tragic story of his murder by the man who was now posing as the King, and of his appeal to deliver him from the sorrows of the well in which he had been confined for three years.

"With regard to the finding of the seal," he continued, "my servant Hing, who is present, will describe how by the supernatural powers with which he is endowed, he descended the well only this very morning and discovered it on the body of your father."

"We have this absolute proof," he said, "that the vision I saw only two nights ago was not some imagination of the brain, but that it was really the King who appealed to me to deliver him from the power of an enemy who seems bent upon his destruction.

"We must act, and act promptly," he went on, "for the man who is pretending to be the ruler of your kingdom is a person of unlimited ability, and as soon as he gets to know that his secret has been divulged, he will put into operation every art he possesses to frustrate our purpose.

"What I propose is that your Highness should send back the greater part of your retinue to the palace, with an intimation to the effect that you are going to spend the night here in a special service to the Goddess, whose birthday it fortunately happens to be to-day. After night has fallen upon the city, Hing shall descend into the well and bring the body of your father here. You will then have all the proof you need of the truth of the matter, and we can devise plans as to our future action."

A little after midnight, Hing having faithfully carried out the commission entrusted to him by Hien-Chung, arrived with the body of the King, which was laid with due ceremony and respect in one of the inner rooms of the temple. With his marvellous wonder-working powers and with the aid of invisible forces which he had been able to summon to his assistance, he had succeeded in transporting it from the wretched place where it had lain so long to the friendly temple of the Goddess of Mercy.

The Prince was deeply moved by the sight of his father's body. Fortunately it had suffered no change since the day when it was thrown to the bottom of the well. Not a sign of decay could be seen upon the King's noble features. It seemed as though he had but fallen asleep, and presently would wake up and talk to them as he used to do. The fact that in some mysterious way the soul had not been separated from the body accounted for its remarkable preservation. Nevertheless to all appearance the King was dead, and the great question now was how he could be brought back to life, so that he might be restored to his family and his kingdom.

"The time has come," said Hien-Chung, "when heroic measures will have to be used if the King is ever to live again. Two nights ago he made a passionate and urgent request to me to save him, for one of the gods informed him that I was the only man who could do so. So far, we have got him out of the grip of the demon that compassed his death, and now it lies with me to provide some antidote which shall bring back the vital forces and make him a living man once more.

"I have never had to do with such a serious case as this before, but I have obtained from the Patriarch of the Taoist Church a small vial of the Elixir of Life, which has the marvellous property of prolonging the existence of whoever drinks it. We shall try it on the King and, as there is no sign of vital decay, let us hope that it will be effective in restoring him to life."

Turning to a desk that was kept locked, he brought out a small black earthenware bottle, from which he dropped a single drop of liquid on to the lips of the prostrate figure. In a few seconds a kind of rosy flush spread over the King's features. Another drop, and a look of life flashed over the pallid face. Still another, and after a short interval the eyes opened and looked with intelligence upon the group surrounding his couch. Still one more, and the King arose and asked how long he had been asleep, and how it came about that he was in this small room instead of being in his own palace.

He was soon restored to his family and to his position in the State, for the usurper after one or two feeble attempts to retain his power ignominiously fled from the country.

A short time after, Hien-Chung had a private interview with the King. "I am anxious," he said, "that your Majesty should understand the reason why such a calamity came into your life.

"Some years ago without any just reason you put to death a Buddhist priest. You never showed any repentance for the great wrong you had done, and so the Goddess sent a severe drought upon your Kingdom. You still remained unrepentant, and then she sent one of her Ministers to afflict you, depriving you of your home and your royal power. The man who pushed you down the well was but carrying out the instructions he had received from the Goddess. Your stay down the well for three years was part of the punishment she had decreed for your offence, and when the time was up, I was given the authority to release you.

"Kings as well as their subjects are under the great law of righteousness, and if they violate it they must suffer like other men. I would warn your Majesty that unless you show some evidence that you have repented for taking away a man's life unjustly, other sorrows will most certainly fall upon you in the future."

The Wonderful Man

THERE IS A CERTAIN prefectural city in the south of China, which has earned a reputation distinguishing it from all such towns throughout the Empire.

In outward appearance this city is very much like every other of similar size. The streets are narrow, and the houses are crowded close up to each other. Every foot of land has been utilized, and no room has been left for sanitation, or for parks and open spaces, where the people may breathe the pure air of heaven. These things are modern inventions of the West and have never yet touched the thought or the life of the East, where sullen heat, fetid atmosphere, and stifling surroundings are the natural inheritance of the men and women who throng the cities and crowd and elbow each other in the great battle of life.

There was one thing, however, for which this city was deservedly celebrated. It had a great reputation for learning, and was famous as the abode of scholars.

In the main thoroughfares, where men with a dexterity begotten of long experience just managed to evade jostling each other, the long-gowned students were conspicuous by their numbers. Their pale intellectual faces, and their gleaming black eyes burning with hidden fires, marked them out distinctly from the farmers and artisans and coolies, with their coarser, heavier features, who moved along side by side with them. And down the narrow alley-ways, where fetid smells and impure airs floated the live-long day, one's ear would catch the shrill tones of more youthful students, who in unhealthy rooms were mastering aloud the famous classics of China, in order that in time they might compete in the triennial examinations for the prizes offered by the Empire to its scholars.

The ambition for learning was in the air, and a belated wayfarer, wandering down the labyrinth of streets in the early hours of the morning, would hear the solemn stillness broken into by the voices of the students, as in their highest tones they repeated the writings of the great sages.

The town was therefore dear to the God of Literature, who has ever been ready to champion the cause of his scholars, whenever anyone has dared to lay a hand upon their privileges.

A legend in which there is widespread belief declares that on one occasion, when the scholars of five counties had assembled at a triennial examination, the Imperial Examiner, who for some reason or other had conceived a spite against the competitors from this particular city, determined that not one of them should pass.

As their essays came into his hands, he carefully laid them in a pile close beside him on the table. The God of Literature, who was sitting in his shrine at the far end of the room, became indignant at the insult that was about to be put on his favourites, and breathed some classic phrases under his breath, to the effect that he would never allow such a wrong to be perpetrated as long as he had power to prevent it.

The last paper had been examined and laid carefully on the top of the others, when, as if by a flash of lightning, the examiner was seized with a stroke of paralysis, and fell to the ground unconscious. That was the answer of the God to his evil schemes.

The greatest dismay was exhibited by the under-officials of the examination. Thousands of students were waiting outside for the list to be issued of those who had passed, but the only man who had the power to prepare this list lay helpless in the grip of paralysis. Yet something must be done, and that speedily. As they looked over the manuscripts lying on the table, a little pile was discovered, evidently placed there by the examiner for some purpose of his own. One of the officials at once suggested that these must belong to the men who had gained their degrees. The idea was enthusiastically accepted as the correct one. There was no need for further delay. The names of the writers were hurriedly copied out and pasted up on the board in front of the Examination Hall.

To the amazement of all the assembled scholars, the only men who had got their degrees were those belonging to the city favoured of the God. This was the God's second answer to the examiner, who would unjustly have excluded them from the honours of the day.

There was another thing for which the people of this city were noted, and that was the pleasure taken by the leaders of society in recognizing those who displayed conspicuous civic virtues.

Outside one of the four gates, and well beyond the streets and houses which had grown up as an overflow from the great city, there was a considerable open space, through the middle of which the main road meandered on its way to the countless towns and villages in the regions beyond, and finally to the far-off capital, Peking, thousands of miles away in the extreme north. It was a busy, much-frequented road, and the tread of human feet and the sound of the voices of passing travellers never ceased from early dawn until darkness had fallen and driven men to the shelter of the city.

The striking feature about the long stretch of uninhabited land which bordered one side of this road was a magnificent series of memorial arches built in close succession to each other for a considerable distance. They were composed of granite slabs, some very plain in their design, whilst others were highly artistic, and had evidently been produced by men who were masters of their craft. The general plan and execution were the same in all, but the ornamentation in some was most elaborate, and filled one with pleasure and delight to look at it.

Every one of these arches had been erected to commemorate some person who had already passed away, but whose virtues in life had been so conspicuous that the community had determined that they should not be forgotten, but that a record of them should be handed down to posterity, not only to keep their memory fragrant, but also to provide beautiful examples for succeeding generations.

Amongst the virtues recorded on these granite slabs, the most common was that of filial piety. A son had distinguished himself by his devotion to his parents, and had sacrificed his very life in faithful service to them. In undying words the story was carved into the stone; and the two mystic characters, "Holy Will," in the centre of the middle arch showed that the Emperor had given his permission for the erection of this memorial to a virtue so admired by the whole Chinese nation.

Other arches, almost as numerous as those raised to dutiful sons, were those setting forth the virtues of widows who had refused to marry again after their husbands had died.

In one case a widow had been left in great straits, and had been compelled to struggle with poverty and privations of every kind. All these she might have avoided had she been willing to listen to the offers of marriage that were made to her. Nothing, however, could make her forget the allegiance which she believed she still owed to the man who had first won her heart, or induce her to neglect her duty to the children of her marriage. She could never consent to let them become the property of another man, who might despise and ill-treat them, and who at any rate would never have for them the kind of affection which would lead him to make the sacrifices necessary to help them towards gaining a better position in life. Accordingly, she struggled on, enduring the greatest sufferings in order to provide for the needs of her sons as they gradually grew up; and eventually, owing to the hardships which she had borne so heroically, they all passed with honour through their examinations into the service of the Emperor.

On her death her story was forwarded to the capital, and his Majesty was so much moved by it that he gave his sanction for an arch to be erected to her memory, in order that for ages to come the crowds passing daily under its shadow might read the record of her self-sacrifice, and might learn how an admiring community had built this imperishable memorial of her wifely and motherly virtues.

But of all the numerous arches spanning the road there was one which attracted more attention than any other in the long line.

This was not because the virtues of the person, in whose honour it was raised, were so conspicuous, or because they so far outrivalled those recorded on the other arches, that men were constrained to stop and ponder over a life so remarkable for its heroism.

On the contrary, no virtues of any kind were mentioned. On the central arch, in large letters cut into the granite stone, were the words: "The Wonderful Man"; and that was all. Not a word of explanation was given as to who this wonderful man was; not a hint as to the special story of his life.

Scholars passing along the dusty road would catch a sight of this brief but cryptic inscription, and would at once be set wondering what a phrase so unclassical and so mysterious could possibly mean. They would walk round to the other side of the arch, to see if any explanation were afforded there. But no, the inscription was simply repeated in the same cold and veiled language; and so they would pass on, no wiser than before.

Farmers, with produce of their own growing suspended from their shoulders on stout bamboo poles, would come along at their accustomed trot, and would gaze at these words, "The wonderful man," with a curious look on their faces. They were not profound scholars, for on account of their poverty they had been compelled to leave school before they had mastered the ancient characters which make up the Chinese written language; but they knew enough to read such simple words as these. But what did the words really mean? They would laugh and joke with each other about them as they sped on their way, and many a witty suggestion would be merrily thrown out as a solution of the mystery.

The story that really lay behind this strange inscription was after all a most romantic and a most pathetic one.

Many years before, in a village beyond the hills skirting the plain on which the city was built, there lived a family of three; that is to say, a man and his wife and their little son. It was a supremely happy home. The husband and wife were devotedly attached to each other, and the ambition of every family amongst the four hundred millions of China had been granted them; for they had a son, who in the future would perpetuate the father's name, and present at his grave sacrificial offerings which would reach him in the Land of Shadows and keep him from starvation there.

The one great sorrow of the home was its poverty. There was no question but that they were exceedingly poor; and every morning, as the dawn broke upon them, they felt that they stood close up to the line beyond which lay hunger and even starvation.

But China is full of homes in such a situation. In this respect, indeed, the country is a land of heroes and heroines, for with vast masses of the people it is a daily struggle for food. Millions scattered throughout the Empire never or very rarely get enough to eat, and yet with splendid and pathetic patience they set themselves to suffer and to die, sternly and uncomplainingly, as becomes an Imperial race such as the Chinese are.

All that this particular family had to live upon were a few diminutive fields, which under the most favourable circumstances could produce barely enough sweet potatoes to keep body and soul together, and a scanty supply of vegetables with which to season them. If the rains failed and the potato vines were parched and blasted in their ridges by the great red-hot sun, then the husband had to look out for some other means of earning enough money to provide the bare necessaries of life for his little home.

Sometimes he would engage himself as a porter to carry the produce of the larger farmers to the great market-town which lay ten miles distant; but even then he could earn only just enough to provide the most meagre fare for his family for a week or two at the very most.

At other times he would secure better-paid employment by carrying a sedan-chair to some distant place, which would take him from home for several days at a time. He would return, it is true, with some goodly strings of cash, which would make his wife's eyes gleam with satisfaction at the possibilities they contained for at least another month of better food for them all; but it was dearly earned money. The man had not been trained as a chairbearer, and so had not learned the knack of manipulating the cross-bars, which rested on his shoulders, in such a way as to make the heavy burden less distressing to him. The result was that every time he returned from one of these expeditions, he was so seriously knocked up that for several days he had to lie in bed and refrain from all work.

Time went on, and the severe strain of his labour, and the poor quality of the food upon which he had to live, and the constant wear and tear of a constitution that never had been very strong, told upon the poor, overworked father. Gradually he became a confirmed invalid, so that he could not perform even the lightest work on his little farm. The shadows of coming misfortune grew darker and blacker every day. Hope began to abandon the hearts of husband and wife, and the sound of the footsteps of cruel Fate could almost be heard, as they drew nearer and nearer. Still these two heroic souls uttered no complaints, and there were no signs of heartbreak, except occasionally when the wife's eyes overflowed with tears, which she brushed hastily away lest her husband should see them and be distressed.

One night the storm was blowing a north-east gale outside, and the wind howled and moaned in such weird and doleful tones around the cottage, that it seemed as though some troubled spirit had been let loose to wail out a solemn requiem over a departing soul.

The Chinese believe that the air is filled with demons who have a mortal hatred of human beings, and who are ever on the watch to compass their destruction. These evil spirits gather round when disaster is about to fall on a home. They stand with invisible forms and peer into the darkened room, where someone lies dying, and they breathe out their delight in unholy sounds that strike terror into the hearts of the watchers.

In her anxiety about her husband the wife had not been able to sleep. Her heart throbbed with an infinite pain, and suppressed sobs now and again showed the anguish of her spirit. She began to realize, during this dreadful night, that her husband was exceedingly ill and might very probably die. The storm which raged outside, and the furious blasts and the uncanny sounds in the air, had terrified her and made her nervous.

It was true that only that day she had gone to the nearest temple, and had been assured by the god that her husband was going to recover; but he had been growing steadily weaker and weaker, and now the tempest had broken her courage and filled her with an unspeakable dread. What a tumult there was outside! Whose were the hideous voices that shrieked round the building, and whose were the hands that tore at the doors and windows until they shook and rattled under their grasp?

At last she could stand it no longer. She felt she must get up and see whether the mad and furious spirits, who had evidently gathered in force around the dwelling, were going to prove to be true prophets of evil.

The room was in darkness, so she lit the tiny wick that lay in a saucer of oil, and, peering into her husband's face, she looked with all her heart in her eyes into his sunken features. He seemed to know her, for a wan and wintry smile flickered round his lips and died out in a moment. She gazed at him with an almost breaking heart, for her instinct told her that the greyness of his face and the sudden paling of his lips were the forerunners of death. A long-drawn sigh, and a sob or two, and the one who was the dearest to her in all the world had left her forever.

After the funeral, which swallowed up everything she possessed, even to the very fields, which she had been compelled to sell in order to meet the expenses, the widow was left almost destitute. She was a woman, however, with a very strong character, and she realized the absolute necessity of making up her mind at once as to her course of action. That she should marry again seemed to everyone the only course open to her; but this she determined she would never do. The memory of her dead husband was too precious to her, and besides it was her duty to rear up her little son to manhood, so that he might take his place amongst the scholars and thinkers of the Empire.

Soon a scheme, as original as it was daring, sprang up within her brain. No one must ever learn what it was. It must be the secret of her life, which she should bury within her own bosom, and which not even her own son should ever know, if she could possibly help it.

Having sold her cottage, she moved away to a quiet suburb outside the great city which was so renowned for learning. Then she discarded her woman's attire and dressed herself as a man. In no other way could she support herself and her child, for in China a woman is always under great disadvantages in the way of earning her own living. As a man, she knew that she could hold her own in any of the unskilled employments which she was capable of taking up. And so it turned out. She could carry as heavy a load as any of the men with whom she had to compete, and she was so civil and so well-behaved and so free from the use of profane language, that employers unaware of her sex used to pick her out in preference to others who offered themselves.

The years went by, and her little son was growing up to be a fine young man. The mother had determined that he should be a scholar. This was the one ambition of her life, and for this she slaved and toiled and denied herself almost the very necessaries of life.

Twenty years had passed since that stormy night. In the neighbouring city, the triennial examinations were just finished and the excitement was intense amongst the thousands of students who gathered round the Examination Hall to learn the names of the successful candidates.

By-and-by the son came home with a light step and with his eyes flashing with delight. His excitement was so great that he could hardly utter distinctly the words which rushed from his lips.

"Father," he cried, "the great desire of your heart and of mine has been granted to us to-day. I have passed, and that too with honours, for my name stands at the very top of the list of those who have been adjudged successful. And now, my beloved father, there will be no more hard work for you. My name will soon be flashed throughout the Province and will be posted in every Confucian guild, and scholars everywhere will speak with admiration of the great success I have won. My fortune has indeed been made, and it is due entirely to your self-denial, and to the sufferings and hardships you have consented to endure, during the long years of the past, that I have at length come into my kingdom, and that I need not be a labouring man, earning but a few cash a day, as you, my dear father, have been willing to do for the love of me."

All the time her son was talking, the mother's face shone with delight, for the hopes and wishes of a lifetime had come to her with a rush that almost overpowered her.

"Ah! if only my husband could have been with us now," she thought, "to share with us the supreme joy of this moment!" And her memory wandered back to that dreadful night, the blackest she had ever known in her life; and the roar of the storm which had thundered round the poor little shanty of a home and the ominous wailings of the spirits of evil which had struck a chill into her very blood, once more sounded in her ears as though the tragedy had happened only the night before.

In the fulness of the new joy which had suddenly transformed his life, the son went on to talk of the plans that he had been mapping out for the future. There would be no lack of money any more, he said, for employment would open up to him in all directions. He would be invited by the wealthy men of the city to teach their sons. He was a notable scholar now, and men of means would compete with each other to secure his services.

Before long too, he would be certain to obtain a government appointment which would bring riches into the home; and then his father would be a gentleman, and would live with him in his yamen, and be treated by all with honour and respect. And so with glowing face and glistening eyes, as the visions of the future rose up before him, the boy talked on with the enthusiasm of youth, whilst his mother gazed at him with admiring eyes.

At last he suddenly stopped. The laughter died out of his countenance, and with a grave and solemn face he exclaimed, "Father, I want you to tell me where my mother is buried. I must arrange to go to her grave and make the proper offerings to her spirit, and tell her how her son has prospered, and how grateful he is to her. That is my duty as a filial son, and I must not delay in performing it."

The young fellow did not notice the deadly pallor that spread over his parent's face as he uttered these words. He did not know that they produced a feeling of despair in the heart of his mother, for she now felt that she had come to the end of her life. She was a true and noble woman, with a high ideal of what a woman's life ought to be, and she dared not face the opinion of the world when it was discovered that she had lived as a man, and for many years had freely mingled with men. She had violated the laws of etiquette which regulate the conduct of women in every grade of society, and now the only thing left for her to do was to die.

Next morning, at sunrise, when the son entered his father's room, as was his daily custom, he found him lying upon his bed, dead, but marvellous to say, dressed in a woman's clothes. That the death was not accidental could be seen at a glance. The body lay prepared as if for a funeral. The clothes and the dressing of the hair, and the other minute details necessary in laying out a body for burial, had all been attended to. No outside hands need touch her, and no curious or unsympathetic eyes be gratified by peering too deeply into the mystery of her life.

The story spread with wonderful rapidity from the suburbs into the city. There it was discussed in every home, gentle and simple. The universal feeling was one of intense admiration for the devotion and heroism which had caused the mother to sacrifice her life for her son, and the mandarins and scholars petitioned the Emperor to issue an edict permitting an arch to be erected in order that the memory of such a noble woman should be kept alive for ever.

This petition was granted; and it was decided that the inscription to be carved upon the arch should consist simply of these words: "THE WONDERFUL MAN."

The God Of The City

ONE EVENING in the distant past a fisherman anchored his boat near the bank of a stream which flowed close by a great city, whose walls could be seen rising grey and rugged in the near distance. The sound of life fell upon his ear and kept him from feeling lonely. Coolies, with bamboo carrying-poles on their shoulders, tired out with the heavy work of the day, hurried by afraid lest the darkness should overtake them before they reached their homes. The bearers of sedan-chairs, which they had carried for many a weary mile, strode by with quickened step and with an imperious shout at the foot passengers to get out of their way and not block up the narrow road by which they would gain the city walls before the great gates were closed for the night.

By the time that the afterglow had died out of the sky and the distant hills were blotted out of the horizon, the fisherman had finished the cooking of his evening meal. The rice sent a fragrant odour from the wide-mouthed pan in which it lay white and appetizing. A few of the very small fish he had caught in the river had been fried to a brown and savoury-looking colour, and he was just about to sit down and enjoy his supper when, happening to look round, he saw a stranger sitting in the after part of the boat.

He was greatly amazed and was about to express his surprise, when something about the appearance of this unexpected visitor kept him spell-bound. For the stranger had a fine scholarly look about him, and the air of a man belonging to a good family. He had, moreover, a benevolent, kindly face, which could not fail to win the confidence of anyone who gazed upon it.

Whilst the fisherman was wondering who his visitor was and how he had managed to come so mysteriously into the boat, the stranger said: "Allow me to explain who I am and to apologise for intruding on you without first having got your permission to do so. I am the spirit of a man who two years ago was drowned not very far from where your boat is now anchored. Many attempts have I made to inveigle others into the river, so that I might be free to leave the spot to which my miserable fate binds me until another unhappy wretch shall take my place."

The spirit of a drowned person is condemned to hover round the spot where his life was lost, until, either by accident or by the wiles of the sufferer, someone else perishes in the water and thus takes the place of the spirit, which then travels with lightning speed to the Land of Shadows.

"I was so dull this evening," continued the stranger, "that I felt impelled to come and have a chat with you for a short time. So I hope you will take my visit in good part, and allow me to sit in your boat until it is time for you to go to bed."

The fisherman, who was greatly taken with his courtly visitor, expressed his great pleasure in receiving him, and invited him to share his evening meal and to make himself quite at home for as long as he liked.

After this the solitary spirit of the river used frequently to come and spend an evening with the fisherman, until quite a friendship sprang up between them. One evening this ghostly visitor appeared with a face covered with smiles and with a glad note of joy in his voice. No sooner had he sat down than he said, "This is the last evening I shall be able to spend with you. The long weary time of waiting is now nearly at an end, and tomorrow another victim to the river will give me my release and you will see me no more."

Now, the fisherman was a deeply benevolent man, and he was most anxious to see what unhappy person was to be drowned on the morrow. About midday, as he was watching by the river-side, he saw a poor woman, weeping and sobbing, come rushing with hasty steps towards the water. Her hair was dishevelled, and her eyes red with tears, and frequent cries of sorrow burst from her lips. Straight as an arrow she made for the stream, and was just preparing to throw herself into it, when the fisherman in a loud and commanding voice told her to stop.

He then asked her what was the matter and what reason there was for her to sacrifice her life in the river.

"I am a most unhappy woman," she replied. "On my way home just now I was waylaid by a footpad, who robbed me of some money that I was taking back to my husband. This money was to pay a debt we owed to a man who threatens us with the severest penalties if we do not give it to him to-day. Far rather would I face death than see the sorrow which would overwhelm my husband if I told him my sorrowful story."

Having asked her how much money had been taken from her, the fisherman presented the woman with the exact amount, and soon she was proceeding with joyful footsteps in the direction of her home.

That same evening the fisherman was again visited by the spirit who had bidden him an eternal farewell the previous evening.

"What did you mean," asked the visitor, "by depriving me of the one chance I had of gaining my freedom?"

"I could not bear to see the sorrow of the poor woman," replied the fisherman, "nor to think of the tragedy to her home had she perished in the stream, and so I saved her." With eloquent lips he proceeded to describe the beauty of benevolence, and urged upon his guest the nobler course of trying to save life even at the expense of his own happiness. In the end the latter was so deeply moved that he promised never again to make any attempt to gain his liberty through another's death, even though this should mean that he would have to spend long ages of misery in the fatal stream.

Years went by, and yet for the imprisoned spirit there came no release. Cases of suicide or accidental drowning in the flowing stream ceased altogether. Many a life that would have perished was saved from destruction by mysterious warnings which came from the sullen water, and which terrified away the would-be suicides as they were about to hurl themselves into it.

At length Kwan-yin, the Goddess of Mercy, moved by the sight of such a generous sacrifice of self in order to save the souls of unfortunate people who had become weary of life, released this noble spirit from its watery prison. Moreover, as she felt convinced that such a man could safely be entrusted with the destinies of those who might appear before his tribunal, she made him a god and decreed that temples should be erected to him in every town and city of the Empire, so that all who were suffering wrong or injustice could have their causes righted at the shrine of one who had shown such profound devotion and sympathy for others in distress.

Such is the story of the God of the City.

Since he is regarded as the representative of the dread ruler of the Land of Shadows, his temple has been erected very much in the same style as the courts of the Mandarins. Its main entrance is large and imposing, and the great gates suggest those of the yamen of some high official.

Within these is an immense courtyard, paved with slabs of granite, and on each side of this there are six life-size statues of the "runners," or policemen, of the god, who stand ready to carry out his decisions, and to pursue and capture by invisible and mysterious processes those whom he has condemned as guilty. The faces of these figures are distorted by passion, and their attitudes are such as men might be conceived to assume in apprehending some notorious criminal whom Yam-lo had ordered to be seized.

At the end of this spacious courtyard is the shrine of the god, but he is so hidden behind a yellow curtain that it is impossible to catch a glimpse of his image. In front of him are statues of his two secretaries, who, with huge pens in their hands, stand ready day and night to take down the petitions and indictments laid before the god by those who are in sorrow or who are suffering wrong.

One afternoon the peace of such a temple was suddenly disturbed by a noisy clamour outside, and the sound of hurried footsteps as of a crowd rushing through the main gates. Two men advanced with rapid, excited strides straight past the demon policeman at the door, who seemed to scowl with added ferocity as they gazed at the actors in a scene with which they would have much to do by-and-by.

The two men were quite young, a little over twenty; and behind them followed a string of idlers and loafers and street arabs, who seem to spring up like magic when anything unusual happens. One of the young men was slightly ahead of the crowd. His face was flushed and his black eyes sparkled with excitement, whilst in his left hand he carried a large white cock. He was the complainant, and his purpose in coming to the temple was to appeal to the god to vindicate his honour.

He took his stand in front of the idol, and the secretaries, with pens in their hands, seemed to put on a strained look of attention as the young fellow produced a roll of paper and began to read the statement he had drawn up. It was diffuse and wordy, as most of such documents are, but the main facts were quite plain.

The two young men were assistants in a shop in the city. Some little time before, the master of the shop, without telling either of them, concealed in a chosen place a sum of one hundred dollars, which he wished to have in readiness in order to pay for certain goods he had purchased. The previous day, when he went to get the money on the presentation of the bill, he found to his horror that it had disappeared. He had told no one of this secret hoard, not even his wife; and therefore he felt convinced that in some way or other one of his two assistants had discovered his hiding-place. For some reason his suspicions became aroused against the man who was now detailing his grievances, and who was appealing to the god to set in motion all the tremendous forces at his command, not only to proclaim his innocence but also to bring condign punishment on the real culprit.

The scene was a weird and fascinating one, and became most exciting as the young man neared the end of his appeal. He called upon the god to hurl all the pains and penalties in his unseen armoury against the man who had really stolen the money.

"Let his life be one long torture," he cried with uplifted hands. "May every enterprise in which he engages end in disaster; may his father and mother die, and let him be left desolate; may a subtle and incurable disease lay its grip upon him; may misfortune pursue him in every shape and form; may he become a beggar with ulcered legs and sit on the roadside and beseech the passers-by, in sunshine and in storm, for a few cash that will just help to keep him alive; may he never have a son to perpetuate his name or to make offerings to his spirit in the Land of Shadows; may madness seize upon him so that his reason shall fly and he shall be a source of terror to his fellow-men; and finally, may a tragic and horrible death bring his life to a sudden end, even as I bring to an end the life of this white cock that I have brought with me."

As he uttered these last words he grasped a chopper, and with one sharp and vicious blow cut off the head of the struggling animal, which wildly fluttered its wings in the agonies of death, whilst its life-blood poured out in a stream on the ground.

He then took his petition, and advancing close up to the secretaries, who seemed for the moment to gaze down upon him with a look of sympathy on their faces, he set fire to it and burned it to ashes. In this way it passed into the hands of the god, who would speedily set in motion unseen machinery to bring down upon the head of the guilty one the judgments which had just been invoked.

The sympathies of the crowd were with the man who had sworn a solemn oath that he was innocent of the theft. The other young fellow, who had said little or nothing during the proceedings, was believed to be the real culprit, but there was no evidence upon which he could be convicted. The god knew, however, and everyone was satisfied that in due time punishment would descend upon the transgressor.

In a few minutes the temple resumed its normal aspect, for with the disappearance of the two principal actors in the scene, the idlers from the street slowly dispersed, each one loudly expressing his opinion as to the merits of the question in dispute. With the dissolving of the crowd, it would have seemed to the casual observer that no further proceedings were to be taken in the matter. The god's face wore its usually placid look, unmoved by the shifting panorama of human life which ebbed and flowed in front of him from morning till night. The ghastly-looking policemen, with their grinning visages and ferocious scowls and contorted bodies, remained in the same unchanging postures by the main entrance.

A week or two had gone by since the appeal had been made to the god, when those who were following the case and were looking out for some grim evidence that the god was at work in bringing retribution on the man whom everyone suspected of being the thief, were startled by a heartrending catastrophe.

This man had a sister, just bursting into womanhood, who was the very light of her home. Her merry laugh could be heard throughout the day, so that sadness could not long abide in the same house. Her face, too, seemed to have been formed to match her sunny smiles, and was a constant inspiration that never failed to give those who looked upon it a brighter view of life.

One morning she went down to the river-bank with several of her neighbours to do the household washing. The stream was strong and rapid in the centre, but the place which these women had selected for their work had always been considered perfectly safe, for it was outside the current and no accident had ever happened there.

They had finished all that they had purposed to do, and were ascending the bank to return home, when they heard an agonized cry and turning swiftly round they perceived that this young girl had stumbled and fallen into the river. They were so horrified at the accident that they lost all presence of mind and allowed the fast-flowing stream to get a grip of her and drag her into the current. When help at last came, her body could just be seen floating on the troubled waters, and before a boat could be launched it had disappeared in the waves of the sea which tumbled and roared about a quarter of a mile further down.

This terrible disaster, which brought unutterable gloom and sorrow upon the home, was unquestionably the work of the god. With bated breath people talked of the tragic end of this beautiful girl, who had won her way into the hearts of all who knew her; but they recognized that her death had been caused by no mere accident, but by the mysterious power of the invisible forces which are always at work to bring punishment upon those who have violated the Righteousness of Heaven.

About a month after this calamity, the monsoon rains began to fall. The clouds gathered in dense masses upon the neighbouring hills, and poured down such copious showers that the mountain streams were turned into roaring avalanches, tearing their way down to the sea with an impetuosity that nothing could resist.

One of these streams, which used to run by the side of the ancestral property of the family of the man who was believed to have stolen the hundred dollars, overflowed its banks and rushing along with mad and headlong speed it swept away their fields, so that when the rains ceased not a trace of them was to be found, but only sand and gravel, from which no crop could ever be gathered in the future. The consequence was that the family was utterly ruined.

This second disaster falling on the homestead was a clear indication to everyone who knew the story of the stolen money that the god was still at work in bringing retribution on the sinner. The fact that other farms had come out of the flood undamaged was proof positive of this.

From this time, too, the young man who really was the culprit began to be troubled in his mind because of the calamities that had fallen on his family. The death of his sister by drowning, and the utter destruction of his home by the flood, which had injured no other farmer in the neighbourhood, were plain indications that the curses which his falsely accused fellow-assistant had prayed the god to bring down on the head of the guilty party were indeed coming fast and thick upon him.

A dread of coming evil took possession of him, and this so preyed upon his mind that he began to lose his reason. He would go about muttering to himself, and declaring that he saw devils. These fits grew upon him, until at last he became raving mad, and had to be seized and bound with ropes to prevent him doing injury to himself or to others. At times he suffered from violent spasms of mania, while at others, again, though undoubtedly insane, he was quiet and subdued. He would then talk incessantly to himself, and bemoan the sad fact that the dread God of the City was sending evil spirits to torment him because he had purloined the hundred dollars belonging to his master.

By-and-by these random confessions attracted the attention of his heart-broken father, who used to sit watching by his side, and they became so frequent and so circumstantial, describing even where the money had been hidden, that at last he determined to examine into the matter. Investigations were made, and the whole sum was found in the very place which the young man had mentioned in his delirium, and was at once returned to the shopkeeper.

As the money had been given back, and the father and mother were dependent upon their only son to provide for them in their old age, the man who had entered the accusation before the god was entreated again to appear before him in his temple and withdraw the charges that he had previously made against his fellow-assistant. Only in this formal and legal way could the god have official knowledge of the fact that reparation had been made for the offence which had been committed; and if this were not done he would still continue to send sorrow after sorrow until the whole family were involved in absolute ruin or death.

Out of pity for the old couple the other young man consented to take the necessary steps. He accordingly presented a petition to the god, stating that he wished to withdraw the accusation which he had made against a certain man who had been suspected of theft. The stolen money had been returned to its owner, and the god was now besought to stay all further proceedings and forgive the culprit for the wrong he had done.

It was evident that this petition was granted, for at once the young man began to recover, and soon all signs of madness left him. He had, however, learned a lesson which he never forgot; and as long as he lived he never committed another offence such as the theft which had brought such serious consequences upon himself and his family.

The Reward Of A Benevolent Life

ON THE BANKS of a river flowing through the prefecture of Tingchow, there stood a certain city of about ten thousand inhabitants. Among this mass of people there was a very fair sprinkling of well-to-do men, and perhaps half-a-dozen or so who might have been accounted really wealthy.

Amongst these latter was one particular individual named Chung, who had acquired the reputation of being exceedingly large-hearted and benevolently inclined to all those in distress. Anyone who was in want had but to appeal to Chung, and his immediate necessities would at once be relieved without any tedious investigation into the merits of his case. As may be inferred from this, Chung was an easy-going, good-natured man, who was more inclined to look kindly upon his fellow-men than to criticise them harshly for their follies or their crimes. Such a man has always been popular in this land of China.

Now the whole soul of Chung was centred upon his only son Keng. At the time when our story opens, this young fellow was growing up to manhood, and had proved himself to be possessed of no mean ability, for on the various occasions on which he had sat for examination before the Literary Chancellor, his papers had been of a very high order of merit.

The rumours of Chung's generosity had travelled further than he had ever dreamed of. Several reports of the noble deeds that he was constantly performing had reached the Immortals in the Western Heaven, and as these are profoundly concerned in the doings of mankind, steps were taken that Chung should not go unrewarded.

One day a fairy in the disguise of a bonze called upon him. He had always had a sincere liking for men of this class. He admired their devotion, and he was moved by their self-sacrifice in giving up home and kindred to spend their lives in the service of the gods and for the good of humanity.

No sooner, therefore, had the priest entered within his doors, than he received him with the greatest politeness and cordiality. The same evening he prepared a great dinner, to which a number of distinguished guests were invited, and a time of high festivity and rejoicing was prolonged into the early hours of the morning.

Next day Chung said to his guest, "I presume you have come round collecting for your temple. I need not assure you that I shall be most delighted to subscribe to anything that has to do with the uplifting of my fellow-men. My donation is ready whenever you wish to accept it."

The bonze, with a smile which lit up the whole of his countenance, replied that he had not come for the purpose of collecting subscriptions.

"I have come," he said, "to warn you about a far more important matter which affects you and your family. Before very long a great flood will take place in this district, and will sweep everything before it. It will be so sudden that men will not be able to take measures to preserve either their lives or their property – so instantaneous will be the rush of the mighty streams, like ocean floods, from the mountains you can see in the West. My advice to you is to commence at once the construction of boats to carry you and your most precious effects away. When the news first comes that the waters are rising, have them anchored in the creek that flows close by your doors; and when the crisis arrives, delay not a moment, but hurry on board and fly for your lives."

"But when will that be?" asked Chung anxiously.

"I may not tell you the precise day or hour," replied the bonze; "but when the eyes of the stone lions in the East Street of the city shed tears of blood, betake yourselves with all haste to the boats, and leave this doomed place behind you."

"But may I not tell the people of this approaching calamity?" asked Chung, whose tender heart was deeply wrung with distress at the idea of so many being overwhelmed in the coming flood.

"You can please yourself about that," answered the priest, "but no one will believe you. The people of this region are depraved and wicked, and your belief in my words will only cause them to laugh and jeer at you for your credulity."

"But shall I and my family escape with our lives?" finally enquired Chung.

"Yes, you will all escape," was the reply, "and in due time you will return to your home and your future life will be prosperous. But there is one thing," he continued, "about which I must entreat you to be exceedingly careful. As you are being carried down the stream by the great flood, be sure to rescue every living thing that you meet in distress upon the waters. You will not fail to be rewarded for so doing, as the creatures you save will repay you a thousandfold for any services you may render them. There is one thing more that I would solemnly warn you against. You will come across a man floating helplessly on the swiftly flowing tide. Have nothing to do with him. Leave him to his fate. If you try to save him, you will only bring sorrow upon your home."

As the priest was departing, Chung tried to press into his hand a considerable present of money, but he refused to accept it. He did not want money from him, he said. The gods had heard of his great love for men, and they had sent him to warn him so that he might escape the doom which would overtake his fellow-citizens.

After his departure Chung at once called the boat-builders who had their yards along the bank of the stream, and ordered ten large boats to be built with all possible speed. The news of this spread through the town, and when the reasons were asked and the reply was given that the boats were in anticipation of a mighty flood that would ere long devastate the entire region, everyone screamed with laughter; but Chung let them laugh.

For weeks and months he sent an old man to East Street to see if the eyes of the stone lions there had overflowed with bloody tears.

One day two pig-butchers enquired of this man how it was that every day he appeared and looked into the eyes of the lions. He explained that Chung had sent him, for a prophecy had come from the gods that when the eyes of the lions shed blood, the flood which was to destroy the city would be already madly rushing on its way.

On hearing this, these two butchers determined to play a practical joke. Next day, in readiness for the coming of the old man, they smeared the stone eyes with pigs' blood. No sooner had Chung's messenger caught sight of this than, with terror in his eyes, he fled along the streets to tell his master the dreadful news. By this time everything had been prepared, and Chung was only waiting for the appointed sign. The most valuable of his goods had already been packed in some of the boats, and now his wife and son and household servants all hurried down to the water's edge and embarked; and remembering the injunction of the priest that there should be no delay, Chung at once ordered the anchors to be raised, and the boatmen, as if for dear life, made for the larger stream outside.

Hardly had the vessels begun to move when the sun, which had been blazing in the sky, became clouded over. Soon a terrific storm of wind tore with the force of a hurricane across the land. By-and-by great drops of rain, the harbingers of the deluge which was to inundate the country, fell in heavy splashes. Ere long it seemed as though the great fountains in the heavens had burst out, for the floods came pouring down in one incessant torrent. The sides of the mountains became covered with ten thousand rills, which joined their forces lower down, and developed into veritable cataracts, rushing with fearful and noisy tumult to the plain below.

Before many hours had passed, the streams everywhere overflowed their banks, and ran riot amongst the villages, and flowed like a sea against the city. There was no resisting this watery foe, and before night fell vast multitudes had been drowned in the seething floods from which there was no escape.

Meanwhile, carried swiftly along by the swollen current, Chung's little fleet sped safely down the stream, drawing further and further away from the doomed city.

The river had risen many feet since they had started on their voyage, and as they were passing by a high peak, which had been undermined by the rush of waters hurling themselves against its base, the boats were put into great danger by the whirl and commotion of the foam-flecked river. Just as they escaped from being submerged, the party noticed a small monkey struggling in the water, and at once picked it up and took it on board.

Further on they passed a large branch of a tree, on which there was a crow's nest, with one young one in it. This, also, remembering the solemn injunction of the priest, they carefully took up and saved.

As they were rushing madly on down the tawny, swollen river, they were all struck with sudden excitement by seeing something struggling in the boiling waters. Looking at this object more attentively as they drew nearer to it, they perceived that it was a man, who seemed to be in great peril of his life.

Chung's tender heart was filled with sympathy, and he at once gave orders for the boatmen to go and rescue him. His wife, however, reminded him of the warning of the priest not to save any man on the river, as he would inevitably turn out to be an enemy, who would in time work his rescuer great wrong.

Chung replied that at such a time, when a human being was in extreme danger of being drowned, personal interests ought not to be considered at all. He had faithfully obeyed the command of the priest in saving animal life, but how much more valuable was a man than any of the lower orders of creation? "Whatever may happen," he said, "I cannot let this man drown before my eyes," and as the boat just then came alongside the swimmer, he was hauled into it and delivered from his peril.

After a few days, when the storm had abated and the river had gone down to its natural flow, Chung returned with his family to his home. To his immense surprise, he found that his house had not been damaged in the least. The gods who had saved his life had used their supernatural powers to preserve even his property from the ruin and devastation that had fallen upon the inhabitants of the city and of the surrounding plain.

Shortly after they had settled down again, Chung enquired of Lo-yung, the man whom he had saved from the flood, whether he would not like to return to his family and his home.

"I have no family left," he answered with a sad look on his face. "All the members of it were drowned in the great flood from which you delivered me. What little property we had was washed away by the wild rush of the streams that overflowed our farm. Let me stay with you," he begged, "and give me the opportunity, by the devoted service of my life, to repay you in some slight degree for what you have done in saving my life."

As he uttered these words his tears began to flow, and his features showed every sign of profound emotion. Always full of tenderness and compassion, Chung was profoundly moved by the tears and sobs of Lo-yung, and hastened to assure him that he need be under no concern with regard to his future. "You have lost all your relatives, it is true, but from to-day I shall recognize you as my son. I adopt you into my family and I give you my name."

Six months after this important matter had been settled, the city was placarded with proclamations from its Chief Mandarin. In these he informed the people that he had received a most urgent Edict from the Emperor stating that an official seal, which was in constant use in high transactions of the State, had in a most mysterious manner disappeared and could not be found. He was therefore directed to inform the people that whoever informed His Majesty where the seal was, so that it could be recovered, would receive a considerable reward and would also be made a high mandarin in the palace of the Emperor.

That very night, whilst Chung was sleeping, a fairy appeared to him in a dream. "The gods have sent me," he said, "to give you one more proof of the high regard in which they hold you for your devotion to your fellow-men. The Emperor has lost a valuable seal which he is most anxious to recover, and he has promised large and liberal rewards to the man who shows him where it may be found. I want to tell you where the seal is. It lies at the bottom of the crystal well in the grounds behind the palace. It was accidentally dropped in there by the Empress-Dowager, who has forgotten all about the circumstance, but who will recollect it the moment she is reminded of it. I want you to send your own son to the capital to claim the reward by telling where the seal is."

When Chung awoke in the morning, he told his wife the wonderful news of what had happened to him during the night, and began to make preparations for his son to start for the capital without delay, in order to secure the honours promised by the Emperor. His wife, however, was by no means reconciled to the idea of parting with her son, and strongly opposed his going.

"Why are you so set upon the honours of this life that you are willing to be separated from your only child, whom perhaps you may never be able to see again?" she asked her husband, with tears in her eyes. "You are a rich man, you are beloved of the gods, you have everything that money can buy in this flowery kingdom. Why not then be contented and cease to long after the dignities which the State can confer, but which can never give you any real happiness?"

Just at that moment Lo-yung came in, and hearing the wonderful story, and seeing the distress of the mother, he volunteered to take the place of her son and go to the capital in his stead.

"I have never yet had the chance," he said, "of showing my gratitude to my benefactor for having saved my life, and for the many favours he has showered upon me. I shall be glad to undertake this journey. I shall have an audience with His Majesty and will reveal to him the place where the seal lies hidden, and I shall then insist that all the honours he may be prepared to bestow on me shall be transferred to your son, to whom of right they naturally belong."

It was accordingly arranged that Lo-yung should take the place of Chung's son, and preparations were at once made for his journey to the capital. As he was saying good-bye to his benefactor, the latter whispered in his ear: "If you succeed in your enterprise and the Emperor makes you one of his royal officers, do not let ingratitude ever enter your heart, so that you may be tempted to forget us here, who will be thinking about you all the time you are away."

"Nothing of the kind can ever happen," exclaimed Lo-yung impetuously. "My gratitude to you is too firmly embedded within my heart ever to be uprooted from it."

On his arrival at the capital, he at once sought an interview with the Prime Minister, who, on hearing that a man wished to see him about a state matter of urgent importance, immediately admitted him to his presence. Lo-yung at once explained that he had come to reveal the place where the lost seal at that moment lay concealed. "I am perfectly ready to tell all I know about it," he said, "but if possible I should prefer to make it known to the Emperor himself in person."

"That can quickly be arranged," eagerly replied the Prime Minister, "for His Majesty is so anxious to obtain information about the seal, that he is prepared at any hour of the day or night to give an audience to anyone who can ease his mind on the subject."

In a few minutes a eunuch from the palace commanded the Prime Minister to come without delay to the Audience Hall and wait upon the Emperor. He was also to bring with him the person who said that he had an important communication to lay before the Throne.

When they arrived they found there not only the King, but also the Empress-Dowager, waiting to receive them. In obedience to a hasty command, Lo-yung told in a few words where the seal was, and how it happened to be there. As he went on with the story the face of the Empress lit up with wonder, whilst a pleasing smile overspread it, as she recognized the truth of what Lo-yung was saying.

"But tell me," said the Emperor, "how you get all your information and how it is that you have such an intimate acquaintance with what is going on in my palace?"

Lo-yung then described how the Immortals in the Western Heaven, deeply moved by the loving character of Chung, and wishing to reward him and bring honour to his family, had sent a fairy, who appeared to him in a dream and told him the secret of the seal.

"Your home," said the Emperor, "must indeed be celebrated for benevolent and loving deeds to men, since even the fairies come down from the far-off Heaven to express their approbation. In accordance with my royal promise, I now appoint you to a high official position that will enrich you for life, for I consider that it will be for the welfare of my kingdom to have a man from a home, which the gods delight to honour, to assist me in the management of my public affairs."

From the moment when the royal favour was bestowed on Lo-yung, it seemed as though every particle of gratitude and every kindly remembrance of Chung had vanished completely out of his heart. He cut himself off from the home he had left only a few days ago, as completely as though it had never existed.

Weeks and months went by, but no news came from him, and the heart of Chung was wrung with anguish, for he knew that Lo-yung's unnatural conduct would in the end bring retribution upon Lo-yung himself.

At last he determined to send his son, Keng, to the capital to find out what had really become of Lo-yung. Attended by one of his household servants, the young man reached his journey's end in a few days. On enquiring at his inn about Lo-yung, he was informed that he was a mandarin of great distinction in the city, and was under the special protection of the Emperor, whose favourite he was.

Hearing this joyful news, Keng, followed by his servant, at once hastened to the residence of Lo-yung, and was lucky enough to meet him as he rode out on horseback from his magnificent yamen, attended by a long retinue of officers and attendants.

Running up to the side of his horse, Keng cried out joyfully, "Ah! my brother, what a joy to meet you once more! How glad I am to see you!"

To his astonishment, Lo-yung, with a frown upon his face, angrily exclaimed; "You common fellow, what do you mean by calling me your brother? I have no brother. You are an impostor, and you must be severely punished for daring to claim kinship with me."

Calling some of the lictors in his train, he ordered them to beat Keng, and then cast him into prison, and to give strict injunctions to the jailer to treat him as a dangerous criminal. Wounded and bleeding from the severe scourging he had received, and in a terrible state of exhaustion, poor Keng was dragged to the prison, where he was thrown into the deepest dungeon, and left to recover as best he might from the shock he had sustained.

His condition was indeed a pitiable one. Those who could have helped and comforted him were far away. He could expect no alleviation of his sorrows from the jailer, for the heart of the latter had naturally become hardened by having to deal with the criminal classes. Besides he had received precise orders from the great mandarin, that this particular prisoner was to be treated as a danger to society. Even if he had been inclined to deal mercifully with him, he dared not disobey such definite and stringent commands as he had received from his superior.

The prison fare was only just enough to keep body and soul together. Keng had no money with which to bribe the jailer to give him a more generous diet, and there was no one to guarantee that any extra expenses which might be incurred would ever be refunded to him.

And then a miracle was wrought, and once more the fairies interfered, this time to save the life of the only son of the man whose fame for tenderness and compassion had reached the far-off Western Heaven.

One morning, as Keng lay weary and half-starved on the blackened heap of straw that served him as a bed in the corner of the prison, a monkey climbed up and clung to the narrow gratings through which the light penetrated into his room. In one of its hands it held a piece of pork which it kept offering to Keng. Very much surprised, he got up to take it, when to his delight he discovered that the monkey was the identical one which had been picked up by his father on the day of the great flood.

The same thing was repeated for several days in succession, and when the jailer asked for some explanation of these extraordinary proceedings, Keng gave him a detailed account of their wonderful deliverance by the fairies, the picking up of the monkey, and the rescue of Lo-yung, now the great mandarin, who was keeping him confined in prison. "Ah!" muttered the jailer under his breath, "the lower animals know how to show gratitude, but men do not."

A few days after this another messenger of the gods came to give his aid to Keng. A number of crows gathered on a roof which overlooked the narrow slits through which the prisoner could catch a glimpse of the blue sky. One of them flew on to the ledge outside, and Keng immediately recognized it as the one which had been saved from the floating branch in the turbid river. He was overjoyed to see this bird, and besought the jailer to allow him to write a letter to his father, telling him of his pitiful condition. This request was granted, and the document was tied to the leg of the crow, which flew away on its long flight to Chung with its important news.

Chung was greatly distressed when he read the letter that his son had written in prison, and with all the speed he could command, he travelled post haste to the capital. When he arrived there he made various attempts to obtain an interview with Lo-yung, but all in vain. The mandarin had not sense enough to see that the threads of fate were slowly winding themselves around him, and would soon entangle him to his destruction.

Very unwillingly, therefore, because he still loved Lo-yung and would have saved him if possible, Chung entered an accusation against him before Fau-Kung, the famous criminal judge.

The result of the investigation was the condemnation of Lo-yung, whose execution speedily followed, whilst Keng was promoted to the very position that had been occupied by the man who had tried to work his ruin.

Women's Words Part Flesh And Blood

ONCE UPON A TIME there were two brothers, who lived in the same house. And the big brother listened to his wife's words, and because of them fell out with the little one. Summer had begun, and the time for sowing the high-growing millet had come. The little brother had no grain, and asked the big one to loan him some, and the big one ordered his wife to give it to him. But she took the grain, put it in a large pot and cooked it until it was done. Then she gave it to the little fellow. He knew nothing about it, and went and sowed his field with it. Yet, since the grain had been cooked, it did not sprout. Only a single grain of seed had not been cooked; so only a single sprout shot up. The little brother was hard-working and industrious by nature, and hence he watered and hoed the sprout all day long. And the sprout grew mightily, like a tree, and an ear of millet sprang up out of it like a canopy, large enough to shade half an acre of ground. In the fall the ear was ripe. Then the little brother took his ax and chopped it down. But no sooner had the ear fallen to the ground, than an enormous Roc came rushing down, took the ear in his beak and flew away. The little brother ran after him as far as the shore of the sea.

Then the bird turned and spoke to him like a human being, as follows: "You should not seek to harm me! What is this one ear worth to you? East of the sea is the isle of gold and silver. I will carry you across. There you may take whatever you want, and become very rich."

The little brother was satisfied, and climbed on the bird's back, and the latter told him to close his eyes. So he only heard the air whistling past his ears, as though he were driving through a strong wind, and beneath him the roar and surge of flood and waves. Suddenly the bird settled on a rock: "Here we are!" he said.

Then the little brother opened his eyes and looked about him: and on all sides he saw nothing but the radiance and shimmer of all sorts of white and yellow objects. He took about a dozen of the little things and hid them in his breast.

"Have you enough?" asked the Roc.

"Yes, I have enough," he replied.

"That is well," answered the bird. "Moderation protects one from harm."

Then he once more took him up, and carried him back again.

When the little brother reached home, he bought himself a good piece of ground in the course of time, and became quite well to do.

But his brother was jealous of him, and said to him, harshly: "Where did you manage to steal the money?"

So the little one told him the whole truth of the matter. Then the big brother went home and took counsel with his wife.

"Nothing easier," said his wife. "I will just cook grain again and keep back one seedling so that it is not done. Then you shall sow it, and we will see what happens."

No sooner said than done. And sure enough, a single sprout shot up, and sure enough, the sprout bore a single ear of millet, and when harvest time came around, the Roc again appeared and carried it off in his beak. The big brother was pleased, and ran after him, and the Roc said the same thing he had said before, and carried the big brother to the island. There the big brother saw the gold and silver heaped up everywhere. The largest pieces were like hills, the small ones were like bricks, and the real tiny ones were like grains of sand. They blinded his eyes. He only regretted that he knew of no way by which he could move mountains. So he bent down and picked up as many pieces as possible.

The Roc said: "Now you have enough. You will overtax your strength."

"Have patience but a little while longer," said the big brother. "Do not be in such a hurry! I must get a few more pieces!"

And thus time passed.

The Roc again urged him to make haste: "The sun will appear in a moment," said he, "and the sun is so hot it burns human beings up."

"Wait just a little while longer," said the big brother. But that very moment a red disk broke through the clouds with tremendous power. The Roc flew into the sea, stretched out both his wings, and beat the water with them in order to escape the heat. But the big brother was shrivelled up by the sun.

How Greed For A Trifling Thing Led A Man To Lose A Great One

ONCE UPON A TIME there was an old woman, who had two sons. But her older son did not love his parents, and left his mother and brother. The younger one served her so faithfully, however, that all the people spoke of his filial affection.

One day it happened that there was a theatrical performance given outside the village. The younger son started to carry his mother there on his back, so that she might look on. But there was a ravine before the village, and he slipped and fell down in the middle of it. And his mother was killed by the rolling stones, and her blood and flesh were sprinkled about everywhere. The son stroked his mother's corpse, and wept bitterly. He was about to kill himself when, suddenly, he saw a priest standing before him.

The latter said: "Have no fear, for I can bring your mother back to life again!" And as he said so, he stooped, gathered up her flesh and bones, and laid them together as they should be. Then he breathed upon them, and at once the mother was alive again. This made the son very happy, and he thanked the priest on his knees. Yet on a sharp point of rock he still saw a bit of his mother's flesh hanging, a bit about an inch long.

"That should not be left hanging there either," said he, and hid it in his breast.

"In truth, you love your mother as a son should," said the priest. Then he bade the son give him the bit of flesh, kneaded a manikin out of it, breathed upon it, and in a minute there it stood, a really fine-looking little boy.

"His name is Small Profit," said he, turning to the son, "and you may call him brother. You are poor and have not the wherewithal with which to nourish your mother. If you need something, Small Profit can get it for you."

The son thanked him once more, then took his mother on his back again, and his new little brother by the hand, and went home. And when he said to Small Profit: "Bring meat and wine!" then meat and wine were at hand at once, and steaming rice was already cooking in the pot. And when he said to Small Profit: "Bring money and cloth!" then his purse filled itself with money, and the chests were heaped up with cloth to the brim. Whatever he asked for that he received. Thus, in the course of time, they came to be very well off indeed.

But his older brother envied him greatly. And when there was another theatrical performance in the village, he took his mother on his back – by force – and went to it. And when he reached the ravine, he slipped purposely, and let his mother fall into the depths, only intent to see that she really was shattered into fragments. And sure enough his mother had such a bad fall that her limbs and trunk were strewn around in all directions. He then climbed down, took his mother's head in his hands, and pretended to weep.

And at once the priest was on hand again, and said: "I can wake the dead to life again, and surround white bones with flesh and blood!"

Then he did as he had done before, and the mother came to life again. But the older brother already had hidden one of her ribs on purpose. He now pulled it out and said to the priest: "Here is a bone left. What shall I do with it?"

The priest took the bone, enclosed it in lime and earth, breathed upon it, as he had done the other time, and it became a little man, resembling Small Profit, but larger in stature.

"His name is Great Duty," he told his older brother, "if you stick to him he will always lend you a hand."

The son took his mother back again, and Great Duty walked beside him.

When he came to their courtyard door, he saw his younger brother coming out, holding Small Profit in his arms.

"Where are you going?" he said to him.

His brother answered: "Small Profit is a divine being, who does not wish to dwell for all time among men. He wants to fly back to the heavens, and so I am escorting him."

"Give Small Profit to me! Don't let him get away!" cried the older brother.

Yet, before he had ended his speech, Small Profit was rising in the air. The older brother then quickly let his mother drop on the ground, and stretched out his hand to catch Small Profit. But he did not succeed, and now Great Duty, too, rose from the ground, took Small Profit's hand, and together they ascended to the clouds and disappeared.

Then the older brother stamped on the ground, and said with a sigh: "Alas, I have lost my Great Duty because I was too greedy for that Small Profit!"

Who Was The Sinner?

ONCE UPON A TIME there were ten farmers, who were crossing a field together. They were surprised by a heavy thunder-storm, and took refuge in a half-ruined temple. But the thunder drew ever nearer, and so great was the tumult that the air trembled about them, while the lightning flew around the temple in a continuous circle. The farmers were greatly frightened, and thought that there must be a sinner among them, whom the lightning would strike. In order to find out who it might be, they agreed to hang their straw hats up before the door, and he whose hat was blown away was to yield himself up to his fate.

No sooner were the hats outside, than one of them was blown away, and the rest thrust its unfortunate owner out of doors without pity. But as soon as he had left the temple the lightning ceased circling around, and struck it with a crash.

The one whom the rest had thrust out, had been the only righteous one among them, and for his sake the lightning had spared the temple. So the other nine had to pay for their hard-heartedness with their lives.

The Magic Cask

ONCE UPON A TIME there was a man who dug up a big, earthenware cask in his field. So he took it home with him and told his wife to clean it out. But when his wife started brushing the inside of the cask, the cask suddenly began to fill itself with brushes. No matter how many were taken out, others kept on taking their place. So the man sold the brushes, and the family managed to live quite comfortably.

Once a coin fell into the cask by mistake. At once the brushes disappeared and the cask began to fill itself with money. So now the family became rich; for they could take as much money out of the cask as ever they wished.

Now the man had an old grandfather at home, who was weak and shaky. Since there was nothing else he could do, his grandson set him to work shoveling money out of the cask, and when the old grandfather grew weary and could not keep on, he would fall into a rage, and shout at him angrily, telling him he was lazy and did not want to work. One day, however, the old man's strength gave out, and he fell into the cask and died. At once the money disappeared, and the whole cask began to fill itself with dead grandfathers. Then the man had to pull them all out and have them buried, and for this purpose he had to use up again all the money he had received. And when he was through, the cask broke, and he was just as poor as before.

The Bird With Nine Heads

LONG, LONG AGO, there once lived a king and a queen who had a daughter. One day, when the daughter went walking in the garden, a tremendous storm suddenly came up and carried her away with it. Now the storm had come from the bird with nine heads, who had robbed the princess, and brought her to his cave. The king did not know whither his daughter had disappeared, so he had proclaimed throughout the land: "Whoever brings back the princess may have her for his bride!"

Now a youth had seen the bird as he was carrying the princess to his cave. This cave, though, was in the middle of a sheer wall of rock. One could not climb up to it from below, nor could one climb down to it from above. And as the youth was walking around the rock, another youth came along and asked him what he was doing there. So the first youth told him that the bird with nine heads had carried off the king's daughter, and had brought her up to his cave. The other chap knew what he had to do. He called together his friends, and they lowered the youth to the cave in a basket. And when he went into the cave, he saw the king's daughter sitting there, and washing the wound of the bird with nine heads; for the hound of heaven had bitten off his tenth head, and his wound was still bleeding. The princess, however, motioned to the youth to hide, and he did so. When the king's daughter had washed his wound and bandaged it, the bird with nine heads felt so comfortable, that one after another, all his nine heads fell asleep. Then the youth stepped forth from his hiding-place, and cut off his nine heads with a sword. But the king's daughter said: "It would be best if you were hauled up first, and I came after."

"No," said the youth. "I will wait below here, until you are in safety." At first the king's daughter was not willing; yet at last she allowed herself to be persuaded, and climbed into the basket. But before she did so, she took a long pin from her hair, broke it into two halves and gave him one and kept the other. She also divided her silken kerchief with him, and told him to take good care of both her gifts. But when the other man had drawn up the king's daughter, he took her along with him, and left the youth in the cave, in spite of all his calling and pleading.

The youth now took a walk about the cave. There he saw a number of maidens, all of whom had been carried off by the bird with nine heads, and who had perished there of hunger. And on the wall hung a fish, nailed against it with four nails. When he touched the fish, the latter turned into a handsome youth, who thanked him for delivering him, and they agreed to regard each other as brothers. Soon the first youth grew very hungry. He stepped out in front of the cave to search for food, but only stones were lying there. Then, suddenly, he saw a great dragon, who was licking a stone. The youth imitated him, and before long his hunger had disappeared. He next asked the dragon how he could get away from the cave, and the dragon nodded his head in the direction of his tail, as much as to say he should seat himself upon it. So he climbed up, and in the twinkling of an eye he was down on the ground, and the dragon had disappeared. He then went on until he found a tortoise-shell full of beautiful pearls. But they were magic pearls, for if you flung them into the fire, the fire ceased to burn and if you flung them into the water, the water divided and you could walk through the midst of it. The youth took the pearls out of the tortoise-shell, and put them in his pocket. Not long after he reached the sea-shore. Here he flung a pearl into the sea, and at once the waters divided and he could see the sea-dragon. The sea-dragon cried: "Who is disturbing me here in my own kingdom?" The youth answered: "I found pearls in a tortoise-shell, and have flung one into the sea, and now the waters have divided for me."

"If that is the case," said the dragon, "then come into the sea with me and we will live there together." Then the youth recognized him for the same dragon whom he had seen in the cave. And with him was the youth with whom he had formed a bond of brotherhood: He was the dragon's son.

"Since you have saved my son and become his brother, I am your father," said the old dragon. And he entertained him hospitably with food and wine.

One day his friend said to him: "My father is sure to want to reward you. But accept no money, nor any jewels from him, but only the little gourd flask over yonder. With it you can conjure up whatever you wish."

And, sure enough, the old dragon asked him what he wanted by way of a reward, and the youth answered: "I want no money, nor any jewels. All I want is the little gourd flask over yonder."

At first the dragon did not wish to give it up, but at last he did let him have it, after all. And then the youth left the dragon's castle.

When he set his foot on dry land again he felt hungry. At once a table stood before him, covered with a fine and plenteous meal. He ate and drank. After he had gone on a while, he felt weary. And there stood an ass, waiting for him, on which he mounted. After he had ridden for a while, the ass's gait seemed too uneven, and along came a wagon, into which he climbed. But the wagon shook him up too, greatly, and he thought: "If I only had a litter! That would suit me better." No more had he thought so, than the litter came along, and he seated himself in it. And the bearers carried him to the city in which dwelt the king, the queen and their daughter.

When the other youth had brought back the king's daughter, it was decided to hold the wedding. But the king's daughter was not willing, and said: "He is not the right man. My deliverer will come and bring with him half of the long pin for my hair, and half my silken kerchief as a token." But when the youth did not appear for so long a time, and the other one pressed the king, the king grew impatient and said: "The wedding shall take place tomorrow!" Then the king's daughter went sadly through the streets of the city, and searched and searched in the hope of finding her deliverer. And this was on the very day that the litter arrived. The king's daughter saw the half of her silken handkerchief in the youth's hand, and filled with joy, she led him to her father. There he had to show his half of the long pin, which fitted the other exactly, and then the king was convinced that he was the right, true deliverer. The false bridegroom was now punished, the wedding celebrated, and they lived in peace and happiness till the end of their days.

The Panther

ONCE UPON A TIME there was a widow who had two daughters and a little son. And one day the mother said to her daughters: "Take good care of the house, for I am going to see grandmother, together with your little brother!" So the daughters promised her they would do so, and their mother went off. On her way a panther met her, and asked where she were going.

She said: "I am going with my child to see my mother."

"Will you not rest a bit?" asked the panther.

"No," said she, "it is already late, and it is a long road to where my mother lives."

But the panther did not cease urging her, and finally she gave in and sat down by the road side.

"I will comb your hair a bit," said the panther. And the woman allowed the panther to comb her hair. But as he passed his claws through her hair, he tore off a bit of her skin and devoured it.

"Stop!" cried the woman, "the way you comb my hair hurts!"

But the panther tore off a much larger piece of skin. Now the woman wanted to call for help, but the panther seized and devoured her. Then he turned on her little son and killed him too, put on the woman's clothes, and laid the child's bones, which he had not yet devoured, in her basket. After that he went to the woman's home, where her two daughters were, and called in at the door: "Open the door, daughters! Mother has come home!" But they looked out through a crack and said: "Our mother's eyes are not so large as yours!"

Then the panther said: "I have been to grandmother's house, and saw her hens laying eggs. That pleases me, and is the reason why my eyes have grown so large."

"Our mother had no spots in her face such as you have."

"Grandmother had no spare bed, so I had to sleep on the peas, and they pressed themselves into my face."

"Our mother's feet are not so large as yours."

"Stupid things! That comes from walking such a distance. Come, open the door quickly!"

Then the daughters said to each other: "It must be our mother," and they opened the door. But when the panther came in, they saw it was not really their mother after all.

At evening, when the daughters were already in bed, the panther was still gnawing the bones he had brought with him.

Then the daughters asked: "Mother, what are you eating?"

"I'm eating beets," was the answer.

Then the daughters said: "Oh, mother, give us some of your beets, too! We are so hungry!"

"No," was the reply, "I will not give you any. Now be quiet and go to sleep."

But the daughters kept on begging until the false mother gave them a little finger. And then they saw that it was their little brother's finger, and they said to each other: "We must make haste to escape else he will eat us as well." And with that they ran out of the door, climbed up into a tree in the yard, and called down to the false mother: "Come out! We can see our neighbor's son celebrating his wedding!" But it was the middle of the night.

Then the mother came out, and when she saw that they were sitting in the tree, she called out angrily: "Why, I'm not able to climb!"

The daughters said: "Get into a basket and throw us the rope and we will draw you up!"

The mother did as they said. But when the basket was half-way up, they began to swing it back and forth, and bump it against the tree. Then the false mother had to turn into a panther again, lest she fall down. And the panther leaped out of the basket, and ran away.

Gradually daylight came. The daughters climbed down, seated themselves on the doorstep, and cried for their mother. And a needle-vender came by and asked them why they were crying.

"A panther has devoured our mother and our brother," said the girls. "He has gone now, but he is sure to return and devour us as well."

Then the needle-vender gave them a pair of needles, and said: "Stick these needles in the cushion of the arm chair, with the points up." The girls thanked him and went on crying.

Soon a scorpion-catcher came by; and he asked them why they were crying. "A panther has devoured our mother and brother," said the girls. "He has gone now, but he is sure to return and devour us as well."

The man gave them a scorpion and said: "Put it behind the hearth in the kitchen." The girls thanked him and went on crying.

Then an egg-seller came by and asked them why they were crying. "A panther has devoured our mother and our brother," said the girls. "He has gone now, but he is sure to return and devour us as well."

So he gave them an egg and said: "Lay it beneath the ashes in the hearth." The girls thanked him and went on crying.

Then a dealer in turtles came by, and they told him their tale. He gave them a turtle and said: "Put it in the water-barrel in the yard." And then a man came by who sold wooden clubs. He asked them why they were crying. And they told him the whole story. Then he gave them two wooden clubs and said: "Hang them up over the door to the street." The girls thanked him and did as the men had told them.

In the evening the panther came home. He sat down in the armchair in the room. Then the needles in the cushion stuck into him. So he ran into the kitchen to light the fire and see what had jabbed him so; and then it was that the scorpion hooked his sting into his hand. And when at last the fire was burning, the egg burst and spurted into one of his eyes, which was blinded. So he ran out into the yard and dipped his hand into the water-barrel, in order to cool it; and then the turtle bit it off. And when in his pain he ran out through the door into the street, the wooden clubs fell on his head and that was the end of him.

Sky O'Dawn

ONCE UPON A TIME there was a man who took a child to a woman in a certain village, and told her to take care of him. Then he disappeared. And because the dawn was just breaking in the sky when the woman took the child into her home, she called him Sky O'Dawn. When the child was three years old, he would often look up to the heavens and talk with the stars. One day he ran away and many months passed before he came home again. The woman gave him a whipping. But he ran away again, and did not return for a year. His foster-mother was frightened, and asked: "Where have you been all year long?" The boy answered: "I only made a quick trip to the Purple Sea. There the water stained my clothes red. So I went to the spring at which the sun turns in, and washed them. I went away in the morning and I came back at noon. Why do you speak about my having been gone a year?"

Then the woman asked: "And where did you pass on your way?"

The boy answered: "When I had washed my clothes, I rested for a while in the City of the Dead and fell asleep. And the King-Father of the East gave me red chestnuts and rosy dawn-juice to eat, and my hunger was stilled. Then I went to the dark skies and drank the yellow dew, and my thirst was quenched. And I met a black tiger and wanted to ride home on his back. But I whipped him too hard, and he bit me in the leg. And so I came back to tell you about it."

Once more the boy ran away from home, thousands of miles, until he came to the swamp where dwelt the Primal Mist. There he met an old man with yellow eyebrows and asked him how old he might be. The old man said: "I have given up the habit of eating, and live on air. The pupils of my eyes have gradually acquired a green glow, which enables me to see all hidden things. Whenever a thousand years have passed I turn around my bones and wash the marrow. And every two thousand years I scrape my skin to get rid of the hair. I have already washed my bones thrice and scraped my skin five times."

Afterward Sky O'Dawn served the Emperor Wu of the Han dynasty. The Emperor, who was fond of the magic arts, was much attached to him. One day he said to him: "I wish that the empress might not grow old. Can you prevent it?"

Sky O'Dawn answered: "I know of only one means to keep from growing old."

The Emperor asked what herbs one had to eat. Sky O'Dawn replied: "In the North-East grow the mushrooms of life. There is a three-legged crow in the sun who always wants to get down and eat them. But the Sun-God holds his eyes shut and does not let him get away. If human beings eat them they become immortal, when animals eat them they grow stupefied."

"And how do you know this?" asked the Emperor.

"When I was a boy I once fell into a deep well, from which I could not get out for many decades. And down there was an immortal who led me to this herb. But one has to pass through a red river whose water is so light that not even a feather can swim on it. Everything that touches its surface sinks to the depths. But the man pulled off one of his shoes and gave it to me. And I crossed the water on the shoe, picked the herb and ate it. Those who dwell in that place weave mats of pearls and precious stones. They led me to a spot before which hung a curtain of delicate, colored skin. And they gave me a pillow carved of black jade, on which were graven sun and moon, clouds and thunder. They covered me with a dainty coverlet spun of the hair of a hundred gnats. A cover of that kind is very cool and refreshing in summer. I felt of it with my hands, and it seemed to be formed of water; but when I looked at it more closely, it was pure light."

Once the Emperor called together all his magicians in order to talk with them about the fields of the blessed spirits. Sky O'Dawn was there, too, and said: "Once I was wandering about the North Pole and I came to the Fire-Mirror Mountain. There neither sun nor moon shines. But there is a dragon who holds a fiery mirror in his jaws in order to light up the darkness. On the mountain is a park, and in the park is a lake. By the lake grows the glimmer-stalk grass, which shines like a lamp of gold. If you pluck it and use it for a candle, you can see all things visible, and the shapes of the spirits as well. It even illuminates the interior of a human being."

Once Sky O'Dawn went to the East, into the country of the fortunate clouds. And he brought back with him from that land a steed of the gods, nine feet high. The Emperor asked him how he had come to find it.

So he told him: "The Queen-Mother of the West had him harnessed to her wagon when she went to visit the King-Father of the East. The steed was staked out in the field of the mushrooms of life. But he trampled down several hundred of them. This made the King-Father angry, and he drove the steed away to the heavenly river. There I found him and rode him home. I rode three times around the sun, because I had fallen asleep on the steed's back. And then, before I knew it, I was here. This steed can catch up with the sun's shadow. When I found him he was quite thin and as sad as an aged donkey. So I mowed the grass of the country of the fortunate clouds, which grows once every two-thousand years on the Mountain of the Nine Springs and fed it to the horse; and that made him lively again."

The Emperor asked what sort of a place the country of the fortunate clouds might be. Sky O'Dawn answered: "There is a great swamp there. The people prophesy fortune and misfortune by the air and the clouds. If good fortune is to befall a house, clouds of five colors form in the rooms, which alight on the grass and trees and turn into a colored dew. This dew tastes as sweet as cider."

The Emperor asked whether he could obtain any of this dew. Sky O'Dawn replied: "My steed could take me to the place where it falls four times in the course of a single day!"

And sure enough he came back by evening, and brought along dew of every color in a crystal flask. The Emperor drank it and his hair grew black again. He gave it to his highest officials to drink, and the old grew young again and the sick became well.

Once, when a comet appeared in the heavens, Sky O'Dawn gave the Emperor the astrologer's wand. The Emperor pointed it at the comet and the comet was quenched.

Sky O'Dawn was an excellent whistler. And whenever he whistled in full tones, long drawn out, the motes in the sunbeams danced to his music.

Once he said to a friend: "There is not a soul on earth who knows who I am with the exception of the astrologer!"

When Sky O'Dawn had died, the Emperor called the astrologer to him and asked: "Did you know Sky O'Dawn?"

He replied: "No!"

The Emperor said: "What do you know?"

The astrologer answered: "I know how to gaze on the stars."

"Are all the stars in their places?" asked the Emperor.

"Yes, but for eighteen years I have not seen the Star of the Great Year. Now it is visible once more."

Then the Emperor looked up towards the skies and sighed: "For eighteen years Sky O'Dawn kept me company, and I did not know that he was the Star of the Great Year!"

The Lady of the Moon

IN THE DAYS of the Emperor Yau lived a prince by the name of Hou I, who was a mighty hero and a good archer. Once ten suns rose together in the sky, and shone so brightly and burned so fiercely that the people on earth could not endure them. So the Emperor ordered Hou I to shoot at them. And Hou I shot nine of them down from the sky. Besides his bow, Hou I also had a horse which ran so swiftly that even the wind could not catch up with it. He mounted it to go a-hunting, and the horse ran away and could not be stopped. So Hou I came to Kunlun Mountain and met the Queen-Mother of the Jasper Sea. And she gave him the herb of immortality. He took it home with him and hid it in his room. But his wife who was named Tschang O, once ate some of it on the sly when he was not at home, and she immediately floated up to the clouds. When she reached the moon, she ran into the castle there, and has lived there ever since as the Lady of the Moon.

On a night in mid-autumn, an emperor of the Tang dynasty once sat at wine with two sorcerers. And one of them took his bamboo staff and cast it into the air, where it turned into a heavenly bridge, on which the three climbed up to the moon together. There they saw a great castle on which was inscribed: "The Spreading Halls of Crystal Cold." Beside it stood a cassia tree which blossomed and gave forth a fragrance filling all the air. And in the tree sat a man who was chopping off the smaller boughs with an ax. One of the sorcerers said: "That is the man in the moon. The cassia tree grows so luxuriantly that in the course of time it would overshadow all the moon's radiance. Therefore it has to be cut down once in every thousand years." Then they entered the spreading halls. The silver stories of the castle towered one above the other, and its walls and columns were all formed of liquid crystal. In the walls were cages and ponds, where fishes and birds moved as though alive. The whole moon-world seemed made of glass. While they were still looking about them on all sides the Lady of the Moon stepped up to them, clad in a white mantle and a rainbow-colored gown. She smiled and said to the emperor: "You are a prince of the mundane world of dust. Great is your fortune, since you have been able to find your way here!" And she called for her attendants, who came flying up on white birds, and sang and danced beneath the cassia tree. A pure clear music floated through the air. Beside the tree stood a mortar made of white marble, in which a jasper rabbit ground up herbs. That was the dark half of the moon. When the dance had ended, the emperor returned to earth again with the sorcerers. And he had the songs which he had heard on the moon written down and sung to the accompaniment of flutes of jasper in his pear-tree garden.

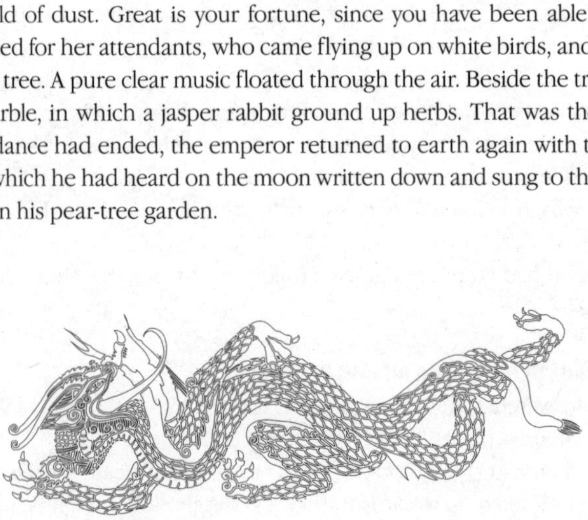

The Ancient Man

ONCE UPON A TIME there was a man named Huang An. He must have been well over eighty and yet he looked like a youth. He lived on cinnabar and wore no clothing. Even in winter he went about without garments. He sat on a tortoise three feet long. Once he was asked: "About how old might this tortoise be?" He answered: "When Fu Hi first invented fish-nets and eel-pots he caught this tortoise and gave it to me. And since then I have worn its shield quite flat sitting on it. The creature dreads the radiance of the sun and moon, so it only sticks its head out of its shell once in two thousand years. Since I have had the beast, it has already stuck its head out five times." With these words he took his tortoise on his back and went off. And the legend arose that this man was ten thousand years old.

The Miserly Farmer

ONCE UPON A TIME there was a farmer who had carted pears to market. Since they were very sweet and fragrant, he hoped to get a good price for them. A bonze with a torn cap and tattered robe stepped up to his cart and asked for one. The farmer repulsed him, but the bonze did not go. Then the farmer grew angry and began to call him names. The bonze said: "You have pears by the hundred in your cart. I only ask for one. Surely that does you no great injury. Why suddenly grow so angry about it?"

The bystanders told the farmer that he ought to give the bonze one of the smaller pears and let him go. But the farmer would not and did not. An artisan saw the whole affair from his shop, and since the noise annoyed him, he took some money, bought a pear and gave it to the bonze.

The bonze thanked him and said: "One like myself, who has given up the world, must not be miserly. I have beautiful pears myself, and I invite you all to eat them with me." Then someone asked: "If you have pears then why do you not eat your own?" He answered: "I first must have a seed to plant."

And with that he began to eat the pear with gusto. When he had finished, he held the pit in his hand, took his pick-ax from his shoulder; and dug a hole a couple of inches deep. Into this he thrust the pit, and covered it with earth. Then he asked the folk in the market place for water, with which to water it. A pair of curiosity seekers brought him hot water from the hostelry in the street, and with it the bonze watered the pit. Thousands of eyes were turned on the spot. And the pit could already be seen to sprout. The sprout grew and in a moment it had turned into a tree. Branches and leaves burgeoned out from it. It began to blossom and soon the fruit had ripened: large, fragrant pears, which hung in thick clusters from the boughs. The bonze climbed into the tree and handed down the pears to the bystanders. In a moment all the pears had been eaten up.

Then the bonze took his pick-ax and cut down the tree. Crash, crash! so it went for a while, and the tree was felled. Then he took the tree on his shoulder and walked away at an easy gait.

When the bonze had begun to make his magic, the farmer, too, had mingled with the crowd. With neck outstretched and staring eyes he had stood there and had entirely forgotten the business he hoped to do with his pears. When the bonze had gone off he turned around to look after his cart. His pears had all disappeared. Then he realized that the pears the bonze had divided had been his own. He looked more closely, and the axle of his cart had disappeared. It was plainly evident that it had been chopped off quite recently. The farmer fell into a rage and hastened after the bonze as fast as ever he could. And when he turned the corner, there lay the missing piece from the axle by the city wall. And then he realized that the pear-tree which the bonze had chopped down must have been his axle. The bonze, however, was nowhere to be found. And the whole crowd in the market burst out into loud laughter.

King Mu of Dschou

IN THE DAYS of King Mu of Dschou a magician came out of the uttermost West, who could walk through water and fire, and pass through metal and stone. He could make mountains and rivers change place, shift about cities and castles, rise into emptiness without falling, strike against solid matter without finding it an obstruction; and he knew a thousand transformations in all their inexhaustible variety. And he could not only change the shape of things but he could change men's thoughts. The King honored him like a god, and served him as he would a master. He resigned his own apartments that the magician might be lodged in them, had beasts of sacrifice brought to offer him, and selected sweet singers to give him pleasure. But the rooms in the King's palace were too humble – the magician could not dwell in them; and the King's singers were not musical enough to be allowed to be near him. So King Mu had a new palace built for him. The work of bricklayers and carpenters, of painters and stainers left nothing to be desired with regard to skill. The King's treasury was empty when the tower had reached its full height. It was a thousand fathoms high, and rose above the top of the mountain before the capital. The King selected maidens, the loveliest and most dainty, gave them fragrant essences, had their eyebrows curved in lines of beauty, and adorned their hair and ears with jewels. He garbed them in fine cloth, and with white silks fluttering about them, and had their faces painted white and their eyebrows stained black. He had them put on armlets of precious stones and mix sweet-smelling herbs. They filled the palace and sang the songs of the ancient kings in order to please the magician. Every month the most costly garments were brought him, and every morning the most delicate food. The magician allowed them to do so, and since he had no choice, made the best of it.

Not long afterward the magician invited the King to go traveling with him. The King grasped the magician's sleeve, and thus they flew up through the air to the middle of the skies. When they stopped they found they had reached the palace of the magician. It was built of gold and silver, and adorned with pearls and precious stones. It towered high over the clouds and rain; and none could say whereon it rested. To the eye it had the appearance of heaped-up clouds. All that it offered the senses was different from the things of the world of men. It seemed to the King as though he were bodily present in the midst of the purple depths of the city of the air, of the divine harmony of the spheres, where the Great God dwells. The King looked down, and his castles and pleasure-houses appeared to him like hills of earth and heaps of straw. And there the King remained for some decades and thought no more of his kingdom.

Then the magician again invited the King to go traveling with him once more. And in the place to which they came there was to be seen neither sun nor moon above, nor rivers or sea below. The King's dazzled eyes could not see the radiant shapes which showed themselves; the King's dulled ears could not hear the sounds which played about them. It seemed as though his body were dissolving in confusion; his thoughts began to stray, and consciousness threatened to leave him. So he begged the magician to return. The magician put his spell upon him, and it seemed to the King as though he were falling into empty space.

When he regained consciousness, he was sitting at the same place where he had been sitting when the magician had asked him to travel with him for the first time. The servants waiting on him were the same, and when he looked down, his goblet was not yet empty, and his food had not yet grown cold.

The King asked what had happened. And the servants answered, "The King sat for a space in silence." Whereupon the King was quite bereft of reason, and it was three months before he regained his right mind. Then he questioned the magician. The magician said: "I was traveling with you in the spirit, O King! What need was there for the body to go along? And the place in which we stayed at that time was no less real than your own castle and your own gardens. But you are used only to permanent conditions, therefore visions which dissolve so suddenly appear strange to you."

The King was content with the explanation. He gave no further thought to the business of government and took no more interest in his servants, but resolved to travel afar. So he had the eight famous steeds harnessed, and accompanied by a few faithful retainers, drove a thousand miles away. There he came to the country of the great hunters. The great hunters brought the King the blood of the white brant to drink, and washed his feet in the milk of mares and cows. When the King and his followers had quenched their thirst, they drove on and camped for the night on the slope of the Kunlun Mountain, south of the Red River. The next day they climbed to the peak of Kunlun Mountain and gazed at the castle of the Lord of the Yellow Earth. Then they traveled on to the Queen-Mother of the West. Before they got there they had to pass the Weak River. This is a river whose waters will bear neither floats nor ships. All that attempts to float over it sinks into its depths. When the King reached the shore, fish and turtles, crabs and salamanders came swimming up and formed a bridge, so that he could drive across with the wagon.

It is said of the Queen-Mother of the West that she goes about with hair unkempt, with a bird's beak and tiger's teeth, and that she is skilled in playing the flute. Yet this is not her true figure, but that of a spirit who serves her, and rules over the Western sky. The Queen-Mother entertained King Mu in her castle by the Springs of Jade. And she gave him rock-marrow to drink and fed him with the fruit of the jade-trees. Then she sang him a song and taught him a magic formula by means of which one could obtain long life. The Queen-Mother of the West gathers the immortals around her, and gives them to eat of the peaches of long life; and then they come to her with wagons with purple canopies, drawn by flying dragons. Ordinary mortals sink in the Weak River when they try to cross. But she was kindly disposed to King Mu.

When he took leave of her, he also went on to the spot where the sun turns in after running three thousand miles a day. Then he returned again to his kingdom.

When King Mu was a hundred years old, the Queen-Mother of the West drew near his palace and led him away with her into the clouds.

And from that day on he was seen no more.

The King of Huai Nan

THE KING OF HUAI NAN was a learned man of the Han dynasty. Since he was of the blood royal the emperor had given him a kingdom in fee. He cultivated the society of scholars, could interpret signs and foretell the future. Together with his scholars he had compiled the book which bears his name.

One day eight aged men came to see him. They all had white beards and white hair. The gate-keeper announced them to the King. The King wished to try them, so he sent back the gate-keeper to put difficulties in the way of their entrance. The latter said to them: "Our King is striving to learn the art of immortal life. You gentlemen are old and feeble. How can you be of aid to him? It is unnecessary for you to pay him a visit."

The eight old men smiled and said: "Oh, and are we too old to suit you? Well, then we will make ourselves young!" And before they had finished speaking they had turned themselves into boys of fourteen and fifteen, with hair-knots as black as silk and faces like peach-blossoms. The gate-keeper was frightened, and at once informed the King of what had happened. When the King heard it, he did not even take time to slip into his shoes, but hurried out barefoot to receive them. He led them into his palace, had rugs of brocade spread for them, and beds of ivory set up, fragrant herbs burned and tables of gold and precious stones set in front of them. Then he bowed before them as pupils do before a teacher, and told them how glad he was that they had come.

The eight boys changed into old men again and said: "Do you wish to go to school to us, O King? Each one of us is master of a particular art. One of us can call up wind and rain, cause clouds and mists to gather, rivers to flow and mountains to heave themselves up, if he wills it so. The second can cause high mountains to split asunder and check great streams in their course. He can tame tigers and panthers and soothe serpents and dragons. Spirits and gods do his bidding. The third can send out doubles, transform himself into other shapes, make himself invisible, cause whole armies to disappear, and turn day into night. The fourth can walk through the air and clouds, can stroll on the surface of the waves, pass through walls and rocks and cover a thousand miles in a single breath. The fifth can enter fire without burning, and water without drowning. The winter frost cannot chill him, nor the summer heat burn him. The sixth can create and transform living creatures if he feel inclined. He can form birds and beasts, grasses and trees. He can transplace houses and castles. The seventh can bake lime so that it turns to gold, and cook lead so that it turns to silver; he can mingle water and stone so that the bubbles effervesce and turn into pearls. The eighth can ride on dragons and cranes to the eight poles of the world, converse with the immortals, and stand in the presence of the Great Pure One."

The King kept them beside him from morning to night, entertained them and had them show him what they could do. And, true enough, they could do everything just as they had said. And now the King began to distil the elixir of life with their aid. He had finished, but not yet imbibed it when a misfortune overtook his family. His son had been playing with a courtier and the latter had heedlessly wounded him. Fearing that the prince might punish him, he joined other discontented persons and excited a revolt. And the emperor, when he heard of it, sent one of his captains to judge between the King and the rebels.

The eight aged men spoke: "It is now time to go. This misfortune has been sent you from heaven, O King! Had it not befallen you, you would not have been able to resolve to leave the splendors and glories of this world!"

They led him on to a mountain. There they offered sacrifices to heaven, and buried gold in the earth. Then they ascended into the skies in bright daylight. The footprints of the eight aged men and of the king were imprinted in the rock of the mountain, and may be seen there to this very day. Before they had left the castle, however, they had set what was left of the elixir of life out in the courtyard. Hens and hounds picked and licked it up, and all flew up into the skies. In Huai Nan to this very day the crowing of cocks and the barking of hounds may be heard up in the skies, and it is said that these are the creatures who followed the King at the time.

One of the King's servants, however, followed him to an island in the sea, whence he sent him back. He told that the King himself had not yet ascended to the skies, but had only become immortal and was wandering about the world. When the emperor heard of the matter he regretted greatly that he had sent soldiers into the King's land and thus driven him out. He called in magicians to aid him, in hope of meeting the eight old men himself. Yet, for all that he spent great sums, he was not successful. The magicians only cheated him.

Old Dschang

ONCE UPON A TIME there was a man who went by the name of Old Dschang. He lived in the country, near Yangdschou, as a gardener. His neighbor, named Sir We, held an official position in Yangdschou. Sir We had decided that it was time for his daughter to marry, so he sent for a match-maker and commissioned her to find a suitable husband. Old Dschang heard this, and was pleased. He prepared food and drink, entertained the match-maker, and told her to recommend him as a husband. But the old match-maker went off scolding.

The next day he invited her to dinner again and gave her money. Then the old match-maker said: "You do not know what you wish! Why should a gentleman's beautiful daughter condescend to marry a poor old gardener like yourself? Even though you had money to burn, your white hair would not match her black locks. Such a marriage is out of the question!"

But Old Dschang did not cease to entreat her: "Make an attempt, just one attempt, to mention me! If they will not listen to you, then I must resign myself to my fate!"

The old match-maker had taken his money, so she could not well refuse, and though she feared being scolded, she mentioned him to Sir We. He grew angry and wanted to throw her out of the house.

"I knew you would not thank me," said she, "but the old man urged it so that I could not refuse to mention his intention."

"Tell the old man that if this very day he brings me two white jade-stones, and four hundred ounces of yellow gold, then I will give him my daughter's hand in marriage."

But he only wished to mock the old man's folly, for he knew that the latter could not give him anything of the kind. The match-maker went to Old Dschang and delivered the message. And he made no objection; but at once brought the exact quantity of gold and jewels to Sir We's house.

The latter was very much frightened and when his wife heard of it, she began to weep and wail loudly. But the girl encouraged her mother: "My father has given his word now and cannot break it. I will know how to bear my fate."

So Sir We's daughter was married to Old Dschang. But even after the wedding the latter did not give up his work as a gardener. He spaded the field and sold vegetables as usual, and his wife had to fetch water and build the kitchen fire herself. But she did her work without false shame and, though her relatives reproached her, she continued to do so.

Once an aristocratic relative visited Sir We and said: "If you had really been poor, were there not enough young gentlemen in the neighborhood for your daughter? Why did you have to marry her to such a wrinkled old gardener? Now that you have thrown her away, so to speak, it would be better if both of them left this part of the country."

Then Sir We prepared a banquet and invited his daughter and Old Dschang to visit him. When they had had sufficient to eat and drink he allowed them to get an inkling of what was in his mind.

Said Old Dschang: "I have only remained here because I thought you would long for your daughter. But since you are tired of us, I will be glad to go. I have a little country house back in the hills, and we will set out for it early tomorrow morning."

The following morning, at break of dawn, Old Dschang came with his wife to say farewell. Sir We said: "Should we long to see you at some later time, my son can make inquiries." Old Dschang placed his wife on a donkey and gave her a straw hat to wear. He himself took his staff and walked after.

A few years passed without any news from either of them. Then Sir We and his wife felt quite a longing to see their daughter and sent their son to make inquiries. When the latter got back in the hills he met a plow-boy who was plowing with two yellow steers. He asked him: "Where is Old Dschang's country house?" The plow-boy left the plow in the harrow, bowed and answered: "You have been a long time coming, sir! The village is not far from here: I will show you the way."

They crossed a hill. At the foot of the hill flowed a brook, and when they had crossed the brook they had to climb another hill. Gradually the landscape changed. From the top of the hill could be seen a valley, level in the middle, surrounded by abrupt crags and shaded by green trees, among which houses and towers peeped forth. This was the country house of Old Dschang. Before the village flowed a deep brook full of clear, blue water. They passed over a stone bridge and reached the gate. Here flowers and trees grew in luxurious profusion, and peacocks and cranes flew about. From the distance could be heard the sound of flutes and of stringed instruments. Crystal-clear tones rose to the clouds. A messenger in a purple robe received the guest at the gate and led him into a hall of surpassing splendor. Strange fragrances filled the air, and there was a ringing of little bells of pearl. Two maid-servants came forth to greet him, followed by two rows of beautiful girls in a long processional. After them a man in a flowing turban, clad in scarlet silk, with red slippers, came floating along. The guest saluted him. He was serious and dignified, and at the same time seemed youthfully fresh. At first We's son did not recognize him, but when he looked more closely, why it was Old Dschang! The latter said with a smile: "I am pleased that the long road to travel has not prevented your coming. Your sister is just combing her hair. She will welcome you in a moment." Then he had him sit down and drink tea.

After a short time a maid-servant came and led him to the inner rooms, to his sister. The beams of her room were of sandalwood, the doors of tortoise-shell and the windows inlaid with blue jade; her curtains were formed of strings of pearls and the steps leading into the room of green nephrite. His sister was magnificently gowned, and far more beautiful than before. She asked him carelessly how he was getting along, and what her parents were doing; but was not very cordial. After a splendid meal she had an apartment prepared for him.

"My sister wishes to make an excursion to the Mountain of the Fairies," said Old Dschang to him. "We will be back about sunset, and you can rest until we return."

Then many-colored clouds rose in the courtyard, and dulcet music sounded on the air. Old Dschang mounted a dragon, while his wife and sister rode on phenixes and their attendants on cranes. So they rose into the air and disappeared in an easterly direction. They did not return until after sunset.

Old Dschang and his wife then said to him: "This is an abode of the blessed. You cannot remain here overlong. Tomorrow we will escort you back."

On the following day, when taking leave, Old Dschang gave him eighty ounces of gold and an old straw hat. "Should you need money," said he, "you can go to Yangdschou and inquire in the northern suburb for old Wang's drug-shop. There you can collect ten million pieces of copper. This hat is the order for them." Then he ordered his plow-boy to take him home again.

Quite a few of the folks at home, to whom he described his adventures, thought that Old Dschang must be a holy man, while others regarded the whole thing a magic vision.

After five or six years Sir We's money came to an end. So his son took the straw hat to Yangdschou and there asked for old Wang. The latter just happened to be standing in his drug-shop, mixing herbs. When the son explained his errand he said: "The money is ready. But is your hat genuine?" And he took the hat and examined it. A young girl came from an inner room and said: "I wove the hat for Old Dschang myself. There must be a red thread in it." And sure enough, there was. Then old Wang gave young We the ten million pieces of copper, and the latter now believed that Old Dschang was really a saint. So he once more went over the hills to look for him. He asked the forest-keepers, but they could tell him naught. Sadly he retraced his steps and decided to inquire of old Wang, but he had also disappeared.

When several years had passed he once more came to Yangdschou, and was walking in the meadow before the city gate. There he met Old Dschang's plow-boy. The latter cried out: "How are you? How are you?" and drew out ten pounds of gold, which he gave to him, saying: "My mistress told me to give you this. My master is this very moment drinking tea with old Wang in the inn." Young We followed the plow-boy, intending to greet his brother-in-law. But when he reached the inn there was no one in sight. And when he turned around the plow-boy had disappeared as well. And since that time no one ever heard from Old Dschang again.

The Kindly Magician

ONCE UPON A TIME there was a man named Du Dsi Tschun. In his youth he was a spendthrift and paid no heed to his property. He was given to drink and idling. When he had run through all his money, his relatives cast him out. One winter day he was walking barefoot about the city, with an empty stomach and torn clothes. Evening came on and still he had not found any food. Without end or aim he wandered about the market place. He was hungry, and the cold seemed well nigh unendurable. So he turned his eyes upward and began to lament aloud.

Suddenly an ancient man stood before him, leaning on a staff, who said: "What do you lack since you complain so?"

"I am dying of hunger," replied Du Dsi Tschun, "and not a soul will take pity on me!"

The ancient man said: "How much money would you need in order to live in all comfort?"

"If I had fifty thousand pieces of copper it would answer my purpose," replied Du Dsi Tschun.

The ancient said: "That would not answer."

"Well, then, a million!"

"That is still too little!"

"Well, then, three million!"

The ancient man said: "That is well spoken!" He fetched a thousand pieces of copper out of his sleeve and said: "That is for this evening. Expect me tomorrow by noon, at the Persian Bazaar!"

At the time set Du Dsi Tschun went there, and, sure enough, there was the ancient, who gave him three million pieces of copper. Then he disappeared, without giving his name.

When Du Dsi Tschun held the money in his hand, his love for prodigality once more awoke. He rode pampered steeds, clothed himself in the finest furs, went back to his wine, and led such an extravagant life that the money gradually came to an end. Instead of wearing brocade he had to wear cotton, and instead of riding horseback he went to the dogs. Finally he was again running about barefoot and in rags as before, and did not know how to satisfy his hunger. Once more he stood in the market-place and sighed. But the ancient was already there, took him by the hand and said: "Are you back already to where you were? That is strange! However, I will aid you once more!"

But Du Dsi Tschun was ashamed and did not want to accept his help. Yet the ancient insisted, and led him along to the Persian Bazaar. This time he gave him ten million pieces of copper, and Du Dsi Tschun thanked him with shame in his heart.

With money in hand, he tried to give time to adding to it, and saving in order to gain great wealth. But, as is always the case, it is hard to overcome ingrown faults. Gradually he began to fling his money away again, and gave free rein to all his desires. And once more his purse grew empty. In a couple of years he was as poor as ever he had been.

Then he met the ancient the third time, but was so ashamed of himself that he hid his face when he passed him.

The ancient seized his arm and said: "Where are you going? I will help you once more. I will give you thirty million. But if then you do not improve you are past all aid!"

Full of gratitude, Du Dsi Tschun bowed before him and said: "In the days of my poverty my wealthy relatives did not seek me out. You alone have thrice aided me. The money you give me to-day shall not be squandered, that I swear; but I will devote it to good works in order to repay your great kindness. And when I have done this I will follow you, if needs be through fire and through water."

The ancient replied: "That is right! When you have ordered these things ask for me in the temple of Laotsze beneath the two mulberry trees!"

Du Dsi Tschun took the money and went to Yangdschou. There he bought a hundred acres of the best land, and built a lofty house with many hundreds of rooms on the highway. And there he allowed widows and orphans to live. Then he bought a burial-place for his ancestors, and supported his needy relations. Countless people were indebted to him for their livelihood.

When all was finished, he went to inquire after the ancient in the temple of Laotsze. The ancient was sitting in the shade of the mulberry trees blowing the flute. He took Du Dsi Tschun along with him to the cloudy peaks of the holy mountains of the West. When they had gone some forty miles into the mountains, he saw a dwelling, fair and clean. It was surrounded by many-colored clouds, and peacocks and cranes were flying about it. Within the house was a herb-oven nine feet high. The fire burned with a purple flame, and its glow leaped along the walls. Nine fairies stood at the oven, and a green dragon and a white tiger crouched beside it. Evening came. The ancient was no longer clad like an ordinary man; but wore a yellow cap and wide, flowing garments. He took three pellets of the White Stone, put them into a flagon of wine, and gave them to Du Dsi Tschun to drink. He spread out a tiger-skin against the western wall of the inner chamber, and bade Du Dsi Tschun sit down on it, with his face turned toward the East. Then he said to him: "Now beware of speaking a single word – no matter what happens to you, whether you encounter powerful gods or terrible demons, wild beasts or ogres, or all the tortures of the nether world, or even if you see your own relatives suffer – for all these things are only deceitful images! They cannot harm you. Think only of what I have said, and let your soul be at rest!" And when he had said this the ancient disappeared.

Then Du Dsi Tschun saw only a large stone jug full of clear water standing before him. Fairies, dragon and tiger had all vanished. Suddenly he heard a tremendous crash, which made heaven and earth tremble. A man towering more than ten feet in height appeared. He called himself the great captain, and he and his horse were covered with golden armor. He was surrounded by more than a hundred soldiers, who drew their bows and swung their swords, and halted in the courtyard.

The giant called out harshly: "Who are you? Get out of my way!"

Du Dsi Tschun did not move. And he returned no answer to his questions.

Then the giant flew into a passion and cried with a thundering voice: "Chop off his head!"

But Du Dsi Tschun remained unmoved, so the giant went off raging.

Then a furious tiger and a poisonous serpent came up roaring and hissing. They made as though to bite him and leaped over him. But Du Dsi Tschun remained unperturbed in spirit, and after a time they dissolved and vanished.

Suddenly a great rain began to fall in streams. It thundered and lightninged incessantly, so that his ears rang and his eyes were blinded. It seemed as though the house would fall. The water rose to a flood in a few moments' time, and streamed up to the place where he was sitting. But Du Dsi Tschun remained motionless and paid no attention to it. And after a time the water receded.

Then came a great demon with the head of an ox. He set up a kettle in the middle of the courtyard, in which bubbled boiling oil. He caught Du Dsi Tschun by the neck with an iron fork and said: "If you will tell me who you are I will let you go!"

Du Dsi Tschun shut his eyes and kept silent. Then the demon picked him up with the fork and flung him into the kettle. He withstood the pain, and the boiling oil did not harm him. Finally the demon dragged him out again, and drew him down the steps of the house before a man with red hair and a blue face, who looked like the prince of the nether world. The latter cried: "Drag in his wife!"

After a time Du Dsi Tschun's wife was brought on in chains. Her hair was torn and she wept bitterly.

The demon pointed to Du Dsi Tschun and said: "If you will speak your name we will let her go!"

But he answered not a word.

Then the prince of evil had the woman tormented in all sorts of ways. And she pleaded with Du Dsi Tschun: "I have been your wife now for ten years. Will you not speak one little word to save me? I can endure no more!" And the tears ran in streams from her eyes. She screamed and scolded. Yet he spoke not a word.

Thereupon the prince of evil shouted: "Chop her into bits!" And there, before his eyes, it seemed as though she were really being chopped to pieces. But Du Dsi Tschun did not move.

"The scoundrel's measure is full!" cried the prince of evil. "He shall dwell no longer among the living! Off with his head!" And so they killed him, and it seemed to him that his soul fled his body. The ox-headed demon dragged him down into the nether regions, where he tasted all the tortures in turn. But Du Dsi Tschun remembered the words of the ancient. And the tortures, too, seemed bearable. So he did not scream and said not a word.

Now he was once more dragged before the prince of evil. The latter said: "As punishment for his obstinacy this man shall come to earth again in the shape of a woman!"

The demon dragged him to the wheel of life and he returned to earth in the shape of a girl. He was often ill, had to take medicine continually, and was pricked and burned with hot needles. Yet he never uttered a sound. Gradually he grew into a beautiful maiden. But since he never spoke, he was known as the dumb maid. A scholar finally took him for his bride, and they lived in peace and good fellowship. And a son came to them who, in the course of two years was already beyond measure wise and intelligent. One day the father was carrying the son on his arm. He spoke jestingly to his wife and said: "When I look at you it seems to me that you are not really dumb. Won't you say one little word to me? How delightful it would be if you were to become my speaking rose!"

The woman remained silent. No matter how he might coax and try to make her smile, she would return no answer.

Then his features changed: "If you will not speak to me, it is a sign that you scorn me; and in that case your son is nothing to me, either!" And with that he seized the boy and flung him against the wall.

But since Du Dsi Tschun loved this little boy so dearly, he forgot the ancient's warning, and cried out: "Oh, oh!"

And before the cry had died away Du Dsi Tschun awoke as though from a dream and found himself seated in his former place. The ancient was there as well. It must have been about the fifth hour of the night. Purple flames rose wildly from the oven, and flared up to the sky. The whole house caught fire and burned like a torch.

"You have deceived me!" cried the ancient. Then he seized him by the hair and thrust him into the jug of water. And in a minute the fire went out. The ancient spoke: "You overcame joy and rage, grief and fear, hate and desire, it is true; but love you had not driven from your soul. Had you not cried out when the child was flung against the wall, then my elixir would have taken shape and you would have attained immortality. But in the last moment you failed me. Now it is too late. Now I can begin brewing my elixir of life once more from the beginning and you will remain a mere mortal man!"

Du Dsi Tschun saw that the oven had burst, and that instead of the philosopher's stone it held only a lump of iron. The ancient man cast aside his garments and chopped it up with a magic knife. Du Dsi Tschun took leave of him and returned to Yangdschou, where he lived in great affluence. In his old age he regretted that he had not completed his task. He once more went to the mountain to look for the ancient. But the ancient had vanished without leaving a trace.

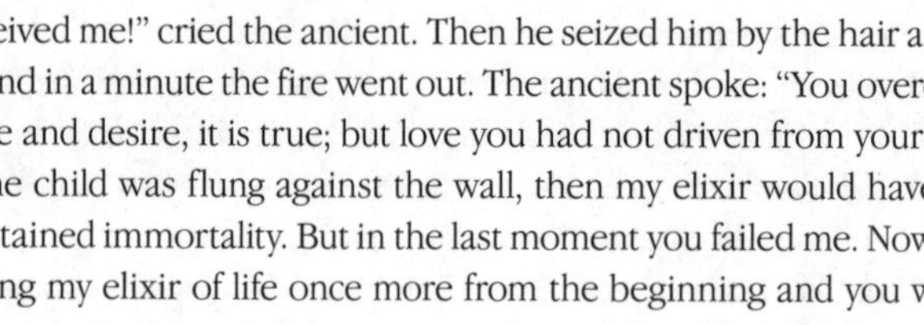

The Flower-Elves

ONCE UPON A TIME there was a scholar who lived retired from the world in order to gain hidden wisdom. He lived alone and in a secret place. And all about the little house in which he dwelt he had planted every kind of flower, and bamboos and other trees. There it lay, quite concealed in its thick grove of flowers. With him he had only a boy servant, who dwelt in a separate hut, and who carried out his orders. He was not allowed to appear before his master unless summoned. The scholar loved his flowers as he did himself. Never did he set his foot beyond the boundaries of his garden.

It chanced that once there came a lovely spring evening. Flowers and trees stood in full bloom, a fresh breeze was blowing, the moon shone clearly. And the scholar sat over his goblet and was grateful for the gift of life.

Suddenly he saw a maiden in dark garments come tripping up in the moonlight. She made a deep courtesy, greeted him and said: "I am your neighbor. We are a company of young maids who are on our way to visit the eighteen aunts. We should like to rest in this court for awhile, and therefore ask your permission to do so."

The scholar saw that this was something quite out of the common, and gladly gave his consent. The maiden thanked him and went away.

In a short time she brought back a whole crowd of maids carrying flowers and willow branches. All greeted the scholar. They were charming, with delicate features, and slender, graceful figures. When they moved their sleeves, a delightful fragrance was exhaled. There is no fragrance known to the human world which could be compared with it.

The scholar invited them to sit down for a time in his room. Then he asked them: "Whom have I really the honor of entertaining? Have you come from the castle of the Lady in the Moon, or the Jade Spring of the Queen-Mother of the West?"

"How could we claim such high descent?" said a maiden in a green gown, with a smile. "My name is Salix." Then she presented another, clad in white, and said: "This is Mistress Prunophora"; then one in rose, "and this is Persica"; and finally one in a dark-red gown, "and this is Punica. We are all sisters and we want to visit the eighteen zephyr-aunts to-day. The moon shines so beautifully this evening and it is so charming here in the garden. We are most grateful to you for taking pity on us."

"Yes, yes," said the scholar.

Then the sober-clad servant suddenly announced: "The zephyr-aunts have already arrived!"

At once the girls rose and went to the door to meet them.

"We were just about to visit you, aunts," they said, smiling. "This gentleman here had just invited us to sit for a moment. What a pleasant coincidence that you aunts have come here, too. This is such a lovely night that we must drink a goblet of nectar in honor of you aunts!"

Thereon they ordered the servant to bring what was needed.

"May one sit down here?" asked the aunts.

"The master of the house is most kind," replied the maids, "and the spot is quiet and hidden."

And then they presented the aunts to the scholar. He spoke a few kindly words to the eighteen aunts. They had a somewhat irresponsible and airy manner. Their words fairly gushed out, and in their neighborhood one felt a frosty chill.

Meanwhile the servant had already brought in table and chairs. The eighteen aunts sat at the upper end of the board, the maids followed, and the scholar sat down with them at the lowest place. Soon the entire table was covered with the most delicious foods and most magnificent fruits, and the goblets were filled with a fragrant nectar. They were delights such as the world of men does not know! The moon shone brightly and the flowers exhaled intoxicating odors. After they had partaken of food and drink the maids rose, danced and sung. Sweetly the sound of their singing echoed through the falling gloam, and their dance was like that of butterflies fluttering about the flowers. The scholar was so overpowered with delight that he no longer knew whether he were in heaven or on earth.

When the dance had ended, the girls sat down again at the table, and drank the health of the aunts in flowing nectar. The scholar, too, was remembered with a toast, to which he replied with well-turned phrases.

But the eighteen aunts were somewhat irresponsible in their ways. One of them, raising her goblet, by accident poured some nectar on Punica's dress. Punica, who was young and fiery, and very neat, stood up angrily when she saw the spot on her red dress.

"You are really very careless," said she, in her anger. "My other sisters may be afraid of you, but I am not!"

Then the aunts grew angry as well and said: "How dare this young chit insult us in such a manner!"

And with that they gathered up their garments and rose.

All the maids then crowded about them and said: "Punica is so young and inexperienced! You must not bear her any ill-will! Tomorrow she shall go to you switch in hand, and receive her punishment!"

But the eighteen aunts would not listen to them and went off. Thereupon the maids also said farewell, scattered among the flower-beds and disappeared. The scholar sat for a long time lost in dreamy yearning.

On the following evening the maids all came back again.

"We all live in your garden," they told him. "Every year we are tormented by naughty winds, and therefore we have always asked the eighteen aunts to protect us. But yesterday Punica insulted them, and now we fear they will help us no more. But we know that you have always been well disposed toward us, for which we are heartily grateful. And now we have a great favor to ask, that every New Year's day you make a small scarlet flag, paint the sun, moon and five planets on it, and set it up in the eastern part of the garden. Then we sisters will be left in peace and will be protected from all evil. But since New Year's day has passed for this year, we beg that you will set up the flag on the twenty-first of this month. For the East Wind is coming and the flag will protect us against him!"

The scholar readily promised to do as they wished, and the maids all said with a single voice: "We thank you for your great kindness and will repay it!" Then they departed and a sweet fragrance filled the entire garden.

The scholar, however, made a red flag as described, and when early in the morning of the day in question the East Wind really did begin to blow, he quickly set it up in the garden.

Suddenly a wild storm broke out, one that caused the forests to bend, and broke the trees. The flowers in the garden alone did not move.

Then the scholar noticed that Salix was the willow; Prunophora the plum; Persica the peach, and the saucy Punica the Pomegranate, whose powerful blossoms the wind cannot tear. The eighteen zephyr-aunts, however, were the spirits of the winds.

In the evening the flower-elves all came and brought the scholar radiant flowers as a gift of thanks.

"You have saved us," they said, "and we have nothing else we can give you. If you eat these flowers you will live long and avoid old age. And if you, in turn, will protect us every year, then we sisters, too, will live long."

The scholar did as they told him and ate the flowers. And his figure changed and he grew young again like a youth of twenty. And in the course of time he attained the hidden wisdom and was placed among the Immortals.

The Spirit of the Wu-Lian Mountain

TO THE WEST of the gulf of Kiautschou is the Wu-Lian Mountain, where there are many spirits. Once upon a time a scholar who lived there was sitting up late at night, reading. And, as he stepped out before the house, a storm rose up suddenly, and a monster stretched out his claws and seized him by the hair. And he lifted him up in the air and carried him away. They passed by the tower which looks out to sea, a Buddhist temple in the hills. And in the distance, in the clouds, the scholar saw the figure of a god in golden armor. The figure looked exactly like the image of Weto which was in the tower. In its right hand it held an iron mace, while its left pointed toward the monster, and it looked at it with anger. Then the monster let the scholar fall, right on top of the tower, and disappeared. No doubt the saint in the tower had come to the scholar's aid, because his whole family worshiped Buddha dutifully.

When the sun rose the priest came and saw the scholar on his tower. He piled up hay and straw on the ground; so that he could jump down without hurting himself. Then he took the scholar home, yet there where the monster had seized his hair, the hair remained stiff and unyielding. It did not improve until half a year had gone by.

The King of the Ants

ONCE UPON A TIME there was a scholar, who wandered away from his home and went to Emmet village. There stood a house which was said to be haunted. Yet it was beautifully situated and surrounded by a lovely garden. So the scholar hired it. One evening he was sitting over his books, when several hundred knights suddenly came galloping into the room. They were quite tiny, and their horses were about the size of flies. They had hunting falcons and dogs about as large as gnats and fleas.

They came to his bed in the corner of the room, and there they held a great hunt, with bows and arrows: one could see it all quite plainly. They caught a tremendous quantity of birds and game, and all this game was no larger than little grains of rice.

When the hunt was over, in came a long procession with banners and standards. They wore swords at their side and bore spears in their hands, and came to a halt in the north-west corner of the room. They were followed by several hundred serving-men. These brought with them curtains and covers, tents and tent-poles, pots and kettles, cups and plates, tables and chairs. And after them some hundreds of other servants carried in all sorts of fine dishes, the best that land and water had to offer. And several hundred more ran to and fro without stopping, in order to guard the roads and carry messages.

The scholar gradually accustomed himself to the sight. Although the men were so very small he could distinguish everything quite clearly.

Before long, a bright colored banner appeared. Behind it rode a personage wearing a scarlet hat and garments of purple. He was surrounded by an escort of several thousands. Before him went runners with whips and rods to clear the way.

Then a man wearing an iron helmet and with a golden ax in his hand cried out in a loud voice: "His Highness is graciously pleased to look at the fish in the Purple Lake!" Whereupon the one who wore the scarlet hat got down from his horse, and, followed by a retinue of several hundred men, approached the saucer which the scholar used for his writing-ink. Tents were put up on the edge of the saucer and a banquet was prepared. A great number of guests sat down to the table. Musicians and dancers stood ready. There was a bright confusion of mingled garments of purple and scarlet, crimson and green. Pipes and flutes, fiddles and cymbals sounded, and the dancers moved in the dance. The music was very faint, and yet its melodies could be clearly distinguished. All that was said, too, the table-talk and orders, questions and calls, could be quite distinctly heard.

After three courses, he who wore the scarlet hat said: "Quick! Make ready the nets and lines for fishing!"

And at once nets were thrown out into the saucer which held the water in which the scholar dipped his brush. And they caught hundreds of thousands of fishes. The one with the scarlet hat contented himself with casting a line in the shallow waters of the saucer, and caught a baker's dozen of red carp.

Then he ordered the head cook to cook the fish, and the most varied dishes were prepared with them. The odor of roasting fat and spices filled the whole room.

And then the wearer of the scarlet hat in his arrogance, decided to amuse himself at the scholar's expense. So he pointed to him and said: "I know nothing at all about the writings and customs of the saints and wise men, and still I am a king who is highly honored! Yonder scholar spends his whole life toiling over his books and yet he remains poor and gets nowhere. If he could make up his mind to serve me faithfully as one of my officials, I might allow him to partake of our meal."

This angered the scholar, and he took his book and struck at them. And they all scattered, wriggling and crawling out of the door. He followed them and dug up the earth in the place where they had disappeared. And there he found an ants' nest as large as a barrel, in which countless green ants were wriggling around. So he built a large fire and smoked them out.

The Little Hunting Dog

ONCE UPON A TIME, in the city of Shansi, there lived a scholar who found the company of others too noisy for him. So he made his home in a Buddhist temple. Yet he suffered because there were always so many gnats and fleas in his room that he could not sleep at night.

Once he was resting on his bed after dinner, when suddenly two little knights with plumes in their helmets rode into the room. They might have been two inches high, and rode horses about the size of grasshoppers. On their gauntleted hands they held hunting falcons as large as flies. They rode about the room with great rapidity. The scholar had no more than set eyes on them when a third entered, clad like the others, but carrying a bow and arrows and leading a little hunting dog the size of an ant with him. After him came a great throng of footmen and horsemen, several hundred in all. And they had hunting falcons and hunting dogs by the hundred, too. Then the fleas and gnats began to rise in the air; but were all slain by the falcons. And the hunting dogs climbed on the bed, and sniffed along the walls trailing the fleas, and ate them up. They followed the trace of whatever hid in the cracks, and nosed it out, so that in a short space of time they had killed nearly all the vermin.

The scholar pretended to be asleep and watched them. And the falcons settled down on him, and the dogs crawled along his body. Shortly after came a man clad in yellow, wearing a king's crown, who climbed on an empty couch and seated himself there. And at once all the horsemen rode up, descended from their horses and brought him all the birds and game. They then gathered beside him in a great throng, and conversed with him in a strange tongue.

Not long after the king got into a small chariot and his bodyguards saddled their horses with the greatest rapidity. Then they galloped out with great cries of homage, till it looked as though someone were scattering beans and a heavy cloud of dust rose behind them.

They had nearly all of them disappeared, while the scholar's eyes were still fixed on them full of terror and astonishment, and he could not imagine whence they had come. He slipped on his shoes and looked; but they had vanished without a trace. Then he returned and looked all about his room; but there was nothing to be seen. Only, on a brick against the wall, they had forgotten a little hunting dog. The scholar quickly caught it and found it quite tame. He put it in his paint-box and examined it closely. It had a very smooth, fine coat, and wore a little collar around its neck. He tried to feed it a few bread-crumbs, but the little dog only sniffed at them and let them lie. Then it leaped into the bed and hunted up some nits and gnats in the folds of the linen, which it devoured. Then it returned and lay down. When the night had passed the scholar feared it might have run away; but there it lay, curled up as before. Whenever the scholar went to bed, the dog climbed into it and bit to death any vermin it could find. Not a fly or gnat dared alight while it was around. The scholar loved it like a jewel of price.

But once he took a nap in the daytime, and the little dog crawled into bed beside him. The scholar woke and turned around, supporting himself on his side. As he did so he felt something, and feared it might be his little dog. He quickly rose and looked, but it was already dead – pressed flat, as though cut out of paper!

But at any rate none of the vermin had survived it.

The Dragon After His Winter Sleep

ONCE THERE WAS a scholar who was reading in the upper story of his house. It was a rainy, cloudy day and the weather was gloomy. Suddenly he saw a little thing which shone like a fire-fly. It crawled upon the table, and wherever it went it left traces of burns, curved like the tracks of a rainworm. Gradually it wound itself about the scholar's book and the book, too, grew black. Then it occurred to him that it might be a dragon. So he carried it out of doors on the book. There he stood for quite some time; but it sat uncurled, without moving in the least.

Then the scholar said: "It shall not be said of me that I was lacking in respect." With these words he carried back the book and once more laid it on the table. Then he put on his robes of ceremony, made a deep bow and escorted the dragon out on it again.

No sooner had he left the door, than he noticed that the dragon raised his head and stretched himself. Then he flew up from the book with a hissing sound, like a radiant streak. Once more he turned around toward the scholar, and his head had already grown to the size of a barrel, while his body must have been a full fathom in length. He gave one more snaky twist, and then there was a terrible crash of thunder and the dragon went sailing through the air.

The scholar then returned and looked to see which way the little creature had come. And he could follow his tracks hither and thither, to his chest of books.

The Sorcerer of the White Lotus Lodge

ONCE UPON A TIME there was a sorcerer who belonged to the White Lotus Lodge. He knew how to deceive the multitude with his black arts, and many who wished to learn the secret of his enchantments became his pupils.

One day the sorcerer wished to go out. He placed a bowl which he covered with another bowl in the hall of his house, and ordered his pupils to watch it. But he warned them against uncovering the bowl to see what might be in it.

No sooner had he gone than the pupils uncovered the bowl and saw that it was filled with clear water. And floating on the water was a little ship made of straw, with real masts and sails. They were surprised and pushed it with their fingers till it upset. Then they quickly righted it again and once more covered the bowl. By that time the sorcerer was already standing among them. He was angry and scolded them, saying: "Why did you disobey my command?"

His pupils rose and denied that they had done so.

But the sorcerer answered: "Did not my ship turn turtle at sea, and yet you try to deceive me?"

On another evening he lit a giant candle in his room, and ordered his pupils to watch it lest it be blown out by the wind. It must have been at the second watch of the night and the sorcerer had not yet come back. The pupils grew tired and sleepy, so they went to bed and gradually fell asleep. When they woke up again the candle had gone out. So they rose quickly and re-lit it. But the sorcerer was already in the room, and again he scolded them.

"Truly we did not sleep! How could the light have gone out?"

Angrily the sorcerer replied: "You let me walk fifteen miles in the dark, and still you can talk such nonsense!"

Then his pupils were very much frightened.

In the course of time one of his pupils insulted the sorcerer. The latter made note of the insult, but said nothing. Soon after he told the pupil to feed the swine, and no sooner had he entered the sty than his master turned him into a pig. The sorcerer then at once called in a butcher, sold the pig to the man, and he went the way of all pigs who go to the butcher.

One day this pupil's father turned up to ask after his son, for he had not come back to his home for a long time. The sorcerer told him that his son had left him long ago. The father returned home and inquired everywhere for his son without success. But one of his son's fellow-pupils, who knew of the matter, informed the father. So the father complained to the district mandarin. The latter, however, feared that the sorcerer might make himself invisible. He did not dare to have him arrested, but informed his superior and begged for a thousand well-armed soldiers. These surrounded the sorcerer's home and seized him, together with his wife and child. All three were put into wooden cages to be transported to the capital.

The road wound through the mountains, and in the midst of the hills up came a giant as large as a tree, with eyes like saucers, a mouth like a plate, and teeth a foot long. The soldiers stood there trembling and did not dare to move.

Said the sorcerer: "That is a mountain spirit. My wife will be able to drive him off."

They did as he suggested, unchained the woman, and she took a spear and went to meet the giant. The latter was angered, and he swallowed her, tooth and nail. This frightened the rest all the more.

The sorcerer said: "Well, if he has done away with my wife, then it is my son's turn!"

So they let the son out of his cage. But the giant swallowed him in the same way. The rest all looked on without knowing what to do.

The sorcerer then wept with rage and said: "First he destroys my wife, and then my son. If only he might be punished for it! But I am the only one who can punish him!"

And, sure enough, they took him out of his cage, too, gave him a sword, and sent him out against the giant. The sorcerer and the giant fought with each other for a time, and at last the giant seized the sorcerer, thrust him into his maw, stretched his neck and swallowed him. Then he went his way contentedly.

And now when it was too late, the soldiers realized that the sorcerer had tricked them.

The Three Evils

ONCE UPON A TIME, in the old days, there lived a young man by the name of Dschou Tschu. He was of more than ordinary strength, and no one could withstand him. He was also wild and undisciplined, and wherever he was, quarrels and brawls arose. Yet the village elders never ventured to punish him seriously. He wore a high hat on his head, adorned with two pheasants' wings. His garments were woven of embroidered silk, and at his side hung the Dragonspring sword. He was given to play and to drinking, and his hand was inclined to take that which belonged to others. Whoever offended him had reason to dread the consequences, and he always mixed into disputes in which others were engaged. Thus he kept it up for years, and was a pest throughout the neighborhood.

Then a new mandarin came to that district. When he had arrived, he first went quietly about the country and listened to the people's complaints. And they told him that there were three great evils in that district.

Then he clothed himself in coarse garments, and wept before Dschou Tschu's door. Dschou Tschu was just coming from the tavern, where he had been drinking. He was slapping his sword and singing in a loud voice.

When he reached his house he asked: "Who is weeping here so pitifully?"

And the mandarin replied: "I am weeping because of the people's distress."

Then Dschou Tschu saw him and broke out into loud laughter.

"You are mistaken, my friend," said he. "Revolt is seething round about us like boiling water in a kettle. But here, in our little corner of the land, all is quiet and peaceful. The harvest has been abundant, corn is plentiful, and all go happily about their work. When you talk to me about distress I have to think of the man who groans without being sick. And who are you, tell me that, who instead of grieving for yourself, are grieving for others? And what are you doing before my door?"

"I am the new mandarin," replied the other. "Since I left my litter I have been looking about in the neighborhood. I find the people are honest and simple in their way of life, and everyone has sufficient to wear and to eat. This is all just as you state. Yet, strange to say, when the elders come together, they always sigh and complain. And if they are asked why, they answer: 'There are three great evils in our district!' I have come to ask you to do away with two of them, as to the third, perhaps I had better remain silent. And this is the reason I weep before your door."

"Well, what are these evils?" answered Dschou Tschu. "Speak freely, and tell me openly all that you know!"

"The first evil," said the mandarin, "is the evil dragon at the long bridge, who causes the water to rise so that man and beast are drowned in the river. The second evil is the tiger with the white forehead, who dwells in the hills. And the third evil, Dschou Tschu – is yourself!"

Then the blush of shame mounted to the man's cheek, and he bowed and said: "You have come here from afar to be the mandarin of this district, and yet you feel such sympathy for the people? I was born in this place and yet I have only made our elders grieve. What sort of a creature must I be? I beg that you will return home again. I will see to it that matters improve!"

Then he ran without stopping to the hills, and hunted the tiger out of his cave. The latter leaped into the air so that the whole forest was shaken as though by a storm. Then he came rushing up, roaring, and stretching out his claws savagely to seize his enemy. Dschou Tschu stepped back a pace, and the tiger lit on the ground directly in front of him. Then he thrust the tiger's neck to the ground with his left hand, and beat him without stopping with his right, until he lay dead on the earth. Dschou Tschu loaded the tiger on his back and went home.

Then he went to the long bridge. He undressed, took his sword in his hand, and thus dived into the water. No sooner had he disappeared, than there was a boiling and hissing, and the waves began to foam and billow. It sounded like the mad beating of thousands of hoofs. After a time a stream of blood shot up from the depths, and the water of the river turned red. Then Dschou Tschu, holding the dragon in his hand, rose out of the waves.

He went to the mandarin and reported, with a bow: "I have cut off the dragon's head, and have also done away with the tiger. Thus I have happily accomplished your command. And now I shall wander away so that you may be rid of the third evil as well. Lord, watch over my country, and tell the elders that they need sorrow no more!"

When he had said this he enlisted as a soldier. In combat against the robbers he gained a great reputation and once, when the latter were pressing him hard, and he saw that he could not save himself, he bowed to the East and said: "The day has come at last when I can atone for my sin with my life!" Then he offered his neck to the sword and died.

How Three Heroes Came by their Deaths Because of Two Peaches

AT THE BEGINNING of his reign Duke Ging of Tsi loved to draw heroes about him. Among those whom he attached to him were three of quite extraordinary bravery. The first was named Gung Sun Dsia, the second Tian Kai Giang, the third Gu I Dsi. All three were highly honored by the prince, but the honor paid them made them presumptuous, they kept the court in a turmoil, and overstepped the bounds of respect which lie between a prince and his servants.

At the time Yan Dsi was chancellor of Tsi. The duke consulted him as to what would be best to do. And the chancellor advised him to give a great court banquet and invite all his courtiers. On the table, the choicest dish of all, stood a platter holding four magnificent peaches.

Then, in accordance with his chancellor's advice, the Duke rose and said: "Here are some magnificent peaches, but I cannot give one to each of you. Only those most worthy may eat of them. I myself reign over the land, and am the first among the princes of the empire. I have been successful in holding my possessions and power, and that is my merit. Hence one of the peaches falls to me. Yan Dsi sits here as my chancellor. He regulates communications with foreign lands and keeps the peace among the people. He has made my kingdom powerful among the kingdoms of the earth. That is his merit, and hence the second peach falls to him. Now there are but two peaches left; yet I cannot tell which ones among you are the worthiest. You may rise yourselves and tell us of your merits. But whoever has performed no great deeds, let him hold his tongue!"

Then Gung Sun Dsia beat upon his sword, rose up and said: "I am the prince's captain general. In the South I besieged the kingdom of Lu, in the West I conquered the kingdom of Dsin, in the North I captured the army of Yan. All the princes of the East come to the Duke's court and acknowledge the overlordship of Tsi. That is my merit. I do not know whether it deserves a peach."

The Duke replied: "Great is your merit! A peach is your just due!"

Then Tian Kai Giang rose, beat on the table, and cried: "I have fought a hundred battles in the army of the prince. I have slain the enemy's general-in-chief, and captured the enemy's flag. I have extended the borders of the Duke's land till the size of his realm has been increased by a thousand miles. How is it with my merit?"

The Duke said: "Great is your merit! A peach is your just due!"

Then Gu I Dsi arose; his eyes started from their sockets, and he shouted with a loud voice: "Once, when the Duke was crossing the Yellow River, wind and waters rose. A river-dragon snapped up one of the steeds of the chariot and tore it away. The ferry-boat rocked like a sieve and was about to capsize. Then I took my sword and leaped into the stream. I fought with the dragon in the midst of the foaming waves. And by reason of my strength I managed to kill him, though my eyes stood out of my head with my exertions. Then I came to the surface with the dragon's head in one hand, and holding the rein of the rescued horse in the other, and I had saved my prince from drowning. Whenever our country was at war with neighboring states, I refused no service. I commanded the van, I fought in single combat. Never did I turn my back on the foe. Once the prince's chariot stuck fast in the swamp, and the enemy hurried up on all sides. I pulled the chariot out, and drove off the hostile mercenaries. Since I have been in the prince's service I have saved his life more than once. I grant that my merit is not to be compared with that of the prince and that of the chancellor, yet it is greater than that of my two companions. Both have received peaches, while I must do without. This means that real merit is not rewarded, and that the Duke looks on me with disfavor. And in such case how may I ever show myself at court again!"

With these words he drew his sword and killed himself.

Then Gung Sun Dsia rose, bowed twice, and said with a sigh: "Both my merit and that of Tian Kai Giang does not compare with Gu I Dsi's and yet the peaches were given us. We have been rewarded beyond our deserts, and such reward is shameful. Hence it is better to die than to live dishonored!"

He took his sword and swung it, and his own head rolled on the sand.

Tian Kai Giang looked up and uttered a groan of disgust. He blew the breath from his mouth in front of him like a rainbow, and his hair rose on end with rage. Then he took sword in hand and said: "We three have always served our prince bravely. We were like the same flesh and blood. The others are dead, and it is my duty not to survive them!"

And he thrust his sword into his throat and died.

The Duke sighed incessantly, and commanded that they be given a splendid burial. A brave hero values his honor more than his life. The chancellor knew this, and that was why he purposely arranged to incite the three heroes to kill themselves by means of the two peaches.

Dschang Liang

DSCHANG LIANG WAS a native of one of those states which had been destroyed by the Emperor Tsin Schi Huang. And Dschang Liang determined to do a deed for his dead king's sake, and to that end gathered followers with whom to slay Tsin Schi Huang.

Once Tsin Schi Huang was making a progress through the country. When he came to the plain of Bo Lang, Dschang Liang armed his people with iron maces in order to kill him. But Tsin Schi Huang always had two traveling coaches which were exactly alike in appearance. In one of them he sat himself, while in the other was seated another person. Dschang Liang and his followers met the decoy wagon, and Dschang Liang was forced to flee from the Emperor's rage. He came to a ruined bridge. An icy wind was blowing, and the snowflakes were whirling through the air. There he met an old, old man wearing a black turban and a yellow gown. The old man let one of his shoes fall into the water, looked at Dschang Liang and said: "Fetch it out, little one!"

Dschang Liang controlled himself, fetched out the shoe and brought it to the old man. The latter stretched out his foot to allow Dschang Liang to put it on, which he did in a respectful manner. This pleased the old man and he said: "Little one, something may be made of you! Come here tomorrow morning early, and I will have something for you."

The following morning at break of dawn, Dschang Liang appeared. But the old man was already there and reproached him: "You are too late. To-day I will tell you nothing. Tomorrow you must come earlier."

So it went on for three days, and Dschang Liang's patience was not exhausted. Then the old man was satisfied, brought forth the Book of Hidden Complements, and gave it to him. "You must read it," said he, "and then you will be able to rule a great emperor. When your task is completed, seek me at the foot of the Gu Tschong Mountain. There you will find a yellow stone, and I will be by that yellow stone."

Dschang Liang took the book and aided the ancestor of the Han dynasty to conquer the empire. The emperor made him a count. From that time forward Dschang Liang ate no human food and concentrated in spirit. He kept company with the four whitebeards of the Shang Mountain, and with them shared the sunset roses in the clouds. Once he met two boys who were singing and dancing:

"Green the garments you should wear,If to heaven's gate you'd fare;There the Golden Mother greet,Bow before the Wood Lord's feet!"

When Dschang Liang heard this, he bowed before the youths, and said to his friends: "Those are angel children of the King Father of the East. The Golden Mother is the Queen of the West. The Lord of Wood is the King Father of the East. They are the two primal powers, the parents of all that is male and female, the root and fountain of heaven and earth, to whom all that has life is indebted for its creation and nourishment. The Lord of Wood is the master of all the male saints, the Golden Mother is the mistress of all the female saints. Whoever would gain immortality, must first greet the Golden Mother and then bow before the King Father. Then he may rise up to the three Pure Ones and stand in the presence of the Highest. The song of the angel children shows the manner in which the hidden knowledge may be acquired."

At about that time the emperor was induced to have some of his faithful servants slain. Then Dschang Liang left his service and went to the Gu Tschong Mountain. There he found the old man by the yellow stone, gained the hidden knowledge, returned home, and feigning illness loosed his soul from his body and disappeared.

Later, when the rebellion of the "Red Eyebrows" broke out, his tomb was opened. But all that was found within it was a yellow stone. Dschang Liang was wandering with Laotsze in the invisible world.

Once his grandson Dschang Dau Ling went to Kunlun Mountain, in order to visit the Queen Mother of the West. There he met Dschang Liang. Dschang Dau Ling gained power over demons and spirits, and became the first Taoist pope. And the secret of his power has been handed down in his family from generation to generation.

Old Dragonbeard

AT THE TIME of the last emperor of the Sui dynasty, the power was in the hands of the emperor's uncle, Yang Su. He was proud and extravagant. In his halls stood choruses of singers and bands of dancing girls, and serving-maids stood ready to obey his least sign. When the great lords of the empire came to visit him he remained comfortably seated on his couch while he received them.

In those days there lived a bold hero named Li Dsing. He came to see Yang Su in humble clothes in order to bring him a plan for the quieting of the empire.

He made a low bow to which Yang Su did not reply, and then he said: "The empire is about to be troubled by dissension and heroes are everywhere taking up arms. You are the highest servant of the imperial house. It should be your duty to gather the bravest around the throne. And you should not rebuff people by your haughtiness!"

When Yang Su heard him speak in this fashion he collected himself, rose from his place, and spoke to him in a friendly manner.

Li Dsing handed him a memorial, and Yang Su entered into talk with him concerning all sorts of things. A serving-maid of extraordinary beauty stood beside them. She held a red flabrum in her hand, and kept her eyes fixed on Li Dsing. The latter at length took his leave and returned to his inn.

Later in the day someone knocked at his door. He looked out, and there, before the door, stood a person turbaned and gowned in purple, and carrying a bag slung from a stick across his shoulder.

Li Dsing asked who it was and received the answer: "I am the fan-bearer of Yang Su!"

With that she entered the room, threw back her mantle and took off her turban. Li Dsing saw that she was a maiden of eighteen or nineteen.

She bowed to him, and when he had replied to her greeting she began: "I have dwelt in the house of Yang Su for a long time and have seen many famous people, but none who could equal you. I will serve you wherever you go!"

Li Dsing answered: "The minister is powerful. I am afraid that we will plunge ourselves into misfortune."

"He is a living corpse, in whom the breath of life grows scant," said the fan-bearer, "and we need not fear him."

He asked her name, and she said it was Dschang, and that she was the oldest among her brothers and sisters.

And when he looked at her, and considered her courageous behavior and her sensible words, he realized that she was a girl of heroic cast, and they agreed to marry and make their escape from the city in secret. The fan-bearer put on men's clothes, and they mounted horses and rode away. They had determined to go to Taiyuanfu.

On the following day they stopped at an inn. They had their room put in order and made a fire on the hearth to cook their meal. The fan-bearer was combing her hair. It was so long that it swept the ground, and so shining that you could see your face in it. Li Dsing had just left the room to groom the horses. Suddenly a man who had a long curling mustache like a dragon made his appearance. He came along riding on a lame mule, threw down his leather bag on the ground in front of the hearth, took a pillow, made himself comfortable on a couch, and watched the fan-bearer as she combed her hair. Li Dsing saw him and grew angry; but the fan-bearer had at once seen through the stranger. She motioned Li Dsing to control himself, quickly finished combing her hair and tied it in a knot.

Then she greeted the guest and asked his name.

He told her that he was named Dschang.

"Why, my name is also Dschang," said she, "so we must be relatives!"

Thereupon she bowed to him as her elder brother.

"How many are there of you brothers?" she then inquired.

"I am the third," he answered, "and you?"

"I am the oldest sister."

"How fortunate that I should have found a sister to-day," said the stranger, highly pleased.

Then the fan-bearer called to Li Dsing through the door and said: "Come in! I wish to present my third brother to you!"

Then Li Dsing came in and greeted him.

They sat down beside each other and the stranger asked: "What have you to eat?"

"A leg of mutton," was the answer.

"I am quite hungry," said the stranger.

So Li Dsing went to the market and brought bread and wine. The stranger drew out his dagger, cut the meat, and they all ate in company. When they had finished he fed the rest of the meat to his mule.

Then he said: "Sir Li, you seem to be a moneyless knight. How did you happen to meet my sister?"

Li Dsing told him how it had occurred.

"And where do you wish to go now?"

"To Taiyuanfu," was the answer.

Said the stranger: "You do not seem to be an ordinary fellow. Have you heard anything regarding a hero who is supposed to be in this neighborhood?"

Li Dsing answered: "Yes, indeed, I know of one, whom heaven seems destined to rule."

"And who might he be?" inquired the other.

"He is the son of Duke Li Yuan of Tang, and he is no more than twenty years of age."

"Could you present him to me some time?" asked the stranger.

And when Li Dsing has assured him he could, he continued: "The astrologers say that a special sign has been noticed in the air above Taiyuanfu. Perhaps it is caused by the very man. Tomorrow you may await me at the Fenyang Bridge!"

With these words he mounted his mule and rode away, and he rode so swiftly that he seemed to be flying.

The fan-bearer said to him: "He is not a pleasant customer to deal with. I noticed that at first he had no good intentions. That is why I united him to us by bonds of relationship."

Then they set out together for Taiyuanfu, and at the appointed place, sure enough, they met Dragonbeard. Li Dsing had an old friend, a companion of the Prince of Tang.

He presented the stranger to this friend, named Liu Wendsing, saying: "This stranger is able to foretell the future from the lines of the face, and would like to see the prince."

Thereupon Liu Wendsing took him in to the prince. The prince was clothed in a simple indoor robe, but there was something impressive about him, which made him remarked among all others. When the stranger saw him, he fell into a profound silence, and his face turned gray. After he had drunk a few flagons of wine he took his leave.

"That man is a true ruler," he told Li Dsing. "I am almost certain of the fact, but to be sure my friend must also see him."

Then he arranged to meet Li Dsing on a certain day at a certain inn.

"When you see this mule before the door, together with a very lean jackass, then you may be certain I am there with my friend."

On the day set Li Dsing went there and, sure enough he saw the mule and the jackass before the door. He gathered up his robe and descended to the upper story of the inn. There sat old Dragonbeard and a Taoist priest over their wine. When the former saw Li Dsing he was much pleased, bade him sit down and offered him wine. After they had pledged each other, all three returned to Liu Wendsing. He was engaged in a game of chess with the prince. The prince rose with respect and asked them to be seated.

As soon as the Taoist priest saw his radiant and heroic countenance he was disconcerted, and greeted him with a low bow, saying: "The game is up!"

When they took their leave Dragonbeard said to Li Dsing: "Go on to Sianfu, and when the time has come, ask for me at such and such a place."

And with that he went away snorting.

Li Dsing and the fan-bearer packed up their belongings, left Taiyuanfu and traveled on toward the West. At that time Yang Su died, and great disturbance arose throughout the empire.

In the course of a few days Li Dsing and his wife reached the meeting-place appointed by Dragonbeard. They knocked at a little wooden door, and out came a servant, who led them through long passages. When they emerged magnificent buildings arose before them, in front of which stood a crowd of slave girls. Then they entered a hall in which the most valuable dowry that could be imagined had been piled up: mirrors, clothes, jewelry, all more beautiful than earth is wont to show. Handsome slave girls led them to the bath, and when they had changed their garments their friend was announced. He stepped in clad in silks and fox-pelts, and looking almost like a dragon or a tiger. He greeted his guests with pleasure and also called in his wife, who was of exceptional loveliness. A festive banquet was served, and all four sat down to it. The table was covered with the most expensive viands, so rare that they did not even know their names. Flagons and dishes and all the utensils were made of gold and jade, and ornamented with pearls and precious stones. Two companies of girl musicians alternately blew flutes and chalameaus. They sang and danced, and it seemed to the visitors that they had been transported to the palace of the Lady of the Moon. The rainbow garments fluttered, and the dancing girls were beautiful beyond all the beauty of earth.

After they had banqueted, Dragonbeard commanded his servitors to bring in couches upon which embroidered silken covers had been spread. And after they had seen everything worth seeing, he presented them with a book and a key.

Then he said: "In this book are listed the valuables and the riches which I possess. I make you a wedding-present of them. Nothing great may be undertaken without wealth, and it is my duty to endow my sister properly. My original intention had been to take the Middle Kingdom in hand and do something with it. But since a ruler has already arisen to reign over it, what is there to keep me in this country? For Prince Tang of Taiyuanfu is a real hero, and will have restored order within a few years' time. You must both of you aid him, and you will be certain to rise to high honors. You, my sister, are not alone beautiful, but you have also the right way of looking at things. None other than yourself would have been able to recognize the true worth of Li Dsing, and none other than Li Dsing would have had the good fortune to encounter you. You will share the honors which will be your husband's portion, and your name will be recorded in history. The treasures which I bestow upon you, you are to use to help the true ruler. Bear this in mind! And in ten years' time a glow will rise far away to the South-east, and it shall be a sign that I have reached my goal. Then you may pour a libation of wine in the direction of the South-east, to wish me good fortune!"

Then, one after another, he had his servitors and slave-girls greet Li Dsing and the fan-bearer, and said to them: "This is your master and your mistress!"

When he had spoken these words, he took his wife's hand, they mounted three steeds which were held ready, and rode away.

Li Dsing and his wife now established themselves in the house, and found themselves possessed of countless wealth. They followed Prince Tang, who restored order to the empire, and aided him with their money. Thus the great work was accomplished, and after peace had been restored throughout the empire, Li Dsing was made Duke of We, and the fan-bearer became a duchess.

Some ten years later the duke was informed that in the empire beyond the sea a thousand ships had landed an army of a hundred thousand armored soldiers. These had conquered the country, killed its prince, and set up their leader as its king. And order now reigned in that empire.

Then the duke knew that Dragonbeard had accomplished his aim. He told his wife, and they robed themselves in robes of ceremony and offered wine in order to wish him good fortune. And they saw a radiant crimson ray flash up on the South-eastern horizon. No doubt Dragonbeard had sent it in answer. And both of them were very happy.

How Molo Stole the Lovely Rose-Red

AT THE TIME when the Tang dynasty reigned over the Middle Kingdom, there were master swordsmen of various kinds. Those who came first were the saints of the sword. They were able to take different shapes at will, and their swords were like strokes of lightning. Before their opponents knew they had been struck their heads had already fallen. Yet these master swordsmen were men of lofty mind, and did not lightly mingle in the quarrels of the world. The second kind of master swordsmen were the sword heroes. It was their custom to slay the unjust, and to come to the aid of the oppressed. They wore a hidden dagger at their side and carried a leather bag at their belt. By magic means they were able to turn human heads into flowing water. They could fly over roofs and walk up and down walls, and they came and went and left no trace. The swordsmen of the lowest sort were the mere bought slayers. They hired themselves out to those who wished to do away with their enemies. And death was an everyday matter to them.

Old Dragonbeard must have been a master swordsman standing midway between those of the first and of the second order. Molo, however, of whom this story tells, was a sword hero.

At that time there lived a young man named Tsui, whose father was a high official and the friend of the prince. And the father once sent his son to visit his princely friend, who was ill. The son was young, handsome and gifted. He went to carry out his father's instructions. When he entered the prince's palace, there stood three beautiful slave girls, who piled rosy peaches into a golden bowl, poured sugar over them and presented them to him. After he had eaten he took his leave, and his princely host ordered one of the slave girls, Rose-Red by name, to escort him to the gate. As they went along the young man kept looking back at her. And she smiled at him and made signs with her fingers. First she would stretch out three fingers, then she would turn her hand around three times, and finally she would point to a little mirror which she wore on her breast. When they parted she whispered to him: "Do not forget me!"

When the young man reached home his thoughts were all in confusion. And he sat down absent-mindedly like a wooden rooster. Now it happened that he had an old servant named Molo, who was an extraordinary being.

"What is the trouble, master," said he. "Why are you so sad? Do you not want to tell your old slave about it?"

So the boy told him what had occurred, and also mentioned the signs the girl had made to him in secret.

Said Molo: "When she stretched out three fingers, it meant that she is quartered in the third court of the palace. When she turned round her hand three times, it meant the sum of three times five fingers, which is fifteen. When she pointed at the little mirror, she meant to say that on the fifteenth, when the moon is round as a mirror, at midnight, you are to go for her."

Then the young man was roused from his confused thoughts, and was so happy he could hardly control himself.

But soon he grew sad again and said: "The prince's palace is shut off as though by an ocean. How would it be possible to win into it?"

"Nothing easier," said Molo. "On the fifteenth we will take two pieces of dark silk and wrap ourselves up in them, and thus I will carry you there. Yet there is a wild dog on guard at the slave girl's court, who is strong as a tiger and watchful as a god. No one can pass by him, so he must be killed."

When the appointed day had come, the servant said: "There is no one else in the world who can kill this dog but myself!"

Full of joy the youth gave him meat and wine, and the old man took a chain-hammer and disappeared with it.

And after no more time had elapsed than it takes to eat a meal he was back again and said: "The dog is dead, and there is nothing further to hinder us!"

At midnight they wrapped themselves in dark silk, and the old man carried the youth over the tenfold walls which surrounded the palace. They reached the third gateway and the gate stood ajar. Then they saw the glow of a little lamp, and heard Rose-Red sigh deeply. The entire court was silent and deserted. The youth raised the curtain and stepped into the room. Long and searchingly Rose-Red looked at him, then seized his hand.

"I knew that you were intelligent, and would understand my sign language. But what magic power have you at your disposal, that you were able to get here?"

The youth told her in detail how Molo had helped him.

"And where is Molo?" she asked.

"Outside, before the curtain," was his answer.

Then she called him in and gave him wine to drink from a jade goblet and said: "I am of good family and have come here from far away. Force alone has made me a slave in this palace. I long to leave it. For though I have jasper chop-sticks with which to eat, and drink my wine from golden flagons, though silk and satin rustle around me and jewels of every kind are at my disposal, all these are but so many chains and fetters to hold me here. Dear Molo, you are endowed with magic powers. I beg you to save me in my distress! If you do, I will be glad to serve your master as a slave, and will never forget the favor you do me."

The youth looked at Molo. Molo was quite willing. First he asked permission to carry away Rose-Red's gear and jewels in sacks and bags. Three times he went away and returned until he had finished. Then he took his master and Rose-Red upon his back, and flew away with them over the steep walls. None of the watchmen of the prince's palace noticed anything out of the way. At home the youth hid Rose-Red in a distant room.

When the prince discovered that one of his slave-girls was missing, and that one of his wild dogs had been killed, he said: "That must have been some powerful sword hero!" And he gave strict orders that the matter should not be mentioned, and that investigations should be made in secret.

Two years passed, and the youth no longer thought of any danger. Hence, when the flowers began to bloom in the spring, Rose-Red went driving in a small wagon outside the city, near the river. And there one of the prince's servants saw her, and informed his master. The latter sent for the youth, who, since he could not conceal the matter, told him the whole story exactly as it had happened.

Said the prince: "The whole blame rests on Rose-Red. I do not reproach you. Yet since she is now your wife I will let the whole matter rest. But Molo will have to suffer for it!"

So he ordered a hundred armored soldiers, with bows and swords, to surround the house of the youth, and under all circumstances to take Molo captive. But Molo drew his dagger and flew up the high wall. Thence he looked about him like a hawk. The arrows flew as thick as rain, but not one hit him. And in a moment he had disappeared, no one knew where.

Yet ten years later one of his former master's servants ran across him in the South, where he was selling medicine. And he looked exactly as he had looked ten years before.

The Golden Canister

IN THE DAYS of the Tang dynasty there lived a certain count in the camp at Ludschou. He had a slave who could play the lute admirably, and was also so well versed in reading and writing that the count employed her to indite his confidential letters.

Once there was a great feast held in the camp. Said the slave-girl: "The large kettledrum sounds so sad to-day; some misfortune must surely have happened to the kettledrummer!"

The count sent for the kettledrummer and questioned him.

"My wife has died," he replied, "yet I did not venture to ask for leave of absence. That is why, in spite of me, my kettledrum sounded so sad."

The count allowed him to go home.

At that time there was much strife and jealousy among the counts along the Yellow River. The emperor wished to put an end to their dissensions by allying them to each other by marriages. Thus the daughter of the Count of Ludschou had married the son of the old Count of Webo. But this did not much improve matters. The old Count of Webo had lung trouble, and when the hot season came it always grew worse, and he would say: "Yes, if I only had Ludschou! It is cooler and I might feel better there!"

So he gathered three thousand warriors around him, gave them good pay, questioned the oracle with regard to a lucky day, and set out to take Ludschou by force.

The Count of Ludschou heard of it. He worried day and night, but could see no way out of his difficulties. One night, when the water-clock had already been set up, and the gate of the camp had been locked, he walked about the courtyard, leaning on his staff. Only his slave-girl followed him.

"Lord," said she, "it is now more than a month since sleep and appetite have abandoned you! You live sad and lonely, wrapped up in your grief. Unless I am greatly deceived it is on account of Webo."

"It is a matter of life and death," answered the count, "of which you women understand nothing."

"I am no more than a slave-girl," said she, "and yet I have been able to guess the cause of your grief."

The count realized that there was meaning in her words and replied: "You are in truth an extraordinary girl. It is a fact that I am quietly reflecting on some way of escape."

The slave-girl said: "That is easily done! You need not give it a thought, master! I will go to Webo and see how things are. This is the first watch of the night. If I go now, I can be back by the fifth watch."

"Should you not succeed," said the count, "you merely bring misfortune upon me the more quickly."

"A failure is out of the question," answered the slave-girl.

Then she went to her room and prepared for her journey. She combed her raven hair, tied it in a knot on the top of her head, and fastened it with a golden pin. Then she put on a short garment embroidered with purple, and shoes woven of dark silk. In her breast she hid a dagger with dragon-lines graved on it, and upon her forehead she wrote the name of the Great God. Then she bowed before the count and disappeared.

The count poured wine for himself and waited for her, and when the morning horn was blown, the slave-girl floated down before him as light as a leaf.

"Did all go well?" asked the count.

"I have done no discredit to my mission," replied the girl.

"Did you kill any one?"

"No, I did not have to go to such lengths. Yet I took the golden canister at the head of Webo's couch along as a pledge."

The count asked what her experience had been, and she began to tell her story:

"I set out when the drums were beating their first tattoo and reached Webo three hours before midnight. When I stepped through the gate, I could see the sentries asleep in their guard-rooms. They snored so that it sounded like thunder. The camp sentinels were pacing their beats, and I went in through the left entrance into the room in which the Count of Webo slept. There lay your relative on his back behind the curtain, plunged in sweet slumber. A costly sword showed from beneath his pillow; and beside it stood an open canister of gold. In the canister were various slips. On one of them was set down his age and the day of his birth, on another the name of the Great Bear God. Grains of incense and pearls were scattered over it. The candles in the room burned dimly, and the incense in the censers was paling to ash. The slave-girls lay huddled up, round about, asleep. I could have drawn out their hair-pins and raised their robes and they would not have awakened. Your relative's life was in my hand, but I could not bring myself to kill him. So I took the golden canister and returned. The water-clock marked the third hour when I had finished my journey. Now you must have a swift horse saddled quickly, and must send a man to Webo to take back the golden canister. Then the Lord of Webo will come to his senses, and will give up his plans of conquest."

The Count of Ludschou at once ordered an officer to ride to Webo as swiftly as possible. He rode all day long and half the night and finally arrived. In Webo everyone was excited because of the loss of the golden canister. They were searching the whole camp rigorously. The messenger knocked at the gate with his riding-whip, and insisted on seeing the Lord of Webo. Since he came at so unusual an hour the Lord of Webo guessed that he was bringing important information, and left his room to receive the messenger. The latter handed him a letter which said: "Last night a stranger from Webo came to us. He informed us that with his own hands he had taken a golden canister from beside your bed. I have not ventured to keep it and hence am sending it back to you by messenger." When the Lord of Webo saw the golden canister he was much frightened. He took the messenger into his own room, treated him to a splendid meal, and rewarded him generously.

On the following day he sent the messenger back again, and gave him thirty thousand bales of silk and a team of four horses along as a present for his master. He also wrote a letter to the Count of Ludschou:

"My life was in your hand. I thank you for having spared me, regret my evil intentions and will improve. From this time forward peace and friendship shall ever unite us, and I will let no thought to the contrary enter my mind. The citizen soldiery I have gathered I will use only as a protection against robbers. I have already disarmed the men and sent them back to their work in the fields."

And thenceforward the heartiest friendship existed between the two relatives North and South of the Yellow River.

One day the slave-girl came and wished to take leave of her master.

"In my former existence," said the slave-girl, "I was a man. I was a physician and helped the sick. Once upon a time I gave a little child a poison to drink by mistake instead of a healing draught, and the child died. This led the Lord of Death to punish me, and I came to earth again in the shape of a slave-girl. Yet I remembered my former life, tried to do well in my new surroundings, and even found a rare teacher who taught me the swordsman's art. Already I have served you for nineteen years. I went to Webo for you in order to repay your kindness. And I have succeeded in shaping matters so that you are living at peace with your relatives again, and thus have saved the lives of thousands of people. For a weak woman this is a real service, sufficient to absolve me of my original fault. Now I shall retire from the world and dwell among the silent hills, in order to labor for sanctity with a clean heart. Perhaps I may thus succeed in returning to my former condition of life. So I beg of you to let me depart!"

The count saw that it would not be right to detain her any longer. So he prepared a great banquet, invited a number of guests to the farewell meal, and many a famous knight sat down to the board. And all honored her with toasts and poems.

The count could no longer hide his emotion, and the slave-girl also bowed before him and wept. Then she secretly left the banquet-hall, and no human being ever discovered whither she had gone.

The Monk of the Yangtze-Kiang

BUDDHISM TOOK ITS rise in southern India, on the island of Ceylon. It was there that the son of a Brahminic king lived, who had left his home in his youth, and had renounced all wishes and all sensation. With the greatest renunciation of self he did penance so that all living creatures might be saved. In the course of time he gained the hidden knowledge and was called Buddha.

In the days of the Emperor Ming Di, of the dynasty of the Eastern Hans, a golden glow was seen in the West, a glow which flashed and shone without interruption.

One night the emperor dreamed that he saw a golden saint, twenty feet in height, barefoot, his head shaven, and clothed in Indian garb enter his room, who said to him: "I am the saint from the West! My gospel must be spread in the East!"

When the ruler awoke he wondered about this dream, and sent out messengers to the lands of the West in order to find out what it meant.

Thus it was that the gospel of Buddha came to China, and continued to gain in influence up to the time of the Tang dynasty. At that time, from emperors and kings down to the peasants in the villages, the wise and the ignorant alike were filled with reverence for Buddha. But under the last two dynasties his gospel came to be more and more neglected. In these days the Buddhist monks run to the houses of the rich, read their sutras and pray for pay. And one hears nothing of the great saints of the days gone by.

At the time of the Emperor Tai Dsung, of the Tang dynasty, it once happened that a great drought reigned in the land, so that the emperor and all his officials erected altars everywhere in order to plead for rain.

Then the Dragon-King of the Eastern Sea talked with the Dragon of the Milky Way and said: "To-day they are praying for rain on earth below. The Lord of the Heavens has granted the prayer of the King of Tang. Tomorrow you must let three inches of rain fall!"

"No, I must let only two inches of rain fall," said the old dragon.

So the two dragons made a wager, and the one who lost promised as a punishment to turn into a mud salamander.

The following day the Highest Lord suddenly issued an order saying that the Dragon of the Milky Way was to instruct the wind and cloud spirits to send down three inches of rain upon the earth. To contradict this command was out of the question.

But the old dragon thought to himself: "It seems that the Dragon-King had a better idea of what was going to happen than I had, yet it is altogether too humiliating to have to turn into a mud salamander!" So he let only two inches of rain fall, and reported back to the heavenly court that the command had been carried out.

Yet the Emperor Tai Dsung then offered a prayer of thanks to heaven. In it he said: "The precious fluid was bestowed upon us to the extent of two inches of depth. We beg submissively that more may be sent down, so that the parched crops may recover!"

When the Lord of the Heavens read this prayer he was very angry and said: "The criminal Dragon of the Milky Way has dared diminish the rain which I had ordered. He cannot be suffered to continue his guilty life. So We Dschong, who is a general among men on earth, shall behead him, as an example for all living beings."

In the evening the Emperor Tai Dsung had a dream. He saw a giant enter his room, who pleaded with hardly restrained tears: "Save me, O Emperor! Because of my own accord I diminished the rainfall, the Lord of the Heavens, in his anger, has commanded that We Dschong behead me tomorrow at noon. If you will only prevent We Dschong from falling asleep at that time, and pray that I may be saved, misfortune once more may pass me by!"

The emperor promised, and the other bowed and left him.

The following day the emperor sent for We Dschong. They drank tea together and played chess.

Toward noon We Dschong suddenly grew tired and sleepy; but he did not dare take his leave. The emperor, however, since one of his pawns had been taken, fixed his gaze for a moment on the chess-board and pondered, and before he knew it We Dschong was already snoring with a noise like a distant thunder. The emperor was much frightened, and hastily called out to him; but he did not awake. Then he had two eunuchs shake him, but a long time passed before he could be aroused.

"How did you come to fall asleep so suddenly!" asked the emperor.

"I dreamed," replied We Dschong, "that the Highest God had commanded me to behead the old dragon. I have just hewn off his head, and my arm still aches from the exertion."

And before he had even finished speaking a dragon's head, as large as a bushel-measure, suddenly fell down out of the air. The emperor was terribly frightened and rose.

"I have sinned against the old dragon," said he. Then he retired to the inner chambers of his palace and was confused in mind. He remained lying on his couch, closed his eyes, said not a word, and breathed but faintly.

Suddenly he saw two persons in purple robes who had a summons in their hands. They spoke to him as follows: "The old Dragon of the Milky Way has complained against the emperor in the Nether World. We beg that you will have the chariot harnessed!"

Instinctively the emperor followed them, and in the courtyard there stood his chariot before the castle, ready and waiting. The emperor entered it, and off they went flying through the air. In a moment they had reached the city of the dead. When he entered he saw the Lord of the High Mountain sitting in the midst of the city, with the ten princes of the Nether World in rows at his right and left. They all rose, bowed to him and bade him be seated.

Then the Lord of the High Mountain said: "The old Dragon of the Milky Way has really committed a deed which deserved punishment. Yet Your Majesty has promised to beg the Highest God to spare him, which prayer would probably have saved the old dragon's life. And that this matter was neglected over the chess-board might well be accounted a mistake. Now the old dragon complains to me without ceasing. When I think of how he has striven to gain sainthood for more than a thousand years, and must now fall back into the cycle of transformations, I am really depressed. It is for this reason I have called together the princes of the ten pits of the Nether World, to find a way out of the difficulty, and have invited Your Majesty to come here to discuss the matter. In heaven, on earth and in the Nether World only the gospel of Buddha has no limits. Hence, when you return to earth great sacrifices should be made to the three and thirty lords of the heavens. Three thousand six hundred holy priests of Buddha must read the sutras in order to deliver the old dragon so that he may rise again to the skies, and keep his original form. But the writings and readings of men will not be enough to ensure this. It will be necessary to go to the Western Heavens and thence bring words of truth."

This the emperor agreed to, and the Lord of the Great Mountain and the ten princes of the Nether World rose and said as they bowed to him: "We beg that you will now return!"

Suddenly Tai Dsung opened his eyes again, and there he was lying on his imperial couch. Then he made public the fact that he was at fault, and had the holiest among the priests of Buddha sent for to fetch the sutras from the Western Heavens. And it was Huan Dschuang, the Monk of the Yangtze-kiang, who in obedience to this order, appeared at court.

The name of this Huan Dschuang had originally been Tschen. His father had passed the highest examinations during the reign of the preceding emperor, and had been intrusted with the office of district mandarin on the Yangtze-kiang. He set out with his wife for this new district, but when their ship reached the Yellow River it fell in with a band of robbers. Their captain slew the whole retinue, threw father Tschen into the river, took his wife and the document appointing him mandarin, went to the district capital under an assumed name and took charge of it. All the serving-men whom he took along were members of his robber-band. Tschen's wife, however, together with her little boy, he imprisoned in a tower room. And all the servants who attended her were in the confidence of the robbers.

Now below the tower was a little pond, and in this pond rose a spring which flowed beneath the walls to the Yellow River. So one day Tschen's wife took a little basket of bamboo, pasted up the cracks and laid her little boy in the basket. Then she cut her finger, wrote down the day and hour of the boy's birth on a strip of silk paper with the blood, and added that the boy must come and rescue her when he had reached the age of twelve. She placed the strip of silk paper beside the boy in the basket, and at night, when no one was about, she put the basket in the pond. The current carried it away to the Yangtze-kiang, and once there it drifted on as far as the monastery on the Golden Hill, which is an island lying in the middle of the river. There a priest who had come to draw water found it. He fished it out and took it to the monastery.

When the abbot saw what had been written in blood, he ordered his priests and novices to say nothing about it to any one. And he brought up the boy in the monastery.

When the latter had reached the age of five, he was taught to read the holy books. The boy was more intelligent than any of his fellow-students, soon grasped the meaning of the sacred writings, and entered more and more deeply into their secrets. So he was allowed to take the vows, and when his head had been shaven was named: "The Monk of the Yangtze-kiang."

By the time he was twelve he was as large and strong as a grown man. The abbot, who knew of the duty he still had to perform, had him called to a quiet room. There he drew forth the letter written in blood and gave it to him.

When the monk had read it he flung himself down on the ground and wept bitterly. Thereupon he thanked the abbot for all that the latter had done for him. He set out for the city in which his mother dwelt, ran around the yamen of the mandarin, beat upon the wooden fish and cried: "Deliverance from all suffering! Deliverance from all suffering!"

After the robber who had slain his father had slipped into the post he held by false pretences, he had taken care to strengthen his position by making powerful friends. He even allowed Tschen's wife, who had now been a prisoner for some ten years, a little more liberty.

On that day official business had kept him abroad. The woman was sitting at home, and when she heard the wooden fish beaten so insistently before the door and heard the words of deliverance, the voice of her heart cried out in her. She sent out the serving-maid to call in the priest. He came in by the back door, and when she saw that he resembled his father in every feature, she could no longer restrain herself, but burst into tears. Then the monk of the Yangtze-kiang realized that this was his mother and he took the bloody writing out and gave it to her.

She stroked it and said amid sobs: "My father is a high official, who has retired from affairs and dwells in the capital. But I have been unable to write to him, because this robber guarded me so closely. So I kept alive as well as I could, waiting for you to come. Now hurry to the capital for the sake of your father's memory, and if his honor is made clear then I can die in peace. But you must hasten so that no one finds out about it."

The monk then went off quickly. First he went back to his cloister to bid farewell to his abbot; and then he set out for Sianfu, the capital.

Yet by that time his grandfather had already died. But one of his uncles, who was known at court, was still living. He took soldiers and soon made an end of the robbers. But the monk's mother had died in the meantime.

From that time on, the Monk of the Yangtze-kiang lived in a pagoda in Sianfu, and was known as Huan Dschuang. When the emperor issued the order calling the priests of Buddha to court, he was some twenty years of age. He came into the emperor's presence, and the latter honored him as a great teacher. Then he set out for India.

He was absent for seventeen years. When he returned he brought three collections of books with him, and each collection comprised five-hundred and forty rolls of manuscript. With these he once more entered the presence of the emperor. The emperor was overjoyed, and with his own hand wrote a preface of the holy teachings, in which he recorded all that had happened. Then the great sacrifice was held to deliver the old Dragon of the Milky Way.

Miss A-Pao, or Perseverance Rewarded

IN THE PROVINCE OF KUANG-SI there lived a scholar of some reputation, named Sun Tzu-ch'u. He was born with six fingers, and such a simple fellow was he that he readily believed any nonsense he was told. Very shy with the fair sex, the sight of a woman was enough to send him flying in the opposite direction; and once when he was inveigled into a room where there were some young ladies, he blushed down to his neck and the perspiration dripped off him like falling pearls. His companions laughed heartily at his discomfiture, and told fine stories of what a noodle he looked, so that he got the nickname of Silly Sun.

In the town where our hero resided, there was a rich trader whose wealth equalled that of any prince or nobleman, and whose connections were all highly aristocratic. He had a daughter, A-pao, of great beauty, for whom he was seeking a husband; and the young men of position in the neighbourhood were vying with each other to obtain her hand, but none of them met with the father's approval. Now Silly Sun had recently lost his wife; and someone in jest persuaded him to try his luck and send in an application. Sun, who had no idea of his own shortcomings, proceeded at once to follow this advice; but the father, though he knew him to be an accomplished scholar, rejected his suit on the ground of poverty. As the go-between was leaving the house, she chanced to meet A-pao, and related to her the object of her visit. "Tell him," cried A-pao, laughing, "that if he'll cut off his extra finger, I'll marry him."

The old woman reported this to Sun, who replied, "That is not very difficult;" and, seizing a chopper, cut the finger clean off. The wound was extremely painful and he lost so much blood that he nearly died, it being many days before he was about again. He then sought out the go-between, and bade her inform Miss A-pao, which she did; and A-pao was taken rather aback, but she told the old woman to go once more and bid him cut off the "silly" from his reputation. Sun got much excited when he heard this, and denied that he was silly; however, as he was unable to prove it to the young lady herself, he began to think that probably her beauty was over-stated, and that she was giving herself great airs.

So he ceased to trouble himself about her until the following spring festival, when it was customary for both men and women to be seen abroad, and the young rips of the place would stroll about in groups and pass their remarks on all and sundry. Sun's friends urged him to join them in their expedition, and one of them asked him with a smile if he did not wish to look out for a suitable mate. Sun knew they were chaffing him, but he thought he should like to see the girl that had made such a fool of him, and was only too pleased to accompany them.

They soon perceived a young lady resting herself under a tree, with a throng of young fellows crowding round her, and they immediately determined that she must be A-pao, as in fact they found she was. Possessed of peerless beauty, the ring of her admirers gradually increased, till at last she rose up to go. The excitement among the young men was intense; they criticised her face and discussed her feet, Sun only remaining silent; and when they had passed on to something else, there they saw Sun rooted like an imbecile to the same spot. As he made no answer when spoken to, they dragged him along with them, saying, "Has your spirit run away after A-pao?" He made no reply to this either; but they thought nothing of that, knowing his usual strangeness of manner, so by dint of pushing and pulling they managed to get him home. There he threw himself on the bed and did not get up again for the rest of the day, lying in a state of unconsciousness just as if he were drunk. He did not wake when called; and his people, thinking that his spirit had fled, went about in the fields calling out to it to return. However, he shewed no signs of improvement; and when they shook him, and asked him what was the matter, he only answered in a sleepy kind of voice, "I am at A-pao's house;" but to further questions he would not make any reply, and left his family in a state of keen suspense.

Now when Silly Sun had seen the young lady get up to go, he could not bear to part with her, and found himself first following and then walking along by her side without anyone saying anything to him. Thus he went back with her to her home, and there he remained for three days, longing to run home and get something to eat, but unfortunately not knowing the way.

By that time Sun had hardly a breath left in him; and his friends, fearing that he was going to die, sent to beg of the rich trader that he would allow a search to be made for Sun's spirit in his house. The trader laughed and said, "He wasn't in the habit of coming here, so he could hardly have left his spirit behind him;" but he yielded to the entreaties of Sun's family, and permitted the search to be made.

Thereupon a magician proceeded to the house, taking with him an old suit of Sun's clothes and some grass matting; and when Miss A-pao heard the reason for which he had come, she simplified matters very much by leading the magician straight to her own room. The magician summoned the spirit in due form, and went back towards Sun's house. By the time he had reached the door, Sun groaned and recovered consciousness; and he was then able to describe all the articles of toilette and furniture in A-pao's room without making a single mistake. A-pao was amazed when the story was repeated to her, and could not help feeling kindly towards him on account of the depth of his passion. Sun himself, when he got well enough to leave his bed, would often sit in a state of abstraction as if he had lost his wits; and he was for ever scheming to try and have another glimpse at A-pao.

One day he heard that she intended to worship at the Shui-yueh temple on the 8th of the fourth moon, that day being the Wash-Buddha festival; and he set off early in the morning to wait for her at the roadside. He was nearly blind with straining his eyes, and the sun was already past noontide before the young lady arrived; but when she saw from her carriage a gentleman standing there, she drew aside the screen and had a good stare at him. Sun followed her in a great state of excitement, upon which she bade one of her maids to go and ask his name. Sun told her who he was, his perturbation all the time increasing; and when the carriage drove on he returned home.

Again he became very ill, and lay on his bed unconscious, without taking any food, occasionally calling on A-pao by name, at the same time abusing his spirit for not having been able to follow her as before. Just at this juncture a parrot that had been long with the family died; and a child, playing with the body, laid it upon the bed. Sun then reflected that if he was only a parrot one flap of his wings would bring him into the presence of A-pao; and while occupied with these thoughts, lo! the dead body moved and the parrot flew away.

It flew straight to A-pao's room, at which she was delighted; and catching it, tied a string to its leg, and fed it upon hemp-seed. "Dear sister," cried the bird, "do not tie me by the leg: I am Sun Tzu-ch'u." In great alarm A-pao untied the string, but the parrot did not fly away. "Alas!" said she, "your love has engraved itself upon my heart; but now you are no longer a man, how shall we ever be united together?" "To be near your dear self," replied the parrot, "is all I care about." The parrot then refused to take food from anyone else, and kept close to Miss A-pao wherever she went, day and night alike.

At the expiration of three days, A-pao, who had grown very fond of her parrot, secretly sent some one to ask how Mr. Sun was; but he had already been dead three days, though the part over his heart had not grown cold. "Oh! come to life again as a man," cried the young lady, "and I swear to be yours for ever." "You are surely not in earnest," said the parrot, "are you?" Miss A-pao declared she was, and the parrot, cocking its head aside, remained some time as if absorbed in thought. By-and-by, A-pao took off her shoes to bind her feet a little tighter; and the parrot, making a rapid grab at one, flew off with it in its beak. She called loudly after it to come back, but in a moment it was out of sight; so she next sent a servant to inquire if there was any news of Mr. Sun, and then learnt that he had come round again, the parrot having flown in with an embroidered shoe and dropped down dead on the ground. Also, that directly he regained consciousness he asked for the shoe, of which his people knew nothing; at which moment her servant had arrived, and demanded to know from him where it was. "It was given to me by Miss A-pao as a pledge of faith," replied Sun; "I beg you will tell her I have not forgotten her promise."

A-pao was greatly astonished at this, and instructed her maid to divulge the whole affair to her mother, who, when she had made some inquiries, observed that Sun was well known as a clever fellow, but was desperately poor, and "to get such a son-in-law after all our trouble would give our aristocratic friends the laugh against us." However, A-pao pleaded that with the shoe there as a proof against her, she would not marry anybody else; and, ultimately, her father and mother gave their consent. This was immediately announced to Mr. Sun, whose illness rapidly disappeared in consequence. A-pao's father would have had Sun come and live with them; but the young lady objected, on the score that a son-in-law should not remain long at a time with the family of his wife, and that as he was poor he would lower himself still more by doing so. "I have accepted him," added she, "and I shall gladly reside in his humble cottage, and share his poor fare without complaint."

The marriage was then celebrated, and bride and bridegroom met as if for the first time in their lives. The dowry A-pao brought with her somewhat raised their pecuniary position, and gave them a certain amount of comfort; but Sun himself stuck only to his books, and knew nothing about managing affairs in general. Luckily his wife was clever in that respect, and did not bother him with such things; so much so that by the end of three years they were comparatively well off, when Sun suddenly fell ill and died. Mrs. Sun was inconsolable, and refused either to sleep or take nourishment, being deaf to all entreaties on the subject; and before long, taking advantage of the night, she hanged herself. Her maid, hearing a noise, ran in and cut her down just in time: but she still steadily refused all food.

Three days passed away, and the friends and relatives of Sun came to attend his funeral, when suddenly they heard a sigh proceeding forth from the coffin. The coffin was then opened and they found that Sun had come to life again. He told them that he had been before the Great Judge, who, as a reward for his upright and honourable life, had conferred upon him an official appointment. "At this moment," said Sun, "it was reported that my wife was close at hand, but the Judge, referring to the register, observed that her time had not yet come. They told him she had taken no food for three days; and then the Judge, looking at me, said that as a recompense for her wifely virtues she should be permitted to return to life. Thereupon he gave orders to his attendants to put to the horses and see us safely back."

From that hour Sun gradually improved, and the next year went up for his master's degree. All his old companions chaffed him exceedingly before the examination, and gave him seven themes on out-of-the-way subjects, telling him privately that they had been surreptitiously obtained from the examiners. Sun believed them as usual, and worked at them day and night until he was perfect, his comrades all the time enjoying a good laugh against him. However, when the day came it was found that the examiners, fearing lest the themes they had chosen in an ordinary way should have been dishonestly made public, took a set of fresh ones quite out of the common run—in fact, on the very subjects Sun's companions had given to him.

Consequently, he came out at the head of the list; and the next year, after taking his doctor's degree, he was entered among the Han-lin Academicians. The Emperor, too, happening to hear of his curious adventures, sent for him and made him repeat his story; subsequently, summoning A-pao and making her some very costly presents.

Giauna the Beautiful

ONCE UPON A TIME there was a descendant of Confucius. His father had a friend, and this friend held an official position in the South and offered the young man a place as secretary. But when the latter reached the town where he was to have been active, he found that his father's friend had already died. Then he was much embarrassed, seeing that he did not have the means to return home again. So he was glad to take refuge in the Monastery of Puto, where he copied holy books for the abbot.

About a hundred paces west of the monastery stood a deserted house. One day there had been a great snowfall, and as young Kung accidentally passed by the door of the house, he noticed a well dressed and prepossessing youth standing there who bowed to him and begged him to approach. Now young Kung was a scholar, and could appreciate good manners. Finding that the youth and himself had much in common, he took a liking to him, and followed him into the house. It was immaculately clean; silk curtains hung before the doors, and on the walls were pictures of good old masters. On a table lay a book entitled: "Tales of the Coral Ring." Coral Ring was the name of a cavern.

Once upon a time there lived a monk at Puto who was exceedingly learned. An aged man had led him into the cave in question, where he had seen a number of volumes on the book stands. The aged man had said: "These are the histories of the various dynasties." In a second room were to be found the histories of all the peoples on earth. A third was guarded by two dogs. The aged man explained: "In this room are kept the secret reports of the immortals, telling the arts by means of which they gained eternal life. The two dogs are two dragons." The monk turned the pages of the books, and found that they were all works of ancient times, such as he had never seen before. He would gladly have remained in the cave, but the old man said: "That would not do!" and a boy led him out again. The name of that cave, however, was the Coral Ring, and it was described in the volume which lay on the table.

The youth questioned Kung regarding his name and family, and the latter told him his whole history. The youth pitied him greatly and advised him to open a school.

Kung answered with a sigh: "I am quite unknown in the neighborhood, and have no one to recommend me!"

Said the youth: "If you do not consider me altogether too unworthy and stupid, I should like to be your pupil myself."

Young Kung was overjoyed. "I should not dare to attempt to teach you," he replied, "but together we might dedicate ourselves to the study of science." He then asked why the house had been standing empty for so long.

The youth answered: "The owner of the house has gone to the country. We come from Shensi, and have taken the house for a short time. We only moved in a few days ago."

They chatted and joked together gaily, and the young man invited Kung to remain overnight, ordering a small boy to light a pan of charcoal.

Then he stepped rapidly into the rear room and soon returned saying: "My father has come."

As Kung rose an aged man with a long, white beard and eyebrows stepped into the room and said, greeting him: "You have already declared your willingness to instruct my son, and I am grateful for your kindness. But you must be strict with him and not treat him as a friend."

Then he had garments of silk, a fur cap, and shoes and socks of fur brought in, and begged Kung to change his clothes. Wine and food were then served. The cushions and covers of the tables and chairs were made of stuffs unknown to Kung, and their shimmering radiance blinded the eye. The aged man retired after a few beakers of wine, and then the youth showed Kung his essays. They were all written in the style of the old masters and not in the new-fangled eight-section form.

When he was asked about this, the youth said with a smile: "I am quite indifferent to winning success at the state examinations!" Then he turned to the small boy and said: "See whether the old gentleman has already fallen asleep. If he has, you may quietly bring in little Hiang-Nu."

The boy went off, and the youth took a lute from an embroidered case. At once a serving-maid entered, dressed in red, and surpassingly beautiful. The youth bade her sing "The Lament of the Beloved," and her melting tones moved the heart. The third watch of the night had passed before they retired to sleep.

On the following morning all rose early and study began. The youth was exceptionally gifted. Whatever he had seen but once was graven in his memory. Hence he made surprising progress in the course of a few months. The old custom was followed of writing an essay every five days, and celebrating its completion with a little banquet. And at each banquet Hiang-Nu was sent for.

One evening Kung could not remove his glance from Hiang-Nu. The youth guessed his thoughts and said to him: "You are as yet unmarried. Early and late I keep thinking as to how I can provide you with a charming life companion. Hiang-Nu is the serving-maid of my father, so I cannot give her to you."

Said Kung: "I am grateful to you for your friendly thought. But if the girl you have in mind is not just as beautiful as Hiang-Nu, then I would rather do without."

The youth laughed: "You are indeed inexperienced if you think that Hiang-Nu is beautiful. Your wish is easily fulfilled."

Thus half a year went by and the monotonous rainy season had just began. Then a swelling the size of a peach developed in young Kung's breast, which increased over night until it was as large as a tea-cup. He lay on his couch groaning with pain, and unable to eat or to sleep. The youth was busy day and night nursing him, and even the old gentleman asked how he was getting along.

Then the youth said: "My little sister Giauna alone is able to cure this illness. Please send to grandmother, and have her brought here!"

The old gentleman was willing, and he sent off his boy.

The next day the boy came back with the news that Giauna would come, together with her aunt and her cousin A-Sung.

Not long after the youth led his sister into the room. She was not more than thirteen or fourteen years of age, enchantingly beautiful, and slender as a willow-tree. When the sick man saw her he forgot all his pain and his spirits rose.

The youth said to his sister Giauna: "This is my best friend, whom I love as a brother! I beg of you, little sister, to cure him of his illness!"

The maiden blushed with confusion; then she stepped up to the sick-bed. While she was feeling his pulse, it seemed to him as though she brought the fragrance of orchards with her.

Said the maiden with a smile: "No wonder that this illness has befallen him. His heart beats far too stormily. His illness is serious but not incurable. Now the blood which has flowed has already gathered, so we will have to cut to cure."

With that she took her golden armlet from her arm and laid it on the aching place. She pressed it down very gently, and the swelling rose a full inch above the armlet so that it enclosed the entire swelling. Then she loosed a pen-knife with a blade as thin as paper from her silken girdle. With one hand she held the armlet, and with the other she took the knife and lightly passed it around the bottom of the ring. Black blood gushed forth and ran over mattress and bed. But young Kung was so enchanted by the presence of the beautiful Giauna that not only did he feel no pain, but his one fear was that the whole affair might end too soon, and that she would disappear from his sight. In a moment the diseased flesh had been cut away, and Giauna had fresh water brought and cleansed the wound. Then she took a small red pellet from her mouth, and laid it on the wound, and when she turned around in a circle, it seemed to Kung as though she drew out all the inflammation in steam and flames. Once more she turned in a circle, and he felt his wound itch and quiver, and when she turned for the third time, he was completely cured.

The maiden took the pellet into her mouth again and said: "Now all is well!" Then she hastened into the inner room. Young Kung leaped up in order to thank her.

True, he was now cured of his illness, but his thoughts continued to dwell on Giauna's pretty face. He neglected his books and sat lost in day-dreams.

His friend had noticed it and said to him: "I have at last succeeded, this very day, in finding an attractive life companion for you."

Kung asked who she might be.

"The daughter of my aunt, A-Sung. She is seventeen years of age, and anything but homely."

"I am sure she is not as beautiful as Giauna," thought Kung. Then he hummed the lines of a song to himself:

"Who once has seen the sea close by,
All rivers shallow streams declares;
Who o'er Wu's hill the clouds watched fly,
Says nothing with that view compares."

The youth smiled. "My little sister Giauna is still very young," said he. "Besides, she is my father's only daughter, and he would not like to see her marry someone from afar. But my cousin A-Sung is not homely either. If you do not believe me, wait until they go walking in the garden, and then you may take a look at them without their knowing it."

Kung posted himself at the open window on the look-out, and sure enough, he saw Giauna come along leading another girl by the hand, a girl so beautiful that there was none other like her. Giauna and she seemed to be sisters, only to be told apart by a slight difference in age.

Then young Kung was exceedingly happy and begged his friend to act for him in arranging the marriage, which the latter promised to do. The next day he came to Kung, and told him amid congratulations that everything was arranged. A special court was put in order for the young pair, and the wedding was celebrated. Young Kung felt as though he had married a fairy, and the two became very fond of each other.

One day Kung's friend came to him in a state of great excitement and said: "The owner of this house is coming back, and my father now wishes to return to Shensi. The time for us to part draws near, and I am very sad!"

Kung wished to accompany them, but his friend advised him to return to his own home.

Kung mentioned the difficulties in the way, but the youth replied: "That need not worry you, because I will accompany you."

After a time the father came, together with A-Sung, and made Kung a present of a hundred ounces of gold. Then the youth took Kung and his wife by the hand, and told them to close their eyes. As soon as they did so off they went through the air like a storm-wind. All Kung could notice was that the gale roared about his ears.

When some time had passed the youth cried: "Now we have arrived!" Kung opened his eyes and saw his old home, and then he knew that his friend was not of human kind.

Gaily they knocked at the door of his home. His mother opened it and when she saw that he had brought along so charming a wife she was greatly pleased. Then Kung turned around to his friend, but the latter had already disappeared.

A-Sung served her mother-in-law with great devotion, and her beauty and virtue was celebrated far and near. Soon after young Kung gained the doctorate, and was appointed inspector of prisons in Shensi. He took his wife along with him, but his mother remained at home, since Shensi was too far for her to travel. And heaven gave A-Sung and Kung a little son.

But Kung became involved in a dispute with a traveling censor. The latter complained about Kung and he was dismissed from his post.

So it happened that one day he was idling about before the city, when he saw a handsome youth riding a black mule. When he looked more closely he saw that it was his old friend. They fell into each others' arms, laughing and weeping, and the youth led him to a village. In the midst of a thick grove of trees which threw a deep shade, stood a house whose upper stories rose to the skies. One could see at a glance that people of distinction lived there. Kung now inquired after sister Giauna, and was told that she had married. He remained over night and then went off to fetch his wife.

In the meantime Giauna arrived. She took A-Sung's little son in her arms and said: "Cousin, this is a little stranger in our family!"

Kung greeted her, and again thanked her for the kindness she had shown him in curing his illness.

She answered with a smile: "Since then you have become a distinguished man, and the wound has long since healed. Have you still not forgotten your pain?"

Then Giauna's husband arrived, and everyone became acquainted. And after that they parted.

One day the youth came sadly to Kung and said: "We are threatened by a great misfortune today. I do not know whether you would be willing to save us!"

Kung did not know what it might be; but he gladly promised his aid. Then the youth called up the entire family and they bowed down in the outer court.

He began: "I will tell you the truth just as it is. We are foxes. This day we are threatened by the danger of thunder. If you care to save us, then there is a hope that we may manage to stay alive; if not, then take your child and go, so that you are not involved in our danger."

But Kung vowed that he would share life and death with them.

Then the youth begged him to stand in the door with a sword in his hand, and said: "Now when the thunder begins to roll you must stand there and never stir."

Suddenly dark clouds rose in the sky, and the heavens grew gloomy as if night were closing down. Kung looked about him, but the buildings had all disappeared, and behind him he could only see a high barrow, in which was a large cave whose interior was lost in darkness. In the midst of his fright he was surprised by a thunderbolt. A heavy rain poured down in streams, and a storm wind arose which rooted up the tallest trees. Everything glimmered before his eyes and his ears were deafened. But he held his sword in his hand, and stood as firm as a rock. Suddenly in the midst of black smoke and flashes of lightning, he saw a monster with a pointed beak and long claws, which was carrying off a human body. When he looked more closely he recognized by the dress that it was Giauna. He leaped up at the monster and struck at him with his sword, and at once Giauna fell to the ground. A tremendous crash of thunder shook the earth, and Kung fell down dead.

Then the tempest cleared away, and the blue sky appeared once more.

Giauna had regained consciousness, and when she saw Kung lying dead beside her she said amid sobs: "He died for my sake! Why should I continue to live?"

A-Sung also came out, and together they carried him into the cave. Giauna told A-Sung to hold his head while her brother opened his mouth. She herself took hold of his chin, and brought out her little red pellet. She pressed it against his lips with her own, and breathed into his lungs. Then the breath came back to his throat with a rattling noise, and in a short time he was himself once more.

So there was the whole family reunited again, and none of its members had come to harm. They gradually recovered from their fright, and were quite happy: when suddenly a small boy brought the news that Giauna's husband and his whole family had been killed by the thunder. Giauna broke down, weeping, and the others tried to comfort her.

Finally Kung said: "It is not well to dwell too long amid the graves of the dead. Will you not come home with me?"

Thereupon they packed up their belongings and went with him. He assigned a deserted garden, which he carefully walled off, to his friend and his family as a dwelling-place. Only when Kung and A-Sung came to visit them was the bolt drawn. Then Giauna and her brother played chess, drank tea and chatted with them like members of the same family.

But Kung's little son had a somewhat pointed face, which resembled a fox's, and when he went along the street, the people would turn around and say: "There goes the fox-child!"

Rose of Evening

ON THE FIFTH day of the fifth month the festival of the Dragon Junk is held along the Yangtze-kiang. A dragon is hollowed out of wood, painted with an armor of scales, and adorned with gold and bright colors. A carved red railing surrounds this ship, and its sails and flags are made of silks and brocade. The after part of the vessel is called the dragon's tail. It rises ten feet above the water, and a board which floats in the water is tied to it by means of a cloth. Upon this board sit boys who turn somersaults, stand on their heads, and perform all sorts of tricks. Yet, being so close to the water their danger is very great. It is the custom, therefore, when a boy is hired for this purpose, to give his parents money before he is trained. Then, if he falls into the water and is drowned, no one has him on their conscience. Farther South the custom differs in so much that instead of boys, beautiful girls are chosen for this purpose.

In Dschen-Giang there once lived a widow named Dsiang, who had a son called Aduan. When he was no more than seven years of age he was extraordinarily skilful, and no other boy could equal him. And his reputation increasing as he grew, he earned more and more money. So it happened that he was still called upon at the Dragon Junk Festival when he was already sixteen.

But one day he fell into the water below the Gold Island and was drowned. He was the only son of his mother, and she sorrowed over him, and that was the end of it.

Yet Aduan did not know that he had been drowned. He met two men who took him along with them, and he saw a new world in the midst of the waters of the Yellow River. When he looked around, the waves of the river towered steeply about him like walls, and a palace was visible, in which sat a man wearing armor and a helmet. His two companions said to him: "That is the Prince of the Dragon's Cave!" and bade him kneel.

The Prince of the Dragon's Cave seemed to be of a mild and kindly disposition and said: "We can make use of such a skilful lad. He may take part in the dance of the willow branches!"

So he was brought to a spot surrounded by extensive buildings. He entered, and was greeted by a crowd of boys who were all about fourteen years of age.

An old woman came in and they all called out: "This is Mother Hia!" And she sat down and had Aduan show his tricks. Then she taught him the dance of the flying thunders of Tsian-Tang River, and the music that calms the winds on the sea of Dung-Ting. When the cymbals and kettledrums reechoed through all the courts, they deafened the ear. Then, again, all the courts would fall silent. Mother Hia thought that Aduan would not be able to grasp everything the very first time; so she taught him with great patience. But Aduan had understood everything from the first, and that pleased old Mother Hia. "This boy," said she, "equals our own Rose of Evening!"

The following day the Prince of the Dragon's Cave held a review of his dancers. When all the dancers had assembled, the dance of the Ogres was danced first. Those who performed it all wore devil-masks and garments of scales. They beat upon enormous cymbals, and their kettledrums were so large that four men could just about span them. Their sound was like the sound of a mighty thunder, and the noise was so great that nothing else could be heard. When the dance began, tremendous waves spouted up to the very skies, and then fell down again like star-glimmer which scatters in the air.

The Prince of the Dragon Cave hastily bade the dance cease, and had the dancers of the nightingale round step forth. These were all lovely young girls of sixteen. They made a delicate music with flutes, so that the breeze blew and the roaring of the waves was stilled in a moment. The water gradually became as quiet as a crystal world, transparent to its lowest depths. When the nightingale dancers had finished, they withdrew and posted themselves in the western courtyard.

Then came the turn of the swallow dancers. These were all little girls. One among them, who was about fifteen years of age, danced the dance of the giving of flowers with flying sleeves and waving locks. And as their garments fluttered, many-colored flowers dropped from their folds, and were caught up by the wind and whirled about the whole courtyard. When the dance had ended, this dancer also went off with the rest of the girls to the western courtyard. Aduan looked at her from out the corner of his eye, and fell deeply in love with her. He asked his comrades who she might be and they told him she was named "Rose of Evening."

But the willow-spray dancers were now called out. The Prince of the Dragon Cave was especially desirous of testing Aduan. So Aduan danced alone, and he danced with joy or defiance according to the music. When he looked up and when he looked down his glances held the beat of the measure. The Dragon Prince, enchanted with his skill, presented him with a garment of five colors, and gave him a carbuncle set in golden threads of fish-beard for a hair-jewel. Aduan bowed his thanks for the gift, and then also hastened to the western courtyard. There all the dancers stood in rank and file. Aduan could only look at Rose of Evening from a distance, but still Rose of Evening returned his glances.

After a time Aduan gradually slipped to the end of his file and Rose of Evening also drew near to him, so that they stood only a few feet away from each other. But the strict rules allowed no confusion in the ranks, so they could only gaze and let their souls go out to each other.

Now the butterfly dance followed the others. This was danced by the boys and girls together, and the pairs were equal in size, age and the color of their garments. When all the dances had ended, the dancers marched out with the goose-step. The willow-spray dancers followed the swallow dancers, and Aduan hastened in advance of his company, while Rose of Evening lingered along after hers. She turned her head, and when she spied Aduan she purposely let a coral pin fall from her hair. Aduan hastily hid it in his sleeve.

When he had returned, he was sick with longing, and could neither eat nor sleep. Mother Hia brought him all sorts of dainties, looked after him three or four times a day, and stroked his forehead with loving care. But his illness did not yield in the least. Mother Hia was unhappy, and yet helpless.

"The birthday of the King of the Wu River is at hand," said she. "What is to be done?"

In the twilight there came a boy, who sat down on the edge of Aduan's bed and chatted with him. He belonged to the butterfly dancers, said he, and asked casually: "Are you sick because of Rose of Evening?" Aduan, frightened, asked him how he came to guess it. The other boy said, with a smile: "Well, because Rose of Evening is in the same case as yourself."

Disconcerted, Aduan sat up and begged the boy to advise him. "Are you able to walk?" asked the latter. "If I exert myself," said Aduan, "I think I could manage it."

So the boy led him to the South. There he opened a gate and they turned the corner, to the West. Once more the doors of the gate flew open, and now Aduan saw a lotus field about twenty acres in size. The lotus flowers were all growing on level earth, and their leaves were as large as mats and their flowers like umbrellas. The fallen blossoms covered the ground beneath the stalks to the depth of a foot or more. The boy led Aduan in and said, "Now first of all sit down for a little while!" Then he went away.

After a time a beautiful girl thrust aside the lotus flowers and came into the open. It was Rose of Evening. They looked at each other with happy timidity, and each told how each had longed for the other. And they also told each other of their former life. Then they weighted the lotus-leaves with stones so that they made a cozy retreat, in which they could be together, and promised to meet each other there every evening. And then they parted.

Aduan came back and his illness left him. From that time on he met Rose of Evening every day in the lotus field.

After a few days had passed they had to accompany the Prince of the Dragon Cave to the birthday festival of the King of the Wu River. The festival came to an end, and all the dancers returned home. Only, the King had kept back Rose of Evening and one of the nightingale dancers to teach the girls in his castle.

Months passed and no news came from Rose of Evening, so that Aduan went about full of longing and despair. Now Mother Hia went every day to the castle of the god of the Wu River. So Aduan told her that Rose of Evening was his cousin, and entreated her to take him along with her so that he could at least see her a single time. So she took him along, and let him stay at the lodge-house of the river-god for a few days. But the indwellers of the castle were so strictly watched that he could not see Rose of Evening even a single time. Sadly Aduan went back again.

Another month passed and Aduan, filled with gloomy thoughts, wished that death might be his portion.

One day Mother Hia came to him full of pity, and began to sympathize with him. "What a shame," said she, "that Rose of Evening has cast herself into the river!"

Aduan was extremely frightened, and his tears flowed resistlessly. He tore his beautiful garments, took his gold and his pearls, and went out with the sole idea of following his beloved in death. Yet the waters of the river stood up before him like walls, and no matter how often he ran against them, head down, they always flung him back.

He did not dare return, since he feared he might be questioned about his festival garments, and severely punished because he had ruined them. So he stood there and knew not what to do, while the perspiration ran down to his ankles. Suddenly, at the foot of the water-wall he saw a tall tree. Like a monkey he climbed up to its very top, and then, with all his might, he shot into the waves.

And then, without being wet, he found himself suddenly swimming on the surface of the river. Unexpectedly the world of men rose up once more before his dazzled eyes. He swam to the shore, and as he walked along the river-bank, his thoughts went back to his old mother. He took a ship and traveled home.

When he reached the village, it seemed to him as though all the houses in it belonged to another world. The following morning he entered his mother's house, and as he did so, heard a girl's voice beneath the window saying: "Your son has come back again!" The voice sounded like the voice of Rose of Evening, and when she came to greet him at his mother's side, sure enough, it was Rose of Evening herself.

And in that hour the joy of these two who were so fond of each other overcame all their sorrow. But in the mother's mind sorrow and doubt, terror and joy mingled in constant succession in a thousand different ways.

When Rose of Evening had been in the palace of the river-king, and had come to realize that she would never see Aduan again, she determined to die, and flung herself into the waters of the stream. But she was carried to the surface, and the waves carried and cradled her till a ship came by and took her aboard. They asked whence she came. Now Rose of Evening had originally been a celebrated singing girl of Wu, who had fallen into the river and whose body had never been found. So she thought to herself that, after all, she could not return to her old life again. So she answered: "Madame Dsiang, in Dschen-Giang is my mother-in-law." Then the travelers took passage for her in a ship which brought her to the place she had mentioned. The widow Dsiang first said she must be mistaken, but the girl insisted that there was no mistake, and told Aduan's mother her whole story. Yet, though the latter was charmed by her surpassing loveliness, she feared that Rose of Evening was too young to live a widow's life. But the girl was respectful and industrious, and when she saw that poverty ruled in her new home, she took her pearls and sold them for a high price. Aduan's old mother was greatly pleased to see how seriously the girl took her duties.

Now that Aduan had returned again Rose of Evening could not control her joy. And even Aduan's old mother cherished the hope that, after all, perhaps her son had not died. She secretly dug up her son's grave, yet all his bones were still lying in it. So she questioned Aduan. And then, for the first time, the latter realized that he was a departed spirit. Then he feared that Rose of Evening might regard him with disgust because he was no longer a human being. So he ordered his mother on no account to speak of it, and this his mother promised. Then she spread the report in the village that the body which had been found in the river had not been that of her son at all. Yet she could not rid herself of the fear that, since Aduan was a departed spirit, heaven might refuse to send him a child.

In spite of her fear, however, she was able to hold a grandson in her arms in course of time. When she looked at him, he was no different from other children, and then her cup of joy was filled to overflowing.

Rose of Evening gradually became aware of the fact that Aduan was not really a human being. "Why did you not tell me at once?" said she. "Departed spirits who wear the garments of the dragon castle, surround themselves with a soul-casing so heavy in texture that they can no longer be distinguished from the living. And if one can obtain the lime made of dragon-horn which is in the castle, then the bones may be glued together in such wise that flesh and blood will grow over them again. What a pity that we could not obtain the lime while we were there!"

Aduan sold his pearl, for which a merchant from foreign parts gave him an enormous sum. Thus his family grew very wealthy. Once, on his mother's birthday, he danced with his wife and sang, in order to please her. The news reached the castle of the Dragon Prince and he thought to carry off Rose of Evening by force. But Aduan, alarmed, went to the Prince, and declared that both he and his wife were departed spirits. They examined him and since he cast no shadow, his word was taken, and he was not robbed of Rose of Evening.

The Flying Ogre

THERE ONCE LIVED in Sianfu an old Buddhist monk, who loved to wander in lonely places. In the course of his wanderings he once came to the Kuku-Nor, and there he saw a tree which was a thousand feet high and many cords in breadth. It was hollow inside and one could see the sky shining down into it from above.

When he had gone on a few miles, he saw in the distance a girl in a red coat, barefoot, and with unbound hair, who was running as fast as the wind. In a moment she stood before him.

"Take pity on me and save my life!" said she to him.

When the monk asked her what was the trouble, she replied: "A man is pursuing me. If you will tell him you have not seen me, I will be grateful to you all my life long!"

With that she ran up to the hollow tree and crawled into it.

When the monk had gone a little further, he met one who rode an armored steed. He wore a garment of gold, a bow was slung across his shoulders, and a sword hung at his side. His horse ran with the speed of lightning, and covered a couple of miles with every step. Whether it ran in the air or on the ground, its speed was the same.

"Have you seen the girl in the red coat?" asked the stranger. And when the monk replied that he had seen nothing, the other continued: "Bonze, you should not lie! This girl is not a human being, but a flying ogre. Of flying ogres there are thousands of varieties, who bring ruin to people everywhere. I have already slain a countless number of them, and have pretty well done away with them. But this one is the worst of all. Last night the Lord of the Heavens gave me a triple command, and that is the reason I have hurried down from the skies. There are eight thousand of us under way in all directions to catch this monster. If you do not tell the truth, monk, then you are sinning against heaven itself!"

Upon that the monk did not dare deceive him, but pointed to the hollow tree. The messenger of the skies dismounted, stepped into the tree and looked about him. Then he once more mounted his horse, which carried him up the hollow trunk and out at the end of the tree. The monk looked up and could see a small, red flame come out of the tree-top. It was followed by the messenger of the skies. Both rose up to the clouds and disappeared. After a time there fell a rain of blood. The ogre had probably been hit by an arrow or captured.

Afterward the monk told the tale to the scholar who wrote it down.

Retribution

ONCE UPON A TIME there was a boy named Ma, whose father taught him himself, at home. The window of the upper story looked out on the rear upon a terrace belonging to old Wang, who had a garden of chrysanthemums there. One day Ma rose early, and stood leaning against the window, watching the day dawn. And out came old Wang from his terrace and watered his chrysanthemums. When he had just finished and was going in again, along came a water-carrier, bearing two pails on his shoulders, who seemed to want to help him. But the old man grew annoyed and motioned him off. Yet the water-carrier insisted on mounting the terrace. So they pulled each other about on the terrace-edge. It had been raining, the terrace was slippery, its border high and narrow, and when the old man thrust back the water-carrier with his hand, the latter lost his balance, slipped and tumbled down the slope. Then the old man hastened down to pick him up; but the two pails had fallen on his chest and he lay there with feet outstretched. The old man was extremely frightened. Without uttering a sound, he took hold of the water-carrier's feet, and dragged him through the back door to the bank of the stream which flowed by the garden. Then he fetched the pails and set them down beside the corpse. After that he went home, locked the door and went to bed again.

Little Ma, in spite of his youth, thought it would be better to say nothing about an affair of this kind, in which a human life was involved. He shut the window and withdrew. The sun rose higher, and soon he heard a clamor without: "A dead man is lying on the river-bank!" The constable gave notice, and in the afternoon the judge came up to the beating of gongs, and the inspector of the dead knelt down and uncovered the corpse; yet the body showed no wound. So it was said: "He slipped and fell to his death!" The judge questioned the neighbors, but the neighbors all insisted that they knew nothing of the matter. Thereupon the judge had the body placed in a coffin, sealed it with his seal, and ordered that the relatives of the deceased be found. And then he went his way.

Nine years passed by, and young Ma had reached the age of twenty-one and become a baccalaureate. His father had died, and the family was poor. So it came about that in the same room in which he had formerly studied his lessons, he now gathered a few pupils about him, to instruct them.

The time for examinations drew near. Ma had risen early, in order to work. He opened the window and there, in the distant alley, he saw a man with two pails gradually drawing nearer. When he looked more closely, it was the water-carrier. Greatly frightened, he thought that he had returned to repay old Wang. Yet he passed the old man's door without entering it. Then he went a few steps further to the house of the Lis; and there went in. The Lis were wealthy people, and since they were near neighbors the Mas and they were on a visiting footing. The matter seemed very questionable to Ma, and he got up and followed the water-carrier.

At the door of Li's house he met an old servant who was just coming out and who said: "Heaven is about to send a child to our mistress! I must go buy incense to burn to the gods in order to show our gratitude!"

Ma asked: "Did not a man with two pails of water on his shoulder just go in?"

The servant said there had not, but before he had finished speaking a maid came from the house and said: "You need not go to buy incense, for I have found some. And, through the favor of heaven, the child has already come to us." Then Ma began to realize that the water-carrier had returned to be born again into the life of earth, and not to exact retribution. He wondered, though, for what merit of his the former water-carrier happened to be re-born into so wealthy a family. So he kept the matter in mind, and from time to time inquired as to the child's well-being.

Seven more years went by, and the boy gradually grew up. He did not show much taste for learning, but he loved to keep birds. Old Wang was still strong and healthy. And though he was by this time more than eighty years old, his love for his chrysanthemums had only increased with age.

One day Ma once more rose early, and stood leaning against his window. And he saw old Wang come out upon his terrace and begin to water his chrysanthemums. Little Li sat in the upper story of his house flying his pigeons. Suddenly some of the pigeons flew down on the railing of the flower-garden. The boy was afraid they might fly off and called them, but the pigeons did not move. The boy did not know what to do: he picked up stones and threw them at the birds. By mistake one of them struck old Wang. The old man started, slipped, and fell down over the terrace. Time passed and he did not rise. He lay there with his feet outstretched. The boy was very much frightened. Without uttering a sound he softly closed his window and went away. The sun gradually rose higher, and the old man's sons and grandsons all came out to look for him. They found him and said: "He slipped and fell to his death!" And they buried him as was the custom.

The Maiden Who Was Stolen Away

IN THE WESTERN portion of the old capital city of Lo Yang there was a ruined cloister, in which stood an enormous pagoda, several hundred stories high. Three or four people could still find room to stand on its very top.

Not far from it there lived a beautiful maiden, and one very hot summer's day she was sitting in the courtyard of her home, trying to keep cool. And as she sat there a sudden cyclone came up and carried her off. When she opened her eyes, there she was on top of the pagoda, and beside her stood a young man in the dress of a student.

He was very polite and affable, and said to her: "It seems as though heaven had meant to bring us together, and if you promise to marry me, we will be very happy." But to this the maiden would not agree. So the student said that until she changed her mind she would have to remain on the pagoda-top. Then he produced bread and wine for her to satisfy her hunger and thirst, and disappeared.

Thereafter he appeared each day and asked her whether she had changed her mind, and each day she told him she had not. When he went away he always carefully closed the openings in the pagoda-top with stones, and he had also removed some of the steps of the stairs, so that she could not climb down. And when he came to the pagoda-top he always brought her food and drink, and he also presented her with rouge and powder, dresses and mandarin-coats and all sorts of jewelry. He told her he had bought them in the market place. And he also hung up a great carbuncle-stone so that the pagoda-top was bright by night as well as by day. The maiden had all that heart could wish, and yet she was not happy.

But one day when he went away he forgot to lock the window. The maiden spied on him without his knowing it, and saw that from a youth he turned himself into an ogre, with hair as red as madder and a face as black as coal. His eyeballs bulged out of their sockets, and his mouth looked like a dish full of blood. Crooked white fangs thrust themselves from his lips, and two wings grew from his shoulders. Spreading them, he flew down to earth and at once turned into a man again.

The maiden was seized with terror and burst into tears. Looking down from her pagoda she saw a wanderer passing below. She called out, but the pagoda was so high that her voice did not carry down to him. She beckoned with her hand, but the wanderer did not look up. Then she could think of nothing else to do but to throw down the old clothes she had formerly worn. They fluttered through the air to the ground.

The wanderer picked up the clothes. Then he looked up at the pagoda, and quite up at the very top he saw a tiny figure which looked like that of a girl; yet he could not make out her features. For a long time he wondered who it might be, but in vain. Then he saw a light.

"My neighbor's daughter," said he to himself, "was carried away by a magic storm. Is it possible that she may be up there?"

So he took the clothes with him and showed them to the maiden's parents, and when they saw them they burst into tears.

But the maiden had a brother, who was stronger and braver than any one for miles around. When the tale had been told him he took a heavy ax and went to the pagoda. There he hid himself in the tall grass and waited for what would happen. When the sun was just going down, along came a youth, tramping the hill. Suddenly he turned into an ogre, spread his wings and was about to fly. But the brother flung his ax at him and struck him on the arm. He began to roar loudly, and then fled to the western hills. But when the brother saw that it was impossible to climb the pagoda, he went back and enlisted the aid of several neighbors. With them he returned the following morning and they climbed up into the pagoda. Most of the steps of the stairway were in good condition for the ogre had only destroyed those at the top. But they were able to get up with a ladder, and then the brother fetched down his sister and brought her safely home again.

And that was the end of the enchantment.

Black Arts

THE WILD PEOPLE who dwell in the South-West are masters of many black arts. They often lure men of the Middle Kingdom to their country by promising them their daughters in marriage, but their promises are not to be trusted. Once there was the son of a poor family, who agreed to labor for three years for one of the wild men in order to become his son-in-law. At the end of that time the wedding was celebrated, and the couple were given a little house for a home. But no sooner had they entered it than the wife warned her husband to be on his guard, since her parents did not like him, and would seek to do him harm. In accordance with the custom she entered the house first with a lighted lantern, but when the bridegroom followed her she had disappeared. And thus it went, day by day. During the daytime she was there, but when evening came she disappeared.

And one day, not long after they had been married, his wife said to him: "Tomorrow morning my mother celebrates her birthday, and you must go to congratulate her. They will offer you tea and food. The tea you may drink, but be sure not to touch any of the food. Keep this in mind!"

So the following day the wife and husband went to her mother's home and offered their congratulations. Her parents seemed highly pleased, and served them with tea and sweets. The son-in-law drank, but ate nothing, though his wife's parents, with kind words and friendly gestures, kept urging him to help himself. At last the son-in-law did not know what to do, and thought that surely they could mean him no ill. And seeing the fresh caught eels and crabs on the plate before him, he ate a little of them. His wife gave him a reproachful glance, and he offered some excuse for taking his leave.

But his mother-in-law said: "This is my birthday. You simply must taste my birthday noodles!"

With that she placed a great dish before him, filled with noodles that looked like threads of silver, mingled with fat meat, and spiced with fragrant mushrooms. During all the time he had been living in the country the son-in-law had never yet seen such an appetizing dish. Its pleasant odor rose temptingly to his nostrils, and he could not resist raising his chop-sticks. His wife glanced over at him, but he pretended that he did not see her.

She coughed significantly, but he acted as though he did not hear. Finally she trod on his foot under the table; and then he regained control of himself.

He had not as yet eaten half of the food and said: "My hunger is satisfied."

Then he took leave, and went off with his wife.

"This is a serious matter," said the latter. "You would not listen to my words, and now you will surely have to die!"

But still he did not believe her, until he suddenly felt terrible pains, which soon grew unbearable, so that he fell to the ground unconscious. His wife at once hung him up by the feet from the beam of the roof, and put a panful of glowing charcoal under his body, and a great jar of water, into which she had poured sesame oil, in front of the fire, directly below his mouth. And when the fire had heated him thoroughly, he suddenly opened his mouth – and can you imagine what came out of it? A squirming, crawling mass of poisonous worms, centipedes, toads and tadpoles, who all fell into the jar of water. Then his wife untied him, carried him to bed, and gave him wine mingled with realgar to drink. Then he recovered.

"What you ate in the belief that they were eels and crabs," said his wife, "were nothing but toads and tadpoles, and the birthday noodles were poisonous worms and centipedes. But you must continue to be careful. My parents know that you have not died, and they will think up other evil plans."

A few days later his father-in-law said to him: "There is a large tree growing on the precipice which juts over the cave. In it is the nest of the phenix. You are still young and able to climb, so go there quickly and fetch me the eggs!"

His son-in-law went home and told his wife.

"Take long bamboo poles," said she, "and tie them together, and fasten a curved sword at the top. And take these nine loaves of bread and these hens' eggs, there are seven times seven of them. Carry them along with you in a basket. When you come to the spot you will see a large nest up in the branches. Do not climb the tree, but chop it down with the curved sword. Then throw away your poles, and run for dear life. Should a monster appear and follow you, throw him the loaves of bread, three loaves at a time, and finally throw down the eggs on the ground and make for home as quickly as you can. In this way you may escape the danger which threatens you."

The man noted all she said exactly and went. And sure enough he saw the bird's nest – it was as large as a round pavilion. Then he tied his curved sword to the poles, chopped at the tree with all his strength, laid down his poles on the ground and never looked around but ran for dear life. Suddenly he heard the roaring of a thunder-storm rising above him. When he looked up he saw a great dragon, many fathoms long and some ten feet across. His eyes gleamed like two lamps and he was spitting fire and flame from his maw. He had stretched out two feelers and was feeling along the ground. Then the man swiftly flung the loaves into the air. The dragon caught them, and it took a little time before he had devoured them. But no sooner had the man gained a few steps than the dragon once more came flying after him. Then he flung him more loaves and when the loaves came to an end, he turned over his basket so that the eggs rolled over the ground. The dragon had not yet satisfied his hunger and opened his greedy jaws wide. When he suddenly caught sight of the eggs, he descended from the air, and since the eggs were scattered round about, it took some time before he had sucked them all. In the meantime the man succeeded in escaping to his home.

When he entered the door and saw his wife, he said to her, amid sobs: "It was all I could do to escape, and I am lucky not to be in the dragon's stomach! If this sort of thing keeps up much longer I am bound to die!"

With these words he kneeled and begged his wife pitifully to save his life.

"Where is your home?" asked his wife.

"My home is about a hundred miles away from here, in the Middle Kingdom, and my old mother is still living. The only thing that worries me is that we are so poor."

His wife said: "I will flee with you, and we will find your mother. And waste no regrets on your poverty."

With that she gathered up all the house held in the way of pearls and precious stones, put them in a bag and had her husband tie it around his waist. Then she also gave him an umbrella, and in the middle of the night they climbed the wall with the aid of a ladder, and stole away.

His wife had also said to him: "Take the umbrella on your back and run as fast as ever you can! Do not open it, and do not look around! I will follow you in secret."

So he turned North and ran with all his might and main. He had been running for a day and a night, had covered nearly a hundred miles, and passed the boundaries of the wild people's country, when his legs gave out and he grew hungry. Before him lay a mountain village. He stopped at the village gate to rest, drew some food from his pocket and began to eat. And he looked around without being able to see his wife.

Said he to himself: "Perhaps she has deceived me after all, and is not coming with me!"

After he had finished eating, he took a drink from a spring, and painfully dragged himself further. When the heat of the day was greatest a violent mountain rain suddenly began to fall. In his haste he forgot what his wife had told him and opened his umbrella. And out fell his wife upon the ground.

She reproached him: "Once more you have not listened to my advice. Now the damage has been done!"

Quickly she told him to go to the village, and there to buy a white cock, seven black tea-cups, and half a length of red nettlecloth.

"Do not be sparing of the silver pieces in your pocket!" she cried after him as he went off.

He went to the village, attended to everything, and came back. The woman tore the cloth apart, made a coat of it and put it on. No sooner had they walked a few miles before they could see a red cloud rising up in the South, like a flying bird.

"That is my mother," said the woman.

In a moment the cloud was overhead. Then the woman took the black tea-cups and threw them at it. Seven she threw and seven fell to earth again. And then they could hear the mother in the cloud weeping and scolding, and thereupon the cloud disappeared.

They went on for about four hours. Then they heard a sound like the noise of silk being torn, and could see a cloud as black as ink, which was rushing up against the wind.

"Alas, that is my father!" said the woman. "This is a matter of life and death, for he will not let us be! Because of my love for you I will now have to disobey the holiest of laws!"

With these words she quickly seized the white cock, separated its head from its body, and flung the head into the air. At once the black cloud dissolved, and her father's body, the head severed from the trunk, fell down by the edge of the road. Then the woman wept bitterly, and when she had wept her fill they buried the corpse. Thereupon they went together to her husband's home, where they found his old mother still living. They then undid the bag of pearls and jewels, bought a piece of good ground, built a fine house, and became wealthy and respected members of the community.

Yang Gui Fe

THE FAVORITE WIFE of the emperor Ming Huang of the Tang dynasty was the celebrated Yang Gui Fe. She so enchanted him by her beauty that he did whatever she wished him to do. But she brought her cousin to the court, a gambler and a drinker, and because of him the people began to murmur against the emperor. Finally a revolt broke out, and the emperor was obliged to flee. He fled with his entire court to the land of the four rivers.

But when they reached a certain pass his own soldiers mutinied. They shouted that Yang Gui Fe's cousin was to blame for all, and that he must die or they would go no further. The emperor did not know what to do. At last the cousin was delivered up to the soldiers and was slain. But still they were not satisfied.

"As long as Yang Gui Fe is alive she will do all in her power to punish us for the death of her cousin, so she must die as well!"

Sobbing, she fled to the emperor. He wept bitterly and endeavored to protect her; but the soldiers grew more and more violent. Finally she was hung from a pear-tree by a eunuch.

The emperor longed so greatly for Yang Gui Fe that he ceased to eat, and could no longer sleep. Then one of his eunuchs told him of a man named Yang Shi Wu, who was able to call up the spirits of the departed. The emperor sent for him and Yang Shi Wu appeared.

That very evening he recited his magic incantations, and his soul left its body to go in search of Yang Gui Fe. First he went to the Nether World, where the shades of the departed dwell. Yet no matter how much he looked and asked he could find no trace of her. Then he ascended to the highest heaven, where sun, moon and stars make their rounds, and looked for her in empty space. Yet she was not to be found there, either. So he came back and told the emperor of his experience. The emperor was dissatisfied and said: "Yang Gui Fe's beauty was divine. How can it be possible that she had no soul!"

The magician answered: "Between hill and valley and amid the silent ravines dwell the blessed. I will go back once more and search for her there."

So he wandered about on the five holy hills, by the four great rivers and through the islands of the sea. He went everywhere, and finally came to fairyland.

The fairy said: "Yang Gui Fe has become a blessed spirit and dwells in the great south palace!"

So the magician went there and knocked on the door. A maiden came out and asked what he wanted, and he told her that the emperor had sent him to look for her mistress. She let him in. The way led through broad gardens filled with flowers of jade and trees of coral, giving forth the sweetest of odors. Finally they reached a high tower, and the maiden raised the curtain hanging before a door. The magician kneeled and looked up. And there he saw Yang Gui Fe sitting on a throne, adorned with an emerald headdress and furs of yellow swans' down. Her face glowed with rosy color, yet her forehead was wrinkled with care.

She said: "Well do I know the emperor longs for me! But for me there is no path leading back to the world of men! Before my birth I was a blessed sky-fairy, and the emperor was a blessed spirit as well. Even then we loved each other dearly. Then, when the emperor was sent down to earth by the Lord of the Heavens, I, too, descended to earth and found him there among men. In twelve years' time we will meet again. Once, on the evening of the seventh day, when we stood looking up at the Weaving Maiden and the Herd Boy, we swore eternal love. The emperor had a ring, which he broke in two. One half he gave to me, the other he kept himself. Take this half of mine, bring it to the emperor, and tell him not to forget the words we said to each other in secret that evening. And tell him not to grieve too greatly because of me!"

With that she gave him the ring, with difficulty suppressing her sobs. The magician brought back the ring with him. At sight of it the emperor's grief broke out anew.

He said: "What we said to each other that evening no one else has ever learned! And now you bring me back her ring! By that sign I know that your words are true and that my beloved has really become a blessed spirit."

Then he kept the ring and rewarded the magician lavishly.

The Kingdom of the Ogres

IN THE LAND of Annam there once dwelt a man named Su, who sailed the seas as a merchant. Once his ship was suddenly driven on a distant shore by a great storm. It was a land of hills broken by ravines and green with luxuriant foliage, yet he could see something along the hills which looked like human dwellings. So he took some food with him and went ashore. No sooner had he entered the hills than he could see at either hand the entrances to caves, one close beside the other, like a row of beehives. So he stopped and looked into one of the openings. And in it sat two ogres, with teeth like spears and eyes like fiery lamps. They were just devouring a deer. The merchant was terrified by this sight and turned to flee; but the ogres had already noticed him and they caught him and dragged him into their cave. Then they talked to each other with animal sounds, and were about to tear his clothes from his body and devour him. But the merchant hurriedly took a bag of bread and dried meat out and offered it to them. They divided it, ate it up and it seemed to taste good to them. Then they once more went through the bag; but he gestured with his hand to show them that he had no more.

Then he said: "Let me go! Aboard my ship I have frying-pans and cooking-pots, vinegar and spices. With these I could prepare your food."

The ogres did not understand what he was saying, however, and were still ferocious. So he tried to make them understand in dumb show, and finally they seemed to get an idea of his meaning. So they went to the ship with him, and he brought his cooking gear to the cave, collected brush-wood, made a fire and cooked the remains of the deer. When it was done to a turn he gave them some of it to eat, and the two creatures devoured it with the greatest satisfaction. Then they left the cave and closed the opening with a great rock. In a short space of time they returned with another deer they had caught. The merchant skinned it, fetched fresh water, washed the meat and cooked several kettles full of it. Suddenly in came a whole herd of ogres, who devoured all he had cooked, and became quite animated over their eating. They all kept pointing to the kettle which seemed too small to them. When three or four days had passed, one of the ogres dragged in an enormous cooking-pot on his back, which was thenceforth used exclusively.

Now the ogres crowded about the merchant, bringing him wolves and deer and antelopes, which he had to cook for them, and when the meat was done they would call him to eat it with them.

Thus a few weeks passed and they gradually came to have such confidence in him that they let him run about freely. And the merchant listened to the sounds which they uttered, and learned to understand them. In fact, before very long he was able to speak the language of the ogres himself. This pleased the latter greatly, and they brought him a young ogre girl and made her his wife. She gave him valuables and fruit to win his confidence, and in course of time they grew much attached to each other.

One day the ogres all rose very early, and each one of them hung a string of radiant pearls about his neck. They ordered the merchant to be sure and cook a great quantity of meat. The merchant asked his wife what it all meant.

"This will be a day of high festival," answered she, "we have invited the great king to a banquet."

But to the other ogres she said: "The merchant has no string of pearls!"

Then each of the ogres gave him five pearls and his wife added ten, so that he had fifty pearls in all. These his wife threaded and hung the pearl necklace about his neck, and there was not one of the pearls which was not worth at least several hundred ounces of silver.

Then the merchant cooked the meat, and having done so left the cave with the whole herd in order to receive the great king. They came to a broad cave, in the middle of which stood a huge block of stone, as smooth and even as a table. Round it were stone seats. The place of honor was covered with a leopard-skin, and the rest of the seats with deerskins. Several dozen ogres were sitting around the cave in rank and file.

Suddenly a tremendous storm blew up, whirling around the dust in columns, and a monster appeared who had the figure of an ogre. The ogres all crowded out of the cave in a high state of excitement to receive him. The great king ran into the cave, sat down with his legs outstretched, and glanced about him with eyes as round as an eagle's. The whole herd followed him into the cave, and stood at either hand of him, looking up to him and folding their arms across their breasts in the form of a cross in order to do him honor.

The great king nodded, looked around and asked: "Are all the folk of the Wo-Me hills present?"

The entire herd declared that they were.

Then he saw the merchant and asked: "From whence does he hail?"

His wife answered for him, and all spoke with praise of his art as a cook. A couple of ogres brought in the cooked meat and spread it out on the table. Then the great king ate of it till he could eat no more, praised it with his mouth full, and said that in the future they were always to furnish him with food of this kind.

Then he looked at the merchant and asked: "Why is your necklace so short?"

With these words he took ten pearls from his own necklace, pearls as large and round as bullets of a blunderbuss. The merchant's wife quickly took them on his behalf and hung them around his neck; and the merchant crossed his arms like the ogres and spoke his thanks. Then the great king went off again, flying away like lightning on the storm.

In the course of time heaven sent the merchant children, two boys and a girl. They all had a human form and did not resemble their mother. Gradually the children learned to speak and their father taught them the language of men. They grew up, and were soon so strong that they could run across the hills as though on level ground.

One day the merchant's wife had gone out with one of the boys and the girl and had been absent for half-a-day. The north wind was blowing briskly, and in the merchant's heart there awoke a longing for his old home. He took his son by the hand and went down to the sea-shore. There his old ship was still lying, so he climbed into it with his boy, and in a day and a night was back in Annam again.

When he reached home he loosened two of his pearls from his chain, and sold them for a great quantity of gold, so that he could keep house in handsome style. He gave his son the name of Panther, and when the boy was fourteen years of age he could lift thirty hundred weight with ease. Yet he was rough by nature and fond of fighting. The general of Annam, astonished at his bravery, appointed him a colonel, and in putting down a revolt his services were so meritorious that he was already a general of the second rank when but eighteen.

At about this time another merchant was also driven ashore by a storm on the island of Wo-Me. When he reached land he saw a youth who asked him with astonishment: "Are you not from the Middle Kingdom?"

The merchant told him how he had come to be driven ashore on the island, and the youth led him to a little cave in a secret valley. Then he brought deer-flesh for him to eat, and talked with him. He told him that his father had also come from Annam, and it turned out that his father was an old acquaintance of the man to whom he was talking.

"We will have to wait until the wind blows from the North," said the youth, "then I will come and escort you. And I will give you a message of greeting to take to my father and brother."

"Why do you not go along yourself and hunt up your father?" asked the merchant.

"My mother does not come from the Middle Kingdom," replied the youth. "She is different in speech and appearance, so it cannot well be."

One day the wind blew strongly from the North, and the youth came and escorted the merchant to his ship, and ordered him, at parting, not to forget a single one of his words.

When the merchant returned to Annam, he went to the palace of Panther, the general, and told him all that had happened. When Panther listened to him telling about his brother, he sobbed with bitter grief. Then he secured leave of absence and sailed out to sea with two soldiers. Suddenly a typhoon arose, which lashed the waves until they spurted sky-high. The ship turned turtle, and Panther fell into the sea. He was seized by a creature and flung up on a strand where there seemed to be dwellings. The creature who had seized him looked like an ogre, so Panther addressed him in the ogre tongue. The ogre, surprised, asked him who he was, and Panther told him his whole story.

The ogre was pleased and said: "Wo-Me is my old home, but it lies about eight thousand miles away from here. This is the kingdom of the poison dragons."

Then the ogre fetched a ship and had Panther seat himself in it, while he himself pushed the ship before him through the water so that it clove the waves like an arrow. It took a whole night, but in the morning a shoreline appeared to the North, and there on the strand stood a youth on look-out. Panther recognized his brother. He stepped ashore and they clasped hands and wept. Then Panther turned around to thank the ogre, but the latter had already disappeared.

Panther now asked after his mother and sister and was told that both were well and happy, so he wanted to go to them with his brother. But the latter told him to wait, and went off alone. Not long after he came back with their mother and sister. And when they saw Panther, both wept with emotion. Panther now begged them to return with him to Annam.

But his mother replied: "I fear that if I went, people would mock me because of my figure."

"I am a high officer," replied Panther, "and people would not dare to insult you."

So they all went down to the ship together with him. A favorable wind filled their sails and they sped home swiftly as an arrow flies. On the third day they reached land. But the people whom they encountered were all seized with terror and ran away. Then Panther took off his mantle and divided it among the three so that they could dress themselves.

When they reached home and the mother saw her husband again, she at once began to scold him violently because he had said not a word to her when he went away. The members of his family, who all came to greet the wife of the master of the house, did so with fear and trembling. But Panther advised his mother to learn the language of the Middle Kingdom, dress in silks, and accustom herself to human food. This she agreed to do; yet she and her daughter had men's clothing made for them. The brother and sister gradually grew more fair of complexion, and looked like the people of the Middle Kingdom. Panther's brother was named Leopard, and his sister Ogrechild. Both possessed great bodily strength.

But Panther was not pleased to think that his brother was so uneducated, so he had him study. Leopard was highly gifted; he understood a book at first reading; yet he felt no inclination to become a man of learning. To shoot and to ride was what he best loved to do. So he rose to high rank as a professional soldier, and finally married the daughter of a distinguished official.

It was long before Ogrechild found a husband, because all suitors were afraid of their mother-in-law to be. But Ogrechild finally married one of her brother's subordinates. She could draw the strongest bow, and strike the tiniest bird at a distance of a hundred paces. Her arrow never fell to earth without having scored a hit. When her husband went out to battle she always accompanied him, and that he finally became a general was largely due to her. Leopard was already a field marshal at the age of thirty, and his mother accompanied him on his campaigns. When a dangerous enemy drew near, she buckled on armor, and took a knife in her hand to meet him in place of her son. And among the enemies who encountered her there was not a single one who did not flee from her in terror. Because of her courage the emperor bestowed upon her the title of "The Superwoman."

How Monkey Became Immortal

MONKEY HAD BEEN BORN from a stone egg on top of the Mountain of Fruit and Flowers, and had received many special powers from the stone. He had led his tribe of monkeys to a safe home behind a waterfall on top of the mountain of his birth, and become their beloved king, ruling wisely for hundreds of years. Their way of life was extremely pleasant, they had all they needed to eat and drink, and were safe from enemies. Yet Monkey was not content.

"However happy we are here," he told his followers, "we still have Death to fear. One day Lord Yama of the Underworld will send for us, and we will have to obey. I have heard of Lord Buddha and the other Gods who cannot die, and I intend to find them and learn the secret of immortality."

Monkey set off for the world of men, and soon learned the whereabouts of a holy man, Master Subhodi, who knew the way to eternal life. Subhodi knew in advance of Monkey's coming, and realizing this was no ordinary animal, accepted him as a pupil, and gave him a new name: Sun, the Enlightened One. Monkey spent twenty years with Master Subhodi, learning of the road to eternal life, and many other skills. He learned to change his shape as he pleased, and to travel thousands of miles in a single leap. And armed with this knowledge he returned to his home.

There he found that a demon had taken control of his tribe, and although he conquered the demon, Monkey realized he needed a proper weapon for the future. He seized upon the iron pillar of the Dragon King of the Eastern Sea. This could be changed at will, from an eight-foot staff for fighting, to a tiny needle that Monkey could carry behind his ear, and he kept it with him at all times.

One day two men came for him with a warrant of death from Lord Yama, and tried to drag his soul to the Underworld. Monkey cried out in vain that he knew the way to eternal life, for the men only tied him more tightly. With a desperate struggle, Monkey freed himself, and taking the needle from behind his ear, turned it into a staff, and knocked the men to the ground. Then, incensed with rage, Monkey charged into the Underworld itself, beating anyone in his way with his cudgel.

"Bring out the register of the dead," he demanded. The book was brought to him by the terrified judges, whereupon he found the page with his name on, and the names of all his tribe, and ripped it from the register, tearing it into a thousand pieces. "Now I am free from your power," he cried, and charged back out of the Underworld to his own land. The other monkeys assured him he had been asleep, and must have dreamt all this, but Monkey knew in his heart that it had really happened, and that death held no more sway over them.

Appalled by the trouble Monkey was causing, the Jade Emperor, the most powerful God, offered him high office in Heaven, so that the Gods could secretly keep him under their control. Monkey gladly accepted and was made Master of the Heavenly Stables, but he soon realized this was a derisory post, created only to tame him, and he stormed out of Heaven and returned home. The Jade Emperor sent guards to recapture him, but Monkey defeated them, and the Gods sent to seize him. Eventually the Jade Emperor appeased him by offering him a magnificent palace in Heaven, and a proper position as Superintendent of the Heavenly Peach Garden.

Now Monkey knew that the peaches in this garden, which ripened only once every six thousand years, conferred immortality on anyone who ate them, and so he ignored the order not to touch any of them, and devoured a huge number. Unstoppable now, and furious too that he had not been invited to the great Feast of Peaches, given to the Gods by Wang-Mu, Goddess of the Immortals, Monkey was intent on revenge. So, when the preparations were complete, he put all the servants under a spell, and ate and drank all the food and wine prepared for the guests. Dizzy with drink, Monkey staggered into the deserted palace of Lao Chun, where he stumbled across the five gourds in which were kept the seeds of immortality, and, ever inquisitive, he ate them all. Assured doubly of immortality, Monkey returned home.

The Jade Emperor and all the Gods and Goddesses were furious with monkey, but none could defeat him in battle. Until, that is, the Jade Emperor's nephew, Erlang, aided by Lao Chun and the celestial dog Tien-Kou, managed to chain him, and bring him, securely bound, back to Heaven. Monkey was sentenced to death, and placed in Lao Chun's furnace, in which the seeds of immortality were made. But Monkey was now so powerful that he burst free from the crucible, stronger than ever, and proclaimed himself ruler of the Universe.

At this, Buddha appeared, and demanded of Monkey what powers he had that entitled him to make such a claim. Monkey replied that he was immortal, invulnerable, that he could change shape at will, and could travel thousands of miles in a single leap. Buddha smiled, and taking Monkey in the palm of his hand, said, "If you can jump from out of my hand, I will make you ruler of the Universe and all it contains."

Monkey laughed at this, and in two mighty leaps found himself opposite the five red pillars that mark the edge of the Universe. Delighted, he wrote his name on one of them as proof that he had been there, and returned to the Buddha.

"I have been to the ends of the Universe in two bounds," he bragged. "And now I seek my reward."

"The ends of the Universe?" asked the Buddha, "You never left the palm of my hand." And Buddha showed Monkey his fingers, on one of which was Monkey's name in his own writing. Monkey realized the five pillars were merely the five fingers of the Buddha, and that the whole Universe was contained in his hand, and that he could never be defeated. Afraid for the first time in his life, Monkey tried to run away, but Buddha closed his hand over him, and changing his fingers into the five elements of earth, air, fire, water and wood, created a great mountain in which he imprisoned Monkey.

"There you must stay until you have fully repented and are free of your sins," Buddha told him. "At that time someone will come and intercede for you, and then you may be free." And crushed under the mountains the dejected Monkey was forced to stay.

The Pair of Fools

ONCE, A POOR VILLAGER called Lin unexpectedly found ten pieces of silver, riches beyond anything he had ever owned before. After his first flush of exhilaration at finding such wealth, Lin realized that he must hide the money, as he worked in the fields all day, and it could so easily be stolen from him. He looked despairingly around his sparse, mud-walled hut for a hiding place for the silver, but there was no furniture, no secret cupboards, nothing. Then suddenly he thought of the wall itself, and pausing only to check through the door that no one was coming, he hollowed out a cavity in the mud wall, and poured the silver pieces into it. He quickly covered the hole with fresh mud, and guarded his door against all visitors until the mud had dried and there was no sign of the hiding place.

However, the next morning, before he left for the fields, Lin had another attack of nerves. If someone did come into his hut looking for money, there was only one place it could be hidden. There was no furniture, no secret cupboards, only the wall itself. It would be the first place any thief would look. Then Lin had a flash of inspiration, and picking up his brush and ink, he wrote on the wall: "There are no silver pieces hidden in this wall." Reassured, he went off to the fields for his day's work.

A few hours later Lin's neighbour, Wan, came to look for him. Seeing no sign of Lin, his eyes were drawn to the writing on the wall, and he chuckled to himself: "Of course there are no silver pieces hidden in the wall, why should there be?" Then a second thought struck him: Why would Lin say there weren't any, unless there actually were?

Pausing only to check through the door that no one was coming, Wan attacked the wall with vigour and found the ten pieces of silver almost immediately. Delighted, he ran home with them to his own hut, where he was struck by an attack of nerves. What if they searched his hut and found the money, and he was taken before the Judge and tortured until he confessed, and then sentenced to death? He must stop anyone from suspecting his guilt. Suddenly, Wan had a flash of inspiration, and picking up his brush and ink, he wrote on the front of his door: "I, Wan, an honest man, did not steal the ten silver pieces from the hole in the wall of Lin's hut."

The Silkworm

MANY CENTURIES AGO a certain man was called up to fight for his Emperor, in the war that was raging on the Chinese borders far, far from his home. The man was distraught at leaving his wife and family, but, being a loyal subject he promptly went away to fulfil his duty. As he left, he instructed the family to look after their farm as best they could, and not to worry unduly as to his fate in the battles that were to come, as all life is in the hands of the Gods.

Try though they might to obey his parting instructions, the family missed him terribly, none more so than his daughter. In her loneliness, the young girl took solace in tending the family's horse, a creature that had been her father's for many years, and one that he loved dearly. Every day she would tenderly groom its fine coat, brush its silky mane, and make sure it had clean hay and enough oats to eat, talking to it all the while about how much she missed her father, and how she prayed nightly for his return. However, what little news reached them from the borders became more and more alarming, and the family began to doubt in their hearts if they would ever see their husband and father again.

One day, the daughter was in the stable tending the old horse and thinking of her father, barely able to hold back her tears in her fear for his safety. "If only you could gallop from here to the wars and rescue him from his peril," she murmured. "If anyone could do that, I swear that I would gladly marry him at once, and serve him joyfully all my days, whatever his state or situation in life."

Immediately the horse reared up violently, and with a loud whinny, tore at the leash that held him, breaking it in two, although it was made of the strongest leather. With a mighty kick of its powerful front legs, it splintered the stable door and galloped across the courtyard and out of sight before the startled girl could stop it, or even call out to the servants. When it became clear that the horse was not going to return, she made her way sadly to the house to tell of its disappearance, not mentioning the oath she had sworn in front of the animal.

Many days later, the runaway horse reached the Chinese borders, and despite the confusion and destruction caused by the war, managed to find its owner in the camp where he was billeted. The man was astonished to see his old horse, and even more surprised when he could find no message from his family on the animal. Immediately, he feared the worst, and became convinced that some disaster had befallen them, and although he was a brave and true subject, his fears for his family overcame his loyalty.

He secretly saddled up the horse, and under cover of darkness he eluded the guards and galloped as fast as possible back to his homeland, and to his farm.

His family were amazed and delighted to find him home again; tears of joy rolled down their cheeks seeing him alive and unharmed by the horrors of war. Only his daughter seemed less than overwhelmed by his return, and avoided his gaze whenever he looked at her, and answered his questions briefly, without emotion. The man was surprised to find nothing amiss in the household, after all his fears and misgivings, but presumed that the horse had come to fetch him out of devotion, and an understanding that his family missed him so much. In gratitude he lavished attention on the faithful beast, gave it the best oats and hay and the finest stable, and groomed it himself. The horse, however, refused all food and kindness, and just moped in the corner of its stall, making no sound at all. Only when the daughter of the house came near, which she did as rarely as possible, did the animal seem to come alive; then it would rear up, and whinny and froth at the mouth, so that it took several servants to restrain it.

The father became increasingly worried about the horse, which was becoming distressingly thin. Noticing the effect his daughter had on the beast, he asked her one day if she knew why the animal was behaving in so peculiar a fashion. At first the young girl lied, and said she has no idea of the cause of the problem, but eventually, because she was an honest girl, she told her father of the promise she had made in the stable to marry whomsoever would return her father to her, whatever his state or station in life. The father became extremely angry at her lack of sense and modesty, and confined the girl to her room in the house. He forbade her to so much as peep out of the door if the horse was in the courtyard, so as not to disturb it further; for although the man was very grateful to the horse for its years of service, and its intelligence in finding him in the front lines, he still could not imagine allowing a dumb animal to marry his daughter.

The horse continued to pine and mope, and deprived of even a glimpse of the girl, wasted away more and more, day by day. Eventually the father realized there was only one thing he could do, and sadly he took up his bow and arrow and shot the horse to put it out of its misery. The animal gave a piteous whimper, and died, still looking at the house in which it knew the daughter was imprisoned. The man took off the horse's skin, and placed it in the sun to dry, and then went to tell his daughter what he had been compelled to do. She was thrilled to hear that her problem was solved, and that she would not have to marry a horse, and ran into the courtyard to greet the sun for the first time in days. As she passed the dead creature's hide, it suddenly lifted as if on a gust of wind, and wrapped itself tightly around the girl's shoulders, and then her whole body, and started to spin her round like a top. Whirling faster and faster, the girl cried out, but no one could stop her, and she disappeared out of the farm and into the countryside, carried away on the wind, her cries growing ever fainter.

Appalled, her father ran after the whirlwind his daughter had become, and followed it for many days, although it appeared to get smaller and smaller the further it travelled, until it was barely visible to the naked eye. At last, the whirlwind stopped by a mulberry bush, and breathlessly, the exhausted father rushed up to it. There, on a mulberry bough, he found a small worm feeding on the leaf, and seeing that this was all that was left of his daughter, he took it home, grieving in his heart. He and his wife cared for the worm with tenderness, feeding it thick mulberry leaves every day, and after a week the worm produced a fine thread that glistened and shone, and was soft and cool when woven, and more beautiful to look at than any cloth they had ever seen. They called it silk, and bred more and more of the worms, which became famous throughout the land. And in time silk became one of China's most acclaimed and desired products, and many people profited through its sale, so that in years to come silk weavers throughout the country worshipped thankfully the silkworm girl who had given them such a great treasure through her love for her father.

The Crane Maiden

TIAN KUNLUN was a bachelor, who lived alone with his elderly mother whose one desire in life was to see her son happily married before she died. It was a desire that Tian keenly shared, but they had little money, and he had little chance of finding a suitable bride.

Not far from their home was a beautiful pool of clear, fresh water, shaded by willows, and fringed with rushes. One day, as Tian was on his way to the fields, he heard the sound of girls' laughter coming from the pool, and creeping as silently as he could through the rushes, Tian edged nearer to the water to see whose voice sounded so sweet. Before him he saw three of the loveliest maidens he had ever set eyes on, playing and splashing in the pool, their clothes piled on the bank near him. Entranced, Tian watched for a while, gazing at their beauty, when suddenly he sneezed loudly.

Instantly the three young women turned into three white cranes, and beating their fine wings, they flew from the water. Two of them swooped and picked up their clothes and soared away, up and up into the clear sky, but the third was not fast enough, and Tian managed to reach her clothes before her. The bird circled him for a moment, and then returned to the water, again taking on the form of the beautiful maiden Tian had seen first. Bashfully, she begged him to return her clothes, but first he insisted on knowing who she was.

"I am a daughter of the High God, and those were two of my sisters," the girl answered. "Our father gave us the clothes to pass between Heaven and earth; without them I cannot return to our home." Again the girl pleaded with Tian to return them, adding, "If you do give them back I shall gladly become your wife."

Tian accepted the offer, thinking what a perfect wife the daughter of the High God would make any man, but he feared that if he returned her clothes, she would simply fly away, and he would never see her again. Instead, he gave her his own coat and leggings, and carried her clothes home with him; the crane maiden unwillingly following behind him.

Tian's mother was thrilled that her son was to marry such a beautiful and high-born girl, and their wedding feast was long and lavish, all their friends and neighbours sharing in their joy. The couple lived together, and learned to love each other, and after a time they had a son, whom they called Tian Zhang, and on whom they both doted.

Some years later, Tian was called away to fight in the wars on the borders of China, many many miles from his home. Before he left, he called his mother to him and showed her his wife's celestial clothes and begged her to keep them well hidden, so that she could never put them on and fly away to Heaven. She promised she would, and found a safe hiding place. Tian then said a tearful farewell to his wife and son, and set off for the wars.

After his departure, the young wife asked her mother-in-law every day for a look at her old clothes, just one quick look.

"If you will let me see them only the once I shall be happy," she told the old lady. Seeing how desperate the girl was to see them, and fearing for her health if she continued as she was, the woman relented. She fetched the clothes from the bottom of a large chest in her own room, and showed them to her. The crane maiden wept with joy to see them and hugged them to her breast. Then, in a flash, she threw off her human clothes, put on the celestial garments, and, instantly was transformed into a beautiful white crane. Then she flew out the window before the old lady could stop her, up, up into the clear sky.

When Tian returned from the wars, his mother told him the news of the crane maiden's flight, but both knew that there was nothing they could do to bring her back. Tian readily forgave his mother, but his little son was inconsolable, always crying out her name, and looking longingly out of the window, hoping she would return. He wandered the fields looking for her, weeping, and would accept no comfort from his father or grandmother. One day his cries were heard by a wise old man who sat beneath a willow, and who knew the cause of the boy's grief.

"Go to the pool near your home," he told the child, "and you will see three ladies all dressed in white; the one that ignores you will be your mother."

Tian Zhang did as he was told, and sure enough, there were three girls all in white silk, as the wise man had said. There was the crane maiden, who had so missed her little son, that she had begged her sisters to accompany her back to earth to see that he was happy and well cared for, and to look once more at his face. Tian Zhang boldly walked up to the women, and two of them cried out, "Sister, here is your child to see you," but the crane maiden looked away, her eyes wet with tears of guilt and joy intermingled. The boy then knew that this was his mother, and ran to her, and seeing this, the girl broke down and took him in her arms, embracing him as if she would never let him go, weeping, and crying, "My son, my son."

After some time, one of the sisters said, "Sister, it is time for us to go. If you cannot bear to be parted from the child, we will take him back to Heaven with us."

Between them they lifted the child and flew up, up into the clear sky, all the way to the palace of the High God. He was delighted his daughter was no longer unhappy, and also greatly taken with his grandson, whom he taught personally, telling him of all the things of Heaven and earth. The child was quick to learn, and after a few days the High God gave him eight books, and sent him back to earth with these words: "Study well, my son, for all knowledge is in these, and you may use them to give great benefit to the earth."

So Tian Zhang returned to earth, where he found that not a few days, but twenty years had passed on earth, and that he was a young man. He tried to find his earthly family, but his grandmother had died, and his father left for the mountains of the West in grief for having lost mother, wife and child. So Tian Zhang devoted his life to studying the eight books, and armed with the knowledge the High God had given him, he became a renowned scholar and judge. He was granted a high place at the Emperor's court, and was famed throughout the land for his wisdom and his desire to help mankind.

And thousands of miles away, in the mountains of the West, the aged Tian heard of his son's fame, and was content.

The Cuckoo

THERE WAS ONCE A GOD called Wang, who lived in Heaven, but whose love for the earth and its people was so great that he used to visit it regularly, using his powers to help struggling humanity, and to right wrongs. On one such visit he met a woman, like him an immortal, who had been forced from her original home at the bottom of a deep well, and was now living in the kingdom of Shu, which we would now call Sichuan. The two immortals fell instantly in love with each other, and were soon married; Wang left his home in Heaven and came to live in Shu with his new bride, where they reigned together as king and queen.

Wang and his wife were excellent rulers, kind and caring. Wang taught the farmers how to get the most from their land, which crops would grow best, and how to observe the seasons, so that soon the whole kingdom prospered. Amid all this peace and happiness, only one thing still troubled Wang, the one thing over which he had no power to help his people. Every year the mighty Yangtze river would flood, breaking its banks and destroying vast tracts of farming land, sweeping across all before it, crops, livestock, and people alike. Try as he might, with all the powers of an immortal, Wang could do nothing to control this force of nature, and he bitterly grieved over his impotence.

One day a messenger came to Wang's palace to report a miracle: a corpse had been found floating in the great Yangtze, but floating upstream against the current. Moreover, as soon as the body had been pulled out of the river, it had revived and asked to see the king. Amazed at this report, Wang had the stranger brought before him, and asked him his story. The man said that he came from Chu, several thousand miles downstream from where they now stood, and that he had tripped over a log and fallen into the river. He was unable to explain why he had drifted upstream, but he impressed Wang enormously with his knowledge and understanding of the river and its ways, and he talked of the methods they used in Chu to control the floods, and the damage they could cause. Wang immediately asked the stranger if he could help with their problem, and when the man agreed to try, Wang made him Minister of the River, and accorded him much honour at court.

Not many weeks had passed before the river came into flood again, and the new Minister journeyed far along its banks to try and determine the cause. It did not take him long to find his answer: in the higher country the river ran through a series of ravines too narrow to take the flood waters caused by melting snow on the mountain peaks. This made the river break its banks. He instructed engineers to bore drainage channels through the rock from the main channel, allowing the water to disperse safely, and so preventing flooding further downstream in the valuable farmlands.

Wang was so ashamed that he had not thought of this himself, and so impressed by the stranger's abilities as an engineer, that he decided the stranger would make a better king for his people than himself. Accordingly, he gave over the kingship to the Minister and secretly left the court to go and live in isolation in the mountains of the West. He had been there a very short time, however, when rumours reached him of a disturbing nature. It was said that while the man from Chu had been in the mountains, Wang had seduced his wife, who had come to court only recently, and that the stranger, on his return, had found the two of them together. The rumour told that Wang had handed over the throne in shame and guilt, in return for the man's silence, and had been banished to a life in exile.

So stricken was Wang on hearing this vile and ungrateful gossip, and so regretful of his act of generosity in handing over the throne for the good of his people, that he wasted away in his mountain retreat, and died broken-hearted. The Gods turned his spirit into a cuckoo, whose mournful cry in Chinese calls out 'Better return', reminding people for all time, and especially in the Spring at the time of planting, of Wang's grief at leaving his people, and the land of Shu that he loved.

The Wooden Bridge Inn

THERE WAS ONCE A travelling merchant called Chao, whose trade took him all over China, and who prided himself on knowing all the roads, and all the inns on those roads, throughout the country. One day, however, finding himself in a strange district with his donkey tiring by the mile, he had to admit his ignorance of the area, so he stopped to ask a farmer where he could find accommodation for the night, and, if possible, purchase a new donkey as he had much further to travel.

The farmer replied that travellers always stayed at the Wooden Bridge Inn, run by a woman called Third Lady.

"And does this Third Lady sell donkeys?" Chao asked the man. "Oh, yes. Best donkeys in the district," the man replied. But when Chao asked where these fine animals came from, the man looked uneasy, and would not look Chao in the eye. "Better ask her that," he said, "I have absolutely no idea, I'm afraid." And without further comment, he returned quickly to his field, and did not look back.

Chao walked his weary animal the mile or so to the Wooden Bridge Inn, which was an inviting and comfortable building, presided over by a young woman who greeted Chao warmly. She introduced herself as Third Lady, and invited him to join the six or seven other guests, who were already drinking cups of wine. Chao stabled his donkey around the back, and joined the others for a delicious dinner of fish, vegetables and rice. While chatting to the other merchants, he admired their capable hostess's ability to make them all welcome, plying her guests with wine until they were quite drunk. Chao, however, was not a drinking man, and left the wine alone, preferring to drink only tea.

As midnight approached, the other guests soon fell into a drunken slumber, and Chao was given a clean and comfortable bed alongside a rush partition, where he lay for a while, musing on his fortune in finding such a pleasant resting place. Just as he was about to drift into sleep, he was startled by a low rumble on the other side of the partition, and fearful that someone might be doing harm to his hostess, he peered through a chink in the rush matting. There was Third Lady, alone, dragging a large trunk across the floor of her room, and Chao watched as she knelt before it, opened the lid, and took out a little wooden man. Intrigued, Chao watched as she next brought out a little wooden ox and a little wooden plough, hitched them together and set the man behind the plough. Then, from a small phial, she sprinkled water over the figures, and to Chao's utter amazement, they began to move, and in no time at all had ploughed up the floor of the room.

Third Lady then gave a tiny seed basket to the little man, who proceeded to sow the field that the floor had become, and immediately green shoots of wheat sprang from the soil, ripened, and were harvested by the tiny farmer, who gave the crop to his mistress. Third Lady quickly ground the corn into flour, and under Chao's astonished gaze, made cakes from it, which she put into the oven to bake. She returned the now lifeless figures to the trunk, and pushed it back to the corner of the room. She then retired for the night, leaving Chao to lie alone in the darkness, wondering at what he had witnessed.

When dawn broke, the guests arose, and Third Lady courteously offered them a breakfast of tea and freshly baked wheat cakes. Chao thanked her profusely, but was determined not to eat his cake, hiding it up his sleeve instead. He then went to fetch his donkey from the stable, ready for the next stage of his journey. As he left the Wooden Bridge Inn, he happened to glance through the door, and he froze in astonishment. The other guests, finishing off their cakes, all suddenly became frenzied, their clothes turning into rough animal hair, their ears growing absurdly long, their voices changing to a grating bray. Within minutes the room was filled with six or seven donkeys, which Third Lady promptly herded with a stick out of the back of the Inn, towards the stables.

Chao hurried his donkey on its way, grateful to have escaped such a terrible fate; he went on to the capital where his business was, saying not a word to anyone about what he had seen. And when he had concluded his trade, he prepared to return home, stopping off only to buy some wheat cakes identical to the ones Third Lady had made for her guests.

On his return journey, he again stayed at the Wooden Bridge Inn, where the hostess welcomed him warmly. This time Chao was the only guest, and Third Lady cooked him an excellent dinner, and bade him drink the wine freely, which he again declined. At midnight, he retired to the same comfortable bed, and was roused again some time later by the same low, rumbling noise of the trunk being pulled into position. Chao did not even bother to look through the partition, he just allowed himself to drift away into a deep sleep.

The next morning, Third Lady again offered him tea and wheat cakes, but Chao, bringing out those he had bought in the city, said, "Gracious Lady, please try one of these, they are from the capital, and are said to be particularly fine," and he handed her the cake of her own making that he had taken a few days before. Third Lady had little option but to thank him, and eat the cake. She took only one bite and immediately her hair grew rough, her ears grew absurdly long, and she turned into a donkey. Chao examined the beast, and was delighted to find it was a strong, powerful beast, infinitely superior to his own decrepit animal, which he promptly set free. Staying only long enough to open the trunk, take out the figures and burn them, so they could do no more harm, Chao then spurred his new mount homewards.

For five years Chao had excellent service from his strange donkey, until one day he was riding through Changan. An old man came up to him, and looking at the donkey, cried "Third Lady of the Wooden Bridge Inn! I would hardly have recognized you. How you have changed!" Then turning to Chao, he said, "I congratulate you on preventing her from causing more grief, but she has served her penance now. Please let her go free." Chao dismounted, and unloaded the beast, which brayed loudly in gratitude. The old man took his sword, and split the creature's stomach in two, and out sprang Third Lady. With a cry of shame, and without looking at Chao or the old man, she ran into the wilderness, and no living person ever saw or heard from her again.

The Three Precious Packets

IN THE FREEZING DEPTHS of a particularly severe winter, a poor student called Niu was travelling to the capital to take his law examinations, so that he could start on the ladder of success that might eventually lead to him becoming a magistrate. As the snow fell, and night darkened around him, Niu stopped at a small inn for some food and shelter. His meagre finances allowed him a bowl of noodles, and some hot rice-wine, and he sat contentedly warming himself in front of the fire.

Suddenly, the door of the inn was thrown open, and in a flurry of snow, an old man staggered into the room. He was dressed in rags, had no shoes on his feet, and was clearly half-frozen, his teeth chattering too much to allow him to speak. Without waiting to be asked, Niu leapt from his seat and offered the man his place in front of the fire, which the wretch took with a grateful nod. Soon he began to recover, but when the landlord asked him what he wanted, he replied, "I only have money for a bowl of tea, and then I will be off again." The landlord grunted and went off to get the tea, but Niu, poor though he was, could not bear to think of the man having to face the freezing weather again that night without food. He insisted that the man share his noodles, and when they were rapidly eaten, he ordered more, and then more still, until the stranger had eaten five full bowls. He then stood to go, but Niu insisted he share his bedding and get a good night's rest before facing the winter's anger in the morning. Once again, the man gratefully accepted, and fell asleep almost immediately.

In the morning, Niu settled up with the landlord, using up almost all his money in the process, and was about to leave, when the stranger woke and said, "Please wait, I have something to give you." He took Niu outside the inn, and said, "Although I am in beggar's rags, I am actually a messenger from the Underworld; for your kindness to me last night, when you could ill afford it, I would like to give you these in return," and from his pocket he took three small, folded packets. "When you are faced with impossible difficulties, you must burn incense and open one of these; it will help you, but only when your circumstances seem hopeless." Niu took the packets, and all at once the stranger disappeared on the wind.

Niu continued on his way to the capital, not really believing what the man had said. There he continued his studies and waited for the examinations, but the city was terribly expensive, and he was soon forced to cut down on food to the point where he was close to starvation, his studies suffering badly as a consequence. He was about to return to his village in despair, when he remembered the three packets and, lighting a stick of incense, he opened the first of them. Inside was a slip of paper which read, "Go and sit outside the Bodhi Temple at noon." The Bodhi Temple was some miles distant, but Niu went there through the cold, and sat in the freezing snow outside the building, all the while thinking that he must be wasting his time. After a time a monk came out and asked him what he wanted. Niu replied that he just wanted to sit there for a while, and taking pity on this strange man, the monk brought him some tea, and started talking to him. He asked Niu his name, and when Niu told him, the monk reeled backwards in astonishment.

"Are you related to the late Magistrate Niu of Chin-Yang?" he asked, and Niu replied that he was the man's nephew. After asking a few further questions, to assure himself that Niu really was the dead man's relative, the monk said, "Your uncle was a great benefactor of this temple, but he also left three thousand strings of coins with me for safe keeping. When he died, I was at a loss as to what to do with them, but now that you have miraculously come here, you must take them as his next of kin."

The astonished Niu was now a very wealthy man, able to live in complete comfort, and concentrate entirely on his studies. However, try as he might, he could not pass the examinations necessary to fulfil his ambition of becoming a Magistrate, and he began to despair. After failing for the third time, Niu was about to give up and return to his village, when he again remembered the three packets, and quickly finding the remaining pair, he lit a stick of incense and opened the second. Inside was a slip of paper which read, 'Go and eat in Shu's restaurant.' Rather baffled, Niu did as he was told. He ordered tea, and sat in the restaurant, wondering what he was doing there. Then, from behind a partition on his right, Niu heard two men in a private room talking, and he could not help overhearing their conversation. "I am worried," said one, "that the questions are too easy. After all, this is an important examination, and we do not want to let standards slip."

The other replied, "Tell me the quotations you have set, and I will tell you what I think." The first man then ran through the list of quotations that were to be set as exam topics, and the astonished Niu realized that he was being told exactly what would be required of him at the next round of examinations. Rushing home, he wrote down all he had heard, and when the time came for the exams he passed with flying colours.

So impressive were his results that he was given an important official post, and very soon became a Magistrate, as he had always wished. He became famous for his fairness and wisdom, and also for his kindness, never turning away any person in need. He always carried with him the last of the three packets, but felt that he would never have to open it, so great was his good fortune. However, when still in middle age, Niu fell ill, and nothing that the doctors or the priests could do seemed able to cure him. At last, with his strength failing, Niu decided to open the last packet. He lit a stick of incense and opened the packet; inside there was a slip of paper which read, "Make your will."

Niu knew now that his life was ending. He carefully put all his affairs in order, and said farewell to his family and friends. Then he died, peacefully, and full of contentment at a life well spent, mourned by the whole city, and remembered with love and admiration by the entire population.

The Dragon's Pearl

MANY HUNDREDS OF YEARS AGO a mother and her son lived together by the banks of the Min river in the province of Shu, which we now call Sichuan. They were extremely poor, and the young boy had to look after his mother, who was very old and very ill. Although he worked long hours cutting and selling grass for animal food; he barely made enough to support them both, and was always afraid that ruin lay just around the next corner.

One summer, as the earth grew brown through lack of rain, and the supply of good grass became even more sparse than usual, the young boy was forced to journey farther and farther from home to make any living at all; higher and higher into the mountains he went in search of pasture. Then one day, tired and thirsty, the boy was just about to set out empty-handed on the long homeward journey, when he came across a patch of the most verdant, tall grass he had ever seen, waving in the breeze, and giving off a pleasing scent of Spring. The boy was so delighted that he cut down the whole patch, and joyfully carried it down the mountain to his village. He sold the grass for more than he often earned in a week, and for once he and his sick mother were able to eat a good meal of fish and rice.

The next day the boy returned to the same area, hoping to find a similar patch of grass nearby, but to his complete amazement, the very spot which he had harvested the day before had grown again fully, as green and luscious as before. Once again, he cut down the whole patch and returned home. This happened day after day, and the boy and his mother were delighted by the upturn in their fortunes. The only disadvantage was the distance the boy had to travel every day, a long, hazardous journey into the mountains, and it occurred to him that if this was a magic patch of grass, it should grow equally well in his village as it did in the mountains.

The very next day he made several journeys to the mountains, and dug up the patch, grass, roots, soil and all, and carried it back to a spot just near his house, where he carefully re-laid the plot of earth. As he was doing so, he found to his wonder and delight, hidden in the roots of the grass, the largest, most beautiful pearl he had ever seen. He rushed to show it to his mother, and even with her failing sight, she realized that it must be of enormous value. They decided to keep it safely hidden until the boy could go to the city to sell it in the market there. The old woman hid it at the bottom of their large rice jar, which contained just enough to cover the stone, and the boy went back to re-laying the magic grass patch.

The next day he rushed out of bed to go and harvest his crop, only to find that, far from luxuriant pasture he had expected, the grass on the patch was withered, brown, and obviously dying. The boy wept for his folly in moving the earth and destroying its magic, and went inside to confess his failure to his mother. As he was going into the house, he heard his mother cry out, and rushing to her, found her standing in amazement over the rice jar. It was full to the brim with rice, and on the top of the jar lay the pearl, glinting in the morning sun. Then they knew that this must be a magic pearl. They placed it in their virtually empty money box, and sure enough, the next morning, they discovered that it too was absolutely full, the pearl sitting on top of the golden pile like a jewel on top of a crown.

Mother and son used their magic pearl wisely, and became quite wealthy; naturally in a small village this fortune did not go unremarked, and the neighbours who had been kind to the mother and son in their times of hardship now found themselves handsomely repaid, and those in need found ready relief for their distress.

However, the villagers were curious as to the source of this new wealth, and it did not take long for the story of the fabulous pearl to become known. One day the boy found himself surrounded by people demanding to see the stone. Foolishly he took it from its hiding place and showed it to the assembled throng. Some of the crowd grew threatening, jostling and pushing, and asking why the boy should be allowed to keep such a lucky find. The son saw that the situation was about to turn ugly, and without thinking, he put the pearl into his mouth to keep it safe. But in the uproar he accidentally swallowed it with a loud gulp.

Immediately, the boy felt as if he was on fire, his throat and then his stomach was consumed with a heat so intense he did not know how to endure it. He ran to his house and threw the contents of the water bucket down his throat, but it had no impact on the searing pain; he dashed to the well, and pulled up bucket after bucket of water, but to no avail. Although he drank gallon after gallon he was still burning up, and in a frenzy of despair he threw himself down on the banks of the Min and began to lap up the river as fast as he could, until eventually he had drunk it absolutely dry. As the last drop of the mighty river disappeared down his throat, there was a huge crack of thunder, and a violent storm erupted. The earth shook, lightning flashed across the sky, rain lashed down from the heavens, and the terrified villagers all fell to the ground in fear. Still the boy was shaking like a leaf, and his frightened mother grabbed hold of his legs, which suddenly started to grow. Horns sprouted on his forehead, scales appeared in place of his skin, and his eyes grew wider, and seemed to spit fire. Racked by convulsions the boy grew bigger and bigger. The horrified mother saw that he was turning into a dragon before her very eyes, and understood that the pearl must have belonged to the dragon guardian of the river. For every water dragon has a magic pearl which is its most treasured possession.

The river was now filling up with all the rain, and the dragon-boy started to slither towards it, his weeping mother still clinging to his scaly legs. With a powerful jerk, he managed to shake her free, but even as he headed for the torrent, he could still hear her despairing cries. Each time she called out, he turned his huge body to look at her, each writhing motion throwing up mud-banks at the side of the river, until, with a last anguished roar, he slid beneath the waves for the last time and disappeared for ever. And to this day the mud banks on the Min river are called the 'Looking Back at Mother' banks, in memory of the dragon-boy and his magic pearl.

The Foolish Old Man and the Mountains

THERE WAS ONCE a very old man, more than ninety years old, called Yu Gong. He lived with his family in the mountains of the West and their house stood right in front of two great peaks, Taihang and Wangwu. Every time the old man went anywhere, he had to cross the two peaks, and he hated them with all his soul for always exhausting him.

Eventually he could stand it no longer, and calling his family together, told them that they were going to move the peaks out of the way.

"Where will you put all the earth?" asked his wife, who thought the whole plan insane.

"We'll just carry it all to the shores of the great lake," replied Yu Gong. And all the men of the family set to work, right down to his youngest nephew.

They carried bucket after bucket, sack after sack of earth and rock away, all the way to the shores of the great lake, but still the mountains seemed no smaller, the climb in the mornings no less strenuous. The wise old man who lived nearby saw all this and laughed at Yu Gong.

"This is madness," he cried. "You are old, Yu Gong, your life is like a candle guttering in the wind; stop this nonsense now."

"Stop now?" replied Yu Gong. "Don't be absurd. When I die my sons will carry on the work, and their sons after them. The work will continue on down the generations until the great task is finished. You really are no wiser than my youngest nephew."

And the wise man kept silent, as he had no answer to this.

Now it so happened that a God overheard this exchange, and he went to the High God to warn him of the old man's ambition, fearing the two peaks might one day actually disappear. But the High God was so impressed by Yu Gong's fortitude and determination that he sent two giants to help the old man, and they took the mountains away, one to Yongnan in the South, and the other to Shuodong in the East. And the old man was able to live out his remaining years without ever again having to climb over the twin peaks.

The Guardian of the Gate of Heaven

IN BUDDHIST TEMPLES you will find a figure of a man holding a model of a pagoda in his hand. He is Li, the Prime Minister of Heaven and father of No-cha. He was a general under the tyrant Chou and commander of Ch'en-t'ang Kuan at the time when the bloody war was being waged that resulted in the extinction of the Yin dynasty.

No-cha is one of the most frequently mentioned heroes in Chinese romance; he is represented in one account as being Yu Huang's shield bearer, sixty feet in height, his three heads with nine eyes crowned by a golden wheel, his eight hands each holding a magic weapon and his mouth vomiting blue clouds. At the sound of his voice, we are told, the heavens shook and the foundations of the earth trembled. His duty was to bring into submission all the demons which desolated the world.

Li Ching's wife, Yin Shih, bore him three sons, the eldest Chin-cha, the second Mu-cha, and the third No-cha, generally known as 'the Third Prince'.

One night, Yin Shih dreamed that a Taoist priest entered her room. She indignantly exclaimed: "How dare you come into my room in this indiscreet manner?" The priest replied: "Woman, receive the child of the unicorn!" Before she could reply the Taoist pushed an object to her bosom.

Yin Shih awoke in a fright, a cold sweat all over her body. Having woken her husband, she told him of her dream. At that moment she was seized with the pains of childbirth. Li Ching left the room, uneasy at what seemed to be inauspicious omens. A little later two servants ran to him, crying out: "Your wife has given birth to a monstrous freak!"

Li Ching seized his sword and went into his wife's room, which he found filled with a red light and a most extraordinary odour. A ball of flesh was rolling on the floor like a wheel; with a blow of his sword he cut it open and a baby emerged, surrounded by a halo of red light. Its face was very white, a gold bracelet was on its right wrist and it wore a pair of red silk trousers, from which came rays of dazzling golden light. The bracelet was 'the horizon of Heaven and earth', and the two precious objects belonged to the cave Chin-kuang Tung of T'ai-i Chen-jen, the priest who had bestowed them upon him when he appeared to his mother during her sleep. The child itself was an avatar of Ling Chu-tzu, 'the Intelligent Pearl'.

Then next day T'ai-i Chen-jen returned and asked Li Ching's permission to see the newborn baby. "He shall be called No-cha," he said, "and will become my disciple."

At seven years of age No-cha was already six feet in height. One day he asked his mother if he might go for a walk outside the town. His mother granted him permission on condition that he was accompanied by a servant. She also told him not to remain too long outside the wall, for his father should become anxious.

It was in the fifth moon: the heat was excessive. No-cha had not gone far before he was sweating profusely. Some way ahead he saw a clump of trees. He decided to go there and, settling himself in the shade, opened his coat and breathed the fresher air with relief. In front of him he saw a stream of limpid green water running between two rows of willows – the water gently flowing round a rock. The child ran to the banks of the stream and said to his guardian: "I am covered with perspiration, and will bathe from the rock." "Be quick," said the servant; "if your father returns home before you he will be anxious." No-cha stripped himself, took his red silk trousers and dipped them in the water, intending to use them as a towel. No sooner were the magic trousers immersed in the stream than the water began to boil and Heaven and earth trembled. The water of the Chiu-wan Ho river ('Nine-bends River') turned completely red and Lung Wang's palace shook to its foundations. The Dragon king, surprised at seeing the walls of his crystal palace shaking, called his officers and asked: "How is it that the palace threatens to collapse? There should not be an earthquake at this time." He ordered one of his attendants to go at once and find out what evil was causing the commotion. When the officer reached the river he saw that the water was red but noticed nothing else except a boy dipping a band of silk in the stream. He called out angrily: "That child should be thrown into the water for making the river red and causing Lung Wang's palace to shake." No-cha replied, "Who is that who speaks so brutally?"

Then he jumped aside, realizing that the man intended to seize him. He took his gold bracelet and hurled it in the air. It fell on the head of the officer and No-cha left him dead on the rock. Then he picked up his bracelet and said smiling: "His blood has stained my precious horizon of Heaven and earth." He then washed it in the water.

"How is it that the officer does not return?" inquired Lung Wang. At that moment attendants came to inform him that the messenger had been murdered by a boy.

Ao Ping, the third son of Lung Wang, immediately placed himself at the head of a troop of marines, and with his trident in his hand he left the palace precincts. The warriors dashed into the river, raising on every side waves mountains high. Seeing the water rising, No-cha stood up on the rock and was confronted by Ao Ping mounted on a sea monster. "Who slew my messenger?" cried the warrior. "I did," answered No-cha. "Who are you?" demanded Ao Ping.

"I am No-cha, the third son of Li Ching of Ch'en-t'ang Kuan. I came here to bathe and refresh myself. Your messenger cursed me, and I killed him."

"Rascal! Do you not know that your victim was a deputy of the King of Heaven? How dare you kill him and then boast of your crime?" Ao Ping then thrust at the boy with his trident, but No-cha evaded the thrust.

"Who are you?" No-cha asked in turn.

"I am Ao Ping, the third son of Lung Wang."

"Ah, you are a blusterer," jeered the boy. "If you dare to touch me I will skin you alive, you and your mud eels!"

"You make me choke with rage," shouted Ao Ping, at the same time thrusting again with his trident.

Furious at this renewed attack, No-cha spread his silk trousers in the air. Thousands of balls of fire flew out of them, felling Lung Wang's son. No-cha put his foot on Ao Ping's head and struck it with his magic bracelet, causing Ao Ping to turn into his true form of a dragon.

"I am now going to pull out your sinews," he said, "in order to make a belt for my father."

No-cha was as good as his word, and Ao Ping's escort ran and informed Lung Wang of the fate of his son. The Dragon king went to Li Ching and demanded an explanation.

Being entirely ignorant of what had taken place, Li Ching went to No-cha to question him.

Li Ching found No-cha in the garden, busily weaving the belt of dragon sinew. "You have brought the most awful misfortunes upon us," he exclaimed. "Come and give an account of your conduct." "Have no fear," No-cha replied; "his son's sinews are still intact. I will give them back to him if he wishes."

When they entered the house he saluted the Dragon king, made a curt apology, and offered to return his son's sinews. The father, moved with grief at the sight of the proofs of the tragedy, said bitterly to Li Ching: "You have such a son and yet dare to deny his guilt, though you heard him admitting it! Tomorrow I shall report the matter to Yu Huang." Having said this, he departed.

Li Ching was overwhelmed at the enormity of his son's crime. His wife, hearing his cries of grief, went to her husband. "What obnoxious creature is this that you have brought into the world?" he said to her angrily. "He has slain two spirits, the son of Lung Wang and a steward sent by the King of Heaven. Tomorrow the Dragon king is to lodge a complaint with Yu Huang, and two or three days from now will see the end of our existence."

The poor mother began to weep. "What!" she sobbed, "you whom I suffered so much for, you are to be the cause of our ruin and death!"

No-cha, seeing his parents so distracted, fell on his knees. "Let me tell you once for all," he said, "that I am no ordinary mortal. I am the disciple of T'ai-i Chen-jen. The magic weapons I received from him – it is they that brought on me the undying hatred of Lung Wang. But he cannot prevail. Today I will go and ask my master's advice. The guilty alone should suffer the penalty; it is unjust that his parents should suffer."

No-cha then left for Ch'ien-yuan Shan. He entered the cave of his master T'ai-i Chen-jen, to whom he told of his adventures. The master considered the grave consequences of the murders. He then ordered No-cha to bare his breast. With his finger he drew on the skin a magic formula, after which he gave him some secret instructions. "Now," he said, "go to the gate of Heaven and await the arrival of Lung Wang, who plans to accuse you before Yu Huang. Then you must come again to consult me, so that your parents may not be molested because of your misdeeds."

When No-cha reached the gate of Heaven it was closed. He searched in vain for Lung Wang, but after a while he saw him approaching. Lung Wang did not see No-cha, as the formula written by T'ai-i Chen-jen rendered him invisible. As Lung Wang approached the gate, No-cha ran up to him and struck him so hard with his golden bracelet that he fell to the ground. Then No-cha stamped on him, cursing him.

The Dragon-king now recognized his assailant and sharply reproached him with his crimes, but the only reparation he got was a renewal of kicks and blows. Then, partially lifting Lung Wang's cloak and raising his shield, No-cha tore off about forty scales from his body. Blood flowed copiously and under stress of the pain the Dragon king begged his foe to spare his life. To this No-cha consented on condition that he relinquished his purpose of accusing him before Yu Huang.

"Now," went on No-cha, "change yourself into a small serpent so that I may take you back without fear of your escaping."

Lung Wang took the form of a small blue dragon and followed No-cha to his father's house. After entering the house Lung Wang resumed his normal form and accused No-cha of attacking him. "I will go with all the Dragon kings and lay an accusation before Yu Huang," he said. Then he transformed himself into a gust of wind and disappeared.

"Things are going from bad to worse," sighed Li Ching, His son, however, consoled him: "I beg you, my father, not to let the future trouble you. I am the chosen one of the gods. My master is T'ai-i Chen-jen. He has assured me that he can easily protect us."

Next No-cha went out and climbed a tower that overlooked the entrance of the fort. There he found a wonderful bow and three magic arrows. No-cha did not know that this was the spiritual weapon belonging to the fort. "My master informed me that I am destined to fight to establish the coming Chou dynasty; I ought therefore to perfect myself in the use of weapons. This is a good opportunity." So he seized the bow and shot an arrow toward the south west. A red trail indicated the path of the arrow, which hissed as it flew. At that moment Pi Yun, a servant of Shih-chi Niang-niang, happened to be at the foot of K'u-lou Shan (Skeleton Hill), in front of the cave of his mistress. The arrow pierced his throat and he fell dead, bathed in his blood. Shih-chi Niang-niang came out of her cave, and examining the arrow found that it bore the inscription: "Arrow which shakes the heavens." She knew that it must have come from Ch'en-t'ang Kuan, where the magic bow was kept.

The goddess mounted her blue phoenix, flew over the fort, seized Li Ching and carried him to her cave. There she made him kneel before her. She reminded him how she had protected him so that he might gain honour and glory on earth before he attained to immortality.

"And this is how you show your gratitude – by killing my servant!"

Li Ching swore that he was innocent; but the tell-tale arrow was there, and it could only have come from the fortress. Li Ching begged the goddess to set him free so that he might find the culprit and bring him to her. "If I cannot find him," he added, "you may take my life."

Once again No-cha frankly admitted his deed to his father and followed him to the cave of Shih-chi Niang-niang. When he reached the entrance the second servant reproached him with the crime, immediately after which No-cha struck him with a heavy blow. Shih-chi Niang-niang, infuriated, threw herself at No-cha, sword in hand; one after the other she wrenched from him his bracelet and magic trousers.

Deprived of his magic weapons, No-cha fled to his master, T'ai-i Chen-jen. The goddess followed and demanded that he be put to death. A terrible conflict ensued between the two champions, until T'ai-i Chen-jen hurled his globe of nine fire-dragons into the air. This fell on Shih-chi Niang-niang, enveloping her in a whirlwind of flame. When it had passed they saw that she had changed into stone.

"Now you are safe," said T'ai-i Chen-jen to No-cha, "but return quickly, for the Four Dragon kings have laid their accusation before Yu Huang, and they are going to carry off your parents. Follow my advice, and you will rescue your parents from their misfortune."

On his return No-cha found the Four Dragon-kings on the point of carrying off his parents. "It is I," he said, "who killed Ao Ping and I who should pay the penalty. Why are you molesting my parents? I am about to return to them what I received from them. Will it satisfy you?"

Lung Wang agreed, so No-cha took a sword and before their eyes cut off an arm, sliced open his stomach and fell unconscious. His soul, carried on the wind, went straight to the cave of T'ai-i Chen-jen, while his mother busied herself with burying his body.

"Your home is not here," said his master to him; "return to Ch'en-t'ang Kuan, and beg your mother to build a temple on Ts'ui-p'ing Shan. Incense will be burned to you for three years, at the end of which time you will be reincarnated."

During the night, while his mother was in a deep sleep, No-cha appeared to her in a dream and said: "My mother, pity me; since my death, my soul, separated from my body, wanders about without a home. Build me, I pray you, a temple on Ts'ui-p'ing Shan, that I may be reincarnated." His mother awoke in tears and related her vision to Li Ching, who reproached her for her blind attachment to her unnatural son – the cause of so much disaster.

For five or six nights the son appeared to his mother, each time repeating his request. The last time he added: "Do not forget that by nature I am ferocious; if you refuse my request evil will befall you."

His mother then sent builders to the mountain to construct a temple to No-cha, and his image was set up in it. Miracles were not wanting, and the number of pilgrims who visited the shrine increased daily.

One day Li Ching was passing this mountain with a troop of his soldiers. He saw the roads crowded with pilgrims of both sexes. "Where are these people going?" he asked. "For six months past," he was told, "the spirit of the temple on this mountain has continued to perform miracles. People come from far and near to worship him."

"What is the name of this spirit?" inquired Li Ching. "No-cha," they replied. "No-cha!" exclaimed the father. "I will go and see him myself." In a rage Li Ching entered the temple and examined the statue, which was the image of his son. By its side were images of two of his servants. He took his whip and began to beat the statue, cursing it all the while. "It is not enough, apparently, for you to have been a source of disaster to us," he said; "but even after your death you must deceive the multitude." He whipped the statue until it fell to pieces; he then kicked over the images of the servants, and went back, telling the people not to worship so wicked a man, the shame and ruin of his family. By his orders the temple was burnt to the ground.

When he reached Ch'en-t'ang Kuan his wife came to him but he received her coldly. "You gave birth to that cursed son," he said, "who has been the plague of our lives, and after his death you build him a temple in which he deceives the people. Do you wish to have me disgraced? If I were to be accused at Court of having instituted the worship of false gods, would not my destruction be certain? I have burned the temple, and intend that that shall settle the matter once and for all; if ever you think of rebuilding it I will break off all relations with you."

At the time of his father's visit No-cha was absent from the temple. On his return he found only its smoking remnants. "Who has demolished my temple?" he asked. "Li Ching," the spirits of his servants replied. "In doing this he has exceeded his powers," said No-cha. "I gave him back the substance I received from him; why did he come with violence to break up my image? I will have nothing more to do with him."

No-cha's soul had already begun to be spiritualized. So he decided to go to T'ai-i Chen-jen and beg for his help. "The worship given to you there," replied the Taoist, "had nothing in it that should have offended your father; it did not concern him. He was in the wrong. Before long Chiang Tzu-ya will descend to inaugurate the new dynasty, and since you must throw in your lot with him I will find a way to help you."

T'ai-i Chen-jen had two water lily stalks and three lotus leaves brought to him. He spread these on the ground in the form of a human being and placed the soul of No-cha in this lotus skeleton, uttering a magic spell as he worked. There emerged a new No-cha full of life, with a fresh complexion, purple lips and keen glance, who was sixteen feet tall. "Follow me to my peach garden," said T'ai-i Chen-jen, "and I will give you your weapons." He handed him a sharp fiery spear and two wind-and-fire wheels which, placed under his feet, served as a vehicle. A brick of gold in a panther-skin bag completed his magic armament. The new warrior, after thanking his master, mounted his wind-and-fire wheels and returned to Ch'en-t'ang Kuan.

Li Ching was informed that his son No-cha had returned and was threatening vengeance. So he took his weapons, mounted his horse and went to meet him. They joined in battle, but Li Ching was soon overcome and compelled to flee. No-cha pursued his father, but as he was on the point of overtaking him Li Ching's second son, Mu-cha, came on the scene. Mu-cha criticized his brother for his unfilial conduct.

"Li Ching is no longer my father," replied No-cha. "I gave him back my substance; why did he burn my temple and smash up my image?"

Mu-cha prepared to defend his father, but took a blow to his back from the golden brick. He fell, unconscious. No-cha then resumed his pursuit of Li Ching.

His strength exhausted and in danger of falling into the hands of his enemy, Li Ching drew his sword and was about to kill himself. "Stop!" cried a Taoist priest. "Come into my cave, and I will protect you."

When No-cha arrived he could not see Li Ching. He demanded his surrender from the Taoist. But he had to do with one stronger than himself, no less a being than Wen-chu T'ien-tsun, whom T'ai-i Chen-jen had sent in order that No-cha might receive a lesson. The Taoist, with the aid of his magic weapon, seized No-cha, and in a moment he found a gold ring fastened round his neck, two chains on his feet, and he was bound to a pillar of gold.

At this moment, as if by accident, T'ai-i Chen-jen appeared on the scene. His master had No-cha brought before Wen-chu T'ien-tsun and Li Ching, and advised him to live at peace with his father. But he also rebuked the father for having burned the temple on Ts'ui-p'ing Shan. This done, he ordered Li Ching to go home and No-cha to return to his cave. The latter, overflowing with anger and with his heart full of vengeance, started again in pursuit of Li Ching, swearing that he would punish him. But the Taoist reappeared and prepared to protect Li Ching.

No-cha, bristling like a savage cat, threw himself at his enemy and tried to pierce him with his spear. At that moment a white lotus flower emerged from the Taoist's mouth and arrested the course of the weapon. As No-cha continued to threaten him, the Taoist drew a mysterious object from his sleeve which rose in the air and, falling at the feet of No-cha, enveloped him in flames. Then No-cha prayed for mercy. The Taoist exacted from him three separate promises: to live in harmony with his father, to recognize and address him as his father, and to throw himself at his (the Taoist's) feet, to indicate his reconciliation with himself.

After this act of reconciliation had been performed, Wen-chu T'ien-tsun told Li Ching that he should leave his official post to become an Immortal. That he should place his services at the disposal of the new Chou dynasty, shortly to come into power. In order to ensure that their reconciliation should last forever, and to place it beyond No-cha's power to seek revenge, he gave Li Ching the wonderful object that had caused No-cha's feet to have been burned, and which had been the means of bringing him into subjection. It was a golden pagoda, which became the characteristic weapon of Li Ching, and gave rise to his nickname, Li the Pagoda-bearer. Finally, Yu Huang appointed him Generalissimo of the Twenty-Six Celestial Officers, Grand Marshal of the Skies, and Guardian of the Gate of Heaven.

A Battle of the Gods

IT IS THOUGHT that during the wars that preceded the accession of the Chou dynasty in 1122 BC, a multitude of demigods, Buddhas and Immortals took part on one side or the other, some fighting for the old dynasty, some for the new. They were wonderful creatures, gifted with marvellous powers. They could change their form at will, multiply their heads and limbs, become invisible, and create – by simply uttering a word – terrible monsters who bit and destroyed, or sent forth poisonous gases, or emitted flames from their nostrils. In these battles there is much lightning, thunder, flight of fire dragons, dark clouds that vomit burning hails of murderous weapons; swords, spears, and arrows fall from the sky on to the heads of the combatants; the earth trembles and the pillars of Heaven shake.

One of these gifted warriors was Chun T'i, a Taoist of the Western Paradise, who appeared on the scene when the armies of the rival dynasties were facing each other. K'ung Hsuan was gallantly holding the pass of the Chin-chi Ling; Chiang Tzu-ya was trying to take it by assault – so far without success.

Chun T'i's mission was to take K'ung Hsuan to the abode of the blessed, his wisdom and general progress having now reached the required degree of perfection. This was a means of breaking down the invincible resistance of this powerful enemy and at the same time of rewarding his brilliant talents.

But K'ung Hsuan did not approve of this plan and a fight took place between the two champions. At one moment Chun T'i was seized by a luminous bow and carried into the air. While enveloped in a cloud of fire he appeared with eighteen arms and twenty-four heads, holding in each hand a powerful talisman.

He put a silk cord round K'ung Hsuan's neck, touched him with his wand and forced him to reassume his original form of a red one-eyed peacock. Chun T'i sat himself on the peacock's back and it flew across the sky, carrying its saviour and master to the Western Paradise. Brilliantly variegated clouds marked its track through space.

On the disappearance of its defender, the pass of Chin-chi Ling was captured and the village of Chieh-p'ai Kuan was reached. This place was the fort of the enemy's forces. It was defended by a host of genii and Immortals, the most distinguished among them being the Taoist T'ung-t'ien Chiao-chu, whose especially effective charms had so far kept the fort secure against every attempt on it.

Lao Tzu himself had descended from dwelling in happiness, together with Yuan-shih T'ien-tsun and Chieh-yin Tao-jen, to take part in the siege. But the town had four gates and these heavenly rulers were only three in number. So Chun T'i was recalled, and each member of the quartet was given the task of capturing one of the gates.

Chun T'i's duty was to take the Chueh-hsien Men, defended by T'ung-t'ien Chiao-chu. The warriors who had tried to enter the town by this gate had all paid for their temerity with their lives. The moment each had crossed the threshold a clap of thunder had resounded, and a mysterious sword, moving with lightning speed, had slain him.

As Chun T'i advanced at the head of his warriors terrible lightning filled the air and the mysterious sword descended like a thunderbolt on his head. But Chun T'i held up his Seven-Precious Branch.

Thousands of lotus flowers emerged from it, which formed an impenetrable barrier and stopped the sword in its fall. This and the other gates were then forced, and a grand assault was now directed against the chief defender of the town.

T'ung-t'ien Chiao-chu, riding his ox and surrounded by his warriors, for the last time risked the chance of war and bravely faced his four terrible adversaries. With his sword held high, he threw himself on Chieh-yin Tao-jen, whose only weapon was his fly whisk. But there emerged from this a five-coloured lotus flower, which stopped the sword thrust. While Lao Tzu struck the hero with his staff, Yuan-shih T'ien-tsun warded off the terrible sword.

Chun T'i now called for the spiritual peacock to help. He took the form of a warrior with twenty-four heads and eighteen arms. His mysterious weapons surrounded T'ung-t'ien Chiao-chu, and Lao Tzu struck the hero so hard that fire came out from his eyes, nose and mouth. Unable to ward off the assaults of his adversaries, he next received a blow from Chun T'i's magic wand, which felled him. He took flight in a whirlwind of dust.

The defenders now offered no further resistance. Yuan-shih T'ien-tsun thanked Chun T'i for the valuable assistance he had given in the capture of the village. Afterwards the gods returned to their palace in the Western Heaven.

But T'ung-t'ien Chiao-chu swore to have his revenge. He called to the spirits of the twenty-eight constellations for help, and marched to attack Wu Wang's army. The honour of the victory that followed belonged to Chun T'i, who disarmed both the Immortal Wu Yun and T'ung-t'ien Chiao-chu.

Wu Yun, armed with his magic sword, attacked Chun T'i; but the latter opened his mouth and a blue lotus flower came out and stopped the blows aimed at him. Other thrusts were met by similar miracles.

"Why continue so useless a fight?" said Chun T'i at last. "Abandon the cause of the Shang and come with me to the Western Paradise. I came to save you, and you must not compel me to make you resume your original form."

An insulting flow of words was the reply; again the magic sword descended like lightning, and again the stroke was averted by a timely lotus flower. Chun T'i now waved his wand and the magic sword was broken to bits, with only the handle remaining in Wu Yun's hand.

Mad with rage, Wu Yun seized his club and tried to fell his enemy. But Chun T'i summoned a disciple, who appeared with a bamboo pole. This he thrust out like a fishing rod, and on a hook at the end of the line attached to the pole dangled a large golden-bearded turtle. This was the Immortal Wu Yun, now in his original form of a spiritual turtle. The disciple sat himself on its back, and both disappeared into space, returning to the Western Heavens.

To conquer T'ung-t'ien Chiao-chu was more difficult, but after a long fight Chun T'i waved his Wand of the Seven Treasures and broke his adversary's sword. The latter, disarmed and vanquished, disappeared in a cloud of dust. Chun T'i did not trouble to pursue him. The battle was won.

A disciple of T'ung-t'ien Chiao-chu, P'i-lu Hsien, 'the Immortal P'i-lu', seeing his master beaten in two successive engagements, left the battlefield and followed Chun T'i to the Western Paradise, to become a Buddha. He is known as P'i-lu Fo, one of the principal gods of Buddhism.

Chun T'i's festival is celebrated on the sixth day of the third moon. He is generally shown with eight hands and three faces, one of the latter being that of a pig.

The Cursed Temple

THE REIGN OF CH'UNG CHENG, the last monarch of the Ming dynasty, was troubled both by internal quarrels and by wars. He was constantly threatened by Tartar hordes, though these were generally beaten back by the celebrated general Wu San-kuei. The country was in a constant state of anarchy and confusion, being overrun by bands of marauding rebels; indeed, so bold did these become under a chief named Li Tzu-ch'eng that they actually marched on the capital with the intention of placing their leader on the Dragon Throne. Ch'ung Cheng, on hearing this startling news, with no one that he could trust in such an emergency (as Wu San-kuei was absent on an expedition against the Tartars), was at his wits' end. The insurgents were almost in sight of Peking, and at any moment might arrive. Rebellion threatened in the city itself. If he went out boldly to attack the oncoming rebels his own troops might go over to the enemy, or deliver him into their hands; if he stayed in the city the people would probably open the gates to the rebels.

In such dire straits he resolved to go to the San Kuan Miao, an imperial temple situated near the Ch'ao-yang Men, and ask the gods what he should do. He would decide his fate by 'drawing the slip'. If he drew a long slip, this would be a good omen and he would boldly march out to meet the rebels, confident of victory; if a middle length one, he would remain quietly in the palace and passively wait for whatever might happen; but if he should unfortunately draw a short one he would take his own life rather than suffer death at the hands of the rebels.

On arriving at the temple, in the presence of the high officers of his Court, the sacrifices were offered up and the incense burnt, previous to drawing the slip on which hung the destiny of an empire. Meanwhile Ch'ung Cheng remained on his knees in prayer. At the end of the sacrificial ceremony the tube containing the bamboo fortune-telling sticks was placed in the Emperor's hand by one of the priests. His courtiers and the attendant priests stood round breathless in suspense, watching him as he swayed the tube backwards and forwards. Finally one fell to the ground. There was a deadly silence as it was raised by a priest and handed to the Emperor. It was a short one! Dismay fell on everyone present, no one daring to break the painful, horrible silence.

After a pause the Emperor, with a cry of rage and despair, threw the slip to the ground exclaiming: "May this temple built by my ancestors evermore be accursed! From this time on may every suppliant be denied what he entreats, as I have been! Those who come in sorrow, may that sorrow be doubled; in happiness, may that happiness be changed to misery; in hope, may they meet despair; in health, sickness; in the pride of life and strength, death! I, Ch'ung Cheng, the last of the Mings, curse it!"

Without another word he left, followed by his courtiers. He went at once to the palace and went straight to the apartments of the Empress. The next morning he and his Empress were found suspended from a tree on Prospect Hill. 'In their death they were not divided.'

The scenes that followed; how the rebels took possession of the city and were driven out again by the Chinese general, assisted by the Tartars; how the Tartars finally succeeded in establishing the Manchu dynasty, are all matters of history. The words used by the Emperor at the temple were prophetic; he was the last of the Mings. The tree on which the monarch of a mighty Empire closed his career and brought the Ming dynasty to an end was ordered to be surrounded with chains; it still exists, and is still in chains. Upward of two hundred and seventy years have passed since that time, yet the temple is standing as of old; but the halls that at one time were crowded with worshippers are now silent, no one ever venturing to worship there; it is the home of the fox and the bat. People at night pass it shudderingly – "It is the cursed temple!"

The Maniac's Mite

AN INTERESTING STORY is told of a lady named Ch'en, who was a Buddhist nun celebrated for her virtue and austerity. Between the years 1628 and 1643 she left her nunnery near Wei-hai city and set out on a long journey in order to collect subscriptions for casting a new image of the Buddha.

She wandered through Shantung and Chihli and finally reached Peking, and there – subscription book in hand – she stationed herself at the great south gate in order to take money from those who wished to lay treasures for themselves in the Western Heaven. The first passer-by who took any notice of her was a friendly maniac. His dress was made of coloured shreds and patches and his general appearance was wild and uncouth. "Whither away, nun?" he asked. She explained that she was collecting subscriptions for the casting of a great image of Buddha, and had come all the way from Shantung. "Throughout my life," remarked the madman, "I was ever a generous giver." So, taking the nun's subscription book, he headed a page with his own name (in very large characters) and the amount subscribed. The amount in question was two cash, equivalent to a small fraction of a penny. He then handed over two small coins and went on his way.

In course of time the nun returned to Wei-hai-wei with her subscriptions, and the work of casting the image was begun. When the time had come for the process of smelting, it was observed that the copper remained hard and intractable. Again and again the furnace was fed with fuel, but the shapeless mass of metal remained firm as a rock. The head workman, who was a man of vast experience, volunteered an explanation of the mystery. "An offering of great value must be missing," he said. "Let the collection book be examined so that we can see whose subscription has been withheld." The nun, who was standing by, immediately produced the madman's money, which on account of its minute value she had not taken the trouble to hand over. "There is one cash," she said, "and there is another. Certainly, the offering of these must have been an act of the highest merit and the giver must be a holy man who will someday attain Buddhahood." As she said this she threw the two cash into the midst of the cauldron. Great bubbles rose and burst, the metal melted and ran like the sap from a tree, clear as flowing water, and in a few moments the work was accomplished and the new Buddha successfully cast.

The Painted Skin

AT T'AI-YUAN THERE lived a man named Wang. One morning he was out walking when he met a young lady carrying a bundle and hurrying along by herself. As she moved along with some difficulty, Wang quickened his pace and caught her up, and found she was a pretty girl of about sixteen. Much smitten he inquired whither she was going so early, and no one with her. "A traveller like you," replied the girl, "cannot alleviate my distress; why trouble yourself to ask?" "What distress is it?" said Wang; "I'm sure I'll do anything I can for you." "My parents," answered she, "loved money, and they sold me as concubine into a rich family, where the wife was very jealous, and beat and abused me morning and night. It was more than I could stand, so I have run away." Wang asked her where she was going; to which she replied that a runaway had no fixed place of abode. "My house," said Wang, "is at no great distance; what do you say to coming there?" She joyfully acquiesced; and Wang, taking up her bundle, led the way to his house. Finding no one there, she asked Wang where his family were; to which he replied that that was only the library. "And a very nice place, too," said she; "but if you are kind enough to wish to save my life, you mustn't let it be known that I am here." Wang promised he would not divulge her secret, and so she remained there for some days without anyone knowing anything about it. He then told his wife, and she, fearing the girl might belong to some influential family, advised him to send her away. This, however, he would not consent to do; when one day, going into the town, he met a Taoist priest, who looked at him in astonishment, and asked him what he had met. "I have met nothing," replied Wang. "Why," said the priest, "you are bewitched; what do you mean by not having met anything?" But Wang insisted that it was so, and the priest walked away, saying, "The fool! Some people don't seem to know when death is at hand." This startled Wang, who at first thought of the girl; but then he reflected that a pretty young thing as she was couldn't well be a witch, and began to suspect that the priest merely wanted to do a stroke of business. When he returned, the library door was shut, and he couldn't get in, which made him suspect that something was wrong; and so he climbed over the wall, where he found the door of the inner room shut too. Softly creeping up, he looked through the window and saw a hideous devil, with a green face and jagged teeth like a saw, spreading a human skin upon the bed and painting it with a paint-brush. The devil then threw aside the brush, and giving the skin a shake out, just as you would a coat, threw it over its shoulders, when, lo! it was the girl. Terrified at this, Wang hurried away with his head down in search of the priest who had gone he knew not whither; subsequently finding him in the fields, where he threw himself on his knees and begged the priest to save him. "As to driving her away," said the priest, "the creature must be in great distress to be seeking a substitute for herself; besides, I could hardly endure to injure a living thing." However, he gave Wang a fly-brush, and bade him hang it at the door of the bedroom, agreeing to meet again at the Ch'ing-ti temple. Wang went home, but did not dare enter the library; so he hung up the brush at the bedroom door, and before long heard a sound of footsteps outside. Not daring to move, he made his wife peep out; and she saw the girl standing looking at the brush, afraid to pass it. She then ground her teeth and went away; but in a little while came back, and began cursing, saying, "You priest, you won't frighten me. Do you think I am going to give up what is already in my grasp?" Thereupon, she tore the brush to pieces, and bursting open the door, walked straight up to the bed, where she ripped open Wang and tore out his heart, with which she went away. Wang's wife screamed out, and the servant came in with a light; but Wang was already dead and presented a most miserable spectacle. His wife, who was in an agony of fright, hardly dared cry for fear of making a noise; and next day she sent Wang's brother to see the priest. The latter got into a great rage, and cried out, "Was it for this that I had compassion on you, devil that you are?" proceeding at once with Wang's brother to the house, from which the girl had disappeared without anyone knowing whither she had gone. But the priest, raising his head, looked all round, and said, "Luckily she's not far off." He then asked who lived in the apartments on the south side, to which Wang's brother replied that he did; whereupon the priest declared that there she would be found. Wang's brother was horribly frightened and said he did not think so; and then the priest asked him if any stranger had been to the house. To this he answered that he had been out to the Ch'ing-ti temple and couldn't possibly say; but he went off to inquire, and in a little while came back and reported that an old woman had sought service with them as a maid-of-all-work, and had been engaged by his wife. "That is she," said the priest, as Wang's brother added she was still there; and they all set out to go to the house together. Then the priest took his wooden sword, and standing in the middle of the court-yard, shouted out, "Base-born fiend, give me back my fly-brush!" Meanwhile the new maid-of-all-work was in a great state of alarm, and tried to get away by the door; but the priest struck her and down she fell flat, the human skin dropped off, and she became a hideous devil. There she lay grunting like a pig, until the priest grasped his wooden sword and struck off her head. She then became a dense column of smoke curling up from the ground, when the priest took an uncorked gourd and threw it right into the midst of the smoke. A sucking noise was heard, and the whole column was drawn into the gourd; after which the priest corked it up closely and put it in his pouch. The skin, too, which was complete even to the eyebrows, eyes, hands, and feet, he also rolled up as if it had been a scroll, and was on the point of leaving with it, when Wang's wife stopped him, and with tears entreated him to bring her husband to life. The priest said he was unable to do that; but Wang's wife flung herself at his feet, and with loud lamentations implored his assistance. For some time he remained immersed in thought, and then replied, "My power is not equal to what you ask. I myself cannot raise the dead; but I will direct you to someone who can, and if you apply to him properly you will succeed." Wang's wife asked the priest who it was; to which he replied, "There is a maniac in the town who passes his time grovelling in the dirt. Go, prostrate yourself before him, and beg him to help you. If he insults you, shew no sign of anger." Wang's brother knew the man to whom he alluded, and accordingly bade the priest adieu, and proceeded thither with his sister-in-law.

They found the destitute creature raving away by the road side, so filthy that it was all they could do to go near him. Wang's wife approached him on her knees; at which the maniac leered at her, and cried out, "Do you love me, my beauty?" Wang's wife told him what she had come for, but he only laughed and said, "You can get plenty of other husbands. Why raise the dead one to life?" But Wang's wife entreated him to help her; whereupon he observed, "It's very strange: people apply to me to raise their dead as if I was king of the infernal regions." He then gave Wang's wife a thrashing with his staff, which she bore without a murmur, and before a gradually increasing crowd of spectators. After this he produced a loathsome pill which he told her she must swallow, but here she broke down and was quite unable to do so. However, she did manage it at last, and then the maniac crying out, "How you do love me!" got up and went away without taking any more notice of her. They followed him into a temple with loud supplications, but he had disappeared, and every effort to find him was unsuccessful. Overcome with rage and shame, Wang's wife went home, where she mourned bitterly over her dead husband, grievously repenting the steps she had taken, and wishing only to die. She then bethought herself of preparing the corpse, near which none of the servants would venture; and set to work to close up the frightful wound of which he died.

While thus employed, interrupted from time to time by her sobs, she felt a rising lump in her throat, which by-and-by came out with a pop and fell straight into the dead man's wound. Looking closely at it, she saw it was a human heart; and then it began as it were to throb, emitting a warm vapour like smoke. Much excited, she at once closed the flesh over it, and held the sides of the wound together with all her might. Very soon, however, she got tired, and finding the vapour escaping from the crevices, she tore up a piece of silk and bound it round, at the same time bringing back circulation by rubbing the body and covering it up with clothes. In the night, she removed the coverings, and found that breath was coming from the nose; and by next morning her husband was alive again, though disturbed in mind as if awaking from a dream and feeling a pain in his heart. Where he had been wounded, there was a cicatrix about as big as a cash, which soon after disappeared.

The Unnatural People

Introduction

LEAVING BEHIND the countless gods, goddesses, immortals, heroes and saints, we turn now to some unusual myths surrounding the curious people supposed to inhabit the regions on the maps represented on the nine tripod vases of the Great Yu, first emperor of the Hsia dynasty.

The Pygmies

THE PYGMIES INHABIT many mountainous regions of the Empire, but are few in number. They are less than nine inches tall, but are well formed. They live in thatched houses that resemble ants' nests. When they walk out they go in companies of from six to ten, joining hands in a line for mutual protection against birds that might carry them away, or other creatures that might attack them. Their tone of voice is too low to be distinguished by an ordinary human ear. They occupy themselves in working in wood, gold, silver and precious stones, but a small proportion are tillers of the soil. They wear red clothing. The sexes are distinguishable by a slight beard on the men and long tresses on the women, the latter in some cases reaching four to five inches in length. Their heads are unduly large, being quite out of proportion to their small bodies. A husband and wife usually go about hand in hand.

The story goes that a Hakka charcoal burner once found three of the children playing in his tobacco box. He kept them there and afterward, when he was showing them to a friend, he laughed and drops of saliva flew from his mouth and shot two of them dead. He then begged his friend to take the third and put it in a place of safety before he should laugh again. His friend attempted to lift it from the box, but it died on being touched.

The Giants

IN THE COUNTRY OF THE GIANTS the people are fifty feet tall. Their footprints are six feet in length. Their teeth are like those of a saw. Their fingernails resemble hooked claws, while their diet consists wholly of uncooked animal food. Their eyebrows are of such length as to protrude from the front of the carts on which they ride, large though it is necessary for these vehicles to be. Their bodies are covered with long black hair resembling that of the bear. They live to the advanced age of eighteen thousand years. Though cannibals, they never eat members of their own tribe, confining their indulgence in human flesh, specifically to enemies taken in battle. Their country extends some thousands of miles along certain mountain ranges in North Eastern Asia, in the passes of which they have strong iron gates, easy to close but difficult to open. For this reason, though their neighbours maintain large standing armies, they have so far never been conquered.

The Headless People

THE HEADLESS PEOPLE inhabit the Long Sheep range, to which their ancestors were banished in the remote past for an offence against the gods. One of the said ancestors had entered into a controversy with the rulers of the heavens, and they in their anger had transformed his two breasts into eyes and his navel into a mouth. They removed his head, leaving him without nose and ears, thereby cutting him off from smell and sound. They then banished him to the Long Sheep Mountains, where with a shield and axe, the only weapons given to the people of the Headless Country, he and his posterity were compelled to defend themselves from their enemies and provide their subsistence. This, however, does not in the least seem to have affected their tempers, as their bodies are wreathed in perpetual smiles, except when they flourish their war-like weapons on the approach of an enemy. They are not without understanding, because, according to Chinese notions of physiology, "their bellies are full of wisdom."

The Armless People

IN THE MOUNTAINS of the Sun and Moon, which are in the Centre of the Great Waste, are the people who have no arms, but whose legs instead grow out of their shoulders. They pick flowers with their toes. They bow by raising the body horizontal with the shoulders, so turning the face to the ground.

The Long-Armed and Long-Legged People

THE LONG-ARMED People are about thirty feet tall, their arms reaching from the shoulders to the ground. Once when a company of explorers was passing through the country that borders on the Eastern Sea they inquired of an old man if he knew whether or not there were people dwelling beyond the waters. He replied that a cloth garment, in fashion and texture not unlike that of a

Chinese coat, with sleeves thirty feet in length, had been found in the sea. The explorers fitted out an expedition and the discovery of the Long-armed Country was the result.

The natives subsist for the most part on fish, which they obtain by wading in the water and taking the fish with their hands instead of with hooks or nets.

The arms of the Long-legged People are of a normal length, the legs are developed to a length corresponding to that of the arms of the Long-armed People.

The country of the latter borders on that of the Long-legs. The habits and food of the two are similar. The difference in their physical structure makes them of mutual assistance, those with the long arms being able to take the shellfish of the shallow waters, while those with the long legs take the surface fish from the deeper localities. The two therefore gather a harvest otherwise unobtainable.

The One-Eyed People and Others

A LITTLE TO THE EAST of the Country of the Long-legs are to be found the One-eyed People. They have only one eye, rather larger than the ordinary human eye, placed in the centre of the forehead, directly above the nose. Other clans or families have but one arm and one leg, some having a right arm and left leg, others a left arm and right leg, while others have both on the same side and go in pairs, like shoes. Another species not only has one arm and one leg, but is of such fashion as to have just one eye, one nostril and beard on only one side of the face, there being as it were rights and lefts. The two in reality are one, for it is in this way that they pair. The Long-eared People resemble Chinese in all except their ears. They live in the far West among mountains and in caves. Their pendant, flabby ears extend to the ground and would impede their feet in walking if they did not support them on their hands. They are sensitive to the faintest sound. Still another people in this region are distinguished by having six toes on each foot.

The Feathered People and Others

THE FEATHERED PEOPLE are very tall and are covered with fluffy down. They have wings in place of arms and can even fly short distances. On the points of the wings are claws, which serve as hands. Their noses are like beaks. Gentle and timid, they do not leave their own country. They have good voices and like to sing ballads. If a man wishes to visit this people he must go far to the south-east and then inquire. There is also the Land of the People with Three Faces, who live in the centre of the Great Waste and never die; the Land of the Three-heads, east of the K'un-lun Mountains; the Three-body Country, the inhabitants of which have one head with three bodies, three arms and only two legs; and yet another where the people have square heads, broad shoulders and three legs, and the stones on the land are all gold and jade.

The People of the Punctured Bodies

ANOTHER COMMUNITY is said to be composed of people who have holes through their chests. They can be carried about on a pole put through the orifice, or may be comfortably hung on a peg. They sometimes string themselves on a rope and walk out in file. They are harmless people. They eat snakes that they kill with bows and arrows. They live for a very long time.

The Women's Kingdom

THE WOMEN'S KINGDOM, the country inhabited exclusively by women, is said to be surrounded by a sea of less density than ordinary water, so that ships sink on approaching the shores. It has been reached only by boats carried there in whirlwinds, and only a few of those wrecked on its rocks have survived and returned to tell of its wonders. The women have houses, gardens and shops. Instead of money they use gems, perforated and strung like beads. They reproduce their kind by sleeping where the south wind blows over them.

The Land of the Flying Cart

SITUATED TO THE NORTH of the Plain of Great Joy, the Land of the Flying Cart joins the Country of the One-armed People on the south west and that of the Three-bodied People on the south east. The inhabitants have only one arm and an additional large eye in the centre of the forehead, making three eyes in all. Their carts, though wheeled, do not run along the ground. Instead they chase each other in mid-air as gracefully as a flock of swallows. The vehicles have a kind of winged framework at each end, and the one-armed occupants, each grasping a flag, talk and laugh one to another in great delight during what might be called their aerial recreation were it not for the fact that it seems to be their sole occupation.

The Expectant Wife

A CURIOUS LEGEND is told regarding a solitary, weird figure which stands out from a hill top in the pass called Shao-hsing Gorge, in Canton Province. This point of the pass is called Lung-men, or Dragon's Mouth, and the hill the Husband-expecting Hill. The figure itself, which is called the Expectant Wife, resembles that of a woman. Her bent head and figure down to the waist are very lifelike.

The story, widely known in this and the neighbouring province, goes as follows. Centuries ago a certain poor woman was left by her husband, who went on a journey into Kwangsi, close by, but in those days considered a wild and distant region, full of dangers. He promised to return in three years. The time went slowly and sadly past, for she dearly loved her husband, but he never appeared. He, an ungrateful and unfaithful spouse, had fallen in love with a fair one in Kwangsi, a sorceress or witch, who threw a spell over him and charmed him to his destruction, turning him into stone. To this day his figure may be seen standing near a cave close by the river that is known by the name of the Detained Man Cave.

The wife, broken by grief at her husband's failure to return, was likewise turned into a stone, and it is said that a supernatural power will one day bring the couple to life again and reward the ever-faithful wife.

The Wild Men

THE WILD BEASTS of the mountain have a king. He is a wild man, with long, thick locks, fiery red in colour. His body is covered with hair. He is very strong: with a single blow of his huge fist, he can break large rocks to pieces; he can also pull up the trees of the forest by the root. His flesh is as hard as iron and is invulnerable to the thrusts of knife, spear or sword. He rides on a tiger when he leaves his home; he rules over the wolves, leopards and tigers, and governs all their affairs. Many other wild men, like him in appearance, live in these mountains, but on account of his great strength he alone is king. These wild men kill and eat all human beings they meet. Other hill tribes live in terror of meeting them. Indeed, who of all these mountain people would have been left alive had not some men, craftier than the wild men, devised a means of overpowering these fierce savages?

This is the method referred to: On leaving his home the herb gatherer of the mountains arms himself with two large hollow bamboo tubes, which he slips over his wrists and arms. He also carries a jar of very strong wine. When he meets one of the wild men he stands still and allows the giant to grasp him by the arm. As the giant holds him fast, as he supposes, in his firm grasp, he quietly and slowly withdraws one arm from the bamboo cuff, and, taking the pot of wine from the other hand, quickly pours it down the throat of the stooping giant, whose mouth is wide open with laughter at the thought of having captured his victim so easily. The potent wine acts at once, causing the victim to drop to the ground in a dead sleep. Then the herb-gatherer can kill him with a thrust through the heart, or leave the drunken tyrant to sleep off the effect of the wine, while he returns to his work of collecting the health-restoring herbs. Because of this the numbers of these wild men became less and less, until at the present time when now just a few remain.

The Jung Tribe

THE FINAL TALE in this collection is about why the people of the Jung Tribe have heads of dogs. It is thought that the wave of conquest that swept from north to south in the earliest periods of Chinese history left on its way, like small islands in the ocean, certain remnants of aboriginal tribes which survived and continued to exist despite the sustained hostile attitude of the flood of foreign settlers around them.

Not many miles inland from the city of Fuzhou, up in the mountainous country, there was once the settlement of one of these tribes. It was that of the Jung tribe, the members of which wore a large and peculiar headgear constructed of bamboo splints resting on a peg inserted in the chignon at the back of the head. The weight of the structure in front was counterbalanced by a pad, serving as a weight, attached to the end of the splints, which projected as far down as the middle of the shoulders. This framework was covered by a scarf of red cloth which, when not rolled up, concealed the whole head and face. The following legend explains the origin of this unusual headdress.

In early times the Chief of a Chinese tribe was at war with the Chief of another tribe who came to attack his territory from the west. The Western Chief so badly defeated the Chinese army that none of the generals or soldiers could be persuaded to renew hostilities and try to drive the enemy back to his own country. This distressed the Chinese Chief very much. As a last resort he issued a proclamation promising his daughter in marriage to anyone who would bring him the head of his enemy, the Chief of the West.

The people in the palace talked a great deal of this promise made by the Chief, and their conversation was listened to by a fine large white dog belonging to one of the generals. This dog, having thought about the matter, waited until midnight and then crept over to the tent of the enemy Chief. The latter, as well as his guard, was asleep; or, if the guard was not, the dog succeeded in avoiding him in the darkness. Entering the tent, the dog gnawed through the Chief's neck and carried his head off in his mouth. At dawn he placed it at the Chinese Chief's feet and waited for his reward. The Chief was soon able to verify the fact that his enemy had been slain, for the headless body had caused so much distress in the hostile army that it had already begun to retreat from Chinese territory.

The dog then reminded the Chief of his promise and asked for his daughter's hand in marriage. "But how," said the Chief, "can I possibly marry my daughter to a dog?" "Well," replied the dog, "will you agree to her marrying me if I change myself into a man?" This seemed a safe promise to make and so the Chief agreed. The dog then stipulated that he should be placed under a large bell and that no one should move it or look into it for a period of 280 days.

This was done, and for 279 days the bell remained unmoved, but on the 280th day the Chief could not restrain his curiosity any longer, and tilting up the bell saw that the dog had changed into a man all except his head, the last day being required to complete the transformation. However, the spell was now broken and the result was a man with a dog's head. Since it was the Chief's fault that, through his over-inquisitiveness, the dog could not altogether become a man, he was obliged to keep his promise. The wedding duly took place, the bridegroom's head being veiled for the occasion by a red scarf.

Unfortunately the fruit of the union took more after their father than their mother and they had exceedingly ugly faces. They were therefore obliged to continue to wear the head-covering adopted by their father at the marriage ceremony. This became so much an integral part of the tribal costume that not only has it been worn ever since by their descendants, but a change of headgear has become synonymous with a change of husbands or a divorce. One account says that at the original bridal ceremony the bride wore the red scarf to prevent her seeing her husband's ugly features, and that is why the headdress is worn by the women and not by the men, or more generally by the former than the latter, though others say that it was originally worn by the ugly children of both sexes.

This legend explains the dog worship of the Jung tribe, which now consists of four clans, with a separate surname (Lei, Chung, Lang, and Pan) to each, has a language of its own, and does not intermarry with the natives. At about the time of the old Chinese New Year (somewhere in February) they paint a large figure of a dog on a screen and worship it, saying it is their ancestor who was victorious over the Western invader.

THE
END

Biographies

Herbert A. Giles

Herbert Allen Giles (1845–1935) was a British diplomat and sinologist, working in Mawei, Shanghai, Tamsui and finally as British Consul at Ningpo. In 1897 he became professor of Chinese language at Cambridge University, a post that lasted for 35 years. He published many writings on Chinese language, as well as on literature and religion, such as his *Chinese-English Dictionary* (1891), and several translations of classic Chinese tales, including Pu Songling's *Strange Stories from a Chinese Studio* (1880).

Lafcadio Hearn

Patrick Lafcadio Hearn (1850–1904, also known as Koizumi Yakumo) was a journalist and writer whose wandering life led him eventually to find a home in Japan, which would prove to be his true inspiration. He wrote about the country and, especially, its legends and ghost stories. His books about Japan include *Japanese Fairy Tales* (1898) and *In Ghostly Japan* (1899). His intriguing *Some Chinese Ghosts* (1887) retells Chinese ghost stories through a Japanese lens, aided by his writer's artistry.

Davide Latini

Foreword

Davide Latini is currently a PhD student at SOAS. He obtained his BA in Foreign Cultures and Languages at Carlo Bo University of Urbino, and focused on classical Chinese studies during his MA at Ca' Foscari University of Venice. His field of research revolves around the symbology of ancient Chinese mythology and its relationship with the ideological and textual context in which the narratives are inserted.

Rev. J. Macgowan

John Macgowan (1835–1922) was born in Belfast and became a missionary to China with the London Missionary Society, where he helped to found the anti-footbinding Natural Foot Society. He was author of many books about Chinese culture and history. As well as *Chinese Folk-Lore Tales* (1910), his works include *English and Chinese Dictionary of the Amoy Dialect* (1883) and *Men and Manners of Modern China* (1912).

Frederick H. Martens

Frederick Herman Martens (1874–1932) was an author, lyricist and translator, whose work includes a translation of Pietro Yon's 1917 Christmas carol 'Gesu Bambino', a biography of the musician A.E. Uhe (1922), *A Thousand and One Nights of Opera* (1926), *Violin Mastery* (*Talks with Master Violinists and Teachers*) (1919), and fairy-tale translations in *The Chinese Fairy Book* (ed. Dr. R. Wilhelm).

Norman Hinsdale Pitman

Norman Hinsdale Pitman (1876–1925) was an author and educator, born in Lamont, Michigan. His works include: *The Lady Elect: A Chinese Romance* (1913), *A Chinese Wonder Book* (1919), *Chinese Fairy Tales* (1924) and *Dragon Lure: A Romance of Peking* (1925).

Pu Songling

Pu Songling (1640–1715) was a private tutor and writer in Qing Dynasty China, best known as the author of *Strange Stories from a Chinese Studio* (*Liaozhai Zhiyi*), a collection of classical Chinese stories often of a fantastical or supernatural character which implicitly criticise contemporary societal issues.

E.T.C. Werner

Edward Theodore Chalmers Werner (1864–1954) was a sinologist specialising in Chinese superstition, myths and magic. He worked as a British diplomat in China during the final imperial dynasty, working his way up to British Consul-General in 1911. Being posted to all four corners of China encouraged Werner's interest in the mythological culture of the land, and after retirement he was able to concentrate on his sinological studies, of which *Myths & Legends of China* (1922) was one result.

Dr R. Wilhelm

Richard Wilhelm (1873–1930) was a German theologian, missionary and sinologist. He is best known for his works of translations of philosophical works from Chinese into German, including his translation of the *I Ching* and *The Secret of the Golden Flower*. He also edited *The Chinese Fairy Book* (1921).

Text Sources

A large proportion of the tales in this book come from E.T.C. Werner's thorough *Myths & Legends of China* (George G. Harrap & Co. Ltd., 1922). A number each are from *Chinese Folk-Lore Tales* by Rev. J. Macgowan, D.D. (Macmillan and Co. Limited, London, 1910); *Some Chinese Ghosts* by Lafcadio Hearn (Roberts Brothers, Boston, Mass., 1887); *A Chinese Wonder Book* by Norman Hinsdale Pitman (E.P. Dutton & Co., New York, 1919); and *Strange Stories from a Chinese Studio*, Vols I & II, by Pu Songling (earliest pub. 1740), translated by Herbert A. Giles (Thomas De La Rue and Co., London, 1880). Another sizeable proportion derives from *The Chinese Fairy Book*, edited by Dr R. Wilhelm, translated after original sources by Frederick H. Martens (Frederick A. Stokes Company, New York, 1921). Remaining contributing authors include O.B. Duane and N. Hutchison.